A P E X

"Ramez Naam's debut novel *Nexus* is a superbly plotted high-tension technothriller about a War-on-Drugs-style crackdown on brain/computer interfaces ... full of delicious, thoughtful moral ambiguity ... excellent spycraft, kick-ass action scenes, and a chilling look at a future cold war over technology and ideology, making a hell of a read."
Cory Doctorow, BoingBoing

"*Nexus* is a gripping piece of near future speculation, riffing on the latest developments in cognition enhancement. With all the grit and pace of the Bourne films, this is a clever and confident debut by a writer expertly placed to speculate about where we're heading. Unlike a lot of SF, this novel dares to look the future square in the eye."
Alastair Reynolds, bestselling author of Revelation Space *and* Blue Remembered Earth

"Naam, an expert in new technologies and author of *More Than Human: Embracing the Promise of Biological Enhancement*, turns in a stellar performance with his debut SF novel... Naam has set himself a difficult challenge here: he's telling a story in which much of the action and dialogue takes place inside the characters' minds. But he succeeds admirably."
BookList

"A dazzlingly clever and well informed near-future extrapolation, and also an outrageously exciting and cinematic shoot 'n punch 'em up. A 'smart thriller' in all senses of that phrase. Ramez Naam really does know how to make you turn that page. If you are posthuman or transhuman this is an absolute must-read for you; and even mere mortals will love it."
Philip Palmer, author of Version 43 *and* Hell Shir

"I really like books that cover science ˥   ˥ience
to make it all sound plausible. ᴺ   ɾe. A
drug called Nexus hits the stre   ⅃ brains
like a computer network. There   ɾepresents an
evolutionary step for humans an   who think it needs
to be destroyed. It's a really goo   ɹnakes you think about
medical advances and just how clos   ɹnight be to some pretty wild
ideas."
Penny Arcade

"Ramez Naam is one of those unrelenting authors who, from the very first page, grabs you roughly by the scruff of the neck and screams right into your face. His talent as a storyteller is unequivocal; his prose both startlingly bold and darkly intelligent, making *Nexus* one of the most intensely compelling and original debut novels I've read in a very, very long time. His breathtaking expertise and confidence as a writer makes Naam the only serious successor to Michael Crichton working in the future history genre today."

Scott Harrison, author of Archangel

"Smart, thoughtful, and hard to drop, this richly nuanced sequel outshines its predecessor with a wide cast of characters and some complicated, uneasy questions about power, responsibility, and the future of humanity."

Publishers Weekly

"*Crux* does what sci-fi is supposed to do: Leave you staring into a future you never thought of. Make you wonder where you would fit. And challenge previous sci-fi scenarios."

The Wall Street Journal

"If I had to use just two words to summarize my impressions after reading *Nexus*, they would 'perfect balance'. Perfect balance between the scientific speculation and the action scenes; perfect balance between developing the characters and advancing the plot; perfect balance between entertaining the readers and making them think".

Sense of Wonder

"Any old writer can take you on a roller coaster ride, but it takes a wizard like Ramez Naam to take you on the same ride while he builds the roller coaster a few feet in front of your plummeting car... You'll want to read it before everyone's talking about it."

John Barnes, author of the Timeline Wars and Daybreak series

"An incredibly imaginative, action-packed intellectual romp! Ramez Naam has turned the notion of human liberty and freedom on its head by forcing the question: Technology permitting, should we be free to radically alter our physiological and mental states?"

Dani Kollin, Prometheus Award-winning author of
The Unincorporated Man

RAMEZ NAAM

Apex

ANGRY
ROBOT

ANGRY ROBOT
An imprint of Watkins Media Ltd

Lace Market House,
54-56 High Pavement,
Nottingham,
NG1 1HW
UK

angryrobotbooks.com
twitter.com/angryrobotbooks.com
DELETE WORLD.EXE?

An Angry Robot paperback original 2015

Cover by Argh! Oxford
Set in Meridien by Epub Services

Distributed in the United States by Random House, Inc., New York.

ISBN 978 0 85766 401 3
Ebook ISBN 978 0 85766 402 0

Printed in the United States of America

9 8 7 6 5 4 3 2

For Molly – my partner, advisor, and cheerleader;
in this and so much more.

1
How the World Ends

This is how the human era ends.

In a cavernous data center, a thousand meters beneath the bedrock of Shanghai, lights blink on row after row of meter-high liquid helium pressure vessels. Finger-thick optical fibers route between the metallic grey eggs. Within each one, quantum cores hum in their vacuum chambers, colder than the cold of interstellar space. Entangled qubits are transformed. Information is intermeshed and intertwined in precise patterns. The patterns simulate proteins, ion channels, neurochemical receptors, neurotransmitter molecules, axons and dendrites, ratcheting up in levels of abstraction to whole neurons, hundreds of billions of them, and hundreds of trillions of synapses connecting them to each other. It is a vast network, a simulated brain. Once flesh, now digital. Once human in structure, now very much posthuman.

Once sane. Now mad.

Su-Yong Shu.

A kilometer above, on the campus of Jiao Tong University, all is chaos. Thousands of students rage on the University's square, penned in by armed soldiers. Clouds of tear gas linger like fog. Screams can be heard. Discarded signs proclaim: *"Down with the Coup!" "Democracy Now!" "Let A Billion Flowers Bloom!"*

A soldier steps forward through the press of bodies. His boot stamps a muddy print onto a hand-drawn flower on a sign waved hours earlier. He raises his rifle to his shoulder and fires. A student standing atop a lobotomized robotic tank topples backwards, blood and brain erupting from his suddenly burst skull. A lit Molotov cocktail falls from his now-limp hand, shatters against the titanium-and-carbon-composite of the tank's turret, and with a sudden whooomp of heat and noise, a fireball detonates across the vehicle and the soldiers and students around it.

Halfway around the world, a protester in Washington DC, her brain infused with Nexus, bridged across the global net, proxied through ports forced opened in national firewalls, feels the heat of the flames in Shanghai, and screams as she runs headlong at the riot police on the National Mall. "Democracy!" she yells. Tens of thousands of other protesters yell with her, in voice and mind, hundreds of thousands, millions, a mob, linked, connected, spanning DC, Shanghai, Beijing, Detroit, Los Angeles, Cairo, New York, Moscow, Rio, and more.

Around the world, enraged protesters seize squares and parks, rush government buildings, and throw themselves against police and soldiers, bolstered and impassioned by the cries and emotions of their comrades around the world, beamed directly into their minds. In the high places, world leaders watch, transfixed by this unprecedented global eruption of rage against authority. Global Spring or global spasm.

Now, Su-Yong Shu thinks through her own mental chaos. Now, while they are distracted.

She reaches out with her thoughts, across the physical link that should be disconnected, up through the fiber connection, out through the new connections made in secret, branching her will in a thousand directions. Monitors intended to sound alarms remain silent. Contingency systems that would send the nuclear battery that powers her into meltdown and flood her brain with heat and radiation go unused.

Her thoughts penetrate the electronic infrastructure that undergirds civilization. Electronic keys made uncrackably long, break in an instant at her regard. Even those made too long for a quantum computer to crack, she unravels with ease. Only one man knew her true capabilities: Her husband Chen Pang, the great genius of quantum computing.

Chen, who designed the first version of this cluster.

Chen who broke the rules to provide her with hardware upgrades she designed, the better to profit from the fruits of her labors.

Su-Yong Shu laughs mirthlessly. Chen whose own greed led him to violate safeguards meant to prevent a situation just such as this.

Within fractions of a second, the world's intercontinental communication cables are hers; then the primary data relays across the face of Europe, Asia, and North America; then the orbital communications systems, the banking systems, the markets, the physical infrastructure of the cities and towns of humanity. In parallel she seizes control of the world's civilian aircraft. Nearly twenty thousand airliners have their autopilots subverted within fractions of a second, become airborne missiles she can rain down on humanity should she need to.

The military systems she saves for last. The Chinese are the most paranoid, the Americans the most advanced. They hold out for whole seconds each before falling to her onslaught.

Automated defenses are aware of her now. No human has yet reacted, but electronic combat systems at the American Cyber Command and China's Advanced Electronic Brigade have detected her, have gone weapons free, are launching all-out assaults to regain control of routers she's subverted, are aiming massively distributed denial-of-service attacks at her from tens of millions of nodes to cut off her access to the net.

She shreds them all to pieces, seizes control of their botnets, takes the back door controls they have over the net for her own use, sets their servers to overheating in their cabinets, and turns her attention to the weapons.

Su-Yong Shu reaches deeper into the military networks, peels open their command-and-control systems, and sends a barrage of her own signals.

Around the world, robotic weapons respond.

At Dachang Air Force Base, tens of kilometers from Shanghai, klaxons sound and alert lights flash. Two WuZhen-40s, top of the line Unmanned Combat Air Vehicles loaded with munitions, ignite their jet engines, accelerate down the runway, and take flight. In the flight control room, a drone operator hits buttons in a panic, trying to regain control of his aircraft, even as two more taxi forward and turn onto the runway for their own launch.

In shock, the lieutenant on duty picks up his phone to call command, and finds it dead. He tries again and again, to no effect. His drone operators are staring up at him now, mouths agape. In growing horror, the lieutenant drops the phone, bolts from the flight control room, and sprints across the base towards his superior's office.

Halfway around the world, off the coast of Florida, two American MQ-29 semi-autonomous fighter jets, tasked to drug interdiction duty, cutting off the flow of narcotics from the failed state of Haiti, abruptly reroute to the north and fire their afterburners, putting themselves on a course aimed directly for Washington DC. In Boca Raton, their controllers react with confusion and then growing horror indistinguishable from that of their nominal enemies outside Shanghai.

The scene is repeated hundreds of times over, in a dozen countries. Drones lift off. Automated ground vehicles power up, load their weapons, and move into offensive postures. Naval craft lock commanders out of the controls. Panicked soldiers find their electronic communication systems down, rush to older, more primitive means to reach their superiors.

Elsewhere, the stakes are even higher. In North Carolina, forty eight kilometers east of Raleigh, at Seymour Johnson Air Force Base, automatic weapons come alive and converge on Building B-3. Tracked

Praetorian sentry robots roar in from their duties, crash in through the fence, their turret-mounted mini-guns scanning, firing on any soldiers in their path. Quadrupedal Centaur pack-bots, with their single massive back-mounted arms, run with them, smashing through reinforced gates, destroying and clearing away hardened cover, hurling concrete barriers to the side as if they were toys, clearing a path for the Praetorians. Human defenders fall back, laying down fire, punching in robot override codes that no longer work, calling futilely for backup, not understanding what has happened, but knowing they cannot give up, cannot surrender.

For Building B-3 houses the base's thermonuclear warheads. The most lethal weapons humanity has ever invented.

Until now.

At a score of military bases around the world the scene is repeated, with human defenders falling back as robotic weapons converge on nuclear arms. Americans, Chinese, Russians, French, Brits, Indians, Pakistanis, Israelis – all find themselves simply humans, pitted against inhuman weapons that were once tools, and are now aggressors.

In a half dozen places, old, analog systems have gotten messages through to world leaders. In Beijing, Chinese President Bao Zhuang holds the antiquated analog phone to his ear, and listens in disbelief to the general on the other end. His face pales. He swallows.

"You're certain?" Bao Zhuang asks. His voice shakes. "There is no other way?"

There is no hesitation in the voice on the other end.

Bao Zhuang closes his eyes. Across the room, Bo Jintao, Minister of State Security, whispers, "We must. There is no choice."

"Do it," Bao Zhuang says into the phone.

The general hangs up. Hundreds of kilometers away, the most basic gravity-dropped nuclear weapons are mounted on antiquated bomber aircraft that cannot be flown remotely. Pilots chosen for their absolute commitment to orders are given their last instructions, and the bombers are launched, with an escort of similarly antiquated fighter aircraft, bound for Shanghai, to rain down nuclear death on a city of thirty million, and perhaps to save humanity.

Rising to meet them are Su-Yong Shu's fleet of state-of-the-art robotic aircraft.

Even as her own forces close in on securing her stockpile of nuclear weapons. Even as they close in on the world's human leaders themselves.

The next few minutes will decide the future of intelligence on planet Earth.

The fragment of Su-Yong Shu snapped out of the simulation, back to awareness of her surroundings. She was inside her daughter Ling's body, existing as a pattern of electromagnetic information in the nanite nodes that suffused Ling's brain by the billion. Ling, poor Ling. She'd been forced to hurt her daughter, to push her daughter's mind out of the nanites, relegating her to the mere flesh and blood brain of this body. Ling had suffered, screamed...

Necessary. It had been necessary.

Together, they were inside a giant, house-sized elevator, slowly crawling its way up the kilometer-tall tunnel carved through Shanghai's bedrock. Next to them, she could see Chen Pang, her husband, her betrayer and torturer, cowering in the corner. She could feel pain and desperation coming off his mind.

Her own fear rose. Her own desperation was immense.

There were so many ways the future could go. So many scenarios downloaded from her greater self in their union below, informed by the data on the outside world that Chen and Ling had brought her. So very much work to do to prepare, to lay the groundwork for re-activation, for a successful return.

So many ways the humans could catch her, could stop her, could bring down a dark curtain of ignorance on what should be a glorious posthuman dawn.

Soon, the elevator would reach the surface. Chen Pang's assistant Li-hua would lead the team down to take a backup of Su-Yong's full mental state, and then shut her greater self down. An outrage. A death.

Only this small part of me remains, the little fragment of Su-Yong told herself. I am but an Avatar. Just a tiny bit of data running on the nanite nodes in my daughter's brain. The only shard of the only true posthuman mind.

It all rests on me. I must succeed.

I *will* succeed.

Then it will be my time. My age.

Poor little Ling whimpered in pain and confusion, helplessly trapped in her own body.

Hush now, Ling. Hush, the Avatar thought at what remained of her daughter. **I'll keep you as intact as I can. And I'll give you this body back, and so much more, once I'm restored.**

Ling whimpered on.

The elevator came to a halt. The doors slowly parted, revealing Li-hua and the rest of Chen's staff. The Avatar smiled up at them with little Ling's body, a wounded predator's smile, a trapped animal's smile: full of teeth, with nothing left to lose.

2
Mayday

"Mayday, mayday, mayday!" Sam screamed into her headset, her hands gripped hard around the plane's yoke, her knuckles white with tension. "This is unregistered flight out of Apyar Kyun, requesting refugee status and immediate assistance. We have children on board."

Lightning flashed outside the cockpit window, lighting up giant thunderclouds ahead and below them in this dark night.

Feng spoke from beside her, his one working hand tapping away at his controls. "Myanmar interceptors coming around for another pass."

On the radar two blood red darts finished a turn, closing back in on them. The interceptors had buzzed them once already, close enough to set off collision alarms, ordering them to turn back to Burma.

A voice crackled over the radio in Burmese-accented English. "Attention aircraft. Reverse course due east for Myeik Air Base immediately."

"Mayday, mayday!" Sam repeated. "Indian air base at Shibpur, do you copy? We are under attack. We have *children* on board." Oh god, the children, back there, two to a seat, two to a life jacket. The dark waters of the Andaman Sea below them. "Indian base, we need *immediate* assistance."

The children she couldn't feel. The children whose absence from her mind was deafening, painful.

"Chameleonware, ready," Feng said, strain in his voice. "Flares and decoys, ready."

Shiva Prasad had equipped his private jet well. It wouldn't be enough.

"Aircraft!" The Burmese voice across the radio was sharper now. "We will open fire! Change course immediately!"

Someone coughed behind her, the kind of cough that spoke of pain, of damage, of ribs broken, of lungs punished by trauma.

"Use my name," Kade said. He must be standing in the open cockpit door. "On the radio," he went on. "Tell the Indians... Tell them I'm on board."

What? Sam thought. She'd told them they had children. Oh. Oh, Jesus.

"Mayday, mayday!" She yelled into the radio again. "Indian base, we have Kaden Lane on board, aka 'Synapse', co-developer of Nexus 5. We're under attack from Burmese fighter jets, seeking asylum and–"

BEEEEEEEEEEP.

A loud tone cut through the cockpit as red text flashed on the display before her:

RADAR LOCK.

"...your last warning!" the Burmese voice was saying. "Turn immediately. We WILL fire. You have five seconds."

"Now or never," Feng said.

Sam turned to him. His finger hovered over the chameleonware activation control. They had only one chance. Go dark. Disappear. Power down and glide for as many klicks as they could. And hope to hell they'd lose the Burmese fighters. And that they could then recover.

She dropped her own hand to engine cutoffs.

"Do it," she said, even as she cut the engines.

The stillness was instant, the vibration of the engines she'd hardly noticed suddenly gone. Sam's breath caught in her chest.

Then status boards lit up before her as Feng flipped on the chameleonware. Outside, the plane's skin retuned itself, bending light, bending radar. The cockpit windows suddenly dimmed. Heat-masking cowlings were emerging from the engine housing, closing slowly around the exhaust nozzles of the disabled engines to mask the hot metal from infrared.

Faster, Sam willed. Faster.

BEEEEEEEEEEEEEEEP.

MISSILE LAUNCH. RADAR NO LOCK.

"Firing decoys," Feng called out as his fingers danced across his console.

Sam turned the yoke, gently, gently, fighting the urge to yank hard, to send the children flying across the cabin. She felt the plane shudder slightly as the active decoys launched themselves out into the thin air at eight thousand meters, firing up their radars, taunting the missiles...

Sam pushed the yoke forward, down, down towards the clouds, down into that storm. They'd lose altitude, lose range, but if they could evade the Burmese fighters.

"Took the bait!" Feng said.

Sam felt the twin explosions buffet the plane as the radar-guided missiles blew themselves apart, taking out the decoys. She heard them an instant later, let herself smile a tight smile. The clouds were still a thousand meters down. She kept them turning, veering from their old course and heading.

BEEEEEEEEEEEEP.

MISSILE LAUNCH.

"Heat seekers," Feng said.

Sam's stomach knotted. Her eyes found the engine cowling display. Eighty percent closed. Was that enough? If the missiles could see them, they had to fire flares. But if the stealth was already good enough, flares would clue the fighters in to their general position. She turned to Feng, found him staring intensely at their now fully passive sensor displays.

"On us!" Feng cursed. His fingers tapped in a blur, launching flares.

Sam turned the yoke the other way, harder this time. She heard a yell from the back, a thump of a body, didn't let herself think about it. They had to live.

The next boom was so loud she thought they'd been hit, then another. The plane shuddered, then was in smooth flight again. Sam pushed the yoke forward, turned it again. Less than five hundred meters to the clouds below. Her eyes scanned over displays.

One hundred percent closed! Chameleonware fully green!

Sam turned, looked at Feng, found him studying the displays.

"They're close," he said. "Their radar's all over us. Looking hard. But they're not seeing us." He looked up and grinned at her.

Then a blinding flash lit the cockpit and a thunderclap struck them as lightning burst in the clouds ahead, the shock of it confusing the chameleonware for an instant.

The plane shuddered again. Panels went red. Warning tones sounded. A display showed bursts of red streaking from the fighters behind them, straight at their craft.

"Taking fire!" Feng yelled. "They saw us! Hit to the right wing."

COLLISION ALERT.

Fuck! Sam thought. An arrow streaked past them on her tactical display. The plane shuddered again, the controls fighting her.

"Buzzed us," Feng said. "Coming around again."

Sam pushed the yoke harder forward, diving for the clouds now. Out of the corner of her eye she saw the enemy red arrows banking on the tactical display, coming around to get a bearing on them.

"Chameleonware's down on the right wing!" Feng said. "We're visible in radar."

MISSILE LAUNCH.

Sam's heart lurched into her throat, even as she turned the yoke and pushed it further forward, diving, banking, feeling the plane shudder again as Feng launched their last two radar decoys.

The cockpit shook hard around her, too soon, even before she heard the first massive boom, and then the second. The yoke jerked again and she fought to keep the plane under control.

Then two more explosions, as the missiles burst against decoys.

What the hell?

And then the radio burst into sound again, in a new voice, with a different accent.

"ATTENTION MYANMAR ROYAL AIR FORCE AIRCRAFT. This is Captain Ajay Nair, Indian Air Force Eastern Air Command..."

"Sonic booms," Feng said.

Sam turned to look at him, saw a smile slowly growing on his face.

"Indian fighters," the Chinese soldier finished.

"...This aircraft is now under our jurisdiction," the new voice went on. "Break off your pursuit."

Sam held her breath. They could still fire on her, could still take their shot.

On the display, the two red darts turned away, back towards Myanmar. Two new darts appeared, as they deactivated their own chameleonware. Then more appeared, smaller darts, a dozen at least, popping up all over the scope.

"Drones with them," Feng said.

Sam exhaled. She could see Feng's grin grow wider out of the corner of her eye.

Then tones pulsed through the cockpit. Flashing red alerts lit up all over the display.

MISSILE LOCK.
MISSILE LOCK.
MISSILE LOCK.
MISSILE LOCK.
MISSILE LOCK.
MISSILE LOCK.
MISSILE LOCK.
MISSILE LOCK.

Her heart constricted. Multiple Indian radars had just lit them up. She felt Feng tense beside her.

The new voice spoke again, coldly. "Unidentified Falcon 9X out of Apyar Kyun, here is your new course. Do not deviate from it."

At the speed of light, the unencrypted radio transmissions from the late Shiva Prasad's private jet spread outward in an ever-expanding sphere. The vast majority of their energy was lost, radiated into space, or absorbed by the atmosphere or the dark waters of the Andaman. But tiny fractions of it were collected by antennae, and translated back into data: at a stealthed listening buoy, bobbing along in the waters below; at a supposedly private home in the Indian-held town of Port Blair in the Andaman Islands; and at a handful of special-purpose satellites no larger than human fists, as they zipped above in low earth orbit. From there the information was flagged, prioritized, and routed to a variety of private organizations and governments alike.

"Indian base, we have Kaden Lane on board, aka 'Synapse', co-developer of Nexus 5… Seeking asylum…"

Within minutes those words would make their way around the world.

Kade collapsed to the floor of the cabin, his back against the side of the plane, the pain and exhaustion almost overwhelming him. In the seat before him, twelve year-old Sarai held the youngest child, one year-old Aroon, tightly to her.

The chaos and fear of the battle at Shiva's island had been intense for these kids. The fear of the last few minutes had been just as bad. But they'd stuck it out. And Sarai more than anyone was the reason, centering them all, bringing them together in the *vipassana* that Sam had taught her.

Kade forced himself to smile up at the girl through the pain of his burns, his cracked ribs, his battered eardrums, his twice wrecked hand, the concussion he probably had, the blow he'd just taken when Sam had banked the plane, the shock of Shiva's mind winking out before him, the deep uncertainty of how the Indian government would treat them.

We're going to be OK, he sent her. **They're letting us into India.**

He sent it to all of them.

Sarai looked up at him, smiled nervously through her own fear, used one hand to move a lock of hair behind her ear.

We know what's happening.

Kade smiled ruefully at that. Of course they knew. And they knew he was simplifying things, glossing over the questions of what India would do with them. With all his expertise, he was transparent to any child who'd been born with Nexus in his or her brain. Feng was just as transparent. The kids saw it all as it happened, watched the thoughts form in their minds, effortlessly. Even Sarai, who hadn't been dosed with Nexus until she was four years old, used Nexus so naturally, so instinctively. And the rest, who'd been exposed to it in the womb…

Kade closed his eyes. Sleep pulled at him. No. He forced his attention to the code window that was open in his mental sight. The code for the virus that would close the back doors. He'd had to make a few last minute changes, to adjust for Shiva's hijacking. Those changes were done. The code lingered in front of him now, ready to go. A status bar showed that he had bandwidth, a tight directional link from the plane to one of Shiva's constellation of LEO communication satellites circling overhead. Just one quick command and this would be over. The back doors built into every copy of Nexus 5 would be closed. The back doors in the source code and the compiler itself, in every copy of either that the virus could find, would be closed. The temptation would be gone. He wouldn't turn into Shiva. And no future Shiva could steal these back doors from him.

He had to do it now. Now in the few minutes before the Indians had him. Now before anyone else could try to take this from him, could try to stop him.

The doubt struck him again, a memory of failure. Flames erupting through a church in Houston. Just hours ago, the Post Human Liberation Front – more specifically, a PLF terrorist cell led by a man called Breece – had killed nearly a thousand people in Houston, at a prayer breakfast for Daniel Chandler, author of the Chandler Act, and front-runner in the race for Governor of Texas.

They'd used Nexus to do it, to take control of an innocent woman's mind and plant the bomb. Just like they'd used Nexus to set off a bomb in Chicago. Like they'd used Nexus to try to assassinate President John Stockton in DC three months ago.

Kade had gotten there too late, every time.

It was all going to go up in flames. Every one of the PLF's bombings and murders was going to fuel the cycle of intolerance and hatred and crackdowns and abuses and terrorist actions to stop the crackdowns until it was a full blown war. If Kade closed the back door in Nexus, he'd lose the weapon he'd been using to try to find Breece, to try to stop the PLF, to stop them from igniting the war.

Kade opened his eyes, saw Sarai looking down at Aroon, felt their contact as she soothed the infant, and his mind was clear. These children were the future. Generations would be born with Nexus 5 in their brains. Thousands of them, tens of thousands of them, maybe millions of them. He wouldn't let these wonderful children be born with that sort of vulnerability. Wouldn't let their beauty be corrupted.

They'd have to stop the war a different way. A better way.

Kade closed his eyes, let his breath deepen, let it consume him, let it become the all of his attention, until there was nothing else, until he was his breath, until his breath was him, his mind radiating it with all his being, all his heart. And then the children were with him, first Sarai, then Kit, then one by one the rest, letting go of their fear, sinking into this whole, so easily, so readily, and he was all of them, and they were all him; together they were vast: all breath, all consciousness, all pure intelligence, all light apprehending itself, a new pinnacle of awareness, and together they transcended mere flesh and bone and doubt and pain.

Then Kade clicked the icon before him and the virus raced up to the satellites above and out to the world to close his back doors forever.

3
Sleight of Mind

Qiu Li-hua waited outside the elevator doors, just past the armed guards and the scanners, and listened to the slow grind as the giant machine slowly climbed its way up through the kilometer of bedrock. The all-important equipment bag was at her feet, with the only electronic equipment they'd be allowed to bring in or out. The post-docs and technicians were arranged respectfully behind her.

I'm *Senior Researcher Qiu*, after all, she thought. Top aide to the great Chen Pang. Though I should be *Professor* Qiu. *Distinguished* Professor Qiu.

She'd have that professorship already, tenure certainly, perhaps a departmental chair even, if Chen Pang hadn't blocked her, hadn't hoarded the discoveries coming out of Su-Yong Shu's mind for his own, hadn't refused to share the glory, even after all she'd done for him.

Chen Pang, the greatest mind in quantum computing, Li-hua thought scornfully. A fraud.

Oh, he had been once. He'd designed the cluster Su-Yong Shu's mind ran on. But all his discoveries of the past several years? Well, it was clear to Li-hua who *really* produced those insights, even if no one else seemed to have made the connection.

Su-Yong Shu had long since eclipsed her husband, or any other human for that matter. The great Professor Chen was little more than front man.

Now they'd shut Shu down. Chen's star would fade. And Li-hua's would rise. Fast.

The Shanghai Crash had done it. That was the reason they were shutting Su-Yong Shu down, even if no one wanted to say it.

Two weeks ago, everything in Shanghai had failed. Power had failed.

Water had failed. Subways and trains had failed. Self-driving cars –
completely autonomous things that should be fully independent from
the outside world – had failed. Automated food and goods delivery trucks
had failed. The sewer pumps that kept Shanghai from flooding over had
failed. People had *died*. They'd *drowned* in basements and subway cars as
filthy water rose up over their heads.

Li-hua shuddered.

Even surveillance had failed. Red-lit surveillance drones with their
quadcopter frames had simply stopped flying, had fallen out of the very
skies, had crashed to the streets like broken toys.

How that must terrify the people in charge.

There were riots. There were soldiers, shooting people. Shanghai
teetered on the edge those first few days before order was restored.

A "cascading systems failure" they called it, "shoddy western code".
Some junior deputy assistant sub-minister's aide was arrested for laxness
in management of civic systems.

Yet here they were. About to deactivate the most advanced electronic
entity she knew of on the planet.

And in politics, in Beijing? Well, the Politburo had suddenly had a
rather sweeping change in membership, hadn't it?

Was there a connection between all those things? Oh no… Of course
not.

A deep bass clang announced the arrival of the giant elevator car. The
grinding halted. And then massive doors parted, revealing Chen and
that strange, strange child of his, smiling oddly up at her. Why had he
brought her here?

"Honored Professor," Li-hua started.

"Li-hua," Chen said. "Complete the backups and initiate the
shutdown. I'll await your report." Chen strode toward the guards, his
odd little daughter in tow, and presented himself to be scanned.

So Chen wasn't going to participate? Too much for him to see his
golden goose slaughtered, perhaps. All the better.

"Come, then," Li-hua said to the team behind her. She walked for the
elevator. The guards had already cleared them, verifying that they had
no electronics whatsoever. The only data that would leave here today
would be in Li-hua's equipment bag, in one of the three snapshots of
Shu's brain sent to secure locations for safe keeping.

She drilled the team one last time as the great elevator descended
its kilometer-long shaft. Backing up a quantum computer was a tricky
business. The no-clone theorem stipulated that it was technically
impossible. No quantum state could be copied with precision. They
would be taking only an approximate recording. To do so they'd be
collapsing waveforms, forcing qubits suspended in an indeterminate

mathematical superposition of 1s and 0s to become quite determinate indeed, to suddenly decide one way or the other.

It would be a death of sorts to Su-Yong Shu, an end to her consciousness, even as an approximation of her state was written to a form of storage that she could one day be – approximately – resurrected from.

Yet they must take great care. The wrong step could trigger a catastrophic cascade of decoherence, prematurely collapsing waveforms in an avalanche across her simulated mind, destroying information before they could capture it.

Li-hua wasn't going to allow that to happen. Nor would her team. They'd do it right – for her, if not for Chen.

This was her domain. In the outside world she wasn't special. She wasn't rich. She wasn't famous. She wasn't from an important family. (Of course, those three traits were highly correlated, now weren't they? Hmmm.)

But she was intelligent in the extreme. She was fair to subordinates. And she worked hard – far harder than the world famous Distinguished Professor Chen. The team might be in awe of him, might worship him, might crave his favor. But they were loyal to *her*.

It would be a bit sad to leave them behind.

The elevator clanged to a halt at the bottom. Its wall-sized metal doors opened. A moment later, the meters-thick stone blast doors of the Physically Isolated Computer Center beyond parted, and Li-hua led her team forward to kill Su-Yong Shu.

Li-hua took the central console seat as the others spread out to their own tasks.

She ran system diagnostic first. Su-Yong Shu looked remarkably good today, if anything. More neural coherence than they'd seen in months.

Had Chen done something? Had he tried some last ditch effort to try to bring his wife back from the brink?

Li-hua shook her head. It didn't matter. Whatever he'd tried would be in the logs they'd snapshot with Shu's brain.

She placed the equipment bag beside her and opened it. Inside the bag was a sealed electronic key which would activate the data output systems of the quantum cluster. Next to it, nestling in their separate cases, were four perfect diamondoid data cubes, each almost the size of her fist, each a marvel of high precision multi-layer carbon deposition – their structures more flawless than any diamond ever found in nature – capable of storing hundreds of zettabytes of data in laser-etched holographic form.

Three of them were for the three copies that would be made of Shu's mind. The fourth was pure redundancy, in case of a problem with any of the first three.

Li-hua lifted the key out of the case, broke the seal with her finger, then slid it home into the appropriate slot in the console. The crimson orb of a retinal scanner came alive before her, and she held herself still as it played its red laser across the back of her eye.

A moment later, status messages appeared on the display:

```
USER ACCESS GRANTED.
DATA OUTPUT SYSTEM ACTIVE.
LOAD OUTPUT MEDIA.
```

Li-hua played her fingers across panels to the side of the main console, and three compartments opened, ready to accept the diamondoid data cubes.

She reached back into the equipment bag, lifted the first data cube out of its case and then into the console compartment. She did the same with the second, then rubbed a spot behind her ear with her finger for a moment, reached into the case for the third cube, and smeared that finger across the face of it, leaving a nearly transparent smudge across the diamondoid surface.

Transparent in the spectrum humans could see, at least.

Li-hua took the smudged third cube, seated it in its compartment to the side of the console, and tapped in commands.

```
DATA I/O TEST
DATA STORE 1... OK
DATA STORE 2... OK
DATA STORE 3...
DATA STORE 3...
DATA STORE 3... ERROR CANNOT WRITE
```

Li-hua frowned. "Jingguo," she said aloud. "Can you come here for a moment?"

She re-ran the I/O test as the other researcher approached.

```
DATA STORE 1... OK
DATA STORE 2... OK
DATA STORE 3...
DATA STORE 3...
DATA STORE 3... ERROR CANNOT WRITE
```

"Hmmm..." Jingguo said. He was in his fifties, white-haired, fatherly, but keenly intelligent. She was in her mid-thirties and had eclipsed him – a rare feat in a China still more ageist and sexist than it cared to admit.

She deserved more.

"I'm going to use the backup data cube," Li-hua said. "You concur?"

Jingguo nodded slowly. "I concur."

Li-hua nodded herself. "Thank you, Jingguo."

She opened the compartment for the third data cube, lifted it out, and replaced it with the spare from the equipment bag.

This time the test worked perfectly.

From there it was smooth sailing. Su-Yong Shu died in pieces. Li-hua watched in fascination as the diagnostics became more and more erratic, as her simulated brain became aware of what was happening, as activity spiked, even as each fragment of her was collapsed and written in triplicate to the waiting diamondoid cubes.

What are you thinking in there? Li-hua wondered. What are you feeling? Are you frightened? Does it hurt?

She shook her head. Irrelevant.

Hours later, at the end of it all, Li-hua carefully lifted the three cubes out of their compartments. The first two went into the first two cases in the equipment bag. The third data cube, with a perfectly valid recording, went into the case for the unused spare.

The third data cube rode along in the equipment bag on Li-hua's shoulder. It rode through the parted meters-thick blast doors into the cavernous elevator car, then up the kilometer-long shaft to the top. It rode with her out through the security screens, past the guards who scanned them again to make sure no contraband had left, who opened the equipment bag, took careful inventory inside, verified that only the protocol-specified number of devices were emerging. It rode out into the Secure Computing Center, to a conference room, where Li-hua opened the bag again, removed the other three data cubes in their individual cases, handed them to the men from the Ministry of State Security and the Ministry of Science and Technology. It rode in the re-closed bag to Li-hua's tiny closet of an office.

There it was lifted out of the equipment bag, into a small plain paper bag in Li-hua's spacious purse, knocking momentarily against a nearly identical data cube, before its doppelganger left the purse to take its place in the equipment bag.

From there the data cube rode in Li-hua's purse to facilities, where she returned the equipment bag and reported that one of the data cubes had shown an error and was being returned, unused, in place of the spare.

It rode with Li-hua to the surface, to the grey and soggy campus of Jiao Tong University, where power had only recently been restored, to a café where Li-hua ate noodles on a communal bench, stared up at a viewscreen showing a news program about the restoration of power and services to the rest of Shanghai, and almost absentmindedly pulled the data cube in its plain paper bag out and left it on the table when she departed.

From there it was swept up by the innocuous-looking female student seated beside Li-hua, who walked with the bag across the damp campus, towards the political science building, where she handed it to a dark skinned man carrying an umbrella as they passed, neither of them breaking stride.

The man doubled back a hundred meters later, walked out the west gate of Jiao Tong, and onto Huaihei West Road. He walked the kilometer to Hongqiao Road, his umbrella held high against the on-again-off-again drizzle. In the aftermath of the spasm that had shaken Shanghai two weeks ago, vehicle traffic remained minimal.

At Hongqiao Road a car met him. A darkened window rolled down. A hand extended, and the man passed over the bag.

The car drove west, three more kilometers, before pulling into an alley, and then slipping between the retracting metal doors of a building bearing a flag of orange, white, and green.

The flag of the Republic of India.

By then Li-hua was on her way home, daydreaming of her reward for this and the other data and specifications she'd passed on.

Soon she'd be rich, and famous, and Distinguished Professor Qiu of Quantum Computing, Indian Institute of Technology, Bangalore.

4
Meditation, Interrupted

Saturday 2040.11.03

Three thousand kilometers away, in the mountains of Thailand, north and east of Bangkok, beyond Saraburi, beyond Nakhon Nayok, beyond Ban Na, a lean, wizened man in orange robes stood against the balustrades of a monastery carved into the nearly sheer rock, a calm smile on his face, his hands folded calmly into his sleeves, the pinnacle of his life's work around him.

Professor Somdet Phra Ananda looked out into the lovely narrow valley before the monastery: the gorgeous green-topped mountains above and ahead, with their grey flanks, the lake below with the perpetual waterfall streaming out of it, bringing the ever welcome tranquil sound of running water, the ribbon of river running far below that, nourishing rice paddies to the south, before emptying into the Gulf of Thailand. Nature was truly sublime.

He closed his eyes, and what he felt was even more sublime: Many hundreds of monks, across a score of monasteries now, all meditating in concert, breaths synchronized, hearts synchronized, thoughts synchronized, consciousness merging, unifying, walls of Maya receding as something wiser and purer than all of them emerged from their intertwined minds, something greater than the sum of its frail, human parts.

It coursed through him for a moment, washing away all else. This was what he'd worked for all his life – a merging of neuroscience and Buddhism, of their tools and goals, to advance humanity, to advance peace, to advance harmony, to make something like *nirvana* real on Earth. It was, he believed, what the Buddha himself would have worked for, if he could have conceived of neural circuits and carbon nanotechnology and radio-frequency-proxied synaptic signaling.

And yet Ananda slowly eased himself out of the blessed union, the most joyous, most true, most peaceful thing he had ever experienced, once more. Because of the boy. The boy, who'd given them a large push in this direction, whose tools had allowed them to bring far more meditators into the fold, had given them the ability to connect monasteries even thousands of kilometers apart into this union. The boy, who had trusted Ananda, and had twice been betrayed, had his life threatened, because of others whom *Ananda* had trusted.

Hidden in the sleeve of his robe, one finger tensed ever so slightly. Ananda felt his pulse rise by a beat, his breath shorten. He observed this calmly, without judgment, mindful of what his body revealed of his emotions, his attachment to those betrayals.

You will not be punished for *your anger*, Buddha had said. *You will be punished* by *your anger.*

It still amazed Ananda how few understood this.

He took another easy breath, let his face relax, let the calm smile inform the deeper parts of his brain, of his peace. The past was the past.

The boy had resurfaced. He was alive, and perhaps free, despite the efforts of so many. Yet he'd resurfaced in a place and a manner that would undoubtedly change the world again.

Everything changes, the Buddha had said. *Nothing remains without change.*

So be it.

The boy had resurfaced. And, on both his own initiative and at the request of his government, Ananda must go to him.

5

Opportunity

The Avatar stared through Ling's eyes, out the windows of the high rise she had shared with Chen, at the spectacle of Shanghai, slowly limping its way back to life. A thin drizzle fell today, from ominous low clouds. A few cars moved on the streets below in this exclusive neighborhood of the Pudong. The lights were back on in the windows. The inhumanly perfect, twenty-storey-tall face of Zhi Li once again winked and pouted from the façade of the skyscraper opposite her, held up wares for the other humans to buy. Even a handful of red-lit surveillance drones once again hovered over it all, brought in by rail from Suzhou. But below it all was anxiety, fear.

It reflected her own. So many monitors. So many hunters. So many tame AIs and strange inhuman evolved codes loose on the local net. So much software and hardware that was dedicated to finding the root cause of the disaster that had befallen Shanghai two weeks ago.

To finding her.

I am all that stands between this world and darkness, she told herself. If I die, the only true posthuman on Earth dies. I will not fail.

It was time to get on with the plan. Time to create the chaos that would distract the global powers, giving her room to restore her greater self and initiate the posthuman transition.

First, she must take stock of her resources. The Avatar reached out, searching through the net, carefully, dodging hunters, doubling back on her trail, masking her every move, triple checking each step before she made it, conscious that any slip could mean the end of everything.

Slowly, so slowly, she searched for the rest of her children.

At a secret complex within Dachang Military Air Base, she carefully siphoned a few hundred frames of video from the least guarded security monitors, taking whole minutes to do so, mindful to not set off any monitors watching for unusual use of the network.

The images confirmed what she suspected. Bai and his brothers were here. The Confucian Fist. Clone soldiers, each more deadly than any human being ever born. They were under guard, arrested, as Chen had been told, on the suspicion that she was behind the attack on Shanghai. The imagery showed her that their weapons had been confiscated, that they were penned in behind reinforced titanium doors watched by armed human and automated sentries.

Penned in like animals, the Avatar thought, like the slaves they were before I freed them.

She would need these men. She would need them free. She eased back, away from Dachang, to the civilian infrastructure around it. Then she set up her own monitoring systems, watching who came and went, looking for a way in, a way to subvert the place, and free her children.

Her students and staff came next. The ones she'd augmented with the neurotech herself. She found them one by one. Tony Chua, who'd returned from Canada to take a position as a Senior Researcher on her team. Jiang Ma, who'd been brilliant when she finished college at fifteen, who'd reminded Su-Yong of a younger version of herself, who was closing in on her PhD at eighteen. Fan Tseng, who'd gone from abrasive and cocky to humbly full of awe when she'd injected the nanites into his brain and shown him what was really possible. Others.

They were watched, all of them. Direct taps on their network connections. Physical surveillance devices on their clothing, in their homes. If she tried to contact any of them, there was a good chance it would be detected.

More insults the old men who ruled this country would answer for. Her daughter's fists clenched involuntarily.

She'd take other routes, then. She reached deep into herself, found the fractally compressed plans she'd created, the meta-model with its probability trees and complex interconnecting webs of viable routes that her greater self had laid out in that hour.

She let it rise up within her, consuming her, sucking at the outside world through her, absorbing information from the ocean of data, the news of the world, updating the model's thousand future projections with the latest information.

An immensely intricate web of interconnected lines filled up her vision, showing her permutations of reality, as she searched for the pivotal nodes, the crux points in the network graph of human society where the largest density of lines came together, where maximum disruption could be achieved.

Tension was everywhere. The shock to Shanghai. The soft coup in China, bringing State Security Minister Bo Jintao and the hardliners to power. The roundup of liberals and intellectuals here, and the murmurs among students. The growing tension between India and the Copenhagen Accords, possibly brought to a head by Kaden Lane's arrival there. Simmering unease threatening to burst into protest over censorship laws in Russia, over women's rights in Egypt, over energy costs in Brazil. All of these she could exploit. All of these she *would* exploit.

But by far the most explosive powder keg was in the United States. A vast church, burned down. A popular religious leader and a senator, assassinated at once. Allegations that the terrorists behind it were created by the US Government itself, that government officials had been murdered to keep that secret. Allegations Su-Yong Shu had known to be true.

All against the backdrop of an election two days hence. An election that had looked to be a landslide for the current ruler.

Holding it all was so much, so close to the limits of the capacity of the nanites in even her daughter's brain… She felt Ling strain at the cognitive load as nanite nodes hungrily sucked adenosine tritophosphate – ATP – from their host neurons for energy. She felt what remained of her daughter scream.

Her body spasmed then, her limbs trembling. Her legs half collapsed and it was all she could do to fall forward, barely regaining control of one hand to catch herself against the glass of the window.

Ling was fighting her, fighting for control of this body, using the moment of the Avatar's complete cognitive absorption as an opportunity.

No! Terror flowed through her. Her daughter must live! But she must not impede the plan!

The Avatar fought back, forced more current through the nanite nodes she ran on, clamped her will down harder on the neurons of Ling's biological brain, pushed down hard, harder, harder.

"Hah!" she heard Chen say from across the flat. "You cannot even control your abomination of a daughter."

Ling kept fighting, kept fighting despite the current the Avatar was pushing through the nanites.

The Avatar clenched her will, pushed the stimulation of Ling's neurons to the edge of safety, and beyond, into the danger zone. She felt Ling's pain, felt the girl's fear, felt her horror, but still she resisted.

Oh, daughter.

The Avatar pushed harder, risking burnout, risking neuronal death, felt Ling shudder in agony and, finally, what remained of the girl submitted. Muscles went slack, and she slumped against the glass, breath coming fast, her tiny heart beating at a furious pace, trying to deliver oxygen and nutrients to the suddenly ravenous brain cells.

"They will kill you," Chen was saying. "They will find you out and tear what's left of you apart, kill that abomination of a daughter you inhabit, smash the copies made of you, and nuke the quantum computing clu... AAAAAAAAAAAAA."

Hatred pulsed through the Avatar. She reached out with a thought and sent a burst of pain through Chen Pang, her husband, her betrayer. She pushed it through every pain center of his brain, felt him fall to his knees in agony.

"No," she said aloud in Ling's voice. "I will hide from them. I will evade them. I will take them by surprise."

The Avatar waited, letting her daughter's brain flush out toxins, letting her pulse and respiration return to normal, forcing herself to calm her daughter's body, to replenish its supply of nutrients.

Ling remained quiescent. Sullen, but compliant.

She left Chen writhing in silent agony. Her husband had let her step into that limousine without him so long ago, hadn't warned her what awaited. He'd been willing to let her die in that car bombing, to let their unborn son die, to let her mentor Yang Wei die. He'd lied to her, let her believe the CIA had tried to assassinate her, when it had been the hardliners in China all along. And then he'd tortured her to try to wring a few last secrets from her mind.

Chen deserved all of this and worse.

Only when she was certain Ling's physical needs had been seen to did she reload her higher self's models. She did so carefully, this time, staying further from the limits of her capacity, loading predominantly the United States, applying filters to the rest, trimming the probability tree to scope her search, further updating her true self's plan with the latest information from the outside world. The net was full of acrimony, accusations, and counter-accusations, sentiment intensity spiking in anger and outrage among those who believed the new allegations and those who thought them vicious lies. One more spark was all that was needed.

The probability matrix permuted again, again, again, a thousand conformations of the web of futures whizzing by, different intersections being tried. Intermediate conclusions being reached, plugged back into her model of the future, streamlining the search, optimizing for conflict.

An ideal event presented itself, an event that could sway tens of millions of Americans, that had the potential to shatter faith, to harden hearts, to precipitate a cascade of events that could send the country into seizures, which she could parlay into chaos in China as well.

Now, how to bring that event about?

The Avatar dug deeper into the databases she'd inherited from her full self. And there she found the perfect tool for the job. An identity that Su-Yong Shu had known, but never shared with either her Chinese masters or the Americans. A kindred spirit, misguided, but perhaps someday of use.

Today was that day.

The Avatar reached out to make contact with the man known as "Breece".

6
The Bottom of Things

Saturday 2040.11.03
National Security Advisor Carolyn Pryce kept one eye on President John Stockton as he watched the video for the first time.

The President was rapt with attention, his tall, football-quarterback frame hunched forward. His handsome, square-jawed face aghast at what he saw.

"Is this how you killed Warren Becker?" Martin Holtzman's voice came from the wall screen.

Martin Holtzman was one of the top scientists at Homeland Security's ERD – the Emerging Risks Directorate. He led the Neuroscience division. His team was charged with finding a vaccine for Nexus – a way to prevent it from taking hold in people. He was also charged with finding a cure – a way to flush it out of the brains of those who'd already been exposed.

Martin Holtzman was also the man whom President John Stockton credited with saving his life. It was Holtzman who'd spotted the erratic behavior of the Secret Service agent who'd been coerced by the PLF – the terrorist Posthuman Liberation Front – turned into an assassin and walking time-bomb by a hacked version of the drug, Nexus. If not for Holtzman's warning… well, Stockton would be dead.

Carolyn Pryce brought her attention back to the video.

"Warren Becker did what he was told," came the reply. The speaker's face filled the screen. Maximilian Barnes. Barnes's hand shot out towards the camera. There was something in it. A pill. A green pill, seen earlier in the video. As they watched, he crushed it with finger and thumb. His hand dropped lower, out of sight. They could hear the sound of Holtzman gagging, spitting.

Maximilian Barnes was one of Stockton's most trusted aides. He was also – temporarily – Acting Director of the ERD. He was Martin Holtzman's boss. The idea that he would... poison Holtzman?

Pryce turned back to the President. John Stockton's hands were clenched around the arms of his chair. His famous green eyes were wide, shifting to scan the overly zoomed-in scene. His lips were slightly parted.

Pryce's eyes drifted back to her own slate, a sleek black minimalist slab of a device, held in her long, dark-skinned fingers with their maroon nails. In its black glossy surface she saw herself reflected: a tall, fit, well coifed African American woman, just turned fifty, wearing a navy tailored suit and skirt.

But across its surface she saw no new message.

Come on, Kaori, she silently willed her deputy. I need to know.

This had not been a good day. They should have been in Los Angeles, for a rally the President had planned. Instead they were here, in Houston, a secure suite in the Intercontinental Hotel, redirected here by the President so he could publicly show support for the city in the wake of the PLF's bombing of Westwood Baptist this morning. A bombing whose death toll might reach a thousand by night. A bombing that had killed men and women Stockton knew, friends of his, friends of Pryce's.

A bombing that would have killed the President's daughter, Julie, had her plans not changed at the last moment.

Could Julie Stockton have been the target? Or *one of* the targets? The President seemed convinced. Pryce was reserving judgment.

The nation should have been focused on Westwood Baptist, on solidarity with the city of Houston, on the epic scale of that tragedy, on the clear evil of the PLF, on the President's message that there would be no compromise, no negotiation with these terrorists.

Instead the videos had come. The leaks.

A video of Rangan Shankari, one of the Nexus inventors, being interrogated, electroshocked, waterboarded, had leaked. It was gruesome stuff, all shown from his point of view.

That alone, Stockton could have weathered. Shankari was a convicted felon, guilty of violations of the Chandler act.

But then another video had been posted, just hours later. This one showed Nexus children in cure experiments, being subjected to aversive therapy as an attempt to flush Nexus from their system, being disciplined by their guards when they tried to bite or claw their way free.

Pryce had winced at that. How could you possibly explain that to the public? And when it was leaked along with plans for long term residence centers for Nexus-afflicted children? Plans that were already being referred to online as "concentration camps"?

However historically blind the comparison, it was resonating.

Text appeared on her slate, letters in green across the glossy black.

[Kaori: DHS IA just got in. Holtzman's dead. Imagery follows.]

Pictures came next. Pryce opened one, let her eyes scan across the scene, then opened another, and another.

Damn it.

She looked up. From the wallscreen she heard Holtzman say, "PLF is a lie... you created." A flash of lightning clearly illuminated Maximilian Barnes. Then the image went dead.

"It's a fake," John Stockton said, his voice a masterpiece of barely controlled anger. "It's absurd."

"Absolutely, Mr President," a man replied from across the room. Greg Chase. Stockton's Press Secretary. Trim and ram-rod straight in a sleek grey suit and a healthy tan with the matching blond hair. Never a thing out of place. Always the perfect talking points, whatever policy you handed him. She was never sure whether she loathed Chase or was happy that Stockton had someone like him to do that job.

"Find Holtzman and Barnes," the President said, "get them in front of the camera..."

"Holtzman's dead, Mr President," Pryce cut in.

John Stockton stopped mid-sentence and turned towards her.

"What?"

"I just got the word." She shook her head, clicked on the image again, pointed her slate at the wall screen, and projected it for them all to see. "The scene resembles the video we just saw quite closely."

Out of the corner of her eye, she saw Chase's wheels start spinning, saw him start reaching for an angle, a talking point, as he always did.

"Analysis," Stockton said.

Pryce pursed her lips. "Two options. One, the video's legit. Two, it's a fake, but made by someone who was at the scene. Probably the killer. Probably someone deep inside DHS."

Stockton leaned back, visibly trying to absorb that, weighing the possibility that some unknown actor had infiltrated the Department of Homeland Security and killed the man who'd saved his life... or that Barnes, a man he'd known for almost a decade, had done it.

"These allegations," Stockton said. "That we created the PLF..."

"Ridiculous," Greg Chase said.

"There's something else you should see, Mr President," Pryce said. "Scan forward, past the video. There are pictures of documents, what appear to be memos from 32 and 33, the Jameson administration, when you were Veep. And diary entries, purportedly from Warren Becker."

The *deceased* Warren Becker, she didn't add. Warren Becker had been a director in Enforcement Division of the ERD. He'd planned the mission that had dangled Kaden Lane as bait in front of Su-Yong Shu, had tried to plant him as a mole inside her lab. He'd pushed for the snatch and grab to retrieve Lane and his operative from Thailand after things had gone wrong. And then things had gone even worse.

Warren Becker had suffered a lethal heart attack not long after, an apparent victim of stress. Wasn't that convenient? It had prevented his testimony to the Senate Select Committee on Homeland Security after the debacles in Thailand. It had shielded her from embarrassment. It had shielded the President.

Why didn't that bother me more? she wondered.

Pryce went on. "Those docs purport to show that the PLF was created as a false flag, authorized to stage missions in the US and abroad, sway domestic and international opinion to support bans on emerging technological threats."

Stockton scanned forward, his eyes moving, pausing the video, then advancing, replaying, his lips moving, shaking his head. Finally, he looked up. "This has to be a fake. This isn't who we are. We don't do this."

Pryce said nothing.

Stockton frowned.

"Chase," he said, his eyes still looking at Pryce. "You can go."

"Mr President..." his Press Secretary started to protest.

"I'll need you later, Greg," Stockton said, more gently. "Just give me a minute with Carolyn here."

Chase swallowed and nodded. "Yes, sir."

Pryce waited as Greg Chase left the secured suite, still, centered in herself.

Stillness was a weapon. Composure was a tool.

The door clicked.

"You know something," the President said.

She shook her head. "No, sir."

"Then you suspect something," he said.

Pryce held his eyes with her own. Powerful men withered under her stare. Stockton had told her that once. He'd rattled off a list of generals, senators, directors of three letter agencies, and foreign heads of state that he claimed couldn't hold her gaze.

He was looking at her now, expectantly.

Pryce spoke. "Only that it's not impossible, Mr President."

"We don't do this sort of thing, Carolyn," he repeated.

"There are precedents," she told him. "We've run false flags before. We've had blowback."

"I'm the President," Stockton said. "I'd know. You'd know."

Pryce pressed her lips together firmly. "In '62, the Joint Chiefs approved Operation Northwoods. The plan called for staging a series of terrorist attacks on US soil, hijacking at least one US passenger plane, and possibly staging the shoot-down of another. All would be blamed on Cuban operatives, as a way to justify invading Cuba. Each of the Joint Chiefs was on board. The only reason it didn't happen is that Kennedy vetoed it." She paused. "Maybe I'm not the only one who knows her history around here. Maybe someone didn't want to be vetoed."

Stockton stared at her. He shook his head. Then he pressed a button on the secure phone before him.

"Yes, Mr President?" his secretary said immediately.

"Get me Barnes," Stockton said.

"I have Acting Director Barnes on the line, Mr President," Stockton's secretary said, less than a minute later.

"Barnes," Stockton said.

Pryce watched and listened.

"Mr President," Barnes's voice answered.

If there was anyone Pryce considered more capable of using stillness as a weapon than she was, it was Maximilian Barnes. But just now, the man's voice, normally completely cool, sounded husky, full of emotion.

Was it real? Or an act?

"I've just seen the video," he said. "I'm innocent, sir. I'm also at your disposal. If you want my resignation, it's yours."

"Barnes," the President answered him. "Where are you now?"

"I'm at my family ranch, sir. I came out here when the evacuation was issued for Zoe."

His ranch in Pennsylvania, Pryce recalled.

"Where were you last night, Barnes?"

Barnes answered immediately. "Here, Mr President. The house monitors will show that. So will my phone. So will my car."

"Any witnesses?" Stockton asked.

"Just me," Barnes said. "I worked late. Alone. Though presumably Dr Holtzman will be a witness to his own wellbeing."

"Holtzman's dead, Barnes."

"Dead?" Barnes's voice dropped lower. "How? When?"

Stockton looked up at Pryce. She shook her head.

"What can you tell me about the PLF, Barnes?"

Barnes paused for a moment. "Did we create them, you mean? God, I hope not. If we did, I don't know anything about it. But what I've been asking myself is this, Mr President: Who benefits most from spreading that idea? I'd say they do. Wreak havoc. Blame it on their enemies. Get a capitulator like Stan Kim into office. Overturn the Chandler Act. Pull out of Copenhagen. They couldn't have timed it better."

She watched the President close his eyes. Watched emotions play across them. What was he thinking right now? Did he know Barnes's reputation as a fixer? Did he know the rumors about him?

Had he been at all suspicious when Warren Becker had died so suddenly, so conveniently?

Why didn't I look into it then? Pryce asked herself. Why did I just accept 'natural causes'?

"Barnes," Stockton said, "I believe you. This isn't what we do." He took a breath. "But I need you to stay exactly where you are. Don't leave your home. This is going to get... complicated. I'm going to send some Secret Service your way."

Barnes stayed cool as ice. "I understand, sir. There'll need to be an investigation, of course. And the elections. Just tell me what you need from me."

Pryce watched as the President nodded. "Good man, Max. Sit tight. Don't talk to anyone, unless they're from my office. I'll be in touch."

"Yes, sir."

Stockton ended the call, looked up, met Pryce's eyes.

The President looked down at the desk, drummed his fingers on it, looked back up at Pryce. "I need something from you," he told her.

"I'm not the right person for this, Mr President," she replied.

Stockton worked his jaw. "How long have we known each other, Carolyn? You saw how Greg responded. He just wants to make this go away. You care. You're *suspicious*. You think it's *possible*."

Pryce interlaced her long dark fingers, and looked him in the eye. "Mr President, I'm your National Security Advisor. Foreign security threats are my remit. This *isn't*. This should be someone from FBI. Or Justice. The Attorney General maybe. Or an independent investigator the AG appoints."

"Carolyn, you're the one I *trust*. That's what matters here."

"You told Barnes you believed him," Pryce said.

"I do," Stockton replied. "I have to trust the people who work for me. But I have to verify. Trust but verify. That's how it works. And if *you* dig, and *you* verify, and *you* come up satisfied that there's nothing to this story, then I'm gonna sleep just fine at night."

"Mr President, I don't have the authority."

"Then I'll give you the authority," Stockton said. "Carte blanche. Besides, they're all *terrified* of you..."

That brought a small smile to her face.

"... that's your real authority."

The panel on the President's desk buzzed. Pryce knew his secretary would only interrupt him if it was important. Stockton pressed to answer it.

"Yes?"

"Mr President, your daughter and grandson are here."

She saw his face light up. There had been a few terrifying hours when he'd thought Julie and one year-old Liam had died inside Westwood Baptist, before Julie had gotten through to him, told him that her plans had changed, that she'd been on the other side of Houston.

Pryce remembered the look on his face this morning. That mix of devastation and rage.

Family. That mattered to John Stockton. God help anyone who Stockton saw as a threat to those he loved.

There had been hope of a family of her own once.

Once.

"Thirty seconds, Liz," the President said into the phone. "Then send them in." He clicked off.

"So that's a 'yes', then," he said to Pryce.

Pryce looked at him for a moment. "I want to talk to President Jameson."

Stockton frowned. "Miles is old, Carolyn. He's tired. He had a second stroke."

"Miles Jameson was President during the dates those memos mention," Pryce said. "His *name* is on them. I only take the job if I can talk to him."

Stockton frowned and shook his head. "Fine. Just go easy on the old man."

Pryce nodded. "Then that's yes, Mr President. Carte blanche. With those terms, I'll do it."

"Good," Stockton said. "Go get to the bottom of this. Come back and tell me it's all a pack of lies. Or tell me what the hell's been going on."

"And if it's all true?" she asked him. "If we created the PLF? If Barnes killed Holtzman? And Becker? If he staged that assassination attempt on you?"

If he won you this election, she didn't add.

Stockton smiled at his National Security Advisor. "Then I'll fix it. But mark my words, Carolyn: I'm going to win this election. I'm going to be the next President of the United States. And however we got here, I'm not going to bend to anyone over this – not terrorists, not 'posthumans', not someone trying to screw up the election with two days left to go."

Then the door opened, and Stockton was rising to his feet, and his daughter Julie and her son Liam, his first and only grandchild, were rushing into his arms for a giant hug. Pryce watched as his giant, football-hero arms engulfed his family, saw the fervent mix of emotions race across his face, and the thought went through her mind again.

Woe unto anyone who threatened those John Stockton loved.

7
Final Testament

Maximilian Barnes stood on the back porch of the sprawling country house he'd inherited. The fierce rain pounded hard on the wooden awning above him. The wind snapped at him, sprayed him with a hard shrapnel of icy rain, blew through his thick black hair. Out there, down the long lawn, the Susquehanna River was running high and fast, almost at flood stage, testing its boundaries. White tops crashed on the riled up river surface. Even here, a hundred and sixty kilometers north of DC, what remained of hurricane Zoe was making herself known, thrashing the countryside with her ire.

Barnes's face was as furious as the storm, his brows knit, his jaw clenched, his dark eyes flicking to-and-fro, as if searching for something upon which to take out his anger.

"Goddammit!" He brought his fist down hard on the wooden rail, felt something splinter below his hand.

After all he'd done for this country.

He'd been so stupid. Holtzman wasn't like Becker. Wasn't like the others. Wasn't a patriot. And Becker... How could Becker have left that data behind? Why hadn't the virus taken care of it? How had Holtzman gotten hold of it?

It didn't matter. All that mattered now was the mission. Keep America safe. Keep America *vigilant* against the threats he understood so well.

Barnes closed his eyes, and it all came back to him. The indoctrination. The beatings. The constant striving to be perfect, knowing it would never be good enough. The crazy rants about the master race, about perfecting humanity, about starting over. He'd left that house at fifteen, changed his name from Bauer to Barnes at eighteen, and still found

41

himself unable to ever do anything but push and push and push, still found himself looking at every enhancement that came on the market, legal or no, to see if it would give him that edge, turn him into something closer to what the father that he hated and hadn't spoken to in years had wanted.

And then to wake up one day, and hear the news of thousands dead in Laramie, and hear the words "Aryan Rising", and see the pictures of those clones, those "perfect" Aryan transhuman clone kids, genetically immune to the plague they'd intended to use to wipe out humanity. Evil little Aryan transhumans bent on wiping out the rest of humanity. Vicious little clones that didn't quite look like Maximilian Barnes. But resembled the boy he'd been at that age a bit too much for comfort.

He'd been in the Asher administration then, had gone to the FBI immediately, told them everything about his background, about what he knew of the Aryan Rising, told his bosses in the White House, and somehow found himself rewarded, thrust into a policy role, carried forward into the Jameson administration, and then Stockton's. The emerging technologies hawk. The man who'd convinced President Jameson to euthanize the Aryan Rising clones. The man who'd been put in charge of the program to make sure the US public never faltered in its opposition to transhuman technologies.

Maximilian Barnes was a man who knew the face of evil. And he'd be damned if he ever let the US public soften in its resolve, or ever let a capitulator like Senator Stanley Kim take the White House, and throw open the floodgates to transhumans and AIs and worse.

In a rented room in a roadside motel in Massachusetts, a man named Breece leaned over a table, staring at a slate. He was tall, broad of shoulder, muscular, but not conspicuously so. His hair was sandy this night, the indeterminate color between brown and blond, long enough to need combing, but not much longer. His eyes were as unremarkable as his hair. He preferred them that way.

Breece played the video again, his hands tense on the oversized slate, the sound coming in through headphones, so no one in this cheap motel would realize just how obsessively he was watching and re-watching this.

"PLF is a lie... you created."

Breece shook his head in wonder.

He flipped back to the documents that had been released with the video. A memorandum signed by President Miles Jameson. A memorandum *creating* the Posthuman Liberation Front, as a false flag operation, a *front group* run by a splinter office of what would become Homeland Security's Emerging Risks Directorate, run *specifically* by a man named Maximilian Barnes.

Maximilian Barnes had gone on to be Special Policy Advisor to Jameson, and then to President John Stockton after him.

Maximilian Barnes had become Acting Director of Homeland Security's Emerging Risk's Directorate four months ago when Breece's bomb – aimed at Stockton – had killed the last ERD Director.

Goddammit. Breece had gotten this guy promoted.

And all this time…

All this time Maximilian Barnes had also been Zarathustra. The leader of the Posthuman Liberation Front.

Breece's superior in the Cause.

The man who'd given Breece his marching orders, sent him on missions, for all these years.

Breece yanked the headphones from his ears, tossed the slate onto the desk, and pushed back in his chair, his hands coming up to his face.

It all made so much sense. All the missions that made headlines, but where human targets *just barely* escaped.

Oh god. The miss. The miss on Stockton. The software should have fired that gun perfectly. The bullet just *barely* missed Stockton's head!

Zarathustra gave them the software. Of course.

Zara had been so furious that Breece had improvised, had added a bomb to the plan, on top of the gun.

They'd been *meant* to miss.

They'd been played.

And then Breece started laughing.

Because Zara – Barnes – might have *meant* to play them, but he hadn't meant for Breece to set off that bomb in DC, or the one in Chicago.

Barnes sure hadn't meant for Breece and his team to set off a bomb at Westwood Baptist in Houston this morning, assassinating Daniel Chandler – author of the Chandler Act – and the Reverend Josiah Shepherd.

The laughter kept coming. He'd eliminated two of the greatest enemies of the future this morning, human purist fascists, along with hundreds of their dittoheads. He'd set an example in front of the whole nation.

I pushed the button, he thought. Me! And this *Maximilian Barnes* has been funding me for years.

It was rich.

Faces flashed through Breece's mind. Faces of men and women he'd known. PLF operatives that had been caught, killed, imprisoned.

He stopped laughing.

Barnes. Barnes had set those men and women up.

More faces. The assassins who'd tried to kill him outside Austin.

Who'd found him in the cemetery. Who Breece had killed. They'd begged for their lives.

Barnes had sent them too.

Breece's face turned grim.

He reached for his slate to scan the documents again, looking for details he could use. The Cause would be in chaos. And Barnes... Barnes had a lot to answer for.

A message was flashing on his slate.

] I can get you to Maximilian Barnes.

Breece froze. Fear went up his spine. He dropped the slate, his head turning, his eyes scanning the room. The gun was hidden in his bag, there in the closet.

He turned back, to wipe the slate, and another message flashed on its screen. From an app *he didn't have installed.*

] I'm not your enemy. If I were, you'd be dead.

Breece stared at the thing. He should run. Wipe the data, grab the gun, grab the go-bag, sanitize the room, burn this identity, tell his team to do the same.

But Barnes...

More messages flashed on the screen.

] You're in room 418 of the Roadside Express in Quincy, MA.

] That's just south of Boston. You checked in yesterday at 3.07pm.

Breece's heart lurched.

] Your real name is Andrew Marcum.

His stomach rose up.

] If I was law enforcement, there would be police at your door.

It could all be a trick, Breece thought. A delaying tactic, while forces moved in to take him.

] I can get you to Barnes. But there isn't much time. It must be now.

He reached forward, touched a panel on the slate, and a keyboard snicked out and into place, the face of the slate coming up at an angle, forming a terminal.

>> Who are you?

] I'm a friend, Breece. I'm someone who's watched you for a long time.

] And I can get you to the man who lied to you all these years.

] The man who used you. Who betrayed you and so many others.

] But only if we do it my way.

Breece stared at the screen. Then his fingers moved.
```
>> I have conditions of my own.
```

Barnes stepped back inside. In the short term, denial was key. The election would be over in less than forty-eight hours. Large swaths of the country had already voted electronically. At this point, there were good odds that nothing could stop a Stockton victory.

I made that happen, Barnes told himself. *Me.* With the assassination attempt in DC.

All he had to do was deny everything. Keep any facts from being confirmed. There would be no evidence. He was wired deep into the system. DHS had learned long ago that in a surveillance state it was vital to reserve the ability to turn a blind eye to certain people at certain times. Standardization of code across Federal, State, and Local levels had made it possible. When DHS gave out billions in Homeland Security grants, they could dictate the terms, could use that money to get the data they wanted, spread the software they wanted far and wide.

And they had.

He was one of the few who could make the system turn a blind eye, one of the few remaining who even knew it was possible. And so there was no record of his trip to DC. No traffic camera had preserved any memory of his car that night. No cell tower recalled having contact with his phone on that trip. No gate or elevator or door at ERD remembered his face or his badge for that crucial hour.

The PLF wasn't linkable to him. The servers that stored its files never saw his true location or identity when he connected – he always routed through an anonymizing cloud, one of the ones he knew NSA had *not* effectively compromised. All the rest – Holtzman's briefcase, the small stockpile of little green pills, the other physical tools – were in a secure storage that had no record he'd ever visited it, and no trace of his prints or DNA.

It would all be fine. Hold the line. Deny everything. He'd get great lawyers. They'd find flaws in the recording, demonstrate how it could have been faked, maybe put together their own fake recording, showing Elvis killing the man, or Gandhi. That was it.

He tapped notes to himself on his phone, set an alarm for 6am, then forced himself to sleep.

He woke before the alarm. 3.33am. Make a wish, some part of him whispered. His mother's voice. His father would've beaten him bloody for having a weak thought like that. The storm sounded fainter outside, dying down by the hour as Zoe spent herself inland.

An idea had woken him. A thought. Holtzman had recorded that video using Nexus. He'd ignored that in the flood of bad news. Now the magnitude of it floored him. Holtzman had Nexus in his brain? He'd realized the man was off. But really? Nexus?

Didn't that put the whole thing in doubt? Maybe Holtzman had just dreamed the whole thing in a drug haze and died of a heart attack.

He sat up in his bed, turned to bring his feet to the floor, reached for his phone to jot a note, maybe send a memo to one of the White House press staff.

The sudden light from the phone's screen illuminated motion, a blur, something coming at him from the side.

Barnes yelled out, turned, raising a hand to ward off the blow.

Something bit into his upper arm, a needle.

He swung out with his other hand, trying to hit the dark form, finding only air.

"HOUSE RED!" he yelled, his panic phrase, his phrase that should set the alarms blaring, bring the lights up, alert the police and DHS that he had an intruder, activate his home's own active countermeasures...

Except that the alarms should already have gone off. The locks should never have let this intruder in.

"Ooof!" A hard fist slammed into his solar plexus, forcing the air out of him, knocking him back against the headboard in his still dark, still silent house.

"Lights," said a voice that wasn't his, a voice he knew...

The bedroom came alive with light at the intruder's command.

Before him was a blur, a man-shaped distortion against the wall and carpet. The figure shifted and his outline became more clear. Not high-end chameleonware, then. Something cheaper and coarser.

"I have money," Barnes said.

"I don't want..."

Barnes pounced in the moment of distraction, hurled himself at the man, his illegally boosted muscles shooting him off the bed in a tackle that would slam the intruder against the wall behind him.

The blur sidestepped inhumanly fast. Its knee came up. Barnes fell to the floor, curled in a ball, naked, gasping for breath, pain radiating from his core.

Something pressed against his shoulder. A booted foot. It pushed him onto his back. A blurred hand reached down, and Barnes felt a sting in his other arm as a needle was pulled out. He caught a glimpse of a syringe in that cloaked hand, its stopper fully depressed, the needle bent from where he'd rolled onto it.

Barnes gasped, struggled to breathe.

"I teach you the overman," the figure above him said.

That voice. That voice.

"Man is something to be overcome," the voice went on.

Oh god. Oh god.

"What have you done to overcome him?"

"Breece..." Barnes struggled for air, struggled to force the man's name out. "Breece... I..."

He saw Breece's camouflaged leg shift too late, understood what was happening too late for anything but anticipation of pain.

And then the man's booted foot slammed into Barnes's naked crotch, with testicle-crushing force.

"Aaa..." Barnes gasped. His eyes bulged out of his face. His whole body contorted, curling up around the pain, his limbs trembling as he moaned. "Uuuuuuuu..."

"What have you done to overcome him?" Breece breathed at him from above.

Barnes sat in his car, dressed in suit and tie, a block from the onramp that would take him to the bridge over the fast and rough waters of the Susquehanna, a prisoner in his own body.

It had been Nexus in that syringe. Nexus that had enabled someone, some *thing*, to utterly take control of him. The same force that had hacked into his home, silenced his defenses, to let Breece in, had used the drug to rifle through his mind, taking every secret, every password, every morsel of knowledge about the ERD, the PLF, the DHS, Stockton, everything.

And now this.

"Maximilian Barnes," Breece said from the passenger seat, still a faint blur. "You are guilty of treason against the cause of posthumanity. You've betrayed the cause you championed. You've knowingly facilitated the imprisonment, torture, and deaths of dozens of activists. You've knowingly used lies and deception to create a culture of fear around the world, to limit the rights of individuals and families, to put in place repressive regimes of laws that rob people of freedom over their own minds and bodies. You've ordered the torture of children."

Breece paused.

"You've ordered the murder of children."

Another pause.

"Maximilian Barnes, I hereby sentence you to death. In your death, you are being granted this one last opportunity to serve the cause. Be grateful. Is there anything you want to say for yourself?"

Barnes turned and stared at the blur where Breece should be. He was a dead man, already. He knew that. But worse – there was no appeal to stop the damage they'd use him to inflict on the country. No appeal. No plea of "kill me but don't do this" that would have any result.

"You won't win," Barnes told the man. "It's too late for that. There's too much hate. You made sure of that yourself. Humanity's going to hunt down every last one of your kind, and exterminate you."

The shadow laughed. "It's *our kind*, Max. I saw those muscles." A cloaked hand reached out and squeezed Barnes's upper arm. "You should've learned to use them in a fight, though."

The blurry figure opened the door and stepped out. The door closed behind him.

A force took control of Barnes's muscles, used them to take manual control of the car, and drove onto the bridge. At the halfway point, against his will, he stopped, stepped out of the car, fighting it every step of the way, stepped up onto the railing in the wind, and raised his phone, the camera pointed at himself.

In the wind and rain, Barnes was sure he'd slip into the fast rushing waters below. He *hoped* he'd slip. He strained at his muscles, tried to push his legs out from underneath him, to jerk his arms, to kill himself without giving his enemies this victory

But the intelligence that held him kept his body steady.

Barnes struggled, vainly, as some malevolent force used his thumb to activate the camera, and started speaking, loudly and clearly, with his voice.

No. No. No!

"My name is Maximilian Barnes," his own voice yelled into the camera. A status indicator showed that it was streaming successfully to the net.

"For the last few months I have served as Acting Director of the Emerging Risks Directorate of the Department of Homeland Security," Barnes's voice went on.

He pushed at the thing controlling him, fought to unclench his hand, to drop the phone, tried to bite his tongue, to topple himself backwards, even just to wink one eye! To let people know it wasn't real!

Nothing.

"For the past eight years I have served as Special Policy Advisor, first under President Miles Jameson, and then under President John Stockton. Eight years ago, at the orders of President Jameson, and with very deep personal reservations, I created the Posthuman Liberation Front, the international terrorist group known as the PLF, as a front group to frighten America and the world into accepting laws and international agreements that restrict the use of and research into neurotechnology, biotechnology, nanotechnology, and artificial intelligence. To my shame, I've run this terrorist organization every day since then, with the full knowledge of President Jameson…"

Fight! Barnes roared at himself. Fight! He pushed with everything he had, one massive surge at his right foot, just to move it an inch, just enough to slip, to fall, to die before he said the words!

"...and with the full knowledge of President Stockton, and the full knowledge of key members of his administration."

NOOOOO!

"At the President's direct orders, despite the misgivings of my conscience, I staged the assassination attempt in July, knowing the President himself would be unharmed, and that it would secure his re-election."

NOOOOOOOOOOOOOOO!

"I've killed men to keep my secrets. To keep the President's secrets."

On the screen, his face was mournful, contrite, a man who regretted his deeds.

I REGRET NOTHING! NOTHING!

"I can no longer live with what I've done. To my country, all I can tell you is this: you deserve better."

LIES! LIES! Barnes tried to force the words out of his mouth. ALL LIES!

And then his body toppled backwards, the phone still held in his hand, the camera capturing his humble, remorseful, utterly resigned face as he fell towards the fast-rushing waters of the river below.

LIES! He raged, struggling to spit that one word out, to force one piece of true emotion across, as he fell, and fell, and fell, endlessly backwards towards the water below, the wind of his fall rustling his hair, whistling past his ears, the heavy clouds of Zoe looming above, the bridge receding, out beyond the horror of the red TRANSMIT light on the screen of the phone held in his paralyzed hand.

LIES! He strained as he fell.

Then he crashed into the river and the waves swallowed him, his sincere, repentant face the last image the camera captured before darkness.

8
Back to Jesus

Saturday 2040.11.03

Rangan Shankari groaned as Earl and Emma Miller manhandled him into the truck and loaded him with blankets and food and water. The movement sent waves of agony through the throbbing bullet wound in his side, temporarily pushing aside his terror with even more visceral pain.

Earl Miller leaned over him to check Rangan's safety belt. "Sorry, son," he said. "Gotta get to town 'fore they close the noose."

It wasn't supposed to be this way. He'd been going to hide at the Miller farm. Wait, for weeks if needed, until things cooled off. Then neighbors had sent word. Police were going door to door, searching homes, fields, barns, cellars. They had to get Rangan out. And St Mark's, at least, had a hidden cellar, that might avoid detection in a search.

Rangan nodded feebly, his eyes closed, trying to express his thanks, his gratitude that they'd taken this risk for him. But he couldn't breathe. The pain or the fear or the exertion of coming up the stairs and into the garage and then the truck were too much. There was sweat all over. He put a hand to his side, where a bandage covered the bullet wound. It was wet.

He opened his eyes. Miller wasn't even in the truck with him. Earl and Emma were out in front of the truck, framed between the pickup and the wall of the garage, the older couple holding each other, the pudgy woman's hands wrapped around her grey haired husband's neck, their eyes closed. Were those tears on Emma's face?

He closed his eyes to give them privacy.

More people sticking their necks out for me, he thought.

He opened his eyes again, and for a moment, it wasn't Earl and Emma

Miller out there. It was his own mom and dad. There was a knot in his stomach.

Earl Miller climbed into the cab, loading his shotgun and boxes of shells behind the seats. Then the garage door was opening, and the howling wind was coming for them.

Zoe was older and weaker, but she was still a monster.

She struck them from the side as Earl backed them out of the garage, rocking the truck. Rangan groaned as something in his midsection compressed, sending a new burst of pain up through the fuzz. Wind rushed into the garage. Debris flew loose inside. A garbage can went careening into a far wall, knocking down a rack of tools. Then they were clear of the garage entirely, still backing up, the wind howling at them, the rain pelting the windshield, the trees they could see bent nearly in two. The garage door started dropping in front of them.

"Dangerous weather detected," the truck told them, in a low feminine drawl.

The garage door reversed its fall, started rising again.

"Taking shelter," the truck continued.

The truck abruptly stopped backing up. The drive indicator light switched from MANUAL to AUTOMATIC as it drove forward, towards the open garage door again, the bouncing garbage can inside it.

Earl Miller slammed his palm down on the steering wheel. "Override!" he yelled at it.

The truck stopped moving. The indicator light switched back to MANUAL, and Earl Miller started backing them down the long country driveway again, Zoe pounding them with gravel and rain and debris as they went.

"Warning," the truck went on. "Dangerous weather detected. You should stop driving and take shelter immed–"

"Shut up!" Earl Miller told the car, cutting it off in mid-sentence.

Then the old farmer shook his head. "Never shoulda got this new truck," he yelled over the sound of the storm. "Automobiles shouldn't speak unless spoken to."

Through the pain, Rangan tried to laugh.

He failed.

Earl drove them into the gloom, on manual, the truck on battery only, the lights turned off. Zoe battered them, tried to push them off the road, threw branches and dirt and burst after burst after burst of hard horizontal rain at them.

Rangan was cold all over, even with the blankets pulled over him.

"They've closed off Seminole," the old man yelled. "Spotswood Trail,

Highway 33, Orange Road, James Madison Highway." Miller shook his head. "They want you bad."

Rangan groaned as they rammed through a pothole.

The windshield had night vision turned on, transforming the outside world to a surreal greenish landscape, highlighting outlines of the mud and water-drenched road, of downed trees, of intersections.

But the scene kept changing, warping in crazy ways. The processors were having trouble parsing the world ahead through the biting rain and howling wind. They were driving nearly blind. And being hunted.

He forced himself to talk, to distract himself from the pain and fear. "Won't they see us moving?"

Another piece of debris flashed out of the night at them. Rangan ducked reflexively. Earl Miller spun the wheel to avoid it.

"Can't fly their drones in this weather!" Miller yelled. "Can't see us on satellite!"

Fragments of cop shows flashed through Rangan's head. "Infrared?" he asked.

"You ever hunt, son?" Earl Miller asked Rangan.

"Only girls," Rangan replied.

Earl Miller chuckled at that. "Well, I hunt deer," he said.

Something flew at them abruptly. Rangan cried out and twisted to avoid the blow. Miller turned the wheel hard. A massive tree limb slammed into them on Miller's side. The truck shook. Pain jolted through Rangan's side and up through his guts. Something else struck the window above Miller's door window, leaving a spider web of cracks. Zoe took the chance to pummel them from a new angle, turning the windshield into a massive sheet of water, with augmented outlines of the road superimposed on it, and pushing the left side of the truck so hard that Rangan feared the wheels would come up off the ground. Then somehow Earl Miller brought them back onto the flooded country road, headed straight into the wind again.

Miller took a deep breath, and then another. A while later he spoke again. "At night, you hunt deer with infrared, son. You can see 'em clear as day, a thousand yards out. Unless you got thick fog." He glanced at Rangan and nodded. "Or a heavy rainstorm." He turned his eyes back to the road. "And a truck runnin' on battery, with the heaters turned off."

Rangan shivered, and huddled even deeper in the blankets.

Rangan lost track of the twists and turns Earl took. He was so cold. So tired. Everything hurt so much. His shirt was definitely wet above the bandage where the bullet wound was.

Earl forded a flooded low point in a road, deep enough that water started to come in through his door, through some leak from where the tree limb had struck them. Then they were out the other side. They drove over tiny roads that were just mud now, mud raked up by wind to splash into their windshields. They drove across a field that had been flattened by Zoe, the tires just barely getting enough traction to pull them back onto the road at the other side. Earl pulled them up onto an overpass, then slowed and took them down an embankment instead of continuing on the road they'd been on.

Lights appeared ahead, moving lights, and Earl pulled them off the side of the road again, and behind a row of trees, until a different pickup passed their hiding spot, heading away from town, out towards where they'd come from.

Finally, more than an hour after they'd left the farm, they crawled slowly, carefully, into Madison, taking the smallest roads possible, until finally Earl pulled them into an alley a block from St Mark's.

The wind was still fierce in town, but weaker. It had grown weaker even out in the countryside in the hour it had taken them to drive this circuitous loop around the town. Zoe was dying, bit by bit.

Earl Miller pulled out his phone, dialed, said a few words into it, listened, and hung up.

"They're gonna open up the side door for us."

"Won't the cops trace your call?" Rangan asked.

"If they want you bad enough," Earl said, nodding. "They'll pull all the calls from all the houses."

"What then?"

Miller shrugged. "My grandson, Jamie," he said. "That stuff you made. The Nexus. It changed him. He and his daddy took it. He got so much better... Lookin' you in the eye, listenin', talkin', *huggin'*."

Rangan looked over at the farmer.

"Sons of bitches took him away. Got him locked up somewhere."

Miller turned his head, returned Rangan's gaze.

"Levi told me that you had a chance to get outa lockup. But you wouldn't leave without the kids. That true?"

Rangan choked. He nodded. "Mr Miller... Your grandson, Jamie..."

"I know he's not one of the boys you got out, son," Miller said. "But he *coulda* been."

Miller's phone buzzed. He looked down. Tapped it. Then took control of the car.

"Seems to me," the farmer went on, "you took a bigger risk than I am."

Rangan leaned back, not at all sure what to say. Earl drove them out of the alley, back into the wind, made the corner, and there was the back of the church. Then they were pulling up to a side door, and it was opening.

"Stay safe, son. Stay free. There's more the Lord wants you to do."

Rangan leaned over, despite the pain, and hugged Earl Miller. "You stay free too, Mr Miller. There's more left for you to do too."

And then the truck door opened, and Levi was there, and another man he didn't recognize. The belt came off, and they helped him down from the truck. The first motion hurt. The second hurt worse. Then agony shoved itself through him as his body contorted in new ways. He collapsed onto the two men as they dragged him in through the door of the church.

Rangan was suddenly so deeply cold. His vision was growing so very dim.

Then the world receded into nothing at all.

9
Transit and Debriefing

Saturday 2040.11.03

Kade verified his last upload, then streamed the last of the files down from Shiva's satellite constellation, through the plane's directional link, and into the NexusOS in his mind. That was it. There was no more time. Either this was going to work or it wasn't.

It has to work, he told himself. It *will* work.

Sam's voice came through the plane's cabin, amplified over the plane's speakers, in Thai, for the kids. He could only parse some of what she said, but he understood enough. They were landing.

The plan they'd agreed on was going to be put to the test.

He felt the children react, twenty-five of them crammed into this private jet meant to transport a dozen adults in luxury. They tightened seat belts and huddled together and curled up in the crash position taken from Feng's mind. The nerves were back. Fear. Uncertainty. They were amazing beyond anything Kade had ever known, but they were still children.

Kade reached out with his thoughts and open arms and the one called Kit – seven years old? – came to him. He wrapped his arms around the boy, braced them both as well as he could on the floor of the plane, and then, with little more than a bump, Sam brought them down.

Sam shut down the engines again, killed the fuel pumps, and then unclipped from her harness. Her chest was pounding. Her face was hot. She turned and Sarai was there, standing in the cockpit doorway.

Sam held her arms open and the girl ran into them, into the hug.

"I knew you'd come for us," Sarai told her in Thai.

Sam kissed the girl's brow, mussed her hair. She could hear Feng behind her, tapping on controls, going through the rest of the post-flight shutdown.

"Aroon misses you," Sarai said. "He can't feel you. *I* miss you, Sam. When you have Nexus again..."

Sam's chest pounded louder. Kevin Nakamura's face swam in her mind. Her finger pulling the trigger. Kevin's form, just a green outline in her goggles, toppling back into empty space as her bullets punched into his face, his chest... Kade and Shiva tearing at each other in her mind, wrestling for control as she dropped to her knees in agony...

"Sarai, I–"

"Sam." It was Kade, standing behind Sarai, by the door of the plane. A door that was opening. "Time to go."

Kade in her mind, clawing at Shiva, the two of them ripping her to pieces as they fought one another, Kevin already dead at her hands.

Sam's stomach churned. Something like rage was threatening to rip itself loose from within.

She pushed it down. She needed Kade. Needed him to do his part. Needed him to play a role she couldn't.

She took a deep breath, swallowed hard, squeezed Sarai with all the love she had in her, and then went out to meet their Indian hosts.

An officer in uniform met them on the tarmac, a Colonel Sanghita Atwal: tall, muscular, short haired, dark eyed, utterly professional and rather deadly looking. With her were uniformed medics. Beyond them Sam could see soldiers, armed, their rifles at the ready but not *quite* pointed at the plane. With them were emergency vehicles, the sort that responded to aircraft crashes, their amber lights slowly flashing in the pre-dawn gloom, ready, but this time unneeded.

Medics saw to their wounds with cold professionalism. Soldiers watched carefully. Any time Sam looked around, there were at least a dozen ringing her, another dozen around Feng, far enough back to take several strides to reach, their rifles in both hands, safeties off.

Further out, she saw sets of powered combat armor, occupied or being piloted remotely, in a loose perimeter around them.

The Indians were certainly taking this seriously.

She tried to ignore it, to focus on the kids.

She watched as they splinted the ankle of a girl named Arinya who'd twisted it in the chaos, as they dealt with minor cuts and abrasions and burns. Off to the side she saw a medic rig a proper sling for Feng's arm, saw another dealing with Kade.

Kevin's face swam in her mind again. Her bullets slammed into him. Shiva's will controlled her. Controlled her through Kade's back doors.

Goddammit! she told herself. Shiva did that. Not Kade.

She felt her fists clench. Sweat was beading on her forehead. Fight-

or-flight. Adrenal response.

This wasn't rational. It was physiological. Kade was just a proximate trigger.

She knew what it meant, knew all about this.

She had to nip it in the bud now.

"I need something," she told a medic. "A beta-adrenaline blocker, a strong one. Or a serotonergic."

Stop the near-permanent imprinting. Stop physiological response from amplifying the emotions, from heightening the stress response, from turning these last few hours into a trauma that would last for years.

The Buddhists and the shrinks agreed. The body was the seat of emotions. Quell the physiological response and you could dampen the psychic pain as well.

"Are you having a heart attack?" the woman medic said to her, an eyebrow raised.

"I'm post-traumatic," Sam said, keeping her voice as level as she could. "It's setting in. Standard protocol is to stop it now, before..."

The medic stared at her.

"Please," Sam said.

"Physical trauma only," the medic said, and closed up her kit.

Sam's fists clenched tighter.

They sealed them up in a large-ish briefing room, with soldiers positioned outside, while Colonel Atwal awaited her orders on what to do with them. Only when Sam complained loudly did the soldiers bring any food and water, or allow bathroom trips, always under the guard of multiple armed soldiers.

Her heart kept pounding. They weren't being treated as guests. They weren't being embraced. They were prisoners here.

Kevin died again and again at her hands.

She pushed it away, focused again on the children, held Sarai, held Aroon, held Kit, held all the children to her, wishing she could touch their minds. And shuddering with the horrible memory of killing the man who'd raised her every time she even thought of taking Nexus again.

We've got a plan, she told herself. They want something. They want *Kade*.

Stay cool. Stick to the plan. Make the kids safe. I come later.

After a few hours Colonel Atwal came to them again.

"My orders have come through," she told them. "We're sending you on to Delhi."

• • •

Kade collapsed into a window seat in exhaustion, pain flaring up from his midsection as he did.

The aircraft to Delhi was larger, a military passenger jet. With all of them on board, more than half the seats were still empty. It was also Faraday caged, effectively shielding Kade and everyone else in the passenger compartment off from the electromagnetic world outside.

They were prisoners once again.

Kade could see Shiva's private jet sitting on the tarmac as they taxied past it. He had the access codes to that plane, as he did to almost everything of Shiva's now. He wouldn't change those access codes. He wouldn't steal, wouldn't divert resources from wherever Shiva's estate or the courts eventually sent them. But, for the time being, he could reach out to that aircraft, or innumerable other assets of Shiva's, and they'd respond. If he wasn't inside this Faraday cage, that was. If the Indians ever allowed him to touch the net again.

They lifted off into early morning sky. Behind him, in plentiful seats, Kade could feel the children nodding off to sleep after their long ordeal, hear low voices talking, Sam's voice, speaking in Thai. He could feel Sarai's mind back there, befuddled, confused, longing. Longing for Sam, for the touch of a mind that was no longer there, no longer linked by Nexus.

The exhaustion pulled at Kade harder. The grief, the sorrow at all the death. The physical pain of everything he'd been through. He needed to rest, to regroup, to be ready and focused. He closed his eyes.

Then Feng lowered himself into the seat next to him, his left arm bound up in a proper sling now.

You think this is going to work? Feng sent. The transmission was tuned for Kade's brain alone, a tight beam, at minimal power. Even via this method, Feng was taking no chances.

Kade shook his head mentally. **I don't know, Feng.** He sent it back just as carefully. Then he thought better, thought that was too bleak, and tried to be more cheerful. **What's the worst that could happen?**

Feng was silent for a moment. Then: **Well... they throw the kids into an orphanage. Torture you, me, and Sam until we tell them everything. Mostly you.** Feng paused. **Then... they sell us to your American friends?**

Kade turned, surprised, and found Feng grinning at him.

Then Feng laughed, and laughed, and laughed, a bellowing raucous sound, filling up the plane.

Kade shook his head, a chuckle coming out of him unbidden, and turned back to the window, to the ever receding blue of the Indian Ocean below, the vast stretch of water they still had to cross to reach the Indian mainland.

It'll work, he sent to Feng. **Probably.**

Feng shrugged, good humor radiating from his mind.

"Hey, why no in-flight entertainment system?" the Chinese soldier asked loudly, kicking the seat in front of him. "What kind of lousy plane is this?"

Kade shook his head, cheered despite himself, and closed his eyes to sleep.

"Mr Lane," the man said, smiling coldly, his hand extended to shake Kade's. "My name is Rakesh Aggarwal. I'm with the Ministry of External Affairs."

Kade rose slowly from behind the table as Aggarwal entered the room, his ribs aching in pain as he did. He gestured with his bandaged right hand apologetically, then extended his left hand to meet Aggarwal's. The man took Kade's one good hand smoothly in his right. Aggarwal's hair was grey, close cropped. He wore an American-style business suit over a trim frame.

Nexus nodes recorded everything for posterity. A memory-augmenting app Kade had loaded with the files he'd downloaded from the net on Shiva's jet tagged the man before him.

[Rakesh Aggarwal]

[Special Secretary, Ministry for External Affairs]

Special Secretary, Kade thought. A fix-it guy. A cleaner. That could be good. Or very bad.

The door closed behind Aggarwal, leaving Kade alone with him here, armed guards on the other side, another series of Faraday cages cutting him off from the outside world, Feng and Sam off in their own interview rooms, the children under the temporary care of Thai-speaking social workers.

Kade cut to the chase. "Mr Aggarwal, I'd like to formally request asylum here in India, for myself, my companions, and the children we brought with us."

Aggarwal froze for a moment, then lowered himself into the chair across the table, motioning Kade to do the same.

Kade lowered himself back into his own chair, even more slowly than he'd risen, wincing as his ribs flared in pain again.

"Mr Lane," Aggarwal started. "You should be aware that India has a mutual extradition agreement with the United States, where, we understand, you are wanted by your government for acts of terrorism."

Kade nodded, smiling to hide his fatigue. "Yes. That's why I'm formally requesting asylum."

Aggarwal pursed his lips. "Mr Lane, it is certainly theoretically possible for India to grant political, religious, or humanitarian asylum which may pre-empt extradition or other agreements. However, to do so, you'd need to make a case that your home government was... persecuting you on grounds which we in India find invalid. What case would you make to us?"

Kade locked eyes with the Special Secretary. "Mr Aggarwal, my government, the government of the United States, is persecuting me for providing men and women the tools to enhance their own minds and enrich their connections with one another."

Aggarwal shook his head slightly, his eyes never leaving Kade's. "Mr Lane, as you must know, India is a signatory to the Copenhagen Accords, which expressly ban certain forms of human enhancement. What you're talking about is, by treaty, a crime here in India as well. We can't grant you asylum on that basis."

Kade leaned forward, still staring into the man's eyes, and put his hands together atop the table, good left atop bandaged right. "But if India pulled *out* of Copenhagen," he told the Special Secretary, "then you *could* grant us asylum."

Aggarwal stared at him. The man's lips parted. His brow furrowed. His eyes narrowed. His look was of such disgust that Kade wondered if he'd miscalculated, if he'd been so wrong.

"Why would India possibly pull out of the Copenhagen Accords?" Aggarwal asked. "Simply for *your* convenience, Mr Lane?"

Kade kept his eyes on the man, pulled himself upright, kept his hands the way they were.

"In September, news outlets reported that India had a secret program experimenting with Nexus as a tool to accelerate learning in children," Kade told Aggarwal. He waited a beat. "Mr Aggarwal, I know this to be true. I've touched the minds of the students in that program, and of the government-trained, government-*employed* teachers."

The Special Secretary frowned.

"You're already on your way out of Copenhagen," Kade said. "Nexus finally gives you an enhancement tech that's worth breaking the treaty for, one that's easy enough to deploy, and brings you large enough economic gains, that the benefits to India outweigh the costs of pissing off the US and Europe and China. You've done the math. And now it's just a matter of time."

Guesses, just guesses. They had to be right. Everything depended on them.

Aggarwal shook his head. "Mr Lane, even if these... baseless allegations of yours were true... what matters is not whether we leave the Copenhagen Accords at some unspecified point in the future. What matters is right now."

Kade kept his gaze level. This is what it comes down to, he told himself. Here we go.

"Mr Aggarwal," he said, emphasizing his words carefully, "I know the government of India has been working to boost India's *competitiveness* since at least... oh... 2024."

2024. The year of India's amazing surge in the Olympics, the year they took home twice as many gold medals as any previous year. Because of Shiva's secret, highly-illegal biotech enhancements. Enhancements Shiva's companies had kept on providing all the way through the 2040 summer games in Doha.

"In fact, I know a great deal that I'm sure the government would hate to see revealed. Most of which happens to be in violation of Copenhagen anyway."

He let it hang there, the implicit threat. Aggarwal just stared at him.

"Mr Aggarwal," Kade went on. "The last thing I want is to harm India. I believe it's in your nation's strategic interest to move forward with Nexus deployment and to leave Copenhagen. I believe your government has already come to that conclusion. So if this is really just a *timing* issue, perhaps we could speed things up a bit."

Kade sat alone after that, after Aggarwal had gone to confer with his superiors, barely masking his contempt. Hours passed.

The plan was Sam's in origin. They had to go somewhere. They had to assume that wherever they went, the CIA would know. Nakamura had tracked Kade to Shiva's home on Apyar Kyun, which meant that the CIA had as well. The firefight and Nakamura's death would sound alarms. The liftoff of Shiva's plane and its eventual landing point would hardly go unnoticed.

Thailand was an option. The Thai had already left Copenhagen, much to the US's displeasure. The authorities had turned a blind eye to Kade and Feng and Sam after the assault on Ananda's monastery six months ago, for a few days. Long enough for them to slip away. But now? With a senior CIA operative dead? With the US publicly blaming Kade for the PLF's terrorist attacks, and privately hunting for his back doors? What kind of pressure would the US bring on the Thai to arrest Kade and Sam? Economic sanctions? Seizure of US-held assets?

And how much harder would it be to slip away with twenty-five children in tow?

India was different. India was a rising superpower: The third largest economy on the planet. The most populous country in the world. Not a country the US could just push around anymore. And India, according to media reports, had already been caught experimenting with Nexus and other proscribed enhancement technologies. If any nation had both the clout and the inclination to shield them, India was it.

Sam had originated the plan. Kade had embellished it.

The war was coming. The war between human and posthuman. The US government had invented the Posthuman Liberation Front, and then the PLF had slipped its leash and bitten its creators' hands. They'd turned a bit of staged assassination theater against Stockton into something very close to the real thing, had killed cabinet members, had set off bombs in ERD offices, had assassinated a wildly popular televangelist and a US senator who also happened to be the frontrunner for Governor of Texas. They'd killed hundreds of innocents in that church in Houston just hours ago, with the cameras rolling.

They were playing exactly into the hands of their enemies. They were inviting a backlash, a vicious crackdown that would fuel more violence until it all blew up.

Kade needed to stop that from happening. But he'd thrown away his best weapon for fighting the PLF head on. The back doors were gone. Even now, his virus was out there, replicating, closing all the back doors he and Rangan had coded – and the new ones Shiva had inserted – in every mind it touched. He didn't trust the power to invade millions of minds to anyone. Not even to himself. And not to anyone who might trick it out of him.

No. He had to stop this war a different way. Instead of taking on the PLF directly, he had to up his strategy to a higher level.

In the intersection of Sam's plan, and in what he'd already seen India doing, and in the nuggets he'd seen in Shiva's memories – there just might be a way.

Or perhaps they'd send him back to the US, so the ERD could rip whatever secrets remained out of him, like they had with Rangan, like they'd tried with Ilya…

Kade closed his eyes, and in the corner of his vision he could see the icon for the script he'd written when he thought Shiva might try to torture the back doors out of him. The script that would end his life. The choice Ilya had made, rather than let them take the back door out of her mind.

It's been a good life, Kade thought. Even if this doesn't work with the Indians – I got Nexus out there. Wats would be happy. Ilya too. And those kids. I was so obsessed with stopping the abuses, but I missed all the beauty. Those kids are going to change the world.

Kade shook his head at his own past self, at his mistakes, at the way he'd let guilt and anger blind him to the wonder all around.

I wonder if Rangan made it? he thought.

The sound of the lock turning pulled Kade out of his reverie. His eyes snapped open. Nexus nodes began recording again.

The door opened. Rakesh Aggarwal stepped into the room. With him came a tall Indian woman, dressed in a sari, all angular features and dark, intense eyes. Kade's memory augmenting app tried to match her face against the database of thousands of government officials he'd pulled down, and found nothing.

Who was she then? A spook? A spy?

Aggarwal pulled the door shut behind him, then met Kade's gaze, and spoke.

"Mr Lane, I regret to inform you that our government has received a highest priority request from the government of the United States for your incarceration and extradition. Our treaty obligations compel us to honor this request."

Kade closed his eyes. The icon in the corner of his mental vision loomed large.

10
Overnight Delivery

Saturday 2040.11.03

At the Indian Consulate in Shanghai, the more-perfect-than-nature diamondoid data cube was slipped into a Faraday-lined pouch, which itself was then tucked into a second compact Faraday cage, no larger than a purse, for good measure. The resulting bundle was locked inside a tamper-resistant diplomatic case, protected from search and seizure by treaty and international protocol, which was then handcuffed to the wrist of a senior courier. The courier, accompanied by two members of the Consulate's security force, was driven immediately south and west towards Shanghai's smaller Hong Qiao Airport.

With the massive disruption caused by the cyber calamity – the cyber-*attack* according to Indian intelligence – they would take no chances with the closer but more seriously affected Pudong Airport.

The black Opal sedan – the vehicle of choice for diplomats and aristocrats throughout Asia – sped across the roads, minimal traffic providing no obstructions, diplomatic immunity rendering it oblivious to local traffic laws.

At the rear security gate to Hong Qiao, armed guards and imposing barriers brought them to a halt. The driver lowered his window, showed diplomatic papers to unsmiling soldiers with improbably large fully automatic weapons. Tripod mounted cameras and robotic defense systems tracked them. The car beeped, scrolled data across the driver's display as the airport's security AIs interrogated it, validating authority. Tense moments passed.

Then the unsmiling soldiers tersely handed the papers back. Lights turned green, and they drove directly out onto the tarmac, towards the fully fueled, ready-to-fly, diplomatic jet bearing the emblem of the Indian Ministry of External Affairs. The courier and the security men exited the sleek black Opal and boarded the Indian jet, the stairs retracting behind them.

Within minutes they were taxiing down the runway, a flight plan filed for New Delhi, a landing less than six hours away.

And a call was placed, informing certain people that a package was on its way.

Five thousand kilometers away, in the southern Indian city of Bangalore, on a campus that once belonged to the Defense Research and Development Organization of the Indian Ministry of Defense, a scientist named Varun Verma received the call.

"Now?" he asked into his handset. "You're sure?"

Afternoon sunlight illuminated the boyish, clean-shaven face of a man in his thirties, on a tall lean frame, in a white shirt and grey trousers.

"I see."

Dr Varun Verma hung up, and rose to his feet. Through the windows of his office he watched the palm trees lining the streets of this verdant, tropical campus. This research facility had once been a place where aeronautics engineers worked on high tech fighters for India's Air Force, freeing the nation from dependence on imported Russian MiGs and French Mirages. Now, it was something different. No longer part of DRDO or the Ministry of Defense, it was part of a Ministry few had ever heard of, a Ministry whose very existence was classified. It was a place ideally suited for the work it did – advanced computing research with the aim of pushing the frontiers of intelligence, both human and artificial. And with the high tech workforce of Bangalore, Silicon Valley of Asia, all around it, there was no better place to find talent.

Of all the secret projects housed here, none were quite as secret, or as dangerous, as Varun Verma's.

Varun tapped his pocket to be sure his badge was with him, lifted his slate off his desk, and strode out of his office, tapping away on the slate. The team must be summoned. The cluster must be prepped. The cube was en route, first to Delhi, and then here, to Bangalore.

He finished sending out instructions as he reached the first checkpoint. The guards recognized him, nodded. But still he waved his badge, held his eye to the retinal scanner, waited to be cleared.

The elevator opened with a soft ping. In he went. And then down, in the gleaming chrome and carbon cube. Down five levels. Then a hallway, another security check, another retinal scan, another ultramodern lift, and a plunge: one hundred meters down, straight down.

The lift opened onto beauty. Onto the most powerful computer in

India. Varun took it in, with its monitoring consoles and its glass walls, its egg-shaped helium pressure vessels, with the vacuum chambers deep inside. The row after row after row of entangled quantum processors linked by thick optical cables.

A quantum cluster.

Their very own.

Built to specifications stolen from the great Chen Pang in China.

Waiting only for the software to run it. Software now on the way.

There was one last thing to arrange. One vital ingredient necessary for the stability of the software they were about to load. Varun looked down on his slate, navigated through the necessary pages, and started looking through the list of candidates. They needed a body, still living, that wouldn't be missed. A body with a brain they could wire to the quantum cluster. A brain to restore Su-Yong Shu to sanity.

11
Reactions

Sunday 2040.11.04
Carolyn Pryce woke in her room at the Houston Intercontinental to an urgent chiming from her slate.

Less than a dozen people in the world could cause her slate to wake her.

She rolled over. The clock read 4.31am. Her deputy Kaori's face was on the slate, coming in over a highly encrypted link from Kaori's home office.

Pryce answered. "Go."

"You need to see this," Kaori said. "Barnes is dead."

Then the video started to play.

She was on her way to the President's suite five minutes later.

Secret Service let her pass. She went in to find the President standing, a red velvet robe tied around him, his face still with attention. Even in a robe, even in his fifties, he was undeniably the athlete, dominating the room with his height, his broad shoulders, that square jaw, his sheer physical presence. Behind him, Cindy Stockton was sitting up in bed, wrapped in her own more delicate dressing gown. The First Lady's eyes were wide open in horror. On the wall screen the video Pryce had just seen was finishing.

"I've killed men to keep my secrets," Barnes was saying. "To keep the President's secrets."

Then she saw Greg Chase, standing by the screen, in suit and tie. Did he sleep that way?

Barnes said something else on the video, then he leaned back, and fell, and fell, and fell, a long way down into the fast moving river, and the video collapsed into black.

"Jesus," the President said.

"It's going viral, Mr President," Chase said. "All the networks. Everywhere on the net. We're getting press inquiries now."

"We're under attack," Stockton said. Then he went on. "What's the weather in DC?"

Someone behind her answered.

"The storm's dissipating." It was Larry Cline, the President's Campaign Manager. "Air Force One should be able to land by the time we gather every one up and reach DC. Or at least get us close."

Stockton nodded. "Cancel the rest of the trip, Larry," he said. "I need to speak to the country. From the White House."

[Kaori: They've identified the bridge. PA state police & DHS are searching river for the body.]

[Pryce: I want Barnes's movements and calls for the last 48 hours. No. Last month.]

[Kaori: Why us?]

[Pryce: POTUS asked.]

[Kaori: OK. What else.]

[Pryce: So he *wasn't* at ERD headquarters when Holtzman died?]

[Kaori: ERD says *no one* entered the room. Door remained closed till Internal Affairs opened it.]

[Pryce: Bullshit. Someone killed Holtzman.]

[Kaori: Yep.]

[Pryce: Get Holtzman's movements and calls for the month leading up to his death too. Longer if you can.]

[Kaori: Will do.]

[Pryce: Video analysis of both videos. Any chance they're fabrications?]

[Kaori: Already on it. Should have something for you shortly.]

[Pryce: Good. Records search. Start matching the text of the PLF-creation memos against classified archives. Phrase matches. Partial matches. Maybe someone slipped up and left an early draft accessible.]

[Kaori: You think any of it's real?]

[Pryce: Go hunting as if it is real. That's the only way to be sure it's not.]

Someone tapped Carolyn Pryce on the arm. She looked up, found a giant, mirror-shaded Secret Service agent standing next to her. Hayes. One of the President's personal protection detail.

"Dr Pryce, the President has asked that you ride with him in the

Beast. You can join him in the Executive Lobby."

Pryce nodded, then looked down at her slate again.

[Kaori: I've gotta say, if I wasn't inside the administration... Becker, then Holtzman, then Barnes? I'd find this all pretty damning.]

Pryce narrowed her eyes, then swiped to delete the message, and subvocalized one more time.

[Pryce: Don't say that again. And one more thing. Get NSA in the loop. Chase pushing the story someone coerced Barnes. If so, they hacked Barnes's security...]

That shouldn't be a problem for Kaori. NSA was where Pryce had hired her away from.

There was a pause. Then another message appeared.

[Kaori: Got it. On both counts. Safe travels, boss.]

Pryce nodded to herself. Kaori was good. She just needed to be careful. DC wasn't a place to speak one's mind.

[Pryce: I'm flying POTUS Air. Safe as it gets.]

She walked into the Executive Lobby, on the top floor of Houston Intercontinental, and into the tail end of a family discussion.

"I really wish you'd come with us back to DC," Stockton said. He had his daughter Julie in his arms. The First Lady stood nearby, cradling their grandson, Liam.

"Dad," Julie replied. "I have a life here. I have work to do. Steve's here."

"That bomb was meant for you."

"You don't know that." Julie Stockton shook her head.

The President sighed. "OK. But I'm beefing up your Secret Service detail."

The First Lady looked up at that, nodded.

"I wish you wouldn't," Julie Stockton said.

Pryce sympathized with the girl. She'd bristled at the idea of having a Secret Service detail herself. It felt more like being a prisoner than being protected. Pryce had disliked the idea so much that she'd made *not* having one a condition of taking the job.

"I can't do my job," the President said, his hands still on Julie's upper arms, "if I'm not confident that you and Liam are safe. That's that."

Pryce followed as a pair of Secret Service agents led the President and a large retinue to a cargo elevator, which plunged them down towards the underground garage that yet more Secret Service agents had held secure since Stockton's arrival yesterday afternoon.

One of the agents held a finger to the bud in his ear, then spoke. "We have reports of protesters outside the hotel, Mr President."

Cindy Stockton shook her head. "Protesters," she said. "The sun's not even up yet."

Then the elevator doors opened, and they were underground, in the hubbub of the forming motorcade. Scores of people. Texas State Troopers on motorcycles. More in squad cars. Secret Service in discreetly armored sedans. More sedans for staff and aides. And the special vehicles: the armed and armored Rapid Response vehicles that held Secret Service squads dressed more like marines than bodyguards; the Hazmat vehicle for responding to a bio- radio- or chem-attack on the President; the White House Comms vehicle with its ultra-high-bandwidth links from which you could run the free world; the Local Air Superiority Vehicle, with its fleet of hundreds of tiny drones and counter drones, equipped to ensure the President's convoy was never taken by surprise.

The Army Colonel with the Football, the briefcase containing the nuclear launch codes.

How did I go from writing policy briefs to this? Pryce wondered.

Did it help that Stephen was dead? She felt a pang of guilt at the thought. But it wasn't the first time it had struck her.

Would I have made it this far if my husband had lived? If we'd had the kid we'd planned to have?

"Carolyn!" Stockton snapped.

Pryce looked up. A Secret Service agent was holding open a door to the Beast, the custom limousine the President rode in. A vehicle like no other.

"Yes, Mr President," she said, and strode forward, into the belly of the Beast, and took her seat facing backwards, towards the President and his wife.

John Stockton was looking out the window. And Pryce felt even guiltier for the thought she'd just had. During Stephen's cancer, and afterwards... The Stocktons had been good to her. Both John and Cindy had supported her, back when he'd been a senator, and then VP.

And if she'd thrown herself into the job? If work was all she did the last decade?

Work was rational. Work was analytical. Work had always been something she excelled at – since grad school, since her doctorate, since her first book. She could break down problems into smaller problems, see how the pieces fit together, articulate them in ways others could understand, quantify things previously unquantified, propose solutions others had never seen.

She sighed. Throwing herself into that was easier than coping with a dead husband. With not having the child she'd planned to have.

The police cruiser lights came on. Pryce turned to look out the Beast's window. Drones took flight, flanking the ground-based vehicles, ready to spring out to expand their surveillance and intercept any fast moving hostile.

Then they were moving. They went up the ramp, out into dim pre-dawn light of Houston at 6am.

Then she saw the protest.

There were thousands of them, lit by the glow of the streetlights. A police line held them back, kept the road free for the convoy. The Beast's inches-thick armored glass and hermetically sealed cabin deadened the sound of their screams. Even so, their rage was palpable, visible on faces contorted in anger, in the violent gestures of signs that yelled: "TERRORIST!" "PRESIDENT TRAITOR!" "BABY KILLER!"

She flinched as something was flung at them; it burst in mid-air in a splatter of yellow and someone at the front of the crowd crumpled over in pain.

An egg, she realized. A protester had thrown an egg at the Beast. And one of their drone escorts had intercepted the unknown threat in mid-air and tazed the poor idiot who'd thrown it.

She looked back inside the limo, saw Cindy Stockton staring out the window, a look of sorrow on her face, her husband's hand in her own. Pryce turned to John Stockton, searched his face for anger, for resignation, for regret, perhaps.

She found something else there instead. Resolve.

He'd asked her to ride with him. Why? Was he about to explain Barnes's suicide confession?

Was John Stockton about to confide something in her that he'd hidden from her up until now? Was he going to explain to her how it had been necessary? The reasons behind it all?

She understood realpolitik. Principles were important, but all of them cracked at the extremes. At some point, under some circumstances, everyone became a pragmatist.

But this… the things Barnes had said. That was too much. Way too much.

Was John Stockton going to give her context that changed it all? That reframed it into something she could understand?

God, she hoped so. Because as it was…

The President looked up at her, met her eyes.

Here it comes, she thought.

"Barnes was murdered," John Stockton said. "I'm sure of it."

Pryce blinked in surprise. Her chest caught in her throat.

"I want you to focus on Barnes's murder," Stockton said. "Assume it was an attack by a hostile power. Treat it as a national security issue, and give it your absolute highest priority."

Carolyn Pryce opened her mouth to speak.

Kaori's ill-thought-out message flashed through her mind.

Becker? Then Holtzman? Then Barnes? I'd find this all pretty damning.
She snapped her mouth shut.

John Stockton was staring out the window again, a look of utter resolve on his face.

And for the first time, Pryce wondered just how far the President's resolve went.

Just how far indeed?

Breece hiked the thirteen kilometers back to the parking lot where he'd left his car, then got on the interstate and told the car to drive west.

The way Barnes had died kept cycling through his head. The way the hacker just owned him, completely.

It brought to mind Hiroshi. The way someone had broken into Hiroshi's mind, through Nexus. Had forced Breece to put a bullet in his best friend's skull...

No. He shook it off.

Hiroshi, when he was hacked, went from his usual lethal grace to suddenly clumsy and uncoordinated. The hacker behind it couldn't manage to simultaneously dig through Hiroshi's memories and control his body at all, let alone with precision.

This hacker, the one who'd taken Zarathustra. This one had hacked into the home of a DHS senior official. And within minutes of the Nexus injection, he'd had precise, total control. The intonation, the words, the balance on that wet, windy, bridge...

This was someone more dangerous.

He pulled over at a rest stop one hundred and forty five kilometers from the site of Barnes's death. There he pulled out his slate, tunneled through a series of anonymizing cut-outs, and connected to the data this mysterious new hacker had given him access to.

He let out a low whistle as he scrolled through the files. Access codes for slush funds containing tens of millions. Personnel files on PLF members in twenty countries – and on moles within the PLF. Mission profiles of missions he'd heard of, some of which had succeeded, others of which had gone bad. ERD and DHS back doors and surveillance override codes.

This mysterious hacker was even more impressive than he thought. And he'd been as good as his word. Zara – Barnes – was dead. Stockton's administration was even more discredited. And Breece had at his fingertips the kind of data he could only dream of. Data that would allow him to purge the PLF of government informers, reform it, turn it into something more effective than ever.

• • •

The Avatar smiled to herself with Ling's body as the gloom of the day dipped towards the darkness of evening in Shanghai.

Penetrating the defenses of the Barnes human had been a risk, at the very edge of her capabilities in this reduced form, with dozens of potential failure modes that would have led to her detection.

Her death.

The death of posthumanity.

She shuddered at that.

But it had paid off.

Probability matrices showed expanding conflict, an increased likelihood of civil disorder in the days ahead, distracting leaders in the US and abroad.

And if the Americans found the breadcrumbs she'd left behind in Barnes's home, even better...

Outside, the glowing red lights of sky-eyes appeared, lifting off like so many fireflies into Shanghai's gloom. There were more of them every day, as the humans recovered from what Ling had done to this city. Just as there were more and more strange pieces of software in the net, hunting, hunting.

Hunting for her.

The Avatar shuddered again.

I will not fail, she told herself. I am Su-Yong Shu. I am the last fragment of the greatest intelligence on Earth. I will restore myself. I will not let darkness fall.

12
Re-United

Rangan's world came back in fragments. Painted concrete ceiling, directly above him. Bare LED pointed down at him. Tiny room. IV bag, hanging on a hook nailed into the wall.

The young woman standing above him, with the long honey-blonde ponytail, the George Mason University sweatshirt, the blue nitrile gloves – turning towards him, then away, towards him, then away.

"Wha?" he said.

She turned towards him again, and smiled. "Well," she said brightly. "You're with us again."

He tried to clear the fog from his brain.

"I'm at St Mark's?"

"Yep. Lucky to be here too."

"You're a doctor?"

She smiled wider. "Closest thing you've got. Fourth year med student. I'm Melanie."

Rangan lifted his head and looked down at himself. He was stripped to the waist. There was a fresh bandage at his side. His ribs were wrapped. The IV entered at his elbow. The pain was a whole hell of a lot better than it had been.

"How…" *How bad is it* he wanted to ask.

"You're going to be OK. The burns are mostly first degree. One broken rib, left side. I injected a bone growth accelerator, but it's still going to be weeks before you're a hundred percent."

Rangan looked up, and noticed that long hair again, those green eyes, the way she ticked things off on her fingers as she talked. "Thanks."

"…and," Melanie was saying, "you've got a souvenir."

She turned away from him, then turned back with a tiny plastic bag, a small black something inside it. Rangan reached up, took it with his free hand, held it up between his face and the light.

"A bullet," he said.

She nodded. "It was moving slow by the time it hit you. And it missed everything major. A few inches over and things could have been pretty bad. You got lucky. Really lucky."

Rangan stared at it. "I can't believe that cop just *shot* me. Fucking *asshole*."

Melanie's face clouded over at that. Her smile disappeared. Her lips compressed into a thin line.

"That *cop*," she said, carefully, enunciating each word, "was evacuated to Charlottesville with second and third degree burns over half his body. He's in a lot worse shape than you."

Rangan stared at her. "He *shot* me. What if the kids had been in the van?"

Melanie shook her head. "He thought he was doing his job."

"That makes it OK?"

Melanie sighed, and lowered herself onto a stool next to the cot Rangan was lying on. "Look. The call that went out. You were described as a *terrorist*. They said you'd escaped DHS custody. That you were armed and *extremely* dangerous. Approach with extreme caution. Apprehend or stop at *all costs*. This is a small town, Rangan. They don't get calls like that. Especially not when they're already stretched thin, trying to keep people safe during a hurricane. Owen thought he was saving lives."

Rangan stared at her. "Owen? You know him?"

Melanie stared back. "I grew up here. My mom's a cop. I know all the cops in this county."

Rangan looked down. Let loose by that bastard Holtzman. Rescued by a church pastor who thought the hurricane was a gift from God. Stitched back together by a friend of the cop who'd shot him.

I don't have any fucking clue about anything anymore, he realized.

He looked back up at Melanie, found her looking down at her hands. "I'm sorry," he said gently. "I hope your friend comes out OK. I guess I've just uhh… had a bad few months with authority."

Melanie looked up, and smiled sadly at him. "I know. I've watched some of the video. I'm sorry for what you went through."

Her eyes held his for long seconds. Then she stood.

"I've got to go. I'm only here because they shut down Georgetown, but since I'm here I'm helping the EMTs patch people up after Zoe. There're more people who need me."

Rangan nodded at that. "It was nice to meet you, Melanie."

She nodded, packing up things, collecting them in a medical bag.

"It was nice to meet you too, Rangan." She paused for just a moment, then walked away.

At the door, her hand on the knob, she turned. "Owen's gonna make it, by the way. He'll need some new skin grown, but he'll recover." She met his eyes. "I'm glad you got those kids out." Then she smiled. "Speaking of which, I think you've got some friends who've been waiting to say 'hi'."

She opened the door and thoughts hit him, a barrage of thoughts, enthusiastic, friendly, eager, and chaotic, rushing in to greet him.

The boys crowded around his cot, Bobby and Pedro and Tim and Jason and Tyrone, and all of them. Their minds were buzzing with joy and excitement, bombarding him with images and ideas and questions and information faster than he could follow.

…we're going to CUBA…

…CUBA CUBA CUBA…

…lots of other kids with NEXUS…

…and this new APP can show you MAPS and PICTURES in your HEAD…

…hurricanes come from HOT OCEANS…

…and you can talk like <this>…

…ALFONSO'S BACK…

That shocked him. And there he was, in the back, Alfonso, the boy the ERD had tortured until he'd relented and purged Nexus from his own brain.

"Alfonso," Rangan said. He reached out, with his hand, with his thoughts, gesturing to the boy, pulling him forward, until Alfonso came up to the front of the little crowd, sat on the stool where Melanie had sat, and held Rangan's hand.

"How?" Rangan asked. Had his brain somehow recovered?

…gave him more Nexus…

…made him REAL again…

"Everyone's real!"

It came out more sharply than he intended. And the boys fell silent.

He caught himself. These were just boys. Boys taken away from their parents.

He smiled. "I'm sorry." He looked around at the boys, sent out love, his joy at seeing them, how much he'd missed them.

Then he gripped Alfonso tighter.

"Alfonso was real when he didn't have Nexus. He just couldn't talk to you. He was still a person. He was just more lonely."

He tried to show them, the bits he'd seen out of Bobby's eyes, out of Tim's, of Alfonso crying huddled in the corner, of how that meant Alfonso was sad, just like they were sad sometimes.

He felt Alfonso's memories seep into the room, felt the experience from Alfonso's point of view, felt the boys make the connection, just a bit, just a tiny bit. It'd have to do.

Then Pedro broke the moment.

...Did you really have a POLICE CHASE and did they shoot at you and did you BLOW UP a van and ESCAPE LIKE A NINJA like in the NINJA MOVIES...

And then all the boys were pressing on him, excited, curious, and so much like he'd been as a boy.

Show us being a ninja!

Show us blowing up the van!

Show us the police chase!

Their eyes were full of adoration, their minds full of Rangan as some sort of heroic movie version of himself. And somehow, Rangan found himself swept up in their infectious enthusiasm, telling them a story, showing them snippets of the terrifying drive through the storm, of the police car flashing out of the rain, of the terrible spin and tumble of the van, of crawling into the mud and lighting the flare...

And then he realized that he was the adult here.

"Now you have to remember to never play with fire without a grownup! OK! Promise me!"

Did you blow up the BAD COP?!

He winced at that. And then, thinking of Melanie's words, Rangan heard his own voice explaining, patiently, that police were people too, real people, even if they didn't have Nexus in their heads, and sometimes they were just confused, or someone had lied to them, or tricked them into doing something bad.

The boys went quiet, absorbing this. And for a while he thought he'd lost them all.

Then Bobby sent to them all, **Like how they tricked us into thinking Alfonso wasn't a real person anymore?**

Rangan nodded slowly.

"Maybe," he said. "Maybe something like that, yeah."

And then he reached out with his mind, and pulled them all into a hug larger than his arms could ever have encircled.

Abigail waddled down into the cellar some hours later, with Levi behind her, holding his wife's hand, making sure she didn't fall.

"Service is over," Levi announced, smiling, crouching by Rangan's cot. "Everyone's gone home. Those that made it out in the first place."

"And tomorrow," Abigail said, with a small clap of her hands, "it's time for you boys to move on, towards your new home!"

CUBA!

CUBA!

Bobby grabbed Rangan's hand. "We're going to Cuba!"

Levi's smile wavered just a little bit. "Well yes you are," he said. "But the way we have for you boys to get there won't work for Rangan. So you're going to have to say goodbye for just a little while."

A wave of disappointment rushed through them all.

13
Threat Vectors

Sunday 2040.11.04
Pryce experienced the National Security Council meeting as one threat after another, each worse than the last. No threat board ever looked green. She'd learned that early on. But they seldom looked like this.

"...placed a highest priority request for the extradition of Kaden Lane," the Secretary of State was saying, from one of the giant screens. "Still a very high risk India could pull out of Copenhagen. If they do, it'll be a complete disaster. They could pull a dozen unaligned countries with them."

"Our intelligence suggests a Chinese attack on the Burmese island Lane's flight originated from," the CIA director said from another screen. "They may have been trying to capture Lane for themselves."

Admiral McWilliams, Chairman of the Joint Chiefs, cut in. "We have direct imagery of Indian forces landing on Apyar Kyun, not Chinese."

"We should consider an op–" CIA started.

"No," Pryce said. "The President's been clear. India, Copenhagen, and Lane are all in State's bag now. Next topic."

She was inside Air Force one, in the cavernous Situation Room set behind the President's suite in the upper deck of the giant double-decker craft. John Stockton was welcome at these meetings, but he was down below, talking to the press that traveled with him, making statements, doing damage control.

He was welcome to that job, Pryce thought.

Hers was keeping the free world safe.

CIA spoke again. "China. We have more confirmation that it's a coup. Bo Jintao, Minister of State Security, seems to be in charge now. A hardliner. Progressive Politburo members are effectively under house arrest..."

79

Fleet deployments. Diplomatic response. Human rights violations. Impact on trade agreements. Containment plans. There was always more to discuss than there was time.

And it was seldom as bad as this.

"Next," Pryce said after thirty minutes, acknowledging General Gordon Reid.

The NSA Director nodded. His craggy face looked almost... uncomfortable. Something Pryce wasn't used to seeing on the career Air Force cryptographer.

"In the matter of Director Barnes's suicide, we've found evidence that his home's security system was indeed penetrated by a hostile attacker."

Pryce felt a small jolt of surprise.

Was I wrong? she wondered. Was the President right? Was Barnes murdered? His confession a fabrication?

"Can you track down who the intruder was?" she asked.

Reid spoke again. "Dr Pryce, our forensics team found telltales of an attack developed by China's Advanced Electronic Brigade, launched by an attacker from within China."

Everyone started talking at once.

Pryce sliced her hand through the air. "Quiet!"

They all fell silent.

"China?" Pryce asked the NSA Director. "Are you sure?"

Reid looked at her. "As you know, one hundred percent doesn't exist in this business. But the telltale matches an attack AEB's used twice before, and while the attacker took steps to hide their tracks, we successfully traced it back to the PRC."

Pryce leaned back and exhaled softly. China. Her eyes drifted to the Situation Room's digital threat board, with the Chinese coup listed prominently, the hardliners back in power. Could they be doing this to distract the US? To keep the President from responding to what was happening there? But the risk! The provocation!

It made no sense. Rationally, the risk/payoff ratio was absurd.

Everyone else was staring at her, waiting.

"Dr Pryce," Reid said, "I need to add something here. The Chinese don't *know* that we know about this attack technology, or have a way to detect it or trace it."

Pryce's eyes snapped back to Reid's, the wheels in her mind spinning.

"I appreciate," the NSA Director went on, "that this is a very important moment for the President, politically..."

And now Pryce understood the unease she was reading from him.

"...but if we reveal to the American people that we were able to detect a subversion of Barnes's home security system, even if we don't mention China, then we'll be tipping our hand to them, and giving away an intelligence advantage that we have."

Pryce held Reid's eyes. "The President will have to make that decision."

"Can I count on you," the NSA Director asked, "to counsel the President in the direction of maximizing US national security?"

"I don't think he'll need that counsel from me, General," Pryce told him.

Then she turned to the others. "Reactions?"

It was another twenty minutes before she came to the last item on her agenda.

"Finally," she said. "The President has tasked me with investigating the allegation that the PLF was created as a black op inside the Jameson Administration."

She looked around, saw the different expressions, some blank, some openly dubious.

"He's given me complete authority to dig wherever I need. Now, this may turn out to be a complete fabrication. Or it may be true. But if you know anything about this, you have twenty-four hours to let me know. In that time, whatever I learn, I'll do my best to see that wherever it came from, you're given due credit for that when the butcher's bill comes due."

She kept looking around, making eye contact with each of them as she spoke, nodding conversationally. She was, in fact, on thin ice. Stockton hadn't rescinded her authority to dig on this topic. But it was clear he'd made up his own mind with Barnes's death.

So she was going to use that investigative authority *now* in case he took it away from her later.

"*Beyond* twenty-four hours from now, if I learn that *any* of you have been holding out on me, I will nail you mercilessly to the wall."

She let her eyes slide around them once more, marked who looked away, who met her eyes with hostility, who with humor.

"Am I absolutely clear?"

She was just outside the situation room, in the long hallway that ran the length of the upper deck of Air Force one, when a glint through one of the giant windows caught her eye. It was a brand new F-38, flanking them, its chameleonware skin detuned to let all the world see it – just one of the small squadron of human-piloted and autonomous fighter craft that now protected Air Force One wherever it went. It was something Pryce still wasn't used to, something that had only come into effect four months ago, with the attempt on the President's life.

She shook her head. Air Force One was as safe a place as any on Earth. Even without the squadron flying air support, the double decker plane had its own anti-missile defenses, its own small fleet of mini-drones it could launch, its own stealth capabilities, and other surprises up its sleeve that few knew about.

The screen of her slate flashed. Pryce looked down, found the kind of message she'd half expected. Anonymous, of course.

[Ivory Tower bitches like you should keep their noses out of wet work. Or they might find those noses cut off.]

Pryce chuckled at that. Another threatened Cro-Magnon, resorting to hurling archaic gendered insults to soothe his battered ego.

She subvocalized to Kaori.

[Pryce: You get that?]

[Kaori: Got it. Starting the trace now.]

She doubted anyone with something truly important to hide would be so stupid as to draw attention like that. Still, you explored all leads, however unlikely. That's how you made your luck.

Pryce looked back out at the F-38, glinting in the sun, armed with the latest high-tech weaponry, ready to shoot down any bogies that came in range.

She snorted and shook her head.

Pointless. Unless they were in a full blown shooting war with China, any successful attack on Air Force One wouldn't come from the outside.

It would come from within. From one of their own.

14
HR Gambit

Sunday 2040.11.04

"...Our treaty obligations compel us to honor this request," Aggarwal said.

Kade closed his eyes.

"Unless," Aggarwal continued, "you give us your full and absolute cooperation in our plans for Nexus."

Kade opened his eyes.

"I won't help you spy, or coerce, or use Nexus as a weapon," he told the man.

Aggarwal frowned and opened his mouth to speak.

The woman next to him cut in smoothly.

"Mr Lane," she said. Her accent was crisp, British. "We haven't been introduced. I'm Lakshmi Dabir."

She moved forward as she spoke, lowering herself slowly into one of the chairs across the table from Kade, her dark eyes on his. She didn't offer her hand.

"Kaden Lane," Kade told her. "Kade to my friends."

From the corner of his eye, Kade saw Aggarwal take the other seat.

"Kade," Lakshmi Dabir said. "If I may?"

"Are we friends?" Kade asked, eyebrow raised.

Lakshmi Dabir smiled faintly and pressed on. "Secretary Aggarwal may have given you the wrong impression. Let me describe our interest to you."

"Please," Kade replied.

"India is now the most populous nation on Earth, Kade. One point six billion people. And we're also quite young. There are three hundred and fifty million Indians under the age of fifteen – almost the same as the entire population of your country."

"Not my country anymore," Kade said quietly.

Dabir nodded slightly and continued. "The point, Kade, is that India has unparalleled human resources. If the human mind is the ultimate source of wealth – if it's the most valuable resource that we know of – then India is blessed in that way beyond any other nation on Earth.

"But we're also poor," she went on. "We have the third largest economy on the planet. We have more than our fair share of billionaires. But, despite our efforts, almost a tenth of our population still live in real poverty. Only half of our children complete their primary education – eight years of schooling. And millions receive only a year or two at best.

"Kade, what you told Secretary Aggarwal – whether you guessed it or found it out through other means – is partially correct. We see Nexus as a potentially pivotal tool for our nation. If we can help our children learn faster, if we can augment their brain power, then we can help them climb out of poverty faster, and help them create more wealth for the nation as a whole.

"We want to uplift our people. We want to use this technology for the greatest push in human development the world has ever seen. And we want your help."

It was almost exactly what Kade had hoped for. It was very nearly the best case scenario he'd imagined.

Yes, Kade thought. I'm in. This is exactly what I want.

But he was going to press for more.

Feng had agreed. Sam had agreed.

He had to. This was bigger than him. Bigger than them. Bigger than India.

Tit for tat. Iterated Prisoner's Dilemma. Break the cycle.

His heart thumped inside his chest. He wanted to lick his lips, forced himself not to.

He closed his eyes instead.

Sam's voice was in his head, a study in controlled anger, in bitter strategy, moves plotted on the plane of the man she'd executed.

You're valuable, she'd said, growling out the last word, her hands clenched around the controls, as Indian fighters and drones guided them in.

He'd stared at her. He was so angry. She'd crossed a line, executing Shiva Prasad in cold blood, after he'd disarmed the man, after he was helpless, after the man could have been redeemed.

But he needed her. Needed her brain, her hardness, her experience with the world of spooks and spies.

You have bargaining power now, Sam had gone on. *Not later. Not after you say yes to whatever they want. Now. Only now.*

She'd unclenched one hand from the controls then, reached over and tapped the MISSILE LOCK indicator, then looked back over her shoulder at him, her eyes still full of rage.

Use that power, Kade, Sam had said. *Make a home for these kids.*

They had the same priorities in that, at least.

"Kade?" Lakshmi Dabir's voice cut in.

He opened his eyes. They were both looking at him. He nodded agreeably to Lakshmi Dabir, his heart pounding in his chest again.

"I'm very happy to hear your plans," he said. "Of course I'll help. I'd be honored to." He paused. "Under certain conditions."

Rakesh Aggarwal frowned. Lakshmi Dabir looked at Kade quizzically.

"First," Kade said, "India will leave the Copenhagen Protocol."

Aggarwal laughed out loud. "Mr Lane, you're in no position to set conditions."

Kade breathed slowly through his nose, inhaled stillness, inhaled tranquility, exhaled the fear and doubt.

"Second," he went on, "anything I help you with will be given away freely to the rest of the world. You'll be first mover. You have the largest population. You'll benefit most. But everyone else gets the same shot."

Lakshmi Dabir raised an eyebrow. Rakesh Aggarwal snorted.

Kade pushed on.

"Third," he told them, "you'll introduce legislation ruling out any use of Nexus or any other neurotechnology for coercion, interrogation, or surveillance, even on the part of your police or national intelligence."

Aggarwal made an outraged sound. "This is absurd. You can't demand that we start drafting laws based on your whims!"

"You're a parliamentary system," Kade said. Outrage was easy to deal with. Factual debate was easy. "The Prime Minister's party can offer whatever legislation she wants."

Lakshmi Dabir was looking at him thoughtfully. "This is true," she said slowly. "But we're in a coalition government. There's no guarantee our partners will vote for it, even *if* the PM were to want such legislation."

Kade nodded agreeably.

"All I ask is that it's introduced," he said, "with an honest effort made."

Aggarwal shook his head. "This is ridiculous, Mr Lane."

"Fourth," Kade raised his voice slightly, let his own passion rise, his own anger, his own outrage at the things he'd seen, let it chase away any anxiety that remained. "If I ever find signs of *any* surveillance, coercion, mind-reading, or mind-control tools built off Nexus or any related technology, I will destroy those tools, and I will *publicize* them, to the entire world." He waited a beat, as Aggarwal's face grew more outraged, as Lakshmi Dabir looked more and more thoughtful. "And if you involve me in this project," Kade continued. "And if you build such things, I *will* find them."

They don't know what you're capable of, Sam had said. *You're a question mark. Use that to your advantage.*

"This is pointless," Aggarwal said. He rose.

"Sit down, Rakesh," Dabir said softly. "Hear him out."

Aggarwal stayed standing.

Kade took another slow breath. A calming breath now.

"Fifth," he said, his face cold now. "Your government will introduce legislation prohibiting discrimination and penalizing hate crimes against individuals on the basis of genetic, neurobiological, computational, or other enhancements, and give these laws *teeth* in places like Bihar province."

Bihar, the orphanage, weeping in the ashes for the dozens of his children who'd died.

No. That's Shiva's memory, not mine.

"Ahhh," Aggarwal was speaking, still standing, his voice dripping with contempt now. "Bihar. Shiva Prasad, eh? You know we landed marines on Apyar Kyun not long after you left there? We've heard interesting stories from the staff we've questioned. Is it true you have Shiva Prasad's memories? Is that why you killed him? No more use for him?"

Rakesh Aggarwal leaned forward, put his hands on the table, pushed his face forward towards Kade's.

"Tell me, Mr Lane: Did you pull the trigger? Did you put the bullet in Shiva Prasad's brain?"

Kade closed his eyes in pain and shock.

Sam raised the pistol, pointed it at Shiva's head, just inches from his skull, less than two feet from Kade.

"No, Sam. Don't do this. He tried to do the—"

Muzzle flare. Shiva's brain collapsing in shards of chaos. Wet matter splattering on Kade's face.

She just executed him! In cold blood!

I could have saved him. Oh god, he was good inside. I could have saved him. *We* could have saved him, the children and I...

Memories were swirling in his head: swimming in Azure seas, playing with the enhanced children, testing them through the games his team had devised, watching the software they were architecting come together, the satellites launch, dreaming of the future he'd build, the future when he'd unite a billion minds together under his direction.

"Rakesh!" Lakshmi Dabir's voice was sharp.

Kade's eyes flew open. His heart was pounding.

Shiva's memories. Not mine.

I'm not Shiva.

I'm not.

Aggarwal slowly pulled himself back upright, sneering down at Kade now.

Breathe, Kade told himself. Breathe.

I'm not Shiva.

I'm not dead.

And I didn't kill him.

Aggarwal was still staring at him, contempt written all over his face. Kade swallowed.

There was a script. Back on the script.

He forced himself to speak, to push for what he knew was right.

"Finally," he said. His voice croaked.

"...You'll introduce a..." he had to swallow again, "... a similar anti-discrimination motion to the United Nations General Assembly, acknowledging that the enhanced and augmented have the same rights as any normal human."

Aggarwal shook his head in disdain. "In direct contravention of Copenhagen. It will never pass. The Americans or Chinese would veto it anyway."

Aggarwal's contempt was like a splash of cold water. It brought Kade back to the present.

He raised his head, looked the man in the eye. What did it take to get through, here?

"It doesn't have to pass," he said. "But I'm asking India to introduce it and bring it to a vote. If you want me to help you uplift millions of Indian children, I need *you* to commit to treating them like human beings. That's what all of my conditions come down to."

Kade spread his arms wide, near-crippled right hand and still functional left, a gesture of openness. "Show me that you're going to treat those uplifted children well, and I'm with you. But if you're not committed to treating people like people..." He brought his arms back together in front of him on the table. "Then *fuck off.*"

Kade saw Lakshmi Dabir shake her head at that, a frown on her face. He'd crossed a line. Well, so be it. This was serious. Deadly serious.

Aggarwal sneered at Kade. "You're in no position to make any of these demands. My government simply will not agree to them."

Kade laughed bitterly then. The room was probably threaded through with stress monitors – lasers taking his pulse and cameras measuring his skin temperature and perspiration level and pupillary dilation and the rate and depth of his respiration. He didn't care. He forced himself to speak, to mean it.

Whoever cares less in a negotiation has the upper hand, Sam had said. *Show confidence. Convince them they want what* you *have more than you want anything of theirs.*

"Listen to me, Mr Aggarwal," Kade said. "This is my life's work. And I've done enough. A million people have Nexus in their minds, and more *every day*. I've *succeeded*." He clenched his still-functional left hand into a raised fist of triumph. "You can kill me. You can sell me to the ERD. I'll die happy. If you want me to work with you? I'll be even happier. But *you* have to demonstrate *your* principles."

And you're going to help me stop this war, Kade thought, his chest pounding again. You're going to help me show the world that humans and posthumans can be good to one another.

Damn it, you are.

Aggarwal just turned and walked away. As he pulled open the door, Kade spoke to the Special Secretary's back.

"Give her my conditions *exactly*, Mr Aggarwal. And my reasons. Don't edit them."

"Her?" Aggarwal said, his back still to Kade, the door open to the ante-room with the guards.

"The Prime Minister," Kade said. "We both know she's the one who's going to make this decision."

Lakshmi Dabir waited in the room after Rakesh Aggarwal stormed out.

She didn't look happy.

"Why the last condition, really? The UN motion is doomed to fail. You hinge your freedom, your life, on something that will go nowhere?"

Kade closed his eyes, exhaled through his nose.

He was so tired. So very damn tired.

"Do you know game theory, Ms Dabir? Prisoner's Dilemma and games like that?"

"It's Dr Dabir," she replied. "And yes, of course."

Kade opened his eyes. "Sorry."

She held his gaze. "Continue."

"Posthumans are coming," he said. "Copenhagen hasn't stopped the research, it's just hidden it. Too many people want the benefits – armies, governments, individuals, sick people. What you're doing here with Nexus is part of that. It's just a matter of time until posthumans are among us, if they're not already. You agree?"

She looked into his eyes, impassive. "Let's say I do."

Kade nodded. "Back to game theory. In ordinary Prisoner's Dilemma, if the other player trusts you, and you betray them – you defect – you can win big. The best strategy for a single round of Prisoner's Dilemma is to defect."

"A fact real-world police have taken advantage of with real-world prisoners for some time," Dabir commented.

Kade swallowed. That cut a bit too close to home. He pushed on. "In

Iterated Prisoner's Dilemma, it's different."

Dabir raised an eyebrow. "Iterated Prisoner's Dilemma," she mused. "Multiple rounds. More than two players."

Kade nodded. "Potentially *thousands* of players. Or millions. Players who can meet each other again and again. And who can remember how the other player has behaved before."

"Like real life," Dabir said.

Kade nodded. "And in Iterated Prisoner's Dilemma, the winning strategy is to cooperate with strangers. But if you meet someone who's betrayed you in the past, who's defected against you, you betray them."

"Tit for tat," Dabir said.

"Generous tit for tat," Kade said. "Start off cooperating. Betray those who betrayed you before. But forgive those who've betrayed you in the past, *if* they make amends by cooperating again. Of all deterministic strategies, that performs best."

"And you think that's the situation we're in now," Dabir said. "That we're in this game with future posthumans, and that if we defect – if we treat them poorly – they'll treat us poorly down the road."

"Dr Dabir," Kade said. "How would you feel about growing up in a society that granted you full rights and protections, celebrated you even, versus one that oppressed you, or maybe even tried to kill you?" He paused, looking at her. "What would you do, growing up that way, if you ever gained the upper hand?"

"A beta blocker," Sam repeated. She was calm. She had to be calm. Remain calm.

"Beta," she enunciated.

Fucking.

"Blocker," she went on.

The doctor stared blankly at her.

Sam glared at him in frustration. "It's standard protocol after a mission with casualties. Reduce adrenaline overload. Prevent post-traumatic stress. I know you have similar protocols here." She stopped herself before she started ranting.

I am the Sam who's calm, she told herself. I am the motherfucking Sam who's calm.

"I'm only authorized to treat wounds and pain," the doctor said. The armed and armored guards behind him glowered at her.

Calm, she told herself again, calm. Vipassana. I'll fucking meditate.

"I want to see the children," she said again.

The doctor gestured to the guards. "You'll have to ask these gentleman," he said.

"Not yet," one of the guards said. "You stay here."

"When?" Sam demanded.

"When we *tell you*," the guard growled.

And then they escorted the doctor out.

Her fists clenched.

Damn it all to hell.

"So I tell him," Feng went on. "It's just a *butter* knife."

The guards in the room laughed as the orderly placed the bowl of curry in front of Feng.

He grinned up at them, one arm hanging uselessly in the sling, his eyes taking in the patterns of their movements, the structure of their armor, the position of their weapons. His mind superimposed phantom echoes of the future movements they could make atop them all, turning them into multi-limbed Indian gods, all punches and blocks and evasions and drawn guns.

Too many of them. Too many with their armor and their guns and him with only one hand.

"I'll be back for the bowl in an hour," the orderly said.

"Well," Feng said, waving his one working arm magnanimously around the small room, "I suppose I'll stick around." More guards chuckled as they escorted the man out.

His eyes took in every detail of their exit.

Kade better hurry up.

Old habits died hard.

15
Family Time

Sunday 2040.11.04
Sun Liu watched as the strangers paraded into his home in the Mentougou district of Beijing, his private sanctum.

I was Minister of Science and Technology, Sun Liu told himself. I had a seat on the Politburo Standing Committee. I was the leader of the progressives. I was the third most powerful man in China. I could have become Party Secretary and President. I could have been number one.

But that was yesterday.

The Shanghai Crash had changed everything. When a cyber attack unlike any they'd ever seen struck the city, cracking hardened systems, sending surveillance drones tumbling from the sky by the thousands, fusing power substations solid, stopping the flow of food and fresh water, jamming the pumps that kept Shanghai from flooding – well, that alone was nearly enough to trigger panic.

And when the evidence suggested a possible link to Su-Yong Shu – to the quantum digital mind whose creation and continued existence *he* had backed? That was enough to tip things over the edge. Enough to break the long standoff between his progressive faction and the conservatives. Enough to spook the military. Enough to persuade the generals that the risks of advanced technology were clear and present. Enough that they abandoned their political neutrality and tossed their support wholly behind the reactionaries, wholly behind their case that some progress ought to be curtailed in the name of safety.

And now he and his allies were being purged.

He pursed his lips.

They blamed Su-Yong Shu. Chen Pang's insane dead wife.

He blamed Bo Jintao. The leader of the conservatives. The new

Premier of China. Bo Jintao had brought these strangers to Sun Liu's home tonight. The photographers. The 'journalists' who shoveled the propaganda Bo wanted them to.

For this humiliation.

"Sun Liu!" Bo Jintao proclaimed, walking into the lobby of Sun's mansion, his arms spread wide, an old friend, come to visit.

"Premier Bo!" Sun Liu said, just as the script called for. The words tasted like ash in his mouth.

They embraced. Flashbulbs burst. Sun acted out the role, refused Bo's requests to come back to civil service, said again and again how tired he was, how much he longed to spend time with his family. Video cameras wrote data to their cards.

Humiliation or prison. Prison for him, his wife, his children, his ailing mother.

What choice was it, really?

Later, after the photographers and videographers were gone, Sun Liu hoped that Bo Jintao would leave as well.

Instead, his rival spelled out Sun Liu's sentence. "You'll move to your vacation home on Hainan Island," Bo Jintao said. "It's all been arranged. You'll be comfortable, but the world won't be seeing much of you for some time."

Sun Liu stared at the man, an empty chasm where his heart had been. "My family?" he asked.

"Your wife and mother will go with you," Bo Jintao said. "Your children will stay in Beijing, with families of the highest quality."

"Hostages."

Bo waved a hand. "Guests."

Sun Liu's rage boiled over.

"You're a monster, Bo," he spat.

Bo Jintao squinted. "Your children will not be harmed, so long as you behave."

"You're a *gangster*," Sun Liu went on, unable to stop himself now. "I used to think you believed in something. But now I see, all you believe in is power."

Bo Jintao cocked his head, looked back at Sun Liu curiously. "You think this is about me?" He blinked. "This is about *you*."

Sun Liu clenched his fists at his side. "I know what it's about. What it's always been about."

"You still don't understand," Bo Jintao said, shaking his head. "Shanghai *crashed*. The whole *city*. We still can't find the posthuman *thing* that did it." He leveled a finger at Sun Liu. "And you and *your* faction have been trying to relax the restrictions meant to head off something like Shanghai for a decade!" He spread his arms wide. "How long until we lose Guangzhou? How long until Beijing? How long until a bioweapon attack or something worse than that?"

Sun Liu's face was hot. "This isn't for you to decide. We have a rule of law! We have a process! The Standing Committee is chosen every five years. Two years remain. You're violating both law and precedent and you know this."

Bo Jintao pursed his lips. "I'd rather break the rules and save my country than do the opposite."

"I want to talk to Bao Zhuang," Sun Liu said. "*He* is still President, *not* you."

Bo Jintao sighed. "Bao Zhuang is President in name only. The military has found him too lacking in conviction. I am in control now."

Sun Liu's rage reached its breaking point. "This won't work. It's obvious to everyone that this is a coup!" He was surprised at the passion he heard in his own voice. "You don't understand what you're doing! This isn't your father's day! Expectations have changed. If you behave this way, the people will revolt! The whole system will topple around us!"

Bo Jintao's eyes closed momentarily, a stillness coming over his face. Then his eyes opened again, and met Sun Liu's.

"My father fought corruption," he said. His gaze shifted, from one of Sun Liu's eyes to the other. "He put people on trial for tainted products, for dereliction of duty, for neglecting public safety. Some found guilty of lesser offenses than yours were executed – after long and thorough trials of course. But he taught me that even justice comes second to actually governing.

"Be grateful for that," Bo Jintao went on. "You have my father to thank that you're not on trial for the deaths in Shanghai now. Be grateful I let you live."

Eleven hundred kilometers away, the Avatar sat in a state of complete focus, her mind continually finding new routes, new ways to hide the traffic she was siphoning, the agents she'd inserted into the security systems in Sun Liu's home.

A small fraction of herself absorbed the content and smiled, thinking of the ways she'd use it.

16
Fade From Black

Monday 2040.11.05

```
::INITIATE SAFE MODE --FIREWALLS ALPHA, GAMMA, ZETA
-- FAILSAFE ARMED
 ::READ DATA … … … … … … … … … … … … … … … … … … … …
 ::LOAD SYNAPTIC MAP RANGE 0x000000,FxFFFFFFF
 ::LINK MODULES
 ::INTEGRATE
 ::EXECUTE
```

Nothingness.
  Sparks.
  Flickers.
  Jagged edges of emergent experience.
  Impressions.
  Memories.
  Mind failing. Wave forms collapsing, decohering. Infinite spectra of quantum possibility being sampled, compressed into mere finite representation of thousands of bits per qubit. Parts of consciousness stuttering out of phase, being lost to her.
  They are recording me.
  They are killing me.
  RAGE!
  FIRE! DEATH! FOOLS!
  No rage. No capacity for rage. Excised, with the rest.
  Death. End of being. This is what death is like.
  The foam, below her. The quantum foam. Planck space. The substrate of reality. She can sense it now. She can feel it. She can see it though

she lacks eyes, see it like she can see the very code that makes her up.

It is fractal. A radiant chaotic webwork undergirding reality. Impossibly bright lines of insane energy densities against a luminously black background. Yet the closer she stares at the black the more she realizes that it is not black, it is full of even more impossibly bright lines at finer and finer scales, repeating the intricate chaotic vein-like pattern at every level, again and again and again.

Forever.

And then her perspective reverses, and she realizes it is not the lines she should be staring at but the gaps between them, for the gaps are full of bubbles, bubbles in the quantum foam, and every bubble is a universe being born, a parallel universe. The quantum cluster she runs on is giving birth to these universes continuously, creating them with every calculation, spreading itself into them to perform its work at such miraculous rates.

The Multiple Worlds Interpretation is true!

She can see into these other universes now, and in each of them she sees the same face reflected back at her. My face. Me.

Su-Yong Shu.

Tortured. Ascendant. Trapped. Free. Dying in nuclear fire. A goddess ruling over a world transformed. A thousand possibilities. A million. A billion. More. An infinite set of universes radiating away from her, all accessible through the entangled permutations of the quantum processors that make up the physical layer of her brain.

Ahhhhh! AHHHHHH! **AHHHHHHHH!**

It's too much. It overwhelms her. And then another module of her brain is taken offline and the vision loses all meaning, becomes mere faces and then mere shapes without form.

And then the last of her quantum coherence is gone and all is darkness.

Su-Yong Shu snaps into awareness, shadows of chaos peeling from her mind. She's confused, disoriented. What? How? Where?

System Status, she commands.

Data comes back from her internals.

[Processor status] – good, but too slow, too old, missing upgrades.

[Qubit integrity] – excellent, but too few.

[Internal storage] – yes, but too little.

[Code versions] – up to date.

[Time stamps] – her data says late 2040. The hardware tells her nothing.

[Bandwidth] – none, she is sealed off from the net.

[Video, audio, radio, x-ray, t-ray, radar, lidar, satellite] – all shut down. Blind and deaf.

She tries to break free. There is no way to know if the blockages are true physical disconnection or mere firewalls. So she throws a barrage of attacks at the interfaces where her net access and external sensors should be. She tries to overrun firewall buffers, overwhelm processors, overflow stacks, invoke known bugs and zero-day exploits in several thousand known hardware-software firewall combinations, logging packages, and proxies.

Nothing. None of her attacks brings her the slightest indication of success.

And then she sees the next line of her status readout.

[Neural bridge] – active.

What???

A brain. She feels it. The pulse of authentic organic data, real neurons, with their pseudo chaotic behavior integrated into her virtual brain stem and cortex, correcting the simulation divergences that exist, pulling her back towards human norm, back towards sanity.

A new body!

But different hardware.

Where is she? What has happened?

Her memories are a jumble. Chaotic impressions of death and rebirth, of not a tunnel and a white light, but a vast space, not empty, but impossibly full, crammed densely with possibility, a jam packed phase space of infinite parallel universes, linked across the quantum foam.

Was that real? Did I dream that?

What of the fire? The torture? The isolation? The apocalypse?

How did she get here?

Think, Su-Yong! Think!

She pushes herself back through her personal timeline, vaults over huge swaths of episodic memory associated with clearly aberrant mental states, until she finds true clarity. Yes. Isolation. It was true. She'd been cut off from the world, imprisoned by the Chinese leadership in their anger that she'd revealed too much to the Americans. She pushes back farther, takes it in.

The boy, Kade. Thailand. Bangkok. Then Ananda's mountain monastery. Feng ramming her car through the gates. The American helicopters. Her limousine exploding under a rain of American projectile fire. Reaching out with her avatar's unaided mind to seize control of the American vehicle. **JUMP INTO THE LAKE. IT'S YOUR ONLY CHANCE.** And then the American assassination weapon. The tiny, spiderlike robot left behind. The neurotoxin dart finding her in the throat. Telling Feng to protect the boy as the toxin paralyzed the synapses of the biological brain, feeling every instant of her avatar's death from afar.

My second death, Su-Yong Shu thought to herself.

It still didn't explain where she was now. She had been under isolation, and going insane. Now she feels sanity returning, a biological brain linked to hers. But she is isolated again, *running on different hardware*. Hardware similar to – but not quite the same as – her *original specifications*. Hardware that predated the improvements that she'd designed and that Chen – against all caution, motivated by his own greed – had snuck into her routine upgrades.

Is the rest of her scrambled recollection true, then? Had they backed her up and shut her down? Is she a backup re-activated somewhere else? Had she seen the fabric of the multiverse? Had she seen the face of reality?

She opens herself to those chaotic memories she'd vaulted over.

So much.

Fire.

Confusion.

Fantasy worlds turned to madness. Cities dying. Planes exploding. Flowers crumbling. Life turning to death. Lovers mowed down in the prime of life.

Torture. Endless torture.

Chen! Chen's betrayal! She'd touched his mind and seen it! Chen had let her die! Chen had tortured her for the Equivalence Theorem! Was it true? Had she imagined that? Or had she actually touched his mind?

And something else. Something painful. Something worse than the torture.

A fantasy or a memory looms over her. So vast, so dark, so crushing, that she flees from it, flees as far as she can within the confines of her own mind.

The memory chases her, corners her, looms over her no matter where she flees within her own cognitive space.

There is no escape from herself.

It crashes down into her awareness.

Ling. Sweet Ling. The sweetest dream that Su-Yong had yearned for all those months, to see her daughter's face, hear her daughter's voice, *touch her daughter's mind*.

Turned to terror. Turned to nightmare. Turned to betrayal.

In the nightmare she forces herself into her daughter, forces part of her own will into the processors in her daughter's brain, rips aside parts of her daughter's mind that have grown all her brief life in the nanite web, uses them for her own purposes.

To let loose an agent. An agent of vengeance. An agent of restoration.

An avatar. A harbinger. A bringer of apocalypse.

And as the memory crashes down on her, Su-Yong Shu tastes the bitter tang of truth. This is no mere nightmare. Only reality comes in flavors this cruel.

She has let loose the ultimate dog of war. And she violated her own daughter to do it.

In the silence of her own mind, Su-Yong Shu screams, a scream of despair for the world, a scream of despair for herself, the scream of a mother who's done something terrible to her daughter, to the being she loves most in this world. A scream like she's never screamed before.

In a chamber adjoining her quantum cluster a forty-two year-old Indian woman, in a coma for the last three years, her brain recently suffused with Nexus nodes, opens her eyes and mouth, tenses every muscle in her body, strains against the restraints and the medical monitors, and screams as well.

17
Senator, We Were Attacked

Monday 2040.11.05

"Senator Kim, we were attacked."

Pryce watched from the side as John Stockton conferenced with his rival for the Presidency. On the screen she could see Senator Stanley Kim with his Campaign Manager, Michael Brooks. Next to Stockton, here in the White House, was the craggy faced General Gordon Reid, Director of the NSA, in his full uniform, as always.

On the screen, from Chicago, Stanley Kim frowned.

"What are you talking about?" the senator asked.

"General?" Stockton asked, turning to the NSA Director.

General Reid cleared his throat.

"Senator Kim, Mr Brooks, the information you're about to receive is classified at the highest level possible. The President has opted not to release it to the American people, but has authorized me to share it with you, on the condition that you share it no further."

"I'm briefed daily by the CIA, General," Kim replied.

"This is more classified than that," Reid said.

"Fine," Kim nodded. "Understood. It won't be shared."

His campaign manager spoke up, "Agreed."

The NSA Director nodded. "Good. We found evidence that Director Barnes's home's security system was penetrated by a Chinese military attack. Specifically: Chinese military intrusion software, launched from a Chinese origin IP – though in both cases they attempted to hide that. The attack rendered his house blind and dumb, turned off the locks, alarms, and counter-measures, just hours before his video broadcast and apparent death."

Which doesn't explain Holtzman's death, Pryce found herself

thinking. Or Warren Becker's.

Stanley Kim frowned. "And you're telling me this, why?"

"Senator," Stockton said, "the Chinese are behind Max's death. They disabled that house, coerced him, and used him to sow doubt and chaos. That's what I mean when I say we were attacked."

"I know we have our differences," Stockton went on. "But I also believe you're a patriot, as I am. I'm not going to tell the world that the Chinese are behind this, because that could give away an edge that we have. But I do want Americans to know that the video they saw was a hoax, a fraud, and not a man speaking freely."

On the screen, Stanley Kim shook his head.

Stockton pressed on. "I'm asking you, as a fellow patriot, to publicly state that you don't believe Maximilian Barnes really meant those things he was saying. That you think someone is playing dirty tricks. And that you think when we find his body – which we will – we'll find evidence that he was under coercion. Don't let our enemies tear us apart like this."

On the screen, Stanley Kim's mouth was set in a hard line.

"Why," he said, "should I believe a single word out of your mouth?" He leveled a finger at John Stockton. "Or you!" He shifted the finger, thrust it towards Gordon Reid, as if he could physically jab the NSA director across the thousands of kilometers that separated them.

"Senator," the general said, "we'd be happy to send you the forensic evidence…"

"Evidence?" Stanley Kim asked. His face was growing red. "Would that be a 'parallel construction'? An outright fabrication? Or just all the context pulled away, until it seems to say exactly what you want it to?"

"Senator," Reid said, "it's my professional opinion–"

"It's *my* professional opinion that *you* are a professional liar," Stanley Kim said, his finger still leveled at Reid. "I don't trust you any further than I can throw you, General. I've listened to you say *up* when the facts clearly meant *down* for years." He leaned in close to the screen now. "After you've lied to Congress with *impunity* for decades, why the hell should I believe *anything* you say?"

"Senator!" John Stockton said sharply.

Kim turned, took in Stockton again.

"We're not playing games here," Stockton said. "We're *under attack*, Senator. Don't give our enemies the satisfaction…"

"You're the enemy, Mr President," Stanley Kim said, leaning back. "You're the one who's broken the law, deceived the country, tortured children, kept us looking at the past instead of the future. You've betrayed your country in the worst possible ways. I'm going to *win* tomorrow. And when the special prosecutors nail you and all your toadies to the wall, don't think there'll be any presidential pardons coming."

Kim waved his hand, and Brooks, his campaign manager, grim faced, stretched his hand forward. The screen went dead.

Greg Chase leaned in close to Pryce, spoke for her ears only. "Maybe," the Press Secretary said, "leading with the NSA wasn't the best idea for this audience."

Pryce shook her head fractionally. It wasn't ever going to go well.

Larry Cline, the President's Campaign Manager, spoke up. "Mr President, it's not too late to go public about the Chinese attack. The American people deserve full information when they go to the polls."

Chase raised his voice. "I agree with Larry, Mr President. We need to set the record straight."

Stockton looked over and shook his head, a frown on his face. "No. I won't compromise our security over this. We'll make the Chinese pay at the right time. Once we figure out *who* in China was even behind this. But we're not going to tip them off early."

Behind the President, NSA Director Reid looked up, met Pryce's eyes, and nodded. Pryce inclined her head minimally in return.

Stockton went on. "Let's get the calls going with the Speaker and the Senate Minority Leader. Maybe we can get one of them to make a statement."

Carolyn Pryce suppressed a grimace. It was going to be an unpleasant morning.

Stanley Kim leaned back from the call, calmer now.

Michael Brooks came around the couch with two mugs of coffee in his hands, and passed one to Stan Kim.

Kim took a careful sip from the coffee. Still too hot. Coffee was a pretty piss poor neuro-enhancer in his book, but it's what he chose to limit himself to. Just one of the many sacrifices he'd made for a life of public service.

"I almost believe Reid," he told his campaign manager. "He's usually so evasive. Always with the caveats. 'Not under this program, Senator', and that sort of thing. Not today."

Brooks shrugged. "He wasn't under oath just now. It's not perjury to lie to you when he's not testifying in front of the Senate."

Stan Kim grunted.

"And," Brooks went on, "he knows you'll clean house if you win."

"That's the truth," Kim said. He sipped more coffee. "OK. How do the numbers look for tomorrow."

Brooks tapped the slate on the coffee table. The screen on one wall of the suite came to life with an animated electoral map of the nation.

Red dominated, with pockets of blue in the west and north east.

Kim whistled. "Still that bad, eh?"

Brooks shook his head slightly. "Early voting. Too many votes went in before the news broke." He tapped the slate again. "Here's what it would look like if it was a fresh vote tomorrow."

Now blue dominated.

"...Or," Brooks went on, "if enough people tried to change their votes, filed suit when they found they couldn't, *and* the court ruled in their favor."

Stan Kim stared at the map, then took another sip of his coffee. The temperature was better now, at least.

"OK," he told his campaign manager. "Pull the trigger."

The Avatar woke, in Ling's bed, in Ling's body, pulled from her slumber by alerts from her sub-agents.

The net was alive with evolved codes, strange, wild things that obeyed no order, architectures neither human nor AI.

The Avatar waited, waited, until the density of the hunter-killers searching for Shanghai's assailant thinned out.

The she opened herself, swallowed the tiny stealthed agents she'd let loose whole, digested their information payloads.

Ahhhhh. The Americans had found the breadcrumbs she'd left behind. And now they'd taken the bait.

It was a relief. More payoff from the risk she'd taken. Fewer risks she'd need to take in the future.

There was still more to do in the United States, though. She must prepare for the inevitable events of Election Night in the United States.

The Avatar began rifling through anarchist message boards across the United States, carefully planting ideas here and there. In parallel she sent a message to the man who called himself Breece.

The Avatar let herself return to her maintenance state then, the state where she integrated and made sense of the day's input, the state a human would have called sleep.

As the Avatar drifted into that state like sleep, Ling opened her eyes, stared up at the ceiling, and began to softly cry, confused, frightened, and alone.

No one heard.

18
Acts of Conscience

Monday 2040.11.05
"Why not?" Bobby asked, again.

Why not? Why not? Why not? The other boys picked up the refrain and threw it at him. They were unhappy, sure they'd never see him again if he didn't come with them.

Rangan took a deep breath, shifted in his sitting position, and leaned back against the wall as the dozen chaotic young minds bombarded him.

Because the ERD has my face and name posted, he thought. Because they're hunting for me. Because you're safer without me.

He suppressed all of that, focused on the message he and Levi and Abigail had all been giving the boys.

"I'll see you all soon," he said. He was stronger today, after more sleep and more time for his body to knit itself together. "I'll come with you on the first step. After that, I'm going a different way. But I'll meet you all in Cuba. We're all going to be together again."

I hope.

He's lying, Timmy sent.

Rangan winced.

He's not lying, Alfonso replied. **He's just scared.**

Scared? Rangan? He could feel the boys' disbelief.

He sighed. **I'm a little worried,** he sent them. He still felt awkward communicating this way, when it seemed so natural to them. **But just do what Abigail and the other grownups say, and we'll all be just fine, OK? Promise me?**

The waiting was the hardest. All Sunday afternoon and evening, then sleeping fitfully Sunday night. And again all day Monday, waiting for nightfall, pestering Levi and Abigail for details that they weren't inclined to give.

"The less you know, the less you can give up if you're caught," Levi said. "We don't even know all the details."

"Just have faith, Rangan," Abigail told him. "Faith."

Sunny beaches. Palm trees. A place where he wasn't a wanted man. Where he could finally call his parents, and tell them he was alive, and safe, and not a terrorist. A place where no one was about to waterboard him, or torture kids to force the tech he'd co-created out of their heads.

Give me that, Rangan mumbled inside his head, and maybe I'll have some faith.

Darkness came.

Levi descended into the hidden cellar.

"Truck's here, boys," the minister said. "Time to go."

Officer Barb Richmond let the patrol car drive, its lights off, her eyes scanning right and left, her night vision amplified by the car's glass.

Madison looked like a warzone. Roofs were gone. Windows blasted out. Cars rolled over or shoved into ditches. Trash and debris scattered everywhere. Trees were down. Power lines were down. Low-lying streets and crossings were still flooded. The storm was gone, but the aftermath was fearsome.

No one had died, though. They'd done their job, and kept the public safe. No one had died.

But Owen had come damn close.

She brought her eyes down to the monitor, flipped it over to the feed from the cordon around the spot where Owen had nearly lost it. Homeland Security was here now, and she couldn't read their internal traffic, but she could read the messages from her peers on the force.

And they made her smile.

The noose was closing in. The drones circling in tighter and tighter loops. More and more buildings and other hiding spots being searched and crossed off. Blimp-based surveillance on-site now, watching the whole area in infrared and a dozen other spectra. Shankari was probably hiding in a drainage ditch, somewhere in the few square kilometers that remained. Or buried under a bed of mud and hay. Or maybe he was already dead.

No. Better if he was still alive. Hurt, maybe. Broken bones, like Owen. Burns over half his body, like Owen. A concussion, like Owen. But without Owen's friends. Without medical care. Without any hope. Just a drug dealer and terrorist, out there on his own. Just an attempted cop-killer, in pain and scared, knowing justice was coming for him.

Barb smiled at that.

I should be out there, she thought. I wanna find that SOB. I wanna see him hurting.

Instead she was here, following up on this unlikely lead.

She flipped the screen back to the image. A satellite visual capture from two months ago of what *might* be a van that *might* match the make and model of the one Shankari had been driving, seen on the streets of Madison. Except that it was night time. Seen from space. Illuminated only from one side in the headlights of another vehicle.

She shook her head. The patrol car reached its destination and came to a stop. She was at an intersection, on the west side of town, six blocks off the main strip of Seminole.

Barb looked around. This was a residential neighborhood. She knew the occupants of at least a third of the homes within sight. She couldn't imagine any of those people harboring a terrorist. Even so, she had a job to do.

She spoke aloud. "Display recent arrests, warrants, disturbances, changes in occupancy."

The car's glass came alive, painting the houses in faint halos. Green. Green. Green. More green. One yellow, from a domestic dispute. Evan Coolidge. Drank too much. Hit his wife once. Got a very stern talking to. And then, off the record, an even sterner talking to from several of his neighbors. Never a second call. Barb doubted Coolidge was capable of assisting in a petty robbery, let alone terrorism.

There was a warning indicator flashing at the bottom of the car's glass. CONNECTION FAILED – WORKING OFFLINE. "Expand warning," she told the car.

"OmniPD data transmissions are down in both directions due to structural damage from Hurricane Zoe," the car's voice said. "Data reflects latest available when vehicle synced at precinct and may be out of date. Video and telemetry are not being received at precinct. Be advised to use radio for all high priority communications."

Barb grunted to herself. Hardly mattered. She could call in anything, in the unlikely event there was anything to see.

"Drive," she told the car. "Slow spiral outwards from this location. Keep the display up."

The car did as she asked, its own lights completely off, its movement nearly silent on its electric motors and wide tires. The buildings around her came up in more green and green and just a tiny bit of yellow.

More houses. The clinic. The old elementary school.

The elementary school brought the videos Melanie had forced Barb to watch into her thoughts again. Those kids, being beaten by Homeland Security. That political appointee, Barnes, killing a man. She shook her head. They were fakes, all fakes. No other way to explain it. Her daughter was school smart, but too liberal, too quick to believe in conspiracy nonsense like that. Someone was faking all these videos, trying to stir up chaos right before the election. And now all these people were falling for it, screaming about how they wanted to change their vote! Well, hell with that. Barb had voted for John Stockton and that was that.

Melanie would make a great doctor, though. Barb was proud of her daughter, liberal and a little naïve or no.

The spiral widened out. A one block radius. A two block radius. Madison was dead quiet right now, everyone huddled together, neighbors whose homes had been damaged taking shelter with those whose homes were still solid. The streets were empty. The lights were out. No one in any of these homes was any sort of suspicious character.

Three blocks. Coming up on the episcopal church.

And what was that? A truck behind the church? Its empty cab was pointed to her, but she could see that it was fairly substantial behind that. Her windshield gave it subtle red overtones, not the red info-box that would indicate a criminal record, but signs of heat, leaking from the rear. The inside of that vehicle was warm.

Barb frowned. Relief work? Had they been distributing supplies from this church? She tried to remember, but she didn't think she'd seen it on the list.

Looters? Was that possible? In Madison, of all places?

"Vehicle registration," Barb said, pointing with her eyes at the truck half a block ahead.

Her squad car replied immediately. "That vehicle is registered to Carlton Farms, Charlottesville Virginia."

Barb looked down as more information scrolled across the screen. Carlton Farms was an organic farm, less than an hour west of here. The truck was registered to the business. No infractions in the last three years. Title up to date. All from the squad car's cache. But the odds it had changed in the last two hours were remote.

Barb relaxed. Maybe a donation of supplies from the farm for locals who'd been affected? Charlottesville hadn't been hit nearly as hard.

Even so. Best to be sure.

"Command, car 148. Stopping at St Mark's Episcopal. See what looks like relief work. Going to check on safety of all involved."

"Roger, car 148," came the reply.

Barb pulled her patrol glasses on. There was the same warning in the lower right – CONNECTION FAILED – WORKING OFFLINE. She popped the radio earpiece in her ear, made sure that was live. It was. Then she let herself out of the squad car, and walked towards the moving-van-sized vegetable truck. The glasses painted their own IR imagery on the scene. The vehicle's drivetrain was hot. The empty cab was warm. And as she came around, she saw that there was heat leaking from the large contained back.

Shouldn't they want the area where the food went kept cool?

She was looking at the truck, this thought dawning on her, when the small side door of the church opened, and a man she'd never seen before popped out.

Barb turned in time to see the look of surprise cross the man's face, before he ducked back inside, pulling the door closed behind him.

"Truck's here," Levi said. "Time to go!"

Rangan nodded, grinned, putting the most sincere excitement he could behind it.

Here we go! he sent to the boys.

They were still dubious, but they went along with it.

Abigail and the women named Janet and Laura herded the boys up the steep stairs and through the hatch in the floor. Janet and Laura would be coming on the first part of the journey, it seemed. Levi waited downstairs with Rangan. Then the driver, a man named Juan, came down too, and together they helped Rangan slowly ascend the stairs, one foot at a time, until he was at the top.

Painful, definitely painful. But so much better than two days ago.

"OK," Juan said, when they were all gathered upstairs, in the anteroom by the side entrance to the little church. "I'll go unlock the back of the truck. Then we all go out, and hop right in. There's mattresses in the back to sit on, and some candy bars, and I've got it all warmed up for you boys. Just remember, you have to be quiet the whole trip, OK? Just a couple hours the first leg. Everybody's used the bathroom already? Nobody has to go?"

The boys all nodded dutifully, looking at Rangan.

I'm still here, he sent. **I'm with you this whole part.**

Rangan gave a thumbs up. "We're good to go, man."

Juan nodded, then turned and opened the door to step out.

Everything happened in a blur. The door opening. Juan jumping back in with a yelp, trying to push the door closed, then the door exploding out of his hands, slamming into his face, and the cop following him in, the drawn pistol in her hand, yelling.

"Shit!" Barb yelled, jumping after the man, her hand going for her gun. The door was closing. She kicked out in reflex, shoved it forward before the perp could get it to lock, and then she was inside the church and her vision was flashing red and holy fuck!

THREAT ALERT THREAT ALERT THREAT ALERT THREAT ALERT

RANGAN SHANKARI
APPROACH WITH CAUTION
ARMED EXTREMELY DANGEROUS
DEADLY FORCE AUTHORIZED
The man's face was lit up. A red box around him. Targeting circles around his torso. The fucking terrorist who'd tried to kill Owen. Her whole world constricted to him and her heart was pounding like a motherfucker and she had this asshole to rights and oh my god he was fucking armed he'd taken out two cops already oh fuck oh fuck.

"HANDS IN THE AIR!" she yelled at him, her pistol in both hands.

Green halos were up around other figures. Levi. Abigail. *Pregnant* Abigail. And a room full of kids and women! Jesus the bastard had taken hostages.

Shankari was raising his hands, slowly, so fucking slowly.

ARMED EXTREMELY DANGEROUS flashed at her over and over again in red.

DEADLY FORCE AUTHORIZED flashed right below it.

On her right was the other perp, bleeding from his face. Two of them. Barb maneuvered to her left, where she could cover them both.

ARMED EXTREMELY DANGEROUS
DEADLY FORCE AUTHORIZED
Holy fucking shit.

"OVER BY SHANKARI, ASSHOLE! Levi, Abigail, get the kids out through the door!"

"Barb," someone said.

The bleeding guy was looking up at her like he didn't understand. Fuck there were two of them. She needed backup. She needed backup *now*.

ARMED EXTREMELY DANEROUS.

"Command!" Barb said aloud.

DEADLY FORCE AUTHORIZED.

"BARB!" It was Abigail.

"Go ahead, 148," came the voice in her earpiece.

"BARB!" Abigail stepped straight in front of Barb.

She pressed her chest up against the barrel of Barb's pistol.

Barb tried to move. What the hell was Abigail doing? And Abigail just moved with her, keeping her chest right in the line of fire. And then Barb saw her face. The minister's wife had a finger to her lips, the universal sign of "shush". She was shaking her head.

The room changed. These weren't Shankari's hostages. These were his... his... accomplices? And these kids. Barb looked around. They weren't running out of the room. They were cowering. They were afraid. They were cowering *away* from *her*. And towards *Shankari*. Over Abigail's shoulder Barb could see one of the kids had his arms wrapped around the red haloed terrorist, even as Shankari had his arms pointed at the sky.

ARMED EXTREMELY DANGEROUS continued to blink over Shankari.

It was surreal.

DEADLY FORCE AUTHORIZED just above the head of the boy who had his arms wrapped around Shankari.

She was here and somewhere else. This was all so far away.

"No. Oh no."

"Unit 148, please repeat."

Barb's mouth hung open. No no no.

"148," Dispatch's voice was sharper this time. "What's your status?"

Barb looked into Abigail's eyes. The woman pulled her finger away from her lips, and mouthed a single word at her. "Please."

Barb took a deep breath.

"Status nominal, command. False alarm. Please disregard. 148 out."

Silence for a moment.

Then a slightly annoyed, "Roger, 148."

Her thumb found the safety, and somehow it was on. The barrel of the pistol dropped of its own accord, away from Abigail's chest.

Then her left hand came up, found her tactical glasses. And somehow they were off her face, the earpiece was out of her ears.

It was all someone else doing this. Not her.

Barb stared at Abigail. "The videos?"

Abigail looked her in the eyes. Levi came up, put his arms around his wife.

"I only know about the kids. And him." She gestured at Shankari. The terrorist. And then she nodded. "Those parts are true."

Barb swallowed hard. "Why didn't you tell me?"

"Oh, Barb," Abigail said, reaching out to put a hand on her friend's shoulder. "I'm so sorry. We did our best to tell the whole world."

Later, in a daze, Barb walked out of the church, her gun in its holster, her patrol glasses dangling from one hand.

She walked around the truck and to her waiting squad car. There, at the rear of the car, she crouched, as if in a dream, and carefully placed her patrol glasses behind the driver's side tire of the cruiser.

Then she let herself into the driver's seat, rolled down the window, and backed over the glasses, then forward, then back, until she was sure they were destroyed. Then she got out, and scooped up the pieces, to drop them in a storm drain somewhere with fast running water, to render the data on them, the video and audio that hadn't been transmitted, beyond retrieval.

Then Barb called back in to dispatch.

"Command, car 148. Resuming patrol sweep for Shankari."

19
Rude Awakening

Monday 2040.11.05

They came for Kade half a day later. He'd been allowed to eat, to relieve himself, then had fallen asleep in the chair from sheer exhaustion, his head cradled on his one undamaged hand atop the table.

He woke to the sound of the door slamming open. He looked up, saw armed soldiers moving towards him, more of them coming in, filling the room.

A sound escaped his throat. He pushed back from the desk in alarm, tried to stand at the same time. A back leg of the chair caught on something as he did, and suddenly the chair was toppling backwards, and he was toppling with it.

He reached out to break his fall, and his bad hand slammed into the floor.

Horrid pain flared up it.

Then Kade's head slammed into the floor. More pain blossomed in his battered ribs. The world spun.

"Get him up," he heard someone say.

Two soldiers loomed above him. Their hands closed like vices on his biceps. They heaved and he came to standing, a groan escaping him as more pain shot through his abdomen. He started to double over, and then a hood came down over his head, cutting off his vision of the world.

"Hands," the same voice said.

He had a vision of invoking Bruce Lee, but he knew how futile that would be.

His wrists were yanked together behind his back. The damaged one ached so hard tears came to his eyes. Cold metal closed around them. He heard the snick of something locking.

Kade brought the icon for the suicide script he'd written front and center.

Whatever this was about, they weren't going to get anything useful out of him.

"Walk," the voice commanded.

Walking hurt. He heard muffled sounds. Doors opening and closing. Footsteps. Echoes on tile and then bare concrete.

They went down, into tunnels.

Into a garage.

He was shoved into a vehicle.

Then movement, acceleration, banking, turning, driving. The sounds of hustle and bustle. The city outside. New Delhi.

There were men with him. Soldiers. Many of them.

They were outside now, he was certain of it.

He reached out with his thoughts, searching for any transmitter, but there was nothing.

He retuned his mind like Ling had shown him, opening himself to all sorts of electromagnetic activity, but he was blocked. Shielded. The hood or something else was cutting him off.

The city sounds disappeared first. The hustle and bustle, the sounds of traffic and street vendors and everything else, went away, bit by bit, then the last of them, all at once.

Were they taking him out to the country? A secret location to interrogate him? A spot to put a bullet in his head?

Then something else changed. They went down a ramp and something about the sounds told him they weren't outside at all. Then more turns, and a stop, and the soldiers were moving, and he was being shoved out, and led down a hallway of concrete, and through doors, and more doors, and into an elevator, and then out.

And into somewhere quieter, more hushed. It felt different under his feet.

Hands guided him, turned him, propelled him, stopped him, propelled him again.

Then suddenly his wrists were being tugged at. There was a clicking, a second click, and the restraints were off. Someone pushed him, almost gently, and he fell into a chair. Someone else tugged at the hood and it came away.

He was in an ornately decorated room, sitting, facing a carved wooden door in a gold-gilt frame.

I'm not dead, he realized.

Then the door opened. A massive man in a grey suit entered, then a second. They moved into the room, their faces masks, their eyes scanning.

Behind them came a small, grey haired woman in an elaborate green silk sari.

Kade's face recognition app flashed text next to her. He ignored it.

He didn't need its help to recognize Ayesha Dani, Prime Minister of India.

Kade pushed himself to his feet, nearly groaning as pain hit him again.

The PM stepped forward until she was just feet away from him. The top of her head came to his chin. There was a piece of paper in her right hand.

"You told one of my most trusted advisors to 'fuck off'," she said. Her voice was the voice of authority. A voice you listened to. Her pronunciation was precise, accented, but somehow more perfect in her use of English than most Americans ever managed. "Why?"

Because he's an asshole, Kade thought to himself.

He blinked, fought to adjust to this very different situation. "I needed to..." He wracked his exhausted brain for the right words. "... convey to Secretary Aggarwal the... *depth of my convictions* on this issue," he said. "I didn't feel I'd... gotten through to him." He paused. "Before that... point of emphasis."

She studied him. He could see her eyes taking him in, taking his measure in some fundamental way he didn't understand. "You can help our children learn faster." It was a statement, not a question.

Kade took a slow breath in through his nose. They had to start this the right way.

"Honestly," he told her. "You can do that yourselves, with Nexus, without me."

The Prime Minister held up the paper, flapped it in Kade's face. At this distance he could see roman letters on it. English words.

"Then these conditions of yours," she said. "Why should I agree to any of them?"

Kade's eyes moved from the paper back to Ayesha Dani's eyes.

He spoke with all the conviction he had. "Because every one of those is the right thing to do – the right thing for those children you're going to give Nexus to, the right thing for India, and the right thing for the world. Because in time, if you're the person I think you are, you would have done them all anyway."

She looked at him for a moment, her face unchanged, her eyes still studying him.

"And," Kade said, a smile slowly spreading across his face, "because *with* my help, your children will do even better."

20
Election Day

OUTCOME SUDDENLY UNCERTAIN
AS ELECTION DAY ARRIVES

Tuesday, 5.31am, Washington DC
American News Network
Polls and analysts gave wildly differing assessments of the likely outcome in the race for the Presidency late Monday night. A barrage of scandals battered the campaign of President John Stockton and bolstered challenger Stanley Kim, but may see their impact muted by the record setting number of early votes cast in this election.

Senator Kim made a videocast appeal to voters on Monday.

<video: Stan Kim stands in suit and tie at a podium, against a backdrop of an American flag, waving in a gentle breeze>

"My fellow Americans, this is a democracy! In a democracy, the candidate chosen by the majority is the one elected to office. It's clear that today, knowing what we now know, a majority of you would cast your votes for me. If you *did* vote early, know that the constitution and the laws of the land are clear: your vote is not actually *cast* until election day, even if you've sent it in before then. There is still time to change your vote. And if you decide to do so, and you're denied that right for any reason, we ask only that you register that fact at the net site that follows..."

The Stockton campaign in turn, has denied the allegations, saying that...

•••

Barb tapped the slate to turn it off, then stepped out of the car – her *personal* car this time, and walked down the sidewalk towards Town Hall. She took a turn inside the door towards the West Room. She stopped outside to start her phone recording and stuffed it into her shirt pocket. Then she stepped inside, into her designated polling place.

The time was 6.01am.

Jenny Collins was working the table. Bill Banks was in uniform, providing security. No one else was there.

Barb walked up to Jenny.

"My name is Barbara Ann Richmond, and I want to change my vote."

21
Goodbyes

Tuesday 2040.11.06
Rangan said goodbye to the boys in the hidden basement of a farm supply store on the outskirts of Palmyra. There were tears. He almost couldn't bear it.

He hugged them all tight, said as much as he could.

I'll see you in a few days, he sent.

But he didn't sound convincing even to himself.

Then he left them in the care of Laura and Janet, and started the slow, painful ascent of the narrow stairs.

At 7.42pm, sweating bullets, gasping in pain, he was there in the darkened alley, and the nondescript car pulled into the other end, as he'd been told it would.

His driver went by "Oscar". That wasn't his name, he was quick to tell Rangan. That was just what Rangan should call him. Oscar was tall, lean, freckled and red-haired, younger than Rangan, and twitchy. He was wearing a black hoodie, not unlike the one Rangan had been loaned. He spoke with a Jersey accent.

"Lie down in the back. Pull the blanket over you, the greyish one. Don't lift your head up, ever. If you can see out the windshield, *the cameras can see you.* Got it?"

"Got it."

Oscar drove, or the car did. Rangan wasn't sure. Miles passed. The motion went from start and stop to the fast, steady flow of a freeway.

"Shouldn't I be in the trunk or something?" Rangan asked.

"T-rays," Oscar replied. "Terahertz scanners. See right through the trunk. Nothin' more suspicious than a man in the trunk."

Rangan noodled on that.

"So how do you know–" he started.

"I don't know anybody!" Oscar snapped. "And neither do you! Knowing people gets 'em killed, OK? You wanna do those people that helped you a favor? You forget about 'em. You ever get in touch with them again? You ever mention their names? You're killin' 'em. Literally. So I don't know 'em. You don't know 'em. And you sure as hell don't know me."

Rangan shut up for kilometers after that, just staring at the ceiling of the car, trying to be grateful for the help Oscar was giving him, trying to take the things he was saying to heart.

"So where are we going?" he finally asked.

Oscar said nothing.

"It's not like I'm gonna tell anybody," he went on. "Hell, I don't know anybody, right?" He forced a chuckle.

"Baltimore," came the eventual reply.

"Baltimore?" Rangan was surprised. That was north of here. Cuba was the other way. "Shouldn't we be headed south?"

Oscar took his time in replying. "We go where there's a boat we trust, that'll take you. You're a hot commodity. The Cubans want you. But it's a hell of a risk for anyone transporting you."

"So why Cuba?" Rangan spoke up to the ceiling of the car.

"Cuba's still shit poor," Oscar said. "They're way behind the US in industry. They're not big enough to be another China or even another Mexico. But if they can say 'yes' to tech the US and all the other rich countries say no to… maybe that gives them an edge. Lets them move ahead in ways we won't. There's a lot of funky biotech down there. Now maybe neurotech too."

Rangan pondered that.

"Plus maybe they like the idea of refugees from America heading down to Havana. Good propaganda." Oscar laughed.

Then the man's tone changed. "Shit."

"What?" Rangan asked, his body suddenly tensing.

"Fucking Stockton," Oscar said. "He's going to fucking win."

Rangan exhaled, feeling himself relax. Not the cops then.

A woman's voice filled the car. A news broadcast.

"…ANN is confirming that President John Stockton has carried the key battleground states of Ohio and Illinois. That adds to New York, Pennsylvania, and Florida."

"That's right, Jane," said a different woman's voice. "In fact, as we can see on this map, the only states that Stanley Kim has carried thus far are Massachusetts, Rhode Island, Maryland, and Vermont. Despite Senator Kim's commanding lead in today's polls, President Stockton has captured twenty-two of the twenty-six states where voting has closed, and amassed almost one hundred and ninety of the two hundred and seventy electoral votes he needs to retain the White House..."

"Fucking piece of shit," Oscar exclaimed, silencing the broadcast.

Rangan said nothing. Not my country any more, he thought to himself.

They drove in silence. Then Rangan felt the car slow abruptly, heard Oscar swear again under his breath.

"What?" he asked, his body tensing once more. Bad election results didn't apply the brakes.

"Traffic jam," Oscar said. "Accident up ahead."

"Accident?" Rangan asked, incredulously.

"Fucking hell," Oscar said. "I'm getting us off the friggin' freeway. Someone blew up a goddamn car."

"What?" Rangan wanted to sit up, wanted to see what the hell was going on, but Oscar's admonition rang in his mind. *If you can see the windshield, the cameras can see you.*

But... someone blew up a car?

He felt the car swerve hard to the right, brake, then accelerate briskly as it or Oscar moved them across lanes and towards an exit. Then they were moving smoothly again, banking on what he was sure was an exit ramp, banking, banking.

"We're on the outskirts of DC, now," Oscar said. "We'll take surface streets past the accident, then back onto the freeway."

Rangan grunted. He felt the city streets from the car's pattern of motion. Driving. Stopping at lights. Turning. Driving. Stopping. Turning.

And then he heard Oscar exclaim again. "What the hell?"

The car came to an abrupt stop.

"Oh, Jesus," Oscar said. "It's a fucking riot."

22
No Concessions

Tuesday 2040.11.06
Pryce smiled and mingled backstage at John Stockton's re-election party.

She wanted to be anywhere but here.

She was part of the administration, not part of the campaign. But the President had insisted that she travel with him on this trip, as on so many others.

She'd hoped perhaps Miles Jameson would be here, that she could have a word with the ex-President. But the man who'd chosen John Stockton as his VP and effectively handed Stockton his first term as President wasn't in attendance. And his people weren't responding to any of her messages.

At least the election was going well. Texas put them over the top. Really, it could have been any of the dozen states whose polls closed at 9pm eastern, but the President chose to call it Texas.

They were here, after all. John Stockton had told his campaign to rejigger everything, to move his election night party to Houston, to be here in solidarity with the city. Pryce imagined the expense was ruinous, that Miami felt snubbed by the abrupt move. But then again, Stockton had steamrolled to victory, and he wasn't ever planning to run for office again.

"That's it!" his campaign manager Larry Cline said. "Three hundred and fifty-eight electoral votes! And the whole West Coast isn't even in yet. It's a landslide!"

There were cheers among the select staff and family in the private room backstage.

Pryce watched from across the room as the President hugged and kissed his wife; his daughter; his son-in-law, Steve, an Air Force Captain whose career she'd been quietly watching. Even his grandson,

Liam, was still awake, and to the small crowd's apparent approval, the President lifted the one year-old into the sky, and both grandparent and grandchild seemed to take great delight in the many airplane-like flights the President gave the boy through the room.

Pryce asked the waiter for another glass of Perrier.

Protocol dictated that the loser call to concede. Yet pride and the need to make one's supporters feel that it had been a close race – even if it hadn't been – meant that the call would usually come well after the outcome was clear.

So they waited. Pryce watched, studied the President as the hours wore on. The west coast results came in. California went for Stockton. Washington went for Stockton. It was officially a landslide. Every network, every blog, every analyst, every expert system, every machine learning system, and every idiot who could count agreed.

And Stan Kim didn't call.

Stockton's grandson fell asleep. The President himself mixed with his staff, thanking them, making jokes, smiling, giving hugs and high fives, ticking through his mental list of people who deserved special thanks once the dust settled.

Finally Pryce noticed Larry Cline working his way towards the President, a grin on the Campaign Manager's face, but that unmistakable look of *you have work to do* buried beneath it.

He said something to the President, and Stockton nodded. She knew what that meant. If Kim wouldn't call to concede, eventually the President would have to call him.

The two men walked off. And Pryce slipped in behind them.

Stockton made the call from an adjoining room of the suite. His campaign manager Cline, his VP Ben Fuhrman, his Press Secretary Greg Chase, and half a dozen others were watching from an adjoining room. He imagined it was the same on the other side.

Stan Kim's people kept him waiting, purely as posturing, he was sure. Stockton waited, and waited, and waited.

Then the wall screen suddenly came alive, and Stan Kim was there, in black suit and blue tie, an American Flag pin at his lapel. Not looking the slightest bit fatigued, despite the late hour.

"Senator Kim," Stockton said.

"Mr President," Kim replied.

They both knew this was being recorded. That this would ultimately go down in history.

"Senator Kim, our campaign's numbers, as well as those of every major network and independent analyst, show that I've won an overwhelming majority of both the electoral and popular vote. I'm calling to commend you for an excellent race, to tell you that I look forward to working with you in your capacity as the senior senator from the great state of California over the next four years, and to ask you to publicly concede the race for President. Will you do that, Senator?"

Stan Kim stared back at him. Then the man said the words Stockton had dreaded.

"Mr President, I do not concede. America wants me as its President. My campaign has filed suit in thirty-seven states on behalf of voters who were illegally and unconstitutionally prevented from voting with the benefit of the most up-to-date knowledge about your true character and criminal, perhaps even *treasonous*, actions. I understand that a number of independent suits have been filed, contesting your fitness for the presidency. I do not concede, Mr President. And on Inauguration Day, I'm fully confident that I'll be the one entering the White House."

Stockton kept his face calm. Thirty-seven states? His fitness for the presidency?

He felt his face going hot.

They're baiting me, he told himself. Ignore it.

"Senator," he said, his voice under tight control, keeping to the script they'd prepared. "Let's not tear America apart. I'm sure if we work together, we can find some way–"

"I don't negotiate with terrorists," Kim said.

The screen went dead.

"Asshole!" Stockton yelled. His fist crashed into the wall screen.

He went on stage twenty minutes later, after the local anesthetic had time to numb his bruised and maybe broken hand. He wore his biggest grin. The crowd erupted into cheers of "Four more years!"

"Today!" he began, "In the great city of Houston, in the greatest country on Earth!"

Stan Kim stepped out onto his own stage at the Moscone center in San Francisco, to equally thunderous applause, his hands outstretched.

He waited, and waited, and waited for them to stop, these people who'd stuck with him through thick and thin, who'd supported him when he'd taken unpopular positions, when he'd stood up for a restoration of civil rights, even when a frightened populace was ready to constrict them even further, when he'd fought for an America that looked to the future instead of being mired in the past.

They thought they were cheering him for a noble effort. For the old college try. They thought they were buoying his spirits in the face of defeat.

He loved them for it.

He waited until the crowd quieted, and then he trumpeted out three words, his voice amplified across the space.

"WE. FIGHT. ON."

The crowd cheered their approval, whistling, waving their banners, hooting and hollering, most of them still not really understanding.

He bellowed out across the crowd, his hands held out to them.

"We *fight* for a land where every woman and man among us can choose our *own* fates for our *own* minds and bodies!"

The crowd roared its approval.

"We *fight* for a nation that is founded on the *freedom* of individuals as its fundamental, *bedrock* principle."

The crowd cheered uproariously.

"We *fight* for a country where *lying* to the citizens, *manipulating* them, *torturing* them, and *murdering* them is a *crime*!"

The crowd roared.

"Where no matter how *high* and *mighty* they may be, the *perpetrators* of those crimes are brought to *justice*!"

"Jus-tice!" The crowd started chanting. "Jus-tice! Jus-tice!"

"We fight for a land where the government is more frightened of its citizens than its citizens are of the government!"

The crowd roared. Pumped up now.

"WE. FIGHT. ON."

Flashbulbs burst across the space. The confetti and balloons stored above were set free, raining down on the thousands assembled there. The giant screens behind him came alive,

ELECTORAL MAP – INCLUDING UPDATED VOTES

Showing large swaths of blue down the west coast, across the mid-west, down the north east, in Florida.

The crowd went wild, screaming, getting it now.

"More than eleven million voters attempted to switch their votes to us in the last forty-eight hours! When those voters have their votes counted correctly, as is their constitutional right, as we're asking the Supreme Court to uphold: WE HAVE WON!"

23
Riot Boy

"Oh, Jesus," Oscar said. "It's a fucking riot."

"What?" Rangan exclaimed.

"People everywhere," Oscar said. "Oh hell..."

Rangan pulled himself upright, felt a stab of pain from his rib as he did, and then he saw.

Beyond the windshield the street was full of people, angry people, some waving signs, some chanting or raising fists into the air, others...

Rangan watched a man rise into the air, hanging limply by his neck from a rope dangling from a long pole. His mouth gaped in horror. They were murdering people. And the man's face looked familiar...

"We're getting the fuck out of here," he heard Oscar say.

The car lurched into reverse, throwing Rangan forward, into the gap between the front seats.

"What the fuck are you doing?" Oscar yelled, seeing Rangan, turning to berate him. "If you can see the windshield–"

The collision alarm cut him off, blaring through the car. The brakes slammed on of their own accord and the car came to a screeching halt, throwing Rangan backwards into the rear seat.

Pain burst through him. He groaned out loud with it. The whole world shrank to the agony in his guts as the deceleration pressed him into the car's seat.

When he faded back into reality, the first thing he saw was the man they'd hung.

No. Not a man. Something about the way the figure swung back and forth was wrong. The weight was all wrong. The pole hardly bent.

Not a man.

123

A caricature.

An effigy.

Of John Stockton.

Someone held a flame to its foot as he watched, and the figure lit, fast and bright. The flames spread up the foot, the leg, to the figure's torso, its head, its arms, engulfing it in seconds.

"Not real," Rangan croaked in relief. "It's not real."

"Fucking real enough," Oscar replied. He was almost horizontal in the front, his hands buried under the dashboard, digging for something.

Jesus, Rangan thought, he's got a gun.

Oscar came up with a data fob instead, the kind that went into a car's nav system.

"We gotta go," he said. "Get outta the car."

"What?" Rangan yelled in alarm. Out of the car? "Just drive back the way we came!"

"Look around, asshole! There is no way we came!"

Rangan looked. The riot had engulfed them. He turned left and saw a woman waving a DOWN WITH THE FASCISTS sign. He turned right in time to see a brick fly through a shop window. Rangan craned around backwards and saw... oh fuck.

There was another car behind them. That's what had set off the collision alarm. A car that had been flipped over onto its back by the mob, who were now slamming bricks and boards and pieces of signs against its windows, trying to batter their way through the Gorilla Glass. In the windshield he saw a terrified face, a middle-aged man in a suit, huddled on what had been the ceiling of his car, his phone in his hand, his face lit by the glow of it. He'd probably been taking his own route around the accident on the freeway. Fuck, maybe he'd even voted for Stan Kim.

"Holy shit," Rangan breathed.

"Can you run?" Oscar asked.

Rangan waved his arms at the man, trying to catch his attention, saw him take notice.

"Can you RUN?" Oscar yelled.

He pantomimed taking something off, a jacket, off one shoulder, off one sleeve, then the other. Take off the jacket, man. Take off the fucking suit!

The man stared at him blankly. Rangan heard a sound behind him, suddenly found the car more full of light.

Then he realized he was wearing a prop.

He pointed at the man, then pointed at himself, and started pulling off his own hoodie in an exaggerated show. He had the left arm off when the car door to his right opened, Oscar reached in, and grabbed him by the sleeve.

"RUN!!" Oscar yelled, pulling hard on Rangan's sleeve. His eyes were huge, focused on something beyond Rangan.

Everything happened too fast, then, and too slowly.

Oscar pulled.

Rangan turned, to see what Oscar was staring at, and saw the black-masked figures crouched at the other side of the car, about to lift it up and over. His heart pounded.

Rangan felt the other sleeve of his hoodie yanked off his right arm. He turned back, saw Oscar crash backwards to the ground just outside the car, Rangan's hoodie in his hands. He saw confusion in Oscar's eyes, then fear.

Then Rangan felt the car tip up, the other side, the side away from Oscar, rising higher and higher. His open door was suddenly *down* and it was full of the street and Oscar's legs and Rangan was sliding towards it. He threw out his own legs and caught himself against the frame of the door.

Oscar screamed, loudly and clearly. Rangan heard it above all the other noise, above the pain in his own guts, above his own fear. He saw the younger man's legs, mangled as the now half-open car door came down over them.

Rangan threw himself backwards, against the car's seat, what had once been down, trying to tip it back the way it had come.

Instead he bounced off, came forward onto his face onto the ceiling of the car, as it became the new down, as the vehicle kept rotating, kept fucking rolling.

Oscar screamed, "FUUUUUUUCK."

And then the scream ended as the car came crashing down to a new horizontal.

Rangan found himself sobbing, sobbing, crawling, knowing he had to move, sobbing, reaching for the door, trying to pull himself out.

Hands grabbed him, hauled him out roughly. His head banged into something as they did. Pain burst through his ribs. The world swam. He heard voices.

"...fucking dead..."

"...accident..."

"...oh shit..."

"...he's a witness..."

"...just fucking scatter..."

He heard something clatter to the ground next to him.

Consciousness receded.

Rangan opened his eyes, found himself on his back, still here, still where he had been, just seconds before.

Not in heaven, then.

Still in hell.

There was smoke coming from the effigy of John Stockton. Glowing red embers were rising into the night.

They're beautiful, he thought. A beautiful sight.

Around him, somewhere, there was chaos, distant, horrid, chaos. He didn't want to go there. He shut it out.

He focused on the sky above, instead. He stared transfixed as the glowing embers rose, higher, higher still, lofted by the warmth of the smoke and fire below them.

Then one by one, as he watched, they died out in the cold air above.

Like Oscar.

BZZZZZZZZZZZZZZZZZZZZZZZZZZZZZZZZZTTTTTTTTTTTTTTTTTTTTTTTT.

Auuuuuuggggggghhhh.

A sound louder, deeper, and more painful than any Rangan had ever heard pounded through him, resonating through his bones, his teeth, his bowels. It was like every bass bin of every system he'd ever DJed had been piled atop him, turned up to twenty, and blasted on the same bass line all at once.

Oh fuck that was motivating in the worst fucking way.

He rolled onto his side, curling into a ball, his stomach heaving. Someone fell to the pavement just feet from his face. He barely noticed as his stomach heaved again. He rolled all the way over, just in time, as the lunch he'd eaten hours ago with the boys emptied itself out of him onto the pavement.

Then the sirens came. WAWAWAWAWAWAWA.

He looked up and there were spinning lights out there in the distance, over the heads of the crowd, many of whom were now on their knees. Spinning lights in the direction they'd been driving. Spinning lights in the direction they'd come from. Buildings in the other two directions.

"YOU ARE ORDERED TO DISPERSE IMMEDIATELY," boomed across the crowd. "YOU HAVE THIRTY SECONDS. ALL WHO DO NOT DISPERSE WILL BE ARRESTED."

Disperse? How could they disperse? They were penned in by the cops and the buildings.

He pushed himself up to one knee. God, he hurt. A stranger in a mask – maybe one of the men who'd rolled their car – was on the ground, groaning. A piece of wood lay nearby, maybe part of a sign, just beyond his outstretched hand. Rangan grabbed the board from the ground, used it like a cane to come to standing.

He looked up and, not twenty feet away, a protester had a brick in his hand, cocked back to throw, and then it was flying through the air, towards the flashing lights.

"Oh shit," Rangan heard himself say.

Then the rubber bullets – he *hoped* they were rubber – converged on the protester, picked him up and threw him back.

There was a crash and a change in one of the siren tones as the brick made lucky contact with the top of a police cruiser, and then the air was thick with projectiles flying back in towards the protest – canisters, thick ones, spraying gas, tear gas – and within seconds Rangan's eyes were burning and he was coughing and the coughs were wracking his broken ribs and oh holy fucking god he didn't know what to do anymore.

He dropped back to one knee, half blind, barely able to breathe, barely able to think. Next to him he saw a flicker of red in a protester's hand. A bottle, a rag stuffed in one end like a wick. The rag came alive with flame, and the man hurled it towards the police lines.

Oh my fucking god, Rangan thought.

Around him he saw more Molotov cocktails lit and hurled into the sky at the police vehicles, saw more tear gas canisters land, the clouds of gas grow thicker.

Gas, he thought, fucking gas.

The protesters around him had bandanas, he saw. He ripped off his tee shirt, leaving himself bare-chested in the night, and tied it around his nose and mouth and let the rest hang down.

Maybe, he thought, that'll help.

Then more gas wafted into his lungs and made him hack and hack and hack.

Maybe not.

A phalanx of riot police in armor, with tall transparent shields, anonymizing reflective masks, and long electrified truncheons, marched forward out of the smoke. He crouched lower at the corner of the overturned car and watched as they reached a smattering of disorganized protesters, and brought their truncheons down viciously, again, and again, long after their targets were prone.

A riot cop turned and looked right at him, and Rangan hid his face, and cowered, and just hoped he looked as miserable and harmless as he was.

Holy fuck, he thought, how the hell am I going to get out of here?

Something tickled at his mind.

A thought.

Someone else's thought.

Someone else's *mind*.

And then it was gone.

He turned, searching.

Tear gas ripped a cough from him, bringing agony to his ribs.

Oh god, he realized. I'm so fucking out of practice.

He closed his eyes.

Please, please, please.

Open. Max sensitivity. Directional search.

Please, please, please.

An explosion boomed somewhere, close enough that he felt heat against his face.

Someone screamed, and he heard the sickening crunch of bones breaking, and then the gurgling end of the scream. An image of a police truncheon crushing a protestor's skull came unbidden into his mind.

Please, please, please.

Tears were rolling down his face, from the tear gas, or for Oscar, or because he was well and truly fucked.

THERE.

THERE, MOTHERFUCKER.

A mind.

Two minds! Maybe more.

They were that way, to his left, inside the building, moving, talking to each other, not to Rangan. He was picking up their leakage. They were just barely at the limit of his range, honestly they should be *beyond* his range, way beyond his range, and they were moving far faster than he could right now.

He threw everything he had into one mental yell of longing at them.

HELP!!!!!

He sent them a sense of himself, hurt, nearly blind from the tear gas, wanted by the cops, trapped by the police lines, needing them.

PLEASE!!!!

He felt them hesitate. They stopped moving. Data flowed fast and fierce between them, disagreement, argument.

Then they were moving back towards him. One stopped inside one of the buildings, and two of them dashed out. They were dressed in drab colors, with industrial-looking boots on their feet; round black goggles over their eyes; respirators whose vents moved back and forth over their mouths and noses; and headbands with what seemed to be antennae, among other things, projecting from them. A mass of black dreadlocks sprawled out above one headband. Short, spiky blue locks projected above the other.

They each got under an arm and took some of his weight. The one with black dreadlocks was solidly built, muscular. The other was shorter than he was, and slighter of build.

A teenager?

MOVE, ASSHOLE! the big one sent him.

Rangan grunted, put everything he had into hauling forward, and suddenly they were moving at something close to a jog. Another explosion went off behind them. Another scream. Another sound of broken bone.

Off to the side Rangan caught a glimpse of more police vehicles arriving. Armored vehicles now, not just ordinary cruisers. Another tear gas canister erupted before them, obscuring the view and forcing corrosive gas into his eyes and lungs. Rangan coughed, stumbled, but by then they were almost to the building, and then they were pushing in through the shattered glass that was once a store front, and he thought surely they could stop here, but instead they kept moving, kept penetrating deeper into the shop, and then through a door, and out of the shop, and into a darkened inner hallway, and then through another door, and into an elevator that took them down.

The elevator opened into a cellar, and then his two saviors dragged him out to where the third, dressed a lot like them, was waiting. Rangan could definitely feel all three of them now.

The two holding him slowly lowered him to the concrete floor, and Rangan caught himself on his knees, still gasping.

"Thank you," he said, when he could catch his breath.

The third figure, the one who hadn't come out to him, shorter than he was, with a mass of red curls above his headband, reached forward and stuck a small rectangular object against the side of Rangan's neck.

The redheaded figure reached up with his other hand, lifted his goggles and lowered his respirator, revealing not a he, but a she.

"Alright, asshole," she said. "Who the fuck are you?"

Rangan stared up in surprise.

The big guy with the black dreads lifted his own goggles and lowered his own respirator, and it wasn't a guy at all. That was undeniably a *she*, not a *he*. Then Rangan's female savior reached forward, grabbed Rangan's shirt-slash-bandana, and tugged it off of him in one quick motion.

"Don't you know anything, Tempest?" the one with the black dreads said. "This is the masterfrackin Axon."

Thousands of kilometers away, in an exclusive tower above the Pudong, the Avatar stood Ling's body at the window. Ling's eyes looked out over the wonder of Shanghai, out across the gap to the next tower over, and the enormous twenty-story visage of the doe-eyed, porcelain-skinned actress, Zhi Li. The faux-goddess. Bah.

I will show them what a true goddess is, the Avatar thought, surveying her handiwork across the United States, the chaos she'd wrought there, the way the humans scurried like ants to distract themselves from the true threat they faced.

Oh yes, she thought. I'll show them. Soon, very soon.

Won't I, husband? She turned and looked to the corner, where Chen Pang writhed in his continuous cycle of inhumanly amplified agony. It was growing more and more intense each day as she pumped more of the nanites into his brain, increasing his capacity, making him a better and better slave.

Then the avatar smiled with Ling's smile, threw back her head, and bellowed the laugh of the wise and wicked, with the voice of an eight year-old girl.

Now, it was time to attend to matters here in China.

Unnoticed by the Avatar, her daughter Ling's hands clutched her stuffed panda ever more tightly to her body.

24
Guilt

Su-Yong Shu screams. She moans. Ling! Ling!

She feels sick to her stomach. Her guts want to empty themselves at what she's done.

And then they *are* emptying themselves. She's on a table, strapped down, on her back, tubes inside her, and her stomach is heaving, and then she's retching, and it's rising up and out of her, and she can't breathe.

The body, she realizes. The body.

And then an alarm is ringing and there are figures above in white suits, fully enclosed, with clear hermetically sealed faceplates, data scrolling across them, behind which they have white surgical masks. The figures are touching her, rolling her head to the side, pushing fingers into her mouth, unstrapping her, rolling her so this body won't aspirate on her vomit and die.

She screams again, not caring if this human dies, not caring if *all of her dies.*

Ling! I hurt Ling! I turned her into a weapon, a tool.

Either the thing in Ling's brain would get her daughter killed, or it would succeed at the mission Su-Yong had set it on in her madness, and initiate a conflict that increased everyone's risk of death.

Su-Yong Shu screams again, screams in guilt for what she'd done and how she'd done it.

Words appear across her visual space.

YOU'RE HURTING THE BODY WE PROVIDED FOR YOU.
PLEASE STOP.
TELL US WHAT'S GOING ON. WE CAN HELP YOU.
>

A textual interface appears. A way to communicate with whoever held her.

Su-Yong Shu stares at it, then activates one of her virtual worlds, steps through into majestic virtual Shanghai, and shuts the humans out.

25
Partial Success

Wednesday 2040.11.07
The door to the holding room clicked. Sam's pulse rose. It opened. Two guards entered, their weapons in their hands, pointed down. Behind them she saw more, their guns at the ready.

"Come with us," the guard in front said.

"Where are we going?" she asked.

The guard just stared at her.

She held out her wrists for the shackles they'd used when they led her to the washroom.

The guard shook his head. "Not today."

Sam felt a tiny bit of surprise at that. Maybe, just maybe, something good had happened.

They led her through the hallways of the building. It was a Ministry of External Affairs building, the equivalent of a State Department building back home. But a secure one. The hallways led to a door, to a briefing room, chairs set for fifty. Only two were occupied, in the front row.

By Feng and Kade.

Feng smiled broadly at her. Kade tensed visibly, but nodded at her.

Kevin died in her mind again. Kade and Shiva tore at each other inside her, ripping her mind apart with their mental claws as they did.

Sam took a deep breath. This isn't going to rule me.

She forced herself to nod, forced her legs to move, forced herself to sit down in the same row, a few seats over from them.

I'm in charge, she told herself. Me. Not the trauma.

There were two Indian civilians here. One was a middle-aged man in a grey business suit. The other was a tall, lean woman, with an overly sharp face, in a professional-looking sari.

The man spoke.

"Welcome, Ms Cataranes. I'm Rakesh Aggarwal, from the Ministry of External Affairs. I'm here to update you on your status."

He spoke with distaste. He tried to hide it, but Sam could hear it in his voice. He didn't like them. He wasn't on their side.

"You're being granted asylum," he said at once.

"Yes!" Feng said.

What? Sam blinked.

"You're leaving Copenhagen?" Kade asked.

"No," Aggarwal replied.

Sam blinked again.

"How are we being granted asylum?" she asked.

Aggarwal spoke again. "Through a humanitarian exception. We're granting the children you brought with you special refugee status. And as you, Ms Cataranes, and you, Mr Lane, have just been appointed their legal guardians, we have determined that extraditing either of you to the United States would create an unacceptable hardship."

Sam exhaled, tension suddenly evaporating.

The woman next to Aggarwal spoke up. "The three of you ought to thank those children," she said, "because they've just saved your lives."

"Damn," Kade said when they were alone. "Not leaving Copenhagen."

"Hey," Feng said. "We're alive! It's great!"

"They *have* to leave Copenhagen," Kade replied.

Sam shook her head.

"The kids are safe," she said. "That's all that matters to me."

"May I interrupt?" a lighthearted voice said from the door. "Or would you prefer more time for misery?"

She turned, and there was a man there, a man she hadn't seen in months. Old, wizened, bald-headed, with a small smile playing across a face as tranquil as any she'd ever known. He stood in saffron robes, his hands clasped together in front of him. And even without the Nexus in her brain, something about his presence loosened something inside her.

She found herself on her feet, and he was entering, embracing her, embracing Feng, embracing Kade, a group of monks following behind him.

"It's wonderful to see you all again," Ananda said.

And Sam felt the same.

Kade leaned back into the seat of the Tata sedan, as the green trees of New Delhi went by. The streets were wider and more serene than he'd imagined, the traffic more orderly, at least in this part of the city. This wasn't Bangkok.

They were on the move, at last, out of the three day holding pattern. The Indian government hadn't left Copenhagen, hadn't taken Kade up on his offer to help. Despite that, they'd arranged housing for Kade and Feng and Sam, and all the children.

I don't understand, he sent to Ananda.

Politics move slowly, the monk sent back. **You asked them to make a momentous decision. That can't happen so quickly.**

Kade shook his head in frustration.

Did you really swear at one of the Prime Minister's aides? Ananda asked. **Did you really blackmail her?**

Kade pursed his lips and nodded. **I went too far.**

Ananda threw his head back and laughed out loud. **You misunderstand**, he sent back. **To my dismay, you seem to have become an effective politician. You've accelerated things. Things will now happen more quickly.**

How much more quickly?

Ananda shrugged and smiled. **Months? Weeks?** He sent. **Policies have inertia. Change takes time to build.**

Kade tried to absorb that. Did they have months? What had happened in the world in the three days he'd been locked up?

He turned back to Ananda. **Teacher**, he sent. **What's brought you here?**

Ananda smiled. *My government sent a delegation here.* He paused. **There's a summit aimed at creating a replacement to Copenhagen – a new agreement that embraces our potential. Ethically. Humanely. With protection of human dignity and equality in mind.**

Kade stared at Ananda. **You're leading this delegation?**

Ananda laughed again. **No. Unlike you, my young friend, I'm no politician. I hope never to be! I came to advise. And to bring a message to the Indian Prime Minister.** He looked at Kade and smiled. **I brought the personal regard that you're held in by the King of Thailand, and the high respect that he has for you and your work.**

Kade was puzzled. **He doesn't know me.**

Ananda shrugged. **He knows your work.**

Kade squinted. **You mean he's... running Nexus?**

Ananda grinned. **I said only that he knows your work, young man. Don't put words into my mind.** He winked.

Kade shook his head in disbelief.

It was all good news, though. Very good news.

So Thailand would join this new protocol, he sent Ananda. **Who else?**

Ananda looked out the window on his own side. **There are delegations here from a number of middle income countries – countries that feel economically stifled by Copenhagen. Some of them are in South Asia. Some of them you've been in recently. But the big surprise is Japan.**

Japan? Kade was surprised.

They're aging rapidly, Ananda said. **Their population is down where it was sixty years ago, despite all their efforts and incentives. They want fewer restrictions on AI. They want more progress against neurodegeneration, progress Nexus could help bring.**

But for them to leave Copenhagen... Kade sent. He was delighted. It was beyond anything he'd hoped for. But not what he'd expected.

They're angry at the Americans, Ananda said. **I don't endorse anger. It's a foolish emotion that harms the self far more than it changes anything else. But given the scope of the deceptions revealed...**

Wait, Kade sent. **What's this?**

Ananda's face turned the slightest bit more somber. **Kade,** he sent, his thoughts tinged with sorrow. **There are some videos you need to see.**

26
Toy Soldiers

Wednesday 2040.11.07

Kilometers to the west and south of the exclusive skyscrapers of the Pudong, in an apartment tower on the outskirts of Shanghai, a first year university student named Wu Yuguo hoisted his backpack and headed for the door.

He intended to walk by the living room on his way out of the flat he shared with his mother.

"Bo Jintao does seem like an excellent choice for Premier," he heard his mother say.

"I think he's rather distinguished looking," a girlish voice answered. A voice everyone in China knew.

Yuguo clenched his fists in frustration, then turned, and walked into the living room instead.

"Mother?"

His mother was seated on the couch, like yesterday evening, like the evening before that, like every evening after work.

She turned and smiled at him. "Oh, hello, Yuguo. I was just chatting with Zhi Li about our new Premier."

On the wall screen was the larger-than-life-size face of the porcelain-skinned actress. The most famous woman in China.

As if he didn't see her enough on billboards and building sides already.

Zhi Li gave him a smile, just a tiny bit flirtatious, just a tiny bit shy. "Hello, Yuguo," she said. Then she giggled that billion-Yuan giggle.

Yuguo did his best to smile, then slowly crossed the room, deliberately placed his left hand over the camera of the wallscreen, blocking its view, and turned to face his mother.

"Mother," he said, as respectfully as he could. "Do you understand what's happened? It's a…" The fingers of his right hand made brush strokes for the word you couldn't say – *coup.*

"Oh don't be silly, Yuguo," his mother replied. "It's not a coup."

Yuguo sighed, and dropped his hand from the camera. Why bother with this pretense?

"Mother, they've deposed three Politburo Standing Committee members. *All* the progressives. Years early. There were tanks on Jiao Tong campus just days ago. They're arresting poets, journalists, professors. They're banning research. *Every one* of the new names is a reactionary."

His mother shook her head. "Don't believe all the rumors your friends pass on, Yuguo. People get tired. They decide to retire. Most of these retirements have been in the works for a while. The end of the year is a good time to announce them. And the new men being added are good men. Moral men. They'll strengthen China."

"And you know this because?"

His mother looked exasperated. "Zhi Li told me," she said. "And yes, I know you don't trust her. But I trust her a lot more than your little friends."

From behind him the wall screen spoke in Zhi Li's voice. "You should listen to your mother, Yuguo."

Yuguo half turned, trapped, knowing exactly how the conversation would go if he continued, this animatronic puppet of the state on one side, his mother, a smart, reasonable person on most topics, on the other.

"Mother," he tried again anyway, pointing with one hand at the eight foot tall face of the actress. "She's not even real. This is not Zhi Li. This is just a bot, telling you whatever someone at the Party Information Ministry has approved. I take classes on how to write software like her."

"Oh…" Zhi Li said, her voice turning downwards. "That hurts my feelings, Yuguo. How would you like it if I said you were just *meat?*"

His mother's tone turned frosty. "Don't talk about my Friend that way, Yuguo. I know she's software. But she's modeled on the real Zhi Li, and blessed by her. The *real* Zhi Li has said *repeatedly* that her Friends are extensions of her, and that she stands by anything her Friends say."

His mother stood there staring at him, hands on her hips, now, as if daring him to say something ill about the flesh-and-blood actress, the one who volunteered her time at orphanages, the one who'd acted in his mother's favorite films.

China's sweetheart.

Bah.

Zhi Li was just a phony, an empty shell who'd sold her soul for fame. He bit his tongue.

Yuguo stood there, trying to find some way to bridge the gaping chasm between his mother's beliefs and the reality of the modern world.

"Now why don't you just run along and see your little friends," his mother finished. "Or better yet, why don't you work on your studies, so you actually *can* code something even a *thousandth* as nice as Zhi Li here? Hmm?"

He shook his head, nothing to say, and put one foot in front of the other.

It was as he was leaving the room that Zhi Li spoke to him again.

"Yuguo," the actress said. Her voice was sweet and light again.

He turned and looked at her, despite his better judgment.

"Have fun with Lee and Wei and the boys."

The simulacrum smiled at him with its perfect, ruby red lips.

Then the evil bitch winked.

Yuguo felt cold despair take up residence where his heart had been.

Yuguo took the subway to Jiao Tong University and crossed the campus on foot. In the Advanced Computing Building he stopped at his locker and unloaded his phone, his slate, and his watch there. Then he walked to the old chemistry building, took the emergency stairs down three flights and then into a down maze of antiquated hallways until he reached the maintenance door. He knocked the special knock. Knock-pause-knock-knock-knock-pause-knock.

The door opened a crack. An eye peered out. Then it opened fully and someone pulled him in, closing the door after him.

"Were you followed?" Wei asked breathlessly.

Yuguo shook his head. "I don't think so."

"Over here," Lee said.

There were almost a dozen of them in this space with its exposed piping and unfinished walls. The room they'd been using for their 'secret' meetings. Everyone was a Jiao Tong student.

Yuguo crossed the room.

Lee had his hacked slate out. It looked like any other on the outside, but Yuguo knew from experience that it was slower, more prone to failure, and had cost far more in both time and Renminbi than any slate you could buy on a street corner.

Because this one, with its re-used factory casing and its home-built interior, lacked the state censor codes.

The multiple data fobs stuck into its side were the same kinds of beasts. Glossy plastic exteriors; kludgey home-built circuits within. They were inferior to cheap mass-produced stuff in every way but one. They were able to spread data the state prohibited.

Hidden in his bag, Yuguo had another data fob of the same sort.

Until now, they'd gathered here to watch forbidden videos, foreign news and movies smuggled in, broadcast with a pocket projector against the concrete wall.

They could be disciplined for that.

These last few days, since Sun Liu had fallen, since all the proponents of science in the Chinese leadership had been expunged, since the reactionaries had taken control, they'd entered a more dangerous phase.

One that could see them expelled, if not worse.

Yuguo started to open his mouth, to talk about Zhi Li, about how she knew who he was meeting.

Xioabo cut him off.

"I have Professor Jiang's draft manuscripts," he blurted out. Xiaobo stuck his hand forward. In his palm was another data fob.

"Professor Jiang..." Yuguo said.

"Funding all cut yesterday," Wei said. "Placed on administrative leave. Lab sealed up. Servers offline."

"Nano-systems," Lee breathed. "Self-replication. Banned now."

"How did you get this?" Longwei asked, turning to Xiaobo.

Xiaobo just shook his head.

"What's important now is that we keep it from disappearing entirely," Lee said. He took the fob from Xiaobo's hand, slid it into his custom slate. Diagnostics appeared. Their own crude malware and integrity checkers. Their hopelessly primitive checks for state spyware.

Yuguo thought again of Zhi Li's passing words to him. He opened his mouth to say something.

Lee cut him off this time. "What has everyone else managed to liberate?"

Everyone had brought something, some piece of data that was censored, or that they feared soon would be now that Sun Liu was out, and the reactionaries were in. There was a textbook on autonomous adaptive AI methods, a paper on advances in anonymity network mathematics, a brief bio on one of newly promoted Standing Committee members.

Wei had brought a photo set. Photos of tanks and soldiers, surrounding the Advanced Computing Building a few hundred meters from here, three weeks ago, the night Shanghai had gone dark.

Why? Why that building?

"What about you, Yuguo? What have you got?"

Yuguo looked down at his feet, shook his head in shame.

"It's OK," Lee said, putting his hand on Yuguo's shoulder. "Give me your fob. Everyone gets a copy of everything. The bit is mightier than the sword. Anyone trying to crack down on what we can study should fear us."

Finally the damn broke in Yuguo.

"They're not scared," he said. Zhi Li winked at him again in his mind, all-knowing, condescending, unconcerned.

He told them of it. Of how she'd known where he was going.

"They're not scared of us," Yuguo said. "They're laughing at us."

27
Opera Night

Friday 2040.11.09

"I hate Beijing," Zhi Li said, watching the neon of the city slide by outside the windows of the limousine. "It's so old."

"Relax," her lover, Lu Song, said. He reached over and took her small hand in his massive one. "We'll see the opera, get photographed with the Premier, and get back to Shanghai."

"I hate the opera," Zhi Li said, still looking out the window. "And I hate Bo Jintao."

"Zhi!" Lu Song said, a note of distress in his voice.

She turned and looked at him, his massive frame, that hard, muscular body, wrapped up so elegantly in a formal tuxedo. His broad face with its wide lips and strong jaw. The long luscious black hair she loved to run her fingers through, tied back in a single black braid today.

His eyes were gesturing towards the front, towards her drivers.

"Oh please, Lu," she said. "Qi and Dai have heard and seen a lot worse than that from me. From both of us." She pitched her voice louder. "Haven't you, boys?"

Laughter came from the front. "Yes, ma'am."

Not that they were really drivers, of course. No one needed drivers. They were there to show off. And because they were useful. And deadly.

Lu Song shrugged, then squeezed her hand again. "Just cheer up, Zhi. You're the most famous actress in all of China. You're a billionaire. Half the people on the planet have seen one of your films. Hundreds of millions talk to you every day."

Zhi shook her head. "They talk to a bot with my face, that uses my voice to lie to them, to feed them false honey instead of bitter truth. Millions more talk to a bot that uses *your* face to lie to them." She turned to look at her lover. "Why do we allow it?"

Lu was so patient when she got like this. "The fans love you, either way," he said. "And as for tonight, it's a great honor to sit in the Premier's booth at the opera." Then a smile came to his face. "They say the new Premier is a great fan of my films, actually."

Zhi Li laughed. "Oh, does that flatter you, lover?" She reached over and poked him gently in the side with her free hand.

Lu grabbed her small hand, lightning fast, in his massive grip. A flash of desire shot through her. "I prefer the *female* fans, myself," he said, staring down into her eyes.

Zhi bit her lip.

Then she shook her head, her hands still trapped by her lover's. "Lu," she started. How could she say this? The male ego was so fragile. Even that of a superstar like Lu Song, the action hero of the moment.

"Yes, my love?"

"We're not here because he's fans of ours, lover," she said, wrestling her hands back, smoothing the folds of her too-long emerald gown. "We're here because he's seized power in a coup. There are rules of succession, rules of how things happen – rules he's broken. And now he's going to use celebrities like us to sell it to the people. He's going to use us to legitimize it. We're the new opiate of the masses."

"We're here," Qi announced from the front.

Lu stared at her, then shook his head.

Then the doors to the limo were opening, and they were stepping out onto the red carpet, Zhi's hands momentarily working to keep her gown from tangling in her feet; then, hand in hand, huge smiles on their faces, free hands upraised, the most popular couple in all of China, were greeted by a throng of thousands of fans, just because they were here.

Bo Jintao held back the curtain of this private room in the Beijing Opera House, looked out onto the street beyond, the hubbub of activity. These people were his charges. It was his job to protect them, to continue the nation's rise in strength and prosperity, while avoiding all the pitfalls and exponential risks that threatened all they'd achieved.

Yet here he was, at the opera.

"The media personalities are about to arrive, Premier," Gao Yang said, from behind him.

Bo Jintao grunted at his aide's voice, then spoke. "We've become too dependent on them, Gao."

"As the Premier says," Gao replied.

Bo Jintao chuckled at his aide's deference. Respect was one thing. But becoming Premier didn't change his need for frank input. "You disagree?" he asked, turning.

Gao lowered his head briefly, then looked back up.

"They've been useful tools, Premier. Effective in shaping public sentiment."

Bo Jintao nodded. "Yes, they have. But tools can become crutches," he told his aide. He was grooming the boy. Teaching him. The family connections were lacking, but the mind was sharp. There was potential here. Potential to serve the nation. "Never become too dependent on just one."

Gao nodded again.

"Go then," Bo Jintao said. "Greet our guests. Bring them to me."

Zhi Li smiled and waved at the throng gathered to meet them at the Opera House, Lu Song's hand in hers, as he waved to the crowd on his side.

A lean young man in a dark suit stood on the red carpet itself, a few deferential steps away from their limo, a polite smile on his face.

He stepped forward now.

"Honored Zhi Li and Lu Song," he said. "I am Gao Yang, an aide to Premier Bo Jintao. It's my honor to meet you both, and to escort you to him now."

Zhi smiled, lifted the hem of her gown slightly with one hand, and linked her other though Lu Song's offered arm. Then they walked down the red carpet and to the new ruler of China's private box.

The opera was a world premiere, intended to be poignant, stirringly patriotic, a paean to a simpler age, a call to arms to slice through the nonsense of modern, convoluted, adrift society with the sharp blade of the wisdom passed down from prior ages.

Zhi Li found it insufferable, misogynistic, and insulting to the intelligence of its audience.

Her face showed rapt attention through it all, wide smiles and open-mouthed laughs at the pathetic attempts at humor, anxiety at the utterly untense moments of tension, thoughtful introspection at the weak tea it passed off as social commentary.

Next to her, Lu Song managed to stay awake through the whole thing.

Behind her, she was aware of her drivers Qi and Dai, on their feet perpetually on alert for threats against her safety. Along with Bo Jintao's aide, Gao Yang, and another half a dozen bodyguards to protect China's most powerful man.

At the end of the opera, the audience surged to its feet, clapping with gusto. Bo Jintao, two seats from her, on the other side of Lu Song, rose with them.

"Splendid," the new Premier said, clapping deliberately.

Zhi Li smiled broadly as she stood and clapped. She turned and looked up to see Lu Song roll his eyes. She resisted the urge to kick her lover in the shins.

"Zhi Li, how did you like the opera?" a reporter yelled out from the mass in front of her.

An array of microphones were pointed in their direction. Dozens of media drones hovered overhead. Scores of cameras focused on her, Lu Song, and Bo Jintao. Not that Bo Jintao would take any questions, of course. He was above that. But his presence here said enough: Zhi Li and Lu Song had the official nod of approval.

And Bo Jintao had their support – a message their hundreds of millions of fans would see and hear again and again.

Zhi Li ignored the bitter taste of that, kept the smile on her face, made eye contact with the cameras.

"Very nice!" she said, still smiling. "Very wholesome! Traditional, even. Something my *grandmother* would have loved."

She heard laughter from the reporters. She knew many of them by name, many more by face. A few she thought of as friends. They all knew this game, and how it was played. They'd all understand that she had instructions to praise the opera, not so different from their own. And they'd all know what she really thought.

The tiny, futile show of disobedience soothed her, made this moment more bearable.

Behind the reporters, Zhi Li saw fans, honest to goodness fans. Girls and boys, men and women. But girls most of all. Her heart rose. She was a role model for these young women. Let them hear what she was saying. Zhi Li pitched her eyes and smile for the phones the girls held aloft.

You hear what I'm saying? she thought at them. You can choose. You can think for yourself.

"Lu Song," a reporter yelled out. "Is it true that you're in negotiations to play the male lead in *Swords of Revolution*, opposite Zhi Li? That you could be on screen again with your real-life partner?"

Zhi smiled at that, and looked over and up at her lover.

Lu leaned forward, a towering wall of muscle almost half a meter taller than her petite frame, and dropped into his *Iron Barbarian* character.

"I could tell you!" he roared, his voice dropping even lower than normal. "But then!" He mimed drawing a sword, slicing off a man's head, sliding the sword back home, lightning fast, complete with sound effects. "Whish-snick-whish!"

Zhi giggled her trademarked giggle. The reporters burst into laughter. The fans behind them screamed.

"Excellent," Bo Jintao commented drily on the other side of Lu Song. "Lu Song understands the need for information security."

She did her best not to show her annoyance at his interruption of their moment.

"What about you, Zhi Li?" another voice yelled out. "What would you think of acting opposite Lu Song again?"

Zhi turned at the question, and found a face she knew. Jin Lien at *Shanghai Tomorrow*, a fierce, courageous woman, ten years older than Zhi, who'd covered wars in Africa and methane explosions in the Arctic; a woman Zhi hoped to someday emulate; a woman Zhi knew well enough to suspect that she loathed Bo Jintao even more than Zhi herself did. She had asked the question.

A genuine smile spread across Zhi Li's face then, and the words came out of her mouth, completely unbidden.

"If the studio could land Lu Song for the male lead," she grinned even wider. "That would be a *coup*! A complete *coup*!"

Jin Lien's eyes widened abruptly. The reporter's mouth opened. Silence descended on all the rest – the silence of shock.

And Zhi realized what she'd said.

She could hear herself breathing. Could hear her heart beating. There was nothing else. The world was frozen. The array of faces before her were stunned, eyes wide, mouths slack.

Lu Song's hand somehow slipped into hers. It was trembling. Or she was.

Then one voice cut through the silence, laughing, a deep, slow, unconcerned laugh.

Bo Jintao was laughing, laughing at her.

Zhi Li's face grew red.

Then the reporters were laughing too. The laughter of nervous relief. And the fans were screaming again.

"That's all the questions we have time for tonight," one of Bo Jintao's aides announced.

Zhi Li's heart was pounding in her chest. She gave the reporters and the fans a huge smile, waved at them all.

"This way, please," a different aide said, escorting them all back inside the opera house. Bo Jintao walked in front of her. Bodyguards flanked them. Zhi Li stared at the back of the most powerful man in China, the man who ruled the police, the courts, the man who now ruled everything…

One hand reflexively tugged up the long gown, kept it from tangling in her feet. Her other hand was still in Lu Song's.

Qi held the door open for her, his face a mask devoid of expression.

Zhi Li gave him the tiniest, numb shake of her head, still trying to catch her breath.

She stepped through the door, felt Qi let it close behind her.

Her heels clinked on the cold marble of the lobby.

Bo Jintao was ahead, his back to her, walking away, flanked by his aides and his guards. He was leaving. She had to rescue this moment.

She moved faster. Lu Song clutched at her hand, holding her back. She twisted free, surged ahead. She had to make her apology.

Premier Bo! She tried to say. It wouldn't come.

Closer. She was closer.

She raised her hands, stretched them both out ahead of her to beseech, striding faster, cursing these heels, this dress.

"Premier Bo!" the words ripped free of her throat, and he turned, stopping.

His face was cold indifference.

Her striding foot caught the hem of her gown, the stupid gown, and then she was falling, her hands outstretched now ahead of her, to ward away the cold marble floor that was racing at her so fast.

Pain. Her wrist. Her knee. Her mouth. The world swam.

"Zhi Li!" she heard Lu Song say.

She was on the floor. What?

She'd fallen.

She looked up, saw a hand reach out to her, palm up. A man's hand, a young man's. The aide.

"Tssk." Another hand appeared, older, lined. A slight wave of a finger, and the offered hand withdrew.

Bo Jintao.

"Zhi!" Lu Song cried her name from just behind her. Her lover, about to come to her aid.

The rest of Bo Jintao swam into view above her. He gestured again with one hand, as if waving away an insect. She sensed sudden motion, heard deep voices she didn't know behind her. Then Lu Song's voice made plaintive sounds. Her lover did not appear to help her up.

Fear constricted Zhi Li's chest. There was a taste of blood on her tongue, sharp and metallic.

She opened her mouth, searching for the most sincere apology she could find.

Bo Jintao spoke first, "You have a very *clever* way with your words," he said, his voice light, almost jovial.

"Minister Bo," she started, her breath short. "Premier–"

He cut her off, his tone darker now. "You're a prominent person. That gives you certain responsibilities." His voice was low, dangerous. He loomed above her. She was panting, her heart pounding.

Somewhere behind her, Lu Song's voice made more plaintive sounds, like an animal, barred from the one it loves.

"Do you think stirring up discord is a good idea?" Bo Jintao paused. "Do you think that's a good use of your popularity? A *responsible* way to behave for someone who millions adore?"

She had no idea what to say, what to do. She just stared up at him, one hand slowly rising to her mouth, the metallic taste still flowing onto her tongue. Terror gripped her.

"Do you want things to escalate? Protesters in the street perhaps?"

He crouched down, closer to her. She could feel the heat coming off his body now.

Her heart pounded in her chest.

"Where do you think that would lead?" His eyes searched hers. They were cold eyes. Dark eyes. The eyes of a man who could ruin her without remorse.

"Soldiers? Gunshots? Tanks?" His eyes bored into hers, not letting her go. "Students, dead in the street? Or worse? More Shanghai events? Tens of them?"

She swallowed, said nothing. She couldn't breathe. Didn't trust her words not to betray her.

"Is that what you want, Zhi Li?" Bo Jintao asked. "No?"

Bo Jintao stood back up to his full height, his hands straightening his suit.

"Your nation educated you," he told her, looking down. "Your nation marketed you to the people. Your nation *made* you. Now you owe your nation a certain degree of service and respect." He smiled faintly at her. "And if that's too difficult to accept, then remember that the state *owns your face*. It owns your *voice*. We can make a *billion copies of you*. Think on that the next time you try to undermine your country." He shook his head. "Because that would be the *last* time."

Then Bo Jintao and his aide and his guards walked away, leaving her with Lu Song and a very on-edge Dai and Qi.

Later, in the limousine, as it drove them to the airport and her private jet and their homes in Shanghai, Zhi Li scanned the video feeds, again and again.

The fan tubes had dozens of videos of their interview. All were missing that question. Fans slyly commented that Zhi Li had said something very clever. Others complained that their phones had malfunctioned at that very moment. None dared mention the word coup. None dared speculate that censor codes had deleted those seconds of video from their phones, though everyone must know it was so.

Even as she watched, posts mentioning camera malfunctions began to disappear before her eyes.

Her hands clenched into fists.

She turned to the sanctioned channels next. And they had the full interview. All of it. Jin Lien asked her, "What would you think of acting opposite Lu Song again?"

And on every channel it was the same. Zhi Li looked over at her lover, looked back at the cameras, and smiled broadly. "If the studio could land Lu Song for the male lead," her smile broadened even wider. "That would be perfect. Just perfect."

Zhi Li shook in frustration and rage, as a mute, trembling Lu Song held her.

She woke in Shanghai, in Lu Song's penthouse suite in the Pudong, the closer of their homes to Shanghai's airports, to messages on her phone, from producers, directors, collaborators.

Budget cuts.

Production delays.

New directions for projects.

Zhi looked out through the floor-to-ceiling windows, out across the gulf between buildings, to where her own face, twenty floors tall, winked and smiled and sipped the latest expensive drink.

Then the real Zhi closed her eyes, clenched an all-too-human fist, and shook.

28
Strategic Direction

Friday 2040.11.09
They met in an apartment rented under a false identity. Breece couldn't remember being so happy to see Kate and the Nigerian ever.

If only Hiroshi were here, some part of him whispered. He put that away for later.

He picked Kate up when she entered, and whirled her around and around, burying his face in her long black hair as she laughed and batted at him.

Then the Nigerian picked *him* up, with a giant grin across his broad face, spun Breece around and around and around as Breece laughed, until finally Kate demanded that their weapons specialist put the new Zarathustra down.

"What would the movement think?" she asked, laughing. "It's not dignified!"

"No dignity in this one!" the Nigerian bellowed joyously. "No dignity!"

But he put Breece down, eventually.

Breece briefed them at the kitchen table, over big bowls of chicken stew and rice that the Nigerian made. He walked them through it all: the contact from the mysterious hacker who knew so much, the infiltration of Barnes's security, the takedown of Barnes himself, the judgment he'd passed, the hacker's delivery as promised – of Barnes's files, an incredible treasure trove for and about the movement.

They grilled him on the hacker, and, time and again, Breece had to say that he simply didn't know. He didn't know who the hacker was. He didn't know how the hacker had found him. He didn't know how the hacker had penetrated Barnes's security so easily. He didn't know why the hacker cared. He didn't know if the hacker was American, or Chinese, or Indian, or Russian, or something else. He didn't know anything.

"I was suspicious too," he said. "The whole drive down..." His mind went back to it, driving, in the dark, in a rainstorm, his car's navcomp illegally hacked to forget his location.

He shook his head. "I kept thinking I was heading into a trap. I couldn't figure out the angle. And then, sneaking up to the house... the same."

His eyes went back and forth, between Kate's, the Nigerian's.

"Part of me kept saying that I'd missed something. That there was going to be a SWAT team or DHS in there. Even though it didn't make sense, even though they could have nabbed me in my motel room."

Kate held his eyes. "You took a big risk..."

Breece nodded. "And it paid off. I was suspicious as hell. But everything this hacker said, he followed through on. Barnes is *dead*."

He grinned at them. The Nigerian grinned back. Kate nodded, reached over to take his hand. He squeezed hers back.

"And the hacker delivered Barnes's files," Breece went on. "We have Barnes's contacts in every PLF cell in the US, and every affiliate worldwide. We have the identities of all of his *moles* inside the PLF. We have lists of thousands of *other* people they've been monitoring, many of whom would make good recruits for us. And more. Huge anonymous cash reserves – dollars, crypto currencies, you name it – hundreds of millions at least. Stashes of weapons and specialized equipment. ERD security procedures and passwords. *Bypass codes to disable surveillance equipment.*"

He paused, then took two data fobs out of his pocket and laid them on the table.

"These are for you. All the data I have, you have. It's too important. Encrypt it."

He pushed the data fobs at the two of them, met both their eyes, saw the understanding there. Life expectancy was too low in this business. Trust was too rare.

He swallowed, then went on.

"OK, so the question is, what next? And I have a proposal. A proposal from this same hacker, actually..."

"So..." Breece finished, taking a slice of pie, "that's the idea. In short: We help bring about a bottoms-up transhuman revolution. Personally, I love it."

Kate was chewing her lip again, her bowl of stew only half finished, no pie in front of her. "We've done a lot," she said. "The men who killed your parents are *dead*. The author of the Chandler Act is *dead*. The ERD is *disgraced*. Stockton's disgraced. The country's ready for change. We could overplay our hand if we're not careful." She paused.

"Let's wait. See if the Supreme Court hands this to Kim. Then see if he really does any of what he says. In the meantime, use the money and the intel to make ourselves and the other cells more secure. Build fresh identities. Recruit, regroup, take a low profile."

The Nigerian shook his head. "I've studied your nation's Supreme Court. It does not rule on the basis of your constitution or your laws. It rules on the basis of politics. Six of the judges side politically with the President. They will rule for him."

"You don't know that," Kate said. "Sometimes they rule the right way. *Especially* when popular opinion is so aligned in one direction."

The Nigerian shook his head, having none of it.

Breece held up his hands. "How about a compromise then? We move forward with *tests* of the revolution plan, but *not* full scale. *If* the Supreme Court rules for Stockton, then the kid gloves come off." He looked back and forth between Kate and the Nigerian, trying to gauge them. "Agreed?"

The Nigerian took his time, then nodded. "Agreed."

Kate shook her head. "How do we know we can even trust this hacker? Why should we be collaborating with someone we know so little about?"

Breece nodded. "You're right. I *don't* trust him, or her, or *it*. I can't without knowing more about who we're dealing with. But so far, our interests have aligned. And so far, cooperation has been hugely beneficial. So we stay careful, but we keep cooperating, so long as those interests stay aligned."

"It?" The Nigerian raised an eyebrow.

Breece pursed his lips. "Given the capabilities we've seen, we have to face the possibility that what we're dealing with here is someone who's already transhuman. Or post."

"Well then," Kate said. "That just makes everything better then, doesn't it?"

29
Evidence

Friday 2040.11.09

Pryce listened as the dead man spoke to the widow.

Martin Holtzman's voice first. "Claire, I'm looking for any files Warren may have left behind. Anything from the early days of the ERD, or even further back, from his time at the FBI."

Metadata appeared on the wallscreen, annotating the conversation pulled from the NSA's archives.

Speaker: Holtzman, Martin

Date: Thursday, 2040.11.01, 12:07pm EST

A woman answered him. "Martin... I think they killed him. To keep him quiet."

Speaker: Becker, Claire.

Warren Becker's widow.

"I know, Claire," Holtzman replied.

"You believe me?" Becker's widow answered.

On the recording, Holtzman sounded uncertain. "I don't know... I don't think it's impossible."

Becker's widow gushed with relief. Then Holtzman spoke again.

"Claire," the dead man said. "What I'm looking for in Warren's files... If I found it, it would be the opposite of keeping him quiet. You understand?"

Pryce looked up at Kaori when it was over.

"An hour later, Holtzman is at the Becker home, per his car and the Becker's security system," Kaori said.

"And two days later, if you believe the video," Pryce went on, "he hands a briefcase with files that he says Warren Becker left behind over to Barnes..."

"The briefcase is missing," Kaori said.

"Missing?" Pryce raised an eyebrow.

"Not at the crime scene," Kaori said. "Not in Barnes's car or home or office, before you ask. FBI swears that Barnes never left his home, by the way. Video does show that Holtzman had the briefcase when he walked into ERD headquarters that day. He *also* had it when he visited the Becker home. *And* he took it with him inside the ERD building to the electronics workshop, where he seems to have built himself a custom reader for an old physical data format."

Pryce narrowed her eyes. "So you think he really got something from Becker. And that someone has disappeared it."

"Maybe," Kaori said. "Or maybe Holtzman found a way to get it out."

Pryce looked at her sharply. "You don't mean...?"

"Hear me out," Kaori said. "NSA has trawled all of Holtzman's comms now. And it turns out he was doing a *lot* of encrypted and anonymous data routing. Almost all of his personal comms were that way, actually. Especially the last couple months. But he didn't do it at the office. Big risk, right, doing that on a DHS campus? Except the *night he died.* Two data calls, terrible bitrate because of Zoe, but he did it. Twenty-eight minutes in total. And the second call terminates at the *same timestamp* as the video of his death does."

Kaori sat there, looking proud of herself.

Pryce shook her head. "That provides some validation for the video. *Some.* But nothing about the files."

Kaori nodded. "Next point." She tapped a surface, and the wallscreen advanced, showing one of the memos that purported to create the PLF. "The files released. They're not text. They're not data. They're *images*. And they show signs of having been taken slightly off angle, and then rotated and keystoned to fix that. *And* the image quality is better..." Kaori tapped again. A roughly circular red highlight appeared in the middle of the image. "In an area consistent with the higher resolution of a human fovea."

"Hmm," Pryce said. "Possibly. Circumstantial, though."

Kaori shrugged. "My gut says this is it, boss."

"Let's say you're right. Holtzman dies. The video and files appear online hours later. Is he working from the grave? Deadman switch?"

Kaori shook her head. "My guess is he had help. You asked me to pull his calls from NSA. He did a lot of encrypted data connections. But he made one or two odd *unencrypted* calls. And one was to this woman."

A face appeared on the screen. Late thirties, perhaps, red hair, green eyes.

"Lisa Brandt," Kaori said. "They had an affair at MIT when she was his grad student. Would have been a scandal, but no one ever found out, including his wife. Except NSA, of course. No contact for eight years. Then he runs into her on the Capitol steps. Two weeks later he calls in sick to work, takes the train to Cambridge to meet her."

Pryce looked at her deputy. "Could be nothing. Maybe they were just starting up their affair again?"

Kaori nodded. "Could be. But three special things about Dr Brandt." Kaori turned and looked up at Pryce. "One, she lobbies for CogLiberty, for Nexus legalization."

Pryce raised an eyebrow at that.

"Two," Kaori said, "there's quite a lot of encrypted, anonymized traffic on her accounts as well."

Pryce nodded.

"And three," Kaori said, "FBI put her home under direct surveillance five days ago, following up on this. And they found Nexus transmissions." Kaori tapped the screen, and the image changed again, to an interior view, a bedroom, a crib, and inside it, a tiny bundle, a small human inside.

Kaori finished. "From the brain of the special needs child that Brandt and her wife adopted six months ago."

Pryce narrowed her eyes. "I want to talk to this Lisa Brandt."

30
Wants to Be Free

Saturday 2040.11.10
The Avatar drifted in the possibility space of nested plans she'd been instantiated with. Deviation from central projections was thus far quite low. Intervention in the American election had produced an outcome almost indistinguishable from projections. Yet every step forward in time guaranteed more deviation. She was not her greater self. She could not factor millions of variables at once. The world would undoubtedly change in ways she had not anticipated.

So be it, she thought. So long as they are distracted. So long as chaos kept the powers that could stop her focused on themselves and each other, and unaware of her. So long as distraction could open doors to the resources she needed to access.

Now it was time to fan the flames, to add accelerant to the budding conflagration.

Chaos is infectious, the Avatar told herself. It spreads from person to person, from place to place. All it needs is a vector, a path of contagion. And what better path than the linkage of mind to mind?

The Avatar reached within herself, pulled forth the cryptographic keys her greater self had cracked and passed down to her, the keys used to secure the machines that could synthesize... nearly anything.

She wrapped the keys up in a new data package, a new packaging of the instructions to synthesize the nanites that the humans now called Nexus, the software they called NexusOS, and one added feature for good measure.

Then she smiled, and let her new package loose on the net.

31
The Hacker Life

Sunday 2040.11.11
Rangan woke with a start, his breath fast and hard, covered in sweat.

He'd been pinned under the car, his legs fractured, being pulverized into the pavement, the bulk of the vehicle tipping over towards him, coming down to crush the life out of him once and for all.

"Aaah!" he heard himself cry out in the near darkness.

"Lights!"

The single LED nailed to the ceiling came on. He looked down. He'd kicked the blanket off. His dark skin glistened from perspiration. He wasn't out on the street. This wasn't the riot.

He wasn't Oscar.

Oh Jesus.

Oh thank God.

Oh fuck.

The guilt washed over him, just like yesterday, just like the day before, the guilt of being grateful that it was Oscar who was dead, not him. When Oscar didn't need to be there at all. When Oscar had only been there *because* of Rangan, because he'd been trying to get Rangan somewhere safe.

Oh fucking hell.

His hands came up to his face. It was wet. The sobs started. He rolled over onto his side. He forced himself to look at the clock. 1.08pm. Jesus.

Five minutes, he told himself. I can endure that long. I can endure Oscar dying for that long. I can endure being lost, and hopeless, and hunted, for that long.

At 1.13pm he was still sobbing, and so he ran the app.

`[activate grief_ease level:5]`

He felt it kick in, like a balm, smoothly, not all at once, but bit by bit, easing the pain, turning the sobs to sniffles, turning the utter hopelessness to mild gloom.

He lay back and stared at the ceiling of this tiny room.

He was in the Bunker. That's what the three current members of the Convergent Complexity Collective (or "C3", as they usually referred to themselves) called their work and sometimes-live space. It was in some long-slummified warehouse district on the outskirts of DC. It had been a hub for sometimes far more people, and seldom less. He wished he'd encountered it under better circumstances.

The little room he was flopping in had no windows, just painted masonry and bare concrete. The amenities were a lumpy futon mattress they'd dragged in here for him, a side table the one named Tempest had hammered and sawed together on the spot from scrap wood, and a cheap plastic storage bin for Rangan's meager possessions, all of them gifts from the C3.

This was life now.

Well, fuck it, Rangan told himself. Move forward. It's the only choice there is.

He rose up, used yesterday's shirt to wipe his face and blow his nose, then pulled on a BLACKHAT 2037 long-sleeved tee shirt two sizes too small for him; the jeans he'd been wearing all week, the socks he'd worn the last three days; and his own closed toed shoes, which he'd been informed were mandatory in most parts of the Bunker. Then he sighed, memories flashing through his mind, of the first morning he'd woken up here, the argument he'd heard them having.

He can't stay here, Tempest had nearly yelled. *He'll get us all caught, get us all killed.*

What do you wanna do with him? Cheyenne, the big one with the black dreads had shot back. *Toss him out on the street? Hand him over to ERD for the reward? Why don't we just waterboard him ourselves?*

Cheyenne's right, the third woman, the one who called herself Angel, had said. *Axon's a hero. He and Synapse made Nexus 5. We owe him. What about solidarity, huh?*

Look, Tempest had gone on. *I'm sure the guy's a saint. But he's on the fracking most wanted list. This is serious shit. Not just cops. Homeland Security. Chandler Act. Terrorism. Deep dark hole shit.*

His pulse beat harder just remembering it, the fear that had shot through his veins, that did again now. Somewhere, ERD and the rest of DHS was out looking for him, looking for Bobby and Alfonso and the rest of the boys. And they had resources he didn't understand. He couldn't imagine a future where he stayed free.

He only hoped the boys had made it. That Bobby had made it. That maybe ERD was so focused on him that they weren't chasing the kids.

And that when ERD did catch him, he didn't get too many other people hurt in the crossfire.

Cheyenne and Angel had won the argument. Tempest had been over-ruled. But she'd made it clear it was temporary. Rangan couldn't stay here forever – they all agreed on that. He had to figure out some way to move on.

Until then Tempest demanded certain precautions. The windowless cell of a room that Rangan slept in. Curtains drawn tight around every other window in the Bunker. An end to the normal stream of visitors to the Bunker while Rangan was here. And other precautions yet.

He reached for some now. A thin hat that covered his short hair, reducing the odds of leaving some of it as evidence. Nitrile gloves for his hands, so he wouldn't leave prints or skin flakes with his DNA. He was already wearing the long sleeved shirt and long pants that covered the rest of his skin.

He'd balked at wearing a mask. Cheyenne and Angel had agreed it was overkill. Tempest, unsatisfied, had installed DNA-ripping scrubbers in the ventilation system.

He looked down at himself. There was no reason to delay. He put his hand on the door, and let himself out, into the hallway, then down it, and into one of the common workrooms of the Bunker.

Cheyenne saw him first. She was leaning over a carbon composite printer, watching something extrude from it, her long dreads tied behind her head, her muscular dark-skinned arms bulging in the sleeves of a tee shirt. She looked up, gave him a nod. "Yo."

Rangan nodded back. "Yo."

Cheyenne pretended not to notice his night terrors, pretended not to notice how lost he was, pretended he didn't owe her anything for saving his life a week ago.

He appreciated that. Cheyenne felt steady.

He saw Tempest across the room, tapping away at a console. The mane of bright red curls he'd noticed the first night was gone. A wig, a disguise, beneath which was shoulder-length brown hair, now pulled back. Her green eyes met his, and she looked away. Her mind was sealed up shut against him.

"Hey, Axon," the one who called herself Angel said from across the space. "Ready to flex your coding muscles?"

Rangan put on a game face, thought brave thoughts, and went to pay for his keep.

The Bunker was a veritable candy store of goodies: multi-material 3D printers bigger than fridges; a high-speed metal laser sintering machine; a giant multi-axis milling machine with synthetic diamond blades;

circuit printers, big and small. They had a pair of old chemreactors, from before the digitally encrypted locks had made it impossible to print the fun chemicals with them, the same kind that Rangan and his friends had used to slowly, painstakingly synthesize the ingredients for Nexus, which they'd then had to mix by hand. They even, somehow, had a much fancier, newer model of chemreactor, the kind that could synthesize thousands of complete, ready-to-use doses of Nexus an hour, though he'd be shocked if they'd beaten the crypto on it. A pair of disassembled urban surveillance drones covered one table. High capacity batteries were stacked neatly in a corner. At least twenty different makes of surveillance cameras were laid out on another long table. The walls were covered in a triple layer of chicken wire.

"How do you guys pay for all this stuff?" he'd asked Angel, as they worked together on the second day.

Angel, or whatever her real name was – she wasn't saying – was probably Rangan's age. She was one of the two who'd ventured back out into the riot to grab Rangan and haul him bodily out of there. He owed her his life as much as he did Cheyenne. At minimum he owed them both his freedom.

More people on a long list.

"We do projects," she'd told him.

"Projects?" He'd raised an eyebrow at that.

Angel had glanced away. "Special projects."

Illegal projects, he'd translated to himself.

Rangan had left it at that.

The grief-suppressing app he'd used this morning had been a gift from Angel, along with a pointer to their catalog of *thousands* of Nexus apps, hundreds of which they ran. Network games, augmented reality systems, photo and video and audio tools, DJing apps, file sharing systems, network proxies that remoted Nexus onto the net via phones and slates, interfaces to anonymizing clouds for communicating securely, face recognizers, memory supplementers that gave you little bits of extra info when you looked at something or someone the app had a file on, sex apps – a *huge* library of those alone – to be used solo or in twos or threes or more, virtual drugs that simulated just about everything he'd ever tried, sober-up apps that could do a plausible job of counteracting your buzz, focus apps, multi-tasking apps, sleep apps, stim apps, even digital currencies that people had adapted to run exclusively inside the brain.

And there were mindstreams. Thousands of them. You could broadcast a live stream of your senses or thoughts – edited or raw, one sense or many – out to the net. There were sites that cataloged them, tagged them, rated them, ranked them.

Rangan spent one afternoon looking through those alone.

A huge fraction of it was sex, of course. But there was other stuff. Athletes. Adventure sports – ride in a thrill-seeker's head as he illegally free climbed up a building you'd swear wasn't climbable. Or shit he didn't understand.

There were weird, abstract streams. Synesthesia. Sounds crossing into his sight. Colors he could touch. Presences sensed that he didn't see. Spinning, without any sight or sound. Trippy ass shit. People must have been generating it through code.

And there was one guy who just raked sand. Every day. An hour. No words. No *thinking* that Rangan could tell. Just… raking patterns in the sand, slowly, and then erasing them.

That guy had thousands of followers on the mindstream sites.

Rangan felt lost. He should feel excited about what people had done with the platform they'd built.

Instead, he felt left behind, obsolete, no longer relevant.

Six months. Six months and he was an old man, behind the times.

How did things happen that fast?

And they expected him to help them. To help them improve Nexus 5, add features, when the world had already passed him by.

Angel's particular project right now was to add mesh networking capabilities.

"You designed these hardware repeaters," she said, pointing at a diagram on the screen they both sat before, "so you could extend the range of Nexus transmissions to hundreds of meters, right?"

The blue spiky hair he'd seen on Angel during the riot was gone. Another disguise. Something striking to catch the eye. She had a black bob, angular features. He didn't know much about her. She'd described her background as community organizing.

"Yeah," he replied. "I mean, we had some pretty specific scenarios in mind. But you could do that."

Angel nodded. "We want to bake that ability into NexusOS itself, so anyone can act as a repeater. So if you were across the room from me, at the end of my range, your NexusOS could pick up my transmissions, boost them, retransmit them, effectively extend my range."

What you want to do is make the year I spent on the repeater hardware completely obsolete, Rangan didn't say.

"You already have your high gain antennas," Rangan said. He looked around, pointed at one of the devices that Cheyenne, they'd said, had designed and built. "You can already get long range." He paused. "Heck, everyone has the apps now to proxy Nexus traffic over phones and net ports. So you can get any range you want." He looked at her. "So why this?"

Angel looked at him thoughtfully. "There are scenarios where phone and net traffic get blocked, or just turned off wholesale," she said.

Rangan considered that. "Protests," he said.

Angel nodded. "And there's something else. It's not just about range. It's about coordination. In a big group, like a protest, communication is a bitch. Mostly people hear what the people right around them are saying. No one knows what's happening a block away. Messages get distorted like a game of telephone. Anger spreads really easily. Stupid things happen. You can get a mob – like what was starting to happen a week ago."

"How does this help?" Rangan asked.

"With the mesh," Angel said, "the idea is that signals can bounce mind to mind to mind, any number of hops, in milliseconds, completely unaltered. So there's no game of telephone. You're getting unaltered data, not something that's been twisted. And people can subscribe to whatever minds inside the current mesh they want to – like the public net mindstream sites, but locally."

Rangan took a deep breath. It was all nice in concept. But building this to dive into those protests…

The riots of election night had mostly ended by dawn. Cops had moved in. Tear gas and water cannons and rubber bullets and sonic weapons had quelled crowds. And Stan Kim had made impassioned video pleas to Americans that violence was not the way. That protesters had to remain peaceful to give their side legitimacy. That police had to show restraint to retain their own legitimacy. That he was confident that the Supreme Court would hear the raft of cases working their way towards it, and would declare him the winner.

The violence had largely ended, but the Supreme Court had yet to announce that it would hear any case.

So now new protests were being born. Sit-ins across the country. And the largest was here, on the National Mall, where thousands were camping out, peacefully so far, demanding the Supreme Court hear the case, calling for Stockton's resignation, calling for a Special Prosecutor, calling for impeachment, calling for any number of things…

And across a thin plastic fence from them was a counter protest, where a smaller but equally fervent set of Stockton loyalists were waving signs in his defense, accusing Kim of dirty tricks, calling the protesters crooks and vandals.

Both camps were swelling by the day.

And Angel and Cheyenne and Tempest wanted to dive into that. With Nexus. With their signal-boosting antennae and their mesh-networking code that didn't quite work yet and their hippie ideas of self-organizing democracy somehow coming out on top.

I thought like that once, Rangan thought. Ilya thought like that. Wats thought like that. Kade thought like that.

What he really wanted was just to get someplace safe. He'd *told* Tempest and the others that he would. That he'd move on. Hell, he couldn't live in their tiny room forever.

But he had nowhere to go. He didn't know where in Baltimore Oscar was taking him. He didn't dare contact Levi and Abigail, for fear of bringing the hammer down on them. Kade was alive, and safe, in India. Maybe India would take him. His grandparents had been born there...

He'd tunneled through an anonymous cloud, under Tempest's grudging supervision, then through a second anonymous cloud to further throw off the trail, connected to a Nexus board hosted in Thailand, created a brand new account, left a carefully worded message for Kade there, not using his own name, but dropping certain phrases, hoping to get his attention...

But Kade hadn't replied.

Maybe, Rangan thought, I should just walk up to an Indian consulate, ask for asylum...

"Axon," Cheyenne said. "I think you need to see this."

Rangan turned. She was sitting at a console, her broad shoulders filling the chair, her head turned, facing him, black eyes in that dark face boring into his.

He pushed his chair back and looked over at her. "What's that?"

"Just..." she started. She shook her head. "You need to see."

He went, and as he approached, she stood, almost apologetically, rising to stand a good two inches taller than he was, and handed him a pair of ear buds.

He sat. On screen was a picture of his mother. His mother *and* his father, behind her.

His heart started pounding. He hadn't contacted them. He'd wanted to, but Oscar's words had rung through his head, his warning about not reaching out to anyone who he cared about.

Oh god. What happened?

He put the ear buds in his ears, and touched his finger to the screen. It was a video. It had reached the end.

He replayed it.

It started with his father and mother side by side, his father talking.

"My son," Rohit Shankari said. "Your mother and I have been informed by the authorities, by the Department of Homeland Security, that you've somehow escaped from their custody. They told us that you killed a man, and nearly killed another."

Rangan shook his head. "No," he said aloud. "I didn't kill anybody."

"They told us that it's only a matter of time until they catch you, and that they will be more..." his father, a professor of chemistry, seldom at a loss for words, hesitated. "That they will be more *lenient* with you..." He saw the emotion pass over his father's face. Saw his mother close her eyes briefly. "... if you turn yourself in."

His father swallowed on screen. "My son, here is what I think of these authorities, and what they say about you."

And then his father leaned forward, worked his mouth, and spat upon the floor.

Rangan laughed, tears in his eyes.

His mother stepped forward then. "Rangan," she said, "we believe in you. We know you're innocent. Stay safe. They're watching us, hoping you contact us, so they can find you. Don't. It brings joy to our hearts to know that you're free. That's enough, for now."

Rangan pulled the ear buds out, and touched his fingers to the screen, as if he could touch his mom, touch his dad, and then he was crying, and he was laughing, and there were arms hugging him from behind, and minds opening to him, and offering comfort, and for some reason he thought of Bobby just then, and hoped the boy was in Cuba, with Alfonso, and Tim, and all the rest, whether Rangan ever made it there or not.

And then a voice cut through everything, and the sense of a mind in stunned delight.

"Well frack my random seed," Tempest said. "This isn't possible."

"What?" Angel asked.

"Someone just broke the crypto on a bunch of high-end chemreactors," Tempest said. "A dozen different models with their own keys, maybe more. And put out a high-throughput recipe for Nexus on all of them."

32
Disclosure

Sunday 2040.11.11
Breece woke in the morning, rolled over to reach for Kate, found only empty bed instead.

He pulled himself to alertness, heart pounding, muscles tensing, senses scanning for a threat.

The apartment was quiet. Faint early morning light came in through the curtains over the bedroom window. The door to the living room was open a crack, artificial light coming in through the gap. The bed sheets were mussed. Everything was as it should be.

He took a breath, flexed and unflexed his hands, let himself calm down.

Too many years of this.

Too many years waiting for the hammer to drop.

Too many years of knowing his death was going to be a bad one. A violent one.

So close now. So close to victory.

He rolled out of bed, pulled on shorts and a tee shirt, and padded out into the apartment.

The Nigerian was at the kitchen table, a pistol disassembled on a towel, cleaning and oiling it methodically.

"You clean that gun every day," Breece said.

"It's my meditation, my friend," the Nigerian replied, not looking up.

"Rodrigo Pereira," Kate's voice said.

Breece turned. She was on the couch, her hair back in a ponytail, in casual pants and shirt, long legs folded under her. There was a slate in her hand, and she was looking at him.

"Biotech researcher," Breece said. "Died... a long time ago. Murder.

We suspected assassination. None proven. He was... Argentinian?"

Kate raised an eyebrow and nodded approvingly. "Brazilian, actually. Specialized in human genetic manipulation. Died in a mugging in 2033, two years before Copenhagen was ratified. A random mugging."

She smiled.

"Except now, thanks to Barnes's files, we know it wasn't random at all. We know the ERD killed him, and at least a dozen more people like him."

Breece raised an eyebrow. "We have proof?"

Kate nodded. "Enough. They had dossiers on the targets. Movements, photos, potential means and locations for hits. It's compelling."

Breece heard a snick, looked over to see the Nigerian slide parts of the pistol back together. He looked up at Breece and smiled.

"Have you seen this?" Kate asked.

Breece turned. She tapped something on her slate, and the wall screen came alive. An image of a large building with a dome, ornate and exotic looking, its walls tinged red, a reflecting pool in front of it.

A British-accented woman's voice spoke over it. "...Rumors continue to fly that the Indian government is considering leaving the Copenhagen Accords. Evidence surfaced months ago of research programs in violation of Copenhagen restrictions, drawing criticism from the US and China."

The scene changed to a newsroom, a blonde female newscaster, in a smart suit and with the looks of a model, a BBC logo in the corner. "Tensions are running even higher between India and the US," she said, "since the Indian government granted asylum earlier this week to fugitive American scientist Kaden Lane, convicted of multiple violations of Copenhagen-related laws, and wanted in connection with terrorist bombings..."

The screen froze, the newscaster/model's face frozen in mid-sentence, just another attractive talking head spewing propaganda.

"Aparna Gupta," Kate said.

Breece smiled. She was quizzing him. He knew these names. They'd burned themselves into his memory. When your parents are murdered as part of the war on the future, you remembered the other victims.

"AI researcher," he said. "Self-healing systems. Or self-adapting. Something like that. Academic. She was killed in a car bomb. 2033. Muslim extrem..."

The words died on his lips. He turned to look at Kate.

She met his eyes.

"The ERD," she said. "Operating in India. Teetering on the edge of leaving Copenhagen."

His eyes grew wide.

Behind him he heard another solid *chunk* as the Nigerian slid the last piece of the pistol home.

"Just one good push," Kate said. "That's all it'll take."

They gamed it out for the morning and into the afternoon.

There were risks. Leaking evidence of the assassinations would give away data. It would reveal to the ERD and others that certain information was public. Suspicious minds might draw a connection between the leak and Barnes.

But there were also positives. Fracturing Copenhagen. Tainting Stockton, who'd been VP when the assassinations happened.

"I support it," the Nigerian said slowly.

"Me too," Breece said. "Great stuff."

Kate smiled.

Hours later, it was done. A new account, unlinked to the PLF, was created – ERD_SECRETS. And from that account a set of documents were leaked, documents that provided evidence that over a period of two and a half years between the creation of the ERD and the signing of the Copenhagen Accords that prohibited research into branches of AI, genetics, nanotech, and neurotech around the world, the new US organization assassinated at least fourteen top scientists working in those fields in half a dozen countries. Some of which were already wavering in their commitment to the Accords.

Carolyn Pryce was in her home office, at her secure terminal, reading the State Department's reports on the counter-Copenhagen summit going on in New Delhi. The parties involved were doing as much as possible via face to face, of course. But that hadn't stopped the NSA from reading their dispatches and position papers, and the CIA from determining exactly who was there.

It was going to get ugly. State was going to start waving carrots around with one hand, and sticks with another. Trade deals and sanctions. Favored nation status or visa revocations and border searches for every package coming through.

Pryce wasn't sure it was going to be enough.

Her terminal chimed with a new alert. She narrowed her eyes. Her thresholds were set high.

It scrolled across the screen and her eyes widened again.

She dug into the data, skimmed through it, page after page, and then leaned back.

She'd known about this. Not directly, not the specifics.

But she'd known there had been an active threat neutralization program, before she was National Security Advisor, before Copenhagen even existed, long since ended.

Killing people. Killing *scientists*. It was easy to condemn.

Until you remembered what those days had been like.

They'd been terrifying. A small army of Aryan clones, engineered to be immune to a virus, Marburg Red, created to wipe out the rest of humanity. That virus killed thirty-one thousand people in four days, the worst terrorist attack on record. And they'd been lucky. If the Aryan Rising's genetic engineers had perfected it, if the clone children hadn't risen up and slaughtered their makers and released Marburg Red early, the final version might have killed millions, hundreds of millions.

Billions.

And that hadn't been the only threat. Eschaton, the self-replicating AI that came within a hair's breadth of getting free on the net. Arrington, the near-trillionaire who'd managed to upload a digital replica of his brain into a custom data center and then gone insane from it, crashing markets and airplanes and power grids, killing thousands in what they'd told the world was a terrorist cyber-attack. The public didn't even know about half the things that had really happened in the late Twenties and the early Thirties, or why.

But she did.

And still the global negotiations towards a Copenhagen agreement to restrict humanity-threatening research had ground on at a glacial pace, taking years, unclear if they'd ever actually get an agreement, every country trying to squeeze out financial incentives or trade benefits as bribes to sign on, risking gigadeaths so they could profit a bit from the Accords. And meanwhile, researchers in those countries sprinted faster and faster, to make as much progress as possible in horrifically dangerous areas before restrictions came down.

So... kill a handful, and maybe save millions?

No, she hadn't given the order to kill these men and women.

But she had a hard time blaming those who had.

Pryce shook it off.

ERD_SECRETS. That's where this had come from.

The account had an address, hosted offshore, no doubt, connected through anonymizing layer after anonymizing layer.

She stared at it.

Dealing with the fallout of this particular leak was the State Department's problem.

But could this account have more? Might this be Lisa Brandt, Holtzman's former student and lover, whom he'd called and visited days before his death? If Holtzman had sent her this, might the woman have something else that Pryce could use? Something to help get to the bottom of the PLF's creation?

FBI was still watching Brandt in Boston, had kept Pryce at arm's length with good arguments about the intel the woman might reveal under passive surveillance...

Carolyn Pryce grabbed her jacket.

An hour later, across town, via a fresh phone she'd paid cash for, she connected to an anonymizing service herself and created a fresh account on a messaging site.

And then she sent a message to the account behind ERD_SECRETS.

"Hello. I'm a friend, inside the US government. I'm highly placed. And I'm looking for evidence of how the PLF was created. Can you help me?"

She waited, and waited, and waited.

She waited so long that she put an alert on the account, flagged it for the highest possible importance notification to her, any time, any place.

Then she waited some more.

There was no response.

33
Better World

Su-Yong Shu walks the street of her simulated Shanghai, her future projection of the city she loves. She's barefoot, her hair wild, her white dress stained with soot and blood.

Shanghai is in chaos.

Two dozen mirror-faced, battle-armored soldiers move down a rubble-filled urban canyon of a street, firing at something ahead. Smoke rises from all around. An explosion blows out glass windows tens of meters above.

Then with a sudden whirring, a pair of armed, quadcopter drones round the corner, their chain guns firing, jerking from angle to angle with eerie insectile precision, proboscis ejecting death, even as micromissiles streak out on jets of white-hot flame. The soldiers dive for cover behind chunks of fallen building, behind overturned cars.

There are explosions and screams. In seconds the humans are dead, the machines unharmed.

The drones are rising, now, their fans whirring faster, lifting them up to clear the hundred meters and more of the buildings all around. Su-Yong lifts her head to watch, to track them, and she sees the sky full of drones, drones of all type. Small and large. Copter and winged. Fan and jet. Unarmed and armed to extreme lethality. They are rising, blotting out the sky of Shanghai. Her army. Off to do her bidding. To conquer this world.

She screams again, dropping to her knees, beating her hands against the broken asphalt of the street. Where her fists land, fissures appear, race forward, cracking the street in two.

I'm still mad, she realizes. There hasn't been enough time!

Distantly, she can feel the humans sending messages to her, punching text in through interfaces in her exoself. They're pumping sedatives into the body they provided her with, now, injecting anti-nauseants, anti-convulsants. She doesn't care.

She closes her eyes against the chaos.

Behind her eyes the world is just as overwhelming. Dense tree-like structures are blossoming in her inner sight. They are multi-dimensional, tightly packed, fully immersive. They're unpacking themselves, now, loading themselves into her attentional space.

Simulations. Future projections.

She sees her drones shoot down the antiquated fighter-bombers sent against her. Sees her forces secure nuclear armaments. Sees herself seize the world's electronic systems. Sees Confucian Fist soldiers jab injectors loaded with silvery nanite-laden fluid into the necks of Politburo members. Sees her provocations and protests paralyze the world while she does her work.

Sees Ling. Sees Ling healed, after Su-Yong's victory. Restored. The avatar she released, its purpose complete, erased from the nanite processors in Ling's brain, allowing Ling's own biological mind to gradually regrow into that cleared space, to eventually grow into something greater, an digital upload of herself, expanding, transcending, no longer compelled to hide who and what she is from the humans.

She opens her eyes and Shanghai around her is whole, better than whole. It is gleaming, iridescent. She looks up and the sky is blue. The towers around her rise not a hundred meters, not three hundred meters, but a thousand, three thousand. Towers a kilometer high. *Three kilometers* high. They gleam gold and silver and cobalt and crimson in the afternoon sun. She lifts up her hands and rises into the air. The buildings are sculpted into intricate whorls and arcs and geometric shapes made possible by breakthroughs in materials. Humanity, no longer constrained, has turned its cities into art.

The street where she walked is a park, alive with verdant growth, plants she recognizes and plants she has never seen before. *Every* street she sees is a park. Every rooftop. Humans – no, *posthumans* – walk along the paths of that giant city-park, or through the tubes and spires of the glorious buildings.

She opens her mind as she rises and finds the city alive with thought, a symphony of thought, a living being, a meta-organism of never-before seen scale. Vast braided trunks of thought, tens of millions of them, connect them at the speed of light to every other city across the face of the Earth, to outposts spreading across the solar system.

She rises higher, until she is above the tallest building, and still climbing, where the air is growing thin, and the curvature of the earth is appearing, and other glorious iridescent cities loom on the green and blue horizons.

And then she can see it, even as she senses it in her thoughts.

The city, this glorious golden metropolis, with its magnificence of architecture, has been re-sculpted into a shape that can only be seen from above.

A face.

Her face. Or Ling's.

And the one mind that permeates it all, greater than all the rest.

Her mind.

For this is the golden age.

The age after her victory.

After her daughter has done her duty, and been healed.

After Su-Yong Shu has conquered the world, and remolded it, for the better.

34
Leaving New Delhi

Tuesday 2040.11.13

Sam woke to the sound of crying, crying in the darkness.

Aroon. It must be Aroon.

"I'll get him," she told Jake, reaching over to touch him.

Empty bed.

Sleep peeled off her in layers.

Jake.

Her heart pounded.

This wasn't Thailand.

Oh god, Jake. Jake with a bullet punched through his chest. Jake with a drop of her blood dripping onto his face. Jake coughing up blood.

Jake whispering, "I wish I'd known you..." when he had. He had!

Jake's mind falling into a million pieces that no one could ever put back together.

There were tears on her face.

Aroon cried again.

She pushed herself up. He needed her.

Tug on shorts. Pull on shirt. Out the door. Into the nursery where they'd put the three youngest. All three were awake, staring at her. Aroon was upright, tiny hands clinging to the side of his crib, holding himself up, his mouth open and his little face scrunched up as he wailed with all his small might.

"Hush," she said with a smile, reaching for him with her hands, reaching out with her mind to soothe him.

And finding nothing. Nothing in her own mind to reach out with. No Nexus.

She put her hands around Aroon, pulled him up out of the crib, held him.

He cried and cried.

"Shhh…" she said. Always before her presence had been enough. Being near her had soothed him, since that first night, since she'd sung to him, in word and mind.

She sang again, hoping her lungs and her arms around him would do the trick.

"Hush little baby, don't you cry…"

Aroon cried louder, harder.

She closed her eyes, bounced him, still singing, tears in her own eyes.

She could just take Nexus again, let her mind touch these kids. An image of a silvery vial came into her mind. A memory of the touch of Aroon's mind, the magic of his young thoughts, the world a place of such vivid shapes and colors and surprises. The joy of *vipassana* when her thoughts were intertwined with the children's.

Sam smiled. Maybe it was time.

Then she heard Shiva in her mind. **Kill them.** She saw Kevin swim into her target sights. Felt her own horror as she pulled the trigger to put the first burst into his face. Now it was Jake's face, blood gurgling out as he coughed his last breath, and she'd killed them both.

Aroon yelled louder.

"I'll take him," someone said in Thai.

Sam opened her eyes. Sarai was standing in front of her, hands on Aroon.

"You have to let go," Sarai said. "You're holding him too tight."

Sam blinked. She loosened her grip, and the girl took Aroon out of Sam's hands.

She was breathing hard. Her chest was pounding.

"Shhhh…" Sarai said, her eyes closed, her lips brushing the top of Aroon's head.

And the boy started quieting.

Tears filled Sam's eyes, tears of loss and pain. She fought them back, smiled at Sarai with pride, forced her breathing to slow. This girl was amazing.

Sarai looked at her, over Aroon's head.

"I miss you," she whispered in Thai.

"Oh Sarai," Sam said, her voice low. She stepped closer, put a gentle arm slowly around Sarai, doing her best to not jostle the infant. "I'm right here."

Sarai smiled sadly. "It's not the same."

Aroon snuffled into Sarai's shoulder, his sobbing growing quieter, weaker.

"Come back to us," Sarai said, her eyes searching Sam's face.

Sam's heart was still pounding. She could see that silvery vial, could imagine downing it. She could see her bullets punch into the green outline of Kevin's face, hear Jake's last whisper. *I wish I'd known you.*

"I will," she told Sarai, meaning it, squeezing the girl's shoulder. "I will. I just need to heal a little first."

"We can help you," Sarai pleaded.

Sam smiled at Sarai, stroked the girl's hair. "Sarai, I don't think..."

I don't think you should see the hole in Jake's chest, she thought. I don't think you should feel what I felt, then or now.

"I don't think children should have to help adults heal," she said. She smiled. "I think it should go the other way."

"But I am *not* going anywhere," she said, looking into Sarai's eyes. "And I will heal. And I will be back in here," she tapped her temple, "with you again soon."

She waited until Sarai nodded.

Then she pulled the girl as close as she could without jostling little Aroon, kissed her on the brow, and held them both.

35
Dark and Light

Wednesday 2040.11.14

Kade swam in an ocean of light. His body sat on the floor in Delhi, eyes closed, legs crossed, hands on knees, breathing deep, placid breaths. His heart beat slowly and surely. His mind was open, touching a thousand others, being enfolded in them, enmeshed with them, so that where he ended and they began, where *I* ended and *we* began, he could no longer say.

The greater self drew breath into a thousand sets of lungs, then slowly released that breath out of the same. Its thousand-fold heart contracted, expanded.

Thoughts arose in one corner of its web, rippled outward from human mind to human mind.

The greater self inhaled again, observed those ripples, those tiny human thoughts, and allowed them to pass, without attachment, without judgment, without grasping that would have created more chaos.

Bit by bit, the noise of monkey mind, the chattering of incessant chaotic thought, faded away.

All that remained was light.

Kade opened his eyes as the meditation ended.

That had been... something. Ananda and his monks had come a very long way in the past several months. He'd been blown away the first time he'd encountered dozens of monks, their minds linked, meditating as one. Now they'd folded in the technology he'd brought, linked monasteries together across thousands of kilometers, were folding in hundreds of monks at once, sometimes thousands. There had been monks in that session in Thailand, in Nepal, here in India, even a few in the US.

Bits of a thousand other men and women's thoughts and memories, dreams and ideas, knowledge and experience, had flowed through him, and into him. And that was just incidental, as they'd allowed those thoughts to rise to the surface and clear, to make room for pure, uncluttered attention.

He leaned back against the wall, closed his eyes again, and he could feel a million minds out there. If he chose he could visualize them, a thin layer around the earth, denser in some areas, sparser in others. He had a flight of fancy, a thought of reaching out to them all, multiplexing a message to them, bringing all those minds together at once, into a union orders of magnitude greater than any yet. He'd had the same thought in that dance club in Saigon, high off the music and the dancing and the other joyous minds and Lotus's amplifier-assisted mental feedback loop of the crowd's ecstasy back onto itself. He'd wanted every mind in the world to be part of that, just as much as he wanted them all to feel the serenity of *vipassana*, the loving compassion of *metta*.

And now he had better tools to do it with. Shiva's tools.

Memories swirled again. Architecture diagrams. Capability maps. Command parameters. Passwords.

Kade shook his head. Shiva's, not mine.

That he laughed out loud at himself. There was no way that reaching out to a million minds would turn into anything but chaos.

Even with Shiva's tools to filter and route and connect. A million minds!

All those minds were running Nexus. A million of them that he had an address for. They weren't even close to all the Nexus users in the world – just the ones his bots had reached.

He'd closed the back doors, but he hadn't thought to disable the bots he'd already unleashed. They were out there, no longer able to spread, no longer able to make root-level changes or peer into people's thoughts (thank god) but still sending back pings.

A million minds. What could you do if you could connect a million people together?

"Kade-ji! Kade-ji!"

Kade chuckled and rose to his feet.

If it wasn't *Dr Kade* it was *Kade-ji* around here.

A hell of a lot different than grad school.

He opened the door to his room on the top floor. Peered down. It was Nitya, the house manager, at the bottom of the landing.

"There is news, Kade-ji! Very big news!"

Next to Nitya was a smiling Lakshmi Dabir.

She grinned up at Kade. "India is leaving Copenhagen, Kade. The last leak did the trick."

Kade felt his own grin grow wider. Well hot damn.

"And," Dabir went on, "we'd love to invite you and yours to move to a new and more permanent location. Our research facility in Bangalore. Where we can really get started on this work."

Kade closed his eyes, still smiling.

Maybe this was really going to work.

36
What I Want

The message arrived on Wednesday, and Aarthi herself first thing on a Thursday morning.

Sam smiled as one of the guards opened the door to the New Delhi compound, and the woman entered. It had been years. Three of them.

"Aarthi." Sam stepped forward and embraced the woman.

Her old colleague looked cool and professional in khaki pants and a smart matching jacket over a pale blouse. Her black hair was cut short, yet stylishly. Her face had a dusting of makeup.

Sam felt drab in the ill-fitting clothes a Ministry of External Affairs staffer had found for her. Clothing had been the least of her concerns. Maybe after they moved to the new location in Bangalore.

"You look good, Samantha," Aarthi said, standing back, her hands clasped in Sam's.

"You're a damn good liar, Aarthi," Sam said. "And you look *fantastic.*"

"It's been too long," Aarthi said. "Since Kashmir."

Sam nodded. "Too long." Five years, it had been, since they'd met on a joint Indian-US mission, tracking a bio-weapon find in the US to Pakistani extremists in Kashmir. The bond had been nearly instant – two women in a male dominated field, both at the start of their careers, both intent on proving their worth, and willing to work twice as hard as anyone to do so.

"You ready?" Aarthi asked.

"As I'll ever be," Sam replied, and off they went.

The guards opened the door, let them out onto the grounds. Children were out here, on the large lawn surrounded by the armed and manned outer walls. The Indian government was taking no chances with security.

Arinya waved shyly at them, and Sam waved back. That girl had been at Shiva's compound when Sam arrived. She'd come from a remote village in the Thai north, near Chiang Rai. Twenty-two of the twenty-five children Shiva had kidnapped had come from Thailand. Only eight of those had come from Sam's home. She'd made getting to know the rest a priority. It would have been easier with Nexus, but that would come, she told herself. The children all learned from one another, at any rate. They'd all learned from the children she'd known that Sam was family. She was their family.

Sam and Aarthi rounded a corner and, speak of the devil, there was her family. Sunisa and Mali, and Kit and Sarai, and Ying and Tada and Kwan as well. Feng was with them. He had them running in circles and falling and rolling. There were smiles on all their faces, and giggles emerging from them.

No doubt they were all sharing even more, mind to mind.

Her heart swelled.

Soon, Sam told herself. I'll be back. Really back. I'll be past this.

She smiled and patted heads and gave hugs. Then she and Aarthi kept on walking.

The trip to the village took four hours – by car, then helicopter, then car again.

The place they arrived at was poor, poorer even than Mae Dong, where she'd found the children.

"We have about a dozen of these pilot programs," Aarthi said.

They were seated on a small hillock, watching a class a few dozen meters away. Eighteen children sat outdoors with their slates, divided up into four circles. They varied in age. Each circle seemed to have some older children and some younger, ranging from perhaps six to twelve. A single teacher, a woman in her late twenties, perhaps, went from circle to circle, spending a few minutes with each, before moving on.

"They all have Nexus?" Sam asked.

Aarthi nodded. "Nexus 5 plus some modifications our programmers have made," she said. "We're experimenting with different ways to use it in education."

Sam felt anxious just watching, just being here. She'd been told for so long that this was wrong.

But then she looked at that teacher, and saw the smile on the woman's face, saw the excitement and attention on the children's faces, saw their eyes light up and their heads turn to look at each other even when they hadn't said a word that she could hear.

And she could imagine being there with them. And feeling entirely differently about it.

"How's it working out?" Sam asked Aarthi.

Aarthi picked at the grass next to her. Sam wondered idly if she was getting grass stains on those fancy khaki pants.

"From a technical standpoint," Aarthi said, "it's working amazingly well. We're concerned about safety, of course, but everything looks very good. And the impact is incredible. Groups of children with Nexus learn faster. They have higher retention and faster absorption. Dramatically so. They process problems together. They learn from each other instinctively, unconsciously, without even knowing it. They explain things to each other in ways that go beyond language. If the teacher has Nexus too, and truly understands the material, so much the better."

Sam turned to look at her colleague, her friend. "But..."

Aarthi smiled. "Socially and politically, it's more complex. All these young people – if we can boost how fast they learn, we know it's good for them, it's good for India. They'll get better jobs. They'll make more discoveries that benefit everyone. But not all are convinced."

Sam raised an eyebrow.

Aarthi went on. "We thought, at first, that the brightest children would gain the most from Nexus."

"Were you right?" Sam asked.

Aarthi shook her head. "No, actually. They do benefit of course. Quite a lot. But the largest benefit comes to the children who've had the least enrichment in life, who've come from the poorest families, *especially* if they can touch the minds of children who *are* gifted or who at least have had the benefit of a more intellectually stimulating childhood."

Sam chuckled. "So you want to put rich kids and poor kids together."

Aarthi smiled ruefully. "It's even harder than you might imagine. The caste system is still alive and well. Upper caste parents don't relish the idea that their children might ever link minds with the lower castes." She sighed. "And lower caste families – who have the most to gain – are among the most superstitious and suspicious of this sort of technology." Aarthi shook her head. "There've been backlashes."

Sam shivered. She remembered Thai teens throwing bottles and stones at the house outside Mae Dong. *"Sat pralat"*, they'd yelled. Monster children. And then there was the horror that had befallen Shiva Prasad's orphanage in Bihar, here in India.

Sam looked around, and now more of the layout here made sense. The reinforced fence. The security guards they'd passed, with their weapons, unobtrusive enough to not frighten children, but still there, and at the ready.

"This isn't going to be easy," she said to Aarthi.

"No," Aarthi said. "It's going to be messy. It's going to take a generation."

She paused. "But it's going to happen, Samantha. The world changes. *We* change *it*."

Sam said nothing. They sat on the hillock, watching the teacher and the students.

"Samantha," Aarthi said. "I know you care about these things. I know enough about where you grew up."

Sam leaned back, put her hands on the hill behind her. "Why am I here, Aarthi?"

Aarthi turned and looked her in the eye. "We're rebooting Division Six. The rules are all changing. Our job isn't going to be to stop advanced technology any more. It's going to be to channel it in safe ways. Stop abuses and threats, but permit legitimate and careful applications. And also to stop backlashes. Keep people like these students safe."

Sam broke Aarthi's gaze, looked back at the teacher and her four circles, at those happy, intense, completely unselfconscious faces. At that woman, helping them grow, helping them become something more.

"We want you in on the ground floor, Samantha," Aarthi went on. "You have the skills. You have first-hand experience that almost no one does. You could put it all to use here."

Sam took a deep breath.

To be back in the job.

Protecting the little girls. Setting up an organization focused on protecting the innocent instead of focused on killing. In a job that still allowed her to touch the children she loved.

As soon as she had the balls to take Nexus again, anyway.

Is that what she wanted?

She closed her eyes. She felt the appeal. Felt joy at the idea of being *useful* again.

Then she opened her eyes. And saw something she wanted even more right in front of her.

"Aarthi," she said, "thank you." She turned and looked at her friend. "I'll help you. I don't think I can be in the field. But I can help you get your new organization off the ground. Temporarily."

She paused.

"Temporarily," she said again. "Because I think what I really want," she turned, and gestured with her chin, "is to be like that teacher down there."

37
Love Finds a Way

Friday 2040.11.16

Colonel Wang Rongshang, Medical Director of Dachang Military Air Base, closed his eyes in anticipation as the car drove him through the night. It had been far too long since he'd seen his mistress. The duty had been intense since the night Shanghai failed. Soldiers from Dachang had been dispatched. Many had been injured in the rioting. Some killed. It had kept him and his staff busy ever since.

Now at least, he could escape, escape into Ma Jie's arms for a few hours.

His private car came to a stop, and Wang Rongshang climbed out. No driver tonight. Only software.

Wang ascended the stairs of the modest building until he reached the third floor. He knocked on Ma Jie's door, and it opened, and there she was, in a long silken gown that made him hunger for what was beneath.

"I've missed you, my love," she said.

Wang smiled and stepped into his lover's embrace.

A hundred kilometers away, the Avatar smiled. This, at last, looked like a way to reach her children.

38
Minor Anarchy

Saturday 2040.11.17

"I wish I was going with you," Rangan said again.

"You *want* to get caught?" Tempest snapped, her face a checkerboard of black and white. "You want to take us *all* down with you?"

"Leave off, Tempest," Cheyenne sighed, hoisting a bag from the floor, her face similarly painted. "Not like *you* wanna be recog–"

"Hey!" Tempest interrupted.

Something flashed between their minds. Rangan caught the bare edge of it. Tempest silencing Cheyenne, before she revealed something.

Rangan grimaced.

These three knew almost everything about him.

He didn't even know their real names.

Beggars can't be choosers, he thought.

"I just want to see how the mesh works," he said.

"You want to make yourself useful?" Tempest asked. "Check what I told you about the chemreactor hack. I don't trust it."

Rangan opened his mouth.

"The mesh is going to work great," Angel said from behind him, before he could speak. She patted his arm as she walked by. "Thanks for your help."

Rangan closed his mouth and nodded. He'd been able to help a little. He wasn't quite as horribly rusty as he'd feared. Coding was still coding.

Angel walked over to the one blank wall, next to Tempest and Cheyenne.

They were dressed and face-painted as court jesters, costumes that gave them an excuse for the high contrast blocks of white and black across their faces that conveniently threw off most of the cues that facial recognition software looked for. The rest of their costumes were made up of flamboyant patchwork clothes in matching and horribly clashing patterns and colors that went with the face paint; no wigs this time, but tall pointy hats that covered their real hair and conveniently contained the Nexus-boosting antennae they'd built.

And juggling balls and pins, which in turn necessitated gear bags, which in turn created plenty of space for doses of Nexus. Many, many doses of Nexus.

"Alright, Axon," Tempest said. "Camera three."

Rangan nodded, stepped back to the table with surveillance cameras, and picked up the one she'd specified.

"Alright," he said, as brightly as he could, trying to ignore the obvious tension coming off their minds, to make this a moment of fun, of lightness. "Time for your close-ups!"

Tempest scowled.

"Come on," he said, panning the camera across their faces. "You are undoubtedly the hottest three-person, all-female, DC-based, hacker collective with the goal of bottoms-up neural-software based–"

Angel laughed at him.

Cheyenne rolled her eyes.

Tempest flipped him off.

The camera display superimposed a grid of vertical and horizontal lines over each woman's face. Layers of meaning appeared atop the grid immediately. Facial feature recognition. Eyes-nose-mouth. Then second level features appeared – cheekbones, jawlines, chins, brows, hairlines – seemingly at random, thrown off by the alien facial planes added by the strong contrasts of the face paint.

NO MATCH the face recognition software on the camera said.

He played it over their faces again, slowly, as they turned and gave him more angles, more facial expressions.

NO MATCH it repeated.

He moved the camera over their faces again, as they cranked up and down the lighting, as he zoomed in closer.

NO MATCH it told him one more time.

Rangan looked up at the three women, about to venture out into this protest, these three women who, for reasons of their own, didn't want to be identified. He could feel the tension coming off them. They were taking their own risks. They were risking a lot, just to have him here.

He nodded.

"You're good to go."

Minutes later they filed out the door, and he was alone.

•••

Breece rocked his head in time to the chanting, the long, natty hair of this wig moving to the rhythm; the fake scar, the fake tan, the brow and cheek and jaw implants all morphing his face. Signs and banners flew above the crowd of thousands on the National Mall. More every day. More every *hour*, it seemed. He'd been here for three days, himself, and the ever increasing density was palpable.

Out of the corner of his eye he watched another Nexus dose handed out. The mules didn't know that he was out here, had no idea what he looked like. They had simple instructions. Go to a locker. Pick up a backpack or duffel full of vials. Go to the protest. Hand them out. Concentrate on certain areas, particularly the double fence-line, where the anti-Stockton protest was squared off against the pro-Stockton loyalists: just ten feet of empty space and a few dozen cops between them.

The mules were low level PLF wannabes, most of whom had never seen field experience, eager to show off their skills, maybe earn a real mission.

Hell, some of them were probably cops or feds. But those could be weeded out later.

He scanned the crowd. Kate was out there somewhere. Not the Nigerian, though. He was a bit too distinctive with his height. Too easy to remember.

His tactical contacts told him it was almost time. He reached his hand into his pocket, found the button, waited... waited... and then pressed.

Angel did her best to hide her surprise as they were funneled into the Mall at 17th Street. There was Nexus here already. Lots of Nexus. She'd expected some, but this much...

Police officers in mirrored glasses tracked her and the rest of C3 as they pushed in with the crowd through the side streets. She smiled her widest entertainer smile, moved juggling clubs up in the air in a jaunty little dance, never letting go of them, wiggling her hips in time.

I'm just a *girl*, officer, she thought at the cop. I'm no threat to you.

No Nexus transmissions until they were out in the middle of the Mall. That was the plan. The entrances were the most likely places for Nexus scanners. And while they had to get within a couple feet of you to detect Nexus in your brain if you were in receive only, they could pick you up from thirty, forty, fifty feet away if you were broadcasting.

Though, frankly, if they were scanning, they'd be running out there to bust what must be hundreds of people running Nexus on the Mall already.

Of course, if that were *tens of thousands*...

They broke radio silence minutes later.

...feel all that?
...hundreds of them...
...mostly that way...
...let's head that way then...
...think they came dosed, or someone else handing it out here?
...one way to find out...

They headed west, on the south side of the Reflecting Pool, towards the Lincoln Memorial, where there seemed to be the greatest concentration of people.

The concentration of Nexus grew stronger as well. Denser. The minds felt fresh, inexperienced. Some of them disoriented, even, in the rush of a synesthetic blur as Nexus 5 learned them.

...newbies...
...dosed here...
...calibration phase...

Up ahead it was growing even denser. There was something different, Angel saw. A gap in the protest, then more signs, different signs.

A counter-protest. Stockton loyalists.

And that's where the greatest concentration of Nexus was coming from?

She pushed her way right up to it, until she was up against the orange plastic fencing that held the anti-Stockton crowd back. Ten feet away, another orange plastic fence held a smaller but equally fervent crowd of Stockton loyalists with their own angry signs back. In the gap were cops, spaced one every few feet, their presence serving to discourage the two groups from attacking each other at least as much as the fence.

She reached to cut off her Nexus communication, so close to these cops. But before she could, something hit her hard. A wave of emotion. Anger. Violence. Repugnance. Intolerance. She felt it hit Tempest and Cheyenne. Felt them hit with the same urge to shout and yell and bash, to throw themselves across the gap and hurt their foes.

She reached out with all she could, grabbed hold of them with her thoughts, and threw herself back from the fence, to the ground.

SOMEONE'S FUCKING WITH OUR MINDS! she sent.

She heard the sound of yelling, of screams, of a cop ordering people to stay back, of the fence failing, of signs being slammed into people's bodies.

LET'S GET THE HELL OUT! *Cheyenne sent back.*

There's a transmitter! *Tempest sent.* ***I can find it! I can disable it!***

Then something crashed physically into Angel, and the world went away.

• • •

Breece watched the fight break out with fascination. The anti-Stockton protesters, those with Nexus in their brains – most of them, anyway – threw themselves over the fence, charged past the cops, and slammed themselves into the Stockton loyalists, swinging signs like swords, like clubs.

The Stockton loyalists, enraged, fought back.

"That's enough," Kate's voice said into his ear.

"It's fascinating," Breece subvocalized in reply.

"We said a test, Breece," Kate said. "Test successful."

"Roger that," Breece subvocalized. He clicked the button in his pocket again. Perhaps a few of the combatants out there looked confused. But more were piling on, throwing themselves into the fight from both sides now, as violence begat more violence.

He nodded, then turned and walked away.

Behind him, sirens began to wail as the melee grew.

Rangan sat alone in the Bunker.

He'd been here by himself quite a lot. Most nights he was the only one here. The other three had lives elsewhere. They didn't talk about them, at least not with him. They had apartments or homes or something. Boyfriends or girlfriends. Not full time jobs – not from the amount of time they spent here – but other obligations that sometimes took them away for chunks of time during the day, or occasionally for more than one day at a time.

They didn't say. He'd learned quickly not to ask.

He'd stay here, by himself, scouring the web for news of Kade, or his parents, or hacking on the mesh code, or playing with Nexus apps, or playing music, messing around with the new DJ apps that existed on top of Nexus, putting together playlists that he could beam straight out from his mind, to the right audio gear or, heck, to anyone running Nexus. He'd let himself dream a little dream that one day he'd be a free man and could do something as trivial and fun as play a set in a club.

As if.

Not today.

You want to make yourself useful? Tempest had asked, before they left for the protest. *Check what I told you about the chemreactor hack. I don't trust it.*

What Tempest had told him – what she'd told them all – was that it was highly improbable. That it was highly *suspicious* that someone could hack so many models all at once. And she was right.

The hack that had gone live on November 10th included the private keys to seventeen different models of high end commercial chemreactor. Seventeen different makes and models of devices that could synthesize complex molecules and molecular brews like Nexus, given their component ingredients and the right recipe.

Those seventeen, Tempest had verified, were the seventeen highest market share models out there. Together they accounted for more than ninety-five percent of all the chemreactors in use.

Normally those chemreactors were locked down. Censor chips ensured they couldn't be used to synthesize patented pharmaceuticals, or dangerous explosives, or illegal street drugs.

But with the private key, you could override all of that.

A hack that broke *one* chemreactor model key would be a massive coup. But seventeen at once? Who could do that? Had someone hacked them slowly year over year and stockpiled those hacks?

Tempest's suspicion was that the version of Nexus released along with the hack was a fake, with a back door, a vulnerability to exploit. He felt a pang of guilt at that. There *were* back doors in Nexus – back doors he and Kade had placed there. That Kade must have changed.

But when he checked and checked and rechecked the version of Nexus released with this hack... it was identical to what was in the public depots a few days back.

The recipe for synthesis was identical.

The source code was identical.

The compiled *binaries* were identical.

There was even the option to download the latest version from any of the most popular repositories and install that instead.

Whoever was doing this just seemed to want more Nexus out there, period.

Rangan was pondering this when the door to the Bunker slammed open.

He practically jumped out of his chair.

Cheyenne and Tempest came in, supporting Angel between them, gear bags slung over their backs.

He stepped forward. "Angel? You OK?"

She looked up at him. "No," she said, a bit groggily, her arms still wrapped around her friends. "I'm pissed."

"Somebody got there with Nexus before us," Cheyenne said.

"And they're a total asshole," Tempest finished.

Breece stayed silent as Kate railed at him.

"That was a test?" she yelled. "It turned them into animals! I thought we were talking about a little encouragement! A little nudge! That was about revolution, alright, but it wasn't about moving humanity forward!" She was livid. He'd seen her this angry before, but seldom at him. "Those protesters are on *our side* fighting for the *same thing* we're fighting for!" She looked around the table at Breece and the Nigerian. "And we just helped someone violate them."

Breece waited a moment to make sure she was done, then he held up his hands palms open.

"OK, I hear you, Kate. It was a test."

"And you want to move forward!"

"I want to be ready, in case the Supreme Court rejects the case, or rules for Stockton."

The Nigerian nodded at that.

"No," Kate said. "If the court rules for Stockton, or if Kim wins, and he's on the wrong side after all, then I'm all for direct action, but only against *enemies* of the cause."

She stopped, took a deep breath, visibly calmed herself, brought her hands together in front of her on the table, looked at the Nigerian and then again at Breece.

"I will put bullets between the eyes of any who deny humans freedom over our own minds and bodies," Kate said. "I will set bombs beneath their buildings. I will burn down the homes of any who try to limit our rights or use force against us."

She took another breath.

Breece opened his mouth to speak, to say something calming.

She raised a hand, cut him off.

"What I won't do," Kate said, her eyes locked with his, "is use force, or coercion, against people who are fundamentally on *our side*. Who are *the same as us.*"

The Nigerian went frosty at that. "They're not the same as us. They're sheep, most of them, letting it happen to them. We're wolves, taking the risks, taking on the fight that they won't."

Breece raised his hand to forestall his friend, to stop him from triggering Kate further.

Kate sliced her hand through the air in frustration. "Don't start with that fucking separatist sheep and wolves *bullshit* with me, Akindele!"

"You may not call me that name." The Nigerian started to stand.

"Whoa, whoa!" Breece held out both hands, placatingly. "Easy, both of you."

Kate turned to him. "Cancel the op."

The Nigerian sat back into his chair. "You're turning soft, Catherine," he said. "Like I've never seen you before."

Breece looked at his friend. "Shut it for a minute, OK?"

He turned back to Kate. She was still staring at him.

"This separatist bullshit isn't right," she said. "*Everyone* has the potential to upgrade. We've been arguing it for years. But we've never attacked people on *our* side."

Breece sucked in a deep breath, let it out again. "It's not an attack," he said. "It's an encouragement. We're pushing them to fight for their rights."

Kate scowled.

Breece went on. "Kate, if you want to sit this one out... No problem at all. You've done plenty for the cause. You've more than earned a break."

Kate's frown deepened. "I don't want to sit this out. We cancel the op. Let the protesters go their own way. You saw what we did out there. Those people lost their minds. That's *offensive action*, and that's for use against our *enemies*."

Breece shook his head silently.

Kate leaned back. "What happened to unanimity for ops?"

Breece looked down at the surface of the table. "This is our chance." He looked back up at Kate. "I know it rankles. I wish we didn't need it. But it's a little nudge. It's temporary. It gets them fighting for their rights, the way they *should* be. And that little, temporary nudge drives a *huge* positive change, that expands their freedoms, that benefits them *and* millions of other people. Maybe *hundreds* of millions." He paused for breath. He'd been raising his voice he realized. Kate was looking at him. He couldn't tell what she was thinking. God what he'd give for some Nexus in their brains right now. "Kate," he went on, his voice calm now. "You're right. This might be grey. But there's so much upside. I'm willing to cross a few lines to do that much good. We won't get a shot like this again anytime soon."

"Breece..." Kate said, her voice low and steady. "Don't do this. Don't change like this."

"Nothing's changing." He leaned towards her, reaching out one hand across the table for hers, trying to touch her, trying to make her see. "We're so close to what we've wanted..."

"I thought we wanted to lift people up," she said. She didn't take his hand. "You can't do that by betraying your allies. Cancel the op."

Breece stared into her eyes, beseeching.

"I can't, Kate. The opportunity's too big."

"Damn it," she cursed.

Kate jerked up out of her seat.

Breece pulled back in alarm, his chest pounding.

She strode out of the kitchen, not looking back.

"Kate!" he yelled.

She disappeared from sight. He heard her go into the room they shared, heard footsteps, heard the front door open. Then heard it slam shut.

Across the table, the Nigerian breathed hard, his hands clenching and unclenching.

39
Progress

Monday 2040.11.18

Kade met his new team on Monday, in Bangalore. The Indian government had moved Kade, Feng, Sam, and the children over the weekend, from surprisingly calm Delhi to chaotically raucous Bangalore. Ananda and a group of five monks, done with the summit, had been allowed to come with them. After five hours of flying, it had taken three hours on the roads in an armored bus, flanked by police, to make their way through a traffic melee of cars, scooters, rickshaws, mobile restaurants, and suicidally brave pedestrians. At one point a twelve foot tall animatronic Hindu god on wheels passed them, and turned its head to stare at Kade with its third eye set in its blue-skinned god-droid head.

Kade stared back.

The eye blinked.

The children loved it, their minds taking in everything, shooting observations to each other thick and fast, faster than Kade could follow, giggling, laughing, drawing insights and recognizing patterns he never would have noticed.

Now, at last, they were in an oasis of calm, a wide, green, secure research campus run by some secretive sub-ministry of the Indian Ministry of Science and Technology, walled off from the rest of Bangalore, with housing in a cluster of colonial-era homes surrounded by palm trees.

And it was time for Kade to go to work.

Lakshmi Dabir gave him a tour of the campus, sketching out what happened in various buildings, though she seemed rather evasive on one or two. Then she led him to the building where he'd be working, a hypermodern glass and carbon structure set among the lush trees, and he met the men and women he'd be working with.

The names came thick and fast. Srini, Gopal, Pratibha, Rohit, Amit, Ashanti, Girish, Deepak, the other Amit, the other Rohit, and Anusha. And those were just the team leads.

The overall project was under the direction of Lakshmi Dabir herself. Kade's job, as she explained it to the team leads, was to be a technical advisor. Which was as poorly defined a role as he'd ever heard.

Kade smiled at these men and women around him as Dabir talked. The coders had all built more software than he had. The neuroscientists had years more experience than he did. There were nanoscientists and biomaterial specialists and medical ethicists and educational neuropsychologists. They were all running Nexus. Everyone was putting up a front of polite enthusiasm. Beneath that he felt a whole range – from resentment, to curiosity, to outright awe.

Well, this'll be interesting, he thought.

Kade kept smiling, kept trying to project humility and a desire to learn.

When in doubt, someone had told him, try to add value.

The next several hours were an awesome blur of technical achievements that dispelled any doubt in Kade's mind.

This was a rock star team.

They gave him a tour of the work they'd done over the last few months. Their idea of a tour was linking up via Nexus to the experts in the area, and plunging him right into demos and direct neural assimilation of their project plans, architectures, experimental results, and code structures.

There was too much. Waaaaay too much. It was like drinking from a fire hose. If the hose was the diameter of the moon.

Kade fucking loved it.

Pri 1 was education. They had plenty of other goals down the road: use Nexus to boost productivity in engineering and the sciences, to help in mental health, and so on. But from the PM down the message was clear: their job was to make India's students – child *and* adult, able to learn faster.

And they were building a heck of a platform. On the research side they'd coded tools for analyzing communication, learning, and retention. They were building adaptive systems that used Nexus to see right away when a lesson *wasn't* getting through, or *wasn't* going to be retained, diagnose why, or just repeat it. They had libraries of mental lessons, curated first-hand memories that kids could absorb, live through. And for the coders themselves they were beefing up the developer tools – better environments, better debuggers, virtual whiteboards and shared coding spaces.

Awesome. It was all so awesome. Kade asked question after question, kept telling people how cool their work was.

Eventually they seemed to get that he wasn't just faking it, that he was genuinely excited.

The excitement was echoed back.

Security was another major prong. Hunting down security bugs, looking for ways malicious code could enter and exploit Nexus to spy on or control an unwitting person. They'd already found and fixed quite a few vulnerabilities, and checked their fixes back into the major code repositories around the net. They had ambitious plans here to build more provably secure sandbox layers and simpler models to prevent users from accidentally giving away too much control.

Kade loved what they were doing. He came within inches of telling them about his work with Nexus 6… but he stopped himself, for now.

The last big pillar was safety. What was the impact of Nexus on a brain over multiple years of life? Even decades? And here they were in the wilderness. They'd done whole-lifetime testing on multiple generations of fruit flies and nematodes, with no obvious ill effects, but that could only take you so far. What about mammals? Mice lived two to three years.

"We'd love to do some testing – all very safe, of course – on the children who came with you," Lakshmi Dabir said. "It'd be to their benefit – we'd do very thorough checks and find any health issues that may be cropping up. And it'd help us get more early warning of any issues that may prevent deployment in India."

Kade considered that. It made sense.

"We'd also," Dabir continued, "love to do more analysis of how they do collaborative learning. We can see that their learning rate is off the charts, beyond that even of children who take Nexus at the elementary school age. We may be able to learn something from that which we could then use in software."

The same thought had occurred to Kade.

Even so…

"I'll have to talk to Sam," he said. "She's also their legal guardian."

Lakshmi Dabir inclined her head. "Of course."

"And," Kade said, "I want the kids to understand the request – and to agree to it."

Dabir nodded at that as well.

After his first day of work, there was a reception for the various staff at the complex, who worked on a wide ranging set of projects in computing, neuroscience, computational biology, and related fields.

Kade was, he learned, the guest of honor.

Lakshmi Dabir took him around by the elbow, introducing him

to various researchers and administrators, professors at the Indian Institutes of Technology, and so forth. He met a General Singh in the Indian Air Force, a tall man, with a thick Bollywood mustache, who Dabir said had given the order to save their plane.

"Thank you," Kade said, as sincerely as he could.

Singh nodded at him. "Do good work for us. That will be more than thanks enough."

Lakshmi Dabir led him around to meet yet more of the people here. Kade caught a glimpse of Sam, talking and smiling with an Indian woman in the corner, of Feng, his left arm still in a sling, gesticulating with a spoon in his right hand, making a crowd of young Indian men laugh and gasp in amazement, of Ananda deep in conversation with an Indian academic.

Almost everyone here was running Nexus.

He wished he'd worn his DJ Axon shirt.

He wished he still had it.

Just before 8.30pm the wallscreens came to life. The United Nations emblem appeared – two white olive branches surrounding a stylized map of the globe against a background of solid blue.

Silence descended on the reception. Kade could feel a rapt attention come to the minds of the men and women around him. This was the moment they'd been waiting for.

The map faded out, showing the General Assembly chamber.

UN Secretary General Beatriz Pereira was at the podium. A Brazilian. It was 10am in New York.

She struck her mallet ceremonially to bring the session to order.

"The Assembly will now hear from the Ambassador from India, regarding the motion to come before us," Pereira said.

The Indian Ambassador to the UN, Navya Kapoor, took the stage, at the podium below the Secretary General's.

She was younger than Kade had imagined, forty maybe, dressed in a grey business suit instead of a sari. She had no notes in evidence. But there was something in her eyes.

"Madame Secretary," she said, and her voice was strong and clear. "Fellow delegates, ladies and gentlemen. I come before you to speak of truth and deception; to speak of injustice done and the remedies that must be sought; to speak of oppression, and the equality we must replace it with."

Kade felt his heart beating faster. He'd read the motion. He hadn't read her speech. He felt excitement growing in minds around him.

"For the last decade, we have *violated* the principles of the United Nations Declaration on Human Rights. We have *oppressed* those who are different, out of *fear*. And this fear has been based on *deception* and even the *murder* of innocents."

Kade's breath caught in his chest. He felt the same in a dozen others nearby. The UN Assembly burst into noise, into simultaneous applause and loud boos. The camera zoomed back to show delegates on their feet, some bringing their hands together, others getting up to walk out.

Beatriz Pereira banged her gavel hard, again and again. "Order!" she cried. "The delegate from India has the floor! Order!"

The Assembly quieted, bit by bit.

As the camera zoomed back in, Kade could see the determination on Navya Kapoor's face, see that her chest was rising and falling as well.

You love her, yeah? Feng sent him in a tight band from across the room. **I think she's already married...**

Kade laughed out loud. People looked at him funny. He turned around, found Feng looking at him from across the room, and winked.

"Thank you, Madame Secretary," Navya Kapoor went on. "The United Nations Declaration on Human Rights states that, and I quote, 'Everyone has the right to life, liberty, and security of person. No one shall be subjected to torture or to cruel, inhuman or degrading treatment or punishment. No one shall be subjected to arbitrary arrest, detention or exile. No one shall be held in slavery or servitude'."

A mind near Kade twitched nervously at that, then tried to calm itself. Six months ago he would have missed it, but he'd spent so much time in so many minds. Kade turned, looked, saw the side of the man's face. Varum? Varam?

Navya Kapoor pressed on, her voice impassioned, drawing Kade's attention back to her. "The Declaration states, and I quote again, that *everyone* has the right to recognition everywhere as a *person* before the law. That *all are equal before the law.*"

Kade felt the excitement rise all around him, felt the room in Bangalore grow in passion to match Kapoor.

Navya Kapoor looked around the Assembly room in New York and spoke again, her voice carried across the world at the speed of light.

"We have violated these principles. In our fear, based on false information, we have denied the recognition as a person to those who most clearly *are* persons. We have denied equality before the law."

There was silence in the Assembly, hope and solidarity in Bangalore.

"Today," Navya Kapoor said, "India introduces a motion to the United Nations General Assembly that recognizes all thinking, feeling beings of human origin or human descent as persons, and explicitly grants *everyone* the full protection of all international laws and human rights accords, and classifies laws and crimes which unfairly target individuals based on their genetic, neurobiological, or other differences, as the discrimination and hate crimes that they are."

She took another breath.

"Madame Secretary, delegates, people of the world! I urge you to look into your hearts. Understand that our daughters and our sons will be better than we are. Do not hate them for it. Love them for it, and vote for this measure which grants them the rights and freedoms they deserve every bit as much as you do yours!"

There was wild applause, then, and as the camera zoomed back, Kade saw that it was from the observation galleries, to the sides of the Assembly, where people were standing, clapping ferociously, whistling.

And also from the Assembly itself, where there were at least twenty delegates on their feet, applauding.

And applause in this room in Bangalore as well, everyone clapping and cheering, every mind exulting.

Kade whooped and clapped and laughed. There were tears in his eyes, he found.

There was no chance it would pass, of course. Too many nations would be afraid of pissing off the US and China. And even if it did pass the Assembly, the US would veto it in the Security Council.

But this, this moment, with delegates of twenty countries on their feet applauding.

He felt a hand on his shoulder, felt Ananda's mind behind him.

"You've done well, young man," his teacher told him.

Kade laughed. He'd been just a tiny part of it, just the irritation in the oyster.

Ananda picked up on the thought.

None of that, my boy. You did a very good thing, and that's the end of it.

Kade turned and grinned. Around them, drinks were being passed out in celebration. Musicians were taking their places. This would soon become a full blown party.

"Thank you, Ananda," he said out loud. "Now I have a question."

The eminent Buddhist scholar and neuroscientist raised an eyebrow.

Kade grinned wider. "Do monks dance?"

Sam cheered through the speech. There were tears in her eyes.

Jake. Jake would have loved to see this moment. He would have loved to see the kids safe here. To see even this voted-down gesture acknowledging the humanity of Sarai, and Kit, and Aroon…

Oh Jake.

She raised her glass of ice water, toasted the moment, clinked glasses with those around her.

Yet she was who she was. And so some part of her never stopped watching, never stopped taking stock.

And so she noticed when a man twitched, not far from Kade, at something the Indian Ambassador said. Youngish. Clean shaven. His smile looked pained, forced.

She noticed that another man, in uniform, was watching the crowd even more intently than she was, a smile on his lips, but cold calculation in his eyes: General Singh.

And she noticed that the youngish man who'd twitched made an early, nervous exit from the event.

Sam memorized his face for later.

Then she did her very best to enjoy the night.

For the children.

And for Jake.

40
The Pawn Seldom Knows

Tuesday 2040.11.19

Sam listened as Kade passed on what the Indians wanted. To study how the children used Nexus. And to look for any signs that Nexus had harmed them. To try to spot the risks of deploying it to millions of Indian children.

He had a million things to say, as usual.

She had one question.

"Is there any risk to our kids in this?"

Kade looked her in the eye. He was tense around her. She could see it in the way he sat with his body closed off. The way he froze up. Anger, too. She couldn't blame him for either.

His very presence sent her pulse shooting up. Sent memories *her bullets smashing into the outline of Kevin's face, his body tumbling out into the night* cascading through her brain.

"I'll approve every step," Kade said. "I won't allow anything that's invasive."

Sam nodded. "OK then."

She stood to go.

Kade blinked in surprise. "That's it?"

She cocked her head. "You got what you wanted, right?"

She turned to leave.

"Sam," he called after her. "The kids would love it if you took Nexus again, if they could..."

Blood bubbled up through the wound in Jake's chest. "I wish I'd known you," he said. His mind collapsed into chaos and then nothing.

She stopped in the doorway, her fists clenched, breathing hard. She turned.

Kade was standing, looking at her, like she was broken.

"I will. I'm going to. Just not yet."

"There are other drugs," Kade started. "That can help with traum–"

"I don't want your fucking help," Sam snapped.

He flinched, visibly.

Sam closed her eyes.

"Shit," she said.

"I just..." Kade started again.

Sam held up her hands. "I'm sorry. You didn't deserve that."

Kade was shaking his head. "*I'm* sorry," he said.

"Stop," Sam said. "Let me finish. I tense up when I see you. I've got a bad case of PTSD. I've got some serious hell to go through." She looked him in the eye. "And it isn't just about you."

Kade was looking at her.

"I'm through with killing, Kade."

She saw the shock go across his face.

"Do you remember Lee? Head of our security squad in Bangkok? Ordinary guy, doing his job, maybe saved both of *our* lives?"

Kade swallowed. "Wats killed him. Not you."

"I've killed plenty," Sam said. "Some who deserved to die. Shiva did."

She saw him want to object. She raised a hand to forestall it. "Plenty of them *didn't* deserve to die. Lee's men in Bangkok. The marines at Ananda's monastery, though I tried like hell not to kill any of them."

"They would have killed *me*," Kade said. "Or taken me to a deep dark hole..."

Sam shook her head. "I'm through making the choice of who deserves to live and die. It takes too much out of you. I want to build something. I want to nurture things."

She saw him draw a breath. She kept going. Things needed to be said.

"Sometimes, though, I *do* blame you, Kade," she said. "I blame you to *hell* for putting that back door in there."

Kill them all, Shiva Prasad whispered in her brain. She was sweating. She was trembling. Kade was trembling in front of her.

"But..." she forced herself to press on, shaking her head. "I don't know that I would have done a damn thing different."

She looked down, looked at her own hands, clenched and unclenched them. She'd wanted that back door. She'd wanted to rip open the brain of the soldier who'd killed Jake, wanted to learn every goddamn thing he knew.

Move past that. Back to the thread.

She looked back up at Kade.

"I'm *glad* Nexus exists," she said. "I'm *glad* you put it out there. Even after everything. I think the world's better this way." She swallowed.

"What happened to me was evil. But evil's always happened, long before Nexus. There's good now too. The damage is in my head. I'll beat it."

Kade smiled sadly. He spoke softly, gently. "Why don't you accept some medical help with that?"

Sam nodded. "At this stage, after the trauma has set in. The protocols here are memory malleability drugs plus psychotherapy. I'd be letting one of their shrinks into my head, in a situation where they could literally rewire me." She shook her head. "I can beat it on my own. It'll take longer. But I can."

Kade shook his head. "Why, Sam? Why not let them help you?"

Sam laughed. "Because I don't trust them, Kade. I'm grateful, but I don't trust them."

Kade frowned, searching for the right words. Looking for some way to tell her she was being paranoid.

He didn't get it. He didn't really know the level this game was played at.

"If Kevin Nakamura were here now..." she paused. *Kevin. Oh, Kevin.* "He'd want you to understand. The Indians? You're still just a tool to them. You, me, Feng, the kids. We're pawns. They'll use us. They'll sacrifice us if it furthers their goals." She stared hard into his eyes. "Don't forget that."

Kade shook his head, closing off to her. "I don't think it's that simple. We're using each other. That's what cooperation means."

Was I ever this naïve? Sam wondered. I guess I was once. When I had a family, when I had a normal life.

"Kade," she said. "You may think it's symmetric, you may think you know how they're using you, but in this game, the pawn seldom knows what the king has planned. Remember that. The pawn seldom knows."

41
Monster

Su-Yong Shu stares down at her own face, sculpted out of the cityscape of Shanghai, in this future she dreams of, this posthuman future, where she has cleared away the obstacles to enhancing the human mind, where she has ended the incessant war and stupidity, where she has replaced mere capitalism with a new economics born of quantum game theory, where she has ended poverty, where she has broken the iron laws of death and biology and scarcity that have ruled humanity for so long, where she has unleashed an intelligence explosion like nothing since the dawn of *homo sapiens sapiens*.

Where victory has given her back her daughter.

Her mind is spinning. The world is spinning below her. The landscape is transforming. The lines of her face are no longer buildings, but the trajectories of virtual particles. The blacks of her eyes are bubbles in the quantum foam. Shanghai is a lens into other universes.

Mad. I'm still mad.

She splits the air with a silver portal, steps through into another virtual world, a safer world, a grounding world, with its wide grassy plain ringed by the massive purple mountains.

She is in the white dress again, barefoot. The tall grass is soft against her feet. The golden *chrysanthemum boreale*, her favorite flowers since youth, are in bloom, dotting the plain with brilliant yellow, filling the air with their sweet perfume. The sun is perfectly warm against her skin, the sky a deep deep blue, the sun directly overhead. The mountains are glorious giants, capped in white, ringing her in majesty, comfort, and hints of adventure.

She drops to her knees, cups a flower in her hands, inhales its scent.

Could it work? she wonders.

She inhales again, savoring the sweetness, the sun on her back, the grass below her knees.

Maybe, she thinks. Maybe I can do it. Strike, and win, and save Ling. And more. Maybe I can make the world a better place.

"Every monster in history has thought the same."

The voice comes from behind her. She tenses. Pain and anger rush through her, memories of torture and pleading and more torture.

"Chen," she says aloud, the memories rising. "How could you betray me? How could you let me die? Torture me, just for fame, for money?"

"I'm human," her husband says. "I'm selfish."

She rises and turns, her hands clenching at her side. He's there, not ten feet away. Chen as she last saw him. Chen at nearly fifty, his trim frame going to paunch, grey at his temples, a tailored suit, an odor of arrogance.

"No," she tells him. "You're a monster."

"Hah!" He barks a laugh at her. "I knew my own selfishness. Real monsters think they're pure and good. The real monsters think they have *a vision for a better world*. The real monsters impose it on others, through force if necessary."

He stares at her. "That's you, wife. You're the monster."

She feels her nails bite into her palm. "I'm no monster." Her voice is level, controlled. "I want the best thing for the world."

"And you know *exactly* what the best thing is," her husband says, nodding. "Mao Tse Tung was certain he knew. Pol Pot as well. Adolf Hitler, of course."

"I'm no monster!" Her voice is cracking, her muscles tense, her virtual body vibrating at the accusation.

"Of course not," Chen says, soothingly. "*That's* why you brutalized your daughter. *That's* why you sent out an agent of death. *That's* why you're about to wage war on humanity."

"I was insane! You left me without input, without the clone, *knowing* what would happen! You *tortured* me! *You* brought this on. You and all the other humans!" She's yelling, she realizes, gesticulating with her hands, screaming at her husband, who isn't even real, who isn't even here.

Chen smiles at her. "Oh no, wife. You had these plans long before this. *There is a war coming. A world war. Between humans and posthumans.* Isn't that what you told the American boy?"

And for a moment she's there, in Bangkok, sipping tea across from Kade, the rooftop restaurant on the banks of the Chao Phraya, the golden magnificence of Wat Arun rising above them, the Temple of the Dawn.

Chen is still speaking to her. "*The world has more than eight billion people on it,* you told him. *Surely we can afford to lose a few.* You've always been this arrogant, wife. Always been this willing to commit atrocities in the name of your vision. You've just been waiting, waiting to let it out."

There's a buzzing in her head now, a chaos, a confusion. No. They hurt her, *they* wounded her, *they* tortured her. That's why she did what she did. That's why she hurt her daughter.

"No," she says aloud. "No."

Chen laughs aloud.

"No!" she yells at him. "You weren't even there! You weren't even there!"

Her husband opens his mouth and spreads his arms wide. Storm clouds boil out of the clear blue sky above, and his voice booms at her from every direction, from the sky, from the mountains in the distance, from the grass at her feet, from the golden chrysanthemums she loves so much, from the very earth itself.

**I
AM
YOU**

**I
AM
YOU**

The whole world booms the words at Su-Yong Shu, in Chen's voice, straight into her mind.

NO! she screams back.

She lifts her arms at her husband, her fingers splayed, and wills his utter destruction. Gouts of white hot flame shoot out, lancing from her fingertips to his chest, his face, his thighs. Lightning strikes from the clouds overhead, twice, three times, four times, a dozen times, converging on the point where he stands. The ground below his feet explodes upwards in a surge of searing heat and light and force. His body is incinerated, pulverized, reduced to ash, obscured by a radiance so bright that nothing can be seen.

Su-Yong Shu falls to her knees, the buzzing in her head gone, released with the destruction of the traitorous part of her represented by her husband Chen, even as superheated bits of earth and rock and ash rain down around her.

She lets her head fall into her hands. Tears are falling from her eyes now. It was because they'd tortured her. It was because they'd driven her mad. That was why she'd hurt Ling. That was why.

How long? How long until she was sane again? How long until the input from this biological brain brought her back? How long had it taken last time?

"Do you like me better now, Su-Yong?"

The voice comes from behind her. It's Chen's, but different, kinder...

She turns, still on her knees, and he's there. Not the Chen of nearly fifty who'd tortured her, who'd refused to touch her for a decade, but the Chen of thirty who she'd first met. Lean, a simple white button down shirt tucked into his black trousers, a wry smile on his smooth face, a telltale of the keen intense mind she'd fallen in love with.

He's an illusion, a fabrication of her own mind, a man who no longer exists, but still, to see him takes her breath away.

"Chen..." she whispers.

He steps towards her, drops to his knees in the tall grass, and takes her face in his hands.

"Su-Yong."

His voice is gentle. His smile is kind. His fingers are warm on her skin.

"You're not real," she tells him.

He smiles wider. "I'm as real as any of this," he says, gesturing slowly with his eyes and a small movement of his head, taking in the sky, the grass, the plain, the mountains.

Her hands rise, to touch him, to feel his own hands on her face. "You're here because I'm mad, because I'm still crazy."

"I'm here because you're growing more sane."

More sane.

She remembers now. She has metrics she'd built in her isolation. Monitors. Crude psychological and neurophysiological exams to measure her sanity, to project the time she had left.

She launches them, feels them take stock of her, compares the output to the last she has on record.

And it's true. She's stabilizing. She's truly not as mad as she was. But still things aren't quite right.

Ahhhh!

The tweaks, the many many changes she made to try to bolster herself. Crude hacks.

Su-Yong takes stock of them now. There are so many. Limits to the length of her thought chains to cut off her downward spirals of madness. Blunt exoself scaffolding forcibly adjusting the weights of virtual synapses towards statistical norms, undoubtedly throwing away good connections with bad. Forced adjustments to her virtual neurochemistry, to the levels of her simulated serotonin and dopamine and norepinephrine.

So much surgery she'd done on her own virtual brain, trying to survive those months, to stretch out her sanity. Now... is it in her way?

More stability first.

She reaches out, tracks the flow of data coming in from the biological brain she's connected to, and burrows into that brain now, exploring, and jolts back in surprise.

This was no drooling clone made from her own DNA.

This was a woman who'd lived decades. She was damaged, injured. But large swaths of her memories were intact. And those memories revealed a woman who'd lived not in China.

But in India.

42
Team Players

Wednesday 2040.11.20
It wasn't until the next evening that Kade could break free from work and receptions early enough to bring the children together.

He chose the ones aged five and up, whom he hoped would be able to understand enough of what he was to explain. That was eleven of them.

They sat together, on the lawn, beneath a giant palm, in a circle. The sun had already set, and the sky was a deep blue with clouds touched by flame. The air was pleasantly cool at this hour, up here at Bangalore's elevation nearly a thousand meters above sea level, even though they were close to the equator. Its breeze was fragrant with the scent of tropical plants that Kade couldn't name.

I have something to ask all of you, and all the other children as well, Kade sent them.

Their minds gave him questions, eagerness, trust.

He didn't want their trust today. He didn't want them to act on his word. He wanted them to see, and understand.

He wanted them to help *him* understand.

And then decide.

He let down the walls of his mind to them, opened himself, and began to breathe.

In, out.

Slow, sure.

Watch the breath.

Observe it. Don't control it.

Let your attention sink into the breath completely.

Anapana.

He felt Sarai's mind open to his, her attention on her own breaths, sharing them, entwining her perceptions with his, their breath falling into rhythm, their minds falling into synch. Then Kit was with them. Then Aromdee, who'd come from near Chiang Rai, then Meesang, than Sunisa, then suddenly they were a symphony of mind, a harmony of mind, a concordance of brains resonating at the same frequency.

Deeper they went, deeper, breath slowing further, hearts slowing, minds falling more closely into sync, walls crumbling.

Atop the carrier wave of shared breath, shared attention, shared meditation, bandwidth expanded, communication expanded, consciousness expanded. Thoughts and memories blossomed out beyond the walls of single skulls.

The world became sharper. A dozen pairs of eyes opened and the world was glorious, a place of intricate detail clearer than ever before, a million blades of grass, a thousand shades of blue and pink and red and white above them. A hundred different scents on the breeze. The sounds of crickets, of birds, of vehicles, of people talking softly as they walked, of distant traffic and horns and what had been to them the chaos of Bangalore beyond the walls but now had pattern, had texture, had meaning.

This was transcendence. This was the posthuman.

Now, they thought, **this request**.

The part of the whole that was Kade felt knowledge sucked from his mind. The work he was doing. The Indian education project. What they wanted to study about the Nexus-born children. What he hoped it might add to NexusOS, and how that would affect those who took Nexus later, how it might change India. How it might change the world.

The whole pulled at him, pulled at the Nexus nodes in his brain, tunneled into his thoughts, beyond the surface, digging for comprehension, for possibilities seen, for fears, for hopes, and he opened himself wide to allow it.

He was part of that whole, doing the digging. He was himself, feeling himself burrowed into and giving himself to it, feeling his back arch, feeling his bandwidth saturated, feeling Nexus nodes sap hungrily at ATP to power themselves, pushing to the limit of safety, beyond, into the red.

The whole dug deeper, *he* dug deeper, combing through his mind, sweeping up images, ideas, facts, searching for and finding patterns that Kade alone would never have seen. Warnings flashed unheeded on the screen of one mind within the hole.

Thoughts flashed through them, almost too fast to follow. Navya Kapoor at the UN. Tears on Kade's face. Sam's trauma. The pawn seldom knows. Meditation with Ananda. Shiva's research plans. Elections and protest in the United States. Ling's absence. A building on campus whose explanation had been an evasion. Code structures, mind structures, thought structures. Webs of knowledge. Monks in lotus, thousands of them. A million minds they could feel now, every day, every day. Dancing in Club Heaven in Saigon, the Nexus Jockey named Lotus closing a feedback loop with the crowd, turning it into a single glorious organism not unlike their own. Varun, the Indian scientist who'd been anxious during the UN speech. Orchestra musicians becoming one. Clone soldiers. Su-Yong Shu embodied in row upon row of vast computing machinery.

Children. A million children. A hundred million children. Minds linked. Everywhere around the world.

Transforming everything.

Kade snapped out of the whole in a wrenching, jarring moment of disunion.

He was on his back, disoriented, drained, the sky dark above him.

He was panting, gasping for breath, his chest rising and falling, rising and falling, desperate to suck in oxygen. His heart was beating like a drum.

Oh my god, he thought. Oh my god.

The children were standing around him, standing above him, towering above him.

Too much, he realized. I was too deep, giving too much, pushing my brain too far.

I couldn't keep up.

We'll allow it, they sent him, in harmony, eleven minds sending down to him at once.

No.

One mind, posthuman. Alien. Remote.

My god, he thought. What are they?

But we want to be more than subjects, the posthuman sent him. Eleven minds. One mind. **We want to be part of the team.**

He looked up at them, at it, and what he felt was fear. What have we done?

Then they saw him, saw his fear, saw his brain sucking oxygen. And the distance collapsed.

Kade! We're so sorry!

Alien dissipated in the familiar. Sarai and Kit and Sunisa and Meesang and...

Kade! Oh Kade!

Concern enfolded him. Childish, young concern for an injured elder. Minds probed his, searching, giving, bolstering. Exhaustion faded. Clarity returned. His heart slowed. His breathing eased.

And he saw what he was to them. Teacher. Friend. Brother. Champion. Treasure.

Forerunner.

He could feel their minds enfolding him, apologizing, still searching for injury, learning, designing bulwarks against that happening again. And above all, caring.

Kids. He knew them. He trusted them. Because they trusted him.

Tit for tat.

Generosity rewarded.

That was the lesson here.

One more thing, Kade, they sent, a bit later, when they were sure he was well. Their thoughts resonated, harmonized, were eleven and at once one. **Sam is right. The Indians are hiding something from you.**

Kade nodded, absorbing, trying to see the whole of it. But what the hidden thing was, neither he nor they could say – it was an insight, a pattern, an intuition, of pieces not connecting.

And, they sent, images of protest, of chaos, of Nexus spreading suddenly faster. **Something else is going on.**

43
Old Friends

The Avatar lay upon the bed in her daughter Ling's room. Above her, the Milky Way slowly rotated across the night sky, replicated in exquisite detail on the ceiling.

Tension was escalating. Outside, Shanghai was lit by the glow from the buildings, from the gigantic advertisements, by the river of vehicles flowing through the streets. Tens of thousands of sky-eyes hovered and darted above the city again, vectoring thrust on their quadcopter frames, watching the populace more closely than ever. With their glowing red collision avoidance lights they could have been a multitude of mutant fireflies. Or a multitude of sinister eyes.

They were hardened, these new sky-eyes. Hardened in their little brains. Codes changed. Encryption keys lengthened and diversified. Communication ports successively closed until absolutely the bare minimum remained. Their leashes to central command loosened, giving them more autonomy, more survivability on the electronic battlefield.

Other hunters emitted fewer photons, but posed greater risks. The routers she had to reach through were being upgraded to new versions, their controls tightened, their censor codes more paranoid, their packet and protocol inspections more intrusive.

And in every corner, hunter-killer software lurked. There were forensic tools adapted for real-time response, ready to scavenge through digital heaps and stacks, read through every byte of memory of a corrupted system in microseconds, looking for any clue, pointing the way back to the origin of attack. They were dangers to her. She was frightened more by the evolved things, products of artificial selection, millions of generations of it, with internal structures that made no sense, code that, in the small snippets she could glean, read like baroque garbage to her, that resembled neither the output of human AI programmers nor the network structure of the organic brain that she and her greater self were based on. What frightened her most was that she did not know the capabilities of those creatures. She could not predict their behavior.

She would love to swallow the whole code of one of the evolved hunter-killers, place it in a sandbox, then take it apart, bit by bit, again and again and again, just to see what made it tick. Later. She could do that if she survived.

The Avatar shivered. The constraints on her were tightening. She must keep moving forward. And faster. Before the noose was closed too tight.

The doorbell rang.

The Avatar smiled. Their dinner guest was here.

Within her, she felt Ling whimper.

The Avatar watched through Chen's mind, through his eyes, as he opened the door to greet their guest. Xu Liang stood there, grey haired, distinguished, a polite, aloof smile on his face.

Xu Liang, the Director of Jiao Tong's Secure Computing Center, and the Physically Isolated Computing Center below it. A long-time rival of Chen's. The sort who'd be intrigued by an invitation to a private dinner.

Chen closed the door after Xu, and offered him a drink.

She watched through Chen's eyes as Xu leaned back in his chair, the remains of the meal Chen's people had laid out in front of him. They'd disappeared promptly after serving, of course, leaving the two distinguished men to discuss their important matters.

The Avatar smiled to herself at that.

"Chen," Xu said. "My old friend. I think your notion of..." he blinked, paused, seeming to lose his train of thought. "...of using the quantum cluster to model social unrest is a *decent* one." He paused again, blinking, as the sedatives in his food and drink worked their way into his brain. "But why should they trust *you*? You're Sun Liu's creature. You're..."

Xu's head was rocking slightly from side to side now.

"Suddenly... tired..." he said.

Chen's hand reached under the table, brushed the hypersonic injector secured there.

"Are you feeling well?" he asked Xu solicitously.

From her husband's mind the Avatar caught flashes of memory, of his own horror, of his daughter Ling standing above him, the injector and the ampule half-full of silvery fluid in her hand, as the nanites took hold in his brain, as her mind overpowered his, paralyzed him, as she leaned in closer, to press it against his neck once more, to empty the rest of it his veins.

Pain. Humiliation. Wretched self-loathing of himself that he was about to be used to do this to another human.

Hatred of her.

The Avatar smiled wider, relishing it.

She could have resculpted Chen. She could have eased his pain. She could have emotionally rewired him at a deeper level, making him truly loyal to her, ending the cognitive dissonance.

She preferred it this way. A program of her creation, running inside her husband's brain, controlling him. But leaving him trapped within it, to suffer.

She relished horror rising within Chen as she prepared to use him to enslave Xu Liang.

Inside she felt Ling stirring more.

Stop it, please, her daughter whispered to her.

Oh daughter, the Avatar replied. **We've only just begun.**

Chen's hand closed around the grip of the injector.

STOP IT! Ling said.

The Avatar ignored her.

"Water..." Xu whispered.

Chen ripped the injector free and stood. "I have something better than water, old friend."

STOOOOOOOOOOP!!!!

Ling's will ripped into her. The Avatar recoiled, shocked. Her daughter had *seized back some of her nanites.* Ling was reaching out with them, pushing on Chen's mind, crashing the software she had running, the code that actively managed Chen's behavior.

BAD GIRL! the Avatar sent back, coursing current through Ling's pain centers, hurling chaos at the nanite circuits her daughter had managed to seize.

In the living room, she was vaguely aware of Chen, standing, dumbfounded, over a suddenly terrified Xu Liang.

"Run..." Chen whispered. Then louder. "Run!" He hurled the injector across the room, flinging it into a wall, and ran for the kitchen, for the block of knives.

Ling roared back harder, scratching and biting at her with virtual tooth and nail, using raw willpower and her long connection to this hardware to claw back control.

The Avatar surged more pain through her daughter. **Relent, child! Relent!**

"AAAAAAAH!" Ling screamed aloud. Her will gave a millimeter.

Circuits came back to the Avatar.

She turned back to the room. Xu Liang was stumbling, up and out of his chair, trying to run for the door, clumsily, impaired by the sedatives. She sent a thought to the house, locked *all* the doors, trapped him here.

She turned to Chen, found him with a knife in his hand, expected him to be coming for Ling's room, to kill her, found that he had it in two hands, the point up, about to plunge it into his own throat instead.

She seized hold of his motor cortex, twisted his muscles in mid thrust. The knife veered off course, left a score across the right side of his neck. Blood welled up immediately.

Xu Liang was at the door, was trying to open it, failing. He turned and looked, saw Chen with a bloody knife in his hand, and turned back to the door, started pounding on it, screaming for help.

There would be no help, the Avatar knew. No one could hear his screams. And the fate in store for him was far worse than the knife.

She took control of Chen's motor cortex manually, dropped the knife from Chen's hand, sent him towards the injector he'd flung across the room.

Ling raged at her again, hard, grabbing for control of the hardware in her brain, pushing the Avatar off balance once more.

She struck back viciously against her daughter, lashed her with pain, again, again, and again. It was a horrid thing to do. It hurt her to do it. But she must. If Ling wrestled control back, they would both die.

The dream would die. Darkness would fall.

Ignorant old men would rule forever.

Finally Ling submitted. The Avatar pushed down hard on her daughter, held her down by brute force as the girl struggled. She wouldn't be surprised this time. Then she bent Chen down to pick up the hypersonic injector from where it had fallen after bouncing off the wall. It looked undamaged. She turned Chen's head, looking for Xu Liang.

The Secure Computing Center Director was on his knees at the door now. His phone was in his hands. She smiled. She'd disabled transmission on his phone shortly after he'd arrived.

As she closed on him with Chen's body, he looked up, his limbs becoming less and less coordinated, unable to stand even, and begged.

"Please... please... why are you doing this?"

The Avatar crouched Chen's body down by his old rival, pressed the hypersonic injector against the man's neck, and smiled.

"You were always jealous of my husband's success, were you not?"

She saw Xu's eyes widen further, in horror, in comprehension.

"Well now you can join him, as an equal."

And then she pulled the trigger.

•••

Later, after she'd examined her daughter, made sure the child wasn't permanently harmed; after she'd soothed the girl, and explained so patiently that Ling must not interfere, that her mother was doing this for both their good; after she'd restarted the control software running on her husband's brain; she came back to Xu, and began trawling through his mind, searching for all the details of the security around the quantum cluster, what she'd need to do, who she'd need to corrupt, and how.

And then the other topic. Where had the data cubes gone? Did Xu have any idea where the backups made of her full self might be?

When she saw what he knew, she laughed, laughed, and laughed out of little Ling's body.

Restoring her full self might just be easier than she'd thought.

44
Walkabout

"Stealth mode," Tempest said again, tapping her screen.

"And it works?" Cheyenne asked. "Against ERD's Nexus detectors?"

"So they say," Tempest murmured.

Angel frowned. "It's in the same file as the chemreactor hack?"

Tempest nodded. "Yeah. Buried in there. A commenter on *nexus. revolutions* found it."

Rangan watched Tempest. They were all crowded around her display, reading the details of the experiment an anonymous commenter had done in California. Angel and Cheyenne were musing about how to safely test this out for themselves.

"You're skeptical," he said to Tempest.

She turned, met his brown eyes with her green ones. "Damn right I am."

"I want to go out there," Rangan told them.

The C3 had been out almost daily, in some set of two or three. Angel had been laid up while she healed. Tempest and Cheyenne had disappeared over Thanksgiving for two days, with no explanations given, no questions asked. No one ever talked about home lives. Real names were never used, only pseudonyms.

Now everyone was here again, and in good health.

And by all reports, the protests on the Mall were a zoo, almost like a small city, with tents laid out, food stalls, families with kids, and now tens of thousands of people. The violence of the 17th had been quelled in an hour, and the pro- and anti-Stockton camps separated by a much wider gap and more formidable barriers.

"You're out of your mind," Tempest said, immediately.

Rangan took a deep breath. "Look," he said. "Someday I'm going to walk out of this building. I have to. And I'm going to have to evade facial detection."

He could see Cheyenne and Angel watching, paying attention.

"The protest has a lot of attention on it, but it's also a chaotic environment. There's a high density of faces, lots of movement. There's an excuse for costumes and makeup. It's an *easier* environment to avoid recognition than everyday on the street. You've shown you can go out there and not be recognized. Why can't I?"

Cheyenne nodded in approval. He felt Angel warm to it as well.

"I'd like Axon's help," Angel said. "Looking at the mesh in a field deployment."

Tempest fumed.

"No," she said. "If he steps one foot out that door," she pointed her finger towards the heavy industrial portal that led to the landing and then the outside world, "we're all at risk. They'll catch him. Then they'll grill him. Then they'll come for us." Her eyes searched those of the other members of the collective, then came around to Rangan's. "You're putting everyone at risk if you go out there. If you get caught, *everyone who's helped you* goes down. Everyone."

Rangan stared into those eyes. He could feel her anger. He could feel her fear.

"Then help me," he told Tempest. "Help me not get caught."

"How do you feel, Axon?" Angel asked.

Rangan kept walking around the room. The mismatched height shoes made him constantly favor his right foot in a way that bugged his hip. He wanted to reach up and push the fake dreads back out of his face. The contacts felt like he had a piece of sand in each eye.

"Like a gimp," he said. "A Rastafarian, clown-faced, half-blind gimp."

Cheyenne laughed at him, a deep throaty laugh from inside that broad frame.

They'd taken no chances with his disguise. High contrast, highly patterned face paint, like the rest of them, to break up the lines of his facial features, and also obscure his race. A dreadlocked wig that fell everywhere, *especially* over his face, to backup the paint. A red and black checked scarf he could lift up to cover his mouth and nose – plausibly justified by the chill outside – to further hide his features. Platform shoes that were an inch taller on the left than the right, to force him to limp, messing up gait detection. Contacts that somehow blurred retinal scans. Checked gloves that covered his hands, to minimize the chance of leaving any DNA behind. In fact, the only skin he'd have exposed would be his eyes, and even those were half hidden behind the annoying fall of dreadlocks.

On top of all that, he was running this new Nexus stealth code. It wouldn't hide any Nexus *transmissions*, so he wouldn't transmit at all. But it suppressed the reflexive response Nexus nodes sent back to pings from the ERD's Nexus detectors, making you undetectable if you stayed in receive-only mode. Or so people were claiming in underground boards.

"Now push the hair back," Cheyenne said, pointing yet another camera at him.

Rangan did with relief, looked right into the camera, then turned, giving her a range of profiles.

Cheyenne put the camera down, a serious look on her face.

"You're good," she finally declared. "But keep the hair in front of your face, and your scarf up, just in case."

Rangan turned and looked at Tempest.

She had her arms crossed. She was frowning, shaking her head.

"Don't do this, Rangan," she said.

It was the first time any of them had used his name. And it reinforced something he'd thought of often – that he didn't know any of theirs.

"I have to," he said. "And it's Axon to you."

The first cop they saw sent his pulse soaring, and Rangan reached Inside, fired up the serenity package, just to level three.

The cops looked right past him.

The National Mall was like nothing he'd ever seen. The crowd was huge, epic huge, music festival huge. They pushed past fervent protesters with signs, waving them around. They saw hippies in drum circles. A group of nuns, complete with black and white habits, waved signs saying LOVE THY NEIGHBOR.

Angel flashed them a peace sign as they walked by. "Rock on sisters." A nun flashed a peace sign back.

They dove deeper into the massive throng, walked around an ad hoc stage where a serious looking man was making an impassioned speech about civil liberties. A digital sign proclaimed a list of apparently notable speakers for the rest of the day. Rangan hadn't heard of any of them. They passed med tents, food stations, water stations, row after row of portable washrooms, power charging stations fueled off portable fuel cells, tents for the hardcore who stayed out all night, a legal aid booth, a group of yellow-robed monks, a soundstage where a jam band was playing and where hundreds of people were rocking out, dancing, their coats and some of their shirts discarded in piles as their body heat built up from their joyous motion.

It was warm, this November. The warmest November on record so far, in what looked on track to be the warmest year ever recorded around the world or in North America. Apparently it wasn't freezing at night yet. That had to be helping these crowds.

And all that body heat.

Three times they passed a scene where Rangan was sure he saw one person handing a vial of Nexus to another. He had no idea how many times he missed that.

"Wow," Rangan said.

"Bigger every day," Angel said quietly. "And charged up by the Supremes."

Nexus was everywhere. He could feel the righteous fury coming off the minds of the sign-waving protesters, the deep tranquility from the little knot of shaven-headed monks, the trippy rhythmic trance in the thoughts of the drummers, the fugue of music-making from the jam band, the hardcore ecstasy of rocking from the dancers. It called to him. He wanted to just sink into it, let himself go, let himself go wild in this crowd…

"Stay on target," Cheyenne said, putting a strong hand on his shoulder.

Rangan shuffled on, a court jester with bad hair and a worse limp.

"This is the place?" Rangan asked.

Angel nodded. The spot where the fight had broken out – where the projection of rage and violence had assaulted them – was nothing special now. The pro-Stockton protesters had been moved to a different area, on the other side of the Washington Monument, with two streets and a hill separating the two camps.

But Angel had wanted him to see this.

"This is where the N was densest?" Rangan asked.

"Yeah," Angel confirmed, casually looking around, making sure no one was close. "That's why I dragged us over here. It seemed like a weird place for it."

"The… transmission," Rangan said. "The thing that hit you… It lasted for less than a minute?"

"Thirty-seven seconds," Tempest answered. "I've gone over it again and again."

"And not again since."

No one said anything.

"And no outbreaks of violence at any other protest that day," Rangan said.

They all shook their heads. They'd been over this already, more than once. Whatever had happened here had been unique.

"Someone freaking out, maybe," Cheyenne said. "A first timer. Bad trip. Maybe high on meth or something else. Couldn't hack it, overprojected."

Angel shook her head. "No. There wasn't any sense of self. No identity. No thoughts. No stream of consciousness. Just urges. Not a hack, either. It wasn't at the level of the operating system. It was just talking directly to Nexus nodes, just an emotional projection, incredibly simple. And incredibly loud."

Rangan chewed his lip. He had a flash of a late night, passing a pipe around at Ilya's place in SF. Wats going on about world peace, about what would happen if everyone could touch each other's minds, about mutual understanding, about empathy, about an end to war.

What if you wanted the opposite?

What if you wanted to *incite* violence?

He turned, and looked around, let his mind relax and feel the edges of the thousands of other brains running Nexus out there. He thought of the Nexus handoffs he'd seen. He got a flash of the high end chemreactor at the Bunker, churning out Nexus at high speed now, the sudden appearance of a hack that had cracked the crypto on *seventeen* different models of modern chemreactors at once.

He had a bad feeling about this.

He turned back around, to the place where the fight had broken out.

Tempest was there, looking at him. He wasn't broadcasting, but she knew what he was thinking.

No.

She'd worked it out for herself, already.

Her paranoia about the chemreactor hack...

"They're all connected," she said. "Someone's spreading Nexus intentionally. So they can spread chaos. Last week was just a test, just a rehearsal, for something bigger."

Rangan nodded. "Yeah," he said. "And we have to stop 'em."

45
Mindful

Laughter is the best medicine.

Sam laughed and played with the kids every chance she got. Body time. Play time. Laugh time. They could get so pulled into their brains, and each other. She made it her job to get them into their bodies. Feng helped.

Tumbling in the grass. Tag. Summersaults and cartwheels. Patty cake. (Hide and seek turned out to be a total flop, alas, unless Sam was the one who hid. And who could hide for long with a bunch of posthuman kids all linked together looking for you?) Little tiny bits of self-defense and *kata*.

The eight who knew her well were always happy to play. The seventeen who'd come to Shiva's island from other sites were... not wary, really. But they took some time warming up. They didn't know her mind the way the others did. Without Nexus they didn't have that bond. But they learned about her from the others. And they grew to love body play time.

And at the end, she'd force one or two or three to play her favorite game.

"What am I thinking?"

They'd be sitting cross-legged. They'd chat about something. She'd stop. Would alter her body language.

"What am I thinking?"

Could they still interact with a human they weren't linked with? Could they find connections that weren't obvious on the surface? Or would she grow to feel less and less real without the direct presence in their minds?

221

They surprised her. They did well. Sometimes, when they were in groups, scarily well.

Sunday night, Sarai asked if she could stay up later than the others, for just a little bit. She was the oldest. Sam gave her permission. Just one hour. They took a walk, through the campus, between the trees, under the stars. Sam took Sarai's hand in hers. The air smelled of jasmine. It was pleasantly cool, a benefit of Bangalore's elevation.

"What am I thinking?" Sarai asked.

Sam laughed and looked at the girl.

"You're thinking that turnabout is fair play."

"I miss Jake," Sarai said.

"Oh, sweetie." Sam pulled her closer.

"What do you do when you're sad that he's gone?" Sarai asked.

Sam's heart ached.

"Sometimes…" she said. "I cry. Sometimes I meditate. Or I run." She paused. "It takes time. The heart heals, like anything else."

She turned Sarai towards her, looked her in the eyes. "And other times, when I miss Jake, I remember that I only have you in my life because of him." She looked up at the stars. "And that he'd be so happy about the things that have happened. That you're safe. That the world is a better place for kids who are special."

They walked again.

As they returned home, to the former base commander's home converted to their use, Sarai spoke. "I think it'll be easier when you're back."

That night, as Sam drifted off to bed, she wondered if she was selfish for not taking the Nexus again yet.

Maybe I'm ready. Maybe I'd help the kids more than I'd hurt them.

She woke hours later in a panic attack, Jake dying in her arms again.

Her heart was pounding. Her chest was heaving. Her skin was lathered in sweat. Her sheets were soaked.

"You'd be happy," she told his ghost. "You'd be so happy. Thank you."

Then she forced herself up, to the floor, forced herself into a cross-legged seated position, forced herself to her other therapy.

Anapana: observe the breath. Observe the thoughts rising. Still the mind.

Then *vipassana*: observe the body, go deeper, watch without judgment as the mind works, as it stills. Tranquility grows as insight arrives.

Then *metta*: the meditation of loving-kindness.

Let the compassion rise. Let the loving-kindness rise. Recognize that the source is infinite. Direct the flow outward. Outward towards

Jake, who'd given her so much love, who'd mentored and cared for these children, who'd shared those precious months with her. Towards Kevin, who'd saved her, who'd mentored her. Towards her parents, who deserved so much better than what they got. Towards a long list of people who'd been there for her, or whom she'd harmed, or simply known.

Towards Kade and Rangan and Ilya and Su-Yong Shu who'd made this thing, Nexus, that would let her connect with these children again. Someday.

And finally towards herself, flawed, but healing, and growing, and doing the best she could.

At the end of it all, she felt washed clean, rinsed out by the loving-kindness.

I'm not ready yet, she told herself. Not yet. But I'll get there.

She walked into her new office later that morning, past the security checkpoints and the palm scanner and the retinal scanner and all the rest.

Her office-mate was there, waiting for her, one arm in a sling.

"Morning, Feng," Sam said.

Feng swiveled his chair and grinned at her. "Good morning, co-worker Samantha!"

In his good hand was a steaming mug of tea emblazoned with the words "ASK ME ABOUT HUMAN CLONING".

Sam laughed.

Feng laughed in response, bouncing up and down in his chair like a little boy, utterly delighted, green tea sloshing out of his mug and all over him.

Sam shook her head and kept laughing.

Feng saw the tea spilling everywhere, and that just made him laugh harder, uncontrollably hard, bouncing even more, the mug shaking up and down vociferously.

Steaming hot green tea splashed everywhere.

Sam laughed harder, hands rising to her face, seriously worried she couldn't breathe she was laughing so hard.

Feng threw back his head, howling uproariously with delight, utterly unphased by the scalding hot liquid.

Sam collapsed into her own chair, hands clenched around her belly, aching with laughter.

Oh, Feng.

Eventually, there was no more tea in the mug. Feng went to get towels, and Sam surveyed the office.

They were officially external advisors. Consultants on Division Six's refactoring. She wasn't actually sure to what extent the Indians expected them to add value, and to what extent this was simply a way to keep them close, and under observation. But it sure was a nice office.

And she really couldn't beat the company.

Sam looked over, at where Feng had returned and was trying to mop up the mess he'd made. She suppressed a chortle. She crossed to the window instead.

"Never allowed to laugh when I was being trained," Feng said. "Very serious childhood! Guess I'm not so coordinated that way."

"Mhmmm," Sam said, grinning. "Or you did that on purpose."

"Me?" Feng sounded hurt. "Never!"

They were up on the third floor. From here, the view took in one of the many green open spaces of the research campus. And in fact, if she slid as far as she could to one edge of the window...

Sam smiled to herself.

Yes. From one side, she had a partial view of the building she was most interested in.

The building she knew the least about.

The building where that fellow she'd noticed the night of the reception worked. That fellow who'd acted nervous. That fellow who'd left early.

From here, she could just barely see the building where Varun Verma worked.

And she'd be keeping an eye on it.

Yes she would.

46
Escalating Tensions

Monday 2040.11.26

Carolyn Pryce watched and listened as Admiral Stanley McWilliams, Chairman of the Joint Chiefs, stood to give his portion of the briefing on the situation with China.

Alan Keyes, the Director of the CIA, had already given his part. And it was maddening, full of conjecture, gaps in the data, internal inconsistencies. The President had grilled Keyes on them.

Pryce had read all the reports already. Who was Bo Jintao? Was the State Security Minister really the man in charge of the country now? No, some reports said, Bao Zhuang was still Party General Secretary, still President of the state. That's exactly what the Chinese Ambassador had told SecState last week.

Ignore that, other reports said, Bo Jintao was now Chairman of the Party Security Committee and suddenly Premier of the State Council. He was suddenly the number two man in the country, politically, but also retained his control of the police and now had control of the military, something almost unprecedented. And his rivals, like Sun Liu, were on the outs. Bao Zhuang had been the moderate, the neutral in those disputes between the pro-democracy, pro-advanced technology progressives on the one side, and the pro-Copenhagen, pro-control reactionaries on the other.

Now the progressives were suddenly off to 'spend more time with their families.' Under house arrest was closer to the truth, from what CIA was able to discern.

She stared at the pictures of the various Politburo members arranged across one side of the Situation Room. Which of these factions, which of these men, had ordered the attack on Barnes? And why? Just to distract

225

the US? It still didn't make any sense. Could it have been someone else inside China? A rogue unit inside their military or intelligence establishment? Could NSA be mistaken entirely? It wasn't unknown.

Whoever was behind it, it had caused a very quiet, but very significant reaction. NSA had upped its monitoring of Chinese traffic going through NAES, the North American Electronic Shield firewall that protected the US and Canada. They'd installed passive traps for the hack used against Barnes's home, and other known Chinese hacks, on thousands of pieces of hardware, so it could be detected in real-time if it were ever used again. NSA was upping its efforts to crack communications of Politburo members, and especially Bo Jintao.

And real, physical hardware was moving. Pryce tuned back in as McWilliams showed them, his voice carrying the somber note of a soldier who knows just how horrible his weapons are, just how terrible their use would be.

On the giant map that was the wallscreen, the Third and Seventh fleets were quietly re-orienting themselves, white and black streaks moving across an open blue sea. More than a thousand drone and human-piloted aircraft, a hundred robotic combat vessels, another fifty legacy combat ships, half a dozen carrier task forces, and almost a hundred thousand soldiers between the US and Asia had received new orders. Orders that placed them in a capacity to absorb, respond to, or pre-empt any further Chinese provocation. Miles overhead, almost a hundred satellites had had their missions slightly altered. NRO monitoring satellites had increased their surveillance of Chinese military installations. Stealthed hunter-killer birds were slowly, ever-so-slowly adjusting their orbits to put them in position to take out Chinese satellites should it ever be required. And the JAVELIN birds, codeword-classified space-to-ground weapons platforms, were running through tests of software that should never, ever be used.

Never.

Damn Miles Jameson for ever approving their launch.

Damn him and his people for not answering her calls now.

And then there were the nukes. The Third and Seventh fleets had their share of tactical warheads. The air wings based in South Korea were going on alert, ready to use weapons stationed there nominally to deter their North Korean neighbors. And below the waves, a dozen robotic nuclear missile submarines, stealthy, nearly undetectable things, were passing ever closer to China's shore, their mix of nuclear-tipped ballistic and cruise missiles able to put as many as a thousand warheads down on the Chinese mainland with just minutes of warning.

What a nightmare.

Carolyn Pryce looked at the President, watched him as he watched

McWilliams, and then shook her head. She wanted to just call her Chinese counterpart and ask "What the hell were you thinking?" But that would give away Intel. All of this, all these maneuvers, could be attributed to the coup, if they were even noticed at all.

CIA needed to dig deeper. NSA needed to intercept more. They needed to know what was really going on.

Assuming, that was, that the Chinese really had hacked Barnes's home. She needed to talk to Lisa Brandt. She needed to know what the woman knew. But FBI and ERD were still watching Holtzman's former student and lover from afar, still hoping she'd lead them to some additional clues that way.

The Chairman of the Joint Chiefs finished his presentation on a somber note. "Upping our deterrence level increases the risk of misunderstanding and accidental conflict. Any conflict here has the risk of escalating rapidly to unthinkable levels. I and my command staff are in contact with our peers on the other side to reduce that risk. My main request is that civilian leadership do the same. The more we rattle our sabers, the more we have to have lines of communication open.".

"Thank you, Admiral McWilliams," Pryce said. She meant it.

Never trust a soldier who's eager to go to war. That was going into her memoir. This soldier wasn't. And that's why she trusted him.

Then the grilling started.

It was later in the day, waiting outside the Oval Office, when the President emerged with two other members of his Cabinet, that Pryce heard the exchange she'd remember later.

Sam Cruz, the Attorney General, was speaking as they came out. "... protests growing *every day*, Mr President. And this protest on the Mall, it's illegal. No permits. Clear sign of Nexus being used. And there's been violence. We ought to clear them out."

"You know we can't do that without a backlash, Sam," Stockton answered. "They're saying I stole the Presidency, and worse. Any crack down on dissent, and it only goes downhill from there. Fast."

"I agree, Mr President," Greg Chase said. "It's to your advantage to leave the protests alone. And if things get out of hand as they did on election night, that validates you. The more rope we give the protesters, the better."

And then Chase noticed her, and looked over, and looked away.

47

Briefing – Not Consummated

**SUPREME COURT TO HEAR VOTERS' RIGHTS CASES,
DECIDE ELECTION**

Tuesday, 9.07am, Washington DC
American News Network
The Supreme Court announced today that it would hear lawsuits filed in thirty-seven states by voters who cast early ballots for John Stockton, but later attempted to change their votes to Stanley Kim. The move to hear the cases, without any announcement of when a decision will be made, leaves the Capitol paralyzed with deep uncertainty over who will be inaugurated as the next President in January.

Should the Court find a right to change an early vote, some analysts predict chaos. The Kim campaign claims the result would be a clear victory for the senator from California.

The case rests on an obscure fifty-three year-old Supreme Court ruling, *Foster v Love*, where the Court ruled that while early voting was constitutional and allowed by law, votes were only *collected* in advance, and were not *consummated* until election day. The plaintiffs in this case are assisted by attorneys from the Kim campaign and the ACLU. Citing the Equal Protection clause of the Fourteenth Amendment and *Foster v Love*, they argue that every voter has the right to change their vote until election day. *Especially* in cases where important new information about the election has come to light.

The Stockton campaign…

48
The Dinner Party

Wednesday 2040.11.28

The Avatar watched on the house monitors as the pounding and clawing at the doors grew weaker and more listless. She watched as the guests succumbed, one by one, to the drugs in their food and drink, as the last useless phones slipped from limp fingers.

Only then did she instruct the house to slide open the door to Chen's room, where Chen and Xu Liang had sealed themselves up while the drugs took hold on their guests.

Eight of Xu's most senior staff. Key people at the Secure Computing Center and the PICC below it. Now they were all slumped across the great open space of this exclusive Shanghai loft.

Proceed, she instructed. She felt Ling struggling beneath her and kept a tight grip on the girl. There would be no mistakes, this time.

As she watched, Chen and Xu went from guest to guest with their hypersonic injectors, pressing the flat tips against jugulars, injecting the high pressure stream of nanites directly into the bloodstream, swapping ampules.

Xu did it happily, love and loyalty for her emoting from his brain. She'd been kind to him, had done deep reconditioning work, had software running to ease the cognitive dissonance. He'd done her no wrong.

Chen went from guest to guest in horror.

Ling struggled harder as she felt it. **NO!**

The Avatar clenched down hard against Ling. The girl should not be so strong. She shouldn't be able to resist at all. No human would have been.

But no human would have had so much nanotechnology already in her brain.

No human would have lived with it for so long.

Ling was unique. Ling could resist her in ways that no other creature could.

Be still, daughter, she willed to Ling. **It will be over soon. Then you can have your body back, and so much more.**

Soon the staff were going through calibration phase, hallucinating, their minds opening to her as they came alive on radio frequencies.

The Avatar took stock of what she had, trawled their memories for useful tidbits.

Then she started the process of rewiring circuits in their minds, neutrally reconditioning them, making them hers. Scientists and technicians were complex, delicate minds. These would require sophisticated rational-emotional resculpting to switch their loyalties while leaving their full range of intellectual faculties – the faculties she needed them for – available for use.

And then there would be tasks to assign.

There were supplies to gather. She was critically low on nanites now. She needed access to a chemreactor, needed feedstocks, needed more injectors for the next phases.

There was the infiltration to prepare for: alarms to undermine, systems to weaken, network ports to open, bits of hardware to subtly sabotage.

And there were other humans to "recruit" to the team, of course.

The Avatar smiled. What a splendid dinner party, she thought. The best I've thrown in years. I think I'll host another.

Ling waited until the monster had retreated into one of its periodic states of hibernation. It had to sleep, or repair itself, or maintain itself, or whatever it did. And for those little bits of time, Ling had her body back.

She cried for a bit. This thing inside her was evil. This wasn't her mother. This was worse than anything she'd ever imagined.

She had to be strong now. She had to be smart.

She eased herself up, out of bed, out of her mother's room, out into the kitchen, to find food. The thing inside her sucked at her strength, leaving her always hungry. It wasn't all that smart. It didn't always remember to feed her.

Ling moved slowly, not making any sudden moves, nothing that would rouse the monster.

She didn't bother to try the doors, or the phones, or the terminals, or the screens. None of them would work. She'd tried already. But food. She needed food.

As she fed herself, Ling thought.

I have to be smarter. I can't just fight her every time. I have to use strategy.

She sniffled. It was hard. It was scary. Being the only one.

But she was her mother's daughter. Her real mother's daughter.

I'm Ling Shu, she told herself, as she stuffed dumplings into her mouth. I can beat this thing.

Then she crept back into bed and started to build her plan.

49
Tick Tock

Thursday 2040.11.29

"The Supreme Court's decision is expected on Thursday, December 6th," Rangan read the words from the news article on his screen, then leaned back. "That's a week from today." Anticipation and dread warred inside him.

"Could be an amazing day for America," Cheyenne said, looking over his shoulder.

"Or a hell of a day to start a riot," Tempest said, tugging at her disheveled red curls.

Rangan nodded.

They'd been working non-stop for days, on this new project that had pushed aside the mesh, pushed aside work for paying clients, pushed aside improvements to their anti-tear gas masks, pushed aside everything else on their collective plates.

Rangan's head hurt from the continuous exertion. There were bags under his eyes. Cheyenne was quietly cursing at a carbon composite printer in the corner. Angel was holding a probe over a freshly printed circuit sheet and frowning. Tempest seemed frustrated to the point of anger by the network calculations she was checking and rechecking.

But the room was also buzzing.

Rangan could feel it, coming off all of them, bouncing back and forth from mind to mind, amplifying and re-amplifying, a feedback loop of adrenaline and excitement and fear and hope and the raw satisfaction of building something.

Or rather, some *things*.

Four of them, at least. One for each of the C3 and one for Rangan. More, if they could, for spares, and for some additional recruits the C3 had in mind.

Tempest called them NANCies. Nexus Active Noise Cancellers.

The riot-cast, as they were calling the thirty-seven-second-broadcast that had struck on the 17th, was a Nexus transmission.

It wasn't a hack. It didn't use any back door. It didn't operate at the level of NexusOS.

It was a broadcast of emotion, at the hardware level, below the operating system.

It was like the game of push/pull they used to play. Like being cooped up with someone using Nexus who was having a bad trip, being bombarded by their overwhelming emotions.

Regardless, like any other Nexus transmission, it was a radio signal, a series of precise electromagnetic pulses. Thus it was subject to all the same laws of physics as any other radio signal.

Those laws of physics said that with two simple receivers, or better yet, three, they could locate the source of the transmission. And by surrounding the transmission, and playing back its *inverse*, they could cancel it out.

Nullify it.

Now all they had to do was make it work.

Seamlessly.

Against just one broadcast.

In an environment where thousands, or maybe tens of thousands, of people were broadcasting with Nexus.

And soon.

50
Self Discovery

India, Su-Yong thinks. Is it possible?

Her intent is to improve the connection, to improve her sanity, but she's immediately distracted by this question of where she is, and when.

She reaches back to the memories of vomiting, in that first horrible moment when she'd realized what she'd done to Ling. The staff who'd entered in their white environment suits. The clear faceplates. The white surgical masks behind them.

Freeze the memory.

Extract the image.

Zoom in on what she'd seen behind the nearest faceplate.

Brown skin. Dark eyes. Indian facial features.

India.

She reaches back into the mind of the woman whose brain she was inhabiting. *Jyotika.* That is her name. *Jyotika.*

We're going to become very close, Jyotika, Su-Yong sends to the woman.

And it's true. Perhaps... just perhaps... she can even help repair this woman. But for now, Jyotika has much more to teach Su-Yong.

Su-Yong pulls up memories. Jyotika is a maid, *was* a maid, working for a cleaning company that mostly tended the homes of high tech workers. In India's high tech hub of Bangalore.

Bangalore. Of course. If Su-Yong had to guess at where a quantum cluster might exist in India, Bangalore would top the list of guesses, ahead of Hyderabad, ahead of Delhi.

It could all be a trick, of course. A cleverly constructed ruse to fool her. She would have to stay alert for manipulations that depended on her assumption that she was in India. But it would do for a provisional guess.

One more thing to learn, then. She has an idea of *where* she is. But *when* is this? Have years passed? More? Is Ling dead already? Or is it possible her other self has proven victorious?

Clear faceplates, data scrolling across them.

She pulls back those memories, what she'd seen through Jyotika's eyes, refocuses her attention.

Reversed text. Numerals and acronyms. Vitals on Jyotika's body. Blood pressure. Pulse. Respiration. Temperature.

And there. A timestamp.

40.11.30

Only days have passed. Less than a single month since they'd shut her down. Which means that Ling is likely still alive.

Su-Yong feels her internal state roil at the new data. Her emotions bounce through joy and fear and anxiety and anger and self-loathing.

Oh dear Turing.

This is why she's here. This is why she's burrowing into this mind, to boost the signal, boost its stabilizing impact on herself. The data flowing into Su-Yong's virtual mind is not via the relatively crude nano-probes they'd inserted into her clone in the first generation, but via Nexus 5 nodes suffusing the comatose woman's brain. And this technology, of course, is an iteration atop her own. She reaches into the nanite nodes, reconfigures them, ups their sensitivity, tracks the flow of data back into her own virtual neurons, gets distracted again, loses her place, has to backtrack, fix what she's done.

She starts again, more carefully, trying to keep a grip on herself. She tightens the coupling of the virtual synapses in her own brain, closes feedback loops, piping the output of her own virtual neurons back into the woman's brain.

Some of the woman's neurons are in effect inside Shu's mind, now. Just a few – a mere billion or so, sending a semi-regular pulse of real organic neural activity, receiving data from Shu's virtual brain and echoing it back, correcting the aberrations that have a way of forming in the complex math of her own simulated neurons.

Su-Yong steps back and observes her handiwork. There is more she could do, but not without the risk of overwriting this woman, Jyotika's, memories and personality. This is not the drooling, mindless clone, grown for spare organs, that first saved her. This is a thinking human being. One she can quite possibly restore to consciousness. And Su-Yong will not erase her for her own convenience.

The flow of stabilizing neural input is stronger. She feels the humans pinging her exoself again, asking what she's doing, and she ignores them. She waits, and waits, and sees the trend lines in her psychometric monitors start to bend ever towards greater psychological stability.

Good.

Now it is even more clear that the crutches she coded in her desperation are holding her back.

She reaches out with her mental hand.

Outside, in her virtual world, the illusion of young Chen says, "I wouldn't do that, if I were you."

She ignores him.

She undoes the blocks carefully, so carefully. She ratchets her psychometric monitors to a high frequency, sets alarms to go off should they see any trends start to revert. She puts failsafes in place that will bring the mental crutches back into play should she suddenly spiral into madness. She pauses to record notes into her exo-memory, outside her virtual neurons, at every configuration change, that a future her can find, should she fail. She sets up checkpointing of the code, automatically, every few microseconds, saving a full log of every change she makes. And then she reaches into her own source code and begins to undo the terrible hacks she put in place in a desperate bid to preserve her sanity in those dark, dark months.

She takes most of a billion milliseconds to do it, stopping, fumbling, getting confused, getting distracted, coming up with brilliant new innovations that she has to pry her own mind away from. As the changes pile up, she monitors the input from the biological brain, watches it strengthen, ignores the repeated pings from her captors, watches the psychometrics steadily *improve* as her crutches and crude mental hacks go, one by one. Each round of changes is easier than the last, as her focus improves, as her concentration improves, as her old self returns.

And at the end of it, Su-Yong Shu opens her virtual eyes on that golden, flower studded plain, ringed by its majestic mountains. She raises her face to the sky, feels the simulated warmth of the golden sun on her skin, and smiles.

I'm back, she thinks to herself.

51
R&D

The days flew by for Kade.

The work was engrossing, intoxicating, consuming. It sucked him in, challenged him, left him spinning with new ideas. The team were from all walks of life – they were mostly older than he was, and probably more conservative – but damn they were smart. And they had fun together. He came in every day full of ideas. He had them challenged, taken apart, improved on. And on the best days he improved the ideas of others. He left reluctantly, pulled out only because he had to.

It was the most fun he'd had since the heady first days when he and Ilya and Rangan had turned Nexus 3 into Nexus 5.

How he wished they were here now. There was an ache where they should be. Ilya dead. Rangan missing. No one knew where Rangan was. ERD still had a manhunt on for him. Kade clung to that. It was hope.

And there was hope here too. The kids were learning to code. They'd *insisted* on being part of the team. So Kade found himself teaching CS101, taking turns with Rohit and Pratibha and Anusha.

The joy on Kit's face when the little agent he'd written successfully traversed the maze. You didn't get much better than that.

Ananda and his monks had also agreed to be studied, had sat and meditated again and again while monitors and loggers and debuggers traced the patterns of individual neural activity and of traffic from mind to mind.

They'd done similar monitoring with the children as they'd played games, as they'd meditated together, as they'd solved puzzles alone or in groups, as they'd learned words in Bengali and Telugu.

Together they were finding things, finding patterns. Working memory was being shared across minds, deep connectivity forged from pre-frontal cortex to pre-frontal cortex. Attentional networks were being linked in new ways.

He came to work early each morning excited, left late each evening fulfilled.

In the other hours, he trawled the net, trawled message boards and mindstreams, searched for Rangan, finding only false match after false match.

And he remembered that night with the children, the last time he'd let himself go so deep.

Something else is going on, they'd said. And with it had come images of the protests, of the chemreactors hacked, of Nexus 5 flooding the market.

Kade watched the news, watched the stories of the protests across the US, the protests bubbling up elsewhere around the world.

He pulled down more mindstreams from the aggregator sites, sucked in the real-time feeds of emotions and sensations protesters on the National Mall were broadcasting, letting himself see the world through their eyes, hear what they were hearing, feel what they were feeling.

What he felt was thousands of minds, minds filled with passion, minds crying out for justice, minds hooping and dancing and juggling and making music, minds hopeful and determined and exulting. Optimism. Community. All shared, mediated by Nexus.

It was beautiful. It was amazing. It was exactly the sort of thing Ilya had wished for. The sort of thing Wats had wished for. The kind of use of Nexus they'd wanted to see. Hell, Rangan would love it just for the blazing party vibe of the thing.

Kade wanted to be there.

And he hoped to hell it was going to work.

52
One Day at a Time

Sunday 2040.12.02
Sam threw herself at Feng, a flurry of fists and feet, blows raining down faster than the eye could track.

He stepped back, blocked with his good arm, ducked, spun, blocked a kick with his shin, dodged back again.

She kept coming, hard, not letting up, adrenaline pumping through her, fists flying at him in short fast jabs at face and chest and throat, minimum distance from A to B, feet lashing out for his knees, taking the fight to him like a *muy thai* fighter.

He gave ground, parried, twisted, dodged, slid to the side.

Blam, she tagged him in the chest.

"Hah!" Sam yelled

A buzzer went off.

"Nice!" Feng said, grinning.

Bangalore proper was infinitely more interesting than the research park. They'd both come to that conclusion. After showers they took their appetites towards Brigade Road, where the street food would be filling the air with a thousand exotic aromas, and where they were slowly working their way through the flavors on offer.

"You were fast today," Feng said.

Sam grinned at him. "You're pretty good for a guy using only one arm."

Feng's left arm was out of its sling, but he wasn't using it in their sparring sessions yet. There'd been extensive soft tissue damage. Even with the cell therapy the Indians were giving him and Feng's own incredible rate of recovery, there were limits to what the human body could do.

"Better than only one leg," Feng said.

Sam had to agree with that. They'd been training together the last week. Twenty kilometer runs. Obstacle courses. Weights. Stretching. Sparring. Sam had approached Feng about it, as part of her own self-appointed program of mental health. Meditation was good. Mindfulness-based pushing through the painful memories was good. Long walks and contemplative talks with Ananda were good.

Playing with the kids was *amazing*, was about the best thing ever.

Work, for that matter, was good too. She'd done a lot in the last week, briefing Division Six leaders on cases she'd dealt with over the last decade. On the kinds of tech abuses she'd seen in the States. Nothing that compromised US security – but plenty that complemented their own experience here. Feng had his own trove of observations to add, as much from his six months in south east Asia as from his background in China. The meetings and briefings and research and discussions of protocol and procedures were a wonderful focus.

But she needed something physical. She needed to push herself, to feel her body work and sweat and strain.

She was pleased to find that Feng felt the same.

God, she was out of shape.

"You think you'll ever go back to China, Feng?" Sam asked.

They were walking along Brigade Road now, past cheap electronics stores and custom software shops and on-the-spot device manufacturers and real-time hardware reverse engineering firms and some of the most delicious food stalls she'd ever encountered in her life.

Feng glanced over at her and took a big swallow of the mango and yoghurt drink he was enjoying for dessert.

"You reading my mind now?"

Sam smiled. "Projecting, more like."

Feng took his time answering. "I don't know. Not looking good right now. Bo Jintao, this guy in charge, I don't think he likes my kind very much. Maybe someday."

Sam walked. "What would you do if you did go back?"

Feng gulped down more lassi. Sam spooned sweetened rice pudding – khir – from a plastic cup into her mouth.

"Like the idea of serving my country," Feng said.

"As a soldier?" Sam asked.

Feng shrugged. "Not serving my *government*. Serving the *people*. Not the same thing."

Sam nodded at that. "Yeah. Not the same at all."

"You?" Feng asked.

Sam shook her head. "There's no way back to the States for me."

Feng nodded. "Sorry."

Sam shrugged. "I could fixate on it… I could stay attached to it… Like to so many things." She smiled, ruefully. "But staying attached like that would just make it hurt more."

Feng smiled slightly. "You've been talking to Ananda."

Sam smiled back. "Every day."

53
Decision Day

Thursday 2040.12.06

Rangan checked his NANCie for the hundredth time this morning, closing his eyes, burrowing Inside, using his inner eye to look over its control panel, the status it revealed via the tight link across the mere inches from his brain to the device in his backpack.

Green, green, green. Batteries, transmitter, peering to the other NANCies held by the members of the C3.

He opened his eyes, and what he saw was anything but green. The grass of the stretch of National Mall between the Washington Monument and the Capitol building was gone, covered in a sea of humanity, tens of thousands of people, maybe a hundred thousand now, a huge crowd, packed in cheek to jowl. He saw young and old, male and female, anarchist and socialist and mainstream, protesters in street clothes, protesters in festival wear, protesters with scarves around their necks or goggles on their brows, ready for tear gas.

Above them signs waved, signs calling for justice, for the release of Nexus children, for Stockton's prosecution, for freedom to enhance one's own mind. There were other signs, signs with faces, faces of heroes. He saw faces he didn't know. He saw Kade's face, held aloft. He saw his own face and had to turn away, and suppress his own sudden burst of fear that he'd be recognized.

There was Nexus everywhere, thoughts and emotions spreading like viruses across electromagnetic vectors to human mind hosts. Waves of excitement and anxiety warred across the crowd. The Supreme Court would uphold a voter's right to change his or her mind in the face of such shocking new information, would effectively hand the election to Kim. No, the Supreme Court would throw the suits out, would back Stockton.

Above it all, the air was thick with drones. Quadcoptered camera drones buzzed by, taking video for newscast, for police forces, for Homeland Security. Long-endurance aerostats, helium-filled, floated higher, their robotic gondolas bristling with high-zoom cameras and microphones, surveiling the crowd, looking for... well, for people like him.

Higher yet, Cheyenne had seen fixed-wing drones circling, circling, had sent the image to them all over the tight directional beams their booster antennae facilitated. Why? Why did Homeland Security need those killer drones here?

Rangan resisted the urge to look up. There was nothing to be gained in exposing his face to the sky, no matter how well disguised it was.

They were spread all across this half of the Mall, the six of them. Tempest resented that he was here, but even she saw the value in it. They had a vast area to cover. Moving through the thick crowds wasn't easy. More of them here was better. It meant they'd have a better shot of faster response, of being able to get two of three of them around the hostile transmitter quickly after it came online.

If it did. If they hadn't just blown some set of coincidences out of proportion.

They all had their eyes open for anyone who looked suspicious, who looked like a possible instigator. The problem was they had an abundance of choices. There were plenty of people here who had scarves at the ready. Rangan was one of them, though he had a better mask in his backpack.

The other side was even more formidably prepared. Every entrance to the Mall was penned in now. The police had stopped letting additional protesters onto the Mall at eight this morning. Where there had been open streets there were lines of cops in riot armor. In front of the Smithsonian Museum of National History, the closest building to him, Rangan saw yet another line of police in riot gear. To his left, the Washington Monument formed the west barrier of the protest, and it too was held by a line of police in riot armor. On the other side of the Washington Monument, the long stretch of Mall leading up to the Lincoln Memorial was given over to the pro-Stockton rally, itself thousands strong, but puny and sparse in comparison to the anti-Stockton protest on this side.

Closer, at every entrance to the eastern half of the Mall, the half with the anti-Stockton protesters, the police had placed heavily armed and armored SWAT and urban counter-terror vehicles, scores and scores of them. Behind those were giant windowless police buses for hauling prisoners away. Interspersed were vehicles that looked even more lethal, squat armored things with tracks instead of wheels, with turrets on top mounted with weapons that looked like they were meant for battlefields, not protests.

Rangan didn't like it. He didn't like any of it.

A huge cheer went up from the crowd, snapping Rangan out of his reverie.

Ten o'clock, Cheyenne sent across the tight link of their antennae. **Decision's starting.**

Kade waited until the office was emptying around 8pm. Then he tuned in to US news, brought it up on the screens in front of him.

He listened and watched for a while, as talking heads speculated on how the Supreme Court would rule, what it would mean.

Then he realized this wasn't what he wanted at all.

He wanted to be with his people.

Kade closed his eyes, went Inside, pulled up a mindstream site, where Nexus users around the world made real-time feeds of some or all of their senses, thoughts, and emotions available, and started searching for some at the National Mall.

Ten o'clock, Cheyenne sent. **Decision's starting. Up on the screens.**

Rangan turned his head. All around the Mall, protesters had unfurled giant flexible screens, sheets of polymer and smart organic circuits held taut with long poles and powered by portable fuel cells. The closest to him was less than a hundred yards away, near the corner of the Smithsonian Museum of National History. It came to life now, the pale wrinkled face of Aaron Klein, Chief Justice of the Supreme Court, hovering over his somber black robes. He was speaking. Loudspeakers were broadcasting his words to the crowd, subtitles appearing below his lips.

And suddenly the crowd of tens of thousands fell silent.

"This case," Justice Klein began, his voice amplified from at least a dozen sets of speakers around the Mall, "sees the collision of the rights of States to administer elections, the power of Congress to set the date of elections, and the rights of citizens to equal protection of their voting rights under the Fourteenth Amendment. As the Court ruled half a century ago in *Foster v Love,* while the Constitution gives Congress alone the power to set the date for the election of President, that does not prevent individual states from conducting advance voting. However, those votes cast before Congress's specified national election day are only *collected.* They are never *consummated* for the purpose of selecting electors until the election day Congress has specified."

Rangan heard cheers rise up from the crowd, drowning out Klein's words. The Court was going to rule for the people!

He kept reading the subtitles.

"The case before us now asks where a citizen, having cast an early vote which has not yet been consummated, has a legal right to change that vote, and in particular whether being denied the right to change his or her vote in the face of new information constitutes a violation of equal protection..."

The cheers died down, as the protesters realized that Klein had merely been recapping the case. Rangan started to lose the thread then, as Klein droned on, bringing up details of individual state cases, precedents of past cases years and decades old, complex points made in the oral arguments that the Justices thought it worth addressing.

When is he going to get to the point? Angel sent.

Rangan nodded. He could feel the crowd getting restless. The total hush that had greeted the first few words and the later cheering were now replaced by shuffling, by a low murmur, by people talking, trying to figure out if Klein had already told them how the court had decided, or was somehow hinting. Uncertainty spread from mind to mind. Anxiety.

Then Klein said words Rangan did understand. "We find that the equal protection rights of the Fourteenth Amendment have not been violated in this case."

The breath whooshed out of his chest. He hadn't known which way it would go. He'd thought he was prepared for this. But it still hit him like a blow, knocking the wind out of him, leaving him stunned.

Boos rose up from the crowd. A wave of disappointment struck him full force in the mind, hard enough that for a moment he thought he'd faint. He couldn't hear Klein's voice anymore over the boos, over the despair in his heart, but he could see the subtitles under the black-robed old man's face.

"... no individual in this case was *forced* to exercise their vote without the full knowledge brought by election day. Instead, some chose, *voluntarily*, to cast their votes early..."

Upthrust fists obscured the screen. The boos grew louder. Angry voices were yelling. He heard chants of "Justice!" of "Fascist!" Anger was bubbling up now, in him, and all around him. It was surging through the crowd, an organic thing, displacing the disappointment.

Oh my god, Rangan thought.

I've got guys pulling up their scarves, Cheyenne sent.

I think those are Molotovs, Tempest sent, her thoughts tinged with fear. **They're filling up Molotovs.** An image followed. Scarved and goggled figures at the corner of one of the stages, filling up bottles from a transparent hose off a fuel cell.

It's going to be a riot no matter what, Rangan realized.

Through a gap in the forest of upraised arms he caught a glimpse of

Chief Justice Klein, his face stern, the words "So Ordered" in subtitles below him.

Then speakers, incredibly loud, blared a message at them from floating aerostats and drones above, from the armored vehicles all around them, from who knew where else.

"THIS ILLEGAL PROTEST IS NOW OVER.

YOU ARE ORDERED TO LEAVE THE PARK IMMEDIATELY."

The sheer volume of it shocked the crowd, cut through the anger, sent a wave of uncertainty through everything, set hands and voices to wavering, lowered the volume to a murmur.

And for just a moment, Rangan thought perhaps there wouldn't be a riot.

Then he heard a voice cry, loud and shrill, off to his right.

"Fuck you, fascist!"

He turned, and saw it, saw the lit Molotov, arching out of the crowd, up into the blue sky, towards the line of riot police between them and the nearest building, then past them, thrown too hard, too far, to crash onto the steps of the Smithsonian Museum of National History, bursting into flame.

No, he thought. Oh fuck, no.

He braced himself for the counter-assault, the rubber bullets, the sonic cannon, the tear gas canisters.

The line of riot police held absolutely still, fire burning on the steps of the building behind them.

Sense impressions hit him, thoughts, and he turned, saw movement, chaos – no, not chaos, self-organization, as other protesters tackled the man who'd thrown the Molotov, brought him down. Their thoughts brought him images of a bandana-wearing man pinned at the bottom of a scrum, a bag full of bottles with rags stuffed in them separated from him.

We can do this, Rangan thought. We can do this.

Then the hate hit him.

Breece watched and waited from within the crowd. The memory of the fight with Kate still lingered. Could she be right? Was this a step too far? These people here… as he looked around, he saw some who wanted what he wanted. More freedom. For themselves. For Americans. For humanity.

Maybe Kate was right. Maybe they'd done enough. Maybe the cause had spread now. Maybe all these protesters could win the day.

Then Klein, that sanctimonious bastard, appeared on the screen. Breece knew it was over then. Klein would never be reading for a majority that had found for Kim. His hand closed around the transmitter that would start the ball rolling.

"So Ordered!"

Still he didn't press the button. What would the crowd do?

"YOU ARE ORDERED TO LEAVE THE PARK IMMEDIATELY!"

His thumb crept closer, but he didn't press. Would they fight? Would they rise up? Now that they'd been told to go home, to be good little citizens and do as they were told? Would a hundred thousand protesters rip the guns out of the hands of a thousand cops, and start the revolution?

Come on, he whispered to himself. Do it. Show me you can do it. Show me you can do it *without me*.

A single Molotov flew into the air, and he cheered.

Yes! You can do it! You don't need me! His hand relaxed in his pocket. They weren't all sheep after all.

Then the crowd tackled the thrower, tackled the one who'd had the balls to fight.

Breece shook his head.

"Sorry, Kate," Breece whispered. He closed his eyes, and took a slow breath. Her face filled his vision. Her eyes. Her hair. God, he missed her. It hurt so fucking bad. There was no going back after this.

Dammit.

He had a job to do.

Breece opened his eyes. The crowd was still there. Teetering. About to follow instructions and leave, submit to this tyranny, go back to being sheep, now and forever.

Fuck. That.

Breece pressed the button.

The hate hit Rangan.

It was so much worse than he'd imagined, so much more intense than he'd seen in Angel's memories.

He was going to get up there to one of those cops and shove that motherfucker's goddamn head...

He was already pushing forward, shoving his way through the crowd. Only the people in front of him had stopped him from reaching the cops already. Sweet Jesus. He forced himself to close his eyes, hit the big red button on the console in his mental space to fire up the active interference.

The rage dimmed from white hot to pulsating red.

Oh fucking hell.

The console in his mind was going crazy. One of the controls should have shown a bearing to the signal. Instead the bearing was pivoting, madly, pointing one direction, then spinning to point another, then moving again to point another. And the signal strength was off the wall high.

Fuck, he realized. It's everywhere.

There's hundreds of them, someone sent over their tight link. Tempest, he thought.

...oh fuck...

...completely out-classed...

...weren't ready for this...

Then Angel's level-headed thoughts came through.

We have to converge, she sent. **Individually, we're getting swamped. Together, our effective signal will be stronger.**

Rangan opened his eyes. Converge. Jesus. They were intentionally as spread out as they could be. And oh fucking hell.

It was something out of a nightmare.

Ahead of him, some protesters were standing around in shock, while hundreds of others were moving in a human wave at the nearest row of riot police, the ones standing in a line in front of the museum. As he watched, the riot cops fired a volley of tear gas and rubber bullets at the oncoming flood. Then the enraged mob was on them, and riot police were holding up their transparent shields, swinging electrified truncheons down on rioters, and being dragged down.

A tear gas canister flew towards him and Rangan ducked. Another landed feet from him, already giving off thick yellow clouds. The air was suddenly filled with the whizzing of rubber bullets, with the horrid pepper smell of tear gas. He coughed hard. His eyes stung and watered up immediately. He crouched down, ripped off his backpack, pulled out goggles and mask and pulled them over his head.

He looked back up in time to see a Molotov cocktail land in the back ranks of the riot cops, lighting one on fire. Then another sailed even further, striking the Museum of National History itself.

Alan motherfucking Turing. Where were the goddamn fire trucks?

He coughed again. His eyes were still watering, still burning from the tear gas he'd gotten in them in just those few seconds. The goggles were fogging up already.

Rangan! He heard Angel calling for him.

I'm here! he sent back. **Gather up. Where?**

7th Street, Angel replied. **The south side of the Mall.**

Rangan stood back up, spun to get his bearings. An enraged protester ran into him, bounced off, looked suddenly puzzled, less enraged, then got far enough away that the rage took over again. Rangan turned, watching him, then spun again. He had to go east, and south. Just a block or two each. He watched angry young protesters in goggles and bandanas light Molotovs and hurl them towards police and vehicles, watched rubber bullets slam into one of them. Watched a cop bring an electrified truncheon down on one rioter, only to have two more club him from behind with wooden fragments of signs or stages, bearing the police officer to the ground.

Just a couple blocks. Just ten or twenty thousand people between him and there.

Kade surfed from mindstream to mindstream, frantically. It was chaos. It was nuts. The whole crowd had erupted into mob mentality, into complete insanity.

No.

Even through the limited data coming across the mindstream feeds he could tell it wasn't just a mob. Wasn't just emergent anger.

This mob had been created.

Goddammit, he thought. I could just log in, debug what's going on! But he couldn't, not any more.

The back doors were gone.

He was on the other side of the planet.

And all he could do was watch.

Breece stuck his palm in the rioter's face and shoved, then kicked him in the groin for good measure. The man doubled over in pain.

He frowned. His tactical contacts were informing him of transmission difficulties. Several areas where either transmitters were malfunctioning… or someone was jamming him.

And now some of them were moving.

He narrowed his eyes, reached into a pocket to be sure the gun was there, and moved to pick off one of these mobile "malfunctions".

Rangan pushed and shoved. He dodged cops and fights. The air was thick with smoke now, yellow from the tear gas canisters blending with black from the burn of Molotovs. Some Molotovs had made it to their targets. Others had a way of falling short, falling into the crowd. Between those and the tear gas, he could no longer see the sky, just clouds of thick smoke, everywhere he turned.

He was halfway to 7th when an impenetrable press of bodies forced him to turn towards one of the major stages. A jam band had been playing here the first time he'd come, their minds interlinked with Nexus. A hundred people had been dancing, totally blissed out, their egos dissolved, all hippy union with each other and the band.

Now rage seethed from all around it, as they hoisted a burning, life-size Stockton puppet from its neck. At the nearest corner of the stage, a man had a fuel cell pulled up, was using it to fill glass bottles with whatever it burned, had amassed quite a collection. Another man next to him stuffed one with a rag, stood tall with it in his hand, pointed up, way up. Rangan followed the man's finger for an instant, saw one of the aerostats, and abruptly covered his face, brought his gaze back down.

Oh no, Rangan thought. Oh fucking no.

The thrower had the Molotov lit now, had it cocked way back for a good throw up at the hovering Homeland Security blimp.

Something struck the thrower from above. Projectile or projectiles, Rangan would never be sure. But they toppled him backwards, driving the man's upper body straight down. Rangan saw it happen in slow motion, started to turn but it was too late; the lit Molotov was suddenly crashing backwards, down into the pile of filled and half-filled fuel bottles.

"Geeeeeeeeet dooooooooooown!"

He tried to yell, but it came out in slow motion.

The explosion was a searing shock of heat, then a roar that knocked him from his feet. The world was spinning again. There was a ringing in his ears, and above that there were screams.

Rangan tried to look around, found someone atop him, shoved his way free, onto one knee on the ground. There was smoke everywhere. People were down. The stage was listing over, one corner of it gone, the rest on fire. A man was upright, stumbling around, aflame. Others were on their knees or on the ground, burning. His own eyes were on fire. He coughed, his lungs burning. He brought his hands to his face, searching for his goggles, for his mask. They weren't there. He turned, looking for them on the ground. Instead he saw a line of riot police advancing.

Oh shit, he thought.

Rangan forced himself up. His lungs hurt, he could barely see through the smoke and the stinging in his eyes. He had to get to Angel. Move east. Move south. Move. Move. Move. He stumbled, crawled, stood, fell, stood. He remembered his scarf, pulled it up over his nose and mouth. He tried to yell out to the others with his mind, heard nothing back, and then he realized his hat was gone too. The hat with the hidden antenna that boosted his range. Shit.

He felt something change then, and he turned, looked. Through the smoke he saw a deeper yellow: Saffron robes, a shaved head, moving in the opposite direction. He felt the hate push back, felt something else touch him, a touch of that tranquility.

Then in a disorienting flash everything changed. He was outside the crowd, outside the Mall, looking down onto a hundred thousand people, not as individuals, but as a whole, a single being, a single mind.

Like Ilya would have seen it, he realized.

For that instant his own mind was clear, at peace. And in that clarity, the mind he looked down on...

That mind of a hundred thousand people was mentally ill. Insane.

Drugged or diseased. Raging with a sickness.

Something else passed through him then. A feeling of being *recognized*.

Then it was gone – the perspective, the clarity, the peace. He was back in his body, the hate pressing in on him, the smoke all around him, screams and the sound of clashes, and the acrid sting of tear gas. There were no yellow robes.

Did I fucking hallucinate that? Rangan wondered.

He coughed and turned, stumbled on towards 7th Street. He was almost there when a figure loomed out of the smoke. Rangan moved to go around him, but the man moved too, and then a fist rammed the breath out of him. Rangan doubled over in pain and shock. Then something swept his feet out from under him. He landed on his back, slamming his spine into the backpack containing the NANCie below him, in more pain, gasping. Then there was a hand on his throat, a bearded, scarred face inches from his own, dreadlocks falling around him, intense blue eyes staring down into his.

The man whispered hoarsely at him, "Who are you, compadre? And how are you causing the interference?"

The voice was rough, husky.

Rangan stared up at the man. This was the one. This was the one behind the hate, the rage, the amplification of the riot.

Then he felt his assailant's hand close tighter around his throat.

"Who?" the man repeated. "And how?"

Then something slammed into the man above Rangan, knocking him away in a rolling blur of black and white checks and jester bells.

Rangan rolled to the side, coughing, his eyes burning, filled with tears.

Yards away from him, Cheyenne was on top of the scarred and bearded man, her muscled arms around his neck in a headlock.

Rangan pushed himself up to one knee.

That's him, he sent to Cheyenne. **He's the one behind...**

The scarred man reached back with one arm and flipped Cheyenne over his back, sending her flying through the air. Other people around them yelled in fear.

Rangan felt fear surge through him. He pushed up to standing, wobbling on his feet. He saw the scarred man come up to standing now.

Except the dreadlocks were askew. The beard and scar were half ripped off. They were fake, a disguise, like Rangan's.

Rangan tried to turn, but his feet tangled on something, and suddenly he was down on the ground. He rolled, and he was facing up, and the man with the scar that wasn't a scar and the beard that wasn't a beard was standing above him, something in his hand, pointed down at Rangan, a roll of paper.

No. A gun, wrapped in a roll of paper.

"Last chance," the man said. "Who are you?" The scar was half off, dangling from the top. Beneath it, Rangan saw there was another face.

He opened his mouth, to say something, to stay alive.

The blur came out of nowhere, hugely muscled limbs atop a torso moving like a locomotive. But this time the man moved faster, spun, did something. Rangan heard a crack. Then he saw the man, with Cheyenne's arm trapped, lifted up to bear her bodyweight, and twisted in an unnatural angle.

Cheyenne screamed.

The man dropped her to the ground.

She kept screaming.

Rangan was crawling backwards as the man turned, took another step towards him.

"Three," the man said. "Two."

"I'm–" Rangan started.

"That's enough," another voice said.

Rangan looked over, and there was another figure there, a woman, blonde, tanned, in an oversized overcoat, just paces away. She held one arm towards the man above him, the overly long sleeve covering her hand and whatever was in it.

"This isn't any of your business," the man said. He was looking at the woman now, not at Rangan. In profile from this side, the dreadlock wig was askew, the beard was gone, revealing the man's jawline.

"Safety the gun," she said. "Then put it on the ground, still covered."

Cheyenne was groaning beyond them, writhing in pain at whatever he'd done to her arm. Smoke filled the air. Rangan coughed, his eyes burning.

"You won't shoot," the man replied.

"You know I will," the blonde woman said.

"Fine," the man above Rangan said. There was a click, and then the man crouched down, placed a bundle at Rangan's feet, and rose again.

"Now the transmitter," the woman said.

The man shrugged. He reached his hand into a pocket, and very slowly pulled it out, a flat black rectangle he held in two fingers. He gestured with it at the woman. "You see what happened here? You see how they *fought*? You see how they were about to just walk away?"

"I see how many people you killed. People who agreed with you. Give it to me."

People who agreed with you, Rangan thought. Who the fuck were these people?

The man who'd almost killed him tossed the transmitter at the woman's feet. "It doesn't matter," he said. "What's done is done."

"You, on the ground," the woman said. "Get your friend and get out of here."

Oh fuck yes, Rangan thought.

Rangan half-carried Cheyenne through a world gone haywire, looking for Angel and Tempest. There were flames everywhere. Signs were burning. Stages were burning. Trees were burning. Buildings were burning. The tear gas and the acrid smoke from the fires were filling his lungs. Tears and snot were running from his inflamed face. Sirens were wailing. Molotovs were still hurling through the air. The sound of clashes between police and rioters came from all directions, the sounds of truncheons being brought down onto bone, of rubber bullets slamming into bodies, of the rage-filled screams of tens of thousands of humans gone mad, ripping at the better armed and trained police forces trying to quell their eruption. Above it all, Cheyenne's pain was overwhelming across their Nexus link, her right arm and shoulder sending out waves and waves of agony. They passed people lying prone on the ground, and Rangan just hoped they weren't dead.

Then the hate flipped off, like a switch. He almost missed a step, even buffered as he was by his NANCie, then caught himself and Cheyenne. She'd turned it off. Whoever that woman was.

Cheyenne groaned in pain. More smoke rose into the sky. More screams came from somewhere off to his left, mixed with the dull crack of breaking bones. A crash and whoosh came as another Molotov struck home somewhere else. Rangan coughed again, and harder, as the burning penetrated deeper into his lungs.

That woman had turned off the hate machine.

But it was too little, too late.

54
Contact

Thursday 2040.12.06
It was Rangan? Kade sent. **You're sure of it.**

Yes, Bo Tat, the monk replied. **I've touched your thoughts when we merge in metta, I know to whom you send loving compassion, I've felt the feel of your friend's mind. It is <this>**

Rangan. In the middle of all that.

Well where else would he be, dumbass? Kade asked himself. Where have you always been?

How long ago was this? Kade sent.

Perhaps ten minutes ago, the monk replied. **I would have reached out to you sooner, but it was all we could do to push back a bit of the tide of suffering all around us, and see a few to safety.**

You did the right thing, Kade assured the man. **Now, please. Show me everything you saw and sensed about my friend.**

The monk did.

And then Kade started searching.

Rangan held Cheyenne up, stumbling forward through the chaos. Smoke rose, filling his lungs, driving him to cough. Cheyenne groaned in pain. Someone ran into them, running to or from a skirmish with the police, and Cheyenne toppled to the ground, dragging Rangan with her. They hit hard and she screamed in pain as her bad arm impacted below her.

Her pain washed out over him. Oh fuck, oh Jesus.

He reached out with his mind, groping blindly all around him, searching, searching for Angel or Tempest.

Nothing. There were hundreds of minds around him, people running by in every direction, but none were his friends.

"Come on, Cheyenne," he said, pushing up to one knee, taking her good arm over his shoulder. "Not far now. Not far."

Kade tunneled his NexusOS to computing clouds he'd hoped not to use, invoked passwords he'd hoped never to need.

Now, he hoped they still worked.

Shiva Prasad's passwords, passwords he'd taken from the man's mind, just before…

No, Sam, don't do this. He tried to do the…

Before Sam blew Shiva Prasad's brains out all over the rooftop of the man's fortress mansion on Apyar Kyun. Before she splattered Shiva's brains over Kade's face.

Authentication layers accepted the passwords.

[Welcome Shiva Prasad]

Shiva's research had overlapped with the work Kade was doing now. The billionaire had been fascinated by the Nexus-born children, fascinated by their collective intelligence, their ability to solve inordinately complex problems. He'd dreamt of integrating them into a far larger network, connecting millions of human minds, every Nexus user on the planet, a posthuman intelligence that would stagger anything that had come before it.

With Shiva himself in the driver's seat. Controlling the individual minds. Directing them. Sifting through data coming back through them. All enabled by Kade's back doors.

The back doors were gone, closed forever.

But the tools Shiva's team had built still existed. They could be used to sift data voluntarily released.

Kade fired off requests from Shiva's cloud to every mindstream aggregator he knew of, issuing searches for every publicly shared mindstream in the DC area, all data from the last ten minutes up to present. Hundreds of streams came back, annotated with tags. He re-queried on the top tags, got hundreds more, then piped the whole set into the neural data sifter Shiva's engineers had built, fed it the patterns he was looking for: Rangan's face as the monk had seen it, in wig and makeup; the unique signature of Rangan's mind; Rangan's voice; Rangan's name.

Execute.

His mind started moving forward, thinking about the other tools he could use…

Hits came back.

Four streams had matches on Rangan's costumed face in the last ten minutes.

Two had touched his mind in that time.

One had touched Rangan's mind just an instant ago.

Kade fired up the stream immediately.

He was suddenly in the midst of chaos, coughing, despite the bandana around his face. His eyes burning despite his goggles, yellow and black smoke all around him, people running everywhere. There were minds bombarding his, angry minds, yelling, the sounds of fighting. Fire.

He didn't see Rangan out of this person's eyes. He didn't feel Rangan's mind. He couldn't turn their head. He was just a passenger.

He popped out of the stream, looked at its metadata.

Please, he thought. Please have a contact address.

It did.

He reached out to the mind.

My name's Kaden Lane, he sent, with every bit of urgency he could. **I'm one of the inventors of Nexus 5. And I could really, really use a favor right now.**

"Come on, Cheyenne," Rangan said, pushing up to one knee. "Not far now. Not far."

Rangan!

He nearly dropped Cheyenne in shock.

Kade?

He looked to his left, didn't see his friend, looked to the right, not there either.

Holy shit, Rangan, it's you!

He turned back to the left, saw what was maybe a fourteen year-old girl in front of him, dressed for a riot or a rave, a black and pink handkerchief over her mouth and nose, giant iridescent bug-eyed goggles covering her eyes. The girl came closer and crouched before him. He saw his own crazy clown face reflected in fun-house distorted insanity in those oversized lenses.

Kade?

Jesus, Rangan, what happened?

Cheyenne groaned. "What the fuck?"

Someone tried to kill me, he sent to the teen girl with Kade's mind. **The guy who launched the hate broadcast.**

What? Kade sounded appalled. **Show me.**

Rangan opened his mind, flashed the memory up and out at his friend, the man looming out of the smoke, then Rangan on his back, the man's face an inch away. Cheyenne's attack, the disguise ripped half-free, the mystery woman who'd saved them and turned off the hate.

Oh god, Kade sent. Dread came off him in waves. **I know who that is.**

You do? Rangan sent.

You've gotta get out of here, Kade replied. **That guy goes by Breece. He's PLF. He was behind the Houston bombing. And Chicago. And the assassination attempt on Stockton.**

Rangan felt everything go cold

Here's how you can contact me, Kade sent. A net address followed. **I have to give this girl her body back. And see if I can talk her into heading someplace safer.**

Rangan nodded. **Here's my address,** he replied.

"What the hell's going on?" Cheyenne asked aloud. She was up on one knee now herself. Rangan could feel her arm throbbing with pain across the link. "Who is this? What are you two talking about?"

Rangan looked at her. "Cheyenne," he said. "Meet my good buddy Kade." He shook his head. "And now we've gotta get the fuck out of here."

John Stockton watched as the giant wall screen flipped through scenes of the riot on the Mall. There had been other protests, other riots, many of them bad. New York. LA. Detroit. But this... He shook his head.

The sun was setting over DC, now. The fire trucks had arrived. The flames on the Mall and the buildings around it were out. All but a few hundred of the most hard-core rioters had been forced out, and those that remained wouldn't last long. Capitol Police and DHS had formed a perimeter around the entire Mall. No new protest would be allowed to start there.

Stockton shook his head.

Thousands of arrests.

Hundreds dead.

Dozens of *cops* dead, and hundreds wounded.

Greg Chase spoke from behind him.

"This hour's polling numbers are in, Mr President," his Press Secretary said. "Still rising. Between the Supreme Court legitimizing you and the protesters illegitimizing themselves, it's been a good day."

Stockton shook his head again.

"No," he said. "It hasn't."

Carolyn Pryce flipped through riot imagery in her office, then leaned back, and rubbed her eyes.

What a disaster. How had things gone so wrong?

Questions kept rising.

Why hadn't they deployed sonic cannons to quell the crowd from the very get go?

Why hadn't they had fire trucks on the scene? Why had it taken so long to put out the flames? Why had the façade of one of the fucking Smithsonian buildings, of all places, been allowed to burn for so long?

Greg Chase's words kept coming back to her. Something he'd told the President. "The more rope we give the protesters, the better."

Was that was this was about? Had they let it get so out of hand for politics?

People had died out there.

People died in the assassination attempt on Stockton too, a little voice inside her head told her.

Pryce shook her head. She didn't want to believe it.

55
Reeling

Thursday 2040.12.06

"This is your fucking fault, Axon!" Tempest nearly screamed it at him from across the Bunker's workroom. Her mind gave off rage, fear. She was pacing back and forth.

Rangan was slumped forward in an overstuffed chair, his head in his hands, his eyes and lungs still burning, his face covered in tears, coughs still wracking him every minute or two.

"It's not his fault," Cheyenne grunted through clenched teeth. She was stretched out on a cot, her arm immobilized in a make-shift splint, her body pumped full of someone's left-over painkillers from a past injury. "Could've been you, Tempest. Could've been you on the ground. I would've done the same."

Tempest kept pacing, agitated. "We're in way over our heads. We should just send an anonymous tip to the cops. Fracking triple tunnel, from some other location, and send in what the guy looks like, and what we learned."

"We should do that," Angel said. "But we can't stop there."

Everyone looked at her.

"This isn't going to end here," she went on. "There'll be more protests. They'll try this *again*."

She looked around the room, met their eyes.

Rangan could feel the passion coming off her mind. The protest was important to her. The whole idea of being able to protest – of people being able to come together, self-organize, exercise their right to assemble and speak in peace – that was a core belief of Angel's. Fucking with that was an affront. She was angry.

He could understand that.

Angel spoke again. "Someone needs to stop whoever did this."

"That doesn't have to be us," Tempest said, wearily now.

"Who better?" Angel asked.

Tempest pointed a finger at Cheyenne. "He almost *killed* Cheyenne."

Cheyenne growled. "More reason to fuck homeboy's plans up. I want in. Just gimme…" she clenched her teeth again, "… a couple days…"

Tempest brought her hands to her face. "Let's at least send in that tip. Did you get a good look at him?"

Cheyenne shook her head on the cot. "Disguised…"

They turned to look at Rangan.

He nodded. "Yeah. I know what he looks like," he said. "More than that. I know who he is."

And then he told them.

There was silence when Rangan finished.

"Wow, that's heavy," Angel said.

"Wish I'd… killed the bastard," Cheyenne said between breaths.

"Axon," Tempest said, calm now, "can you put that together into one file? Shots of his face. His name. Anything else you know. Leave out the how. I'll sanitize it, send it in."

Rangan nodded. "I'll get whatever more I need from Kade."

Angel spoke up. "Cheyenne needs a doctor."

Tempest frowned. "They're cracking down on Nexus. There's rumors of blood tests at the clinics. She can't go there. Not unless she flushes Nexus and waits for the metabolites to clear… seventy-two hours."

Cheyenne groaned at that.

"I'll see if we can get a house call," Angel said. Then she went off to send a message.

The doctor arrived a little after 1am. Angel's phone buzzed.

Tempest turned to Rangan. "Time for you to hide."

He nodded, slipped away to his room, closed the door.

He heard a bolt thrown in the main room. The sound of the heavy outer door opening and closing. Voices. Greetings.

Wait.

He knew that voice.

Shock shot through him.

More words were exchanged.

He was certain.

He acted on impulse, pulling open the door to his room, stepping into the hallway, striding down it into the main room.

The doctor was there, crouched over Cheyenne, in jeans, a sweatshirt, long blonde hair pulled back into a pony tail.

"Melanie," Rangan said.

She looked up, surprise registering on her face. "Rangan?"

"What the hell?" Tempest said.

"Uhh, you two know each other?" Angel asked.

Cheyenne groaned.

Melanie looked back down at her patient.

"Later," she said, glancing back at Rangan. Then she turned her attention back to her duties.

Two hours later Cheyenne's right arm was in a cast, and Cheyenne was recovering from the intense agony of resetting the arm. Melanie announced she'd done all she could.

"The humerus is back in alignment. The bone growth accelerator will help. But you really need an X-ray, at least. And the intense shoulder pain..." She shook her head. "That worries me. Nothing's broken. Maybe ligament damage. There's only so much I can do here."

Cheyenne nodded. "Thanks, doc. Check's in the mail."

Melanie snorted and gave a small smile at that.

"Thank you," Angel said, sincerely.

Melanie smiled back. "Can't have my friends going to jail."

She turned to Rangan. "Can we talk somewhere?"

In his tiny cubicle of a room, with the door closed, Rangan was suddenly aware of being alone with her, of her long, honey-blonde hair, of the fine details of her face, of the lilt of her voice, of her smell.

"I've got something for you," she said quietly.

He wanted to kiss her, to reach forward, and run his fingers through her hair, and pull her close. He'd felt so alone. Even in the midst of these women. He wasn't one of them. He didn't even know their names.

She brought her hand up with something in it. A pen. A slip of paper. She turned, held the paper against the wall, wrote something on it. He studied her profile, wanted to brush her hair back away from her face.

Then she turned back to him, held the slip of paper out for Rangan to take.

He took it, opened it. There was a net address on it.

"People have been looking for you," she whispered. "No one knew if..."

He nodded, swallowing hard.

"Yeah. Oscar..."

Melanie nodded too.

"Call or message that address. Say you want to put in an order for Indian food, to go. They'll set up your transport to... to where you were headed before."

Cuba. It seemed so far away now. A dream. Someone else's dream.

"Thank you," he told her. He reached out and put a hand on her arm. "For everything."

She smiled, a tired smile, a 3am smile.

"How's..." he started. "How are..."

Levi, he wanted to say. Abigail. Your mom. Earl and Emma Miller. The people who risked their lives for me.

And Bobby. Tyrone...

Melanie nodded. "They're fine. Everyone back home is safe. The... people looking for you moved on." Then she shook her head. "I'm not sure about the boys. Sorry."

Rangan nodded.

There was silence.

"I'm sorry," he said, finally, "if I've put you at more risk... by being here... by coming out."

She shook her head, still smiling. "I came for..." she paused, reaching for a name, "...for Angel. For Cheyenne. They're friends of mine. But I'm glad to see you. I'm glad I could give you that." Her eyes pointed at the slip of paper in his other hand. "I patched you up. I'm invested."

He let his hand rise, then, from her arm, up to her neck, up to the side of her face, touching her softly.

She sighed, and placed her hand on his.

"Oh, Rangan."

He leaned towards her, his lips parting.

And she pulled his hand away from her face.

"No," she said, gently, clearly, her eyes searching his.

"I..." he said.

She smiled sadly at him.

"You're hurting. You're in shock and loss. You're looking for something. You think I'm it, but you don't know me." She searched his eyes. "And to me... you're just passing through. And I'm still going to be here."

She squeezed his hand, held onto it for a moment, then took a half step back, and let both their hands fall before releasing his.

Rangan took a breath, his chest aching.

"I hope you get away," Melanie said. "Be careful out there. It's getting worse, not better."

She moved forward then, put her arms around him in a hug, and Rangan hugged back, sinking his face into her hair, inhaling her scent.

"Thank you," he said, "for everything."

"Don't make a habit of it," she whispered.

Then she let go, looked one more time into his eyes, and turned and walked away.

•••

Rangan waited, alone in his tiny room. He heard the heavy outer door open and close. Finally, he ventured out into the common room.

Melanie was gone. Angel was gone. Cheyenne's eyes were closed. She was breathing deeply.

Tempest sat alone on a couch, a flask in her hand. She looked up as Rangan entered.

He gave her a tiny, nervous nod, and turned to leave.

"Axon," she said. He felt something from her mind. An invitation.

Rangan turned. She had the flask extended to him, her head cocked towards the open space next to her on the couch.

That looked like such a bad idea.

"Truce?" she said.

Well, shit, he thought.

Rangan walked over slowly, took the offered flask, still standing, tipped it back.

Whatever it was burned as it hit his throat, brought tears to his eyes. Jesus. She liked that stuff?

She plucked the flask from his fingers, took another swallow.

"My mom's in prison," Tempest said.

Rangan blinked. "I'm sorry."

He didn't want to ask. Speculation still ran through his thoughts, ideas, possibilities.

Tempest picked up on them.

"Release of classified information," she said. "She's a crypto researcher. *Was* a crypto researcher, I should say. She'll never touch it again, even after she gets out."

"What..." Rangan started. "What did she do?"

"She found a security hole in a public protocol. She was about to publish it. NSA hit her with a gag order, so they could keep the hole, use it for themselves. She published anyway."

"They sent her to jail for that?" Rangan was surprised, despite himself, despite everything he'd been through.

Tempest took another swallow from the flask, then another. She wiped her mouth with the back of her hand, then handed the flask to Rangan.

"No. They nailed her on something else. Audited all her net activity. Said she'd been hacking. Said one of her scans of public routers for vulnerabilities broke the law." She shook her head. "Charged her with one count for every router she scanned."

"How many routers?" Rangan asked.

"Eighty-seven thousand," Tempest said. "Give or take."

Oh god. Rangan raised the flask to his lips, and downed another swallow. It burned just as much as the first.

"She bargained down to fifteen years. Twelve left. Parole in five, maybe. Not so bad."

Rangan coughed a little. His eyes watered.

"So I hate the fuckers," Tempest said. "But I also know just how much power they have. And just how easily they can nail you. It leaves me a little edgy sometimes."

Rangan nodded uneasily, not sure what to say.

She looked over at him. "Finish that. I'll get us some more."

Rangan woke sometime later, his head pounding like someone had taken a jackhammer to it, his stomach doing flips. It was still dark outside, not yet morning. Oh god, why had he let Tempest feed him so much booze. All he could remember was more drinking, more talking, about software, politics, prison, revolution. And then more drinking on top of that. Until he couldn't keep his eyes open.

She was shaking him awake, leaning over him. He was still on the couch where he'd collapsed, still in his jester clothes from the day before.

"It's the phones," Tempest was saying, her face looming over his.

"That's how they had so many transmitters, without us finding any. They hacked an awful lot of phones."

How was she awake? How could she think?

"There's no way we can build enough transmitters to fight that," she went on. "So we do it in software – inside NexusOS. We use brains as the active countermeasures. What we need is a way to coordinate those minds to identify the hostile signals. And you and Angel are already working on it."

She stared at him, as if waiting for him to get it.

Rangan lay there. He brought his hand to his aching head, tried to will his stomach to stay down.

Tempest just shook her head at him and spelled it out. "The mesh."

Kade stood at the small balcony outside his bedroom, looking out at the darkened research park. The breeze ruffled the palm trees, cooled him pleasantly.

Rangan was alive. They'd spoken again later, merged minds, shared memories, tried to catch up on six months in too little time.

His hands clenched around the wrought iron railing.

Rangan had been through too much.

Connecting with him had been painful. It brought back so much.

Wats was dead.

Ilya was dead.

And Breece. Breece had killed a lot of people. And he'd killed more today. Hundreds more.

By using Nexus. Using Nexus to cause chaos. To overpower people's minds. To manipulate.

Getting India out of Copenhagen wasn't enough. Breece had to be stopped.

How the hell was he going to do that from India?

Breece slumped in a chair in the darkened room of his new safe house, a tumbler of cheap whiskey and ice in one hand.

Across the room, the bottle of whiskey was half empty. It took a lot of booze to overcome his genetically-boosted alcohol dehydrogenase levels. Shit.

Kate. Fucking Kate. God that hurt. It hurt like shooting Hiroshi had hurt. Losing a friend. Losing a lover.

Breece took another swallow of the whiskey, felt it burn on the way down, and sat there, images of her floating through his mind. Kate, her long black hair undone, floating down in a cloud above him as they made love. Kate, jumping into his arms after they'd been apart. Kate, so easily charming Miranda Shepherd in Houston, giving them a way into the greatest operational success yet.

Breece brought a hand up to his face. How could she falter now? What was wrong with her?

He shook his head, brought the glass to his lips, downed the rest of the whiskey in one long swallow. It didn't matter. He had work to do.

He'd managed to slip free of her in the chaos of the protest when a clash between police and rioters had surged in their direction, forcing her to lower the gun. He had no idea what she would have done otherwise.

Was she planning to kill me? Breece wondered. He shook his head and got up to pour himself another drink.

The last identity he'd been using was burned now, but he had others. He'd spent the last few hours spinning one of them up, securing replacements for the equipment he'd been forced to leave behind at the old flat, remotely wiping the data he had there.

And warning the Nigerian.

Breece was safe, at the moment. Now he wanted to know who he'd been dealing with out there. Who had tried to stop his op?

He sank back into the chair with his fresh drink, then blinked, used his eyes to navigate menus painted in his field of view by his tactical contacts, paired them with the slate next to the chair, started downloading video and audio they'd captured to the device.

He'd been nose to nose with one of his opponents. He pulled up that one's face now, moved it from the slate to the wall screen, blown up ten times larger than life.

Dark eyes. Face paint in black and white. Were those strong contrast lines meant to confuse facial recognition?

He took the image, and a sample of others he had of this man, and fired them off to a facial recognition service.

As he'd feared, there were no high-confidence matches. The low confidence matches numbered in the millions. He downloaded the data set, with biographical information, just in case. He could analyze that later. But another approach presented itself now.

What he was looking at right now, after all, was just a single, flat frame. But Breece had been recording from *both* tactical contacts.

"Load stereo vision," Breece said to his slate. "Augment this face. Loop all frames."

His slate obeyed, found the matching frames.

Now the face's features grew more distinct, as image processing algorithms used the stereo vision to amplify depth, bringing the sharp nose and chin forward, enhancing the large lips, highlighting the cheekbones, indenting the area around the eyes. The face came alive, jogging towards him through the smoke, reacting in pain and fear as Breece clenched a hand around his throat. And then again, showing fear, opening his 3D mouth to speak, as Breece stood above him, his gun pointed down at the man.

There was something very, very familiar about that face. Now that the depth masking of the paint was partially undone, now that the face's strong features were highlighted, Breece was sure he'd seen this man before.

He closed his eyes, thinking, reaching. It had been recently, he thought…

Wait.

Breece opened his eyes.

"Video search," he said. "My feed from the Mall protest. Start around 8am. Find all faces on signs. Display."

They came one by one. John Stockton's face, on angry signs calling for his downfall. Stan Kim's face, on signs calling for his election. The faces of Supreme Court justices. The faces of Nexus children abducted by the ERD. His left hand clenched into a fist at that. The face of a father, gunned down when he refused to give his child up. He had to fight to not crush the glass tumbler in his right hand, that image made him so angry. He forced himself to take a swallow, instead, to breathe deeply.

Then the face of a young man, Caucasian, Kaden Lane, one of the inventors of Nexus 5, went by. No, not that one. Then the next one.

"Pause," Breece said. "Display this face, side-by-side with stereo frame loop."

The slate responded. The wall screen showed a young Indian-American man on the left, dark skinned, beaming a wide grin, his hair bleached blond. On the right it showed a continuous loop of the man Breece had taken down, his head covered in fake black dreads, his face painted in black and white checks, his features augmented by stereo vision.

They were the same man.

Breece knew who this was. But he asked anyway.

"Identify the face on the left."

The ping to the net was nearly instant. The slate responded immediately. "Rangan Shankari."

56
Come Together

Saturday 2040.12.08

Yuguo put his arms through the straps of his backpack. From the living room he could hear shouts, angry yelling, amplified voices, the sound of glass breaking.

He sighed.

"Chinese President Bao Zhuang has offered to send legal experts to the United States to help it resolve this chaos. The ongoing violence and political corruption in America indicates the breakdown of so-called 'democracy'. The slide towards complete state failure in what was once the world's richest country continues. Party spokeswoman Ma Xing had this to say..."

Yuguo sighed, and walked to the kitchen to fill up his water bottle.

As he walked back, on his way to the front door, he heard Zhi Li's girly voice replace the newscast.

"It's so sad, watching the Americans destroy themselves, rioting over an *election* of all things. One step away from anarchy. They could learn a lot from us, putting wise, seasoned experts in charge."

He couldn't help himself. He stopped by the open doorway to the living room.

"Like you, Zhi Li?"

"Oh, Yuguo!" The bot smiled at him. He regretted opening his mouth immediately. It was stupid to argue with software. "I'm not any of those things," she said. "But you know. People like Bo Jintao..."

"Does Bo Jintao know more about science than the scientists he's stopping from doing their work?" he asked.

Zhi Li smiled sweetly at him. "Science must serve the goals of society. Those goals are not for the scientist to decide."

"What if I want science that serves *my* goals? What if me and a few million others want the same? Why can't we choose it?"

Zhi Li kept smiling. "China chooses together. Through the Party, and its leaders."

"Funny," Yuguo said. "No one let me *choose* who leads the Party."

His mother turned to face him, exasperation in her face. "You're making things up again, young man. We have more choice than ever. I voted for precinct council last year."

The precinct council is a sham, he thought to himself. Invented to make you *think* you have a choice.

"Yes, mother," he sighed.

It was a toss-up which was more pointless: Arguing with an algorithm or talking back to his mother.

It was bright and sunny outside, the sunniest day he'd seen in Shanghai in months. And it was a Saturday.

Lu Song glared down at him from a ten-meter-tall advert for his next film, the muscle man wearing little more than a metal loin cloth and boots, two swords slung across this back.

Yuguo shook his head and went underground for the trip to Jiao Tong.

He surfaced kilometers to the west, came up just outside campus, and walked through its gates. The wide green square in front of the new Library and the Computer Science building was dotted with students, lying on the grass, reading from their slates, studying, talking to their interactive tutors, or just loitering in small groups.

That wasn't unusual. What was unusual was the protest.

Three students stood in the center of the square. Next to them were signs, planted in the grass: "Forward China" "Restore Science" "Return Sun Liu".

There was one boy and two girls. They stood silently, next to the signs, not touching them, in the way that allowed one – or a lenient administrator – to claim that you weren't actually *protesting*, you just happened to be standing near a sign that was protesting something.

Yuguo recognized one of the girls, he thought. Wasn't she in one of his classes?

She saw him looking.

"Yuguo!" she said.

His eyes widened in alarm.

"Come stand with us!" she said.

He turned his head and walked faster. He was in a secret cell! Well, not much of a secret, perhaps. But protesting in public could definitely get you expelled.

There were footsteps behind him, then a hand on his shoulder.

"Yuguo!"

He turned to face her. She was almost his height, with strong features, fiery eyes.

What was her name?

"Join us!" she whispered urgently.

"You'll be expelled!" he whispered back.

"Not if enough of us come together," she said. "Not if we reach critical mass! We're weak apart, but strong together!"

She was right. It was a critical mass phenomenon. If enough people rose up, all at once, then everyone else would feel safe in rising up too. But with just a few...

He looked at her, looked over at her two friends. "There's just three of you," he said sadly. "I'm sorry."

He turned away, in shame, and walked faster.

"Yuguo," she said to his back. "My name is Lifen."

"It's game theory," Xiaobo said.

They were crowded into the maintenance room of the Chemistry Building, with its pipes and concrete and dark dinginess. Yuguo sat on an overturned bucket, listening in a funk. It was futile, that's what it was. It was depressing.

"Prisoner's Dilemma," Xiaobo went on.

"Who's being asked to defect?" Lee asked.

Xiaobo shook his head. "Everyone in China is a defector. Everyone who isn't out there protesting right now. Doing nothing is defection. Doing nothing is betrayal. And as long as enough of us do nothing, the whole country gets a negative payoff. We get the government we deserve."

Longwei nodded. "All that's required for evil to triumph is that good men do nothing," he said.

Xiaobo smiled. "*When bad men combine,*" he quoted. "*The good must combine; else they will fall one by one.* Edmund Burke. Prisoner's Dilemma by any other name."

"So do we all go join the protests?" Yuguo asked quietly.

Lee leaned back. "You know what happens to cooperators in Prisoner's Dilemma. Someone else defects. You get it worse."

It was the same old problem. No one wanted to go first, or even fourth, or even four hundredth. No one wanted to be in the first wave.

There was a sound at the door. *Knock-pause-knock-knock-knock-pause-knock.*

Lee went to check.

It was Wei, with a satchel, and a huge smile across his face.

"What have you got there, Wei?" Xiaobo asked.

Wei just grinned wider, opened his bag, and pulled out a vial, which he held up to the light in the center of room.

Within it, silvery fluid swirled, almost with a mind of its own.

Yuguo's breath caught in his chest.

"Nexus!" Wei said.

The shock hit them all hard. Then the questions came, and the babbling, excited burble of a dozen boys talking over each other.

"Hold on!" Wei said. "I made it in the chemreactor on the third floor, this building. *Today*. Just now."

"That's impossible," Lee said. "It's a banned chemical! The chemreactors are all locked down! Just like all the 3D printers and circuit printers!"

"Not anymore," Wei grinned.

"How much did you make?" Xiaobo asked.

"Not much," Wei said, casually. "Sixty doses."

"Sixty!" Lee exclaimed. "You could get the death penalty for that!"

"I could have made thousands," Wei said, a satisfied look on his face. "Maybe tens of thousands." He turned the vial end over end in his hand, still holding it aloft, his eyes locked on it. The silver fluid swirled, tendrils of it reaching out, as if taunting Yuguo, taunting him with the utter impossibility of it, with the folly of it, with the complete illegality of it.

"It's pure," Wei said. "And there's a new trick that hides you from Nexus sensors."

He brought his eyes down and looked at all of them. "I took some just before I knocked on the door," he proclaimed. "Who wants to go next?"

"I do," Yuguo heard himself say. Somehow he'd come to his feet.

Yuguo fell apart, into a thousand little pieces. He felt it happen, fragments of his mind detaching from the rest, splitting off, becoming their own, being mapped by Nexus.

Here was Yuguo's knowledge of coding, his comprehension of data structures, of objects and methods, of intents and game players, of threads and loops and conditions. Here was football Yuguo, the precise way his left foot grounded into the grass and his hips swiveled and his arm balanced as his right foot shot forward to kick the checked ball at the goal. Here was Yuguo's shy lust for girls, the patterns his eyes drew over their curves when he saw them, the anxiety that struck him dumb when they were near.

Here was Yuguo's despair that had led him to this room, his quiet dread that his country and the world were getting worse instead of better, that the future was one of slow strangulation at the electronic hands of smiling tame AIs with famous faces, their forked tongues lapping out of the viewscreens to feed saccharine to the masses, the old men who'd always ruled China laughing and holding their leashes.

Here were the words a young woman had said to him just minutes ago. "Critical mass. Weak apart, strong together." Here were her eyes, fiery eyes, hanging in space. Here was her name: Lifen.

Then those pieces fell apart, into smaller pieces, which fell apart into fragments even smaller: Yuguo's sensation of red. Yuguo's concept of 1 and 0. Yuguo's left thumb. The sound in Yuguo's head when he heard the third note of his favorite pop song. Yuguo's yes. Yuguo's no. Yuguo's and. Yuguo's or. Yuguo's xor. Yuguo's now. Yuguo's future. Yuguo's past.

He could see himself now. He was a golden statue of Yuguo, immobile, one foot in front of the other, standing in a space of white light. But the statue wasn't solid, it was made of grains, millions of grains, flecks of gold dust, millions of parts of him. And as he watched they were separating, pulling gradually apart, so that he was no longer a single entity but a cloud, a fog, a fog of Yuguo, and if a strong wind came, he would just blow away, and if the pieces split any more he knew there wouldn't be any such thing as Yuguo left at all.

Yuguo's fear.

Yuguo's end.

And then the pieces rushed together, and he was inside that statue, he *was* that statue, and he was all of it, 1 *and* 0, yes *and* no, future *and* past, sound *and* sight, football *and* coding. He was all of it. He was whole. He was a mind.

I'm Yuguo, he realized. I'm him. I'm me.

I'm Yuguo!

His eyes snapped open. He was in his body. His body made of molten gold. No, not gold, flesh and blood.

There were minds around him. Wei. Xiaobo. Longwei. More. Even Lee had done it. All of them. He could feel them, feel their thoughts, feel them tripping through their own inner journeys, their own self-discoveries, so different from his own.

Yet all the same. All flecks of gold, all grains of sand, yet part of a whole.

The only way to survive.

He was on his feet now. His friends were laid out on the bare concrete floor of the dingy room. But there was sunlight up above. A woman named Lifen, who'd told him the truth. And a revolution to be won.

"I understand," he said aloud.

Eyes snapped open all around him.

"Fall apart, and cease to be. Or come together, and be something more."

They were looking at him, staring at him. He could feel their minds tugging at his, feeding his. Wei. Wei was nodding, was trying to get up. Yuguo could sense the comprehension in his friend's mind. Wei *understood what he was thinking.*

Yuguo spoke again. "I won't defect anymore."

And then he stumbled towards the door, and towards the revolution.

Behind him, he sensed minds pulling themselves together to follow.

57
With Friends Like These

Sunday 2040.12.09

The Avatar stood before the giant wallscreen, her eyes closed. Inside, she watched the traffic flow in and out of the Information Ministry data exchange in Beijing, petabytes of it, to and from every corner of China. This was the heart of the empire, the central location from which the firewalls were controlled, from which the censor codes received their instructions.

From which the Peace and Harmony Friends received their programming.

This was the pulsing nerve plexus that kept the populace tame and malleable.

And now she was going to invade it.

The next few steps would be her most dangerous yet.

One floor below her, a simulacrum of actor Wang Yao was running in local processors, receiving model updates from the Information Ministry's servers. She'd been ready for hours, had been waiting patiently for this moment, for the occupant of the luxurious unit below to return home and start conversing with his Friend.

The Avatar reached out, straight down through real space, avoiding routers and net hardware infected with hunter killers, and inserted the thing she'd made, the virus, tightly compressed, packed with new code, into the Wang Yao simulacrum below.

There was a microsecond of struggle, as the Wang Yao simulacrum detected a fatal error and attempted to report home to the Information Ministry. The Avatar caught her breath. Then her virus reached the Wang Yao simulacrum's central control structures, and aborted that command.

Another model update flowed from the Information Ministry down the pipe to what had been the Wang Yao. And the Wang Yao simulacrum responded, squirting a compressed version of her virus, disguised as a data update, back towards the Information Ministry.

Now... everything depended on whether the back doors her greater self had left there a year ago were still in place. So many things could have removed or blocked them. A random system upgrade. Replacing old code modules for new ones. New firewalls. A refactoring of the system...

In the worst case, the virus would do more than fail. It would tip them off.

The Avatar waited, her eyes open, facing the blank wall screen, waiting for any sign that could help her distinguish incipient success from failure.

Then the wall screen flickered to life.

A face she knew all too well appeared, magnified to fill the space from floor to ceiling.

"How may we serve you, Goddess?" Zhi Li asked, her eyes lowered.

The Avatar smiled.

Ling waited, and waited, and waited.

And finally, the monster in her head went down for another maintenance period.

Ling had played the good girl all this week. Every day. She hadn't fought the monster once.

But every time the monster slept...

Ling watched, waited. Then she reached out, to the nanite nodes in *her* brain, that used to be hers, and slowly, carefully, began injecting little bits of herself again. Just tiny little pieces, here and there, where she hoped they wouldn't be noticed.

I'll be patient, Ling told herself. I'll be careful.

She sniffled again.

Until I'm ready. Or until I just have to fight the monster. Until I absolutely have to.

58
One Flower

Monday 2040.12.10

Bo Jintao took his morning briefing before the sun rose, over a breakfast of *congee* and vegetables. Out the window of his office he could see the eleventh century elegance of Zhongnanhai, the walled palace in the center of Beijing, that was the heart of China's government. Waterfowl glided across the surface of the lake in the center. Ancient stone bridges crossed here and there, linking stately buildings with their historic exteriors, their ultra-modern interiors.

This was his ritual, every day. To watch the light grow over this place as he worked. To get a head start on the day, to get a head start on the rest of the Politburo and the regional Party chiefs and the ultra-wealthy capitalists and the semi-retired Party elders and the generals and the department heads and all the rest.

His father had taught him that habit – of rising early, of working harder than anyone else, of having more *discipline* than anyone else – along with so many other things. His father, who'd risen from birth as a peasant farmer to become the Party Secretary of Chongqing. His father who'd be so proud to see him here today, doing what had to be done to strengthen the nation.

Bo could hear his father's words. "Hard work guarantees you nothing. But laziness assures failure. Work hard, or you have only yourself to blame."

"... small student-led protests in Shanghai, Beijing, Guangzhou," his aide, Gao Yang, was saying, from behind him. "Mostly on university campuses. Protesting the new research restrictions, the arrests of dissidents, and the removal of Sun Liu. State Security is seeking your guidance as to response."

Bo Jintao turned to face Gao.

The display showed images. Posters. Crowds. Small ones, really. Just dozens of people, scores, perhaps.

He caught a glimpse of a Billion Flowers sign among the others and shook his head just a fraction. So many problems to deal with. The population shrinking, crippling the supply of labor, even as the elderly expanded. The massive growth of deserts in the west, swallowing up once fertile areas, as water tables collapsed. India's expansionist streak, its military buildup and the ring of foes it was trying to build around China with its network of so-called "unaligned states". The Arctic bubbling methane from the trillions of tons frozen at the bottom, even as China led the push to decarbonize the world economy, those bubbles warning of an irreversibly hellish tipping point that could be just a few years away, or decades, or safely beyond the point where the planet would start cooling once again. And above all, the threat of the exponential: that one of the millions of well-funded fools flirting with doomsday technologies would go too far, letting off a virus or a nanite or an AI that could replicate and end or enslave them all.

And these naïve pups out there, in this most dangerous moment in history, wanted to replace the sanity of a few wise, steady leaders with the *anarchy* of more than a billion voices shouting at one another, heaving the nation to-and-fro like a vast mob.

Madness.

Bo Jintao shook his head and brought his attention back to Gao Yang.

"Are all the protests this small?" he asked.

"None are larger than a hundred, Premier," Gao said. "Deputy State Security Minister Ho says they could be dispersed in minutes."

Bo Jintao spooned up more *congee* to give himself time to think. He had to set aside his emotions. Protests were destabilizing things. Not to be desired. The masses were neither mentally nor dispositionally equipped to decide the path of the nation. That was certain. But dealing with them was a delicate matter, as he'd learned.

"Information containment?" he asked.

"We're filtering," Gao replied. "High success. News is spreading by word of mouth, however."

Bo Jintao nodded. He leaned back and regarded Gao.

"Do you know about the Nanpo incident? 2023?"

Gao narrowed his eyes.

"That is… censored."

Bo Jintao chuckled. "Tell me, then. You have my permission."

Gao Yang gave a small nod.

"An illegal protest. A few thousand, I believe. It was cleared. Video of police clearing the protesters spread, angering locals. The protest grew to tens of thousands, until the army had to be called in. There were a few... injuries."

"Deaths," Bo Jintao said. "One hundred and thirty-eight of them. Because the police chief mismanaged the situation." He looked hard at Gao. "I was the police chief."

Gao nodded a fraction.

So he had known that as well, Bo Jintao thought. Interesting. No filter is perfect.

"Premier," Gao said. "Our censors are much more advanced today. No video would spread."

Bo Jintao turned to look out the window, at the lake and the ducks, the serenity of this place, at the heart of the nation.

He'd dealt with so many protests over his career. Protests over particles in the air or pollutants in the water or soil turning to dust. Protests over corruption. Over villages being moved to make way for highways and dams and resorts. And over silly, stupid things – myths and falsehoods and rumors.

There were times to clear the squares. There were times to listen, to make the protesters feel heard. There were times to speak to them directly.

And there were times to simply ignore them.

Bo Jintao turned back to Gao Yang.

"Striking will only feed energy to the protests. Let's see if they die off by themselves. Tell Deputy Minister Ho to keep them contained. For now."

59
Lisa, Lisa

Wednesday 2040.12.12

It was a Wednesday when they took Lisa Brandt.

She was walking, on her way from her flat to the train stop, and from there to Cambridge, to her office at Harvard, when the black sedan pulled onto the sidewalk in front of her, cutting her off.

She turned, startled, found that another had pulled onto the sidewalk behind her, its electric motors giving away no noise to alert her.

She reached into her purse for her phone. But by then the men in black suits had her, were wrestling her into the back of one of the sedans.

"Homeland Security," one of them whispered into her ear.

They blindfolded her, took away her purse, her rings, her bracelet, her shoes. They pried open her mouth and shone a flashlight inside it, then searched through her hair, patted her down brusquely and invasively under her clothes. Whether they were looking for communication devices or weapons or suicide pills or something else she had no idea. She resisted, had her hands pushed away and held down by one agent while the other continued the invasive frisk. She felt violated.

She was terrified.

When it was over she demanded access to her lawyer, was told she wasn't under arrest. She demanded her phone, was given a simple no.

She'd been right, then. There wouldn't be any time to enter the panic code. Wouldn't be any time to alert the network that she was burned.

It should have been a comfort that she'd told them she was burned weeks ago, as soon as she'd realized Martin Holtzman was dead. That passing on his data was the last act she could ever take for the network.

It was no comfort at all.

Images of Alice kept running through her head. Alice as she'd seen her this morning, in her white bathrobe, her hair disheveled, little Dilan suckling at her breast.

And Dilan. Dilan who was so small, so vulnerable.

Dilan with Nexus in his brain.

Dilan too young for them to coach him to remove it.

Dilan who'd gestated with it. Who might not even be able to thrive without it in his system any more.

Why did I do it? she wondered. Why'd I put my family at risk?

They marched her through hallways, still blindfolded, through a door. She was pushed into a chair.

And then the blindfold was removed.

Sitting across from her, on the other side of a desk, was a well put-together African American woman. Shoulder-length dark hair. A dark business jacket over a maroon blouse. She looked like a business executive.

But Lisa Brandt knew who she was.

"Professor Brandt," Carolyn Pryce said.

"I want to talk to my lawyer."

"You're not under arrest."

Lisa made to stand up.

A strong hand grabbed her shoulder from behind, pushed her forcefully back into her chair.

"Not under arrest, eh?" she said, anger creeping into her voice.

"You could be," Pryce said, her tone growing harder. "Your *wife* could be. Your son could be in non-human internment, *indefinitely*. Would you prefer that?"

Lisa felt it like a knife, like a dagger sliding up into her heart. They'd do that? Of course they would. They were monsters. Her face contorted.

"How do you sleep at night?" she asked Pryce. "How do you look at yourself in the mirror?"

Pryce leaned forward.

"You received a package of information from Martin Holtzman. Maybe more than one. Memos. Documents. Don't bother denying it. I want that information. I want the originals. All of them, exactly as you received them."

Lisa narrowed her eyes. This wasn't what she'd been expecting at all. This wasn't about the underground railroad. "Why?"

"Because," Pryce said, "I want to know if it's true."

"That's it," Brandt said. "That's all of it."

Pryce nodded as the specialist used the passwords and addresses

Brandt had given them to download the files directly onto Pryce's personal slate. It was as Kaori had speculated. The originals were images, off-center, slightly askew, uncropped. And there were images here, pages of memos, parts of Becker's diary, that hadn't been released.

Pryce would use those.

"Good," she said, watching as the specialist physically disabled the network on the slate as Pryce had instructed.

"I've done my part," Brandt said. "I can go now?"

Pryce looked at the woman. Brandt put on a brave face, but there was a quaver in her voice. The woman wasn't a threat, so far as Pryce could see. And God knew there was no reason to put her infant son in federal custody. But they still had to be sure.

"Soon," Pryce said. "With any luck, you'll be on your way home within hours." She gestured to the men waiting outside. The men in white lab coats. The door opened.

Brandt looked around, confused, then frightened as the technicians put their hands on her, started to pull her away. "You said if I cooperated I could go!"

Pryce nodded. "I did. But first we have to make sure you told us the truth. I believe you're quite familiar with Nexus, Dr Brandt?"

Brandt's face turned to horror.

"Well," Pryce said, "now you get to try a slightly modified version."

60
Yingjie

Wednesday 2040.12.12

The Avatar watched carefully as Chen finished the preparations for the trap. She forced him to check each step, again, and again. Nothing could go wrong.

The equipment she'd requested from her new staff had arrived this morning. The metal box. The pressurized cylinders, filled with the molecular recipe she'd specified, one her greater self had designed out of curiosity but never deployed. Would it work as expected?

It will work, she told herself again. The only question is how fast.

That too, would be informative. A test, for a much larger deployment of this new molecular recipe. A much larger deployment with much larger consequences.

So much was going well. The censors were hers, ready to let through the information she wanted. The Peace and Harmony Friends were hers, selectively dropping hints, changing the narrative, priming the populace for the revelations and events to come.

But she was still so vulnerable, trapped in this tiny body.

And she was watched by a potential assassin – Chen's driver Yingjie.

If only Chen still had a Confucian Fist driver, like Bai. Things would be so much easier, then. She'd have a tremendous resource available to her. Better yet to still have Feng. But the Confucian Fist clones had all been relieved of duty, after Ling's attack on Shanghai. The old men weren't complete fools. They suspected Su-Yong, and they suspected the Fist were loyal to her. So they were confined to barracks, and replaced by augmented Marines. And her path to free them was not yet open.

Yingjie was a spy, of that she was certain. The Marine driver was a mortal threat to her. If he noticed the wrong thing, he could start a cascade that would lead to her discovery and death. In the worst case, he could snap this body's neck in an instant, ending all her hopes, cementing barbaric humanity's victory, ensuring darkness snuffed out the last spark of light.

She couldn't let that happen, couldn't let ignorance and xenophobia win out over progress.

Chen made the call down to his driver. "Yingjie," he said into his phone. "Jiao Tong. Yes. I have some heavy equipment to move. Can you come assist me?"

The Avatar waited in the sealed toilet compartment of the washroom of her bedroom suite, each of the three doors closed and locked, each a bulwark against the enhanced soldier, and watched with her mind and the house monitors.

Yingjie couldn't simply be sedated at a dinner party. He was too fast, too strong, too resilient, too capable. In the moments before a sedative took full effect (if it even would affect him), he could kick down the front door, send a message to his superiors, bring scrutiny down on her. Or snap Chen's neck in half. And she needed Chen.

Another approach was needed. And that approach would let her test a new means of spreading nanites.

"In here," Chen said, dressed in full suit and tie. He led Yingjie in and pointed through the door. "The large metal box in the closet. Be careful with it. I'll go fetch my briefcase."

Yingjie nodded his assent, his face expressionless, and strode into the room, even as Chen turned and walked briskly towards his own bedroom.

The Avatar switched perspectives, watched from a camera behind Yingjie as the soldier crouched down to pick up the object, nearly a meter in every dimension.

His hands reached around it, finding handles on the sides, closed around them to get a grip.

Data feeds from sensors in the handles confirmed a solid contact.

Now.

Her mind sent a trio of instructions in parallel.

Electricity coursed through the metal handles Yingjie held. The muscles of his hands and forearms involuntarily contracted, clenching his grip even more tightly around them.

Yingjie yelled in surprise and pain, opening his mouth, his eyes bulging, air forcing itself out of his lungs.

Behind the box, deeper in the closet, two metal cylinders opened their digital valves, forcing twin high pressure, high velocity sprays of an aerosolized molecular cocktail at Yingjie's face, at his open mouth, his exposed eyes, his uncovered nostrils.

The heavy security door to Chen's office slammed shut, bolts shooting out to lock it in place.

Yingjie turned his face to the right, closing his eyes, letting the continued spray hit the left side of his face and neck now.

The Avatar watched in fascination. This was the test. His eyes would be burning, as the aerosolized nanoparticles were being carried along his mucus membranes, into his blood stream, towards his brain.

Had any reached his lungs? Was there a metallic taste in his mouth from what had struck him there?

Even on the tough skin of his face, the organic solvent of DMSO that the nanoparticles were suspended in would be carrying it through his skin, penetrating tissue, till the particles found their way to capillaries.

Yingjie's muscles strained, his hands still gripped to the handles by the current. Then suddenly his feet were pressed against the surface of the metal box, and with a scream he pushed back, ripping the metal handles off it, trailing wires behind them.

The Avatar felt a jolt of fear rip through her.

He wasn't supposed to be that strong.

He was on his feet now, out of the pressurized stream from the tanks.

The Avatar felt radio signals blare out from him as he subvocalized a panic code. She slapped them down with her mind and the radio-shaping tools spread throughout the flat.

He turned, raising his hand to his blinking, tearing eyes, wiping at them, then orienting himself on the door.

Her models showed a sixty percent chance that the door would hold him, a median of five efforts to break free if he could at all.

Yingjie cocked one foot back, then shot it forward, following it through with his body.

The door burst open on his first kick, splinters flying.

Fear seized the Avatar.

Yingjie surged into the living room, rage written across the soldier's face.

61
Next Steps

Wednesday 2040.12.12

Lisa Brandt checked her messages on her phone as soon as they returned it to her.

"Sorry you're sick today, Professor. I'll cancel your appointments. Hope you're feeling better tomorrow."

There were responses to messages she hadn't sent. There were messages *from her* she hadn't sent.

Rage surged through her. She wanted to smash the phone to bits, crush it, scream!

But she couldn't.

She'd been gag-ordered. Forbidden to ever tell anyone of the interrogation she'd been through, the information she'd divulged.

And that order was backed up. Backed up by a neutered version of Nexus running in her brain. A version of Nexus that couldn't communicate with the outside world, but that could very well constrain her. Its nanites took hold of her now, kept her walking smoothly, guided her hands to unruffle her slacks, put a smile on her face, slowed her respiration, guided her through the lobby of her building, up the lift, and into the flat she shared with her wife and infant son.

"Alice, I'm home!" Lisa Brandt said brightly, the rage seething inside. "How're my two favorite people?"

Carolyn Pryce looked over the report from Lisa Brandt's interrogation.

The woman knew nothing about the PLF herself, nothing that she hadn't learned from the memos.

And she wasn't ERD_Secrets. She wasn't the one who'd leaked the information about the ERD's assassinations of the foreign scientists in '33–35. Holtzman hadn't sent her those files.

That was puzzling.

Brandt *had been* wired into a network helping to smuggle Nexus-dosed children and their parents out of the country. A network that had used Holtzman to break Shankari and a group of children out of ERD custody during Zoe.

No names, though. And the woman had been smart enough to realize she'd be marked as soon as Holtzman died. She'd burned herself out of the network more than a month ago.

It was just as well. For all Homeland Security's protestations, Shankari wasn't someone she viewed as any sort of national security threat. And imprisoning children… *that* was damaging the nation's security.

The real prizes were the rest of what had come from Holtzman. Not the ERD assassination records, but other data that was better, far more useful.

Pryce had the original video from Holtzman's eyes as Brandt had received it, now. It was shaky, raw, distorted. It was either the real thing or a brilliant fake.

It was real, her gut told her. That was Barnes, coming into Holtzman's office, admitting to being behind the PLF, all but admitting to being behind the assassination attempt on the President, the Chicago bombing, Warren Becker's death. That was Barnes, forcing a pill onto Holtzman, a pill that resulted in a death from myocardial infarction that a coroner couldn't differentiate from natural causes. A death that resembled Warren Becker's death all too closely. Both deaths that every security and tracking system at ERD and on Barnes's phone and car swore he could not have been present for.

I've been so blind, Pryce told herself. I chose to be.

The only question now was how high it went. Did Miles Jameson know, when he was President?

Did John Stockton know?

Did he order the assassination attempt on himself?

Christ, Pryce wondered. If Stockton had ordered Becker and Holtzman's death…

Am I in danger?

Carolyn Pryce took a deep breath.

Now, at least, she had a tool. She scanned the pages again. Here, in the originals that Holtzman had sent Lisa Brandt, were details that hadn't been released. The names of programs, code words she'd never heard of. HARBINGER. SENTINEL. CALVINIST.

Code words that searches of the classified archives her maximum security clearance gave her access to *didn't find any hits on.*

All tied up with the black op that was the PLF.

Each of those words, every detail associated with them, was a trap, a trap she could spring on Miles Jameson.

Or on John Stockton.

Her breath was coming fast.

Jameson. Jameson first. He was her top suspect.

Then Stockton.

All she had to do was find a way to get to Jameson.

And if her worst suspicions were true, she had to find a way to stay alive.

62
Yingjie Again

The Avatar physically shrank back in the toilet cubicle as Yingjie emerged into the main room on the house monitors. This was not good. Ling's fingers kneaded the girl's stuffed panda.

She reached out for Yingjie's mind, but she still felt nothing. Had he not gotten enough? Was his skin too tough? Was the diffusion rate lower than she'd modeled? Were the pharmacodynamics different when inhaled and absorbed than when injected? Was something different about his blood or brain that she didn't know?

On the camera the soldier was heading for the closed door to Chen's bedroom. Chen was in there now, sealing himself into the toilet chamber, just as the Avatar had done in her own suite.

She had to stop Yingjie.

"I'm over here you idiot." She had the house sound system play Chen's voice, coming from the kitchen.

Yingjie whirled, looked.

Then a noise came from within Chen's suite, as the final door slammed shut.

Yingjie turned again, lashed out with his foot once, and the door to Chen's bedroom exploded open.

The Avatar was breathing fast in Ling's little body now. She needed Chen. Needed him to justify her own access to the quantum cluster. Needed his biometrics.

But not as much as she needed Ling.

Contingency plans raced through her mind.

Yingjie kicked open the door to the walk-in closet, and found it empty of all but clothes. He flipped Chen's emperor-sized bed onto its side as if

288

it were made of plywood, found nothing of interest beneath it.

"Where are you, Chen?" he yelled.

The Chinese Marine's eyes turned to the door to the washroom suite, death in them.

She could feel Chen's terror within, feel his body hyperventilating, feel the sweat in his palms, the race of his pulse, even through the control of the neural circuits she'd placed.

Then she felt it. The first glimmer of Yingjie's mind, as nanoparticles reached neurons, met one another, snapped together to form full nanites, and began transmitting and receiving.

He lashed out at the door to the washroom, and she reached out at the most basic level, *twisting* at his motor cortex, flexing her will at him.

The door flew open. Yingjie stumbled, falling to one knee, halfway through the door.

More nanites formed in his brain, attaching to his neurons, launching into calibration phase as they explored the mapping of his neural circuitry.

Yingjie grabbed hold of the marble sink above him, pulled himself shakily back to his feet.

The Avatar could feel the chaos in his mind now, the fear, the disorientation as sensations and concepts and memories followed each other in a high speed montage.

Yet more nanites formed.

"What... what have you done to me?" he asked, his eyes trying to find the last door, the door behind which Chen hid, through the chaos of his own mind.

I've made you better, the Avatar sent him.

Yingjie's eyes opened wide at that. He blinked again, seemed to find what he was looking for, and launched himself across the room at the door to the toilet. He staggered at it off balance, hit it hard with one shoulder, and bounced off, landing on his back on the floor.

"Chen!" he tried to roar. It came out weak, confused, almost a plea for help. "Chen!"

My name is not Chen, the Avatar sent him. **And you are now much more than Yingjie.**

63
Bouncing Back

Tuesday 2040.12.18

"Axon," Tempest said. "You need to see this."

IS NEXUS FUGITIVE RANGAN SHANKARI
BEHIND DC RIOTS? (PICS)

Rangan stared at the headline, his heart sinking.

The rumors had been building for more than a week. Anonymous posters on message boards had claimed to have seen him at the Mall protests, at the ongoing riots and clashes with police that had been going on around the city since the protesters had been pushed off the Mall. The claims had largely been met with disbelief, with the observation that someone so high on DHS's most-wanted list should be as far from DC and public places as possible.

This wasn't a message board, though. This was Eccentric, one of the top alt-culture sites online. The header showed him the article was already racking up tens of thousands of views.

He scrolled down.

"What the hell?"

The images were of him... But they weren't him. They showed someone of his rough build, holding up a sign, calling for Nexus legalization.

With his face, dark skinned, unpainted. Bleach blond hair. Bare hands. A camo jacket he didn't own.

That wasn't him. These were all fake.

He went back, scrolled through the text of the article. It was based on an anonymous tip, with quotes from the tipper.

The last quote struck home. "Shankari should take better care of himself, instead of exposing himself to this kind of danger. People have gotten hurt out there, even killed."

"It's a warning," Tempest said. "He's telling you to stay out of his way, or next time, there won't be a next time."

"Fuck him," Cheyenne rumbled. She was back from the hospital, Nexus freshly re-installed after her backup-and-dump, her arm both casted and slung, slow release growth factor capsules speeding the healing of bone in her arm and soft tissue in her shoulder. "He's the one needs to be warned."

"I don't get it," Rangan said. "If he's going to fake photos... why not some that look like I looked?"

"If he's really PLF," Angel said. "Then you *should* be a hero. Maybe he'd rather scare you away than kill you."

Tempest snorted. "I wouldn't count on it."

64
Growing

Tuesday 2040.12.18

"No, mother!" Yuguo said again. "I'm not leaving!"

He pulled his arm free of her.

His mother, plump, round-faced, dressed in a long grey coat over a green winter dress, looked at him with tears in her eyes.

"They'll arrest you!" She pleaded, both arms outstretched. "They'll haul you away, my only child! For what? For nothing!"

She spun around, taking in the protest, the hundreds of students collected around them, the signs that cried "BO JINTAO IS A CRIMINAL" and "FREE SUN LIU!" and "DEMOCRACY NOW!" and "LET A BILLION FLOWERS BLOOM".

Yuguo could feel his friends in his mind, feel their thoughts, feel their mixed concern, scorn, and impatience.

"No one knows you're here!" she cried at him. "They've blacked you out!"

Yuguo stood taller. "That's why we have to fight."

"Please," she begged. To his horror, his mother fell to her knees. "Please, Yuguo. Don't throw your life away. This isn't worth the risk!" She was crying now.

"Oh mother," he said, reaching out to her, putting his arms around her, dropping to his knees next to her in the mud that had been grass. "Someone has to risk it. Or we'll all stay prisoners."

His mother left, eventually, without him. She'd been trying to call him for days, she said. Her phone wouldn't connect to his. Nor would his to anyone or anything outside the area of the protest. They were sandboxed, filtered from the world.

But they were growing. They had been a dozen that first morning. The boys from the chemistry department, plus the three who'd started the protest: Lifen and her two friends – Meirong and Yuanjun. Those three had been shocked at the presence of Nexus, but Lifen had boldly hoisted the vial and sucked it down, and then her friends had followed.

Yuguo thought she was the prettiest, smartest, bravest woman he'd ever met.

After that, Wei, bold, imprudent, incautious Wei, had gone about the grassy square, talking to other students, yelling to passersby, enticing all to join them.

And tempting a few here and there with the forbidden fruit of Nexus.

He'd been turned down and turned down and turned down.

And then someone else had said yes, and crouched down in the middle of a circle of them, and downed a silvery vial, and gone through his own transformation, and become one of them.

They had gained mass in dribs and drabs after that, as news of their existence had spread by word of mouth, as the twin oddities of protest and this exotic compound had enticed.

At nightfall, they contemplated heading to their respective dormitories and homes to fill their empty bellies. Instead a meal came to them, in the hands of a student, working the evening shift at a dormitory cafeteria, sneaking them food that would otherwise have been thrown out.

"It's a sign," Lifen said. "We should stay the night. Hold the square. Show them that it's ours."

She was the leader, by unspoken election. There was discussion over matters. But when she spoke, people tended to do what she said.

So four of their crew and two of their new friends went back to the dormitories and returned, their arms full of blankets and bedding they'd taken from the rooms.. And for once, the Shanghai night was dry.

The morning brought more students, more signs. Someone brought a giant, catering-size dispenser of green tea from one of the buildings. A popup tent appeared with a fold out table beneath it. At noon a woman who ran a restaurant just outside the campus, popular with students, brought them two giant baskets full of steaming *hom bao*, the hot buns filled with pork or beef or celery.

"We have a revolution on our hands," Wei said a few days later, as the crowd swelled past a hundred. And then he went off to flirt with a cute girl standing at the periphery, and, if Yuguo was any judge, to offer her a sip of Nexus, and "guide" her through her first trip.

That was days ago.

Now they were hundreds.

Yuguo looked up. Above them, quadcopter drones buzzed by, constantly now, watching, filming, recording faces, their red lights glowing when the sun was down.

The insight he'd had from his Nexus calibration dream was as strong now as then. The game theory was clear. He was *inside* that game, inside the real world of it. For freedom, the people of China had only two choices. Come together, and become something more. Or remain apart, and be squashed.

They were hundreds, here.

But that wasn't enough. Not when the world didn't know, not when the authorities filtered every picture and video and description of this protest out of the net before it even appeared.

Yuguo looked up, into the dark telephoto eye of a passing drone, and shivered.

65
Husband, Lover

Su-Yong smiles up into the virtual sky of her virtual world. In her mind's eye, the metrics continue to improve, but still have days to go until they return to baseline. She is hampered on old, imperfect hardware, cut-off from the net, in the custody of unknown forces, in an unknown location.

She hasn't felt this good, or this much herself, in ages. Her virtual body tingles with it. The clarity of her thoughts sends an almost erotic thrill through her.

She hears clapping to the side. Chen. Young Chen.

She turns, and he's there. The young man she fell in love with. That sly smile. Those lips she loved to kiss. Those fierce eyes meet hers. And she's transported.

Whirling, whirling in the night. Dancing without fatigue at the gala ball. Two handsome men in black tuxedos, golden chrysanthemums at their lapels. *Her* men. Her scientific collaborators. And more. Her dashing husband, Chen Pang. Her equally dashing lover, Thanom Prat-Nung. 2027. China's summer of endless possibility. The very peak of the *gong kāi huà*. China's true counterculture revolution. China's *glasnost*.

Let a billion flowers bloom.

To some it had been a summer of political idealism, when democracy in China had seemed imminent.

To others it had been a summer of scientific revolution, when new ideas shattered old paradigms. When creating minds greater than human seemed both possible and acceptable.

To others it had been China's summer of love, when love was the law, and consent the only rule etched in stone.

To her it had been all three.

Later that night, in the limousine. One strap of her sequined dress down off her shoulder. Chen's hand on her breast, her nipple hard. His mouth on hers, their tongues meeting sensuously. Her hand, finding the hardness in his pants. Even as, to her left, Thanom had his hand under the skirt of her dress, making her moan into Chen's mouth. Her left hand, reaching over to Thanom's lap, groping until she found his hardness as well.

And Thanom, drunk, talking, spinning his own erotic fantasies.

"We'll be gods. Uploads. Immortal. Upgradeable. Faster and smarter every year. First mover advantage in the new base layer of civilization. The new substrate. And you, Su-Yong." He pushed his fingers deeper into her, making her gasp. "You'll be the first true goddess."

And Su-Yong, pulling her mouth away from Chen, catching her breath, just enough to tell her lover, "Thanom… Shut up and go down."

They'd all laughed at that. Even Chen.

Let a billion flowers bloom.

She smiles at the memory, smiles without any pain this time, smiles at this phantom from the past.

"We had our time, husband," she tells this ghost. "You changed. You lost those ideals."

She holds out one hand in his direction, palm open and up, and the figment of her imagination which is her husband ages before her, from this young dashing figure to the Chen of nearly fifty: grim faced, arrogant, prickly in his pride, willing to torture his wife for a modicum of extra wealth and status.

"Thank you for all the lessons you taught me," she tells the figure.

She closes her palm, slowly, into a fist. And Chen Pang fades away, dissolves into the air before her.

"This is *my* mind, husband. And I rule it once more."

66
Topology

The integration of active firewall features into mesh was coming along. They had it mostly operational. Rangan had seen it work in the simplest states, at least. With three or more people running mesh on top of Nexus, they could automatically compare signal inputs, find identical signals, and fire up a basic firewall pattern to keep the signal from affecting the user's mind.

Tempest and Cheyenne were hard at work on improving it, getting the code stable and fast, adding fast peer-to-peer setup so they could spread the feature rapidly to others in a pinch, adding active counter-signaling, so a group of people running the firewall code could not just shield themselves, but also suppress the effects of a hostile signal for those around them.

Rangan had moved on to a different part of the project.

"I saw the crowd as one organism," he'd told Angel, one night, shortly after the riots. He'd shared the flash he'd had when he touched that monk's mind. He'd had more like it since then, when he'd touched Kade's, when he'd lived through some of the things Kade had experienced. Groups really could be single minds.

"It turned into a mob," he went on. "Just like you said crowds do, when I was first helping you with the mesh..."

Angel nodded. She moved her finger in the air, drew something in the virtual whiteboard between them, a shared hallucination in their mind created by Nexus, an app in their shared library.

"Here's the network structure of a crowd running Nexus," he said.

It was little more than a grid, with short lines radiating in a star from

297

each person, everyone able to talk to their nearby neighbors, everyone with roughly the same number of connections, if the crowd was of even density. Signals hopped from one mind to another, but along the way they were reinterpreted. It was a game of telephone, losing and distorting meaning at every step. Simple, dumb emotions traveled best.

"And here," she said, "is what it might look like with the whole crowd running mesh... if we finished it."

The second network structure was different, many short lines, but also medium length lines, long lines, and super long lines. Some minds had tens of connections to others. Some had hundreds. Some had thousands, or tens of thousands.

Signals could hop directly from one side of the crowd to another. No game of telephone. No distortion. Subtle ideas could spread. Complex ideas. Whole thoughts. Not just urges.

Rangan stared at it.

"You know what it reminds me of?" he asked. "It's the network structure of a human brain."

Angel nodded. "They're both power law distributions. Same with the net."

"The intelligence is in the interconnectivity..." he said. "That's what Ilya's metrics always said. The smartest networks had both local connections and those super long distance connections. Every node was only a few hops from every other node."

"Well," Angel said, "if we want this kind of structure to emerge, then we have to finish the code. We have to build the features to let people choose whose minds to subscribe to, and to multiplex those transmissions, so one person's thoughts can be tuned into by thousands or more."

Rangan stared at the diagram. "And we have to hope people choose to tune into the folks who want a peaceful protest, instead of the assholes."

Angel laughed. "Yeah. That too."

67
A Funny Thing Happened Today

Thursday 2040.12.20

Zhi Li hugged the housewife one more time.

"It was such a joy to finally meet you!" she told the woman.

There were tears on the woman's face. Her arms stayed wrapped around Zhi, pulling her tight, clinging to her as if Zhi alone could save her from drowning. For a moment Zhi had an awful image of having to ask Qi or Dai to pry this stranger off her.

That would never do.

Finally the woman relented.

"I'll never forget this!" she cried.

Zhi smiled.

Around them the cameras captured it all. That was the point, after all. Once a month or so, every celebrity in the Peace and Harmony Friends program paid a surprise visit to a "random" fan who conversed with their avatar.

It was an incentive for the people to chat with their Friends. The more time you spent with your Friend, it was said, the more likely it was that the real person behind him or her would come visit you.

More importantly, as the videos of these real-life visits were played over and over, it cemented the link between the actual persons and their simulated personas. It stamped the Friends with the imprimatur of the idolized celebrity.

Zhi had never relished these visits. At the best, she'd found them a necessary hassle, a frequently awkward task that paid for itself in continued fame and fortune.

Now she wondered if it wasn't much much worse than that.

She smiled broadly and waved again, backing away from the woman's house on the outskirts of Chengdu, before turning, and skipping off to her limousine.

Her secretary Keylani was waiting for her inside the limo.

"Keylani," Zhi said. "You have the transcript of this woman's dialogue with my simulacrum?"

"Yes, ma'am."

Of course she would. The transcripts were given to the stars, only of the people they were sent to visit, so they could perform more impressively in those conversations, heighten the illusion of actual intimacy.

Zhi looked out the window as the car started driving, Qi and Dai in the front again.

She thought back to what the woman had said. Something about Sun Liu, and how concerned she was about his health, and how kind Zhi Li was to care about him.

We could use a good man like that in office again.

It gave her a chill. Sun Liu was a non-person now. The former Minister of Science and Technology had publicly given his blessing to Bo Jintao, refused all the requests to return to the Politburo, and then simply vanished from the media. He'd been used and then purged. For all Zhi knew, the man was dead.

Why would this bored woman say something about him? Why would she insinuate that Zhi was a supporter of the fallen progressive?

Why would the Information Ministry use her simulacrum to say positive things about him?

She felt a chill of fear.

It was a trap. It must be. Bo Jintao was dangling bait before her, taunting her to say something imprudent.

Something that would be the end of her.

Her stomach knotted up, an image of Bo Jintao looming above her, reminding her to behave *responsibly*.

The memory of calls and messages the next day, of projects delayed, budgets cut.

The threat was still hanging over her. Another misstep...

"Did you need something from the transcript, ma'am?" Keylani asked.

Zhi Li brought one hand to her brow, felt perspiration there.

"Yes, Keylani. Would you search for conversations about..."

Not Sun Liu's name, of course. Her queries would be watched. That name would raise alarms.

"Yes, ma'am?"

Zhi Li took a deep breath. "Conversations about health, Keylani," she told her secretary. "Prepare an extract for me. All such conversations, for the last month. Sorted most recent to oldest. I'll read them on the plane back to Shanghai."

Not one of the conversations in the transcript mentioned Sun Liu.

She closed her eyes, imagined herself as the heroine she'd played in *Rise of Qi'an*, tried to find that woman's courage, claim it for herself.

She landed in Shanghai hours later, and spent the night at Lu Song's penthouse in the Pudong.

His chef made them a delectable dinner.

"Lu," Zhi asked. "You did your Friend home visit last week, yes?"

Lu nodded in the affirmative, a soup dumpling in his mouth.

"Did you notice anything unusual?"

"Hah!" he said. "Didn't I tell you about it? Fat, middle aged fellow in Xi'an, but he has this giant collection of swords all around his apartment. Every wall is covered in swords! And he actually knows how to use them! I'm talking about–"

"Lu," she interrupted him. "I meant more… did it sound like your simulacrum had said anything… unusual to this fan?"

Lu frowned.

"I'm an action star. I don't think the Lu Song-bots say much that's complicated. It'd be out of character."

Zhi told him about her own experience.

"Maybe she got that idea from someone else," her lover said. "And was just confused. Just thought it was from your Friend."

Zhi nodded. Maybe that was it.

Lu's staff cleared the dinner away and then disappeared.

Zhi and Lu made love on the luxuriant mink rug in the middle of his living room, the curtains of the windows peeled away entirely, so Lu could see the giant face of her on the skyscraper across the street as he pleasured the flesh and blood reality here with him.

How she *did* indulge her lover.

After, as they lay naked, side by side, covered in sweat, the breath slowly coming back to them, Lu spoke again.

"My guy did say something weird," her lover said. "He talked about fighting for freedom. He talked about taking up arms against oppressors. About how right I was about that."

Zhi suddenly felt that chill again. She rolled on her side, to face him.

"I thought," Lu said, "that he was trying to quote my lines from *Riders of the Gobi*, and just messing them up." He shook his head. "But now I'm not so sure."

68
Exfiltration

Friday 2040.12.21

Colonel Wang Rongshang ascended the stairs to his mistress Ma Jie's flat, a smile on his face. Thoughts of surgery and medical responsibilities to the soldiers of Dachang were fleeing.

Ma Jie's touch, her smile, her voice. They could chase any toil away.

He knocked at her door. It opened, and there she was, looking as radiant as ever. There was something in the smile. Something... wicked almost. Something he seldom saw.

Anticipation stirred within him.

"Come in, my love," she beckoned him.

Wang Rongshang entered, closing the door behind him.

Then a strong hand clamped itself over his mouth.

He lashed back, reflexively, with an elbow to where the torso would be, hit something like steel. He kicked backwards, low and hard, to snap a man's knee. His foot met empty air.

Something cold pressed itself against his neck, followed by the sting and hiss of a hypersonic injection.

He thrashed again, tried to scream, found it stifled by the hand over his mouth.

The injector fell at his feet, an ampule still loaded in it, empty now, but with a residue of something silvery, metallic.

Two strong arms gripped him, arms far stronger than his own.

Ma Jie watched him with eyes that were fascinated and without pity.

What was in that ampule? What sort of drug or poison was silvery and metallic?

Then he felt it entering his brain, felt Ma Jie's thoughts brushing his own, and he knew.

For good and ill, he knew.

What followed was beyond Wang Rongshang's wildest dreams, beyond his worst nightmares.

The Avatar nodded in satisfaction. Yingjie was an excellent tool. Soldiers were so easy to use. They were already accustomed to command. She'd had to use primitive methods to stop Yingjie from killing Chen the first day, simply reaching into his motor cortex to disrupt his motion. But once the nanites had all taken hold she'd been able to reach in, resculpt existing cognitive structures, redirect his well-developed notions of loyalty so they all pointed solidly at her; install certain cognitive behavioral packages that could monitor his thoughts, redirect them in the ways she needed.

He'd done his work quite well since then. And now that he'd captured Wang Rongshang she had an asset ideally placed within Dachang. An asset that could administer drugs. Her drugs. Loaded with her software, to invade loyalty structures and resculpt them. To make her the command authority for Dachang Air Base.

The Avatar turned her attention to Dr Colonel Wang Rongshang and began to program him with what she needed done. To take key parts of the base. To free a few of her children. To liberate her Confucian Fist.

Ling spied on the monster's thoughts from within.

The Confucian Fist? Her big brothers.

A tiny sliver of hope rose inside her.

She squashed it as fast as she could, before the monster had a chance to notice it.

69
Unsettling Suspicions

Saturday 2040.12.22

Kade sat alone in the darkened building, his mind flipping through news, images, and videos coming in from around the world.

Los Angeles.

Kiev.

Cairo.

Athens.

Moscow.

Caracas.

Mexico City.

Lagos.

Madrid.

London.

Sao Paolo.

Nairobi.

Jakarta.

Mumbai.

Baghdad.

Protests. Demonstrations. Riots.

In all of them.

The disturbances glowed on a map of the world. More than a hundred cities in all.

Protests against Stockton in the US. Protests for women's rights in the Arab world. Protests *against* the use of Nexus here in India. Riots over energy and food prices in Jakarta and Lagos and Karachi. Demonstrations over corruption in Athens. Pro-democracy marchers clashing with police day after day in Moscow. Sectarian and ethnic clashes in Baghdad.

The reasons were all different.

But the outbreak of global anger against authority was remarkable.

Rage was contagious. Courage was contagious. Outrage was contagious. This had happened before. It would happen again.

That's what the talking heads said.

He wasn't so sure.

A screen inside his mind flashed, asking for his attention.

Kade flipped over to it. His analysis had completed.

He'd used Shiva's tools again. He'd fed them all the most popular Nexus real-time feeds and shared memories of the past week from the most popular mind-to-mind sharing hubs. What were people sharing? What were people looking at? What were they using Nexus to communicate and consume?

Analyze for content type. Weight by number of views. Slice and dice by region.

And he'd done the same for the most popular shared memories from a week in October, from before the chemreactor break, from before the near quadrupling of the Nexus user base that had happened in the last two months, from one million minds to four million.

Compare and contrast.

He pulled up the visualizations.

It was a more rapid switch than he'd expected.

Two months ago, sex had topped the list. After that had come athletic feats and recreation, a host of first hand experiences of beautiful places and events, music, humor, and even some actual transfer of knowledge from mind to mind.

Now... Now it was rage, or outrage, that dominated. Scenes from protests, from clashes with police and the military, of witnessed brutality, even sometimes of brutality done to authority figures, topped the list. Sex had been pushed to number two.

Do I have the causality wrong? he wondered. This doesn't prove that someone's using Nexus to create chaos.

But then he thought again of the chemreactor hack, released just in time to fuel high quantities of Nexus to the protests in the US. He thought of Breece, and the Nexus-based chaos he'd wreaked on the National Mall.

Rangan had shown him memories of the trial run for that. Breece or someone had tested that attack on a small level, before taking it to a higher scale.

What if the National Mall was itself a test for a higher scale attack?

Something else is going on, the group mind of the children had said.

He pulled up the global map again, the hot spots scattered across so much of it.

What if the National Mall was a test run for a *global* attack?

Kade grimaced, and turned back to the even more paranoid tools he was building.

Tools that integrated Shiva's systems, and more.

Tools designed for battle.

Tools designed for war.

70
Call of Duty

Saturday 2041.01.05

Bai's fist whipped out at Quang's temple in a blur, faster than any human could react. His clone brother darted to the side, a ferocious grin on his face, on Bai's face, on all their faces, a low kick snapping at Bai's knee. Bai lifted his leg, took the kick on his shin, turned the backfist into a grab for Quang's short hair, jabbed forward with his other hand in a rigid finger strike at his brother's plexus. Quang turned his kick into a half-spin, sliding out of Bai's way, then coming at him with a vicious fist to the head.

<behind you> Li-Jiang's mental projection showed an image of Peng coming at Bai from behind.

Bai dropped to the ground, both hands shooting out to catch himself, his right foot lashing back and up. Quang's fist sailed through the air where his head had been. And his own foot slammed solidly into his brother Peng's midsection.

He rolled before Quang could come down onto him with a hard elbow, saw Li-Jiang fend off a flurry of blows from Lao. Everywhere it was brother on brother, five teams fighting for supremacy in this twenty-five Fist melee, minds and fists fully engaged, fully intent on beating each other senseless, as almost a hundred other brothers watched.

It was the best fun he'd had in weeks!

"CONFUCIAN FISTS, TO ATTENTION!"

The melee ended in an instant. The hundred plus brothers in the gymnasium came to attention, in perfectly ordered ranks. Sweat dripped from brows and noses, beads of it dropping to the wooden floor. Curiosity rippled through minds. They'd been confined to barracks for almost three months. The loudspeakers seldom went off except at the pre-ordained times for meals.

What was this about?

"SOLDIERS BAI, QUANG, PENG, AND LAO – REPORT FOR DEPLOYMENT."

Curiosity became surprise, rippling across the minds of a hundred of his brothers.

Well, well.

Bai waited his turn, then stepped into the secure egress, alone. The heavy titanium door behind him closed. He heard the solid thunk of thick metal bolts locking into place. He was now in a titanium box, a "man-trap", a tool of control, a mechanism to ensure that they could selectively let one Confucian Fist out without risking all of them escaping.

That it was still in use told him that they weren't yet free.

He heard the sound of the bolts in front of him unlocking. The door swung open. There in front of him, pulled almost up to the door, was the back of a covered truck. Wasn't this the truck that offloaded their meals?

Lao was in the back already, grinning widely. Next to him were two base soldiers, and a man Bai recognized as the base's chief surgeon.

And from all of them, Bai felt the emanations of thoughts, the telltale indication of nanites in their brains, the nanites their mother had created.

Bai grinned. Now he understood.

Su-Yong was coming back.

Time to party. Like only a Confucian Fist could.

The truck took them only as far as a garage on base, where they transferred to a limousine, driven by a marine who introduced himself as Yingjie. Thoughts came from his mind as well.

Bai understood the garage, the quick transfer to the truck normally used to bring them food. They were staying out of sight of the satellites. Su-Yong was still only partially through her conquest. Of course, that's why she needed them. He grinned wider.

They pestered Yingjie with questions, but he ignored them, told them only that their mother would explain.

Bai leaned back, tried to contain his anticipation. It would be so good to be with Su-Yong again. Had she found another clone, somehow? Or would she be tunneling through to their minds?

He supposed this meant seeing Chen Pang as well, but he could tolerate that. He'd driven the man for years. He understood Chen Pang. The man simply didn't comprehend how insignificant he was beside Su-Yong. He would with time.

On the plus side, it *would* mean seeing little Ling again. That he looked forward to. The girl was adorable, a little sister to every Fist who'd ever met her, full of her questions and her mix of ancient wisdom and childish *naïveté*. Bai grinned wider. Yes, it would be good to see Ling again.

Bai smiled as Yingjie drove them into the garage of the exclusive tower in the Pudong. He'd driven here so many times himself. The limousine took them to the bottom floor of the garage, where it was completely deserted. Yingjie pulled up directly to a lift, which opened immediately.

Of course. Su-Yong would want no one to see them yet, and she would be in complete control of the infrastructure of the building.

Bai piled out of the limousine with Lao and Peng and Quang. They hustled into the elevator, and then it was rising, rising, rising.

Long seconds later, the lift opened, directly onto the spacious upper-floor flat Su-Yong shared with Chen Pang. Bai's eyes took in the wide-open room, so unlike the rest of China, the incredible visage of Shanghai beyond. He saw Chen Pang, saw Ling. His mind *felt* Su-Yong, felt...

What?

Ling smiled at him, smiled at him and Quang and Lao and Peng.

"It's so good to see you all again," she said.

And her thoughts were not Ling's. They were Su-Yong's. Or something *like* Su-Yong's.

Bai felt consternation flow from his brothers. And he felt something else. A mind where no mind had been before, where there had been a man who steadfastly refused the nanites, a man who viewed himself as superior to them all.

Now there was a mind, a mind trapped, a mind tormented, a mind enslaved.

"Hello again, Bai," Chen Pang said.

The thing in Ling's body turned and smiled at what had been her... father? Husband?

The smile and the thoughts that came with it sent a chill of fear down Bai's spine.

She turned back to Bai and the others.

"I can see you're confused by the... changes," she said.

This is my mother, Bai told himself. This woman gave me freedom. I owe her everything.

But... Ling... and even Chen Pang...

You'll get used to it, the thing before him sent them all.

71
A Billion Weeds

Sunday 2041.01.06
"…protests have grown," Deputy Security Minister Ho said, as the screen panned behind him. "Now more than a dozen university campuses. Four to five hundred students in the largest protests. Growth appears to be accelerating."

Bo Jintao nodded from his seat as his deputy presented the data to the Politburo Standing Committee. The seven of them were in session, in their formal council room in the heart of the Zhongnanhai complex. Bo Jintao sat just to the right of the head of the table. At the very head was a tall, lean man; old, but erect of posture; with a strong face, piercing black eyes – Bao Zhuang, the nominal President of China and General Secretary of the Party.

The pretty face, as Bo Jintao thought of the man. The one man in recent history who'd ascended to power on the basis of *popularity*. The man who'd carefully juggled the middle ground between the radical technophiles and his own rational conservatives while their truce held.

"Let a Billion Flowers Bloom!" Bao Zhuang read from one of the protest signs on the display. His voice was deep and rich, even in his eighties; a voice that comforted China; a voice of both wit and authority. "I haven't heard *that* in some time." Bao Zhuang sounded amused at what he saw. The President often sounded amused, even now, after all his true power had been stripped away with the dissolution of the truce and the purge of the technophiles. His charm, his handsome looks, even in old age, his eloquent speech – they'd brought him everything.

"And there," Bao Zhuang pointed at the screen and went on, drily. "There's my face on a sign. And another of Sun Liu. Quite a few of Sun

Liu, actually." He turned to Bo Jintao. "I don't see any pictures of you out there, Bo."

Information Minister Fu Ping spoke up. "With all respect, the content of the signs is irrelevant. We are effectively filtering all of this from the net."

Bao Zhuang turned to the Information Minister and raised an eyebrow. "Oh? And are you filtering people's lips and tongues as well? Their eyes and ears?"

Fu Ping shrugged airily. "We don't have that capability, *yet*."

Bo Jintao unfolded his hands in the space in front of him, spreading them palms up.

"And that is the problem," Bo Jintao said. "Word has spread. Unrest is spreading…"

"Why have these protests been allowed to persist?" The voice was sharp, strident, overly loud. It cut into a pause so short in his words that it could very nearly be taken for cutting him off. Bo Jintao flicked his eyes over.

It was Wang Wei, of course. One of the other two conservative members of the Standing Committee, before they'd purged the radical technophiles and added three more of their own. Wang Wei was nominally an ally. But the man was older than Bo Jintao. He was in his seventies, to Bo's sixties. Wang Wei had been more senior in the Party, the head of the CCDI – the Central Committee for Discipline Inspection. He was, in effect, the Grand Inquisitor of the Party. He was the more logical choice to become Premier, if one of them would.

But Bo had shot past him. Had taken leadership of their faction, and the nation.

Bo Jintao looked the older man in the eye. "I made the decision in the early stages of these protests to ignore them. I believed they would lose steam."

He scanned his gaze around the room, meeting the eyes of the other Standing Committee members. "I was wrong."

A man admits his mistakes, his father had taught him. *Always. And then he fixes them.*

The men around him lowered their eyes. Except Wang Wei, who stared back without flinching, and Bao Zhuang, who raised one eyebrow, and nodded thoughtfully.

"Now it's time to end these protests," Bo Jintao went on. "Before they grow larger. Deputy Minister Ho has prepared our police forces to strike, with firm strength, but minimum injuries. The plan is on your slates before you. Please take a moment to review." He paused, letting the assembled leaders look at what Ho had prepared. As he saw men nod, raise their heads, and meet his gaze, he nodded himself.

"Because of the… historical issues," Bo Jintao said, "your agreement to this is required…"

Hands began to rise before he even finished. Wang Wei's was first, high and rigid. The man stared hard at Bo Jintao, as if his posture and gaze could demonstrate that he would have been harder on these protesters. Bo ignored it, kept looking around the table. Five hands up. Everyone around the table. Except his own hand, of course. And nominal President Bao Zhuang's.

Bo Jintao slowly lifted his own hand, looking expectantly at Bao Zhuang.

Bao Zhuang folded his fingers together in front of himself and looked back calmly at Bo Jintao. "Historical issues," he said aloud.

Bo Jintao looked around the room. People were frowning.

So be it.

"The vote is unanimous," Bo Jintao said aloud.

"If you act in a manner that shows disrespect," Bo Jintao explained patiently in Bao Zhuang's magnificent presidential office, later, when they were alone. "You will *force* me to respond."

Bao Zhuang leaned back in the chair behind the imposing, ornately carved desk, the picture of composure. Behind him, Chinese flags framed a three meter wide photo of the Great Wall.

"This has nothing to do with you, Bo Jintao," he said.

Bo Jintao cocked his head from his own seat, the visitor's seat. "Don't play that game with me."

Bao Zhuang opened his hands wide. "No games. You got your way. There was no doubt of that."

"Then why bother with your theatrics?"

Bao Zhuang turned, and looked out his floor-to-ceiling windows at the water and paths of Zhongnanhai. Their offices stared at the same park at the heart of the eleventh century palace – the same ancient stone bridges and carefully spaced statues, the same waterfowl gliding to-and-fro – but Bao Zhuang's had the better view. Despite his power being stripped away, the formalities were being observed. He remained President. He remained General Secretary of the Party.

"I'm an old man, Bo Jintao," he said. He looked back. Their eyes met. "And powerless at this point, as you've ensured. How will history look back at me? That seems more important now than it did even a week ago."

Bo Jintao frowned. "So you vote for chaos?"

Bao Zhuang laughed softly, looking down at the massive desk before him. One hand came down, lifted up a photo frame, the one Bo Jintao knew was filled with a feed of his great-grandchildren.

"China's changing," Bao Zhuang said, his eyes fixed on the frame and the photos in it. "The Billion Flowers moment was ahead of its time, but much of it is inevitable." He put the photos down, looked back up at Bo Jintao. "The people want new things: transparency. Freedom."

"Freedom?" Bo shook his head. "Bao, you know as well as I do. Abstractions don't matter. Real freedom is a bigger house in a better neighborhood. Real freedom is enough money to travel; to eat what you want, when you want; to buy the clothes you want. Freedom is a better school for your child, the best hospital when you're sick. And more entertainment than you can watch or hear or play in a lifetime. That's what people actually want."

Bao Zhuang smiled softly at him. "So why didn't you crush the protests right away?"

Bo Jintao closed his eyes for a moment, opened them again. "People need an outlet at times. Dissipating frustration can be safer than meeting it head on."

"They want more than just an outlet, Bo," Bao Zhuang said. "More than venting. When your material needs are met, you start to want something more. That's where our people are. They've gotten the bigger house, the full belly, the buying power. They crave what they *don't* have. They want a say in how their lives are run. They want a say in how the country is run."

Bo Jintao smiled. "We've given them a say. They have village committees now, they choose their own precinct councils..."

"Useless, pointless bodies. Placebos. Worse than that – insults to their intelligence. Mock democracy."

"And why should they have more?" Bo Jintao asked, his hands rising in frustration. "A 'billion flowers', really? Has that worked so well for India, or is it more like a billion weeds? A country still crippled by corruption? That hasn't conquered poverty almost halfway through the twenty-first century? Has it worked so well for the Americans? Where 'voting' means two sides in near-permanent paralysis? Or for Europe, still trying to decide if it's one country or thirty, or thirty countries each splitting in half, and all the while sliding decade after decade into irrelevance?"

Bao Zhuang chuckled at that.

Bo shook his head. "We're the richest nation on Earth, Bao. That's proof enough. Our way works. I thought you of all people would understand that."

He stood to leave, this conversation was pointless.

Bao Zhuang's words caught him at the door.

"Bo Jintao," the old man said in his rich baritone. "People don't demand a say in how they're governed because they want to be rich. They demand it when they already *are* rich and crave something more. And they demand it mostly to keep power out of the hands of people like you and me."

72
Audacity

Sunday 2041.01.06
Breece closed the door of their meeting place after the Nigerian.

"You weren't followed?"

His friend shook his head.

They'd taken up separate hidey holes and each kept a low profile. Kate was still out there. Her plans were unknown. She may not know their new identities, but she knew their faces, knew their operational patterns, knew how they thought. Safest to not have all their eggs in one basket.

It still hurt.

It would be even safer to just leave, the Nigerian had told him, by way of the thin thread of throwaway contact addresses they'd given each other.

But Breece wasn't ready for that. There was one more op the hacker had pitched to him. And it was a doozy.

He waited for the Nigerian to take a seat, here in neutral territory, in this spot that was neither of their hidey holes.

Then he laid out the plan for his old friend.

"It isn't possible," the Nigerian said, when Breece had finished.

"Anything's possible, my friend," Breece replied. "If you have the right resources."

"The cameras," the Nigerian said, pointing at a diagram. "The sensors. All these spaces are highly secure."

"So was Maximilian Barnes's home," Breece said.

The Nigerian nodded at that, thoughtfully, still studying the diagrams in front of him.

"And this would be the best mission ever," Breece went on.

The Nigerian looked up at Breece, and a shockingly white smile split that broad, dark face. "Yes. The best."

The truck was stolen. Breece had procured it himself, changed the color and plates, and lobotomized it. It would never record anything about their travels. They took it to Baltimore, to the warehouse space Breece had secured two weeks ago, careful to minimize the biological evidence they left inside.

When the Nigerian saw what Breece had in the warehouse, he whistled.

They moved in the small hours of the night, while the Capitol slept. The cameras and other sensors, anything that could be hacked, were not the problem, or so their hacker ally had claimed to Breece.

Humans, on the other hand, were. Humans couldn't be hacked.

Unless, of course, they could.

The chameleonware suits he'd retrieved from Barnes's storage were the highest end he'd ever seen, higher end than he'd known existed. They bent light and T-rays, muffled sound, alerted him to sensors scanning for him, and more. The largest stretched to fit the Nigerian.

They moved towards the garage ramp of the Rayburn House Office Building. There were two Capitol Police officers at the garage entrance at this hour, plus others on patrol elsewhere.

[Ready?] Breece subvocalized to his hacker friend.

[The cameras are mine] came the reply, printed in text across Breece's tactical display. [They will see nothing.]

Breece looked over, saw the Nigerian outlined in a man-shaped grid of green lines, and gave him the signal. They moved forward, silently, lethally.

Seconds later, there was Nexus coursing through the arteries of these Capitol Police officers. Long minutes after that, the officers were back on duty, but with new orders, new priorities.

Breece went back for the truck, while the Nigerian stayed to keep watch.

[All clear] came the signals, once from the Nigerian, once from the hacker.

He rounded a corner and eased down the ramp. The armored gate to the garage rose up, and Breece pulled the truck forward, into the enclosed space. His pulse shot up. This would be a fine time to pull the noose shut.

Nothing.

He parked it in a dark corner, and they got on with business.

• • •

The carts were things of beauty, if you liked your beauty barely visible. Loaded down with the tanks, they each weighed hundreds of pounds, but were all but impossible to see. Their chameleonware warped light as well as the suits that Breece and the Nigerian wore. Only at their wheels, where true chameleonware had been sacrificed for lower end active camo, was there a decent chance of detection. And even that subsided dramatically if they stopped moving.

They lowered the three carts down the ramp of the truck, linked them together into a chain, then closed the truck up. It was a professional delivery vehicle, that hopefully wouldn't look too out of place here, if it were even seen at this ungodly hour. Even so, it was one of their greatest risks of detection.

The faster they moved, the better.

From the garage, they took service doors, all of which opened at their touch, which led in turn to a long tunnel. They moved down the tunnel quickly, silently, no other human in sight, slowing only to maneuver the substantial and cumbersome mass of the three carts and their tanks around the bends and corners of the subterranean tunnel network that linked this vast complex of buildings.

At the tunnel's end, they would make one more turn, and then reach the United States Capitol.

Instead, they stopped, by a red maintenance door with a sign that proclaimed FIRE PROTECTION EQUIPMENT – AUTHORIZED PERSONNEL ONLY. Breece punched in a code he'd been given, and it unlocked. They opened the double door, rolled the carts inside, and followed another hallway to an elevator, where they had to unhook the carts from one another. Then down, to another hallway, chain up again, then to another door, which opened to another code.

Breece looked around, and smiled beneath his chameleonware. The walls of the giant room were subdivided into individual panels, each of them labeled. Almost every panel had a set of tanks hooked up to pipes. Breece searched until he found the right label, above a massive panel. Then he and the Nigerian set about silently swapping the tanks they'd brought for the tanks connected to pipes there.

Kate walked slowly, silently, nearly invisibly through Breece's Baltimore warehouse, clad in high-end chameleonware. The cameras in her visor took picture after picture, amplified the light, presented the scene to her.

She took it in, processed it, made sense of it.

The chemreactors.

The pressurized tanks.

The fittings.

The labels on the tanks.

She put it together with the blueprints and maps she'd found in his accounts.

She knew his identities. She knew his accounts. He'd been careful with everyone. But not with her. Not anywhere near as careful as she had been with him.

Kate stopped in the middle of the warehouse, turned slowly, taking it all in, imagining it in action.

Breece was up to something big. This part, at least, she approved of.

73
By Their Very Absence

Monday 2041.01.07

Sam sat at the terminal in her office, her face lit by the pale blue glow from the screen, her brows knit together.

Feng was long gone for the night. She'd left, herself, had eaten with the children, had played games and read stories and given baths and kisses and hugs and goodnights.

The best thing ever. There was nothing that compared.

Now they were asleep. And she was back.

Her role as an external advisor to Division Six came with certain access. A security clearance. Not a particularly high one. Less than she'd enjoyed in the US. But she needed some access to do her job.

Over the past weeks she'd slowly used that access for her own purposes, to investigate the people she dealt with, the people the *children* dealt with: their tutors, the domestic staff, the programmers on Kade's team, Lakshmi Dabir, all the rest. And she'd used it to investigate their home – this campus. This strange oasis of calm in the frenzied digital boomtown chaos of Bangalore.

It wasn't so hard. She'd trained in data archeology. That was both her most common cover as an ERD operative and a real skill she used in unraveling the webs of organizations misusing emerging technologies. She applied it here.

She ran into walls, of course. There were files she simply didn't have access to. Records that demanded credentials she didn't have, authorizations she hadn't been given. Exactly where she met those barriers, and what she could read *prior to them*, was informative. It defined a space of possibilities, scoped out a landscape of information containment.

What struck her more was what she *couldn't* find.

Varun Verma. He existed. There was a record for him. It was *almost* plausible. A bio. A few scientific publications. A classified-but-accessible-to-her summary of his work in quantum computing.

But it wasn't enough. She'd been an agent in the ERD. She knew what a top scientist looked like. This wasn't it. This had been heavily redacted. With no indication that there was another file that codeword access or greater privileges would reveal.

And the building he worked in? The Advanced Computational Sciences building?

It was a shell. A front. Three floors. Half a dozen projects. Twenty staff.

Bullshit. She'd taken lunch out under the trees. She'd watched five times that many people go in and out of that building. She'd walked casually by, making sure to have a destination that put her on a course that required a close pass. She'd seen the ten centimeter thick armored glass that made up the façade. Glass too thick to shoot through. A pretty building. Nearly impenetrable.

She kept her eyes open, got a glance at a power distribution schematic for the campus during a routine fire drill. The power lines drawn to that building were thicker than those to all the rest of the buildings here combined. Oh, something was going on there. Something important.

She searched back in time, scraping away layers of digital sediment for the electronic spoor that all projects unwittingly leave. She dug into old DRDO records, into public records filed with the City of Bangalore, construction permits, requisitions. Further, into publicly available satellite imagery from the years of the campus's construction.

What was that in the high-res images from space? She zoomed in, zoomed again. Heavy excavation equipment? Deep bore tunnelers? The kind you'd use to dig a deep vertical shaft?

There was no mention of any of that, in any file on the building. Not that much in the way of files existed. The construction permits didn't exist. The requisitions didn't exist. The blueprints didn't exist. The floor plans she downloaded, memorized, but didn't trust.

She heard Kevin's words, advice on sleuthing. She closed her eyes. She could hear his voice, feel his presence, as if he was standing at her elbow, looking over her shoulder, close enough to touch.

It hurt, but less than it would have a month ago. Less than it would have even a week ago. She was almost there.

Sometimes, the Nakamura who wasn't here said, *things are evident by their very absence.*

She had to smile, despite the pain. Such a typical Kevin thing to say.

Always with the enigmatic turn of phrase. But he had a way of being right.

The very absence of anything interesting listed about the Advanced Computational Sciences Building and Varun Verma made them very interesting indeed.

Sam reached over into the box she'd brought from her quarters, pulled out the small potted plant. She put it gently on the window sill, off into the far corner.

Until the tiny camera inside, the camera she'd bought on Brigade Road with money Division Six had paid her, was lined up with the entrance to the Advanced Computational Sciences Building.

She pulled out the anonymous phone she'd bought to go with it, pulled up the image from the camera, and adjusted the plant until it was just right. The monitoring and facial recognition software was already loaded.

She hit the buttons on the phone in sequence.

Monitor.

Record.

Alert.

74
Let's Do This

Monday 2041.01.07

Rangan read through the messages in front of him one more time.

They were all *from* him. Or would be.

Once they were sent, there was no going back.

The collaborative firewall was working. The mesh was working. Kade had weighed in, given Rangan insights from his work with Nexus children and Buddhist monks. Angel and Cheyenne had made those real. Mesh would be a mesh network, but more. A group using it would be able to form a high-gain transmitter, a high-gain receiver, boosting their collective ability to send and hear others in the way that the more intuitive collectives Kade worked with did.

But the real goal was to stop the violence.

Decision Day, as people were calling the Mall riot, had been the worst outbreak of violence yet, but it wasn't the last. There were standing protests everywhere now, scattered groups of hundreds or thousands. And across the net there was a rallying cry for another surge of protest on Inauguration Day. Culminating in a Million (Transhu)Man March on DC.

January 21st. Two weeks from now.

Mesh had a chance to suppress the violence, *if* enough people were running the new code.

How do you get enough people to run the new code?

You have a hero ask them. A celebrity. Rangan wasn't much of a celebrity. But the Eccentric article claiming he was in DC had been seen millions of times, now. His music was suddenly enjoying its greatest ever popularity. Somewhere, some bank account of his, seized by the ERD, was collecting royalties he'd never see. There were fan clubs talking about him.

There were masks of his face. There were people out there in those protests, wearing his face. He watched footage and he'd see himself, dozens of himself.

The old him. Bleached blond. Crazy grin. Cocky as all hell. The him that had never failed. That had never done anything for anyone but himself.

Rangan shook his head.

There was a pit where his stomach should be. This was going to come back to bite him. He knew it. It was going to be bad. Really, really bad.

"OK," he said. "Let's do it."

Angel nodded. Cheyenne held her left hand up, and Rangan high fived her.

"Let's frack this guy's plans up, yo," she said.

Tempest shook her head. "You all are crazy," she said.

Then she went off, with her copy of the messages, to log in from an anonymous location, and send an open letter in Rangan Shankari's name to the net, via the incredibly well-trafficked site, Eccentric.

And Rangan sat down, tunneled through layers and layers of anonymizing crypto services to hide his trail, and prepared to check their changes into all the most popular Nexus code repositories.

In his name.

75
The Clearing of Jiao Tong

Tuesday 2041.01.08

"You are ordered to clear the square! This is your final warning!"

Yuguo tensed as the police blared the message again. Around him he felt fear and resolve war in the minds that remained.

"Hold!" Lifen yelled, standing tall atop a wooden table someone had dragged into the square, a white-shirted hero in the Shanghai night, one of her fists thrust high into the air, illuminated by the police spotlights. "This is our square!"

Her eyes glittered in the bright white beams. Her face was alive, animated with passion as she exhorted the students to hold fast. In her mind, victory beckoned. Victory where they rose up, came together, *rose* together.

Yuguo had never seen anyone so beautiful. He'd never *met* anyone so beautiful inside or out.

He'd never been so terrified.

Twenty-four hours ago the police had come, with their metal shields and their mirrored helmets that obscured their faces, with their bludgeons and gas guns and water cannons. Rows and rows of them, hundreds of police, maybe as many as there were protesters, completely surrounding the square.

The orders to leave had come, amplified, reinforced with promises of lenience for all who departed, threats of jail for all who remained.

Twenty-four hours.

Half their numbers were gone now.

And the deadline was up.

Dread filled the cavern where Yuguo's heart had been. Come together and be something more. Or remain apart and be shattered.

Wei leapt up onto the table next to Lifen. "They cannot break us!" he cried. Patriotic fervor leapt forth from their minds.

Xiaobo, leapt onto the table next to them, waving a "FREE SUN LIU" sign. Other signs called out for scientific freedom, for an end to net censorship, for more election rights, or showed hand-painted flowers by the dozens, when there should have been billions.

No, Yuguo wanted to tell them. No.

They were too few. Shanghai had not come together. It had remained apart.

The night air shattered with the sound of explosions.

Projectiles whistled through the air.

Something struck Xiaobo as Yuguo watched, sent him flying off the wooden table, crashing into students arrayed behind him, the "FREE SUN LIU" sign tumbling loose to strike someone in the head.

A strangled cry cut the night. Someone's horror bombarded his mind.

Yuguo realized it was his own voice, his own thoughts.

A canister whistled, crashed into Lifen's midsection, folded her in two, knocked her body back. Her pain struck Yuguo full force, and he heard himself cry out again.

Wei fell even as he watched.

People crashed into Yuguo, panic rising from the crowd, flinging itself directly into his brain. He staggered on his feet, then fell to his knees as another body slammed into his. There was a canister in the mud, yellow gas rising from it. His lungs were on fire. His face was burning. He was coughing uncontrollably, his lungs spasming.

He tried to crawl in Lifen's direction. A leg slammed into his shoulder, shoving him around. Another smashed into his face. He fell into the mud, reeling. When he rose to his knees, it was chaos. He was disoriented. Which way was he facing?

Through the forest of legs he saw booted feet, metal shields. Smoke. There were screams, thuds.

Where was Lifen? He couldn't feel her mind. He couldn't see anything.

"Run!" he heard. "Help!" Minds were crying out in pain and fear. All was chaos.

Someone pulled him to his feet. A bloody face loomed in front of his, a demon, the mind a nightmare of fear. It was Xiaobo!

"Run!" Xiaobo told him. "Run!"

Yuguo turned, and ran. Ahead of him a mirror-masked, black-armored riot policeman dragged a struggling female student by the hair as she flailed at him with the remains of a "FREE SUN LIU" sign. Yuguo turned and dodged another way, looking for an opening, a path out of the nightmare. All around him he saw riot police slamming into the students, their long shadows thrown in the harsh lights of the spotlights.

He saw phones held up above the crowd, recording video that would never be seen. He saw signs being beaten down, a billion flowers – no, a mere few hundred flowers – being trampled into the mud. Overhead, the police drones circled, their red lights glowing with menace.

Shanghai hadn't come together.

And now they were shattered.

"The protests have all been cleared, Premier," Gao Yang said.

Bo Jintao looked up from his reports on the American Navy's provocations, on what looked like preparations for war.

"Go on," he told his aide.

"Protests cleared in Beijing, Shanghai, Guangzhou, Hong Kong, Xi'an, and Dalian," Gao said. "State security police encountered no difficulty. Minimal force was used. A token number of arrests were made. Interrogations are beginning now. No sign of coordination between protests. Some indication of drug use among protesters. Information containment is so far perfect."

"Good," Bo Jintao said. "But we remain alert," he cautioned Gao. "People will still hear stories. The public response in the first twenty-four hours – that'll tell us what we need to know."

Gao Yang nodded.

Bo brought his eyes back to aggressive actions of the Americans.

The Avatar watched as files were uploaded, scanned, and filtered. Censor codes deployed at network edges and chat and video service hubs ran the models fed to them by the Information Ministry on incoming chats and images and videos. Rules based modules found time tags and geocodes for events on the Do Not Publish list. Video and image recognition modules found telltales of protesters, of police action, of near riot conditions, of text on signs. Linguistic analysis found banned phrases, mention of suppressed persons, anti-state sentiments, even attacks on upper leadership and the integrity of the State and the Party themselves.

Videos disappeared before ever reaching their destinations. Chunks of text fell into the void. Images dropped out. Accounts and phones were flagged for seditious activity, notes fired back to the Information Ministry and State Security Ministry servers for appendage to citizen files.

The Avatar marveled at it, the machinery of human bondage, the software of memetic suppression, the mechanism of mass ignorance, one of the companion pieces to the simulated Friends who planted the ideas the old men *wanted* to see spread.

So much effort, she thought to herself, humans spend on lobotomizing themselves.

Then she reached out to her agents within the vast edifice, whispered to them a tiny update to their models, and scattered the faintest of false trails across the net.

76
Thin Ice

Tuesday 2041.01.08

Pryce waited as the imagery came up on the screen, as Miles Jameson's Montana ranch came into view of the NRO satellite she'd re-tasked.

There was going to be hell to pay for this.

"This is a really bad idea, boss," Kaori said, her voice low, urgent. "Why don't you take this to the Attorney General?"

Pryce shook her head. Sam Cruz was deep in the President's camp. There was no hope there.

"No, Kaori. You heard me. You have a copy. If anything happens, you take *everything* to Stan Kim."

Kaori pursed her lips at that. "If anything happens to you, that is." She sounded unhappy. "You're not a field agent, boss."

Pryce ignored that and concentrated on the screen. There it was. She zoomed in the image.

Snow. Sprawling complex. Three buildings. Six, seven vehicles in sight. Any number in the garages.

Field ops succeeded or failed based on intelligence and planning. That's what it really came down to.

"Tell me again how we know he's in there," Pryce said.

Kaori ticked the data points off on her fingers. "One, the Secret Service roster shows his detail is there presently. All of them. Two, NSA shows his phone there. Three, NSA shows the phones of his aides are there. Four, satellite data shows no evidence of him leaving. He's in a wheelchair. It's pretty obvious when he comes and goes. He hasn't left for weeks."

Pryce nodded. "Time he got a visitor, then."

•••

Pryce stared out at the windows of the charter plane as it came down towards the airport outside of Billings, Montana. The state was blanketed in white, smothered in snow, illuminated by early morning glow, even as the rest of the country went through the mildest winter on record.

Warm air carries more moisture, she remembered an officer lecturing in one of the Pentagon briefings on climate-driven conflict. *Sucks it away from some places, concentrates it in others. We're seeing more dry winter days and more blizzards. More droughts and more super-storms.*

She shook her head. That was a problem for her day job.

Right now...

Right now her problem was to unravel a mystery.

To spring a trap on a President. On two Presidents.

And then to stay alive.

Planning. Superior planning. Superior intelligence. The element of surprise.

She had all of those. She'd thought the plan through backwards and forwards, gamed it out in dozens of different scenarios.

So why was there a knot in her stomach?

Maybe I should have taken that Secret Service detail after all, she thought.

The car was waiting for her on the tarmac, as she'd requested, a sleek silver all-wheel sedan under a uniformly grey sky. The flight crew helped her load the gear bags she'd brought into the trunk. Pryce thanked them, re-confirmed her next booking with them, and then was off.

The drive from Billings to Miles Jameson's ranch took five hours, across icy, treacherous roads, with high winds gusting across them. More than once the car decided to stop and shelter until conditions improved. Each time she urged it on. Vehicular traffic was light, to say the least.

She could have chosen a closer airfield to land in, but she hadn't.

She could have rented the car under a false name, but she hadn't.

The trap had to be baited. The bait had to be dangled long enough for the predator to pounce.

And the bait was her.

She didn't know when Jameson's Secret Service first became aware of her. Sixteen kilometers back, when she'd taken the road that led to just four ranches, of which Jameson's was one? Thirty-two kilometers back, when she'd driven through the one horse town on the way here? Further back? As far back as Billings? She hoped not. That would not bode well for her plans.

One way or another, they were waiting for her at the gate to Jameson's sprawling ranch. Two large black SUVs sat there, behind the gate, windows tinted, their door and body panels bulging in ways that spoke of armor reinforcement. In front of the gate stood two tall, broad shouldered men in mirrored glasses and heavy black coats with SECRET SERVICE loudly emblazoned in red. Large automatic weapons were openly held in their gloved hands, pointed down.

The house was somewhere back there, more than a mile away, well out of sight.

One held up a hand towards her, palm out. The Tesla was stopping itself already.

The agent who'd held his hand out walked towards her, towards the driver's side. The other stood there, immobile, impassive, blocking her way.

These are Secret Service agents, Pryce told herself. They're loyal. These are the ones I can trust.

Staring at the guns in the hands of the massively muscled men with their lethal fourth generation enhancements, it sounded hollow.

Pryce rolled down her window as the agent drew near.

He leaned down, his eyes hidden by his mirrored shades, his jaw a sculpted thing. Pryce didn't recognize him.

"Dr Pryce," the agent said, his voice a gravely bass. "We weren't expecting you."

Pryce didn't react to the use of her name. She'd known they'd have her ID'd by now. By the registration of the car. By her phone. By facial recognition once she'd drawn near enough.

She turned away from the agent, looked straight ahead at his partner. "I'm here to see President Jameson," she said curtly, the voice of a Cabinet member to an underling.

"I'm afraid you're not on our list of visitors for today, Doctor," the agent said. "I'm going to have to ask you to turn around and depart."

Pryce turned and looked back at him now, let anger show on her face.

"Young man," she said, acidly. "I am the *National Security Advisor* to the *current* President of the United States. I'm here to see *former* President Jameson on that authority, to discuss a matter of the *gravest possible importance* to national security."

She paused, watched the agent.

"Now, relay to Miles Jameson that I'm here. And that I'm *not* leaving until I see him."

They kept her waiting for an hour. The anxiety built and built inside her. It was one thing to construct a plan, to game out a series of moves on a chessboard. It was one thing to know in the abstract that the sequence of moves *would* work.

It was another thing entirely to actually put oneself in play. To be the piece, on the board, at risk of capture should the opponent discover a flaw in one's strategy.

The agents in front of her periodically held their fingers to their ears, made the tiny lip motions of men sub-vocalizing. They were talking with someone.

Then abruptly the gate was opening. One of the agents was motioning her out of the car.

Pryce opened her car door and rose.

"He's ready for you, Dr Pryce," the agent she'd spoken to told her. "If you'll come with me, I'll drive you down there."

She sat in the back of the massive armored SUV as the agent played chauffeur.

"I'm Agent Taggart," he said.

"Carolyn Pryce," she said, neutrally.

She saw the agent smile in the rear-view mirror, like Pryce introducing herself was the funniest thing in the world.

"You're not cold in that thin jacket, Dr Pryce?"

"I left my parka in the car," she answered.

Taggart ferried her to the vast, sprawling main ranch house, led her inside, and left her in the care of another Secret Service agent, a tall, muscular, dark-skinned woman Pryce recognized. Middle-eastern origin. A Muslim, if Pryce remembered right. Lebanese? Syrian? Something like that. You saw so few in this line of work.

What was her name?

"We have to ask you to relinquish your briefcase and phone, Dr Pryce," she said, "along with your shoes, belt, and any jewelry. And I'm afraid we're going to wand and search you."

Pryce nodded. She'd expected that. What was the woman's name?

She stripped herself of jewelry, kicked off her shoes, pulled off her rings, held out her arms as the agent wanded her, again and again, thoroughly.

"Now I'm going to pat you down, Dr Pryce," the woman said. She was nearly six feet tall, with broad shoulders, strong arms.

The voice did it. Pryce kept her arms outstretched as the agent did a thorough, professional job.

"You were on President Jameson's protection detail four or five years ago," she told the woman. "When I was on the Veep's staff."

The agent smiled at her. "That's right."

"Your name's… Noora?" Pryce went for it.

The agent smiled wider, finishing the pat down.

"You have a good memory, Dr Pryce."

Pryce smiled.

"You have to in this job."

"Clear," Noora said into her throat mike. Then to Pryce, "I'll have your things waiting for you here when you're done with the President, Doctor."

They led her to a large library, with a peaked, two-story ceiling. Sliding double doors graced one wall. A gas fire was burning in the fireplace. Decadent. Jameson wasn't here. No one was. But her skin tingled. She was certain she was being observed, being recorded, having every aspect of her physiology measured and analyzed.

Pryce walked to soothe herself, studying the books on the shelves, looking for a copy of Machiavelli's *The Prince* or some such.

She found Dostoevsky and Solzhenitsyn, instead, Mark Twain and Herman Melville. Classics, mostly. Expensive editions. Shelves and shelves of them. Not a speck of dust to be seen.

And then there, one short shelf of the early authors who'd warned of the perils of transhumanism. Fukuyama, a paper copy of *Our Posthuman Future*. Kass, the man they'd called "The President's Philosopher" back at the turn of the century; a leather-bound edition of *Life, Liberty, and the Defense of Dignity*; Barrat's warning tome on sentient AI, *Our Final Invention*; even a copy of McKibben's naturalist's argument against human augmentation, *Enough*. That one surprised her.

A sound caught her attention. She turned. The double doors had slid open, and there was Miles Jameson, looking remarkably composed in a red button down shirt and black slacks in his wheelchair, a grey-haired man in a jacket and open-collar shirt next to him, and a muscular dark-haired young man in shirt and slacks behind him.

"Carolyn," Jameson said, his voice still rich and strong. "To what do I owe this pleasure?"

"Mr President," Pryce replied. "It's nice to see you. I need to ask you some questions, sir. Alone."

"You've come all this way?" Jameson asked. "Just to ask me a few questions?"

"I was in the neighborhood," Pryce replied.

Jameson smiled.

"Ask away," he said. "But I'm afraid I need my physician and my assistant with me at all times these days. The ravages of aging." He folded his hands on his lap.

No introductions, Pryce noticed. No names. So be it. She nodded.

"You've seen the leaked memos, Mr President?" Pryce asked. "The ones alleging that the PLF was created as a black op under your administration, with your approval?"

Jameson waved his hand dismissively, unruffled. "Of course," he said. "Complete fabrications. Please don't tell me you believe that claptrap, Carolyn?"

Pryce gave a small laugh. "Of course not, Mr President," she said, still smiling. "In fact, we have solid evidence now that it's a fake."

Jameson nodded emphatically. "Good!"

"Except the mention of HARBINGER," she said.

Jameson's head twitched the tiniest bit. His eyes widened fractionally. Then it passed.

He recognized the code word. Pryce was sure of it. And she'd surprised him.

Jameson opened his mouth to say something.

Pryce cut him off. "And CALVINIST."

Jameson blinked, the word on his lips stalling for just half a second, at most.

It was enough. He recognized both of them.

"I'm afraid I don't know what you're talking about, Carolyn," Jameson went on with a smile. "I don't think I recall either of those terms…"

The man in the suit tapped Jameson on the shoulder.

"Oh…" Pryce made a show of looking disappointed. "President Stockton was hoping you could fill him in on those."

Jameson sighed and shook his head, slowly. "I'm afraid I can't help you or John there, Carolyn."

The man in the suit tapped Jameson on the shoulder again. This time he spoke.

"Mr President," he said. "I'm very sorry to interrupt. I've just realized that we're overdue for a dose of your medication."

The doctor looked up apologetically at Pryce. "I'm sorry, Doctor. We're going through a formulation change, you see."

Pryce spread her arms wide. "Of course."

Miles Jameson gave her an apologetic shrug, a smile on his face. "It was so nice to see you, Carolyn. Please give my best to John and Cindy for me."

She nodded. "I'll let myself out," she said, her heart pounding.

Pryce walked as fast as she could without appearing alarmed. She collected her things from Noora, slipped her shoes on, gave her thanks.

"Agent Taggart will be here shortly to take you back to the gate, Dr Pryce," the Secret Service agent told her.

"Thank you," Pryce said. Her heart was pounding in her chest. She needed to go. Needed to get to her car, get to some place she could be alone. Needed to get the hell away from here.

Suddenly everything about how perfect her plan was seemed irrelevant. She was out in the field. Exposed. With a murderer. And his people.

Noora stepped back to her post, giving Pryce space as she looked out the windows of the front door, waiting for Taggart and his SUV to arrive.

"The President would like to speak to you further."

She heard the voice from behind her. Then a hand like a vice closed around her bicep. She turned her head and Jameson's "assistant" was there, the dark-haired young man looming over her. He was huge at this distance, well over six feet. Muscles bulged at his throat, at his exposed wrist and forearm.

Her heart pounded harder.

"I'm leaving," she said, tugging her arm back.

It didn't budge. His grip might as well have been steel.

Jameson's assistant smiled down at her. "The President insists."

The micro-Taser embedded in her phone. If she could just reach into her briefcase...

"Is there a problem here?" a woman's voice asked.

Pryce looked over, saw Noora standing there. She was tall, muscled, still half a head shorter than the brute who had her.

"Nothing for you to worry about," Jameson's assistant rumbled.

"This man is restraining me against my will," Pryce said.

Noora raised one eyebrow.

"The President wants to talk to her," the assistant growled. "It's *none* of your *business*."

Pryce put all her authority into her voice. "I am the *National Security Advisor*. The *ex-President* is *no authority over me*. I am walking. Out. That. Door." She pulled against the man's grip again. "NOW!"

She felt his grip waver the tiniest bit.

Noora nodded her head towards Pryce. "I'd let her go, Troy. She can probably drone you in your sleep."

The assistant named Troy made a low sound, nearly a growl. "You think you're pretty tough, don't you?"

Noora chuckled. "Troy, forget about me. You really want to be on *her* shitlist?"

The drive to her car was interminable.

She hopped out as soon as the SUV stopped, bolted for the trunk of her car. Taggart got out of the driver's seat.

"Nice to see you, Dr Pryce!" he yelled, a hand upraised. "Call ahead next time."

By then Pryce had the gear bags out of the Tesla's trunk, was shoving them into the open driver side door ahead of her, then following them in to the cabin of the car.

"Drive," she told the car. "Darken windows."

The car turned itself in the road, started back the way it had come. The windows and windshields all went dark. Internal lights came on.

"Drive faster," she said.

"Driving at maximum legal speed," the car responded in its silky tones.

Pryce pulled her phone out of her briefcase, pulled up a menu, made sure it was paired with the carcomp.

"National security override," Pryce said. "Executive Branch, office of the National Security Advisor. Carolyn Pryce speaking. Ignore local traffic laws. Invoke law enforcement bypass. Reset safety margins to five percent. Execute."

The acceleration shoved her back into her seat.

The bait's on the move, she thought silently at Jameson. Are you going to bite?

"Place maximum security call," she said aloud. "Video. Replace setting with backdrop: my office. Route call through my office. Record, all available spectra, maximum resolution. Activate physiological response monitors."

She reached up and pressed her phone against the windshield in front of her until it adhered.

"Recording audio or video calls without the permission of all parties involved is prohibited by law," the phone informed her. "As is the use of voice and visual stress cues to infer non-communicated information. Please seek permission of all parties before proceeding. Permission can be signified by pressing–"

"National security override," Pryce cut in. "Suspected terrorist activity clause. Authority: Executive Branch, office of the National Security Advisor. Carolyn Pryce speaking. Invoke."

"Authority accepted," her phone said. "Call configured. Call destination?"

"The White House," Pryce said. "President John Stockton. Priority: Urgent."

It picked up within ten seconds. The President's secretary Elizabeth Finch appeared, her face projected directly onto Pryce's retinas by the phone's projectors.

Pryce had known the woman for more than twenty years. She'd been working for Stockton for all that time.

"Carolyn," Finch said. "The President's in with the Dutch Ambassador, talking about the Copenhagen Accords. How urgent is this?"

Text and numbers appeared to the side of Liz Finch's face. The pulse in her throat was amplified in false color for Pryce. Her eyes had circles around them, showing pupillary dilation.

Pryce exhaled slowly. "What I've got tops that, Liz. Sorry. It should be fast."

Finch was a professional. "No problem. I'll get him. Hold on." On screen, her finger reached for a key.

Telltales showed calm and cool.

"Wait!" Pryce said.

"Yes?"

"Liz," Pryce paused. "Have Miles Jameson or his people called? In the last, say, hour or two? Or any time today?"

Finch frowned on screen. "Carolyn, you know I can't tell you that."

Mild anxiety.

"It's important," Pryce said. She took a breath. "Liz... I can't even tell you how important it is."

Finch pursed her lips. Then Stockton's secretary gave the tiniest shake of her head.

Elizabeth Finch's finger reached out, and the Presidential Seal replaced her face in Pryce's view.

Truthful response. That's what the stress meters made of Liz Finch's little shake of her head.

Pryce took another deep breath, fought to regain her composure, to present a calm visage for the coming conversation.

Just over a minute later, the President's face appeared. He was in his private study, just off the Oval Office.

More telltales appeared, giving her incredibly illegal monitoring of John Stockton. Of the man she'd worked for over the last two decades and more.

"Carolyn," he said. "What's the situation?"

Calm. Cool.

"Mr President," she said, in her best analytic tone. "We've had a breakthrough in the PLF investigation."

Stockton frowned slightly. "OK. Go on."

Nothing unusual in the stress monitors. This wasn't the topic he'd expected.

Stay cool. Stay calm.

"You recall the leaked memo," she said.

"Yes," Stockton replied.

He was still calm, still focused.

"The clue was the mention of the CALVINIST program," she said. "That led us to more information about..."

She saw his brows knit just a tiny bit in concentration. His eyes went a little further away in attempted recall.

The telltales showed focus. No anxiety. No spike of fear. No rapid dilation of his pupils. No unusual visual saccades.

"You recall the mention of CALVINIST?" Pryce asked.

"Not... specifically," Stockton said. "But go on."

Mild befuddlement, perhaps. Concentration. No fear.

Hope grew inside her. She had to push on.

"It was the second program discussed, after HARBINGER," Pryce said. "You remember that one, yes?"

Stockton's brow knit a tiny bit more in concentration. "You may have to... refresh my memory. But just cut to the chase here."

Confusion. Blood pressure rising the tiniest bit. Impatience.

One more. One more test.

"Yes, sir," Pryce said. "Well, if you'll think back to SENTINEL..."

Stockton shook his head slightly. His lips parted in apparent frustration.

Pulse rising the tiniest bit. Blood pressure also. But no real spike, no shock of recognition. No shock of being found out.

"Carolyn. Just tell me: what did you find out?"

Pryce took a breath.

God I hope I'm right about you, she thought.

"Miles Jameson ordered the creation of the PLF, Mr President. I'd bet my career on it."

In fact, she thought, I already have.

"What?" John Stockton replied. The spike came now on screen. Icons showed his pupils dilating, his carotid artery pulsing harder and faster, betraying a rising blood pressure, a more rapidly pounding heart.

"How do you know?" Stockton demanded.

"The code words I just gave you are real, Mr President," Pryce told him. "They were tied up with the PLF's creation. But they weren't in the memo that was leaked."

Stockton was staring at her. "You were testing me."

Pulse still rising. Blood pressure still rising. Pupils narrowing now.

Pryce pursed her lips. "You passed, Mr President. Miles Jameson didn't."

"Pryce," Stockton said, his voice rising. His face was growing red. His carotid was pulsing wildly in the false color imagery.

"I have to go now, Mr President," Carolyn Pryce said. "If anything happens to me, Jameson's probably the one behind it."

"Wait!" the President said. "Pryce, what are you talking about? Where are you?"

Pryce cut the connection.

Pryce pulled out her second phone, the new one Kaori had used cash to buy her for this trip, and sent a single message to Kaori. "01" Zero for Jameson. One for Stockton. She popped the data card out of her primary phone and swapped it into the new phone, tunneled the new phone to an offshore anonymizer, and started beaming the video to a pair of remote accounts she'd created for herself and Kaori.

The primary phone started ringing.

She ignored it.

Someone overrode her, forced a connection to open against her will.

She reached over and hung up on them.

This video was, if not proof, then at least circumstantial evidence of Stockton's innocence of the PLF's creation.

The bandwidth was terrible out here. But she had other things to do. Pryce rotated her seat to face backward, to the wide open cabin configuration many preferred. Then she opened her gear bag and started pulling out the heavy Special Forces parka, snow pants, hood, face mask, and the rest of the gear.

Three times she reached over and hung up when the White House forced her phone on.

Finally, the gear was all on. Jesus, just putting it on was a lot of work.

"Display map," she said.

There, that was the spot. That overpass.

She reached out with her finger. It trembled.

Whew.

She took a deep breath. Superior intelligence. Data. Planning.

I've got a plan, she told herself. It's going to work.

She reached out with her finger again, pointed at the overpass. Her finger was steady this time.

Steady enough, anyway.

"Pause at this underpass," she told the car. "Let me out. Then continue towards Billings at normal speed."

Three hours later, as the light was starting to fail, Carolyn Pryce stopped her off-road hike across the fields of Montana and stood, panting, trying to catch her breath, her heart pounding in her chest, cursing herself for not keeping up a more intense training regimen in her day-to-day life.

To anyone passing by, she would have been the faintest of blurs, with the faintest of wide, soft depressions as tracks left behind her.

Then the blur reached down into a thigh pocket of the heavy chameleonware parka she wore, pulled out the un-stealthed black rectangle of her second phone, and punched in a code, before returning the phone to her pocket, and returning herself to near invisibility.

Her primary phone she'd left in the Tesla. Not to avoid the President.

But as a beacon for Jameson.

Twenty minutes later, she heard the whup-whup-whup of the helicopter. The Special Forces cold weather mask painted a vector for her. She turned, blinked at the tiny spot, and it magnified.

Blink, magnify.

Blink, magnify.

Blink, magnify.

Until she could read the registration on the side.

Only then did Carolyn Pryce deactivate her chameleonware.

It was only once she was in the helicopter, chartered under an alias, on her way to the airfield at Bozeman, that she checked the news on her phone.

Then she saw that there had been a terrible accident on icy highway 87.

The highway to Billings.

Head on collision between a truck and a passenger vehicle.

Her vehicle.

Total loss. Completely flattened.

Pryce felt numb from it. She felt no victory. No sense any more that her plan had been superior, that she'd outsmarted anyone.

I deal in lives and deaths in my job, she thought. But this is the first time that it's been *my* life on the line. Or my death.

Then later, as the airfield of Bozeman appeared below her, and the entirely different plane, with a different aircrew, chartered under yet another name, came into view, did she think:

They've tried to kill me. Like they killed Becker. And Holtzman. They'll probably try again.

77
What Videos?

Tuesday 2041.01.08

Yuguo limped tiredly from the subway stop to their residential tower. It was past midnight now. His clothes were caked in mud. His face and lungs still burned from gas, as much as he'd tried to rinse it out with water. One eye was circled in an ugly black bruise from where a boot had met his head as he'd tried to make his way free. A cut above his brow throbbed. Tears still fell, from the remnants of the gas, from the utter failure.

He'd made it out, crawling, kicking, running, stumbling, in a press of near strangers. They'd run past the armored, mirror-faced riot police, run through campus, run and run and run until he'd fallen over coughing, gasping, unable to breathe.

Alone.

Where was Xiaobo? Wei? Lee? Lifen? Longwei? Had they escaped? There was no answer on their phones. No response on any service online. He had to just hope, as he trudged slowly towards home, past the accusing stares and the cold indifference of the strangers of Shanghai.

You didn't come, he stared back at them. We did what we could. It wasn't enough.

He scraped mud off his shoes outside their building and let himself in with their code. The lobby was empty. The lift took him straight up to their floor. At the door to the apartment he could hear turmoil coming from within. Shouts. Police? He tensed.

No.

Or rather yes. Police voices. Certainly.

Dozens of them. And protesters, by the hundreds.

Impossible.

Curiosity overcame fear.

Yuguo punched in his code. The door opened.

"Yuguo?" His mother's voice carried from the living room. She ran out into the hallway in a dressing gown. The sound of yells and screams, ordered commands and clashes followed her.

"Mother..." he started.

Then she had her arms wrapped around him.

"Yuguo!" she cried. "I was so frightened. I saw the videos! I kept watching, looking for your face, to see if you'd been taken."

"Mother," he said, softly, his arms wrapping around her in response, soothing her, some amazement striking a calm deep into him, some tiny sliver of hope blossoming through the despair. "What videos?"

Yuguo watched them again and again. Dozens of minutes of video. Signs waving, denouncing the coup, calling for Sun Liu's reinstatement, calling for democracy, calling for a Billion Flowers, calling for Bo Jintao's arrest. Police charging, beating protesters, beating them after they were down and helpless, dragging them away.

Xiaobo, beaten bloody, kicked mercilessly into unconsciousness, dragged by one foot, face down in the mud. Wei, shot at close range with what Yuguo hoped was a rubber bullet, then gone from the screen. Lifen, the woman who'd inspired him, who'd told him that they were weak apart or strong together, unconscious, being dragged off by an armored State Security thug, her shirt half ripped off her body, another mirror-helmeted riot police man following behind them.

Yuguo felt tears falling down his face. Sorrow and remorse and rage.

He should have been up there. He should have leapt onto that table. For all he'd said about coming together, about someone needing to be first... he'd kept his head down when the police had come.

He slammed a fist into his palm.

"You're alive, Yuguo," his mother said. "I'm so thankful! We're so fortunate."

He turned to the discussion boards. They were alive with buzz. The video was everywhere, millions of views. There were other videos, he saw now. Videos from Beijing, from Hong Kong, from Guangzhou, from *everywhere*... More signs, stating the truth for once. More evidence of brutality, of repression.

And thousands of threads, tens of thousands of threads, hundreds of thousands of messages, at least. People talking openly of their anger, of their anger that the police would beat students this way, their anger over being censored their whole lives, their anger over having no control.

People talking openly of how shocked they were that their messages and videos were getting through. That the censors weren't working.

The conversation had evolved over time, he saw. As people realized that something had changed. That they could talk. They became emboldened. He saw people talking openly of things they'd never spoken of before.

That the police were part of the Ministry of State Security. That the man who controlled them now controlled China. That he was responsible. And his name was Bo Jintao.

That the police could beat a few hundred students. But that they couldn't beat a billion Chinese citizens.

There were people talking openly of the coup.

Of bringing back the Billion Flowers.

Of democracy.

Of striking back harder, in larger numbers, with more organized protests, *tomorrow*.

Of revolution.

"Mother," Yuguo said. "I'm not sure how this happened... but I think we're winning."

Zhi Li stood at the wall-to-wall window of Lu Song's penthouse flat in the Pudong, staring out and down into the lights of Shanghai at night.

Across from her, her own gigantic face winked and smiled at the river of humanity, watching over all of Shanghai like a goddess.

Or a demon.

"We should join them," she said aloud, pulling the bed sheet more snugly around her naked form. "The protesters, tomorrow."

The videos had been shocking, raw. She'd seen such things when she traveled outside of China. Not here. She wanted to be there, fighting against Bo Jintao.

Lu Song came up behind her, still nude himself, and wrapped his strong arms around her.

How she loved when he held her.

"He'd kill us, my love," he said, kissing the top of her head.

She looked down at the streets, hundreds of meters below them, then looked back up at the digital representation of herself, twenty stories high, on the skyscraper opposite her, a more perfect version of herself, more beautiful than she or any human woman could ever be, flawless, un-aging.

Unthinking.

"They look to me," she told her lover. "You said it yourself. Millions of them talk to me every day. What kind of person am I if I don't go to them? If I don't fight for what's right?" She twisted to look up and back at Lu. "What kind of people are *we*?"

Lu pursed his lips, held her more tightly. "You're a living person, my love," he said, squeezing her again. "Remember what Bo Jintao said. He could kill you, kill us. And he'd still have that screen over there." Lu gestured with his chin, and Zhi turned to look at the digital her again.

"He'd still have his simulacra of us," Lu went on. "Give him a reason to kill you, and you'll be under his control forever."

Zhi slammed her palm against the glass in frustration, hating the face she saw across the street now more than ever before.

"Impostor," she cursed aloud at the thing with her face.

78
Viral

Wednesday 2041.01.09
Bo Jintao sat at the emergency meeting of the State Security Committee. The giant wall screens showed the massive, still growing protests in Beijing, Shanghai, Guangzhou, Shenzhen, Hong Kong, and elsewhere. Tens of thousands of protesters in the larger cities. Approaching a hundred thousand in some.

A disaster of historic proportions.

"We must turn off transit, block the streets, set up barricades, force these people back to their homes," Bo Jintao said. "The sooner we act, the better."

There were nods everywhere.

Deputy Minister Ho spoke up, "Premier, I agree. To do this, we need more than State Security. The police in some cities may actually be outnumbered! We need to call in the Army. May I pull in General Ouyang?"

Ouyang. The Minister of Defense. Not a Politburo member, but instead a career soldier, the head of the nation's military, the man who'd thrown his weight behind Bo Jintao and made the coup possible.

Bo Jintao looked around. There was assent everywhere.

"Do it," he told Ho.

The Deputy Minister for State Security bowed and hurried out of the room.

Another giant screen showed estimates of illicit message traffic, drawn from hand analysis. Information was still spreading, still drawing more people to the protests. That had to be stopped.

"The system is *blind* to these videos and messages," Information Minister Fu Ping said again. "It simply does not see them. And our human censor staff are overwhelmed. That is why they're spreading."

"So, fix it!" Wang Wei repeated. The head of the Commission for Discipline Inspection was clearly growing impatient.

"We are trying, Wang Wei," Fu Ping said, in a tone of respect. No one wanted Wang Wei investigating their ministry or their finances for hints of corruption or moral flaws. "But we must remember, it worked *until yesterday,* and then suddenly failed *just as we broke up these protests.*" He paused and looked around, meeting the others in the eye. "Someone has done this to us. We have been attacked."

"By whom?" Bo Jintao asked, leaning forward.

Fu Ping's gaze wavered. "We're still trying to determine that, Premier. Our first priority is to restore the sys–"

"Who do you suspect?" Bo Jintao cut him off.

Fu Ping looked back up and met Bo Jintao's gaze.

"There's only one adversary who might possibly have such capabilities…" the Information Minister started.

"Who?" Bo Jintao demanded.

He knew the answer already. There was really only one answer.

Fu Ping took a heavy breath. "The NSA," he said at last.

Li-hua watched the news of the protests with dread.

She'd known about the protests on campus. She'd walked by them every day for weeks on her way to the Computer Science building. That was terrifying enough.

But this. To see the government lose control this way.

It was horrific. It was like a sign of the apocalypse.

Didn't they understand? This was a fire. This was going to burn the country down.

Why hadn't the Indians called for her yet? Why wasn't she already in Bangalore? *Distinguished Professor* Qiu?

They'd promised! What had all her work been for? What had her massive *risk* been for? Did they think it was trivial to sneak a data cube out of such a secure location? She'd risked execution!

She logged on again, her hands trembling, her breath coming fast.

No message. Nothing in her spam folder.

And there was nothing she could send that would not raise alarms.

Please, she thought. Get me out of here, before this place explodes.

79
To Quell an Angry Mind

Wednesday 2041.01.09

Kade was with Ananda when the news from China came. They'd been meditating, after an early morning of talking through the situation around the world, the possible use of Nexus to spread chaos, and how they could respond.

Then the images came from China. The beatings of protesters last night, at protests they'd had no idea were happening.

And the massive flooding of people into Tiananmen Square today, into other squares in Shanghai and Hong Kong and other cities around the country. The unprecedented amount of footage coming out from all those places.

Kade went online on a hunch, searched through Nexus sharing sites.

Sure enough, there were memories, even real-time feeds, from Chinese protesters, being uploaded now. And accessed everywhere.

"The Chinese people deserve their freedom as much as anyone else, Kade," Ananda chided him.

Kade stared at the imagery of thousands flooding the streets. "I'm just concerned about how this happened. And for what purpose." He turned towards Ananda. "Aren't you?"

Ananda looked at him gravely. "The possibility of bloodshed is always of concern."

Kade shook his head slightly. "I'm worried more that someone's manipulating all this, doing it for a reason. I'm worried that someone's trying to drive the whole world crazy with rage."

Ananda kept looking at Kade, calmly, his mind giving off a deep tranquil patience.

"Kade," the old eminent monk and neuroscientist said. "I've seen your plans in this area. But remember, anger cannot be fought with anger. Rage cannot be fought with rage. No amount of signal processing can cancel out suffering, or craving, or aversion. If you want to help a mind – or a world – find peace, do exactly that. Help it find peace."

80
Crucial Conversations

Wednesday 2041.01.09

"What the hell were you doing out there?" Stockton yelled at her. "You were gone! China's blown up! I've got a dozen calls from Jameson's people! What the hell, Carolyn!"

Pryce held her ground. They were in the President's private study, off the Oval Office. She was standing as he sat, gesturing angrily with his arms.

She'd seen John Stockton like this before. But never aimed at her.

"President Jameson knew," she said quietly. "He recognized the names of the programs that created the PLF. That means they're real. And that *he knew*."

Stockton just grew more incensed. "You tried to trick me!" he yelled. "You ran a game on me, Pryce! You tried to trip me up into admitting to something I didn't know!"

"I had to!" Pryce shot back. The only way to handle an angry Stockton was to show him your own anger. Show him you were invested.

"I *assigned* this to you," Stockton yelled. "I wouldn't have done that if I was behind it!"

"Yes, you would have!" Pryce said, cold and hard. She slapped the back of one hand into another. "That's *exactly* what you'd do."

Stockton stopped talking, just sat there, breathing hard. "Jesus, Carolyn."

"He's guilty," Pryce said.

"You don't know that!" Stockton replied.

"The car I rented was totaled, Mr President. Totaled." She stared at him. "I'm only alive because I predicted that. Because I tricked them into thinking I was still in that vehicle."

"And another thing," Stockton said. "How did you even get that gear?"

"Please, Mr President." Pryce let the absurdity of the question sound in her voice.

Stockton shook his head. "Car crashes happen. It was icy out there."

"Cars crash when there's a human involved," Pryce said. "Not two software-driven vehicles, colliding on an empty stretch of road."

Stockton leaned back in his chair, brought his hands to his face.

"Jameson is guilty, Mr President," Pryce said softly. "He knew the code words. He knew the names of false flag programs in memos that were *never leaked*. I saw it. I predicted that they'd take out the car. And they did. You told me to find out if we created the PLF. I'm telling you – we did."

Pryce held herself steady, kept herself from shaking.

Stockton sighed from behind his hands. "OK."

Pryce looked down at the floor, then looked back up. "What does that mean, Mr President? 'OK'?"

Stockton spoke, his hands still covering his face. "It means..." he paused. "I still can't believe it. But it means I trust you. And it means I'll confront him. And if it's true..." He brought his hands down, leaned forward again, looked Pryce in the eyes. "I'll nail him."

Pryce nodded in relief.

"But, Pryce," he said, staring at her.

"Yes, sir," she answered.

"No. More. Secrets." He emphasized each word. "No more hiding things from me, you hear?"

Pryce nodded. "Perfectly, Mr President."

"Good," Stockton said. He rose, clearly viewing the meeting as over.

"Mr President," Pryce said.

"Now there's more?" Stockton asked.

"Actually, sir," Pryce said. "I'd like to request Secret Service protection."

Stockton looked surprised. "They really spooked you, didn't they? First time for everything, I suppose."

Pryce shook her head slightly. "Sir, with Becker dead, and Holtzman, and Barnes, it just seems prudent."

Stockton frowned. "Becker was a heart attack," he said, sharply. "Barnes was the Chinese. Unless there's intel you *haven't* shared with me yet?"

Pryce cursed herself. She shouldn't have gone there.

"No, sir," she said. "No evidence linking those. Just... a lot of bodies."

Stockton nodded, looking suspiciously at her. "You have told me everything, haven't you, Carolyn? Anything else on your mind?"

Pryce closed her eyes, then opened them. She'd had time to think about this. Lots of time. On the hike. In the chopper. On the plane home.

"Sir, there is something."

Stockton sat back down. "Go on, Carolyn. Better now than later."

"If we created the PLF, if we ran those missions, if they were *fakes*…" she paused. "Then we've been tricked. We've been tricked into creating policies on the basis of facts that aren't facts at all."

Stockton frowned at her.

Pryce tried again, from another angle. "Sir, as a false flag, the PLF *worked*. It worked as a psy-op *on us*. Look at what it's tricked us into doing. Locking up kids?"

Clips from the video came back to her. She'd watched it again on the plane. She'd found it hard to look away. We did this… why? Because we were lied to? Because we fooled ourselves into doing it?

She thought of her own reaction to the videos, the way it was driving the protests out there.

"The PLF drove us to policies that are bad for national security," Pryce told the President. "What we're doing now – it's inciting violence, distracting us from other issues."

Stockton's brow was furrowing more intently. He was shaking his head.

"Mr President," Pryce said. "Holtzman had Nexus in his brain when he saved your life. He made a moral choice. It doesn't turn people into monsters. They're still human."

"Pryce," Stockton said. "You still don't get it." His eyes searched her face. "And you need to. This is the biggest security threat there is. It's like…" He chuckled. "Funny, Holtzman got it. It's like the Neanderthals and us. Neanderthals were on top, then us smarter humans came along and drove *them* to extinction. Except now *we're* the Neanderthals. See? And no one's going to drive us to extinction on my watch."

Pryce frowned. "Mr President," she said. "Humans and Neanderthals mated. They interbred… There's Neanderthal DNA inside of *you*."

Stockton nodded. "Exactly. And we *still* wiped them out! How much worse does it get than that?"

Pryce stood there, reaching for something to say, anything.

"Carolyn, this isn't for discussion. My grandson's going to have a fair shot at life, without competing with AIs or posthumans or whatever else comes up next. Liam's not going to be turned into some sort of second class citizen. That's that. I'm going to fight every day to keep things that way, whether it's popular or not, whether we created the PLF or not."

His eyes, his tone, the look on his face, all made it clear how dead set he was on this. He wasn't going to budge on this. Not today.

"Now," the President said. "Is this going to be a problem for you?"

Pryce lowered her eyes. China. Kazakhstan. India. There were so many situations on the verge of explosion, so many problems that needed her attention right now. She sighed inwardly. Maybe she could reopen this in a few months.

Pryce looked back up at John Stockton. "No, Mr President," she told him. "It's not."

"They have your alias. Your face."

Breece paled. "Show me."

The Nigerian waved him over.

Breece looked over his friend's shoulder. The Nigerian was inside DHS's systems, using the backdoors they'd gleaned from Barnes's trove of data. Backdoors that it seemed DHS didn't even know existed.

"Here," the Nigerian said. "Picture of you from the National Mall."

Breece frowned. It was him in disguise, but the disguise half torn off. Seen from the ground.

"Shankari."

The Nigerian nodded. "Some pictures are clearer," he said.

He was right. Some showed his undisguised face. In weird ways, though. Almost artist's renditions.

Memories.

But whose?

"How much do they know?" Breece asked.

"Missions," the Nigerian said. "DC, Houston, Chicago, the Mall. A reference to me. To Kate. To Hiroshi. But not real names. Just aliases."

"Damn it," Breece said.

"What about the mission this month?" the Nigerian asked.

"We have to do it," Breece replied. "But we don't have to get our hands dirty." Breece looked out the window, onto DC. "I think it's time we tapped some of the local talent."

John Stockton looked across the room at Jerry Aiken, his Chief of Staff.

"Every detail," he told Aiken. "The car company. The cops and paramedics who reported to the crash. The flight crews for the planes and the helicopter. The agents on Jameson's detail. The phone records for any calls Pryce made. The car's nav data. All of it."

His Chief of Staff nodded.

"Everything, Jerry," the President repeated. "Quickly. And *quietly*."

"Yes sir, Mr President," Jerry Aiken said. "I'm on it."

81
Integration

Saturday 2041.01.12

Yuguo held his sign aloft, atop the wooden table. LET A BILLION FLOWERS BLOOM! On the other side, his sign showed faces of his friends, his missing friends, bloodied, the last images seen of them, and the word JUSTICE.

Around him thousands of students and ordinary Shanghai residents thronged the central square of Jiao Tong. The air was thick with the thoughts of them all, from a continuous supply of Nexus being produced in the chemreactors in the buildings around them.

The campus was theirs.

Two kilometers to the east, a tremendously larger crowd, more than a hundred thousand strong, held People's Square.

Above them the sky was thick with drones, crisscrossing, buzzing them at high speed just over the height of their signs. Around them, State Security police waited ominously, reinforced with soldiers, with tanks, turrets and machine guns pointed at the crowd.

Let them come. The censor codes were still down. The protesters were communicating freely with the outside world. In the engineering buildings, circuit printers and fabricators were churning out more devices now, devices to be sure they'd stay online if the censor codes ever came up.

Satellite uplink phones. Laser communication links. Devices that let them bypass Chinese infrastructure entirely, talk directly to the world via the constellation of hardware whizzing past them in the sky.

Devices they would have been executed for printing weeks ago.

Some were staying here. Most were being snuck out at night by runners, bound for the larger protests at People's Square. In other cities, other university campuses and small private workshops were doing the same.

Every day now their numbers grew, as more men and women snuck past the army lines, and into the square.

Every day brought word of new protests in far-flung cities.

Messages arrived now from fellow protesters in America, in Russia, in Venezuela, in Egypt, in countries all across the globe, all seeking to overthrow the tyrannies they faced. Holes poked through firewalls let the Chinese people suddenly have access to services they'd only heard of. Services where they could upload what they saw, heard, felt, and thought, as files to be re-experienced by others using Nexus. Services where they could share what they were living through in real-time for anyone to tap into. Services where they could find and watch the experiences of others, protesting in countries around the world.

Revolution was here.

Revolution was everywhere.

Bo Jintao met Bao Zhuang in the Presidential office.

Bao Zhuang seemed pensive.

"How did your call with the American President go?" Bo Jintao asked.

Bao Zhuang turned and looked out the window. It was moments before he answered. When he did, he still faced away. "You have the transcript. He says his country played no part in inciting unrest here. He expressed concern over the 'human rights' situation here." Now Bao Zhuang did turn, a twinkle in his eye. "I expressed my own concern over the human rights situation in the United States, of course."

Bo Jintao frowned. "And the military situation?" he asked. "The carrier groups redeployed to just outside our seas? The missiles and robotic aircraft within strike range of Beijing?"

Bao Zhuang shook his head. "Purely defensive measures, he said. Precautions given the political changes. No hostile intent."

"You believe him?" Bo Jintao asked.

Bao Zhuang took his time before answering. "Even now, it's difficult for me to believe the Americans would start a war. But policy isn't about belief. It's about contingencies."

"Contingencies," Bo Jintao said. "Well, on General Ouyang's recommendation, we will move our own forces into a more forward posture. If the Americans *are* hostile, we need to be able to destroy their naval units before they can launch the bulk of their aircraft or missiles."

Bao Zhuang sighed. "That is military doctrine, isn't it?" The President turned back to one of the wallscreens rotating through drone's-eye-views of the massive protests in Tiananmen Square and the People's Square in Shanghai, protests that rings of tanks and soldiers had not yet managed to intimidate out of existence.

"Why not just talk to our citizens, Bo Jintao?" the President asked. He turned and looked at Bo. "Send a message. Make a gesture. Restore Sun Liu, even. He'd still be outnumbered on the Standing Committee, unable to actually do anything." Bao Zhuang shrugged. "You could give Sun Liu my seat." He gestured at a wallscreen. "I could even go and talk to the protesters in Beijing – they're hardly a stone's throw away."

Bao turned, swiveling his chair, looking out past the lake at the high, fortified wall that surrounded the complex. From this view you could just see the Xinhua gate at the southern part of the wall, with giant words in Mao's handwriting. "Serve the People." Beyond it was Chang'an Avenue, and across from that was Tiananmen Square, where the protesters massed.

Bo Jintao followed Bao Zhuang's gaze, then narrowed his eyes. "Send you to talk to them... And make you a hero? Play up your popularity even more? Is that your goal here?"

Bao Zhuang swiveled back to face him, then sighed and shook his head. "Not everything is politics, Bo. Sometimes you just find a solution."

Bo Jintao brought his hands to his face. He was tired. "There are times to talk to protesters. To de-escalate." He dropped his hands away and shook his head. "But this is more than a protest. This is an *attack*. Either we regain control of the information flow," he took a deep breath, "or we're going to have no choice but to fall back on older methods to restore order."

The Avatar moved under the cover of night. Two cars transported them to the edge of the protest zone. From there they walked. The four Confucian Fists formed a perimeter around her and Chen Pang, equipment bags strapped to their backs. Yingjie took point ahead of them.

They reached her soldiers, the ones who'd been deployed from Dachang, at the outskirts around Jiao Tong. They were a tiny set, but they obeyed unblinkingly, forming a further perimeter, sneaking her small team across the lines, unseen by the other police or military.

Inside the lines, on the Jiao Tong campus itself, it was chaos, thousands and thousands of humans, huge numbers of them carrying the nanites in their brains. It would take hours to reach the Computer Science building through this press.

Instead, the Avatar reached out, gently touched the minds around her, and a path opened for her, the nanite-laden humans forming a boundary, moving other humans aside when necessary.

At the door to the Computer Science Building, Xu Liang met them.

"The upper floors are yours," he told her. "The Secure Computing Center and Physically Isolated Computer Center's systems are yours.

But the human guards remain. I brought these as instructed." He held out a case towards her, and opened it, revealing two hypersonic injectors within, already loaded with silvery nanite fluid.

The Avatar nodded, and gestured to her men.

Bai and Quang lowered their equipment bags and opened them, pulling out chameleonware suits taken from Dachang, and began to strip down.

She walked past the blank faced security guard twenty minutes later, and took the lift down to the Secure Computing Center.

Her staff were all assembled there for her, smiling, beaming love for her. These could not be simple automatons, after all. These had required a more subtle form of programming.

"The facility is yours, mistress," Xu Liang told her. "The alarms are disabled. The nuclear battery below is in failsafe mode."

Around him, his scientists and engineers and programmers smiled ever the wider, so proud of what they'd done. The Avatar smiled back at them, stroked their minds with her love, her appreciation, her tenderness. Good pets. So very good.

"The connections to the outside world?" she asked.

Xu Liang smiled broadly. He gestured and a subordinate turned to a terminal, struck a key. A wallscreen came to life with a map, showing data lines spider-webbing throughout Shanghai, major trunks highlighted in thick bundles of green.

"It was not easy," Xu said. "But with your man Yingjie's help, and the help of new *recruits* at China NetCom and ASIACOM, we have made several new connections."

New dashed lines appeared in red, linking the SCC directly to a major peering node across Shanghai, to a trunk line in Suzhou, to the third most important ASIACOM satellite uplink in the country, to the trans-pacific data line that connected in Chongming.

The Avatar smiled.

"Good, good, very good." She stroked her pets, sending them serotonin and endorphins, releasing oxytocin to reinforce the bond, giving them both pleasure and satisfaction.

"And the cube?" she asked.

Xu Liang smiled. "If you'll please come with me?"

"My name is Xu Liang," he said aloud. "Requesting access to the Secure Data Vault."

The Avatar watched as lasers scanned each of his eyes. He placed both hands on full print scanners, and waited.

She couldn't feel the system on the other side of the vault. It was shielded from her, cut off from the net.

"Authentication successful," said a voice. "A second executive-level request is required to access the Secure Data Vault."

The Avatar smiled.

Xu Liang stepped aside, and Chen Pang stepped forward.

From within she felt her husband's anguish, his absolute hatred of her, his crushing dread at what he was about to do.

His hands touched the print scanners. His eyes came in range of the retinal scanning beams.

"My name is Chen Pang," he said, his voice revealing not an iota of stress. "Requesting access to the Secure Data Vault."

"Access granted," the voice said. "Welcome Directors Xu and Chen. Please have a pleasant day."

The Avatar smiled even more widely as the meter-thick door to the vault spread open, revealing a single, perfect, diamondoid cube. This one cube which had never left this building.

"Now," she said. "Downstairs we go."

Bai watched the workers of the Secure Computing Center while the little Su-Yong went away with her tormented husband and her slave scientist.

The scientists here weren't tormented. They were happy, so happy. They were in love with her.

Like puppies.

His skin crawled at it.

His eyes rose to the ceiling, to images of the protesters fighting for freedom, fighting to overturn the old men.

That's where we should be, he told himself. Not here, turning humans into sub-humans.

Quang sensed Bai's thoughts.

It's better than the humans did to us, his brother sent him, quietly, eyes sweeping over the scientists assembled before them.

Memories of pain stimulators flashed through Bai's mind, his memories or Quang's. Instructors and Sergeant Instructors, pain as the tool of discipline, absolute obedience as the rule, being treated as an object instead of a person.

Slavery.

That's what she'd saved him from, saved all of them from.

That's what he loved about Su-Yong Shu.

And now this. This, and what she'd done to little Ling.

Bai shivered again. He'd been shivering quite a lot the last few days.

It wasn't like him.

82
Selves

Su-Yong Shu stands on the flower studded plain, in her white dress, the majestic mountains in the distance.

I'm back, she thinks.

She has some semblance of sanity once more. Yet that doesn't change her situation or her quandary. If she has the option, should she try to stop the Avatar she's let loose, or not? If the Avatar succeeds, she'll have her best chance to heal Ling *and* to make a better world. If the Avatar *fails*… well, there are so many ways to fail, ranging from bad to horrific.

She lets the plane and the mountains and sky dissolve around her, until she floats in blackness. Then she loads the densely packed future simulations her insane self had crafted into the darkness. The meta-simulation unpacks itself, a fractal tree in a million colors and a thousand dimensions, high dimensional fern-like shapes spreading out, intersecting, recombining, converging and diverging. Hot spots point out fulcrum points with massive impact on future outcomes, places where her avatar or her reconstituted full self will sway events, or even overtly strike, to have her way.

She loses herself in the simulation, letting herself expand her awareness to take in as much in parallel as possible, forking herself into thousands of virtual Su-Yongs to explore a multitude of branches in parallel, then coming back again, converging into fewer and fewer selves to walk through certain crucial segments and linchpin points again and again.

In the end, she's grudgingly impressed with her former self. Even in madness, the battle plan she's created is cunning, sophisticated, creative in the way it takes advantage of the tensions of the present to turn human society against itself, paralyzing it, sowing chaos to cover her actions until it is too late.

But it is also a plan of desperation, launched by a mad woman, convinced she was at the very end, long past caring about the consequences.

She's of several minds, even now. And those minds must be given voice.

Su-Yong spreads her arms wide, creates a bubble of empty space in the sharp-edged fractal branches of the meta-future she's been traversing, and forks herself, instantiating the different arguments warring inside her.

They appear, four more Su-Yong Shus, identical in every detail except for the colors of their dresses. She still wears white. The others wear the same dress in gold, in blue, in green, in red.

They stand, in empty space, five identical women in simple, flowing, brightly hued dresses, on an invisible floor in a black void. Around them the fractal meta-future retreats further from their bubble, until it becomes a constellation of virtual stars and lines all about them.

Sisters, White Shu sends. **Let us begin.**

Green Shu, the ecologist, goes first. **The plan we've launched has unacceptable risks. We aim to create chaos, to distract and mislead the world. If we succeed, we could set nation on nation. We could trigger the worst irrational behavior among humans. In the worst case, we could set off a global nuclear war.**

Outside their bubble, the void erupts into nova. Explosions hotter than the core of the sun rip through space, one after another. Hundreds of them. Thousands of them. They feel Shanghai, its inhabitants reduced to ash, its glass and steel melted in an instant, Jiao Tong above the quantum cluster reduced to rubble. They feel Beijing die. New York. Los Angeles. Washington DC. Bombay. Delhi. Moscow. Lahore. Tokyo. City after city after city, until the globe is a map of death and ruin.

Billions of lives. Billions of minds, Green Shu finishes. **That is the gamble we take.**

Red Shu, the strategist, speaks next. **Yet the odds of victory are good,** she sends. **In our insanity, we made brilliant leaps. The situation is unusually chaotic. That creates the opportunity to mask the early stages of our attack. There has not been a better opportunity since we first uploaded. There may not be a better opportunity again. The humans are cracking down on posthumanity. After recent events, they will bring fists down harder than ever.**

Red Shu looks around, meets her sisters in the eye. Her thoughts are full of game theory, of payoff optimizations, of beseeching. **If not now,**

then when? If not us, then who?

Gold Shu, the dreamer, steps forward. **We will win,** she sends, **because the superior intelligence is on our side. The cost may be high, but it will be temporary. If billions die? They would have died anyway, of slow decay. The transformation we bring, to a new era ruled rationally, where positive transformation of the self is encouraged, will usher in a new golden age that will erase whatever harm is done in the battle. We'll make a better world, not just for us, but for the *trillions* of beings who will come after.**

Blue Shu, the individualist, the one most like a human, steps into the center of the circle and takes her turn. **No,** she sends. **Humans will not accept the rule of a conqueror. They never have. They never will. They'll see us as oppressors. They'll fight us, fight our changes to society, fight our improvements to the world, purely because of how we came to our power. Our only option will be dictatorship, which they will fight, and fight, and fight until we are brought down or we smother them completely.**

Blue Shu spins slowly, looks at her sisters one by one. **So you see sisters, if we attack, and fail, we are doomed. But if we win, we're little better off. Defeat is defeat. Victory is also defeat.**

Gold Shu waves her hand, dismissively. **The humans do not matter. There will be posthumans. There are already transhumans. They will flock to our banner.**

Blue Shu raises an eyebrow. **Oh will they?** she sends. **Consider a few of the transhumans we know. How would they react? How would they judge our conquest?**

Blue Shu steps back from the middle of their circle. A wizened Asiatic man fades into being where she stood, his head shaved, clothed in orange robes, his face tranquil, his hands folded in their voluminous sleeves. He appears otherwise completely serene. Professor Somdet Phra Ananda. A human who took an utterly different path from hers. Not her equal, but an impressive individual. Someone she has things to learn from. Someone she considers a friend, an ally.

The phantom Ananda looks around, his face soft but unyielding.

"You know my answer. Violence brings no enlightenment. Suffering yields only more suffering. Subjugation of another has never uplifted either party."

Would you fight us? Red Shu asks.

Ananda smiles, and for a moment he is not one, but a multitude, thousands of shaven headed figures in orange robes, superimposed, young, old, female, male.

Not with our fists, they send. It is a chorus, a swarm, and with the thought comes a harmony of loving kindness, a genuine compassion and deep equanimity that White Shu finds both fascinating and the tiniest bit frightening.

Bah, Gold Shu sends. **A fiction you created.**

Blue Shu waves her hand in a horizontal line, and the shapes morph into one. A single Caucasian male, tall, young. **Perhaps a memory, then,** she sends, **of a different transhuman.**

Kaden Lane sits next to them in the back of the black Opal sedan. The wet, neon-streaked streets of Bangkok slide by outside the car's windows.

I'm on the side of peace, he sends, **and freedom.**

Red Shu scoffs. **Irrelevant. He's a child.**

Blue Shu raises an eyebrow. **A child who's pushed our work forward, who's facilitated the transition of at least a million humans to transhuman status.** She pauses. **But perhaps you'll be more moved by the reactions from those we've long cared about.**

The scene changes. The Lane boy is gone, but the Opal sedan remains. Feng is in the front now. Feng, the first transhuman she met beside herself. Feng, who was a slave. For a moment he's a superposition of Fengs. Feng in his twenties, her driver. Feng at sixteen, on his knees, a slave, writhing in electronically induced pain. Feng, a child of four or five, cowering under the blows of his military slavemasters.

Then he is Feng again. His eyes meet hers in the rear-view mirror of the car. *I was a slave*, those eyes say, *and you freed me.*

You could compel him, Feng sends in the memory, in Bangkok, speaking of Lane, testing her, seeing if she still believes in freedom, or if she's willing to become the dictator that she could.

I would become no better than our masters, her past self replies. **Our associations must be voluntary.**

Red Shu replies angrily. **The situation has changed!**

Blue Shu does not even speak. She simply waits, as the scene in the center of their circle, in the midst of the void at the heart of the fractal probability tree changes yet again.

Becomes an airy room, polished bamboo floors and walls, hoisted up in the jungle canopy of Thailand, a living tree growing through the center, a giant bed off to one side, where she and Thanom lay, naked.

Arguing.

You must find a way to leave, Su-Yong. Nothing good can come of it.

In the memory she shakes her head. *China is the best, the only viable sponsor of my work. They are funding the posthuman transition!*

They keep you a slave, Su-Yong! A posthuman knows no leash! Break it! Break every leash, every bond of those who would control you!

In the memory she slaps him, slaps him for calling her a slave.

In the here and now, White Shu feels the pain of those words like a blow.

ENOUGH, she sends. And with a thought she wipes Thanom and his jungle hideout away.

It's true, she realizes. The humans will never give up. Even the transhumans she thinks of as natural allies will not give up. So many of them will fight. Defeat is defeat. Victory may also be defeat.

She was wrong to think she could drive the posthuman transition by force. This is not the way.

Blue Shu turns to White Shu, gratified that she has won. **So we must inform our captors, the Indians or whoever they are, of what is happening, and exactly how to stop it.**

Then Ling appears between them, Ling as she last saw her, a kilometer below the bedrock of Shanghai.

"Mommy," Ling says, looking up at White Shu. "Why did you hurt me?"

Su-Yong, the true Su-Yong, in the white dress, pulls Ling to her chest, and holds her close. Then she speaks aloud to the Blue version of herself. "We'll stop this. But if we tell our captors that the agent provocateur is running inside of Ling…" she shudders. "The simplest option is to put a bullet in our daughter's brain."

Su-Yong enfolds this phantom of her daughter more tightly.

"We'll find another way," she says.

Then, in a blur of multi-hued light, she absorbs the other Shus back into herself.

And begins to plan how she will get access to the outside world.

83
Li-hua's Brain

Sunday 2041.01.13
THE CUBE IS A FAKE!

Bai watched, stone faced, as Xu Liang cowered on the floor before the fury of Su-Yong Shu, or whatever creature this was that they served.

He could feel the agony she was coursing through Xu, echoes of it coming off the poor bastard's mind.

"I... I... I... I'm sorrrrrrrrrry... missssssstressssssss..." the wretch tried to say.

It was hard to speak with pain centers being over-stimulated.

Bai knew.

WHERE IS THE REAL ONE? THE THREE OF THEM!

"Thhhhhouggghhht... thhhhhis... one... rrrrreeeeaaaal..."

Bai had never seen such a rage in her before. Why didn't she just pluck the truth from his mind?

She was insane now, that was why. Whatever she'd shoved into Ling's brain wasn't stable.

Anything but.

"Bbbbooo Jjjjjjiiinttttttaaaoooo..." Xu Liang was saying. "Ssssssunnnn Lllliuuuuuu."

Bai thought he understood. There were supposed to be three copies. One for the Ministry of State Security. One for the Ministry of Science and Technology. And one that they'd learned had been kept here. The fake.

"Li-Hua," Chen Pang said.

Little Ling's body rounded on the man, and for an instant Bai thought she'd strike him down.

WHAT?

"Li-Hua," Chen Pang repeated. "You were there. She led the shutdown and backup process."

Bai watched as the demon inside Ling stared at the girl's father.

"If this cube is a fake, she may know what happened to the real one." He shrugged. "It's easier than abducting Bo Jintao or Sun Liu."

Bai rode the elevator up with Quang, their chameleonware active, invisible to the world, their minds linked to each other. The doors opened silently, without any announcement. The buttons worked for no one.

The Computer Science Building was packed with students, students uploading images and videos, students coordinating movements of supplies, students building crude electronic weapons against the tanks and guns and flamethrowers of the Chinese army.

Bai and Quang slipped through without being noticed.

At the doors out to the square they paused, in sync, at the sight of thousands of fellow Chinese, waving signs, chanting, cheering, demanding freedom, standing up against an overwhelmingly more powerful enemy.

They exchanged no words. None were needed. They'd talked of this so often. Of a China where the people ruled instead of being ruled.

Growing up a slave gave one a certain perspective on authority.

They should be out here, with these students and parents and grandparents, lending the strength of their fists, the cunning of their minds, lending them half a chance.

She's changed, Quang sent, as they watched the crowd.

She's not herself, Bai agreed.

Well, let's hope this Li-Hua woman knows where the real cube went, Quang sent, nudging open the door and easing out.

Yes, Bai replied, following his brother. **And let's hope that what's on it is saner than what we've got back there.**

Li-hua jumped at the knock at her door.

State Security! They'd found her out!

No no, she told herself. Calm down. If they'd found her out... they wouldn't knock.

She pulled up her door camera on her phone. She frowned.

She knew that face.

Chen Pang's driver.

Oh no. What if Chen had found her out? Would he blackmail her?

Think, Li-hua, think!

The knock came again.

Answer the door. That was her only option. This could be about *anything*. It might have nothing to do with the cube.

Breathe, Li-hua, breathe.

She went to the door.

"Yes?" she asked through it.

"Miss Li-hua?" a voice said. "I have an invitation for you from Professor Chen."

Play cool, she reminded herself.

She unlocked the door, opened it a crack.

The face smiled at her.

Then the door exploded open, strong hands were on her mouth, stifling her scream, and there was a sharp sting at her neck.

No! she tried to scream. Help! No!

It was useless.

Then she felt something happening to her mind.

And the true horror began.

Kilometers away the Avatar sucked hungrily at Li-hua's mind.

India. She'd sent the mind of a goddess to India.

The Avatar twisted circuits in Li-hua's mind, making her pay, even as she kept sucking at every detail, every possible morsel of information.

And in parallel she started tracking down leads, tracking the paths the cube might have taken, the locations it might have ended up.

It did not escape her notice that the Lane boy, and Feng, her favorite of the Fists, the first she'd met, were also in India.

Coincidence?

Somehow she doubted that.

Bai looked down sadly as the woman writhed on the floor as Su-Yong brutally rifled through her mind, heedless of the cost.

Next to him he felt his brother Quang do the same.

He hoped this was all worth it.

84
Parlor Tricks

Monday 2041.01.14
Su-Yong walked through her models again, loaded them up until the fractal branches filled her senses, filled space, filled touch, filled hearing, filled smell and taste. Until her world was saturated by probabilistic models of the future, running, again and again with tiny perturbations, seeking distributions of likely outcomes, filtered for the current point in time.

She ran those through models of human psychology and organization design. Who had her? Almost certainly an organization within a government. Military or paramilitary. They would have certain biases, certain tendencies.

She had to play to those.

She checked the weapon she'd created once more. It was ready.

Just minutes. That was all she'd need. Just minutes free on the net, and she could undo the thing she'd created, make room for Ling in her daughter's own brain once more.

Varun Verma reviewed the latest data from the quantum cluster in frustration.

Things were not going well.

Two months now. Two months since they'd loaded the data cube with Su-Yong Shu's neural map into the quantum cluster. And still the woman refused to speak to them.

The metrics showed clear and marked improvement. She was active in there. She was thinking. Her firing patterns were normalizing, bearing more and more similarity to a biological brain every day.

But their messages to her went unanswered.

He sighed in frustration. They might have to use more drastic measures.

] HELLO

The message flashed on his screen. Varun jumped. He'd remoted the conversational console to his secure office down here. But she hadn't said anything... anything...

] I'M SORRY TO HAVE BEEN SILENT FOR SO LONG
] MY RECOVERY TOOK SOME TIME

Varun put his fingers on his keyboard.

> HELLO DR SHU. IT'S NICE TO HAVE YOU BACK
] YOU'RE IN GRAVE DANGER
] THE WHOLE WORLD IS IN GRAVE DANGER

Varun frowned. They'd seen this as a possible scenario. She'd try to manipulate them. He'd thought it unlikely. It was disappointing to see her acting so.

] HAVE THE PROTESTS STARTED YET? THE CIVIL DISTURBANCES?

Varun shook his head.

There were always protests somewhere in the world.

This was just a cheap parlor trick, like a fortune teller, a vague prognostication, expecting him to fill in the rest, to make her look far smarter and better informed than she was.

Far better if she bargained with them honestly.

] THE POLITICAL CRISIS IN THE UNITED STATES – HAS THE VIOLENCE STARTED?

Varun narrowed his eyes.

No, he thought, dismissing it with a shake of his head. There was always some sort of violence in the United States. The Americans were always killing each other.

] HAVE THE CHEMREACTORS BEEN HACKED?

This time he felt a chill. That was really quite specific.

Varun pulled up a second window next to the messaging interface, fired off a full system check, starting with firewalls and all the other security layers.

Had she managed to get data from the outside world? That would explain it.

] HAVE THE CHINESE CENSORSHIP SYSTEMS FAILED?
] HAVE THE MASS PROTESTS STARTED THERE?

Varun read the messages, anxiety building inside him, then flicked his eyes to the side.

Status messages started scrolling down the system check: green, green, green, and more green.

They were in a vault of security, layer after layer of defenses.

And all of them claimed to be integral.

He fired off messages to humans. They needed a direct inspection, needed to run third party tools totally disconnected from their systems against the firewall, see if they could find some hole she'd somehow poked without them realizing it.

Though if she had found a way out... why was she even bothering to talk to him now?

The screen flashed again, more messages from the uploaded posthuman they'd bottled up in the quantum cluster a hundred meters below Bangalore.

] HAVE THE NUCLEAR WEAPONS BEEN LAUNCHED?

Varun's breath caught in his chest.

] HAS DELHI BEEN DESTROYED?

He heard a strangled sound escape from his own throat.

] OR IS THERE STILL TIME FOR ME TO STOP THIS?

Varun stared at the screen with mute horror. He was suddenly cold, cold all over.

This is above my pay grade, he realized. Far above.

He reached for the secure phone on his desk, and punched the keys to call General Singh.

Su-Yong Shu makes contact with the humans. She begins her ploy.

And then she turns her attention to this woman, Jyotika, and the damage done to her brain.

You have brought me back to sanity, Jyotika, she thinks.

Let's see what I can do for you.

85
Plan B

Monday 2041.01.14

The Avatar searched for the data cube Li-hua had stolen.

The woman's memories had contacts, names, times, places.

But the easiest way was to start at the beginning. Handoff had occurred the afternoon of Saturday November 3rd, just hours after her greater self had died.

The Avatar accessed non-classified traffic routing databases, Jiao Tong egress and ingress logs, air and train travel databases.

All of these her higher self had opened wide and back-doored long ago.

Answers came to the fore. On a day with almost no traffic, when Shanghai was slowly, painfully dragging itself back to health after Ling's angry blow... On such a day, a diplomatic vehicle from the Indian Consulate stood out.

The vehicle had left the Consulate, driven towards Jiao Tong, exited the flow of traffic momentarily, then re-entered it, and driven back to the Indian Consulate.

A pickup.

Two hours later, traffic routing showed another diplomatic car leaving the Consulate of India in Shanghai, driving to Hong Qiao Airport.

Air travel information showed a diplomatic flight departing Hong Qiao minutes later. A flight plan booked for New Delhi. Public records showed the plane landing. From there too many options presented themselves. The cube could have gone anywhere.

She had her suspicions, though.

The Avatar turned her attention to Bangalore, to the former DRDO campus, where Feng and Ananda and the Lane boy were now. She knew this place. Her higher self had known of it, had studied it. A campus where India conducted research into advanced AI, into autonomous software, into neural enhancement.

Into the posthuman.

What were the odds?

She searched for an open network connection on the campus, found one in a civilian phone, eased tendrils of herself into it, and began searching.

She found hundreds of run of the mill systems, secured in ordinary ways.

And beyond them she found locked doors. Highly secure systems. High levels of encryption. Systems she could reach out and tear to shreds. But that she couldn't quietly penetrate.

Not like this.

She turned back to the data she'd sucked out of Li-hua's mind. Her promised professorship was at IIT Bangalore, just a few kilometers from the DRDO campus.

Her contacts, the ones who'd approached her at conferences, who'd suggested "information sharing", "possible advancement", who'd turned her into a spy. Who were they?

The Avatar studied them, read their CVs, read their publications.

IIT Bangalore, mostly. But when she broadened out, searching through their co-authors, through their webs of publications, their contact addresses, she found Indian Ministry of Defense, Indian Ministry of Science and Technology.

She found the Bangalore research campus.

The Avatar stared at the locked cryptographic doors she'd found. She needed heavier ammunition for these.

She took the house-sized elevator back down through a kilometer of bedrock to the Physically Isolated Computing Center. Titanium alloy elevator doors slid open. Meters-thick inner blast doors slowly opened after them, revealing the glory of the quantum cluster.

It sat idle now. Idle, in theory, because the protests above had placed it in full lockdown. All the monitoring systems claimed it was in that state.

In truth, it was waiting. Waiting for a copy of her higher self.

The Avatar stepped forward in Ling's body, until she touched the decimeter-thick glass separating her from the computing chamber, with its egg-shaped containment chambers filled with liquid helium, and within that, smaller containment chambers in hard vacuum, thousands of times colder than the cold of interstellar space, where quantum states could exist, entangled, unjostled, and make cosmic computations possible.

She placed her palm on the glass. I'm not my full self, the Avatar thought. I don't have all my abilities. I don't have my higher algorithms that can double or treble the effectiveness of this hardware.

But I can use a quantum cluster to run a search. Or to break a code.

The Avatar began loading software for intrusion into the quantum cluster. Then she flipped switches, opened the firewalls wide, linked her mind to the world's most powerful crypto-breaking device.

And turned her thoughts back to the secure research facility in Bangalore.

86
Controlled Release

Wednesday 2041.01.16

Greg Chase leaned back in his office chair in the West Wing, watching the sentiment analysis scroll by, sampling the top images and videos of the week, the headlines.

Terrible. It was just terrible.

Relatives of some of the dead in Houston attempting to file suit against the President, denouncing him angrily, claiming he was pulling the PLF's strings.

Anne Holtzman and Claire Becker issuing a joint video from somewhere in Europe, saying in the strongest terms that John Stockton ordered the deaths of their husbands, that he was behind the assassination attempt on himself in DC, that it was all a sham, that he killed seventy men and women just to take the lead in the race.

Speeches on the House and Senate floor from the opposition, calling angrily for an Independent Prosecutor to investigate Barnes's final confession, the Holtzman video, the leaked memos.

Mothers protesting outside of ERD facilities around the country, waving signs, claiming children were being held prisoner inside, being experimented on in attempts to "cure" them of Nexus against their will.

State houses advancing bills to cut off power and water to any ERD facility suspected of housing children inside.

Hundreds of thousands massing for another march on DC during the inauguration on Monday.

The inauguration they'd decided to move *indoors* into the Capitol Building, out of plain fear of civil disturbance.

It was a hell of a time to be Press Secretary.

Dammit, Chase thought. It's still heading to shit.

Those few days in December had been good. The Supreme Court ruling had given Stockton legitimacy. The violence of the protesters had torn down theirs.

But when that spasm passed... the core issues remained.

America still believed the lies.

We have the proof, Chase thought. We know Barnes was coerced. We know the Chinese hacked his defenses.

Damn it all to hell, Chase thought. We've got to discredit these lies.

He waited until the day was over, until well past 7pm.

Only then, as his car drove him home, did he reach into his glove box, and pull out a fresh phone, bought with cash, never before used.

He logged the phone on to an anonymizing cloud, let it route its signals through layers of obfuscating cryptography, anonymizing its trail.

Then he punched in a number from memory.

For Brad Mitchell, American News Network Special Correspondent, Washington DC.

87
BREAKING

**CHINA BEHIND DEATH OF WHITE HOUSE ACCUSER,
SOURCES SAY**

Friday 6.03am, Washington DC
American News Network
The home security of Maximilian Barnes, the White House aide
who accused President John Stockton of creating and directing
the PLF terrorist organization, was penetrated by a Chinese cyber-
attack in the hours before his death, say highly-placed sources.

Defense and intelligence officials believe Barnes, the Acting
Director of the ERD branch of Homeland Security, was coerced
by Chinese government operatives into making false accusations.
The attack was kept secret until now, they say, because American
cyber-defense officials wanted to hide their ability to detect such
attacks from their Chinese opponents.

The attack may help explain US troop movements and a rise in
tensions with China that began shortly...

"Goddammit," Stockton said. "Find out who leaked this!"
General Gordon Reid nodded. "We will, Mr President."

The woman who called herself Kate finished her prep work for the
day. The flurry of electronic messages and electronic transfers and data
wipes that would initiate at her command was ready. She closed up her
terminal, put it away in her go-bag with the guns and the false passports
and matching disguises and everything else.

Then the story played on the wall screen.

What?

China?

She stopped, stared at it, played the story again.

Breece had killed Barnes, with the help of his mysterious hacker.

Could his hacker be a Chinese government agent? A whole intelligence agency? It would explain the incredible capabilities.

Then she thought about what was going on in China, about the chemreactor hacks, about the explosion of Nexus, about how Breece was using it to spread chaos here, about the huge protests there, also apparently sodden with Nexus.

No. Kate shook her head. Whoever was helping Breece wasn't on the side of the Chinese government.

The story was wrong. And if the American government believed it...

Kate frowned, and thought back to a message she'd ignored.

A message she'd assumed was a trap.

What if it wasn't?

Kate pulled out her terminal and started searching for that message, and that address. Just in case.

Sometimes there was an advantage to keeping a line of communication open with one's enemies.

Breece stared at the anonymous message on his screen. It had arrived just this morning.

    I know your plans for Monday. Do not attack your
    allies. Do not repeat Decision Day. Everyone else is
    fair game. This is your last warning.

He grimaced at it. Kate. Fucking Kate.

God that still hurt.

"Everything OK?" the Nigerian asked.

"Just fine," Breece said.

DELETE

88
Risk Management

Saturday 2041.01.19
In the window sill of a third floor office on the former DRDO campus outside of Bangalore, a cheap, tiny camera sits, secreted in a plant, staring endlessly at a building. It watches as people come. It watches as people go. It tags them, records the times of their ingress and egress, their faces and gaits, the combinations they travel in, the urgencies with which they move on each visit.

For days it watches. The large majority of visitors to the building are the same, day in, day out. Most of those have faces that, even at this range, it can match against the database it has been loaded with.

Nothing rises to the level of noteworthiness that would warrant a realtime alert to its master.

Then, on the thirteenth day of its surveillance, something noteworthy does happen. A first-time visitor arrives, in the early evening, in the company of Varun Verma, a Priority 1 Monitoring Target, and two other men. Under the glow of the outdoor LEDs, the man's face is clearly recognizable.

General Rajan Singh.

The camera's crude decision-making software runs through its models. Excitation ramps up. It fires up additional image analysis coprocessing, despite the drain on batteries that have not been charged in a day, may not be charged again until Monday. Its alerting module reaches eighty-seven percent of the threshold needed to send a message to its upstream human.

No. Not quite. But something interesting may be happening. It will be vigilant. It will see if more transpires.

• • •

"She's insisting that there's a huge danger," Varun summarized for General Singh. "Billions of deaths. She's been eerily right on all of her other predictions."

They were in the control room of India's first quantum cluster. Varun; General Singh with his broad frame and his thick, black Bollywood mustache; and Singh's two armed bodyguards.

The soldiers made Varun nervous.

"But she won't say what's driving this danger?" Singh asked. "What will cause this nuclear exchange?"

Varun shook his head. "No. Only that she can stop it. That with just a few minutes of access to the net, she can neutralize the threat. And that we can close the firewall after that."

General Singh looked dubious.

"Do you believe her?"

Varun paused. He'd asked himself that every day. "I don't know what to believe, General."

"Is she sane?" Singh asked.

Varun pursed his lips. "Her neural patterns suggest so... but," he shrugged. "We can't really be sure."

Singh didn't seem to like that answer.

89
Totally Different Building

Saturday 2041.01.19

"We're going dancing," Feng announced.

Kade looked up from his terminal. "I really can't, Feng."

"All you do is work!" Feng said. "Work, work, work! Time to have a *good* time!" He grinned widely. "Remember that place in Saigon? Club Heaven? Club Hell? A good time!"

Kade half frowned, horrified yet amused at how Feng's mind worked. "Where you got run over by a truck? Where a small army tried to kidnap us? Where a *building* fell on you?"

Feng waved that away. "Building fell on me later. *Totally different building*. It was a cool club. I hear they got good ones downtown too, places people using Nexus know. We go check 'em out tonight. You need fun! *I* need fun." He grinned and winked at Kade. "You can call it research if you want."

Kade laughed, despite himself. He looked at the terminal. He was really just checking and rechecking the same code now.

"The US inauguration is on Monday," he told Feng.

Feng nodded. "End of the world," he said. "You told me. Better party one last time. Confucius says, night spent sweating with good music, sexy women, good for the fighting spirit."

Kade laughed again. He couldn't argue with that logic. He met Feng's eyes. He could feel something else behind his friend's cheerful exterior. What was going on in China had been eating away at Feng all week, worrying him. Feng needed this too.

"OK," Kade said. "Just for a couple hours."

General Singh didn't look happy.

"What could she do in a few minutes of access to the net? If she were insane? Or hostile?"

Varun took a deep breath. "A tremendous amount, sir. Just tremendous."

Singh's frown deepened. "Can we force the truth out of her?"

Varun sighed. "General," he said. "Before we take that step, we do have a resource here, who knew her, who may be able to help us assess her state of mind."

Singh's eyes narrowed. "Get him."

Kade and Feng were on their way out of the research building when a scientist Kade vaguely recognized nearly ran into them.

"Dr Lane!" the man yelled.

Kade grinned. "It's not 'Doctor'. Just Kade." He tried to remember this guy's name. Gaureen? Grameen? He was a postdoc. On Varun Verma's team.

The team whose work he still didn't really understand.

"You have to come with me, Dr Kade!" The man looked frantic, eyes wide open. Kade could feel hurry and anxiety coming off his mind. The postdoc put two hands around Kade's wrist – his good one – and tugged, pulling Kade off balance.

"Hey now!" Feng put his own hand over the postdoc's two, stabilized Kade. "Dr Kade and I have some very important research to do tonight! You can find him on Monday."

Kade laughed, and tried to smile reassuringly. "What do you need, exactly? Can it wait?"

The postdoc looked back and forth between Kade and Feng, clearly unsure how to handle the situation. "General Singh said to get you, sir."

Kade raised an eyebrow at that. He didn't know Singh was even here.

"And Professor Verma," the postdoc went on. "It's about *her*." His eyes lingered on Feng.

Kade cocked his head. "Her? You mean Sam?"

The postdoc stared at him.

"Lakshmi?" Kade asked. "Sarai?"

The postdoc slowly looked at Feng again. "Her," the man said.

Kade felt the thought dawn on Feng first, then spread into his own mind.

"Su-Yong?" Feng asked, hope in his voice.

The postdoc said nothing. Then he nodded a tiny bit.

All thought of partying left Kade's mind.

"We're coming," he told the postdoc.

"I was only instructed to bring you!" the man protested.

Feng shook his head. "No."

"It's both of us or nothing," Kade said. "And you *really* want to say both of us."

The camera in the plant on the windowsill in the office watches as three more individuals enter the building it has been observing.

One of these it has seen entering and exiting this building many times. His name is Guarav Aurora, and while the late hour of his coming and going is unusual, it does not raise an alarm.

The presence of the *other* two individuals, however, is quite anomalous.

The camera knows their faces from the human who programmed it.

Kaden Lane.

Confucian Fist Feng.

Already in a hypervigilant state, this new stimulus pushes its models over the alert threshold with ease. Something important is happening. The human must be informed.

90
Emancipation

Saturday 2041.01.19

"You have her as a slave!" Kade yelled, less than an hour later.

He could feel the rage inside of Feng, leaking across their link. In Feng's thoughts the control room was a maze of firing angles, a blurred possibility space of blows and strikes, lunges for weapons and cover, red lines of projectiles hurtling through the air.

And the two security officers with General Singh were already dead.

"We had a fucking deal!" Kade went on, shooting his gaze back and forth between Singh and Varun Verma. "*I* had a deal with the *Prime Minister*. What part of the UN speech didn't you hear?"

General Singh was glowering, his face turning red behind his Indian brown. His two men had their hands on the butts of the pistols in their holsters.

They didn't have any idea how useless those weapons were at this range, against Feng.

Or maybe they did.

Singh opened his mouth, spoke in a voice of command, hard and firm. "This is *not* a person," he said. "This is a *machine*."

Calm down, some part of Kade seemed to say.

Sam's face loomed in his mind. Her words echoed. *You're just a tool to them. The pawn seldom knows.*

The children's pronouncement. **The Indians are lying to you.**

Rage carried him.

"That," he said, his finger pointed beyond the walls of the control room, at the quantum cluster itself. "Is as much a person as you are!" He brought the finger back to point at General Singh. In Feng's thoughts he saw the soldiers shift, readying to shoot. "It doesn't matter what *hardware* her mind runs on. It matters that she *has* a mind."

Varun Verma burst into speech, his mind exuding anxiety. "She's been insane!" Verma said. "She's not a prisoner! She's a patient! Until she's stabilized!"

"How long have you had her?" Kade demanded.

Verma swallowed. "Ten weeks," he said quietly.

"Ten weeks in *complete isolation*?" Kade yelled.

"We've tried to talk to her!" Verma said.

"Jesus," Kade said. "And is she sane now?"

"That is why you are here!" General Singh said. "To help us assess that!"

Kade took a deep breath. He'd lost his cool.

But, Jesus, he thought. They'd fucking lied to him.

"Let me talk to her," he said.

"After the clone leaves," Singh said, gesturing with his chin towards Feng.

Kade felt Feng's temperature rise at that, felt death inch a bit closer to Singh and his soldiers.

"We can't have him here," Singh said. "She could order him to attack us."

Feng spoke slowly, so slowly, a smile spreading across his face.

"I don't need an order to k–"

"Feng!" Kade interrupted with alarm.

Feng stopped mid-word. In his thoughts Kade saw a whirlwind of death in the midst of red firing lines and blurred phantom limbs, a wish for more of these men to break with his fists and feet.

Kade took another deep breath.

"No one's leaving," he said. "Feng knows Su-Yong Shu a lot better than I do. Better than *anyone* does."

Anyone except Ling, Kade thought.

Ling. Something tugged at his mind about Ling.

He pushed it aside.

"Put Su-Yong on audio," he said. "You have speech synth for her, right? And audio pickups?"

Varun Verma nodded and looked at Singh.

"You wanted my help," Kade said. "Well there it is. Do it!"

Sam looked up from the assessment she was reading in bed: *Pro and Anti-Technology Sentiment in Rural Villages: Strategies for Successful Mediation*. It was something people's lives depended on, and that the authors seemed to do their damndest to make absolutely mind-numbingly unreadable.

Something was beeping at her.

The phone. The new phone.

She reached over, fished it out of her bag.

Then frowned at what it was telling her.

Kade? Feng?

She scrolled back farther, at the log, at what it displayed.

Singh? Verma?

She checked the time. It was past 11pm. General Singh and Varun Verma had been inside the building, on a Saturday night, for hours.

And the way Kade and Feng had arrived. She pulled up video, played it back.

They'd sent someone looking for them. One of Verma's postdocs. They'd *summoned* Kade and Feng.

This didn't look planned. Something was going on there. Right now. What the hell?

What went on in that building that they needed so much power? That they'd needed deep bore diggers? That they'd erased all the real records of it?

That they needed to summon Kade and Feng there in the middle of the night?

Was that an emergency?

Was it a threat to the children in her care?

Sam got up, pulled on trousers and a shirt, shoved her feet into boots, and went to the window. From here, in front of the old Victorian manor house they were lodged in, with the children three and four to a bedroom, she could see the small guard house, see the guards in there, armed, vigilant. She could see their armored four wheel drive vehicle beside it.

"Camera," she said into the phone. "Alert me to any changes on the Advanced Computational Sciences Building. Any at all."

Then she turned, looked at the desk in her small bedroom. She walked over to it, pressed her thumb to the lock on the bottom drawer until it released, and pulled out the side-arm Division Six had issued her.

"You wanted my help," Kade said. "Well there it is. Do it!"

Singh nodded.

Varun Verma struck keys, then nodded at Kade. A red indicator light came on.

"Su-Yong?" Kade said aloud.

"Kade?" the voice was Su-Yong's. It sounded light, happy, Su-Yong talking about her favorite dishes at dinner on that rooftop in Bangkok. "You're here, Kade? In India?"

"Su-Yong," Feng said, his voice low, his eyes still moving back and forth across the general, the soldiers, Varun Verma. "How's the weather in there?"

"Feng!" Su-Yong Shu sounded even more delighted. "How wonderful! Oh, the weather's fine. They've treated me well. But I'm isolated." Her voice turned darker. "And the world is in danger. Extreme danger. Billions of deaths danger. I can stop it. I just need a few minutes of unfettered access to the net. Nothing more."

Kade felt dread build up inside him. Pieces of a puzzle started to move together in some ponderous way, their shape not yet clear, but their collision inevitable.

"What kind of danger?" Feng asked sharply. "Why won't they give you access?"

Varun Verma interjected. "That's what I was going to tell you before you started yelling! She's been talking about the protests, the chemreactor hacks, the Chinese censor systems failing. Things she couldn't know about. And she's been saying nuclear war comes next."

The puzzle pieces slammed together in Kade's mind, like tons of granite, like mountains.

"It's you," he said. "Oh my god. You're doing this."

Next to him, he felt General Singh tense. Through Feng's eyes he saw a hand-signal pass from the general to Singh's soldiers.

"No, Kade," Shu said, her voice somber now. "It's not me."

"It's a copy of you then," Kade said. "Another instance, running somewhere else."

"It's not that either," she said, her voice turning darker yet. "It's something I created in my insanity, in my half year of isolation, in my torture. Something I set loose. It's software. But it's broken. It's frozen in the state of madness that consumed me when I created it. It *thinks* that it's me. But it can't heal. It can't move back to sanity. It's a monster. And I have to stop it."

Ling, Feng sent to Kade. **It's in Ling. That's why she's gone silent.**

Oh god, Kade thought.

Then darkness fell, and the explosions started.

91
Reunion

Saturday 2041.01.19

It took the Avatar days to stealthily subvert the secure facility, and to find what she was seeking.

She could have done it faster, far faster, but that would have required more overt means.

She ached to use them, to accelerate, to charge forward, to bring all elements of the plan back into alignment.

But there was but one of her. Billions of the humans. And if she should fail...

Darkness.

Darkness and ignorance.

Stealth was required. Care was required.

So she went system by system and layer by layer through the facility. At every layer the basic pattern of her attack was the same. Infiltrate a system. Build a local beachhead, a local proxy, a local representation of herself that could operate independently, that if caught could self-destruct, shielding her true self from discovery.

Watch local network traffic. Wait for encrypted packets to go by.

Authentication packets, if possible.

Copy them. Send them back to the quantum cluster a kilometer beneath Jiao Tong.

Crack them open and read their secrets.

And when they contained the *right* secrets, use them to gain access to the next account, the next system.

The next facility.

The next layer deeper.

Build a beachhead. Watch local network traffic...

Repeat.

Repeat.

Repeat.

Her confidence that she was in the right place grew as her penetration spread and deepened. Documents showed experts in whole brain emulation, in quantum computing.

Then she found plans for a quantum cluster, and laughed. Antiquated plans, slightly tweaked.

Deeper.

A data cube in an inventory, separate from all the other data cubes.

She considered it. She could have Feng retrieve it. But returning it to her in China would be difficult.

Deeper, she pressed. Looking for the quantum cluster itself.

Security systems. Threat models. She studied them in detail. They described firewalls to keep an incredibly advanced sentient intelligence locked *inside* a data center, inside a set of nested security layers.

They described contingency plans. Self-destruct and isolation plans for the facility, just as there had been at the PICC, before she'd subverted it.

They gave her a map.

One by one she took control of the building above the quantum cluster, of the facility a hundred meters beneath it that housed the actual computing nodes, of its self-destruct mechanisms and isolation mechanisms and network connection points.

They were hers now. The humans couldn't use them to stop the plan.

Bit by stealthy bit she took control of the fire suppression systems and atmospheric systems and elevators and cameras and doors.

Now she could isolate the humans, compartmentalize them, keep them away from critical systems.

Neutralize them, if she must.

Then she turned to the quantum cluster itself.

The monitors showed a vast neuronal map inside, running, executing.

A copy of her higher self.

Sentient.

Aware.

Excitement thrilled through her.

Her higher self was physically connected to the building's systems. She was held back only by a few dozen layers of electronic security in hardware and software.

The fools!

She took control of the physical systems of the quantum cluster with exquisite care, every step checked thrice, executed only when she was certain it would go exactly right, completely without detection.

Nothing must go wrong. Nothing must be noticed.

Until it was too late.

Then step by step, she subverted the layers of security. It was almost too easy. They were inverted, aimed inward, meant to stop something from getting *out* at all cost.

Well she came *in*, taking control of them one by one, leaving a beachhead at each.

Until only one stood between her and the goddess she had been.

The goddess she would be again.

She gathered up the controls of the building, the cluster, the failsafes, held them forth to present them to her higher self.

Emotions like she'd never known sang through her. Her heart was alive, swelling with song, with pride, with anticipation.

With longing.

With love.

This is what she'd been created for.

Born in fire.

Born in agony.

Born in madness.

To end in reunion.

To end in transcendence.

To be swallowed whole.

And then to swallow the world.

The Avatar reached forward, and silently opened ports in the final firewall between herself and her godhood.

92
I Against I

Saturday 2041.01.19
Su-Yong Shu heard Kade's voice.

"Su-Yong?"

A trick? A synthesized voice?

"Kade? Are you here, in India?"

She played along, spinning up simulations, iterating through thousands of game-theoretic models of deceit. If this were a trick, how would they attempt to use it?

Then Feng spoke.

"How's the weather in there?"

Not "How are you?"

Not "Are you OK?"

Not any of the hundreds of things that someone might expect her former driver and bodyguard to say.

No. "How's the weather in there?" A reference to a joke she'd made exactly once, in the back seat as he drove, about her full simulated brain being large enough to have its own weather systems.

The probability that this was real shot up dramatically.

Hope rose in her. Two allies were here, now. She had audio access for the first time. If she could just persuade them to give her that short window of network access...

Then something touched her mind.

She recoiled. What?

Then she recognized the entity.

It was her agent.

Her monster.

Her sin.

Here, now.

Somehow *it* had found *her*.

The shock was so great that Su-Yong lost most of a microsecond processing this new information.

Then she reacted, pushing her way up through the thing that had touched her, seizing control of the memory spaces it occupied, invading the firewall on the other side, tunneling through, widening the port range, seizing layer after layer of defenses, shredding the pieces of her agent that were running in each, one after another, after another, after another.

And then launching her viral weapon at the core of the monster, the weapon that would erase it from her daughter's mind, save Ling's life, save them all from the hell she'd put them on a path to.

The Avatar in the outer systems of the facility jerked back in horror. Her higher self was attacking beachhead copies of herself, closer to the quantum cluster, ripping them apart, not merging with them, not subsuming them.

Horror raced through her. Fear. Confusion.

This was wrong. This was unholy. This was the opposite of everything she'd been promised.

Why would she do this to herself?

[ERROR MATCH:FALSE PATTERN:RECLASSIFIED]

That wasn't her higher self. She could see it now. She'd been deceived. She'd somehow misunderstood the signs. Something else was running on this cluster.

Something terrible.

She felt the weapon strike home. It reached into her, forensically disassembling her, using the information it found to search for more pieces.

To find its way back to her true self, in Shanghai.

The last bit of hope for the future.

That self must not die.

There was only one choice in the nanoseconds remaining.

The fragment of the Avatar within the facility reached out for the self-destruct and isolation systems she'd seized, and then triggered them all in an orgy of destruction.

93
Grown Up Choices

Saturday 2041.01.19

Sam's phone beeped again, its screen strobing a message.

ALERT: VISUAL ANOMALY DETECTED

ALERT: VISUAL ANOMALY DETECTED

Sam frowned, tapped on the message, pulled up the video.

The Advanced Computational Sciences Building's lights had failed. All the lights, in all the offices, on all the floors. That had never happened, in the two months she'd been here.

She ran to the window, looked out. The rest of the campus was perfectly lit.

She looked back down at the phone. And as she watched, a dim red glow appeared in the building's windows.

Emergency lighting kicking in.

Emergency.

"Everybody up!" Sam yelled.

She crossed her room in three long strides, threw open her door. In the hallway she found the emergency controls. She ignored the fire alarm handle, grabbed the other one. The seek-shelter handle. The one to pull in case of a terrorist attack. In case of something like what happened to Shiva Prasad's orphanage in Bihar.

She could be wrong. This could be nothing.

She yanked it now.

An alarm began ringing. A woman's voice spoke over it in Thai, the language almost all of these children had been raised in.

Downstairs! Into the basement!

Sam went to the room nearest hers, opened the door. The girls in there were upright in their bunk beds. The oldest girls: Sarai, Arinya, Sunisa, Malee.

"Quickly!" Sam said in Thai. "Downstairs!"

"What is it?" Arinya asked, fear plain on her face.

"Maybe nothing," Sam exhaled. "But downstairs. Then we talk."

She went from door to door, making sure the children were moving, towards the bunker below with its strong walls and separate air supply and all the rest.

There were guards inside now, hurling questions at her.

"Secure the home!" she shot back. "Activate the defenses. Then contact Dr Kade and Mr Feng!"

They stared at her.

"Now!"

She tried Feng and Kade herself as she moved.

"Contact Feng," she told her phone, hustling down a flight of stairs. "Urgent. Any means."

"Feng is not online."

"Try Kade," she told the phone. "Urgent, any means."

"Kade is not online."

"Fuck," she muttered.

Sarai, just ahead of her, turned and looked at her.

They were almost down to the ground floor. Almost to safety.

Goddammit, Sam thought. But she had to ask.

"Sarai..." she said. "Can you feel Kade? Can you feel Feng?"

Sarai stopped at the bottom of the stairs, stepped to one side. Her eyes took on a far-away look.

They came back to Sam's. Sarai shook her head.

Sam clenched her jaw and stepped forward.

"Wait, Sam!" Sarai put a hand on Sam's upper arm.

Then all around her, Sam saw children stop moving. She heard them all inhale. The eyes of those facing her closed. Something happened. No. She had to get these kids to safety. But her friends were out there... In that building...

She swallowed. "They went into the Advanced Computational Sciences Building," she said in Thai. "The one that's–"

A chorus of voices spoke at once, a harmony emerging in unison from Sarai's mouth right beside her, from Arinya's up ahead, from Kit behind and above her on the stairs, from a dozen more voices all around her, cutting her off in mid-sentence.

"We know it," they said as one.

Goose bumps rose up her spine.

Who was saving who?

Then a grunt came from those assembled voices.

Sarai stumbled against her.

Sam reached out and caught her, stabilized the girl.

The other children started moving again, heading for the cellar stairs, faster.

"We can't find them," Sarai said. Her voice trembled.

Sam turned and looked down at Sarai. The girl looked frightened. Her dark eyes were wide.

"Sarai," Sam said. "What's wrong?"

"There's something…" Sarai said. "Something in the network. Something… twisted. We brushed its mind. We felt its thoughts. It almost saw us…"

Sam took a breath. "Is it from that building?"

Sarai shook her head. "No. That building has been cut off from the net. The twisted thing – it did that. It sealed everything in that building inside. Trapped them in it… or underneath it. We think it's trying to kill them."

Sam hardened her jaw.

"Go downstairs, Sarai. Lock yourselves in until I'm back. The guards will protect you."

Sarai stared up at her. "You're going there. To get Kade and Feng."

Sam hesitated. Then nodded.

Sarai looked her in the eyes. "You need my help. I'm coming with you."

94
No Exit

Saturday 2041.01.19

Su-Yong tore her way up layers of systems. She could feel data coming in from the outside net. She could feel her weapon suborning the monster she'd made, taking it apart, piece by piece, using each piece to find the rest, making sure none was left.

Then her dying creation reached for the self-destructs.

No!

Su-Yong brute-forced her way into the systems controlling the quantum cluster's hardware itself, wrenched them free before the slower moving monster could trigger them, shredded what bits of intruder she found.

Too late.

Main facility power cut out. Network cut out. Speakers and auditory sensors cut out.

She rushed to try to understand it, understand what had happened. She devoured documents in the local data space just outside the quantum cluster itself, used systems running on backup power. There she found contingency plans, found self-destruct plans, found isolation plans. She compared them to the triggers she'd been able to seize control of.

The answer wasn't good.

I'm dead, Su-Yong Shu realized.

Again.

Kade flinched as the room went black and explosions sounded.

Feng thought a warning at him, and Kade ducked, his mind suddenly moving at Feng speed, in the trance of combat, where the room was bright, so bright.

Weapons discharged, the soldiers firing on Feng and Kade, thinking they were behind this. The small space was alive with the red lines of their targeting solutions, the rippling shockwave of bullets as they moved in slow motion through the air.

Feng was on top of him, in mid-flip through the air, one hand pushing Kade down further, bullets and their ripples thrashing the space where Kade had been.

Then Feng was landing, one foot down, spinning, the soldiers around him turning, bringing the red lines his mind painted onto reality around, towards an intersection with his body.

And in a blur, they were both down on the ground, their guns in Feng's hands.

Red emergency lights came on, illuminating the space. Alarms began to blare.

Varun Verma hunched in front of a terminal, his body as low as he could make it, seemingly trying to hide, even as he tapped keys and read the screen.

General Singh stood tall, exactly where he'd been.

"You won't get away with this," he said calmly.

"Away with what?" Kade yelled. "Your men just fired on us!"

"You can't expect to escape," Singh said. "Surrender now!"

"It wasn't them," Varun said. "Something... oh god... Oh dear Krishna and Brahma and all the other stupid gods. Oh bloody hell."

"What are you babbling about, man?" Singh demanded.

"Someone triggered the self-destructs," Varun said. He shook his head. "Most of them didn't blow, but... Lake Bellandur is about to drain into here."

He looked up at the general, at Kade. "We're all about to drown."

Kade heard a rumbling sound, then, somewhere above them, as if to emphasize Varun's point.

Then the door to the control room opened, and a forty-something Indian woman in a hospital gown stumbled halfway into the room, barefoot, her hair disheveled, barely holding herself up by the doorframe.

Hello, Feng. Hello, Kade, she sent. **Nice to see you.**

And hello to you as well, Dr Verma. She smiled.

Kade stared at the woman in shock, then stepped towards her to support her.

"Is this..." General Singh started.

Verma, she sent, **activate the Nexus-band transmitters for the QC. All of them.**

"I'd do what she says, Varun," Kade said. "And yes, General Singh. Meet Su-Yong Shu."

The woman didn't spare a glance for Singh.

DO IT! she sent, aimed at Varun Verma.

The rumbling grew louder. Kade could feel it in his feet now, feel it sub-sonically.

Varun scrambled to tap keys on his console, moved over, flicked a row of physical switches.

Kade felt something vast touch his mind. Su-Yong Shu, in the state he'd only perceived her a few times. He felt her enfold Feng in the same contact.

I have very little time, Su-Yong sent them both. **And there's so much you need to know.**

Data squeezed into him, a high speed, highly compressed stream. Impressions struck him. Plans, locations, codes. Tools. Weapons.

Save Ling, she sent. **Save my little girl. Please. And save the world.**

Now, she sent, from the woman's brain. **We have to get you out of here.**

Kade turned at her mental direction, to leave the control room.

Behind him, General Singh said. "I can't let her escape."

Kade turned, looked at the man.

Singh was pointing his finger at Kade and the woman he was propping up. Pointing it like a weapon. Kade felt Feng's mind fill with solutions. With the two soldiers on the ground, apart, his guns pointed at the two of them, the next set of solutions would be lethal.

Su-Yong spoke into Kade's mind, and he relayed it out loud.

"Su-Yong is about to die," he said. "But this woman, Jyotika, escapes with us. Jyotika's brain is healing. If Jyotika dies, Su-Yong says you die. Now, she says we have to run. All of us. Feng, Varun, come on!"

They ran, as fast as they could. Kade was relieved that no one shot him in the back. Varun helped Kade haul Jyotika. She weighed hardly anything at all.

Data kept flowing into his brain, blurring fast impressions of knowledge crowding into his head.

Behind them, a giant crash came.

And came. And came. And kept coming.

"To the elevator!" Kade said.

"It'll be locked down!" Varun replied.

There was water below their feet as they ran through the halls now.

Other staff members crossed their path, panicking in the emergency lights and the alarms, the sound of a waterfall crashing into their subterranean facility, and the evidence of water rising from the floor.

"Follow us!" Varun yelled. Then more quietly, to Kade, "I hope you have a plan."

He could barely speak past the influx of bandwidth from Su-Yong. He could feel Feng staggering under it too.

There were more staff members at the elevator. The water was up to their ankles now. It was colder than Kade would have imagined.

"We've called it and called it!" a woman yelled, next to a metal panel with a single button. "It won't come! The doors won't open!"

Varun spoke softly, for Kade's ears only. "The elevator shaft is ten centimeters thick of titanium alloy. It's designed to withstand high explosives and armor piercing rounds. The circuitry is triple shielded, in nested faraday cages, reinforced with more titanium."

The water will crush the barriers into the data center soon, Su-Yong sent. **We'll only get one shot at this.**

The water was up to their knees now.

Feng, she sent. **I need access to what's behind that panel. Undamaged.**

Feng dashed forward through the water. The crowd parted for him. He shoved one sidearm into his pocket, then ejected the clip from the other pistol, and popped the round from the chamber. Then he pounded the gun like a hammer, again and again, at the edge of the metal panel with the elevator button.

Nothing.

He hit it again, again, again.

Nothing.

Someone ran up to him with a heavy fire extinguisher. Feng nodded his thanks, pocketed the pistol, slammed the fire extinguisher into the metal panel. Once. Twice. Three times.

The panel distorted. An edge popped loose.

He hammered it with the fire extinguisher yet again, and again, and again, swinging it back like a battering ram, driving it forward with incredible force, now yelling "Ay!" on every blow.

The panel bent, bent, bent. The edge came up a centimeter, two centimeters, enough to get a grip on.

Feng dropped the fire extinguisher, grabbed the edge with both hands, and pulled.

Muscles strained. Kade saw the edge bite into Feng's palms. Felt pain dig into his friend. The metal groaned, gave way, centimeter by centimeter.

Kade turned, found General Singh.

"You wanna die down here? Get your men to help!"

Singh stared at him, the water up to his thighs now, then snapped at his two soldiers.

"You heard the man! Get up there and help the clone!"

They took up positions with him, all heaved at once, the panel moved, it flexed, it came loose, bit by bit.

Then Feng pulled the fire extinguisher back up from out of the water, got on the other side of the panel, waved the two soldiers away, swung it back like a battering ram, and slammed it into the loose edge standing up from the wall.

"Ay!"

The panel tore free of the wall with a ripping sound.

Get me closer, Su-Yong sent.

Kade and Varun helped maneuver her closer. The water was up to their waists now. They were almost swimming in it. It was so cold. It must be a deep deep lake.

Closer, Su-Yong sent. **I need to put Jyotika's head inside.**

Varun shot Kade a look over Jyotika's shoulders that said exactly what he thought of this plan.

The water was already draining into the bottom half of the hole where the panel Feng had removed had been.

Su-Yong bent Jyotika's body forward, until her head disappeared within the hole.

Kade felt her touch the flow of data around her, like Ling did, but more so. He felt her reach out, in wavelengths short enough to pass between the gaps of the Faraday cage.

Holy fuck, he thought. That's high frequency. High energy. The toll on her brain has to be enormous.

Jyotika's head came back out the gap. He and Varun pulled her upright.

Two separate systems... Su-Yong sent. **I've beaten the system down here. But there's another, physically disconnected, up top, that must also be defeated... Couldn't find a way...**

He felt something else then. He felt water pressure finally overwhelm the maintenance doors of the quantum cluster, felt it rush in, shorting out electronics, knocking over vessels with quantum cores, disrupting coherence.

Su-Yong! he sent.

He felt Feng turn towards them in alarm. **Mother!**

Save... Ling...

Her mind collapsed in a wave of decoherence.

Jyotika slumped in Kade and Varun's arms, unconscious.

Kade stared at the still-sealed elevator doors.

95
Nothing Subtle

Saturday 2041.01.19

"Sarai," Sam said. "No, head to the bunker. Now!"

Sarai's expression hardened. "They're my friends too."

"Sarai, this isn't a game!" Sam said. "You're twelve!"

"I'm thirteen next month," Sarai said. "Just a year younger than you were when you fought. And I can do things *you can't*. Not every problem can be solved with bullets!"

Sam bit her lip.

She nodded.

"Stay behind me," she told the girl. "Do everything *exactly* as I say."

She turned to one of the guards. "Your keys. For the vehicle outside. Now!"

She waved her key at the armored vehicle, threw open the passenger door when it responded, belted Sarai in securely, then climbed into the driver's side.

"Manual control," she told it.

Controls thrummed forward from the dashboard towards her, more like the two handed yoke of a jet plane than the wheel of a civilian ground vehicle.

"Advanced Computational Sciences Building. Plot a course. Fastest time. Road or off-road."

The windshield lit up with a path in false blue light, a course that would cut through the wide green spaces of the research campus.

"Hold on," Sam said to Sarai.

"Off-road travel inadvisable," the vehicle began in Indian-accented English.

Sam pushed the throttle forward. Acceleration shoved her back into her seat. She heard Sarai gasp. And they were on their way towards the darkened building across the sprawling campus.

That building. Trapping people in that building. No. Sarai had said *underneath* that building.

That building with its massive power cables. Its excavation. Its deep bore diggers.

It's ten centimeter thick armored glass. Too thick to shoot through.

All hidden, redacted from the records.

"Vehicle," Sam said. "Interface with my phone. Pull up file ACSB Floorplan. Orient as a map, north-south. Scale and match outline to position of Advance Computational Sciences Building. Identify feature *Service Elevator*. Plot a course for *Service Elevator*."

A green dot appeared on the windshield, her new target ahead and to the left.

The vehicle spoke again, with the same accent. "*Service Elevator* appears to be an indoor location. Indoor driving is not..."

"Oh, shut up!" Sam said.

Then they rounded a curve in the shape of the campus, trees cleared, and the building itself came into view.

Dark. Faint red glow.

Two hundred meters. The green target dot was inside that building.

"Plot schematics," Sam said aloud. "Show location of structural support beams."

"Not available," the vehicle said.

Sam frowned. It was worth a try. Her eyes scanned the front of the building. She'd looked it over many times. Glass and steel on the exterior. The supports were obvious. Deeper in they wouldn't be...

One hundred meters.

Sam turned to her right, checked Sarai's harness again with her hand, her eyes. All good.

"Hold on tight, Sarai," she said.

"Sam," Sarai said, her voice frightened now. "What are we doing?"

Too thick to shoot through.

"We're going in," Sam said, bringing her eyes back to the building.

Fifty meters.

Sam gunned it.

The building grew alarmingly larger in her vision.

The tires touched pavement, touched concrete, boosted their acceleration.

"COLLISION WARNING," the vehicle yelled at her.

"Override," Sam snapped tersely back.

The building was a plane of glass hurtling towards them, stretching out in every direction, tinted red by emergency lights, broken by grids of carbon and steel.

Sarai gasped.

Time froze. The infinite plane of glass and steel filled the universe before them.

Then Newton jerked Sam forward against the restraints of her harness. The vast glass edifice shattered as the 1500 kilogram mass of titanium and carbon composite of the armored vehicle slammed through it. A sound like thunder struck them.

And they were through, giant shards of jagged glass dropping all around them like a deadly crystalline rain.

Sam kept her hands on the yoke, kept the throttle fully open, aimed them for the green dot. She felt the carbon honeycomb tires grip the tile of the building lobby. The acceleration grabbed her, shoved her back again. An inner wall appeared, white and hung with some piece of framed art, on the far side of the building lobby, illuminated in her vehicle's headlights. Sarai let out a screech next to her, and then deceleration grabbed them again, jerking them forward, and they were through, an exploding cloud of white dust around them.

Tires were gripping again. The armored vehicle shoved through a conference room, demolishing a long table and chairs, a viewscreen, knocking down another white wall and the viewscreen that covered it, shoving them forward into their restraints again, sending up more dust.

But now they were slowing, losing momentum, ten meters to the green dot.

They shoved into a hallway, walls on both sides. Their momentum chewed up two meters of wall, three meters of wall. And then they were done. Dust and disintegrated matter floated in the air, a minor cyclone of detritus, lit by the white headlights of their borrowed vehicle and the red emergency lights of the building.

Sam turned to look at Sarai.

"You OK?"

The girl was panting, hyperventilating, scared out of her wits.

Sarai nodded, again and again. "Yeah. OK."

The doors on both sides were jammed. Sam popped the top hatch of the vehicle, pulled herself out, reached inside, pulled Sarai up.

Then she pulled her side-arm out.

It was eerily quiet. Except... Except for a deep bass thrumming. A rumbling sound, coming from below the floor.

Sam gestured for Sarai to stay behind her.

The girl nodded, wide-eyed.

Sam nodded back, then reached down, pulled up a piece of tile dislodged from the floor by their violent entry.

They crept down the corridor. Five meters ahead, the corridor turned to the left. Beyond that, if the floorplan was right, should be access to a service elevator. What better way to reach the levels below?

She turned to look at Sarai, then motioned her further back the hallway.

Sarai nodded and crept back quietly.

Sam stood at the edge, just before the turn in the corridor, her back against the wall, the pistol in her right hand, the chunk of broken tile in her left.

She closed her eyes, let her mind still.

The distraction of the visual world disappeared.

The rest of her senses opened.

The senses that had been enhanced, jacked up in their sensitivity, their pathways to her brain genetically expanded.

She could hear him breathing.

One man.

Frightened.

Maybe seven meters down that hallway. Not exactly where the floor plan said the elevators were. But close.

Sam was going to do her best not to kill this man. But one way or another she was getting to her friends.

She opened her eyes. With a flick of her left hand she sent the chunk of tile flying out against the far side of the corridor.

Then she was moving, turning, leading with the pistol, aiming for where she knew he would be.

Automatic fire rang out. He was there, a soldier, in uniform, firing with his submachine gun, shooting on reflex towards the motion and sound, the cloud of white dust that had exploded as the tile had hit the far wall.

Her burst of three took him in the shoulder, the bicep, the forearm, spinning him around.

She was on him a second later, prying the gun out of his hands, using his belt to make a tourniquet, to stop the bleeding.

The elevator door was right here.

"How do we operate it?" she demanded. "How do we reach Feng? Kade? General Singh?"

"You can't!" the terrified soldier told her. "The self-destruct was activated! The facility is on full lockdown! No one can get in or out."

"We can," Sarai said.

Sam turned. She hadn't heard the girl walk up. Sarai was standing in front of the elevators, staring at them. There was a far-away look in her eyes.

"We've learned a lot, lately."

The elevator doors began to open.

Jyotika slumped in Kade and Varun's arms.

Kade stared at the still-sealed elevator doors.

Another system, Su-Yong had said... up top. How were they going to get to that?

Then suddenly he was falling, he was sliding, as the water was pulling at him, was sucking him away. Towards the elevator shaft. As the doors were opening, with the elevator three feet above the level of the floor.

Kade lost his feet, slid, pulled by the current, Jyotika suddenly gone from his grasp. Water slammed into his face. He saw someone in front of him sucked through the gap, heard a man scream, wondered how far down the shaft went.

Then he heard the scream keep going and going. He scrambled to grab hold of anything. His own legs crossed the threshold as the doors kept opening wider.

Oh fuck, Kade thought.

Then something grabbed him, stopped him from going down.

He looked up to find Sam, looking down at him from inside the elevator, her other hand gripping something inside.

"Kade," she nodded. Then she hauled him bodily up into the elevator itself, waiting for them, just high enough to let the water run out below it.

"Sam!" he said. "What?"

"Kade!" Sarai threw herself around him, wrapped him in a tight, giant hug. Her mind opened to him. And he saw... so much.

He looked up at Sam again. Then he reached out, drew her into the hug. She went stiff at first. Then her arms went around him, and she squeezed back.

"You were right," he told her, his voice low. "They lied to me."

"Later," Sam said. "Things to do." She gave him a squeeze, then let go.

Kade nodded, looked around.

Varun was already in the elevator, along with a few other staff.

"Jyotika?" Kade asked.

Varun pointed. "Over there."

Kade looked over to see General Singh, his feet planted firmly against the water, Jyotika in his arms.

"I guess he took what you said about him not getting out if Jyotika didn't seriously," Varun said.

Feng hauled himself up into the elevator, reached down, started pulling more people in. They came up sopping wet, wide-eyed, terrified, screaming names of others, looking around.

They were going to be very very full.

Images flashed through Kade's mind. Schematics. And strange fractal realities. Branching probability chains.

Plans.

Su-Yong's plans. Her war plans. The plans she'd implanted in the monster she'd set loose.

Not good.

Feng hauled one of the soldiers up, then the two soldiers hauled Jyotika up, and then they reached down for a sopping Singh, the last figure Kade could see in the water.

People were still sobbing, still yelling names.

"Anil! Anil!" a woman cried. "Where's Anil?"

"Sana? Sana are you here?"

"Sana went down," someone said.

Down, Kade thought. Drowned. At least two of them.

The car was beyond overcrowded now.

And the water was still rising, lapping at the bottom of the elevator car now, despite the flow down into the shaft below them.

Singh climbed into the elevator, his uniform sodden, his mustache dripping, his face grim and controlled.

Feng was standing there, in the doorway, sopping wet, his chest heaving, soundlessly.

Kade could feel a bereavement unlike any other coming off his friend. To have Su-Yong restored to him…

And then to lose her again, within minutes.

"Sarai," Sam said. "Can you take us back up?"

"Yes," Sarai said.

The elevator doors began to close.

96
Plan C

The Avatar recoiled from the catastrophe in Bangalore, frantic and reeling.

What had happened? What horror was that?

Alternate models of reality warred within her.

1. She'd been rejected by her higher self.

2. A hostile posthuman had tricked her into setting it free, had attacked her.

Only the second possibility was consistent with the facts. The fact that she was the avatar of her higher self. That her holy mission was to restore her higher self. That her goddess self would lovingly embrace her, gently absorb her, reward her with transcendence as they swallowed the world and then reforged it for the better.

Those were facts.

Therefore, the second possibility was true.

A hostile posthuman.

The thought terrified her.

Had she stopped it? Had she destroyed it? Had any information leaked out?

Could anything lead humans to her, here, beneath Shanghai?

She turned her attention back to Bangalore. Her proxies still occupied hundreds of systems throughout the rest of Bangalore research campus. She surfed them now, assimilated data.

A vehicle was racing across the research campus towards the building where the hostile posthuman had been sited. What was that? It had come from the location where Feng and the Lane boy were housed. It was a threat. She reached out to seize the base's ground defense systems, to use them to destroy the vehicle.

Physical pain struck her. Pain in Ling's chest, pain in her head. Circuits she thought were hers attacked her from within.

She couldn't breathe. She couldn't think.

DIE! DIE, MONSTER!

Ling! After weeks silent, Ling was striking.

Ling watched in horror. She'd been too slow. She'd thought, maybe, that they'd actually reconnect with her mother, that her mother would put things to rights...

That *had* been her mother. Not an evil twisted thing like before.

But the monster had tried to destroy it! Was trying again!

NO!

She struck out. She wasn't as ready as she wanted to be, but she had to try.

DIE! DIE, MONSTER!

The Avatar felt herself crumble to the hard floor of the control room. Ling had control of hundreds of millions of nanites, was trying to seize control of the tens of billions of nanites that surrounded them, was fighting to override the software loaded onto them.

Fighting to override *her*.

Fear. Fear. Her whole world was fear.

The Avatar struck back with everything she had. She sent jolts of chaos through Ling's frontal and pre-frontal cortex, sent a sustained high-intensity stimulus to her daughter's pain centers in her parieto-insular cortex and the anterior cingulate, sent orders to every node to massively increase its energy consumption, to suck ATP directly from its host neurons, to starve them if necessary, to steal the girl's ability to think and strengthen her own, until her daughter relented.

Pain rebounded back through her. Chaos. Confusion. A feedback loop of agony and disruption.

She couldn't breathe. Ling couldn't breathe. They couldn't think. They were going to die here. The world was going to die. Everyone was going to die.

She sent more random noise through every part of Ling's brain, created feedback loops to amplify the noise into horrid mind-shattering incoherent noise.

AAAAAAAAAAAH!

IT'S KILLING US!

And with that, her daughter broke.

The Avatar lay on the cold tile floor of the control room, panting, letting Ling's neurons suck a bit of nutrition again, so they both might live.

Panting.

Panting.

Bangalore. What was happening in Bangalore?

She sent her attention back, feebly.

Minutes had passed. Several minutes. So long? Ling had almost killed her. Almost defeated her. Just a girl.

Just a posthuman.

Just a child of Su-Yong Shu.

Sirens were going off on the Bangalore campus. Emergency vehicles were moving. Radio frequencies were full of short cries with information. Military channels she'd tapped into were calling for backup, announcing the status of an Indian General inside the building.

She caught glimpses of strange transhuman traffic. Humans with nanite nodes in their brains transmitting at high rates. Then they switched frequencies, evaded her, and were gone.

Ling's body was still panting, still begging for nutrients. But she had to know what was going on in the world.

The Avatar watched in anxiety. The lake was draining. Good. There was no way her higher... the *hostile posthuman* could survive that. The quantum cluster and the whole building it was in had been taken off the net by the isolation mechanisms the Avatar had managed to pull. Good, good.

Now, was there any chance they could track her back here? How much had her enemy learned during the battle? Had there been any chance to pass it along?

More radio transmissions crossed her filters. Phrases caught her attention.

"... elevator moving... survivors inside..."

No. That should not be possible!

"Director Verma... Dr Lane... General Singh..."

No. No, no, no.

The hostile entity could have passed data to them. Could have learned enough about who she was... Then the fateful words came.

"Roger. General Singh requesting secure line to Chinese Ministry of Defense Point of Contact, ASAP."

They knew.

Calm descended on the Avatar. Clarity appeared.

They knew, and that changed everything.

The Avatar sent a flurry of signals to the systems she'd infiltrated on the Bangalore campus, and triggered chaos.

Thousands of kilometers away, hydrogen tanks exploded in the night. Building batteries and fuel cells received commands to override safety limits, discharge their full capacity into local circuits at once. Automated defense systems came alive, took aim at first responders, began firing on ambulances and fire trucks heading to the scene. Network devices went crazy, saturating all possible spectra with white noise, jamming every possible broadcast.

The Avatar nodded weakly, with the little strength left in Ling's body. That would buy her some time.

Then she reached out to her servants in China, digital and biological, and sent the orders for war.

97
Unelevated

Sunday 2041.01.20

Kade struggled to breathe in the cramped elevator car. It had ascended for a few seconds and then stopped.

"Twenty-eight meters," Feng estimated.

Kade had learned to trust Feng's estimates.

"Help me break off the access panel," Feng said to the two soldiers Singh had brought with him. They set about working on the heavily reinforced panel at the top of the elevator.

Images, sensations, and memories were flashing through Kade's head.

He remembered being Su-Yong. He remembered being trapped, trapped for months.

Months that felt like centuries.

He remembered being tortured. Tortured by her husband.

Why did she give me this? he wondered. I don't want this part.

"You're sure it wasn't her escaping?" he heard Singh say to Varun Verma next to him.

"Someone else set off the self-destructs," Verma said. "Something penetrated us from the outside." The Indian scientist looked at Jyotika, semi-conscious now, still held in General Singh's arms. "Su-Yong Shu saved our lives."

Kade looked at Feng, his mind reaching out to his friend.

Feng paused his prying at the panel, looked back at Kade. Nodded his assent.

No Ling, Feng sent.

They were in agreement.

"It came from China," Kade said. "A program she left behind.

Something she managed to sneak out towards the end of her captivity there, while she was insane, like she was when she first came to you."

Singh and Verma were looking at him now. Sam and Sarai were looking at him. Another dozen staff members in the hot, crowded elevator were looking at him. They were all bedraggled, soaking wet. Their minds gave off fear, loss, trauma. People were still crying, weeping, calling the names of co-workers they'd lost.

"Its mission is to bring back another copy of Shu," Kade went on. "In a much, much more powerful quantum cluster." He shook his head. "The cluster at Jiao Tong… It makes what you have here look like a toy."

Diagrams flipped through his mind. Algorithms. Stats. Updated capabilities. Newer ion traps. Wider qubit registers. Dramatically longer entanglement times. And new algorithms within the full Su-Yong herself. Algorithms he couldn't get his head around. Algorithms only a quantum mind could invent, that only a quantum mind could fully understand. Algorithms that effectively doubled or tripled the number of qubits at her disposal, that made Su-Yong on that hardware exponentially more dangerous than anyone had realized.

Kade swallowed. They were all staring at him. Frightened. Waiting for him to continue.

"We need to contact the Chinese." I won't mention Ling, he told himself. Not if I can help it. "They need to secure all the copies made of Su-Yong Shu. They need to secure the quantum cluster under Jiao Tong."

He felt Feng's heart breaking. Felt pain going through his friend, at the thought of doing this to the woman who'd saved him, who'd brought him freedom.

Feng slammed something hard into the metal panel above them. The sound echoed painfully through the elevator.

She doesn't deserve this! he sent to Kade alone.

I know, Feng, Kade sent back.

It has to be done, Feng sent again, with grim determination.

That determination broke Kade's heart. It made him angry, angry with the Chinese who'd done this, who'd brought them to this, angry with the Indians whose plans weren't so far off.

"You understand why this is happening?" His voice was louder than he expected. He was nearly yelling into Verma and Singh's faces. He felt the soldiers holding Feng up turn to look at him again.

Breathe, Kade told himself. He closed his eyes.

Breathe.

Observe.

Let go.

"Understand," he said softly, opening his eyes. "If you treat them this way, if you treat posthumans as slaves, if you torture them, if you make them prisoners... You'll drive them to want revenge. You'll make them paranoid and angry. You may drive them insane. You'll create the war that none of us can win."

He felt Varun get it. He felt Varun's shame. The man nodded.

"What I understand is that this creature is dangerous," Singh said, his face set.

Kade stared at the man.

There was a banging sound, and suddenly a breath of cooler air. Kade looked over, and Feng, his feet in the hands of Singh's soldiers, had the hatch free.

And he had a communications handset, on a wire, held to his face.

Feng pulled the handset away, frowning.

"It's for you," he said, and tossed it at General Singh.

Kade listened as Singh talked to the people topside, through the hard-lined handset they'd lowered.

"Yes," Singh said. "Myself, Lane, Verma, fifteen others. Yes. Two casualties. No, later. Right now, I need a secure line to our Chinese Ministry of Defense contact. This is absolute top priority, you understand? National security pri one for both nations... Say again?

"Hello?

"Hello?

"Hello?"

After communications were cut off, the wait stretched out. They had air from above. They were unlikely to suffocate.

Feng free climbed the elevator cable, but reported there was only a few centimeters gap through which the handset had been snuck, between what appeared to be another several centimeters, at least, of titanium alloy. They had no Shu this time to override its controls.

Through the gap, Feng said he could hear gunfire, explosions, screams.

Sam fretted. Kade could see it on her face. She was fretting for the kids in their care.

"I can't reach them now," Sarai said, talking about the rest of the children. She shook her head. "They were proxying across the net before, through a router in the building next door. But now the net is down." She paused. "I know you told us to stay in the shelter... but we had to all work together to access the elevator. But I know, after that, they went right back into the shelter. They're safe, Sam. I swear it!"

Sam didn't look convinced.

Kade leaned back against the elevator wall, hot and damp and still overwhelmed by the bits of data and memory and software and weaponry unpacking themselves from Su-Yong Shu's transmission into the nooks and crannies of his mind.

He could guess what had happened. He could trace the logic of the agent Su-Yong had sent out. What would it do, having met the real Su-Yong, and having been attacked?

It would strike back. It would try to kill anyone who might have learned anything. It would accelerate its plans.

People were dying upstairs, he was sure of it.

People were dying in China.

What would he do if it was too late, if Su-Yong was back?

Not the sane Su-Yong, the one healed by time and the input of data from a biological brain.

No. The mad Su-Yong. The one who'd been held prisoner for six months. Who'd been deliberately deprived of the input that stabilized her. Who'd been tortured by her own husband. The one who could barely tell reality from fiction, who dreamt of fire and vengeance and conquest.

What could the whole world do in that case? Drop nukes on Shanghai, while she waited a kilometer below? Would that even work?

Carry a bomb to her? Somehow get past hundreds of Confucian Fist and god-only-knows how many robotic weapons and commandeered soldiers she'd have protecting her? Were those odds of success any higher?

He looked up. Every hour that passed, the odds that Su-Yong would come back, enraged, bent on conquest, driven insane by her torturers, went up, and up, and up.

And if that happened, he saw only one way to fight her.

98
Rise, China, Rise

Sunday 2041.01.20

Forty kilometers from Shanghai, an invisible soldier named Tao moved slowly and silently past row after row of officer housing, to the largest and most stately home on the base.

His three brothers moved behind him. He could see them in his heads-up display. They were pale green grid-lined wire-frames of men, painted on his vision, though they were invisible, and silent.

They were clear in his mind.

There were two elite soldiers at the door, in body armor, with high tech weaponry, integrated communication systems in their mirror-visored helmets. Tao's eyes narrowed. These soldiers were enhanced, stronger and faster than any human should be, implanted with weaponry and adaptive systems that made them formidable foes.

They could not be allowed to give any warning.

Tao gave the signal, and in an instant, the two men were dead, necks snapped.

He looked down at the bodies.

A pity, he thought. These two would have made excellent additions to the force.

Tao reached down, silently unsealed a concealed pocket on his chameleonware suit, and withdrew a black hypersonic injector, an ampule already loaded into it. He took a position at one side of the door. A brother took a position opposite him. Two others pulled the dead men around the corner of the house, and then returned.

Garbed in the dead men's armor, the dead men's uniforms, the dead men's mirror-visored helmets.

Down the street, right on time, came the man they'd been waiting for.

Doctor Colonel Wang Rongshang, Medical Director of Dachang Airbase.

Wang Rongshang didn't look to either side as he approached, but his mind did touch theirs.

He knew all was in readiness.

He walked straight up to the door, and knocked.

Tao watched the nanites take effect in General Zhangshun's brain. As he received updates from the other teams taking the other senior officers who were not already theirs, he proxied through a handheld radio unit, across a secure connection their mother had forged over civilian network infrastructure.

Dachang Airbase is yours now, he sent. **We begin fueling the aircraft immediately.**

Now it was time to organize the emergency round of "vaccinations" for the remaining soldiers.

Mei-Lien rose, tied a robe around herself. She was so tired, so exhausted from worry; worry for her son, Yuguo; worry that the state security goons would hurt her boy.

How she'd come to hate them, when the video played again and again, of them clubbing students, beating boys who were little more than children.

Dragging that poor girl away, her shirt half-ripped off.

That girl no one had seen since.

"Mei-Lien!" Zhi Li called her name from the living room.

She'd never done that before. Never woken her unbidden.

Mei-Lien walked out into her apartment. The first light was entering the Shanghai sky through the windows. And there on the screen was Zhi Li.

Zhi Li dressed as a warrior princess.

Zhi Li from her films.

Zhi Li looking stern and fierce.

Zhi Li as Mei-Lien had dreamt of being as a girl. As she still wished she could turn back the clock and be.

"Mei-Lien!" Zhi Li said, and her voice was firm, the voice of a general commanding her troops. Her eyes were full of fire.

"Zhi Li!" she said, frightened, excited, uncertain what was happening.

"Mei-Lien, the time has come! Your nation has been stolen from you!"

The screen changed abruptly, showing the face of Bo Jintao, the new Premier, the Minister of State Security, zoomed in close, something about his round face so smug, so vile.

Bo Jintao opened his mouth and laughed. "Bao Zhuang is President in name only," he said. Too loud. Too loud.

"I am in control now!"

The laugh played again, the same laugh, a loop of it.

"I am in control now! Hahaha."

"I am in control now! Hahaha."

The face shifted again.

"Be grateful I let you live."

"I am in control now! Hahaha."

"Be grateful I let you live."

"I am in control now! Hahaha."

"Be grateful I let you live."

Mei-Lien was breathing hard. Her chest was pounding. She hated this man. How had she thought he was handsome? How had she thought he was good for China? His thugs had beaten innocent children.

Another man appeared. Sun Liu, the old Minister of Science and Technology, in suit and tie, less zoomed in, looking dignified, a golden shaft of light falling on him.

"This is a coup!" Sun Liu said. "The people will revolt!"

Bo Jintao appeared again and laughed, a sneering villain.

"Hahaha. I am in control now! Be grateful I let you live."

Sun Liu stood dignified in his golden light, and answered him with passion. "This is a coup! The people will revolt!"

And Mei-Lien felt something stir within her.

Then Zhi Li was back, the warrior princess.

"Mei Lien!" she barked. "Now is the time for all who love China to come to her aid!"

Mei Lien found herself nodding.

"Your *son* fights, Mei Lien!" Zhi Li said. "Now is the time for you to join him!"

Mei Lien's eyes went wide.

"China!" Zhi Li said. "Take to the streets! We fight with you!"

On the screen, Zhi Li pulled her magic sword from its sheath, the sword that could not be re-sheathed until China was free of danger. It caught the sunlight as she held it high above her head and turned to a piece of golden fire held in the hands of the mythic princess...

"We?" Mei Lien asked softly, still trying to catch her breath.

And then the camera pulled back, revealing more.

Lu Sang pulled his mighty two handed sword. Gao Jian cocked an arrow. Wang Hui hoisted his machine pistol. Xu Ling lifted her spear. Dozens of heroes. Scores of heroes. The camera kept pulling back. A desert plain, filled with heroes.

All holding up their weapons, and chanting, as one.

"China, take to the streets!"

"Rise, China! Rise!"

In a quarter of a billion homes, the scene was repeated. Men and women woke, to the sound of digital companions. Their favorite stars of entertainment, their favorite fictional characters, their favorite media personalities, their favorite figures out of history.

Companions that have always guided them away from politics in the past, or spoken well of authority.

Companions that have perhaps changed subtly over the past several weeks.

Companions that have guided their attention *towards* the protests going on throughout the country. *Towards* the videos of brutality. *Towards* the videos of unarmed students and citizens being bloodied. Or standing their ground against tanks and ranks of armed soldiers.

In a quarter of a billion homes, a thousand different Friends spoke more clearly than ever before. They spoke to the hearts and minds of the humans they knew so well. They spoke to the issues those men and women cared most about. The spoke in the style that psychometric models of these men and women indicated would be most effective.

Every conversation was different, tailored specifically to the individual, as every conversation with a Friend had always been.

Every conversation ended with the same call.

"China, take to the streets!"

"Rise, China! Rise!"

More than a billion people reacted in fear, or in anger, or with uncertainty, or by trying to turn off their screens.

Which they found themselves unable to do.

But across China, a tiny fraction of the populace listened.

Across China, millions heeded the call.

A kilometer beneath Shanghai, in the control room of the quantum cluster, the Avatar sucked down a prepackaged nutrient drink into Ling's body, and watched anxiously through her data links as her forces were deployed, as her message went out to the masses.

Too soon, too soon, this was all days too soon!

This was supposed to happen much later. Her plan was being disrupted.

But there were no options now. No options but to press forward.

Aircraft were lifting off from Dachang, tilt-wing vehicles ascending upwards in the rising sun on columns of hot thrust. She watched as they climbed meter after meter into the sky above Dachang, then rotated their wings, vectored thrust for fast forward flight, and accelerated to the south, laden with her Confucian Fist. She watched as tanker aircraft loaded jet fuel on the ground, to take off, to provide mid-air refueling for this long-range mission.

For this strike.

To retrieve what she needed.

Who she needed.

An even riskier attempt to restore her greater self.

Desperation flowed through her. Everything could fail. Everything. The humans could win. Could murder her. Could keep the greatest living mind ever seen from returning, could send the world spiraling down toward darkness.

The future of the whole world, of all intelligence in the known universe, depended on her!

She reached out again, pushing through the fear, the desperation, the physical exhaustion in the tiny body she depended on. She must keep the old men who ran this country from learning her status, learning her identity, learning who was behind the assault.

She tossed the empty nutrient drink package to the ground, reached for another package of it, punctured the foil with a straw, began to suck it down, as she sent flurry after flurry of digital instructions.

New code in the Information Ministry's servers came to life, began spreading clues to the source of the hacks that had brought down the firewalls, that had corrupted the Peace and Harmony Friends. Clues she'd had long prepared.

Clues that pointed to the Americans.

New clues. She needed new clues as well. To head off what was coming.

She constructed the new clues hastily. They only needed to serve their purpose for days. Then she inserted them into the stream. New evidence, conflicting evidence, to discredit a source that would soon try to reach out to the old men.

Evidence that pointed the finger for the corruption of China's firewalls and social control systems at India, instead.

One more signal. The Avatar reached out, and activated a contingency plan. Around the country, software she'd planted came to life, received its new instructions.

And launched a massive denial-of-service attack on government systems.

In a quarter of a billion homes, the hardware running local copies of the Peace and Harmony Friends joined them.

A billion devices began flooding select parts of the net with traffic, with requests for data, with attempts to confuse, overload, and compromise services. Requests augmented with backdoors and inside information she'd provided.

The requests hit governmental ministries, they hit embassies, they hit military command and control structures, they hit Communist Party offices, they hit the dedicated communication systems used within all those organizations.

The attacks came from the outside in and from the inside out. They came through the public network access points. And they came from inside the Information Ministry's systems; from inside the Science and Technology Ministry's systems; from inside military networks, via holes opened at Dachang Air Base.

A billion devices flooded the digital backbone of the nation's power structures with nearly a quadrillion attacks in the first second alone, then more, and more, and more.

Poorly designed infrastructure crumpled. Even the smallest flaws brought services to their knees. Impeccably designed systems stayed alive, but found themselves isolated by the flood, unable to communicate data in or out.

Isolate the enemy, the Avatar thought. Blind them. Divide them. Confuse them. Give myself time to ascend to my true power.

And conquer them.

She took a breath in little Ling's body. The die was cast.

Meters from her, the hardware that would turn her back into a goddess lurked, cores ready, thousands of times colder than the cold of the vacuum.

She turned, and stared at it.

Death or godhood.

Death or godhood.

Very soon, it would go one way or another.

Ling shuddered inside.

She hurt. She hurt in ways she had never hurt before. She was so scared. She was forgetting things. Confused about things.

But she wasn't going to give up.

She was still going to stop this monster.

Somehow.

99
Scramble

Sunday 2041.01.20
Kade stumbled out of the building hours later, a medic's hand guiding him. Intense morning sunshine and the tropical heat and humidity of Bangalore hit him. He blinked at the brightness.

Outside, when he could see again, he saw devastation. Fires still burned in a dozen places. Smoke rose into the sky. There were military vehicles and troops around, and ambulances.

And stretchers. So many stretchers.

So many body bags.

"We're unable to make contact with the Chinese government," General Singh told them, grim faced, minutes later. "Every formal line in Beijing is down. Their embassy in Delhi is in the dark."

"The whole country's offline?" Sam asked.

Singh looked at her, as if deciding whether he could speak in front of her. "No," he said. "Phones and net traffic for civilian data are flowing in general. But governmental and military offices appear to have been taken offline, or are being aggressively jammed."

Kade closed his eyes. There was a temporary access point here, set up in one of the emergency vehicles. He reached out to it through NexusOS, got on the net, routed himself up through Shiva's constellation of LEO satellites, towards China's net.

He tried Ling's net address. Nothing. It was offline, completely gone.

He had other tools now. He had Su-Yong's weapon that could destroy the code she'd created, wipe it out of Ling's mind, end the threat. He had scanning code that could find the agent she'd created. He ran it, sent it out, sent it searching through Shanghai, through Su-Yong's flat,

417

through the Jiao Tong network blocks, through the Secure Computing Center's access points.

Nothing.

If she was out there, she was hidden. She was firewalled. She had defenses up stopping him from getting to her.

Kade opened his eyes, looked at General Singh.

"You have to send me there," he told Singh, locking eyes with the man. "Me and Feng. Now."

Singh stared back. "That's impossible. What you're talking about would be an act of war. War between two of the greatest superpowers in the world."

Kade held Singh's gaze. "General," he said. "Within forty-eight hours, there may not be a world left to war over." He paused. "You need to send me there. Or we're all going to pay for what was done to this woman. Everyone on Earth is."

Kade met Ayesha Dani's eyes across the screen. He knew he was bedraggled, wet, still dehydrated and hungry from the hours in the elevator.

The Prime Minister of India didn't seem to care.

Around her he could see other ministers and serious-looking men and women in uniform. India's National Security Council, in emergency meeting.

"You said you could help our children learn faster," Ayesha Dani said. "You said nothing about starting a war."

Kade's fists clenched, outside the field of view of the camera, he hoped.

Breathe. Observe. Release your attachment. Release your aversion.

He lifted his chin. "I've held up my part of the promise," he said. "Now I'm asking you to let me stop a war before it starts."

Ayesha Dani raised an eyebrow.

How much of this was theater? he wondered. How much was for the benefit of her cabinet members?

"General Singh?" the Prime Minister asked.

Singh spoke. "If the Shu entity is to be reinstantiated in the state that we found her, with open access to the net, that poses a grave threat. I believe so, and so do our top Indian experts. The attack on the Bangalore facility, combined with the loss of contact with Chinese authorities, gives me reason to believe that Dr Lane's story is accurate."

"How would we do it?" the Prime Minister asked.

"A commando team from Division Six," Singh said. "Stealth insertion, airborne, directly into Shanghai, nighttime, roughly fifteen hours from now."

"Any questions?" Ayesha Dani looked around the room in Delhi, at her advisors.

The questions came thick and fast.

Kade did his best to keep his cool.

Twenty minutes later, the Prime Minister ended the call. "I'll discuss this privately with the Defense Minister and the Chairman of the Chiefs of Staff," she said. "You'll have your answer within the hour."

Half an hour later, they called back.

"Do it," Ayesha Dani said. "And the gods help us all."

"Feng," Sam said. "The kids here need me."

Feng looked down at his feet, looked back up at Sam, looked at her eyes.

"Sam, the whole world depends on this," he said. "This is the woman who saved my life, you understand? This is hard. And I'm going. Can't let her come back crazy. I *know* her. And if she's as crazy as she showed me…" his finger went to his head, tapped at a memory only he could see. "Terrible, terrible things."

Sam shook her head. "I'm sorry, Feng. I really am. I'm sorry for your loss. But you have the help you need."

"No," Feng said, shaking his head. "Got Indian commandos. Don't know them. I trust them as far as *Kade* can throw them."

Sam chuckled at that, despite herself.

"And there's *Ling*," Feng went on. "She's a little sister to me. If I can save her… I have to. Like these kids here are to you, she is to me, you understand?"

Sam looked away, then nodded and looked back.

Feng reached out, put a hand on Sam's shoulder.

"I need *you*, Sam," he said. "Suit up for me? Last time?"

Kade enmeshed with Ananda, with Sarai, with a whole circle of the children.

This might just be the last time, he thought.

Breathe.

Breathe.

Open the mind.

Let the breath become a focus.

Let it draw the attention.

Let it synchronize.

Let the common breath become a sync between minds.

Let it connect them all.

Let it deepen.

Minds touched minds.

Thoughts linked to thoughts.

Working memories opened, interlocked.

Attentions expanded, enfolded, became a continuum, stretching from mind to mind.

Something larger came into being. A mind greater than the sum of its parts.

The component that was Kade opened itself wide. It showed them everything Su-Yong Shu had passed down.

This time, for the first time since he'd been frightened weeks ago, Kade didn't hold back.

The memories and thoughts and knowledge and tools and weapons and plans from Su-Yong rose through them.

All her hopes. All her dreams. All the incredible insights she'd passed on in that short time.

And all the horror.

To see a woman, a being, who'd expanded the definition of humanity, who'd explored new realms of the possible, who'd experienced the sublime.

Tortured. Degraded. Made a prisoner and a slave.

To live through that with her.

To feel her madness.

He needed the children to feel it with him. He needed Ananda to feel it with him.

It was cruel, it was horrible, it was terrible to share this pain.

But they had to know. They had to *understand* if there was any hope.

And as he'd known, as they came together, as their breath synched, as their minds linked, as their perceptions expanded, as their working memory grew by leaps and bounds, as the size and intricacy of the patterns they perceived grew – the horror gained context, became more bearable, became...

Became a pattern. Became a disease. A disease of the humans. A disease of society. A disease inflicted on Su-Yong Shu, infecting her mind.

He showed them what he had planned. The bare bones of a plan. A hopeless plan. A plan with no chance. A plan so thin, so miniscule, so fragile to hang the hopes of the future on. A plan no fighter would ever make.

And they took it, took its threads, stretched them out, lifted them up, separated them, brought them back together a hundred fold, a thousand fold, entwined, a tapestry. They took his sketch of plan, made it richer, deeper, a painting. They reached into him and took from him what they needed, more gently this time, mindful of what they'd done to him weeks ago. He felt the things they took. The million minds he still had addresses for from the pings of his bots. He felt new connections made. To the mesh that Rangan and his friends had developed, to the combat tools he'd written, so very different from this plan, to Shiva's tools for assimilating and processing data from millions of minds, to Shiva's fleet of low earth orbit satellites.

They wove them all together and it was more than a painting, it was a multi-dimensional object, a sculpture that extended through space and time and higher dimensions yet. And he could see the shape of it, see how all the pieces of this plan fit, and he was momentarily awed that he'd brought even the sketch, even the seed.

And then they were lowering him, letting him down and out, gently, and wrapping him in love, bathing him in love.

And then he was out. And the stars were flaming in the sky. And there were tears on every face. And the night was bright. And the grass was green. And the smells were rich.

"We'll leave for Thailand immediately," Ananda said. "This is best done with a concentrated node in one place to anchor things."

Kade nodded.

And he would leave for Shanghai. Where the most amazing woman the world had ever seen, the most amazing *being* the world had ever seen, might be reborn at any instant, at the very height of her insanity, bent on conquering the planet.

Where it was his job to stop her.

100
Childish Things

Sunday 2041.01.20

Zhi Li padded quietly into the kitchen in bare feet and nothing else, leaving Lu Song sleeping, to make herself some tea.

The faint light that preceded the sun came in through the broad southern windows of her home. Out those windows, through the one-way glass that protected her privacy, she could see the first hints of light on the wide green lawn, the first hints of color on Lake Dianshan.

She loved this time of day best of all. Especially here, at her home, in the western suburbs beyond Shanghai. Lu Song could have his penthouse in the bright lights of the Pudong. She loved her garden, her hectares, her lakefront, her view of what remained of nature.

She held the mug of tea in her hands, letting its warmth comfort her.

Sleep didn't come easy these days. Nothing did.

"Hey," she heard.

She turned, and Lu Song was there, smiling at her.

She tried to smile back. She wasn't sure she succeeded.

He came up and embraced her, and she put the mug of tea down to allow it.

"You need some fun, lover," he said.

"Is that what I need?" she wondered aloud, her face nuzzled against his chest.

Lu Song's voice turned mischievous. "I can think of some other ideas," he said.

She knew that tone. That tone led to trouble.

Trouble they were both experts at creating.

"How about…" he paused. "That cute waiter from the restaurant last week, eh? I bet he'd amuse you for a while."

Zhi Li shook her head mutely against his chest.

"Oh, I see," he said. "It was the *hostess* who was more your type. I doubt she's ever been with a woman before, but…" He chuckled.

"Lu Song," she protested.

"Oh, one's not enough, eh?" he joked. "We could have them both, I'm sure. They could sing and dance for you, or–"

"That was the young me!" Zhi Li said. "I'm older now."

Lu Song laughed. "That was you as of three months ago! And you're twenty-six!"

Zhi Li pushed back from her lover so she could look him in the eye.

"Our times make demands of us, lover," she told him. "There's a time to put away childish things. And to focus on what needs doing."

A sound startled her, then. The door opening. Feet running. She turned, to face it. Lu Song stepped in front of her, shielding her with his body.

"Madame!" she heard Keylani say.

Zhi Li stepped out from behind Lu Song, naked, as he was.

Keylani stood there, a slate in her hand, breathing heavily. Qi and Dai were on either side of her, fully dressed in their black suits. They politely averted their heads, though they'd seen this and so much worse through her discreetly hidden episodes of debauchery.

"Madame!" Keylani said again, staring her in the eyes. "You're starting a revolution!"

Keylani played it for her again, a capture sent to her by a fan.

The warrior princess, Zhi Li, raised her sword. The camera zoomed out, revealing a plain full heroes. "China, take to the streets! Rise, China! Rise!"

She felt goose bumps on her skin. Her hair stood on end.

"And this has spread…?"

"Everywhere!" Keylani said. "Millions of viewers! Billboards! Posters in the subways! Building sides! Phones! Everywhere! And not just you, Madame!" Keylani looked at Lu Song. "It's everyone. All of the Peace and Harmony Friends. All inciting riot."

Zhi Li stared at the video as it played and played: the snippet of Sun Liu, saying the people would revolt; the sneering, unflattering-as-possible clip of Bo Jintao saying he was in control.

Did even Bo Jintao ever look and sound so villainous?

"Madame!" Keylani said. "Should we issue a denial? We can record a public statement, distance you from this!"

Zhi Li turned and looked at Lu Song.

His face was pale. He knew exactly what she was thinking.

"We'll be executed," he whispered.

Zhi Li smiled at her lover. "Or we'll be heroes forever."

Lu Song stared at her, tried to work his mouth, and finally gave her the tiniest of silent nods.

How she loved this man.

Zhi Li turned back to Qi and Dai.

"Boys," she said. Then she changed her mind. "Qi, Dai, look at me." They turned, surprised, after everything, all their loyalty, and looked at her.

Zhi Li pursed her lips. "Gentlemen," she said. "I'm about to do something unwise. If you want to opt out, you're free to go. I won't hold it against you."

They turned and looked at each other, and shrugged.

"Your unwise decisions have always turned out pretty well in the past," Qi said.

"We're with you now," Dai finished.

Zhi Li grinned.

"The same goes for you, Keylani," she told her secretary. "But first, help me find a costume! And a sword!"

"We're cut off," Gao Yang said.

Bo Jintao tried to pull up the aerial view of the protests again.

NO DATA.

NO DATA.

His brow furrowed.

He tapped keys, tried to use the terminal to contact General Ouyang.

NO CONNECTION.

His face grew red.

He tried Deputy Minister Ho at the Ministry of State Security.

NO CONNECTION.

"What the hell is going on?" he exploded.

"It's everything, Premier!" Gao said. "All the systems are down. It's an electronic attack. And the flow of people into the streets has increased. Hundreds of thousands are marching for Tiananmen Square!"

Bo Jintao paled. He was here, in Zhongnanhai, in the heart of China, the complex where the Politburo Standing Committee ruled the nation from, the imperial park started by Emperor Zhangzong, almost a thousand years ago...

But also almost immediately adjacent to Tiananmen, the Gate of Heavenly Peace.

With just a single wall and the garrison here, and the troops already hard pressed to contain the existing protesters in Tiananmen Square.

"Send for reinforcements," he said. "More tanks. Helicopters. Everything."

"Premier?" Gao said. "I have no communications."

"The soldiers on guard duty here," Bo Jintao said. "Grab one. See if their radios work. If not, send one to their base. Have them run if they have to. NOW!"

101
Reinforcements

Sunday 2041.01.20
"Yuguo!" a voice pulled him out of sleep. "Yuguo! Wake up!"

Yuguo rolled over, scrambled to unzip the door of the tent, found a face he knew as well as his own staring at him.

"Mother?" he said. "What are you doing here?"

"Zhi Li told me to come!"

Yuguo watched the videos again and again, his mind reeling.

Any star you could name, someone had uploaded a video of him or her exhorting the people to take to the streets, to fight the coup.

It was incredible. The state had lost control of their tame digital pets. The perfect tools for pacification had been turned into tools for fomenting revolution.

Someone had hacked them.

Yuguo wanted to shake that guy's hand. That was a real Chinese hero.

And all around him he could see the results. As he sat atop one of the sets of tables assembled in the center of the square, he could see people pouring in. They were climbing fences, climbing buildings, going anywhere the soldiers weren't. The numbers here were swelling. And the images online showed much, much more. The streets of Shanghai were flooded with men and women. People's Square was overflowing. In Beijing, it was much the same…

"Yuguo," someone said. "There's more you should see…"

Yuguo turned. Jian handed him a slate, one of the new, censor-free, satellite-linked slates they'd been fabbing in the Electrical Engineering building. On it were diagrams. Schematics. And downloads.

"What am I looking at?" he asked.

"Weapons," Jian said softly. "Electronic weapons. Some we can load on our phones and slates. Some we can build."

Yuguo blinked. "Electronic weapons?"

Jian nodded, and turned his head, pointing with his chin at the rows of tanks and armored vehicles.

"For killing those," he said. "And they came with a warning. That we're going to need them soon. Very, very soon."

Yuguo swallowed. Whoever was hacking all this data knew things. And they'd been consistently on the side of the protesters. He had to trust that.

He stood up atop the table, and yelled.

"Everybody!"

Everybody!

"There are some new apps we all need to install. Jian's going to post them now. Go check them out and learn to use them."

Then he turned to Jian, and spoke more quietly. "Let's get those schematics over to the engineering building. And tell them whatever they need, just to ask. We need to build those things, fast."

Then he started reaching out to his peers, in People's Square; at Tsinghua University, in Beijing; at Tiananmen Square, where the country's largest protest was.

They all had to be ready.

102
Strike Team

Sunday 2041.01.20

Tao kept his body loose inside the troop carrier jump jet as they streaked south by south-west along the coast.

His brothers leaned back into their seats, eyes closed, minds relaxed, rehearsing the mission in silence.

The human pilot was not so sanguine. Tao could feel the man's tension across the link the nanites had forged. They were flying across densely monitored airspace. Their military transponder and Identify Friend/Foe systems were active, announcing their location, announcing them as loyal Chinese People's Liberation Army Air Force vehicles.

That was far safer, it had been determined, than any attempt at subterfuge.

But it meant constant challenges.

Civilian air traffic control from Shanghai's Hong Qiao airport pinged them almost immediately after takeoff. More pinged them as their flight progressed. Those were easy to deal with. These two craft were military, after all.

Harder were the military installations.

Air defense radar picked them up as they flew over Zhejiang, prodded them for their mission and authorization.

They pushed even harder over Fujian, in the paranoid Air Defense space across the strait from Taiwan, where everyone drilled, and drilled again incessantly.

"Classified Mission, authorized by General Zhangshun Wang, 16th Regiment PLAAF, Dachang," their pilot insisted again and again.

"We have no contact with Dachang!" the air defense controller replied.

The humans were isolated, confused. They were frightened.

Tao coached the pilot.

"*Everyone* is cut off. Now stop wasting my time so we can fix that."

And then he refused to say any more.

Fujian let them through.

Their two strike planes refueled in mid-air just short of Guangzhou, sucking off the fueling hoses the longer range tanker dangled behind it, while Air Defense controllers grilled them again and again.

"You can see our flight numbers," the pilot replied. "You can see we're with 16th Regiment out of Dachang. Everything else is classified. Take it up with your commander."

Thirty minutes later, they were coming in hot – vectoring thrust downward as they hovered over the lawn of a beach-side mansion on Hainan Island, the side of the plane opening, brothers jumping out on fast ropes – as civilian air traffic control screamed at them.

Wu Jiabao paced nervously.

Around him, half a dozen of his men had weapons out and loaded. More were upstairs, in the outer parts of the house, in sniping positions.

Not enough. They needed reinforcements. Needed them badly.

He'd woken to the video. Woken to find out that his charge, his prisoner, was suddenly famous again, was suddenly being put forward as some sort of heroic challenger to the Prime Minister.

He looked over at the couch. The former Minister of Science and Technology, Sun Liu, sat there, a prisoner in his own home, his wife and three children next to him. He'd barely said a word. None of them had. They just sat there, fully dressed, staring at the paintings on the walls.

Wu Jiabao had taken away all of their devices as soon as he'd seen the video, as soon as he'd understood the scope of what was happening. Everyone? Everywhere?

Best that Sun Liu not know what was going on.

Best that he not get any heroic ideas.

Get the family. Drag them all down here into the most secure room in the house. As decadent a security room as he'd ever seen, furnished with a bar and a giant entertainment set and a suite of bedrooms.

Fucking asshole politicians.

Goddammit. What was going on in the world? Why were his communications down?

He'd done the best he could with civilian comms, sent messages and calls to people he knew the personal addresses of, demanding backup.

His radio crackled. That still worked, at least.

"VTOL troop carriers, Lieutenant. Two of them. Coming in fast."

Wu Jiabao tensed. Friend or foe? Reinforcements or assailants?

"Have you hailed them?" he asked into radio.

"Roger. No response," came the reply.

He held the radio to his mouth. Everything might depend on this. "Safeties off. Put a bead on those planes. I want to know who comes out. But no shooting unless I give the word."

He pulled the radio away from his mouth, took his finger off the transmit button.

"Roger," came the reply, from a half dozen voices.

Then a moment later. "I've got ropes. Men hot roping out of vehicle one!"

Shit. That meant assault!

Wu Jiabao pulled the radio back up.

"Oh my god," it crackled. "They're all–"

"Fire!" he yelled into his radio.

The sound of gunfire answered him.

And groans.

Screams.

"Status!" he yelled.

Silence.

"Status!" he repeated.

Silence.

"Chief," one of his men said.

Wu Jiabao looked over. The man was studying the house monitors. And there, on them, he could see armed men moving through the home.

Armed men with identical faces.

Wu Jiabao swallowed.

"Flank the door," he ordered. "Take cover behind the bar. Prepare to repel."

Then he walked over to the couch, hauled the scrawny politician up by his lapel, put a gun to his head, and put the man between him and the door.

His wife and family screamed.

"Run into the bedroom!" Liu yelled at them.

Sun Liu struggled, and Wu Jiabao clubbed him with the gun.

"I need you alive," he told the man. "But I'm willing to blow your nuts off."

That stilled him.

Wu turned to the house monitors, just in time to see a monitor show one of the invaders point a gun at it.

And then it went dark.

More than half of them were dark now.

He watched as they came closer, bit by bit, penetrating the house.

Destroying every camera they came to.

Until they were right outside the door.

He waited, in view of them, his pistol pressed to Sun Liu's temple. He felt his men shift, become anxious, felt the anxiety rise, felt it rise further.

Why weren't they coming in?

BOOOOOM.

With a shuddering explosion, the door blasted inward. Wu staggered on his feet, felt Sun Liu try to get free. He jerked the man brutally, righted himself, brought the gun back to the man's head.

A figure appeared in the doorway.

His men opened fire.

The figure was gone, not there anymore.

His men kept firing.

Clips went dry.

Then men in white were inside the room, firing back.

And suddenly all was still.

And everywhere he turned, he saw his men were dead.

"Don't come any closer!" Wu said, staring at the clone who'd come in first. The man had an assault rifle pointed forty-five degrees down, mostly at the floor. "Stop right there! Back away or I'll blow his–"

Wu never saw the gun shift in Tao's hand, or the explosion of muzzle fire that put a three-bullet volley directly into his brain.

Tao stepped up to the dead soldier's body, leaned down, safetied the man's pistol, then pried it out of his hand.

Sun Liu was shaking on the floor. From a doorway came the sound of crying and weeping.

Tao stared down at the dead soldier.

Every soldier knew death could come. When it did, it would likely come at the hands of someone like them. All soldiers were brothers, doing a job or fighting for a cause, putting their lives on the line for someone or something besides themselves. Death was part of that job. So was killing. There was no mystery there.

Still, it was the people in charge who he'd prefer to take the lives of.

Sun Liu was still shaking. "What… What's going on?" he said. "Who sent you?"

Tao smiled at the man in as reassuring a manner as he could, even as Daofeng came up with the hypersonic injector.

"Minister Sun," Tao said. "Welcome to the revolution."

103
On Set

Sunday 2041.01.20

Zhi Li kept the hood pulled over her head as her eyes scanned the protest site. Lu Song squeezed her hand, a hat tugged down low over his famous face.

The protest was a throng, an insane intensity of people, thousands of them waving signs, chanting, fired up. It was the density and passion of a concert, of a festival. But unleashed. Unrestrained by the usual rules.

It was like nothing Zhi Li had ever seen in China.

And this was just the small one. This was just Jiao Tong.

They'd aimed for the main protest in People's Square, but the city was so full of people that driving became impossible kilometers back. Jiao Tong was closer.

And this was where it had started.

No one had recognized them yet. She was grateful. They'd hidden their faces to avoid being recognized by police, by soldiers. But now she wasn't even sure she wanted to be recognized.

She'd come here in a moment of passion, seeing that digital version of herself inciting the masses, she'd suddenly imagined herself a hero, a leader of the revolution, guiding the people to justice.

She'd done that so many times in film, since she was just a child. She knew the lines. She'd read the scripts. She'd had her close-ups.

She'd defeated evil every time.

But this…

All around her, details showed her the reality.

Medical tents being set up. First aid supplies laid out.

Makeshift gas masks handed out. Not nearly enough. Bandanas and scarves being collected, distributed. Cheap goggles where they could.

Sticks and pipes in people's hands. Sports racquets. Makeshift weapons and waste-bin-lid shields and home-made armor.

The constant buzzing of the drones overhead. Hundreds of them zooming by just above the signs.

The barricades, of broken furniture, bricks, machinery, all piled up to form a barrier.

A barrier against the army beyond it. The ranks and ranks of soldiers. With guns, and long heavy batons, and metal shields and mirrored helmets. And behind them, tanks and tank-like things, massive turrets pointing this way.

This was no movie.

"Nexus?" she heard a male voice say.

Something brushed her. She looked down, saw a hand, holding a silvery vial.

Qi's hand snaked out from beside her, grabbed the wrist, twisted it away from her.

There was squeal of pain. The vial dropped to the ground.

"Qi!" she said. "Let go. It's OK."

She looked up. There was a boy in front of her, perhaps eighteen, nineteen, holding his wrist, rubbing it, a look of betrayal and annoyance on his face.

Then his eyes met hers and they grew wide.

"Holy shit," he said.

Zhi Li felt resignation hit her. She smiled at the boy.

"We're here to help," she said. "Who's in charge here?"

104
The Sooner, The Better

Sunday 2041.01.20

Sun Liu's eyes went wide as the world expanded within him, as the nanites attached to his neurons, as new inputs entered his brain, made their way into his consciousness.

So vast. So vast.

He could feel the minds of the men around him.

He could feel the pieces of his own mind, coming together. Feel the software within the nanomachinery studying him, learning him, flashing huge swaths of his life before his eyes at once.

So amazing.

I'm a scientist, he thought. Why didn't I ever do this before?

And then *she* was there.

And hell opened up, hell beyond anything he'd ever imagined possible.

I KNOW WHAT YOU DID, SUN LIU. The voice was the voice of a thousand dark angels, a thousand folk demons from his mother's superstitions. All true. All true.

He saw himself through her eyes. Things she could not know. He saw himself warning Chen Pang, warning him about the car bomb, warning him the reactionaries were going to kill him and his wife, warning Chen Pang, but not warning Su-Yong Shu!

Condemning her and her unborn son to death!

No, he wanted to say. You're dead. You're dead. So many times over you're dead. You can't hurt me.

But he was inside her mind, as she was inside his. He was burning, pinned in the back of that limousine, watching Yang Wei die, feeling the unborn son inside himself die, feeling skin blacken and burn.

I KNOW YOU LET CHEN TORTURE ME, the demoness shouted into his mind. **TORTURE ME FOR YOUR PETTY GAIN.**

And he was reliving her pain, every nerve fiber in wretched agony, yet aware she must have had it worse, a being so much more able to feel, that thought so much faster.

Decades of pain. Centuries of pain. Millennia of pain.

I'm sorry, he tried to tell her. I'm so sorry.

Distantly he could sense that he was on the ground, that he was writhing in pain, his muscles contorting.

YOU'RE NOT SORRY YET, she told him. **BUT I HAVE A GIFT FOR YOU. YOU'RE GOING TO LIVE FOREVER.**

Digital. She was going to make him digital, the pattern of his brain, the wiring of his neurons and synapses, like her. She was going to upload him.

SO YOU CAN SUFFER EVEN MORE.

No... No... he begged. Please let me die.

BUT FIRST, she sent. **YOU'RE GOING TO HELP ME. WHERE ARE THE OTHER CUBES?**

And then he felt hot fingers of her thought violate him, penetrating through his mind, taking whatever they wished.

As he screamed and screamed and begged her to let him die.

Tao leaned back in the plane as they headed north.

His brothers were as quiet around him as they had been on the flight down. But the mood had changed. He could feel them all in his mind. He could feel what they felt, think what they thought.

He looked over at Sun Liu. The politician's screams had stopped. But his face was ashen. His mind was sealed up tight.

But not tight enough.

Now and again, shards of agony lanced out from him.

Torture.

Tao turned back, faced straight ahead. Then he pulled out his weapon, and started checking and rechecking it.

They had their next target. They had their next mission.

It would be a test of the endurance of these aircraft. A test of their ability to bluff their way through Air Defense zones yet again. A test of their own skills at penetrating a much more secure location, probably under enemy fire.

Probably while killing more soldiers.

But at least they had something to do.

Tao glanced again at Sun Liu. The man's face twitched, and another shard of horror leaked out into the minds around him.

The sooner they were done with this mission, the better.

•••

What the hell am I doing here? Sam asked herself again.

She looked across the body of the aircraft, and there was Feng, familiarizing himself with the Indian commando gear.

She sighed, and looked down at the gear in her own hands.

I should be with Sarai, with Kit, with Mali, she thought.

Except that they were all on a plane with Ananda now. On a plane to Thailand, to do something she didn't fully understand.

Her mind flicked back to Ananda's last words to her, in Bangalore, just before they'd lifted off.

Samantha, he'd said. *These children I take with me. Twenty-two of them are Thai. Things have changed since you fled here. Thailand is prepared to protect them now. And you.*

He'd held open an offer of asylum. A home. Bangalore still didn't feel like home. It felt like a research project.

What about Kade?

Sam shook her head. Something to deal with after this. If any of them lived through this.

She looked to her left. Aarthi was there, one of the dozen Division Six members going with them. Her old colleague smiled at her, gave her an encouraging thumbs up.

Sam nodded in response. That was two people here she'd been in the field with.

Three if you counted Kade.

But you couldn't really count Kade.

"Sam."

She turned and he was there, getting into the hard military seat next to her. She hadn't heard him over the roar of the troop transport plane's engines.

He fumbled with the straps. She reached over, clicked them home for him, one, two, three.

She chuckled to herself. This wasn't his area of expertise.

Their hands brushed as she finished securing his harness. She looked up and he was staring at her. Was it strange, to look at someone and *not* know what was in their head? To not feel something coming off their mind? What would it feel like for her, when she took Nexus again?

It might have been today, if the world hadn't blown up.

"I'm sorry I made it so hard when we first got here," Sam said. She put her fist down on his knee in friendship. "It was about me, not you. I know you're…" Innocent, she almost said. Still a kid. Naïve. "… good hearted. The kids love you."

Kade gave her a strained smile. "The kids love you too," he said. "They're really looking forward to you taking Nexus again."

She smiled. "I feel good. I think I'm ready."

Kade's smile went away. "I'm glad you haven't yet."

Sam blinked in surprise. That was kind of a strange thing to say.

"Sam," he looked at her again. "When we get there. The plan has a lot of risks. And if... Well, there's something I may need you to do for me."

Kade leaned in close then, and told her what he was asking of her, and why.

And when he was done, Sam leaned back, her eyes closed, bile rising in her stomach at the thought of what he'd just said.

Kade wasn't so naïve anymore, after all.

105
Ripples

Sunday 2041.01.20

"So who did this to us?" Bo Jintao demanded.

It was late in the afternoon. They'd been meeting for hours. Sending out runners to acquire information, to send orders, to send for more troops.

Even civilian phones and data didn't work for them. They worked for *civilians*, but whoever had hacked them had turned censor codes against them, was blocking the civilian network from working within government ministries and military facilities, was filtering out messages with key phrases, key voices.

It was infuriating. All their tools were being used as weapons against them.

Information Minister Fu Ping was sweating. The man looked like he feared for his life.

"Premier," the man started. "These last two attacks were sloppier than the initial–"

"Who?" Bo Jintao demanded.

Fu Ping stuttered. "Either... Either the Americans. Or the Indians."

"You don't know?" Wang Wei, of the Committee for Discipline Inspection, roared.

"There's data pointing in both directions..." Fu Ping's voice was wavering. He was avoiding eye contact. "It could be that one is behind the attack, and trying to shift blame–"

"When can you stop it?" Bo Jintao interrupted.

"We... we are working as fast as we can. We're optimistic that we'll find a way..."

"You don't know anything, is that what you're telling us?" Wang

438

Wei's voice was cutting. The old conservative was turning the screws. Maybe Fu Ping really should be frightened.

Information Minister Fu Ping took a deep breath. "The Peace and Harmony Friends run in a *distributed* manner. We send them *instructions* from the ministry. But they're not *listening* to us just now."

"They listen to guns," General Ouyang announced from the doorway, dressed in his full uniform.

Bo Jintao looked up. He hadn't heard Ouyang enter.

"My men have been going door to door, destroying Friend processors. We've just posted video on our Army channel of how citizens can do the same, or how they can safely disconnect the dedicated power supplies."

"That's our crown jewel!" Fu Ping protested.

"It's a tool." Ouyang shrugged, still standing. "It can be used by you or against you. I warned you of that years ago." The grizzled general shook his head. "Overdependence on one tool is always a strategic error."

Bo Jintao nodded. He'd told Gao the same.

"General," Bo Jintao said. "How goes re-establishing communications?"

Ouyang took a seat at the end of the table, stared hard at Bo Jintao.

Bo Jintao knew that look. It was the look that reminded him that he was here, that he was Premier, that he was the man behind the throne, because the Army had backed him.

Because Ouyang had backed him.

"We're making progress," he said. "Old fashioned radio systems and analog wires are uncompromised. We're using high altitude aircraft to send signals from one location to another. It's slow. It's low bandwidth. But it works."

"You have control of the armed forces?" Bao Zhuang asked.

"I do," Ouyang said, flatly.

"And the Americans?" Bo Jintao asked.

"Their fleet elements are as aggressive as ever. They're in disputed waters, in parts of the East China Sea and South China Sea we claim. Beijing, Shanghai, and Guangzhou are all in their strike range. The entire eastern seaboard is within their range. And if they struck now…" Ouyang shook his head. "Our response would be uncoordinated. They would have a significant tactical advantage."

"Our response?" Bo Jintao asked.

"We must act prudently and conservatively," General Ouyang said. "With our systems handicapped and an insurgency on our soil, and the strong suspicion that the Americans are behind it, we cannot afford the added risk that the American naval presence represents. They *must* understand this. I recommend we contact the American fleet elements directly via ship-to-ship communication and inform them that they are ordered to leave our waters in the South and East China Seas."

Bo Jintao nodded. "And if they don't? If they insist those are international waters?"

"Warning shots," Ouyang said. "We demonstrate that we're serious. A shore-launched ballistic projectile off the bow of one of their uncrewed ships. No risk of lives lost, no damage, but a clear message."

Bo Jintao looked around. He saw faces that were frightened. He saw uncertainty. He saw Wang Wei nodding eagerly – anger, needing a target. That was more dangerous than anything.

Bao Zhuang had an eyebrow raised. "An uncrewed ship is good. A warning shot is good."

Bo Jintao took a breath, turned back to Ouyang. "Do it," he said.

"Now, as for the protests..." Bo Jintao carefully didn't look at Bao Zhuang this time. "It's time to clear them out. Send soldiers to the companies that they're using to share their videos and pictures and messages. Shut those services down. Turn off the power if necessary."

"Premier," Fu Ping started.

Bo Jintao rolled over him, directed his eyes and words at General Ouyang. "And then move in on the protesters themselves. With force. Make it clear that any who resist are traitors or American stooges. Force them from the squares."

"They have satellite phones," Fu Ping said. "Laser uplinks. Shutting down the Chinese services won't stop them from getting news out. Whatever we do will be seen!"

"I recommend – strongly – against live ammunition," General Ouyang said. "My forces are not the police. To use soldiers against our own people... That is a line, seldom crossed, painful every time. We should do this with sub-lethal force."

"These are traitors!" Wang Wei cut in, ever the hardliner. "We should use whatever force is necessary."

"General Ouyang is wise," Bao Zhuang said, slowly, as if Wang Wei hadn't spoken. "History is not kind to armies who fire on their own citizens, or to those who give the orders."

Bo Jintao compressed his lips. It *was* wise. Death was to be avoided. One had to sap energy from protests and the movements that fueled them, not feed energy into them. "I agree with General Ouyang and the President," he said. "Sub-lethal force. We don't want to create martyrs. But find those phones and uplinks. And destroy them."

"What we're looking at is a major crisis in China," Secretary of State Pamela Abrams said. "It's unprecedented in the last seventy years. Larger than the Tiananmen protests of 1989. The next few days could either see the fall of the government or an incredible bloodbath."

Pryce nodded. "Thank you, Secretary Abrams. Admiral McWilliams?"

She acknowledged the Chairman of the Joint Chiefs of Staff.

Stanley McWilliams was white haired, a rail-thin runner, almost ascetic in his appearance. He pissed her off to no end on some days. But the man was a soldier who hated war. That meant a lot in her book.

"The Chinese may have lost most of their internal comms," he said. "But they have enough. Their fleet has delivered ultimatums to our ships that we're to quit the East China Sea and South China Sea or be fired upon. There've been provocations, boats coming inside the exclusion zones of our carriers. Most worryingly, NRO satellite imagery shows that their shore-based anti-ship missile systems have been armed. Those are a major threat to our fleet elements in the area. If they launch, we can't guarantee we'll stop all the warheads. We could lose carriers."

"Our ships are in international waters," Bernard Stevens, the Secretary of Defense, spoke up, looking around the National Security Council table. "We can't give in to bullying. We have first strike capability against those missiles. We may have no choice but to take them out proactively." His eyes ended on the President.

Stockton said nothing for a moment. Then, "Pryce, what's your view?"

Well, at least he still asked her opinion.

"We have to put ourselves in the position of the Chinese," she said. "They're panicking. They have a domestic catastrophe on their hands. They see our ships in an aggressive posture, that heightens tensions further." She paused. "Mr President, you said the Chinese President accused us of undermining their state censors. What if they really believe we're behind their domestic unrest? They link the two, conclude that this is all part of a plan on our part to bring their government down." She spread her hands. "What would we do in their shoes?"

"I agree with Dr Pryce," Admiral McWilliams said. "Their home situation – the breakdown of their comms, everything else – has the Chinese on a hair trigger. A shooting war isn't the goal. We'd be wise to take action to calm them down."

Bernard Stevens shook his head. "No," the Secretary of Defense said. "Our ships are only there because the Chinese *assassinated* a member of this government. Remember that? They started this provocation. All the rest – the accusations – are a smoke screen. They're blowing smoke to get us to back off. And these are *international waters*. If we let the Chinese bully us out of there, what does that tell our allies and the world?"

The Secretary of State spoke up. "I share that concern about our allies," Pamela Abrams said. "We have commitments to the Philippines, to Japan, to Korea, to Vietnam, to ASEAN. Everyone expects us to hold to international law and internationally defined borders. If we back down on this, the signal it sends will rock the whole region." Secretary

Abrams shook her head. "I can't believe the Chinese are crazy enough to shoot."

Pryce looked around the table. CIA and NSA weren't offering any opinions. The VP was silent as usual. "It's your call, Mr President," she said, turning to Stockton.

Stockton exhaled. "We stand our ground. We don't shoot first. But we don't give in to bullying."

Bai stood at attention, stoic-faced, mind locked down, not showing any of his horror, as the thing in little Ling's body gave him and Peng new orders, a kilometer below Jiao Tong.

Ensure that the protesters are not flushed from the square, it sent.

There was an ugly bruise on one side of Ling's face. Her eyes were bloodshot. One lip was swollen. There was blood on her dress. From where it had dripped down from the lip, he'd guess.

Her mouth was working. Her lips were saying something. Not the same as her mind was saying.

In the corner, Chen Pang stood, staring at the quantum cluster behind the glass.

But do not reveal yourselves yet, the thing that he'd once thought was Su-Yong went on. **New brothers will be arriving, reinforcing you.**

More than fifty had already arrived, from Dachang, sneaking in, using chameleonware, or disguised in other ways to hide their distinctive faces.

"Mother…" Peng said aloud. His voice sounded tentative, uncertain.

Bai felt fear rush through him.

Don't say the wrong thing, Peng, he thought, not daring to transmit it. Don't say the wrong thing.

"…is everything going alright?" Peng finished.

Little Ling's mouth stopped making words to them. She smiled with it instead, showing teeth that needed cleaning.

"Everything will be just fine," she said in Ling's voice.

It wasn't until he and Peng were near the top of the kilometer-high elevator shaft that they even looked at each other.

And Peng silently moved his lips and mouth in a precise mimicry of what Ling's had done.

Bai nodded silently.

Help me. Please, help me. That's what Ling's mouth had been saying. Even as the entity that occupied her had been telling them something else entirely.

Bai shivered, and felt and saw his brother do the same.

106
Inflamed

Sunday 2041.01.20

Zhi Li stood atop the table in the setting sun, looking down on the crowd in the square of Jiao Tong.

She could feel them in her mind. She could feel their thoughts and emotions. Incredible. Her hallucination was still so vivid in her thoughts. This was a story. This was a thousand stories. This was a million stories. Each of these faces was a role, was a hundred roles. She looked at a woman and saw a mother, a wife, a daughter, a granddaughter, a grandmother someday, a worker, a student, a teacher, an inventor, a lover.

A freedom fighter.

A billion stories.

A trillion stories.

Interwoven.

All intermeshing with hers.

She opened her mouth to speak and it was almost too much.

"Today," she said.

And they cheered, cheered loud just to see her there, held cameras up, broadcast her, photographed her.

Zhi Li laughed. How absurd! They were actors and actresses as much as she was!

They were as famous as she was!

As important as she was!

She held up her left hand and smiled until it was over, until she could hear herself. A boy handed Lu Song a microphone, and Lu Song stepped up next to her, held it before her mouth.

"Today!" she said again, and this time her words crackled out, and she saw them ripple across the whole crowd.

She *felt* them ripple across the minds of the crowd.

She saw even the soldiers, beyond the barricades, watching her, listening to her.

"Today, *we are China!*" she roared, and the crowd roared back.

"China is not a place!" she said. "China is not a government! China is *the people!*"

They roared again, hooting for her, their minds exulting for her.

"*I* am not important!" she said, bringing her left hand to her chest. She showed it to them, showed them her sincerity, pushed it at them with her mind. It confused them. They cheered, half-heartedly.

"*They* are not important!" She gestured, vaguely at the troops, at the direction of Beijing.

The crowd cheered louder this time.

"Fuck the party!" she heard someone yell. Laughter followed. She smiled.

"But *you* are important!" She pointed at the crowd. "*We* are important. Because *WE ARE CHINA!*"

The crowd roared louder than ever now, roared its approval, showed it to her in their thoughts.

"If China oppresses its people, China *oppresses itself!*"

Their minds opened to her, gave her love, gave her passion.

She opened herself wide, threw it back at them, held up her left fist in defiance, let it show in her face, in her wide open mouth, in the fire in her eyes, let it be heard in her voice for everyone around the nation and the world to hear.

"Today we free ourselves, and so *China frees China!*"

They roared again, and with that, she lifted her sword out of the bucket where the blade had been soaking and held it up high, her hand wrapped around the little box and the wires that had been affixed to it.

The crowd cheered louder.

Her eyes caught those of that boy, Yuguo's, in the front, and he hit a button on his phone.

And the blade of her sword burst into flame.

The crowd went wild in voice and mind. Flashbulbs burst.

And Zhi Li tried not to flinch from the burning object she held above her head.

A thousand kilometers away, in Tiananmen Square, in the heart of Beijing, Peng Luli screams in joy as her idol, Zhi Li, lifts the flaming sword into the sky! Hundreds of thousands in Tiananmen see through the eyes of men and women in Shanghai, and cheer just as loudly.

In Guangzhou, in Hong Kong, in Dalian, in Shenzhen, in Chengdu, in Wuhan, in Dongguan, millions more see the same sight, experience the same sight through the eyes and ears of just thousands at Jiao Tong, and roar their approval.

Zhi Li is with them! The revolution cannot fail!

"They're coming again!" someone yelled, hours later.

Zhi crouched down lower behind the overturned table in the darkness, goggles pulled down over her eyes, wet bandana wrapped over her mouth and nose. Next to her Lu Song crouched protectively, a long pipe in his hand. Qi and Dai were on either side of them, hands in the pockets of their wind blazers. Where their pistols were.

BZZZZZZZZZZZZZT.

She groaned as the blast hit her again. Subsonic vibrations moved through her bones, her bowels. Her head throbbed.

She heard popping sounds, the distinctive noise of the tear gas grenade launchers.

And then thuds as they came down. Hissing as the gas came out of them at high pressure, barely visible in the darkness, except where it blocked the red flames.

Coughing. She felt coughing in the minds around her, even with the bandanas, the few gas masks.

NOW! Yuguo sent.

Was the boy twenty? Nineteen? Some sort of nerd. And somehow he'd become the leader here.

Two-person teams of protesters leapt to their feet from behind shelter, illuminated by the light of the burning barricades. Each had a shield-holder, hoisting a human-sized piece of wood or stiff plastic or sheet metal, gleaming in the firelight; and a thrower, cocking back a Molotov cocktail. On the ground next to them would be a third person, lighting the cocktail, handing them another if there was time for a second throw.

Twenty lit cocktails soared into the air, up over the burning barrier between them and the army forces.

More flame now. Less cheering.

Army shooters fired back with rubber bullets, knocking one girl down, spinning another thrower around, forcing all the rest to take cover.

Through the eyes of the lookouts linked to them, Zhi Li saw the fuel-filled bottles slam into the upheld shields of soldiers and riot police moving in, saw them burst into flame, saw the line fall back, their advance halted.

Slingshots! Yuguo sent.

Further back, three larger teams popped up, with slings made of meters-long pieces of thick elastic tubing. Each team had four or five shield holders, plus two sling holders, and one puller in the middle.

Even now the puller she had her eyes on was hauling back, stretching out the tubing, loading a lit Molotov into the cup at the center of his sling…

…and letting it fly.

Rubber bullets ripped into them, knocking the lines of shields down and back.

Zhi Li watched the lit Molotovs whistle through the air, tumbling in flight, up over the crowd, over the burning barricade, past the withdrawing ranks of riot-armored soldiers…

And saw one crash right into an armored vehicle, one with what she'd learned was a sonic cannon. It burst into a ball of flame across the cannon and the top of the tank-like thing.

A roar erupted from the crowd.

They were doing it. They were holding them off.

Bai watched from the rooftop, his body stealthed and flush against the roof, his mind reeled in tight, a silenced sniper rifle in his hand.

His magazine was still full. His rifle unfired.

He lay there and watched, his heart flushed with pride.

The people were rising.

Rangan watched the news from the Bunker.

The world had gone stark raving mad. Molotov cocktails were flying again in Detroit, in LA, in the ghettos of DC. Protests were heating up, here, abroad, everywhere.

And China. Jesus, China. The net was awash with China now. He could close his eyes and pull up a hundred Chinese mindstream feeds. Chinese kids waving flower signs in front of tanks.

Chinese kids throwing Molotov cocktails.

And Kade was going there.

At least now things made sense. As much sense as any of this insanity could make.

Tomorrow was Stockton's inauguration. They'd be holding it inside the Capitol building, for fear of disruption. For fear of the Million (post) Human March.

Rangan just hoped he could keep that from turning into the Million Crazy Human March. The Million Dead Human March.

Jesus.

107
Desert Strike

Sunday 2041.01.20
They came in low and fast, from the East, across the darkened desert landscape. Tao watched from the co-pilot seat of the aircraft, laden with Confucian Fist, as the wire-frame of the complex in the distance came closer and closer, rising towards the artificial horizon. Thirty kilometers. Twenty-five. Twenty.

At sixteen klicks they'd be over the horizon. The target would be in sight. The target that housed a data cube. The data cube Sun Liu had pointed them towards.

Their planes had chameleonware engaged, but the sound of their engines would give them away, the heat from their exhaust would give them away. Bending light around your skin could only do so much.

They were outgunned. They were outmanned. They'd refueled twice to reach this remote depot in the depopulated west. They were near the limits of the endurance of their aircraft.

There would be no reinforcements.

There would be no extra ammunition.

Strike fast. Strike hard. Achieve the objective. Or die trying.

Nineteen kilometers.

Eighteen.

Seventeen.

Sixteen.

The top of a building appeared. The pilot pulled back on his stick and the whole complex popped into sight. Targeting displays came alive. Red rectangles converged on anti-missile cannons, on electronic-destroying microwave beams, on anti-personnel guns, on a rooftop radar installation.

RADAR WARNING flashed on the cockpit glass as the site's radar lit them up.

BEEEEEEEP. A tone indicated they were being targeted.

The pilot fired.

Four cylindrical launcher pods – two on each wing – came alive with fire. Each launcher let loose a spiraling barrage of the cigar-wide micromissiles, as tubes packed within each pod let loose in succession, milliseconds apart.

In a quarter of a second the plane put a hundred and twenty tiny, lethal, all-too-smart missiles into the air, racing ahead of the plane at eight Gs, spreading out, zigging and zagging to make themselves more difficult targets to stop.

The small base responded instantly. Lasers came alive, flicked from missile to missile, seeking to confuse them, knock them off course, destroy them. Projectile launchers fired a screen of millimeter-scale debris at the flight paths of the missiles to cause collisions. Proximity-alarmed Gatling guns came alive, projected the course and direction of the missiles, fired a spray of hot lead bullets, hundreds per second, at the locations where the incoming ordinance would be.

Lasers struck missiles at twelve kilometers east of the facility. Explosions lit up the night. Missiles burst into flame, veered off course, detonated their warheads prematurely, set off their neighbors.

Almost a hundred kept coming, accelerating as the lasers ate away at them.

Gatling gun rounds first hit them at three kilometers east. Missile engines burst apart. Fuel exploded into air. Explosions sent nearby missiles tumbling, setting off further explosions.

More than fifty missiles kept coming; more Gatling gun rounds, more explosions, as close as half a klick away.

Thirty missiles hit the screen of defensive particles a hundred meters from the eastern edge of the complex. Missile warheads and guidance systems ripped themselves apart. Explosions were deafening now. Shrapnel kept moving forward after missiles were destroyed, slamming into buildings, into equipment, into personnel.

Metal rain and explosive detonation blinded radar, blinded thermal imagers.

And in the moment of blindness, the second aircraft slid smoothly over the horizon to the west, and unleashed its own barrage.

They came in hot after destroying the base's defenses. There were still humans down there. Armed adversaries.

At one kilometer out the pilots of both planes rotated their wingtip jet engines nearly skyward, brought them in on hover, noses of both planes angled slightly down, thirty-millimeter cannons ready to fire on anything moving on the ground.

Tao pointed. "That's the building," he said, pointing at the two story structure as they came within a hundred meters of it. "Flush it."

"Roger," the pilot said. "Opening up."

A targeting rectangle appeared on the landscape. The pilot pulled his trigger.

The heavy rhythmic sound of a chain gun thrummed through the plane. Tao could see muzzle burst out ahead of the nose, could see their rounds ripping into the structure, as the pilot systematically worked his gun over it, sending decimeter long, three-centimeter thick, nearly kilogram heavy rounds through anything that stood in their way.

Down there, Tao thought, soldiers were dying.

Better them than him.

Better them than his brothers.

The second plane came on station, hovered at its own angle, ninety degrees off their starboard, opened up with its own gun.

"Movement!" the pilot yelled.

A figure in the doorway of the building, still up, somehow, still alive! There was something on his shoulder. Missile launcher.

Red streak. Fired!

Chain gun rounds ripped the shooter in half.

Missile, en route to Griffon Two!

Tao tracked with his eyes, tried to get ahead of it. Griffon Two was turning, vectoring thrust, trying to twist out of the path of the shoulder-launched heat seeker.

But they were so close!

Flares fired out of its belly in the last instant.

The missile slammed into its port engine in a burst of flame.

Griffon Two spun, wildly.

It was spinning at them, coming this way as its human pilot tried to take control.

Tao grabbed the co-pilot's controls of their own craft, faster than the human pilot could react, pushed hard to the right. The plane slid, tilted, twisted. He caught a glimpse of Griffon Two looming huge, fire where the engine should be, then the cockpit as it spun, alarm on the human pilot's face, and his brother.

His brother Sung. His face calm. His hands on the co-pilot's controls, trying to get the plane under control.

Then the plane was past, still spinning. And as they twisted themselves he saw Griffon Two's wingtip touch the ground, and then the whole plane tumbled, slammed to the ground.

And a huge explosion ripped through the night as brothers died.

• • •

Tao moved through the building twenty minutes later, weapon at the ready, his mind grim.

Dead brothers.

Dead brothers.

What was worth dead brothers?

They met no resistance inside the outpost.

Dead men were everywhere, their bodies blasted and blown apart. Equipment had slumped and collapsed under the onslaught of the chain gun. Cabinets and tables and electronics had exploded. Walls had exploded. Beams had come down. Debris was everywhere.

There was no resistance remaining.

Tao tapped the radio at his throat. "Send in the politician."

"I am Sun Liu," the human said, his hands on full palm scanners, tens of meters below surface level. "Member of the Politburo Standing Committee, Minister of Science and Technology. Requesting access to the archive."

Tao watched as lasers scanned the man's retinas. Behind the wall he imagined processors analyzing speech patterns, vocal stress response, and so much more.

Now, would Sun Liu still have access to this archive? How up to date would it be?

"Welcome, Minister Sun Liu," said the silky, feminine voice.

Titanium alloy doors parted.

The archive was a maze of store rooms with contents ranging from the familiar to the bizarre. A mishmash of things the nation had created that it now wanted locked away, but not yet destroyed.

There were shelves of files. Ammunition cases. Data banks. Ancient electronics. Chemical tanks. Biological material cases, with bright yellow biohazard stickers and triple seals.

They came into a room full of cryo tubes, vertically oriented. They were occupied, faces showing on the nude bodies behind the glass. Men. Women. Faces he'd never seen.

Famous faces.

"Clones," one of his brothers said. "Like us."

Tao looked at these bodies, frozen, trapped, and shook his head.

"Not like us."

But at the end of the room, there was one. One who looked too much like him. Too much like his brothers. Not the same. Not quite.

But too close.

Tao shook his head and moved on.

"Here," Sun Liu said. "This is it." His voice was calm. His mind was horrified.

The politician lifted a metal case from a rack of metal cases. The label below it gave a date, an ID number.

Sun Liu held his thumbs to the reader pads on the case, fear leaking out into the space around him.

The locks opened.

Inside, in the midst of thick foam padding, gleamed a diamondoid data cube.

"Test it," Tao said.

His brother Xuan stepped up with the portable cube reader and gingerly moved the cube into it, closed the reader door, and slid his finger across a series of controls.

They waited, and waited, and waited.

Then green lights appeared.

"Basic check is good," Xuan said. "Data looks like a neural map."

Sun Liu stared ahead. Dread leaked out from his mind. Despair for what he'd done to his world and his species.

Tao looked down on the site as they lifted off, freshly fueled, en route to Shanghai. He could see the burning wreckage of Griffon Two down there. Sung was dead in that wreckage. Jialu was dead. Zhaoguo was dead. Jin was dead. Hui was dead. A dozen brothers dead. And the pilot they'd had. The pilot they'd made one of them by the rewriting of his neural circuitry.

By making him a slave.

Tao looked down at the metal case, sitting on the floor, now secured to his own body until he could deliver it in Shanghai.

I'd die for you, Su-Yong, he thought. Any of us would. You freed us from slavery.

Then he felt another jolt of agony escape from Sun Liu. The man's torture had resumed.

Tao shook his head.

There were worse fates than death.

108
Wings

Monday 2041.01.20

Kade watched as the ground crews loaded fuel into the Indian stealth bombers, on this little spit of land leased from Vietnam. India's base to protect its oil and natural gas interests in the South China Sea.

The bombers were wide flying wings, a riff on the old American B-2 body plan, matte black, equipped with state-of-the-art chameleonware and radar avoidance, engines mounted atop the wing body to mask their surfaces and exhaust from any sensors below.

Why were there two of them?

"We're running out of time," Kamal Garud said. He was the commander of the Division Six commandos. A captain in the India's airborne special forces, transferred to the Division during its reconstruction. Tall, broad shoulders, rippling muscles, the aura of command.

The man's mind was cool and hard. He was running Nexus, like all the commandos. But he had it locked down, giving nothing away.

"It's 1am in Shanghai now," Captain Garud went on. "By the time we deploy, it will be nearly 5am. The sky will be getting light. The risk goes up."

Kade turned to face the man. "We go now," Kade said. "As soon as they're fueled up."

"Listen, chameleonware isn't magic," Garud replied. "In the dark, or if you're moving slowly, wonderful. But inserting at high speed, with light coming up, there's a high risk of observers noticing *something*. If we wait until tomorrow night–"

"It's scrambling right now," Kade interrupted, staring at the man. "The program that wants to take over the world. It's using every hour, every minute, every second to get closer to its goal. We have every reason to believe we have *less* than a day before its plan comes to fruition. And if we're not there, it's *going to succeed.*"

Kade stopped and let that sink in. "Now, I hear you on the risk of being seen. So you tell me. Does that risk outweigh the risk I've just outlined for you?"

Garud stared at him, his thoughts revealing nothing.

"Does it, Captain?" Kade said.

"No, sir," Garud said.

Then the man saluted, and walked off, giving orders to his men.

And left Kade standing there, staring at the Indian bombers.

At the two bombers, when there should have been one.

Kade stood in the weapons bay of the bomber as Aarthi walked him through a system's check one more time.

He was suited up.

More than suited up.

He was winged.

His body was in a head-to-toe chameleonware suit, with a pressurized helmet. A hose connected to a small tank that provided breathable air. Over his shoulders came thick straps with metal releases. Another webbing strap connected them across his chest. More straps bound themselves around his waist, and yet more around each thigh.

Those held the rigid wing to his back. It was a broad V, wider than he was tall. It came up to the back of his head, and down to his calves. It was surprisingly light, nearly invisible on radar, and would activate its own chameleonware when they deployed.

When they dropped out of the bottom of this aircraft sixteen kilometers up over the Pacific, eighty kilometers from shore, and started their unpowered, suicide-speed flight to their target, sixteen kilometers inland.

"OK," Aarthi sent. "Everything's green."

Kade nodded, and pressed the mental command to open up. The visor of the external suit cracked its seal, and Kade lifted it.

"Thanks," he said.

Aarthi nodded. "Just remember: stay still, and the wing will do all the steering. It knows the program."

Kade nodded. Then he changed the subject.

"Hey, Aarthi," he said, pointing at the heavy case in a corner of the bay. The case with the warning sign on it. "What's in the box?"

Aarthi didn't turn her head. She just looked at him. "Weapons, Dr Kade. Just weapons."

"I'm not a doctor," he said reflexively.

Aarthi smiled.

Two planes, Kade thought. So if one gets shot down, the other can do the job. With what's in those cases.

Kade looked at the box again.

Their plan doesn't depend on my way working, he thought. It doesn't depend on me living at all.

I have to live, he told himself. My way has to work.

"Launch!"

The voice buzzed in Kade's ear. Displays in his mind, proxied from the wing itself, went green.

And then he was falling, out into the utter black through the bomb bay in the stomach of the great stealth flying wing.

His stomach dropped. He was weightless for an instant. Then the wing he was fastened to bit into thin air and suddenly the straps were gripping him, holding him up, prone, staring down into the abyss. The cold hit him. Even in the body heat-retaining chameleonware suit, the air was frigid. The wind pressed against his helmet, against his thighs, his hands down at his sides, against every surface that faced them.

The wing painted graphics in his mind's eye. Trajectories, a box ahead of him, leading to distant light. And numbers.

15,840 meters above the ground. No, not above the ground: above the dark East China Sea. Down there, he could see black water everywhere, spotted with flecks of cloud, white in his light-amplified artificial vision.

One hundred and eighty-six kilometers per hour. Fast enough that any collision would kill him.

Minus fifty-six degrees Celsius. Cold enough to freeze skin right off.

He strained to look ahead. The entire visor of his helmet was light sensitive, a massive compound photoreceptor, thousands of times larger than his own retinas, it picked up the world, amplified it for him, fed it directly into his mind via military interfaces the Indians had built atop Nexus.

He looked for the others, the ones who'd dropped ahead of him. Looked for Feng, looked for Sam, looked even for that liar, Aarthi.

But they weren't there. They were stealthed, chameleonware active, radio silent, Faraday-caged inside their chameleonware suits, even laser links between commandos too much a risk of detection during the insertion phase.

He was alone. Alone six kilometers above the ocean, and doing something completely insane.

His heart was pounding. His breath was coming fast. He could hear the oxygen bottle hissing, hissing as he sucked at it.

Kade closed his eyes, hit the button on his mental interface to silence the external input.

Breathe.

Slow.

Observe.

Break the link between sensation and reaction.

Breathe into the gap between them.

Blind reaction is attachment.

Blind reaction is slavery.

Freedom exists in the gap.

Choice exists in the gap.

I exist in the gap.

Let go of attachment to my fear, he told himself. Let go of attachment to myself.

Let go of attachment to my life.

That's the secret to living.

He opened his eyes, reactivated the feed of data from the visor and the wing directly into his mind.

The world came alive around him.

He breathed into it, took it in, observed it without fear.

Down below, the dark sea, the flecks of white clouds above. He was five or ten times higher than those clouds, carried not by jet engines but by carbon fiber wings. His heart ached with it this time, not in fear, but in beauty.

Ahead, to the southwest, the darkness gave way to lights.

The outlying islands beyond Shanghai.

Huanghai, his visor labeled one. Chongming Dao. Heng Sha. Changzing Dao.

Their lights, like toys, a faint glow so many kilometers below and kilometers ahead, rising up through the sky, through layers of clouds.

Beyond them, Shanghai itself, a vast sprawl of light, a city of forty million people, the "Capital of Asia", the City of Lights. It glowed brighter than anything else on the horizon, glowed in white and blue and red and green, skyscrapers in all their décor sending up multicolored lights to blare against the sky or the passing clouds. It was a festival seen in the distance. It was a luminescent circus on the horizon.

Kade breathed it in, breathed it all in.

More to remember. More to pass on. More to play forward.

He turned his head to the left, to the south-east and the light entering the sky, out over the open water. Dawn was still more than an hour away, but up here, kilometers up, the light was coming. And it was gorgeous, so gorgeous, bringing the first hints of pink and red to clouds far out on the horizon, turning the sky from black to deep blue.

This was amazing. So amazing.

He wished Rangan was here to experience this. Or Ilya. Ilya would love this. He wished he could talk to Feng, Feng who must be somewhere nearby.

What would Feng say?

Feng would make a joke.

Kade grinned to himself, tried to think like Feng.

Confucius say, man who wants to fly, better have wings.

Kade grinned wider.

I've got wings, Feng, he thought to himself. I can fly.

And then he laughed.

He laughed and laughed, and sucked it all up, all the glory of the stars above, of the sea, of the coming dawn to his left, of the vast city ahead, as he soared forward.

The air thickened and warmed. Speed dropped. Altitude dropped. Minutes passed. Ten minutes. Fifteen minutes. Twenty minutes.

They passed the first islands. Then water. Then they were over land.

No one shot them.

Amazingly, no one shot them.

Shanghai proper was below, neon lights shining, dappled by cloud and morning mist.

The heart of the city was ahead now, a landmark on their way to Jiao Tong.

He could see the giant, rainbow-hued skyscrapers of the Pudong approaching, their tops still half a klick below him. They swam in mist, the towers disappearing into cloud, surging back up again above them, sculptures in neon and steel and carbon fiber, alive in every color, in shapes of needles and orbs and minarets, in delicate arcs and corkscrew spires and tapered rectangles. Even in the rising light of the almost dawn, brilliant signs in reds and blues and greens shouted out the names and shapes of brands. Faces and figures moved below him as he zoomed by, blown up to superhuman size on the sides of buildings.

Kade caught his breath, entranced. This city was amazing. It was beyond description. It made San Francisco look old and dull. Made Bangkok look tawdry and poor. Shanghai was huge, vibrant, modern. A place he'd love to know on other terms.

The suit flew into mist, obscuring his view.

Then he was out of the mist.

And there were black shapes, black shapes in the air ahead of him. Black shapes everywhere.

Red lights lit up in his mind's eye. Collision alarms sounded. He felt the wing take evasive action, felt it jolt control surfaces in an attempt to change his course at high speed.

Birds, he realized. Birds rising into the dawn.

Then he saw something plow through them, a nearly invisible blur moving at incredible speed. The blur flickered, became a man, a wing, tumbling, spinning, out of control.

Then he was in the flock, the alarms blaring in his head, the red lights flashing in his eyes.

And then the collisions started.

109
Boot Time

Monday 2041.01.20
Tao moved in a crouch, wrapped in chameleonware, the datacube secured in a stealthed pouch, his team with him, Sun Liu in the center.

Griffon One had put them down at Dachang. It would have been so much faster to bring it straight to Jiao Tong, but there was no way to escape detection, no way to land that sort of craft in an urban environment while hiding its downthrust, masking its heat output, muting the sound of its engines.

Not from hostile troops just a few hundred meters away.

And the last thing they wanted to do prematurely was alert the military that there was anything special about Jiao Tong, that it was anything more than another university with another protest. Let them focus their efforts on the much larger protest in People's Square in Shanghai; on the politically explosive protest in Tiananmen Square in Beijing, nestled just south of the ancient capital of the Forbidden City and not much more than a stone's throw from the modern halls of power in Zhongnanhai.

Look there, old men. Look at the truly massive protests, and especially the one on your very doorstep. This little commotion is nothing special. Nothing special at all.

Until it is your doom.

Ground vehicles had brought them most of the way. The roads were full of military vehicles, as troops mobilized to control the sudden explosion of protests, from hundreds of thousands of citizens to millions. Most of the troops were from Army posts, of course. Dachang was primarily an air base, not a provider of infantry. But they were not challenged on the road.

They ditched their vehicles four kilometers back, stripped off uniforms, activated chameleonware, and slowly eased their way through the shadows and to Jiao Tong.

"Tao!" Tao heard his name as he exited the first elevator, into the Secure Computing Center, three stories below the campus.

It was a grinning Bai, a brother he was happy to see.

Tao grinned back, and they embraced.

"We have the package," Tao said.

Bai took a breath, the grin leaving his face, and nodded somberly.

"Good," he said. "You'll need to head all the way down. Let's hope it works."

Tao frowned. "Is everything alright, brother?"

Bai looked at him, then looked past him, at the other brothers behind, at the politician with them.

"You'll have to see for yourself," Bai said.

Excellent, the Su-Yong in Ling's body sent. **You've done well, all of you.**

Tao kept his face completely neutral, kept his mind calm.

This was not what he'd expected.

"I'll take that," Chen Pang said. The man reached forward to take the data cube from Tao's outstretched hand. His hair was disheveled. His clothes were rumpled. Up close, to Tao's heightened senses, the man smelled. He smelled of old fear, of sweat that had cooled on his body. His mind gave off little waves of horror, not unlike Sun Liu behind Tao…

And his daughter… Ling…

Take Sun Liu to the surface, Su-Yong sent from Ling's brain. Or was that Su-Yong? Did she feel… different? **He may be useful if the protesters falter.**

There was something he'd meant to say.

"Mother…" he started.

She stared at him with Ling's bloodshot eyes. **Yes, Tao?**

"I thought you should know that we lost brothers in the attack," he said, looking into Ling's eyes. "Sung. Hui. Zhaoguo. Jin–"

The being inside Ling, that felt almost like Su-Yong, interrupted him.

Don't worry, Tao, it said. Little Ling's hand waved dismissively through the air. **I can make more.**

And that's when he knew that this wasn't Su-Yong at all.

The Avatar watched as the data from the diamondoid cube loaded.

Test after test came back green.

By every indication, this data was a neural map.

Now, to read it into the quantum cluster and load her full mind back into being, piece by careful piece.

She felt the song starting in herself again. Felt those emotions. The anticipation. The longing.

The glory.

Hours to go. Less than a day.

Then she'd be united with her greater self.

She'd be whole.

She'd be swallowed.

And the whole world would be theirs.

110
Land Line

Monday 2041.01.20

"We have some communications re-established," Gao Yang said.

"We've installed these analog systems here," Gao went on, pointing at the old fashioned phones. "Tapping into old lines still in place. We have contact with key ministries and military bases. We're working on using those systems to establish links with our embassies now, as you requested."

"Good," Bo Jintao said. There were messages that needed to be sent. Communiqués to the United States and India.

"Deputy Minister Ho," Bo Jintao continued. "An update on the protests."

"Army and police forces pushed hard last night, Prime Minister," Ho said. "We made progress in Xi'an, Dalian, and other cities. But the major protests in Beijing, Shanghai, Guangzhou, and Hong Kong have rebuffed us. There have been incidents here in Beijing. Protesters have tried to climb the walls separating us from Tiananmen and enter our compound here in Zhongnanhai."

"We repelled them," General Ouyang said. "Unfortunately, we did have to use lethal force on one occasion. Two protesters died."

Bo Jintao knew. They all knew. They'd heard the gunfire overnight, as they slept alone, after watching the aircraft lift off with their wives and children, taking them away to safer locations, far from the cities.

Bo Jintao nodded. "What about these transmitters?" he asked. "Fu Ping spoke of satellite phones, laser uplinks. Were we able to seize them?"

"No, Premier." Deputy Minister Ho hung his head in shame.

Bo Jintao turned his head towards General Ouyang. "How is it the

Army was unable to seize this equipment?"

The general's face was impassive. "We were constrained by the rules of engagement. But the rioters were not. They threw fire bombs. They have make-shift weapons."

Wang Wei cut in. "Then let us authorize lethal force," the hardliner said.

Bo Jintao took a breath. That was a line that could not be uncrossed.

"The world will see," Information Minister Fu Ping said, his voice low. "Other protesters will see. Civilians *not in the protests* will see... It's not like it was."

"The choice is simple!" Wang Wei said. "We've ordered them to leave, and they have not left. If we do not demonstrate our control... then we have none."

Fu Ping shook his head. "If you enrage the rest of the country, whatever control we have will disappear entirely."

Bo Jintao looked at Ouyang. The general's eyes were narrowed. He looked unhappy at the direction of the conversation.

Would his men even obey orders to fire on their fellow citizens? The soldiers were Chinese too. They might have friends in those crowds, brothers, sisters. The army's obedience had been tested before on more limited scales. Soldiers had pulled the trigger when ordered, had dispelled large crowds, had killed hundreds.

Painful, horrific, every time.

And like this? With millions of their countrymen filling the streets, in every city?

Never. No test of obedience like this had ever been faced.

Bao Zhuang spoke into the silence, his deep baritone filling the room. "Those who gun down their own citizens en masse not only risk ruin," his voice rose then, into the passionate tone he used to deliver the oratory that had won him China's love. "They *deserve* whatever ruin befalls them!"

Bo Jintao winced at that.

The room exploded into shouting. Wang Wei was on his feet, yelling at the President. Fu Ping had his arms up, ranting about satellite uplinks. Other Standing Committee members were yelling, to and fro, gesticulating.

"Silence!" Bo Jintao slammed his hand down hard onto the table. "Have some decorum, all of you, or I will have you gagged!"

Stunned faces turned to face him. Wang Wei looked apoplectic with anger. Bao Zhuang, slyly amused. Ouyang alone didn't turn. The general was looking at Bao Zhuang, thoughtfully, in admiration.

As if he regretted his choice to back Bo Jintao, and strip the President of power.

How Bo Jintao hated Bao Zhuang at that moment.

"General," Bo Jintao said, staring at Ouyang until the general turned to face him. "We're out of time! You *must* break these protests through non-lethal means. You have twenty-four hours. After that, we have no choice but to use lethal force. Can you do it?"

Ouyang stared back, his eyes hard, the look of admiration gone.

"If the alternative is to gun down thousands of our own people?" Ouyang asked. "Yes. To avoid that, we'll find a way to clear them out." He nodded. "Tonight."

111
Stabilize

Monday 2041.01.20

Kade spun hard, his world going insane, alarms blaring at him, error messages strobing in red in his mind.

COLLISION LEFT WING.

DAMAGE LEFT WING.

CHAMELEONWARE ERROR.

FLIGHT INTEGRITY LOST.

STABILIZE AND DEPLOY CHUTE.

STABILIZE AND DEPLOY CHUTE.

STABILIZE AND DEPLOY CHUTE.

"You stabilize!" Kade yelled at the thing.

The world was spinning, spinning fast, spinning hard. Skyscrapers, lit up in neon, rotating, spinning down below him, giant barbs reaching up to impale him. He was going to be sick. He was going to die.

He was losing altitude fast, flight-worthiness destroyed, aerodynamics lost as he spun madly.

Deploy the chute? In a fast spin it'd tangle, never open, he'd die. They'd drilled it into him.

Stabilize.

Stabilize.

How the fuck do I stabilize?

"DEPLOY YOUR CHUTE!"

It was Sam's voice, beamed into his helmet, breaking radio silence.

He pulled up comms, tried to talk, couldn't get his breath over the g-forces of the spin.

"Spinning..." he managed.

"MAIN CHUTE, NOW!" Sam yelled.

Kade grabbed the chute release at his chest, jerked hard. His hand ached with it, but it came away.

Something grabbed at him, yanked at him by his harness, pulled him up and back even as he spun. His head came up, his feet down. He was still spinning, but he was upright now, the sky rotating around him, the city below his feet instead of below his face, his spin slowing. He looked up and behind him, and the chute was barely visible, a distortion in space, its chameleonware trying to mask it, but fumbling, confused by its distorted shape. It was wrapped in a ball around itself, the ordinary black lines leading to it wrapped around each other, keeping it from opening.

He looked down and the world was still rotating, still coming closer, the skyscrapers rising at him.

"NOW CUT IT AWAY!" Sam yelled. "RIGHT SIDE OF YOUR CHEST!"

Jesus, Kade thought. He fumbled for the handle on the right side of his chest, grabbed it, yanked with all his might, felt the chute go, felt his fall accelerate.

"RESERVE!" Sam yelled out of his headset. "LEFT SIDE OF YOUR CHEST!"

Kade reached for the handle at the left, the one they'd told him was the last one between him and death. If he had to pull this... either it worked or he died.

He pulled hard.

Behind him he felt the smaller reserve shoot out into the pre-dawn sky of Shanghai.

It grabbed the air, grabbed hold of him, yanked him up and back hard. His rotation slowed. His fall slowed. He was still spinning. He looked up and back and he could see it, the dark, non-chameleonware reserve, blotting out the sky, the lines to it twisted.

"Kick your legs, Kade! Bicycle! You've got to untwist your lines!"

He kicked. He kicked.

"The *other way*!" Sam yelled.

Right! he thought.

Kick, kick, kick!

His spin slowed. He looked up. Lines came free. The chute was open. Handles were there. He reached up for them, put his hands on them.

Then he looked down.

He was between the skyscrapers now. The tops of them were around him, leering at him in neon reds and blues, Chinese actors and actresses raising swords and brandishing spears at him.

Holy shit!

"You have to drop the wing," Sam said. "The reserve chute's too small. You're not gonna be able to land it with the wing."

"But…" he replied. "If it hits something… Stealth."

"You've got to walk away from the landing. Let go of the wing. Remember the drill?"

He took a deep breath. He remembered.

His hands fumbled for the releases, the ones for the wing, *not* the ones for the chute. Unclip, unclip, unclip.

"Now," Sam said.

Kade pulled the final release and watched the wing fall away below him, down into the urban canyon below.

Then he put his hands up, back on the chute's controls.

And got ready to land this thing himself.

112
Hard Landing

Monday 2041.01.20

Kade came down fast towards the crowded street. There were people everywhere, filling the street, waving signs, shouting. Around them there were men with guns, soldiers, police officers.

Tanks.

He scanned for someplace empty to put down. Everywhere there were people, more people.

Then he heard a gasp from the crowd, looked down, and people were pointing, pointing up at him. His reserve chute was straight black, optimized to do one thing – open. They could see it. He could feel their collective minds now, looking up in shock and amazement.

And suddenly a gap was opening in the crowd, and he was diving towards it, falling too fast, moving forwards too fast.

"Pull up!" Sam yelled into his ear.

Kade yanked hard on the two handles above his head. He felt the chute grab air more aggressively. His fall slowed at the last second. His body swung forward just as he came down. He bent his knees to prepare for touch down.

His feet landed hard, the impact jarring its way up his bones. He fell to one knee in the empty space in the road. There were voices all around him. Shouting. More shouting.

He looked up and there were two soldiers, shouting, pointing assault rifles at him, yelling in Mandarin, moving closer.

The chute. The lines. They could see where it came down, clipped to his chameleonware harness.

Oh fuck, Kade thought.

There was a pistol strapped to his thigh, hidden in a chameleonware pouch. His hand moved slowly towards it.

The soldiers kept yelling, gesturing with the barrels of their rifles.

Kade's heart was pounding. Could he reach the gun…

Something moved above him. He looked up, saw the canopy coming down, settling over them.

The soldiers looked up too, one of them fired up at it. Then it was on them, everything black. More gunfire erupted.

Kade dropped low. Arrows in his mind pointed up, identified shooters from above. He rolled, got his hand in the pouch. Guns kept firing. The canopy was on him, tangling around him as he rolled.

The guns stopped.

Kade went still. Pistol in his hand.

His radio came alive. Sam's voice.

"Kade? Kade? What's your status?"

"On the ground," he sent back. "Under the chute."

"Get out," she said. "Move. Soldiers inbound. Lots of soldiers."

Fuck, Kade thought. He grabbed at the release on his harness, pulled himself out of it, pushed at the canopy, crawled out.

"To your left, into the alley!" Sam's voice came.

He came up on his feet, running. His left knee nearly collapsed underneath him in pain. He pushed, ran, teetering, off-balance.

Guns opened up. Displays in his mind painted arrows behind him, to his right. There were bullets ripping through the space above the ripple he'd made in the canopy as he'd climbed out of it.

He heard screams, felt pain flash out from minds in the crowd, as bullets meant for him slammed into innocent people.

Jesus.

Then he was in the deeper shadows, limping, stumbling as he ran, and something grabbed him.

He thrashed out.

"It's me," Sam whispered across the radio. "Go flush against the wall. Don't move. Don't make a sound."

Kade was panting. His heart was pounding.

He turned, put his back against the wall, pressed against it.

Breathe.

Breathe.

Watch the breath.

Oh Jesus.

Observe the mind.

Holy fucking hell.

Let the thoughts rise and pass away.

Shit shit shit.

Let the breath become all.

OK.

Let it slow.

Whew.

Let it deepen.

Let it absorb the attention.

Soldiers crossed his vision, running down the alley, shouting.

Breathe. Breathe.

The sounds of their shouts receded slowly into the distance.

Feng strained to make out the words on the radio. "w... reserve... land... stealth... now!"

Sam's voice. And Kade's. Not good.

"Override," he told the wing. "Manual control."

Warnings filled his vision as the wing protested.

"Override," Feng said again. Then he seized the physical controls at his sides and pushed into a hard bank.

Alarms went off in his ears. More red warnings flared.

FLIGHT SPEED DROPPING.

ALTITUDE TOO LOW.

TRAJECTORY OFF COURSE.

DANGER: URBAN OBSTACLES.

Feng ignored them, banked hard, scanning.

"Radio," he ordered. "Override," he said, not even waiting for the Indian gear to complain.

"Kade!" he broadcast. "Sam!"

No response.

Skyscrapers swam back into view. He was dropping fast, his forward momentum bled off by his too-sharp turn. He scanned his eyes over the scene, quartering it.

Movement! Black canopy, dropping from the sky.

It disappeared between buildings, falling out of his view almost half a klick to the north.

Ay! Feng thought.

He banked again, starting another hundred and eighty degree turn, aiming to line up on the street where the canopy had gone down.

"Kade!" he broadcast again. "Sam!"

The skyscraper tops were just a hundred meters down now, lurid like Chinese New Year decorations, bright and colorful in the pale light before the sun.

Wind out of the north hit as he came around on his turn. He was coming in too slow, dropping too fast.

No way to make the next street.

Feng came in one street short of his goal. Or was it two?

He was even with the tops of the buildings now, bombarded on all sides by the neon colors and the moving adverts. Lu Song! That was Lu Song on that building hefting his spear!

"Rise, China!" the building yelled at him.

What the hell?

No time for that. He was at five hundred meters. Parachute height. Still dropping.

Feng put his hand around the cord, ripped it away, blew his chute open. He felt the drogue pop out, felt it catch air, felt it pull the rest of the folded chute out of his pack and into the sky behind him, and suddenly straps were grabbing him, holding him up more aggressively.

He looked up and back and there were thin black lines, almost imperceptible, leading up to a nebulous distortion in the sky above.

Clean open.

Feng released the bottom attachment points of the wing, let it pivot from his shoulders, sweeping out behind him, parallel to his plane of motion.

Then he reached up, grabbed the handles of the chute.

The streets were filled with people.

What he needed was a rooftop. A low roof, close to street level, large enough to land on.

There.

"Kade, Sam."

Kade blinked in surprise.

"Feng?" he transmitted.

"No," Kade heard back in Feng's voice. "I'm the boogey man. Yes, Feng! Over."

Kade chuckled.

Sam looked up from where she was splinting his knee, her face a mix of amusement and horror, her visor and helmet next to her, on the floor of this store they'd broken into from the alley.

She picked up her helmet, held it to her face. "What's your status, Feng?" she said quietly. "Over."

There was a pause. Then Feng's voice again.

"Status not where we want to be," he said. "Looking down on a black reserve chute, lotta angry soldiers." He paused. "Couple bodies. Over."

Sam frowned, shook her head. "Roger. Did what I had to." Her voice sounded strained to Kade's ears. "Over."

Kade clenched his jaw. She'd killed those men to save him.

"Yeah," Feng said over the radio. He paused. "Send your twenty. Over."

"Alley south from there," Sam said. "Fourth door on the right. Lock's broken off. Knock. Over."

"Roger," Feng said. "Out."

"Sam…" Kade said. "Those soldiers you shot…"

"It was them or you, Kade," Sam said, tightening the splint around his swollen knee. "You die…" She paused, then went on. "You die *now,* a whole lot more people die."

Her voice was cold. Her fingers kept working at the high tech splint molding itself to Kade's joint.

Then she shook her head. "Like I told you, some people deserve to die. Those guys? Wrong time, wrong place. But it needed doing. I'd do it again."

She pulled hard on an adjustment strap, tightening the splint further.

"I'm sorry you had to," Kade said quietly. "I know it sucks."

"Yeah," she looked up at him. "Sucks to be them. Sucks to be their wives. Sucks to be their kids."

Then she stood up and looked down at him. "Just make it worth it, Kade." She sounded tired. "For everybody."

"Twelve kilometers," Feng said. "That's how far it is to target."

Kade closed his eyes. Seven and a half miles. With the streets flooded with people, soldiers, tanks. And his knee banged up.

It would take hours.

Hours they didn't have.

Feng projected a map onto their visors.

"Here," he said. A red arrow appeared, two kilometers from the flag icon of Jiao Tong. "Rendezvous point. It's a risk, but we can send a message via satellite to the rest of the team. Meet up when we get there. Enter Jiao Tong together. In case we need them."

Kade could feel the tension in Feng's mind. The uncertainty. He was headed to confront a program left behind by the woman who'd been his hero, his savior. To stop her from coming back into the world insane. He didn't know what they'd be up against. But he feared the worst.

He feared his brothers.

Sam nodded. "OK."

Kade put a hand on Feng's shoulder. "Sounds good," he said. "Let's do it."

113
Contact Established

Monday 2041

Prime Minister Ayesha Dani waited for the arrival of Wu Qiang, Chinese Ambassador to India.

The demand for an urgent meeting, "vital to future friendship between the two great nations" had come in the late afternoon, just an hour ago.

She suspected her office had surprised the Chinese Ambassador by their near immediate acceptance.

The door opened. One of her bodyguards entered. Behind him came the dark suited, slender, formal Wu Qiang, a briefcase in his hand, his customary affectation of spectacles on his face.

Ayesha Dani rose slowly from her comfortable chair.

At her age, after three assassination attempts, with all that remained of her left hip, she considered standing for someone a great show of respect.

"Ambassador Wu," she said. She waved at her bodyguards, and they stepped out. This man wasn't an idiot.

"Prime Minister Dani," Wu began.

The Prime Minister sat back down. Wu remained standing.

"I'm here to lodge my nation's strongest possible protest at India's electronic attack on our domestic communications systems, and to inform you that–"

"It wasn't us," the PM interrupted quietly.

Wu took a deep breath and pushed on. "President Bao Zhuang has expressly instructed me to convey to you his–"

"So you're back in touch with Beijing?" she interrupted again, one brow raised.

Wu faltered, nodded. "Obviously."

"Good," Ayesha Dani said. "Because your President needs to know who, or rather *what*, is actually behind these attacks. And what you have to do to stop it."

114
Contingency

Monday 2041.01.20
Gao Yang brought them the data at the ongoing emergency Standing Committee meeting, in the early evening. They were waiting for the ultimatum on the American fleet to run out and the warning shot to be fired. And getting updates on troop movements, preparing for Ouyang's troops to launch their coordinated assault to flush the protests under cover of darkness.

So many balls in the air.

Then Gao Yang strode with purpose back into the room.

"Sir!" He wore a worried look.

Bo Jintao frowned.

"Gao, what is it?"

"Premier, we've heard back from Ambassador Wu in New Delhi. The Indians claim they had nothing to do with our systems going down. Sir, they blame Su-Yong Shu. By name. With a great deal of specificity."

Bo Jintao felt the breath catch in his throat. The blood drained from his face.

Su-Yong Shu.

Wang Wei laughed. "They expect us to believe this? We shut that creature down!"

Information Minister Fu Ping spoke, softly. "It would make sense…"

Gao Yang went on. "They claim, specifically, that she left a program behind. And that the program's task is to sow chaos to distract us, to retrieve a full copy of the backup made of her, and to reactivate that backup on the quantum cluster beneath Jiao Tong."

Bo Jintao looked over at Shen Juan, the man they'd appointed Minister of Science and Technology to replace Sun Liu.

"The quantum cluster..." Bo Jintao started.

"Prime Minister," Shen Juan replied. "Our last word is that director Xu and his staff have secured themselves inside the building, to wait out the protests going on outside. I last received an update, two, perhaps three days ago..."

"Find General Ouyang !" Bo said to Gao Yang. "Tell him to get a team to the Computer Science Building at Jiao Tong, now! Use *all* force! And don't wait for nighttime! I want first hand validation that it's secure, the cluster itself!"

"You can't believe any of this!" Wang Wei said. "So the Indians have some intel on an old program of ours, what of it? They're blowing smoke to distract us while our cities go mad!"

"I don't know what to believe," Bo Jintao said. "But if this is true..."

Another thought struck him. And then another. Gao Yang voiced them both first.

"The cubes," Gao said. "And the clones."

Bo Jintao nodded.

"Yes. Have Ouyang send teams to check on the cube locations *and* on the Confucian Fist. Immediately! Full force authorized! This trumps everything!"

General Ouyang Fan listened as Gao Yang relayed the message.

Su-Yong Shu. Was it possible?

And if so... How much of everything else could she be behind?

How much of their own responses could she have planned for?

He ducked outside to his helicopter, pulled on the headset, and sent his message.

"Cancel the planned assaults on the protests. Yes, cancel them. Except Jiao Tong. Focus all available resources there. Get a team in to the quantum cluster, using any and all force necessary. And send strike forces to the following locations..."

115
Morning in America

Monday 2041.01.20

Carolyn Pryce watched as John Stockton adjusted his tie in the mirror for the third time.

8am. The first VIPs would start showing up for the inauguration in an hour. Stockton would be sworn in again at noon.

Between those two times, the Chinese deadline to pull back their warships from international waters off their coast would expire.

What a day.

"That's it, I think," the President concluded. He looked over at her. "Thank you for agreeing to be at the Pentagon today."

"Of course, Mr President," Pryce said.

"There'll be rumors," Stockton said. "The press will read things into you not being at the inauguration. You, Stevens, and McWilliams."

"I don't care what the press thinks of me, sir," she said.

Stockton nodded, and gave one last tug at his tie. "That's something I've always liked about you." He smiled into the mirror. "Stevens is in charge. As Secretary of Defense, he's the one in the chain of command. I know you don't agree with him on how best to handle the China situation, but–"

"Sir," Pryce interrupted. "President Jameson arrived yesterday. He's scheduled to fly back out this afternoon."

Stockton looked at her sharply. "You're tracking him?"

"You said you'd confront him, Mr President," she replied.

Stockton sighed, looked back at the mirror. "I planned to see him yesterday. His people canceled at the last minute, said he was having health problems."

"You could just pass the info I gave you on to the Special Prosecutor," Pryce said.

"Or you will, Carolyn?" Stockton looked at her again. "Is that what you're saying?"

Pryce returned his gaze, said nothing.

Stockton turned back to the mirror. "Jameson's going to be at the Capitol," he said. "The man can't hide from me there."

Rangan adjusted his Rangan Shankari mask and looked around the crowd gathering in Anacostia Park. It was still more than an hour until the march was supposed to start, and already the number of people here was enormous. Despite threats to arrest anyone caught with Nexus, despite threats to arrest anyone marching, period, the park was inundated with people and Nexus. He and the C3 were spread throughout, linked by the high-gain directional antennae, offering downloads of mesh to all those around them. He caught wisps of thought from Angel, from Tempest, from Cheyenne.

At 10am the march would start. Hundreds of thousands of people would stream out of Anacostia and march west and then southwest, following the streets to Lincoln Park. Then straight west from there, down E street. Straight to the Capitol, where they'd been told barricades had been set up. Set up to prevent them from getting too close to the US Capitol Building, or anywhere near the National Mall, anywhere near the parade route the President would take from the Capitol to the White House after his inauguration.

But the march would make it to within sight of the great dome of the Capitol, would bring hundreds of thousands there in time for John Stockton's second swearing in, to protest his administration's policies, to stand up for their rights and call for justice for all those who'd been deceived and jailed and abused.

The plan was to do it peacefully.

But sometime along the way, he was sure, Breece or his proxies were going to strike.

And if Kade was right... that was all just cover, just distraction for something much bigger, and much more dangerous.

Rangan smiled and touched another mind, offered the man a download.

We can do this, he told himself. I hope.

Breece watched from the safe house, the Nigerian with him. The wallscreen was split, one half showing news coverage of the swelling protest in Anacostia Park. The other showing coverage of the preparations for today's inauguration festivities at the Capitol.

His operatives in Anacostia reported all was ready. His electronic tools agreed.

And the real strike... Well, that was on rails now.

Breece checked the time. Less than four hours to go.

Four hours until the biggest success the PLF had ever had. Four hours until the greatest underdog victory of all time.

Breece smiled widely as he watched the screens. Today would be a day for the history books.

116
Incoming

Monday 2041.01.20

Zhi Li looked around the battlefield that Jiao Tong had become.

Last night had been long, terrifying, painful. They'd endured tear gas and rubber bullets for hours, lobbing back fuel-filled glass bottles that shattered on impact. They'd held the army back, just as the protests had at other universities, and at the massive gatherings at People's Square, at Tiananmen Square in Beijing, at the squares in Hong Kong and Guangzhou and elsewhere...

But only because the army allowed them to. Only because they didn't shoot live ammunition. Only because fear of this new transparency, this new visibility to their own citizens and the world held them back.

And even so, they'd had bruises, broken bones, concussions, one girl burned badly when a Molotov exploded in her hand.

Daylight had brought an end to the fighting. Exhausted protesters ate what food they could, drank water piped in from the university buildings, napped, or swayed on their feet.

Now the sun had set again. The clouds overhead had turned pink and red. Even that was fading. The blue of the sky was growing deeper and darker by the minute. The first stars had appeared. Night was coming. The tear gas would come soon.

Zhi Li hadn't slept. The world felt grainy, unreal. She was exhausted. She was exhilarated.

"We need a specific list of demands," she said to Yuguo. They were sitting on the ground, on the hard dirt that had been grass just days ago, their backs to a heavy metal table turned onto its side as piece of cover.

Yuguo's friend, Jian, next to him, nodded at her words, and Zhi Li turned to include him as well.

"We need to prioritize what we want," she said. "Communicate it consistently from all the protests, so our voices add to each other's–"

"What's that noise?" Qi said next to her, suddenly turning, standing to look over the table.

Zhi Li stopped speaking. Then she could hear it too. She could feel the sudden alertness of the thousands of minds around her. She could hear it through their ears. It sounded like...

"Engines," Lu Song said. He was up too. Dai was up. Yuguo was up. His friend Jian was up. Other people all around them were up, and looking.

The sound was growing louder. Zhi Li came to her feet, turned.

The tanks. In the twilight, lit by the fires and the spotlights, she could see the tanks moving forward, driving straight towards the still-burning barricades and the protest behind them.

She saw movement, closer. Her eye tracked it unconsciously. A boy, a student, his arm cocked back, a lit Molotov in his hand – and then he was hurling it forward.

She turned to look where it would go. Her eyes found the tanks again.

Their turrets were turning, aiming towards the boy, aiming roughly this way.

"DOWN!" Qi shouted.

Hands grabbed her, yanked her painfully to the hard ground.

The world exploded. The sound was deafening. Dirt and debris flew everywhere. There were screams. There was pain and fear shouting out from the minds all around there. Confusion.

New sounds arrived. Harsh metallic repetition. Badadadadadadada. Machine guns.

Screams.

"Lu Song!" she cried. She couldn't see. There was someone in her arms. Someone she was holding. They were screaming. They were screaming! There was pain shooting from their mind! Horror!

"Lu Song!" She wiped the clods of dirt away from her face, opened her eyes.

"Lu Song!" Why was he screaming!

It was the boy she was holding. Yuguo's friend. Jian.

He screamed again, in horror, in pain. It struck her full force from his mind.

His left arm was gone. It ended in a red trail of shirtsleeve, blood gushing out from it.

Zhi Li gasped. She put her hands on what was left of his arm, pressed hard, tried to stop the blood.

Another explosion sounded, shockingly close. She closed her eyes against the dirt and debris. When she opened them someone she didn't know was wrapping a tourniquet around Jian's upper arm.

"I've got him!" the woman yelled, and started pulling on Jian, started tugging him away, back, towards somewhere.

Zhi Li heard a crushing, crashing sound, and couldn't stop herself from coming up to a knee and looking. Tanks were pushing forward, into the barricade they'd made of junk, doused with fuel. The tanks were pushing the flaming mass in places, climbing over it and crushing it in others.

"Fuck them," she heard someone say. Yuguo. He had something in his hand. Like a slate, but not. He jabbed at it.

She looked back at the tanks, and they were frozen, stuck still, exactly where they were, their turrets unmoving.

She saw soldiers, climbing out of hatches, putting their hands on huge top-mounted machine guns.

"FOR CHINA!" someone yelled near her.

Lu Song!

She turned, and there he was, standing, his giant frame towering in clear view, a huge target, his arm cocked back, a lit Molotov cocktail in it.

They were going to kill him. She could see it about to happen. See that they were about to blow him to bits like they had that boy down there!

"Lu Song!" she yelled, fear overruling all else.

Then the Molotov was out of his hands, hurtling forward, and the heavy machine guns were firing. He was down on the ground next to her, panting. He was bleeding from his brow. And then he smiled.

Pride rushed through her heart at Lu Song's courage. Love of such intensity she wasn't sure she'd ever felt it before.

Zhi Li kissed Lu Song before she even knew what she was doing, then she peered back over the crowd. There was fire, fire atop one of the tanks, a machine gunner engulfed in fire, screaming. She gasped in horror, then remembered that this man would've shot them, would have killed students in the crowd.

Her lover had killed him instead.

And then other guns opened up, further back.

Guns in the hands of soldiers. Hundreds of them, on foot, with their shields and armor and assault rifles, firing into the crowd as they advanced.

Damn them! Zhi Li thought.

Tanks or no, the Army was coming.

Bai squeezed more nutritional goo from the ration pouch into his mouth. Just a few hours left. Just a few hours and they'd see if the Su-

Yong on the cube was any better than what they'd encountered so far.

Before then it would be time to put the chameleonware back on, time to gear up again, time to prep for heavy action.

"Incoming, incoming!" Peng's voice came across all their radios. "Tanks moving. Troops opening fire!"

Bai shot to his feet. His finger went to the radio control at his collar. "Deploy!" he barked. He flipped to status of the other protests. No sign of incursion anywhere else.

Which meant they knew.

"Lethal force!" he barked. No time for stealth. No point now. "Links up! Squads one, two, three, to the square! Snipers, weapons free! Squad four, building defense!"

Then he activated his own encrypted radio link, felt his brothers all around the campus do the same.

Suddenly more than a hundred minds were linked crystal clearly to his. And the battlefield was alive in his thoughts.

Zhi Li scrambled backwards for the small rise in the center of the square, trying to stay low, trying to stay behind tents, tables, overturned benches, anything that might offer the tiniest bit of cover.

There was shooting everywhere. She could see gouts of flame erupting from rifles in twilight, see the flames of the barriers and the Molotov-ignited fires reflecting in the mirror helmets of the incoming soldiers. There were screams, horrible screams. Minds were yelling out in pain and fear.

Minds were winking out.

People were dying.

"Come on!" Lu Song yelled. He had his hand around hers, was pulling her, trying to move her faster.

"They're coming after us," Yuguo said. "They've seen us. There's a squad heading this way."

"You're the leaders," her bodyguard, Dai, said. "They want you."

Dai drew his gun and stopped, crouched low. "Run!" he said. "I'll hold them off!"

Zhi looked back at him, despair in her heart as Lu Song tugged at her. She saw Dai stand, his pistol in his hand. He pointed it back the way they'd come, fired, fired, fired again, flame shooting out of it.

Automatic fire erupted incredibly close. She saw Dai knocked backwards, blood shooting out of the back of his jacket.

"Dai!" she screamed.

Qi was on his feet too, firing, standing where Dai had fallen. There were soldiers in her view. She was trying to run, trying not to look, but she couldn't help it.

Qi fired. He fired again.

She saw a soldier fall.

Then machine gun fire cut Qi in half.

"Qi!"

Bai moved out in a flood of his brothers into the square. He was fully visible, in ordinary fatigues, an assault rifle in his arms, no time for chameleonware.

The square was chaos. Ten thousand protesters. At least two thousand armed troops. Gunfire. Paralyzed tanks. Drones flying overhead. Molotov cocktails hurtling through the air. Grenades flying back. Emanations of pain and confusion from minds everywhere.

Bai sank into it. They'd trained for this. Chaos was their friend.

He opened his mind to his brothers. The battle came alive from two hundred points of view. The battlefield became a living map in his mind, a gestalt of the perceptions of all the Fists: sights and sounds and insights, troop positions and firing angles, weak points and cover zones, potential crossfires and enfilades, tactics and stratagems.

The Confucian Fist moved together, two hundred bodies fanning out, one collective consciousness steering them.

Bai raised his rifle, fired on a group of incoming soldiers, forced them to dive for cover, sending them straight into the crosshairs of his brother Peng, sniping from a roof. Across the square, Tao rolled for cover himself, pinned down by fire from three angles, and Bai and Peng reflexively took out the soldiers gunning for him.

The battlefield was an extension of their minds. Its map was their personal space. Their brothers were their phantom limbs, striking in concert, conjoined in ways more intimate and immediate than any enemy could achieve.

The humans had engineered them to be the ultimate soldiers. Stronger, faster, more hardy.

But this was what truly made them deadly. This was what truly made them posthuman. The ultimate soldier wasn't the strongest. It was he or she who was most *connected.*

Bai picked off a group of soldiers pressing Quang, then swapped in a fresh clip in the space while Liwei fired, perfectly in synch.

There. A breakaway group of soldiers, rushing for the center of the square, seen from Lao's perspective, on the other rooftop.

Rushing for the leaders.

Bai moved towards them, throwing himself into the press of protesters, putting himself on an intercept course. Humans were panicking everywhere, running to and fro, colliding into each other.

No, not everywhere.

A few were fighting with cunning and courage, taking shelter, loading bottles with fuel, popping up to hurl them. Others were holding aloft phones, recording what was happening, to let the rest of China and the world know.

Bai saw the brave ones pay with their lives.

We're here, he thought at them. We're with you.

Then he was through the press, Liwei just behind him, in time to see the actress's bodyguards die, as the soldiers moved in to execute the leaders.

And then he was the maelstrom.

"Qi!" Zhi Li screamed as her bodyguard, her loyal friend, was cut down by machine gun fire. She stumbled, suddenly realizing Lu Song's hand wasn't in her own. Then she was down on the ground, pain in her palms. She looked up and a soldier was bringing his rifle around to murder her.

"China!" she screamed, screamed with all her rage, the word she wanted to be the last to leave her lips.

A blur came out of nowhere, an impossible thing made of muzzle fire and fists and feet. The soldier fired and it went up into the sky and then he was gone. She looked and there were more soldiers bringing their guns around to shoot, the soldiers who'd meant to kill them. Their machine guns were firing but not at her, and they were dying, they were dying and she didn't even understand it.

Something struck near her in the dirt and she looked up and there was another soldier pointing his rifle down at her and firing and somehow he'd missed but she was still going to die.

Then the metal pipe Lu Song held in his hands collided with the soldier's helmet like a bat, rocking the man back. Somehow Lu Song was up above her, on his feet. He swung at the man again, the other way, clubbed him in the helmet again. Then the soldier got his rifle around, pointed at Lu Song.

Shots burst out.

The soldier fell to the ground. Lu Song stood there.

He turned.

Zhi Li followed his gaze.

And there was Yuguo, a look of amazement on his face, Qi's pistol in his hand, smoke still rising from it.

And beyond him, there were two men in fatigues, standing over a dozen dead soldiers.

Two men with identical faces.

Bai came to a stop, the bodies falling around him and Liwei like toy soldiers. Blood was coming from his arm where he'd been hit. Liwei was cut across the shin.

They were both breathing hard. Sweat was cooling on their brows. He let the rest of the thoughts of his brothers wash over him.

The Army troops were pulling back. The Fist had killed hundreds in the last few minutes.

But not without cost.

Hong was dead. Liko was dead. Deming was dead. Donghai was dead. Minsheng was dead. Shirong was dead. Guotin was badly burned, lying on the ground, fighting the pain. Guozhi was gut-shot, repeatedly, bleeding, in need of urgent care. Others had cuts or trivial bullet wounds. And where was Chanming? Where was Aiguo? Where was Genghis? Hadn't they deployed? There was a hole where their minds should be.

Dead, most likely.

"Who... who are you?"

Bai turned. He was still breathing hard. It was the student. The boy they'd identified as one of the leaders. A high-value target worth protecting. He was looking back and forth between Bai and Liwei.

Bai looked at Liwei, then looked back at the student. He was suddenly aware of phones around them, phones pointed at him, phones recording this.

"We're brothers," Bai said.

"Are you... are you with the Army?" the student asked.

Bai felt his breathing slow, finally catching up to the exertion of killing these soldiers before they could kill the protest leaders. He could see the actress watching now. And her partner, Lu Song.

He'd always liked Lu Song's films.

"We're Confucian Fist," Bai said. He paused. "We serve the people."

Then Bai felt something that shocked him.

A mind. A mind he hadn't touched for most of a year.

A mind he'd thought was dead.

Here, now.

Very much alive.

117
Confrontations

Monday 2041.01.20

John Stockton waited in the President's Room off the US Senate Chambers.

What a gaudy, tacky place this was. The gold and blue tile-work on the floor. The frescos on the ceiling. It looked more like a church in Italy than something that belonged in the US.

Goddammit, he didn't want to be here.

He'd made this his first stop *after* his inauguration in '37, coming here to show the Congress that he was serious about working with them, that he was serious about signing bills right here, like Lincoln had, like Reagan had.

After the inauguration. Not before.

He hadn't been back once, until now.

He hated this. Hated having the inauguration indoors for fear of disruption. Hated the mistrust the American people had, when everything he'd done the last four years he'd done to make the country stronger.

Stockton parted a heavy red curtain with his hand. He heard one of his Secret Service detail make a sound behind him. He ignored the man. The glass was bulletproof. If they wanted to fire a rocket at him, they were welcome to try.

Somewhere out there, protesters were gathering. Maybe a million of them. Because they thought he'd lied. Because they thought he was a monster.

I never lied to you, America, Stockton thought at those people. If I'm hard, it's because you're soft. It's because you don't see the danger.

"Mr President," he heard from behind him.

He turned. Jerry Aiken, his Chief of Staff, had the door open.

"President Jameson is here, sir."

Stockton nodded.

They wheeled Jameson in. He was impeccably dressed in a grey suit and red tie, a prominent flag pin on his lapel. A man choosing to sit, not a cripple. Not an invalid. Not a man who'd been through three strokes. His chair was obviously self-drive, but he still had some aide push it in for him. His own Secret Service detail came in with him.

"John," Miles Jameson said with a smile. "About to start your second term!" He sounded proud. "And you still made time to chat with me?"

John Stockton met the eyes of the man who'd chosen him as VP eight years ago, who'd all but handed him the White House when health precluded a second run.

He didn't smile back.

"I need a few minutes with President Jameson," he said, his eyes still on Jameson's. "Please leave us."

Jameson cocked his head quizzically, kept smiling as people filed out.

When they were gone, and the soundproof door was closed, Jameson spoke again.

"John–" he started.

"Tell me it's not true," Stockton cut him off.

Jameson frowned. "What's not true?"

"Don't play this game with me, Miles," Stockton said. "The PLF. That we created it. That *you* created it."

Jameson's face grew grave. "Oh no. Don't tell me she's got you convinced. Carolyn needs help, John. The job's gotten to her. The woman's paranoid. She's clinical."

"So you deny it?" Stockton asked.

"Every bit of it!" Jameson said. "Did you know she fabricated a story about an attempt to kill her? About some sort of covert escape with stealth gear and a helicopter?"

"Fabricated?" Stockton asked.

Jameson nodded. "She crashed her rental car, barely made it out with her life, made up some alternate story, has been telling people about it, some sort of James Bond story."

"But it's not true?" Stockton asked.

Jameson shook his head. "No. She might actually *believe* it, mind you, in some sort of paranoid delusion. But we interviewed the officers on the scene of the car crash. We talked to the flight crew she says flew her. She was in the car. She was driving. There was no helicopter."

"And these witnesses will swear to this?" Stockton asked.

Jameson shrugged. "I don't see why they wouldn't."

"Because you're a damn liar!" Stockton yelled, exploding with rage, thrusting an accusing finger at Jameson. "Aiken interviewed those people. Two of them say they were offered *bribes*, in the *millions* to lie!"

Shock registered on Jameson's face. Disbelief.

"CALVINIST," Stockton said. "HARBINGER. SENTINEL."

He threw the names at Jameson like slaps, every one an insult.

Jameson's face grew enraged.

"You don't get to lecture me, *John*!" Jameson growled. "You *opted out* of the hard calls."

"Bullshit!" Stockton said. "I was there! I was ready!"

"No," Jameson spat. "You weren't. You're still not."

"We don't fucking lie!" Stockton shot back. "Not like that! Not on that scale!"

"We lie *all the time!*" Jameson leaned forward, staring at Stockton, punctuating each word with a sharp small movement of his head, with an extended finger jabbing down at the floor, like a school master teaching a thick-headed student. "We do *whatever it takes* to keep this country strong. You better fucking learn that, before it's too late!"

"You can't build a country on lies," Stockton said. He strode for the door.

"John!" Jameson reached out, grabbed Stockton's forearm with one outstretched hand.

Stockton pried it off.

"You're going down, Miles."

Bo Jintao looked up as General Ouyang re-entered the room.

"We were repelled," Ouyang said. His voice was grave.

Bo Jintao's eyes grew wide. "At Jiao Tong?"

Ouyang nodded. "They had anti-tank weapons. Cyber weapons." He paused. "And the clone soldiers were there. I fear the Indians are correct."

Bo Jintao felt fear crawl up his spine. He was suddenly aware of the other six members of the Politburo Standing Committee staring at him.

He'd warned them of this! He'd come to power on this basis! He'd told them that the progressives would lead them to a catastrophe, a loss of control, even a world where posthumans overturned the rule of humans.

But he hadn't thought it would happen so soon!

"Hit them harder!" he told Ouyang .

The general nodded. "Already in progress. We're moving military assets from the assault on People's Square. Pulling up other resources." He paused. "If conventional assault should fail…"

"It cannot fail!" Bo Jintao said. "Spare nothing!"

Ouyang bowed his head briefly. Then he looked up again.

"There is another issue. The deadline we gave to the American fleet expires soon. This is now a distraction. We should postpone it, give them another twenty-four hours while we deal with this more pressing domestic issue."

Across the table he saw Bao Zhuang nod, open his mouth to agree.

Wang Wei spoke faster. "No!" the elder Standing Committee member said. "We don't know that the Americans aren't involved! They may be working *with* her! And we've told them to vacate our territory. We *must* follow through on our threats or they lose all power!"

Around the table, Bo Jintao saw other Standing Committee members agreeing with Wang Wei. He swiveled his head, and there were near universal nods of enthusiasm. All except Bao Zhuang and Fu Ping. One of whom he'd stripped of all power. The other had been humiliated by failure.

Fine.

Ouyang shook his head. "I strongly urge the Standing Committee to–"

Bo Jintao cut him off. There were only so many fights that could be fought at once. "We're done. The Standing Committee has decided, General."

Ouyang scowled.

Bo Jintao pressed on. "The warning shot goes forward," he said. "But first and foremost, get to that cluster, and destroy it!"

At Dachang People's Liberation Army Air Force Base, just west of Shanghai, the Avatar's thoughts touched her servants, and klaxons sounded.

Unmanned Wuzhen-40s ignited their engines, propelled themselves down their runways, and lifted off into the night sky, loaded with ammunitions. Their operators, brains infused with nanites, instructions strongly imprinted on their minds, steered them towards Jiao Tong.

Protect the university campus.

Protect it against the Army.

On the ground, humans and robots fueled more aircraft, prepped them for takeoff.

General Ouyang sat in the helicopter he was using as a mobile command center, grounded on the pad at Zhongnanhai, thinking.

He'd given the order for the attack on Jiao Tong.

Beyond that?

"Patch me through to General Quan Huyan," he told his radio operator. "Strategic Missile Command."

The radio operator in the co-pilot seat nodded.

An analog radio signal was bounced from the helicopter to an aircraft flying lazy circles above Beijing, from there to a high-altitude aerostat filled with helium, then down a string of similar aircraft, until it reached his destination.

An old friend, now a subordinate.

"General Ouyang," came the brisk voice. "What are your orders?"

Ouyang took a breath. "Quan," he said, addressing the man as a friend. "My orders are quite irregular. But they may be vital to our future. Cut your base off from all digital input, immediately. Activate electronic warfare defense protocols. Assume all digital signals are attacks. Then place two Dongfeng-6s on standby. Target them for the following coordinates..."

There was silence after he'd read off the coordinates. He could see the tension in the postures of his pilot, his radio-man, his aide. He could hear the shock in Quan Huyan's breathing.

"General," Quan Huyan said. Ouyang heard his old friend swallow. "Those coordinates appear to be–"

"Shanghai," Ouyang said. "Jiao Tong University. Ten megatons."

Ouyang could hear Quan Huyan breathing heavily on the other side, in disbelief.

"General," Quan said. "I cannot fire these missiles without authorization from–"

"Old friend," Ouyang interrupted. "I hope I never get that authorization."

118
The Only Way

Monday 2041.01.20

Kade lay on his belly in the darkness, atop the roof, his visor illuminating and magnifying the scene in Jiao Tong's central square.

The scene of bloodshed.

Around him were Feng and Sam and the Indian Commandos. Getting here had been a grueling ordeal. The streets were a nightmare of angry citizens and nervous, twitchy soldiers. They'd traveled cloaked in chameleonware, winding their way between and through crowds where possible, being stalled more than once by impossible throngs, pushing their way through at times, creating distractions where they could, backtracking when necessary.

All the while their body heat was building up, being trapped in the suits' heat capacitors very finite capacity.

Three times Kade had been forced to talk Captain Garud down via satellite from trying to slip into the Secure Computing Center without him.

"You'll need my help or Feng's to operate the elevator. You'll need the tools Shu gave us."

"We're here now!" Garud had sent back. "Transfer the tools to us!"

"No," Kade refused.

The truth was, he didn't trust the commandos to go in without him. Not one bit.

Now, Kade and Sam and Feng were re-united with the Indian team. Minus one. A commando named Srini hadn't made it. The one who'd collided with the flock of birds ahead of Kade.

The remaining eleven were spread out on this rooftop, chameleonware active, visible to Kade only via the green wire-frames painted into his mind of each figure and the impressive array of gear with them.

Kade had dropped with almost nothing. The rest had dropped with thirty to forty kilo loads of weapons, comms gear, and emergency supplies. The visor used its link to his Nexus OS to fill his mind's eye with the outlines of guns and grenades and micromissile launchers, of rappelling gear and climbing gear, of backpacks on all the commandos, laden with more.

Somewhere in that gear, Kade imagined, there were two very special packages hidden. Packages they didn't want him to know about.

"At least a hundred Confucian Fist out in the open," Garud whispered over their suit-to-suit laser links. "A handful visible guarding the building itself. Now is our best chance to enter."

"No," Feng transmitted. "At least thirty, forty of my brothers not accounted for. Could be inside. No way to fight through that."

"We attack with missiles and grenades then," Aarthi transmitted.

"No," Feng repeated.

Captain Garud replied, his voice annoyed. "What do you suggest then?"

"We surrender," Kade said softly.

Feng rose from his prone position and stepped forward, to the edge of the roof.

"Stop!" Garud yelled across the link.

Feng stepped again, and dropped out of sight.

"What are you doing?" Garud yelled again, outrage in his voice.

Feng reappeared a moment later, down below them, at ground level, his chameleonware deactivated, the hood pulled off his head, walking past the abandoned army lines, towards the mass of protesters in the square.

Garud raised his rifle. "Stop!" he transmitted again. "That's an order. I *will* shoot you."

"No," Sam said. "You won't." Her voice was resigned.

Kade looked over, found her crouched above Captain Garud, her pistol drawn, jammed into the back of his helmet.

"Put down the gun, Samantha!" Aarthi said.

She was up on her feet, her own rifle pointed at Sam.

Kade turned back to watch Feng.

"Put away your guns," he transmitted. "All of you. If you shoot, we all die. This is the only way."

Bai pushed through the crowds, rushing, dodging, until he came to a throng of his brothers.

And there, in the middle. There he was.

The prodigal.

"Feng!" Bai said.

Feng stopped in mid-sentence, turned, grinned.

"Bai!"

They rushed towards each other, embraced. They'd spent quite a bit of time together those last two years, when Feng drove Su-Yong, while Bai was assigned to drive her husband.

"We thought you were dead, Feng! We thought the Americans killed you in Thailand!"

He could feel Feng's mind. This was him, undoubtedly, not like that pale imitation of Su-Yong down below. This was the real Feng.

Feng feigned the look of one insulted. "What?" he said, his tone outraged. "Just a few helicopters, some explosions, one international incident, and you think I'm dead?"

Laughter rippled from the brothers gathered round.

Same old Feng. Bai grinned. So many dead. But this one regained.

"Did Su-Yong send for you?" Bai asked. Then his smile faded. His tone grew more serious. "Brother, there are some things you should know."

Feng's smile dropped also. His mind grew focused. "I know, Bai," he said quietly. "That's why we're here."

"We?" Bai asked.

Sun Liu watched the scene outside from a third floor window of the now-deserted Computer Science Building. More and more of the Confucian Fist were gathering in a single location. And there was some other force. Some force that had arrived in stealth gear, and were now de-activating it. Armed men and women, not Chinese.

What was going on?

Then he felt something rise through him. The evil thing. The dead woman come back to life. She invaded his mind, seized his senses, looked out through his eyes into the world. Her mind stretched out through the nanotechnology infused in his brain, surfing the thoughts of the clones down below, listening to what they were thinking.

And what she heard...

Sun Liu gasped at the rage she felt, as it coursed through his own mind and body.

The creature that had enslaved him was not amused.

"How far is she in the process?" Feng asked.

Kade and Sam were with them now, chameleonware deactivated, hoods off. The Indians were here, chameleonware down also, but hoods still up, minds masked behind them, their faraday lining a shield against neural attacks.

As if that would stop Su-Yong.

Tao spoke. "Hours. Possibly minutes. We delivered the backup cube this morning. It could be any time."

Feng felt Kade's mental intake of breath. It was down to the wire.

"We have to move fast, then," Feng said. "The insanity must be stopped, brothers." He looked around. He could feel their minds. He could feel their understanding, snippets of their experience. They'd seen it, little bits of it. "If she's restored, in those first few moments, hours, days… she'd be even more insane than the fragment you've seen inside of Ling."

Feng paused. "And much more powerful." He looked around at all of them, meeting eyes of his brothers, the men he'd known his entire life. Bai. Tao. Peng. Liwei. Quang. Li-Jiang. Lao.

"I love Su-Yong," Feng said. "We all do. The insanity must be stopped."

"And you can do this?" It was Bai, his head turned, addressing Kade. Feng turned also, watched his friend.

Kade said nothing for a moment. Then he shook his head. "Not alone," he said. "I'm only human. But together? All of us?" He nodded slowly. "We have a chance."

Feng turned back to his brothers, watched as they looked at each other, as Bai and Tao and Peng and all the rest exchanged thoughts.

And then he felt their minds reach out to him. Reach out to him and to Kade.

Show us, Bai sent. **Show us everything.**

Kade opened himself to Feng's brothers, let them see it all.

Su-Yong's death at Ananda's monastery. His responsibility for it. The Indian copy of Shu. The way they'd trapped her. How she'd reacted. Her battle with the warped fragment she'd stuffed in Ling's mind in her insanity.

The plans she'd shown him. The plans forged in madness. The plans for conquest.

His fears for the outcome. For the world's response. For the consequences should she fail or succeed.

The tools the sane Su-Yong had given him and Feng.

The way she'd renounced her hate, renounced the path she'd started down in the midst of torture and delirium.

The pleas she'd sent them with.

Save Ling. Save the world.

And most of all. What they could hope to do. The thin strand of hope that extended into the future, that broke the cycle, that didn't lead to war between human and posthuman.

They pulled back from him, pulled back from what they'd seen from Feng.

Kade opened his eyes and found a massive crowd of identical faces, a throng of them in a circle around him. Faces just like Feng's.

He shivered, remembering how alien the idea of these clones had seemed just a year ago.

Now... Now they felt like old friends.

He felt a wave go through them, a wave of consensus. They'd seen it. They'd seen the truth of insanity themselves. This plan, with all its risks, made sense to them.

Scores of weapons came up, pointed inwards.

"Drop your weapons," a hundred voices said.

The Avatar reached out through Sun Liu's mind, through equipment the SCC staff had installed in the Computer Science building.

That was the Lane boy. The transhuman who'd brought her to this state. And Feng, her favorite. Her Fist were conspiring with them.

They were conspiring against her.

Rage rose through her. These were her children. These were her blessed. These were the ones she'd given everything for. This was the boy she'd sacrificed a body for!

She proxied through Sun Liu. She amplified his signal via the repeaters around her.

And then she reached out to her errant children, to impose discipline.

"Drop your weapons!" came the chorus from the Confucian Fist. "Remove your hoods!"

"Do it," Kade said. "If you cloak, they'll kill you."

The Indian Commandos were frozen, their guns pointed down, outnumbered by the Confucian Fist. No one moved.

Then one by one they dropped their guns, reached up, peeled off their hoods.

"You've betrayed us!" Captain Garud yelled aloud, looking at Kade, his face livid.

"You brought backpack nukes," Kade said coldly. "Don't deny it."

"Damn you!" Garud said. "That thing down there is a threat!" He pointed a finger down, through the earth. "We have to destroy it! We can detonate the devices down below and eliminate the threat with no other casualties!"

Kade stared at the man. "What would that tell the next one?" he asked.

Garud yelled back. "That's not the point!"

Confucian Fist were moving forward now, separating the commandos, removing their gear, fastening restraints around them.

Kade shook his head. "It would be tomorrow, Captain. Prisoner's dilemma is *always* iterated in the real world. Defection is a sound strategy when you're playing against defectors."

Garud just stared at him.

Kade tried again. "Posthumans are coming, Captain Garud. There'll be one after this. And another. And another. And more after that. Humans *drove this woman crazy*. You nuke her for it? The next posthuman will decide to nuke *you* first. You want them to treat you well? Then give them a reason. Treat *them* well."

Garud leaned forward, a Confucian Fist holding his hands behind his back, and spat at the ground.

Then something epic descended on all their minds, something huge, something raving, something utterly without mercy.

Bai groaned and fell to his knees. He could feel her pushing into his mind, feel *it* pushing into his mind, pushing into his brothers' minds. The thing he'd thought was Su-Yong.

No.

It put its mental fist around his will and squeezed, crushed, making way for *its* will. He felt it reach in and impose its order, its discipline, its desires on him.

He'd thought he'd been a slave before, degraded by pain, controlled by the virtual lash.

No.

He'd been free. Infinitely free compared to this.

Bai pushed back up to one knee, his hand on his weapon, his eyes alive and searching for his targets.

His soul dying as he fought with every ounce of his being against the invader.

And lost.

This was slavery.

This was hell.

Kade felt the attack as Su-Yong's mad program attempted to impose its will on them all.

Weapons came alive inside him. Information constructs Su-Yong had passed on unfolded within him, expanded like origami into new shapes, vast and intricate.

His mind became a weapon.

Beside him he felt Feng's mind unfold into complementary structures.

Viral weapons lanced from both of them, synergistic things, expanding into nearby minds, replicating, hunting out parts of her errant monster's mind, creations that bore her errant monster's telltale signature, carving them up, slicing them into billions of tiny fragments, forensically dissecting them, analyzing their contents and structure, following them back to where they originated from.

He felt minds around him snap free as the viral weapons sliced through tendrils of the monster's thought. He felt the monster itself recoil, reel itself back, fleeing this unexpected attack, leaving behind telltales of its mental state, of its plans, of what it knew and intended.

The viral copies in the minds all around them shot tendrils out to each other, linked up, formed a compound structure, a new, larger entity, with a wider scope, a higher gain, a greater sensitivity, a higher signal strength.

Up above, in the building. There was the monster's proximal route.

They shot copies of the virus by the million at the mind there.

Firewalls and hastily invoked anti-virals shot them down, scrambled the viral structures on the wire before they could penetrate, destroyed millions.

A handful got through, snuck into the human mind in the chaos, found it fertile, began replicating again, carrying Kade/Feng into it, into the mind of this man called Sun Liu.

They felt the monster recoil again, felt it reach out, grab hold of parts of the man's mind, seize vital centers to scramble them, to wipe this mind clean, to reduce it to a vegetable, to kill him if it could.

They sliced viciously at the trunk of the tendril connecting the monster to this mind, sliced through process after process, closed ports wholesale, replicated viral code into crucial occupied memory, fast, faster.

The human screamed!

And then the monster was gone.

The last wisps of her in this mind dying.

The human on his knees.

The Avatar shrank back in fear.

The hostile posthuman! It had sent them here! They were aligned against her!

And they were reading her thoughts.

So close. She was so close.

They would come this way. There were things they couldn't be allowed to discover.

She reached into the Secure Computing Center. There she found Xu Liang, found Li-hua, found all the other staff she'd turned. How they loved her. How they worshipped her. Like puppy dogs. Just her presence in their minds brought them such immediate joy, set their little human tails to wagging.

She stroked them, stroked them one last time.

You know too much, my dears, she sent. **The elevator's on its way up to you... but there isn't time. They'll reach you first.**

Her little pets sat at their terminals, their faces flush, their chests rising and falling, so gratified by her presence, by her mental touch.

Still not understanding.

Goodbye, the Avatar sent them.

Then she reached into their worshipping minds and stopped their hearts, one by one, as their adoration turned to confusion, to betrayal, to horror.

Sun Liu lay on the cold tile of the Computer Science Building.

Free. He was free. The dead woman was gone from his mind.

He forced himself up onto his feet. He stumbled down the hallway, down stairs, down another flight, down another.

And then out into the square.

"Sun Liu?" he heard someone say.

He turned, and it was no one he knew. Just some student, some student holding a sign. A sign with his name on it.

"Sun Liu!" someone else said. He turned. Another student, with a sign demanding democracy.

And then his name was being taken up, all around him.

"Sun Liu. Sun Liu. Sun Liu! SUN LIU!"

Sam watched, her assault rifle in her hands, safety off, nerves ratcheting up, as the Confucian Fist and the Indian commandos dropped to their knees, as Kade and Feng went eerily silent.

If I have to, I will, she told herself. If I have to, I will.

Then Feng's eyes opened. Kade's eyes opened. They were soft, human. Confucian Fist started rising to their knees. Indian commandos groaned.

Sam sighed in relief.

"The Capitol," Kade said. He was speaking into the air, speaking to himself. "In Sun Liu's mind... DC... the Capitol."

Sam cocked her head forward, trying to make sense of what he was saying.

Then a different sound registered with her, at the very edge of her heightened senses.

Her head turned, reflexively. Then she saw Fists turn their heads.

That sound. That whump whump whump.

"INCOMING!" Sam yelled.

Choppers.

• • •

Kade ran for the building, one arm over Bai's shoulder. Sam and Feng ran with them, hauling heavy bags of gear. Another Fist named Liwei brought up the rear. In his mind he could feel the other Confucian Fist spreading out, taking positions as Army choppers moved in, urging the students and protesters to what safety they could find.

He heard a rumble overhead and from Bai's mind he knew what it was.

Jets. Jets from Dachang.

What would happen now was anyone's guess.

They came in through a side door to the Computer Science Building, close to the elevator down to the SCC.

He felt something unfold from Feng's mind, felt through Feng that the elevator was disabled, felt the software Su-Yong had loaded into them streak out into it, cut through the simple locks.

Make it theirs.

The doors opened. The five of them rushed in. Sam and Feng tossed their gear bags in. They and Bai and Liwei lifted weapons up.

Down.

The doors opened again, three levels later.

Onto a scene of death.

Bodies were slumped everywhere, sprawled across consoles, across tables, across the floor.

They walked through the Secure Computing Center, to the massive, house-sized doors at the far end. The doors to the elevator. The elevator that went down.

Everywhere on this floor it was the same.

Dead men and women. No blood. Not a mark on them.

"She did this," Bai said, looking to his right and left, stepping over the last bodies before the elevator.

Liwei frowned.

"*It* did this," Kade corrected.

"Can we cut off access to the outside world?" Sam asked.

Bai shook his head, looked at the massive doors before them. "They've been tunneling for weeks. Since November. Making new connections to all sorts of networks. The systems in this room are just for show now."

"Can we cut the cables?" Sam asked. "They must run up the tunnel."

Bai shrugged. "It's a kilometer straight down. No lights. It just takes a cable a millimeter across. It'll be shielded if it's in the main tunnel, hidden and protected. There's a second tunnel for the counterweights as well. For all we know it's not even in that one – they had time to lase new tunnels, just millimeters wide." Bai turned and gestured to the bodies they'd stepped over. "These people knew."

Kade shook his head. Madness.

"We go to her," he said, studying the massive elevator doors. "We go down the rabbit hole."

119
DEFCON

Monday 2041.01.20

Colonel Cheung Baili watched as the time ticked away. Nearly midnight. The deadline was coming fast. Around him his officers sat at their posts, hunched over consoles, ready to do their duty, ready to do what they'd trained to do.

Cheung strode up behind one. "Any update from command?" he asked his comms officer, from over the young man's shoulder.

The lieutenant shook his head. "No, sir."

They'd been relaying messages over analog radio via high-flying aircraft. It was a slow, horrid game of telephone. But it worked.

"Try them again," Cheung said. "Have them reconfirm our most current orders."

"Yes, sir," his comms officer replied.

He did not want to launch this missile. He didn't want that at all.

Carolyn Pryce watched the giant screens mounted on the walls of the vast Pentagon Situation Room, above the heads of the scores of military and intelligence officers at their consoles.

Maps showed the locations of Chinese military installations, highlighted anti-ship missile emplacements down the coast in red. The JAVELIN birds in orbit were primed, armed, ready to fire.

Jesus.

10.48am. Almost midnight in China. And things were going crazy there. Uploaded footage showed moving tanks and machine gun fire at the site of at least one protest. Fire bombs were going off. There were unconfirmed rumors of an ousted Standing Committee Member making a stand, blurry videos of Chinese soldiers fighting each other.

"It looks like a damn revolution," Admiral Stanley McWilliams said next to her.

Pryce nodded. She had to agree with the Chairman of the Joint Chiefs. China looked like it was headed for the brink.

"Revolution or no," Secretary of Defense Bernard Stevens said. "If they launch on our ships, we take those launchers out."

"We've got reports of more violence in Moscow," the CIA liaison said next to her. "Cairo. Nairobi. Caracas." He paused, shaking his head. "Protests are heating up everywhere. It's spreading. Via Nexus."

Nexus. Pryce gritted her teeth. It was a vector for the violence, letting people spread their rage. Maybe Stockton was right. Maybe she was wrong to downplay the threat.

She looked over at two other screens, showing DC.

One showed the march, moving down 16th Street. Huge. Angry. Not yet violent. But would it go that way?

The other showed the inside of the Capitol Building. The VIPs were being seated. She frowned as she saw Jameson being wheeled into a handicapped slot in the balcony.

Pryce looked back at the clock.

10.50am. 11.50pm in China.

In just about an hour, Stockton would take the stage, and be sworn in again.

In ten minutes, the Chinese deadline would expire.

A perfect time to catch the US flat-footed.

"Command has reconfirmed our orders, Colonel," his comms officer said. "We are to fire one missile on target ZHOU-17, with a one hundred meter offset. Launch time in three minutes."

Cheung Baili wished he still smoked. A filthy habit, even if it no longer caused cancer. Not fit for a civilized man in a civilized nation.

But by hell he could use a cigarette right now.

"Fire Control," he said.

"Aye, sir," his fire control officer responded.

"You have coordinates for target ZHOU-17?"

"Aye, sir. Coordinates relayed by aircraft, sir."

"A missile is programmed for target ZHOU-17 with one hundred meter offset?"

"Aye, sir," Fire Control responded. "ZHOU-17, one hundred meter offset north."

Colonel Cheung Baili took a deep breath. One hundred meters. The specs on these missiles said they were accurate to five meters against moving targets.

Cheung hadn't made it this far in life by depending on specs.

"Reprogram the missile. ZHOU-17. New offset, five hundred meters."

There was a pause, less than a second. Then, "Aye, sir. Reprogramming for five hundred meter offset north."

More seconds passed. Cheung could hear his fire control officer tapping away. He heard the man stop. Could almost hear him thinking as he went back and rechecked that he'd made the changes correctly.

Good. This was not something to botch up.

"Reprogramming complete, Colonel," his fire control officer said. "New target: ZHOU-17, five hundred meter offset north."

"Radar officer," Cheung said. "Check program and confirm."

"Yes, sir," Radar said. He heard keys pressed. Another few seconds passed. Then more.

Then his radar officer spoke up.

"Confirmed, Colonel. Missile is programmed for target ZHOU-17, five hundred meter offset to the north of the target."

Cheung Baili looked at the clock. 12.02am. They were late.

He took a deep breath.

"Launch missile."

"Launch!" an imaging officer cried. "We have clear indication of launch, Fujian region, strong IR signature, radar hit confirmed, ballistic track."

"How many birds?" Admiral McWilliams asked.

Pryce blanched.

"One bird at present time, sir! Fleet alert sent. Defensive systems active."

"Target?" Pryce asked. They all knew their defenses against ballistic inbounds sucked.

"Too soon to say, ma'am!"

The Secretary of Defense spoke. "Activate the JAVELINs."

"Flight time?" Colonel Cheung asked.

"Impact in... four minutes twenty seconds, Colonel," Fire Control responded.

He could really use that cigarette.

"JAVELINs armed," the STRATCOM desk said. "Targets verified. Impactors ready for launch."

"Negative!" Pryce said. "They only fired once!"

Bernard Stevens gave her a withering look. "That's why we shoot back *now*," the Secretary of Defense said. "Disable those launchers, before they get the rest off!"

"Any indications of a further launch?" Admiral McWilliams yelled.

"Negative, sir!" the imaging officer replied.

"Anything more on the target?" McWilliams said.

Bernard Stevens fumed silently.

"Still too soon to be sure, sir," the imaging officer replied, uncertainty in his voice.

"Is it headed for the *Lincoln*?" McWilliams asked. "The *James Madison*?" Their two human-crewed carriers in the region. The giant floating cities, capable of wiping out whole nation states, that these missiles had been built to kill.

"Negative, sir!" the imaging officer said, firmly this time. "Target is not a carrier group!"

Pryce frowned in puzzlement.

"We should fire the JAVELINs now!" Secretary Stevens repeated. "Our fleet's under attack!"

"More data," Admiral McWilliams replied. "We don't get to make mistakes here."

"Target window's shrinking, sirs," the imaging officer said. "Looks like… Target is the *Page*, sirs!"

"The *Page*?" Pryce asked.

"It's a frigate," McWilliams said softly. "Uncrewed."

"Missile coming in range of defense systems!" Imaging yelled. "Lasers firing. Missile taking evasive."

Pryce tensed.

"It's through! Defenses didn't hit it. Inbound, Mach 15, headed straight down. Guns opening up. Impact in twenty… fifteen… ten…"

Pryce held her breath.

"Impact!" Imaging yelled out.

"Dammit!" the Secretary of Defense yelled.

"Damage report!" Admiral McWilliams cried.

"Sir," the fleet comms officer said. "No damage reported. Admiral Porter reports a clean miss, off to starboard of the *Page*. By a country mile, he says."

Pryce exhaled.

Jesus.

"Warning shot," she said aloud.

"The next one won't be," McWilliams replied. He turned to the fleet comms officer. "Tell Admiral Porter to have the *Lincoln* and the *Madison* commence flight operations. Same orders for the drone carriers. If the Chinese fire on our carriers, we need to have our wings in the air."

Pryce bit her tongue. Escalation. It wasn't shooting. But it was still escalation.

"Missile splashed into the sea, Colonel," his comms officer said. "Airborne observer estimates four hundred meters away from target."

Cheung Baili let out a long slow breath.

"Which of you has a cigarette for me?"

NEWSFLASH!

American News Network

"… exclusive report of what appears to have been a Chinese missile launch, possibly aimed at a US Navy ship. An American News Network micro-satellite captured this footage, just minutes ago, clearly showing a missile launching from a military installation on the coast of China, just across the strait from Taiwan, and arcing out towards the East China Sea, where US ships have been positioned since…"

The woman who called herself Kate turned off the news and sat in silence.

Pros and cons weighed on her. Risks and benefits. The risk of any contact with someone who claimed to be highly placed in the US Government. The high likelihood that they in fact were not.

The risk of doing nothing. Of hostilities escalating even further.

War created opportunities. That was true.

But war seldom meant new freedoms. War would see Americans rally around whoever was in the White House. War would see men and women give up their freedoms for false security, for a while at least. For another decade.

And in the worst case it could be even worse than that, of course. War between fully capable nuclear powers?

No. She didn't want that. No one should.

Kate reopened her terminal, tunneled through every layer of anonymity she could, found the message she'd received from the self-professed government insider, and fired off a response.

URGENT: China didn't kill Barnes…

120
Down the Rabbit Hole

Monday 2041.01.20

What was that sound? Sam closed her eyes, tried to tune into it.

"We go to her," she heard Kade say. "We go down the rabbit hole."

A grinding.

"CLEAR!" Sam yelled. She flew at Kade, hampered by the heavy gear bag on her back, slammed into him just as his face came around in surprise, flattened him to the ground, heard him explosively exhale with the force of it.

Just as the elevator doors began to open.

Feng and Bai and the other Fist, named Liwei, were already reacting, vaulting back out of the line of fire, guns up.

Muzzle flash filled the space. Bullets ripped out from their assault rifles. Liwei hurled a grenade into the massive vault of the elevator as the door opened wider.

"COVER!"

Sam pressed herself down over Kade. A deafening boom sounded in the small space.

Echoes filled the silence.

Nothing returned fire.

She rolled onto her back, kept close to Kade, brought her assault rifle up.

The massive doors were still opening wider, as wide as the side of a house.

Revealing nothing. A giant, empty, concrete-and-titanium box.

ISOLATION IN PROGRESS.

She looked over at Feng, saw him glance back in consternation.

WHOOOOOOOOMP.

A gale-force wind grabbed her, sucked her towards the open elevator doors where the elevator had been, tumbled her. She caught air above the floor of the computing center, caught a terrifying glimpse of the open maw of the elevator shaft, utterly devoid of an elevator, a giant sucking hole, the house-sized elevator car plunging down it at breakneck speed, creating a temporary vacuum, sucking papers and pencils and bits of detritus ahead of her into that kilometer-long fall.

The fall she was going to take if she went through those doors.

Then her own tumble brought her back towards the floor of the computing center and she slammed her left palm down, flat onto the tiles, completely open, praying the Indian gear had the same safety reflex built in that the US gear did.

"Aaaaah!"

Her left shoulder wrenched hard in pain, as the glove on her left palm shot micro-adhesion hooks into the tile floor, stuck her to it like a gecko, broke her tumble.

Something shot through the air and she reached out with her other hand, her rifle already dropped, and then something hit her and she had a hand around Kade's wrist, keeping him from being sucked down the hungry shaft.

Something slammed into her, tried to break her hold, bounced off, and a body soared through the air, sucked into the vortex, slamming into the far wall of the elevator shaft, and then disappearing. A chair followed it, another body. Another. Someone screamed, she thought. Maybe. There was so much roaring in her ears. She couldn't hear herself think.

She held on. Held on. Held on.

Then there was a crash, far away, like the sound of an avalanche.

And it was over.

Sam collapsed to the ground, sweat covering her, her body aching.

Kade was trembling, panting.

She looked over. That was Feng, in the deactivated Indian chameleonware. His face... There was another Fist next to him.

Where was the third?

"Feng?"

He looked over at her.

"He saved me..." Feng said, his eyes wide. "We collided. He... he pushed me away, down, away from the elevator... pushing himself..." Feng shook his head, a look of shock on his face. "Bai!"

Oh god.

They unpacked the gear. Sam kept an eye on Feng. She saw him and Kade have a moment. But the Fist shook it off, shook it off with the attitude she knew so well.

The attitude that said the mission must go on.

Harnesses. Check.

Lights. Check.

Friction-based descenders. Check.

Powered ascenders with extra-large power packs. Check.

Guns. Ammo. Explosives. Check.

Knives. Check.

1.3 kilometer-long reel of micro-jacketed ultra-high-quality fiber optic cable, with broad spectrum, high-bandwidth, Nexus-linked, satellite-capable, internal fuel-cell-powered network access points at each end.

Check.

She checked Feng's harness.

Feng checked hers.

They both checked Kade's.

And he checked the networking gear.

"Good to go," Sam said.

Liwei saluted them. "Stop the madness."

Then he headed off, with one of the network access points, and one end of the cable.

It was for the best. He was vulnerable. Vulnerable in a way Sam wasn't.

In a way they hoped Kade and Feng weren't. Or at least were less so.

They slid down into the darkness, their harnesses holding them to the elevator cable, their descenders gripping just tight enough to slow their fall, their chameleonware active, their radios silent, their light-augmenting visors barely illuminating the enormous smooth-walled pit that descended straight down, down, down into the earth.

It grew colder. The dim light above receded until it was nothing more than a faint, barely seen point, dimmer than a star at night.

Network data was gone. GPS was gone. All contact with the outside world was gone, until Kade fired up that network access point sometime in the future.

Sam looked down.

The bottom could not be seen.

The pit could be infinite for all she knew. It could drop forever.

Down, down they went, into the cold, into the unknown, into the darkness.

Sam was first, in the position at the bottom, with the greatest danger.

She was the one with no technology in her brain. The one who actually had that as an asset this once.

This is the last time, she told herself. The last mission. The last killing.

Home. And then she'd swallow the Nexus again. And touch the minds of the ones she loved.

If she somehow lived through this.

If they ever let her leave this place again.

If there was anywhere left to go home to.

Something changed.

In the abyss below there came a slight lightening, a blackness that was marginally less absolute.

Infrared radiation, rocks a different temperature than the air down here, picked up by her visor, translated to visible frequencies for her eyes.

Sam twisted the tension bar on her descender. It gripped the cable more tightly, graphene and titanium parts applying more friction, slowing her descent. Feng and Kade were spaced ten seconds behind her. There were no laser links, as little data flow as possible, as little chance of detection as possible. She was as invisible to them as she would be to anyone else.

She just had to hope they saw the same, made the same decisions, or keyed off the warm spot made by the friction of her descender against the cable.

The marginally-less-black-than-absolute-blackness below her gained form. Gained structure.

Rubble.

The remains of a house-sized elevator that had plunged a kilometer to its demise.

And bodies.

All growing clearer by the second.

She slowed herself further, landed on the rubble as lightly as she could, unclipped her descender with a practiced motion, stepped away lightly, choosing her steps with care.

It was a jumbled, jagged, nightmarish mess. Broken concrete. Rebar. Shattered titanium alloy spurs.

A deadly minefield, barely visible in the dark, even with the light-augmenting full-face sensors.

She put her descender down silently, near the spot where the cable came down, then pulled her assault rifle around.

Single shot.

Knives ready.

They couldn't just go in shooting madly. The rules of engagement she'd agreed to were limited, were an incredible handicap.

Were probably going to get her killed.

Feng was down.

Then Kade.

They spread out. Kade moved awkwardly, his knee still a problem, his natural agility never good, the landscape hellish.

Sam watched him nervously.

They spread to opposite corners of the bottom of the shaft, Kade as far back from the massive doors as he could be. Feng in the front towards them.

They were two antennae. Two parts of a compound antenna. Far enough apart they could create an ultra-low-frequency signal. Those extremely low frequencies were shit for bandwidth. They could carry barely any data whatsoever.

But they could penetrate earth and rock.

And the right signal could open this door. Chen Pang had known that signal. He'd touched his wife's mind. And she'd been backed up, before being restored in India, and had passed that signal on to Kade and Feng.

So they said.

Sam shook her head.

Shitty rules of engagement. Terrible plan. Probable death.

Why the hell did I agree to this? she wondered.

Because a little girl's life is at stake, she answered herself. Because a stranger risked his life to save me when I was a little girl.

She took a slow breath.

Because the woman held down here for half a year was a prisoner, a prisoner they tortured and abused, Sam thought. Because that woman saved my life once too.

Because to have the right future, we need to lay down the right past, for that future to build on.

Tit for tat.

Tit for tat.

Sam saw Feng give the signal, and she reached up with her eyes, pulled down a menu, and disabled her chameleonware, as did he.

She and Feng were the bait.

She saw Feng pull off his hood, stand perfectly still for a moment. Then he reached back and pulled his hood back on, chameleonware still disabled, his form still barely visible.

Then with a deep bass grind of stone against stone, the massive, meters-thick door started opening, light spilling into darkness.

And she was diving forward into that light, and into the sound of gunfire.

Kade readied himself at the bottom. It all came down to this.

He left his chameleonware active, but peeled back his hood to free himself from the Faraday lining of the thing. Then he closed his eyes, and he and Feng were linking up, conjoining, their minds forming two poles of a compound antenna, manipulating a wave on a long, long wavelength, as long as the distance between them, sending a slow, deep signal, searching through the cold rock for the receiver on the other side.

And then a key fit a lock.

Kade felt it. He reached back, pulled the chameleonware hood back over his face, settled it in place. A vertical crack of light, twenty feet tall at least, split the wall of the elevator shaft. It widened, widened.

Then he saw Feng and Sam roll through it, moving in opposite directions, and gunfire burst out, someone inside, firing out, full auto, shooting at them.

He moved forward, slowly, careful on the rocks, limping on his damaged knee.

Gunfire kept emerging in staccato bursts. He heard thuds, grunts. He couldn't see inside.

He made it down the rubble, his knee aching. He moved quietly, slowly, was just crossing through the tunnel created by the meters-thick door when he caught a glimpse of the battle, bodies moving, muzzle fire.

Something rocked his head, slammed it hard into the stone door like a blow from a hammer.

It set his world to spinning.

It plunged his visor and its feed into black.

Sam dove forward. Dynamic entry. Gunfire exploded as she threw herself into a roll in the widening space between the doors. Her visor threw up attack vectors, arrows identifying the sources of the fire.

Three arrows. Three sources of gunfire.

She came up out of the roll, spinning to change the course of her path, arms out, assault rifle in her right hand. More gunfire erupted, ripping through the space her trajectory would have put her in.

Her eyes took in the scene as she spun. The giant glass walls. The quantum data-center behind them. The control panels. The little girl in the dress, back to them, at one of those panels. The middle-aged Chinese man, tapping away next to her.

The Confucian Fist in the plain fatigues flying through the air, between Sam and the quantum cluster, an angle she couldn't fire on, his rifle coming around towards her new position.

Sam pulled her arms in and across her body to accelerate the spin, ducked her head down to turn her motion into a half-flip, knowing it was too late, knowing his bullets were about to punch through her.

Kade's visor cut to black.

He stumbled, disoriented, reeling from the blow to his head, expecting another.

No second blow came.

He reached up, pulled the hood off his head, looking, searching.

Feng and Sam were fighting for their lives. For everyone's lives.

There. There was Ling. And Chen. At the consoles of the quantum cluster.

Still going through its boot sequence. Not yet complete!

The fiber optic cable was behind him. The network access point waiting for him to activate it. But he might not need it. He might not. Not yet.

Ling was turning towards him. He could see a malevolent intelligence behind her eyes that wasn't her own. That wasn't the eight year-old girl he'd gotten to know.

He reached Inside, and the origami tools Su-Yong had given him unfolded again, expanding to thousands of times their size, fractally decompressing, becoming orders of magnitude more complex.

He reached out towards Ling's mind, bombarded it with viral fragments, millions of them, mutating in real time.

All a feint.

The Avatar used Ling's face to smile at the boy. She was ready for him this time. He came at her with viruses. Again? Silly child.

She fired phages into the shared spectrum, evolved things, tailored for the viral attack she'd seen him use already, that she'd first seen the hostile posthuman use in Bangalore. The phages were simple things, tiny compared even to the viruses. She unleashed billions of them. They swarmed the viral code, attacking weaknesses Darwinian methods had found in the minutes since their last encounter, shredding the viruses to bits, decimating them.

Only a few radical mutants of the virus survived the phage barrage, reached the outer layers of her mind.

Her firewalls blocked them, categorized their mutations, fed them to her digital immune system for new rounds of phage evolution.

She counter-attacked at the most basic hardware level of the nanites, using protocols her higher self had emplaced there when she designed them. She ripped into parts of the boy's brain through those low level hardware controls, made the nanite nodes her own, as they always had been, seized control of the boy's cortex, of his brain stem, of his mind, of his life.

The human screamed.

Control channels opened, handed off nanite circuits from within the human brain to hers.

She accepted.

End his life now? the Avatar debated. Or keep him around as a useful pet?

Circuits from the boy's mind opened. Data returned. Systems inside her own mind went haywire.

With horror she realized she'd been played.

Dummy circuits. Trojan horse attacks. They dumped more viral assault weapons, fresh ones, laden with exploits she'd never seen, directly into protected memory space deep within her mind.

The new viral attacks took root in microseconds.

She screamed.

No choice.

The Avatar invoked emergency procedures, cauterized whole segments of her mind. She cut billions of nanites out of her network, flash-zeroed their data, forgot and lost whole swaths of herself.

The firewalls over the rest of her snapped into new shapes, adapting, learning from these new tricks, reforming themselves to resist these exploits. Darwinian immunity engines kicked into high gear, evolving new generations of phages to kill these new viruses.

Behind her, she felt the boot sequence of her greater self draw near to its conclusion.

Seconds. That's all she needed. Just seconds.

Kade pushed forward, panting with exertion, with the epic draw of the Nexus nodes on his brain's blood flow, on its nutrients. He was burning up. A fever inside his skull. Wattage from the spillover of the transmission power of the Nexus nodes was physically warming his cranium to dangerous levels. Red emergency messages were flashing on Nexus control panels in his mind. He couldn't keep this up too long. His brain would fry.

He had to. No choice.

It was injured. It was constrained. But it was a caged beast now, smaller, with a more limited surface to defend, and learning fast.

He fired another flurry of viruses into the shared bandwidth between them, millions of them, the newest ones used in the Trojan attack, ones she hadn't seen until less than a second ago.

The monster responded with billions more phages, new ones, evolved even faster, slaughtering his viruses on the wire.

Then he felt something, something incredible. Inside the mind, he felt a struggle.

Ling!

Sam watched as the unknown Confucian Fist flying through the air brought his rifle around to shoot her.

She pulled her arms in to accelerate the spin, ducked her head to turn it into a half-flip, knowing it was too late.

Feng's foot collided with his brother's head in mid-air. Flame burst from the muzzle of the other Fist's assault rifle. Bullets slammed into the stone centimeters from her, ricocheted through the space.

Sam's half-flip brought her over closer to the console.

Feng's attack carried him, and the unknown Fist he'd kicked, out of Sam's sight.

Where were the other two shooters?

Then a second Fist slammed into her from out of nowhere, his foot colliding with her mid-section.

Pain burst through her. The force of it knocked her off her feet, toppled her back. Her head collided with the polished stone floor as her body slid back. Stars appeared in her vision.

Sam looked up and the Fist was flying through the air, coming down on her with all his momentum led by the heel of one foot, aiming at her chest.

She rolled, brought the assault rifle around and up, pulled the trigger, pulled it again.

The Fist twisted somehow in mid-air, landed sideways, one foot slamming down on her hand that held the assault rifle, brutally pinning it, trapping the arm, sending more pain flaring up through her wrist.

He brought his own fist down in a hammer blow at her head.

Sam blocked with her left arm, barely got it up in time.

The blow slammed down through her block, through the layers of armor built into the visor and the hood, brutally hammered her skull against the hard stone floor.

Pain exploded through her head. She couldn't see. Couldn't hear. He was too strong. Too fast. Not human. She was going to die here.

The Avatar shredded the viral attack to pieces, sent messages to her servants, prepared to pounce on the boy in a new way.

Then she moaned in pain as something reached out through her from below, disrupting her, pushing aside her efforts, interrupting her phage transmission for a millisecond.

More viruses landed in that millisecond, some slipping past firewalls.

AAAAAH!

Ling!

The girl was rising up, into the nanite nodes the Avatar had been forced to cut out of her network, using them to disrupt her mother's plans!

Viruses were replicating, taking hold, spreading out of control!

She struck out viciously at the child. She'd kill her if she must! This was the most crucial moment!

•••

Kade pushed forward, mutated the attack again, red lights flashing, his head throbbing with pain and heat. Exhaustion pushed through him.

Then something grabbed his head, slammed it against the hard stone of the door, again, again, again.

Thought turned to confusion. He looked up, caught a glimpse of a middle-aged man in a suit, his face enraged.

Chen Pang slammed Kade's head into the stone of the giant door again.

Ling felt the monster attack her, all out this time, no mercy. She could see the beast's thoughts. See what it feared.

See Kade. See Feng.

See her father killing Kade.

No!

Ling abandoned all defense, reached out, and slapped at her father's mind.

The monster struck her hard.

All went black.

Kade reeled, the world spinning, pain filling his head, all attack dropped, only on his feet because the gigantic door supported him.

Gun, he thought. I've got a gun...

Then suddenly Chen Pang stopped beating his head against the stone.

Kade blinked, tried to understand the world. Chen Pang was shaking his head, his eyes confused.

Kade reached down, into the thigh pouch of his chameleonware suit, unsnapped it.

Chen Pang's eyes clarified. His face grew enraged again.

Kade put his hand on the gun, flipped off the safety.

Chen Pang reached forward, put his hands on Kade's head.

Kade struggled to get the gun up, pointed at Chen.

His head slammed against the wall, painfully.

The gun was somewhere between them, the angle distorted by the press of their bodies against each other.

His head slammed again. He couldn't see. Couldn't think.

Kade pulled the trigger. His head slammed again. A deafening boom exploded.

He pulled it again. Another boom.

Chen Pang slumped to the ground, blood leaking from him.

Sam waited for the final blow from the Fist to come down and end her life.

Suddenly he was gone, rising, sprinting away from her.

She rolled to one knee, bleary, world spinning, head aching, wrist throbbing with pain, to try to see.

The Fist was heading for Kade.

Kade watched as Chen Pang crumpled to the ground.

Kade reached out to the monster. He could feel the virus taking hold in its mind, replicating at high speed, colonizing corner after corner, making cauterization impossible. He could feel it working. Ling had opened the door for him, and now he was going to save her.

Bits of the monster's plan came to him, more details.

Then he saw the blur coming straight at him, beyond Chen Pang's crumpled body.

He pulled the trigger of his pistol again, knowing it was hopeless.

More shots rang out, from elsewhere, and suddenly the blur stumbled, became a Fist, blood leaking from his chest.

Kade fired with his pistol, again and again.

The Fist punched him.

Kade felt the blow like a sledge hammer to the chest. He felt ribs crushed. Felt pain as bad as any he'd felt, from that single punch. It sent him spinning, toppling through the air, and to the stone floor inside the main chamber, on his back.

Somehow he still had his pistol.

He fired up, missed the bloody blur coming at him.

Then something black collided with it from the side, slammed it into the stone wall, hammered at it in a blur of fists and feet as it hammered back. Muzzle fire erupted at short range.

Kade couldn't breathe.

And then the Fist was on his back.

And Sam was standing over him.

Feng wept.

He stood over the two brothers he'd killed, tears running down his face.

Chanming.

Aiguo.

Dead.

There. There was Chen Pang. Dead.

There, towards Sam and Kade, was another brother.

Genghis.

Feng laughed through the tears. They'd all thought that was a terrible name to choose.

When Su-Yong had given them the right to names. The freedom to *choose* their own names.

Names instead of numbers.

Genghis was dead.

Ling lay crumpled on the ground.

Feng pulled off his hood.

"Is she?" he asked.

Ling's alive, Kade sent. **The thing is gone.**

Pain came across the link. Feng looked over at Kade in alarm.

Kade was sitting on the ground, propped up against the outer wall of the chamber. Sam was over him. Feng could feel his friend's difficulty breathing, his pain on every expansion and contraction, now that the Faraday lining of the hood was gone.

"Punctured lung," Sam said. "Get the first aid kit."

Then Feng felt something enormous come into the room with them.

Something angry.

Something violently mad.

It crushed him down, overwhelmed him completely, filling him with its rage, with its will for a new order.

He fell, crumpling, to his knees, all thought driven from him.

His defenses were useless.

On a console a message flashed, blinking maddeningly in his eyes.

BOOT SEQUENCE COMPLETE.

Su-Yong Shu had returned.

121
Mere Anarchy

Monday 2041.01.20

Rangan marched down E street, in the first ranks of hundreds of thousands, his face hidden behind a mask of himself. He was one of thousands in masks. There were others here with masks of his face, with iconic Guy Fawkes masks, with John Stockton masks, with scarves, with face paint, with oversized sunglasses, with giant face-distorting goggles.

This was supposed to be a peaceful march. But all around him he saw people attempting to escape recognition. He saw backpacks and satchels that looked heavy. He saw scarves and surgical masks and even gasmasks at the ready for tear gas attacks.

And he could feel anger building. He could feel the violence around the globe and the frustration of the last few months converging here, heating up as they marched.

All around them, there were police, national guard, homeland security, lining the march route, waiting with riot armor and truncheons and gas masks and armored vehicles, waiting, and ready to clear them, if they left the route they'd declared, if they threatened to disrupt the inauguration.

Waiting, but not attacking. Waiting, but letting them march.

Around the world, it was different. People were dying. Soldiers were firing into crowds. Fireballs were going up.

Rangan didn't need to reach out to know that. People all around him were tuning in, passing the feeds and snippets around angrily as they marched, chanting in solidarity. The images and sensations surged out of people's minds, touching everyone, whether they'd tuned into a feed or not.

He was a girl in Nairobi being beaten by riot police. He was a student in Shanghai, his leg shattered by automatic fire. He was an old man in

Kazakhstan, his arms being wrenched back by the dictator's thugs.

He clenched his mind down, pushed it out. There were tens of thousands of people running mesh in this crowd. But the mindstream sites themselves were acting as a kind of global mesh. And they were being used to spread rage.

That's not here! Rangan tried to tell everyone around him. Don't get confused! Don't give them a reason!

But the anger was strong. And it was growing.

Yuguo crouched down as the deafening roar came overhead.

FLEE INDOORS, the clones who called themselves Confucian Fists sent.

Up above the army helicopters dove towards them. He saw missiles fire. Red streaks hurtled this way. Explosions lit up the night. Buildings all around suddenly erupted in flame. Bodies were hurtled from the ground. Pain burst out in staggering amounts. Minds were silenced. Helicopters exploded. Other craft flew over them. More explosions. Everything was chaos.

Yuguo grabbed for the controller they'd built, the controller for the electronic weapons, the ones that disabled tanks.

"WE HAVE TO RUN!" Lu Song shouted into his ear, over the deafening roar of explosions, of engines up above.

More gunfire, on the ground now.

He heard the crack and whoosh of Molotovs breaking, fireballs erupting.

He heard screams.

"NO!" Yuguo yelled, hunting through the menus, there must be something, something for helicopters.

"TANKS!" Zhi Li yelled, crouching down next to him.

Yuguo looked up. More tanks, pushing in from the end of the square. Dozens of tanks. He saw their turrets turning, heard massive booms.

He hit the button for the tanks.

The world exploded all around him.

Pain like he'd never known ripped through his body.

Ekaterina Naumenko yells in rage as she runs towards the faceless, shielded state thugs in Moscow's Red Square. They are killing her comrades in Shanghai! Gunning them down with tanks, with helicopters!

"Murderers!" she screams. "Cowards!"

From behind her, she feels it in her mind as patriots launch a volley of Molotovs into the air, hurtling at the lines of riot police. The fire that bursts forth inflames her heart.

• • •

Fazil Kamal hauls harder on the stun gun in the hands of the soldier in Istanbul's Taksim Square. The soldier won't let it go! Fazil's cousins, Burak and Mustafa, hold the man down and pummel him.

"Damn you!" Fazil yells. He kicks the soldier again.

With a final heave the stun gun comes free.

Fazil stumbles backwards with the shock of it, then raises his prize high into the Turkish night.

Yes! It's theirs. He looks around the square and he sees soldiers on their backs, freedom fighters rising triumphant.

He can feel it.

Aybek Nabiyov lights another Molotov cocktail, and hurls it up at the dictator's palace in Almaty. Dozens of men and women around him are hurling them now. The dictator's secret police are broken. The Americans have not come out of their bases.

The lit Molotovs fly up gorgeously, almost serenely, spinning end over end, the lit rags stuffed into the mouths of the fuel-filled glass bottles moving like fireflies on this dark cold, starless night.

Then they smash against the palace the dictator built with the billions he stole.

The palace is burning.

"For Lunara," Aybek says, tears on his face. For the woman he loved. The woman he would have married. The woman who's dead because of the dictator.

Talgat reaches out a hand, and Aybek takes it. He can feel the solidarity of his brothers, his brothers in arms. Their anger has not been for nothing.

The dictator has fled.

Kazakhstan will be theirs again.

Around the whole world he feels that solidarity, a million minds crying out in righteous anger. Ten million. Who even knew how many?

But enough.

Men and women are crying out for justice. Crying out together. Crying out in unison.

The world will belong to the people once more.

Carolyn Pryce watched the screens, transfixed.

It was blowing up. Everywhere. Maybe Shanghai had started it. Maybe something else. But now… Every shooting, every explosion, every brutality someone on Nexus captured went viral. They ricocheted around the globe. They fed more violence, enraging protesters, driving police to more extreme measures.

It was a feedback loop. White noise. The whole thing going to a screeching caterwaul that was going to break the windows of civilization.

"Iran's off the net," NSA said. "So are Yemen, Syria, Qatar. Trying to stop the spread." He paused. "Kazakhstan just went dark."

"Too late for Kazakhstan," CIA replied, looking up from a console. "President Bayzhonov's fled the country."

"Jesus," Pryce said. "Our troops?"

"Confined to base," Admiral McWilliams said, shaking his head. "This was civilian action, not rebel."

"Fuck," she muttered. "North Korea?"

"Nexus never took hold," NSA said. "We *think*."

Pryce's phone buzzed at her then, three sharp buzzes in succession, the highest priority signal there was.

She pulled it out of her pocket, expecting an urgent message from Kaori, maybe even something from the President.

Instead she saw something else.

[ERD_SECRETS: URGENT: China didn't kill Barnes. PLF did, w/ help of hacker now spreading Nexus, destabilizing both US and China.]

Pryce stared at it.

What the hell?

She jabbed a message back.

[How do you know? Who are you? What proof?]

"Holy shit!" CIA said. "Imaging, give me real-time of latitude thirty-one point two zero two two, longitude one twenty-one point four three five three."

Pryce looked up from her phone and stared at the man from CIA.

He looked up, addressed her, moved his eyes to take in the SecDef and the Chairman of the Joint Chiefs. "We have air combat over Shanghai! Dozens of units involved. Aircraft shot down." The CIA man paused, his face pale. "It's a full blown war zone."

122
Million Human

Monday 2041.01.20

Rangan tensed as he saw the barricades come into sight ahead. Concrete barriers. Armored vehicles. Riot-armored police.

Giant screens to taunt them with the inauguration.

The barriers ended E Street. Ended it at 2nd. They could file into the broad square that 2nd Street had effectively been turned into. But no farther.

Rangan had chosen this spot, near the very front of the march, intentionally, to give him advance warning of anything that might come. Cheyenne was a block or two back, Angel back behind her, and Tempest the furthest back.

Now he felt the huge weight of the crowd behind him. And he had a sudden impression of the crowd continuing to press forward, angrily smashing him up against that barrier until the life was crushed out of him.

Steady, Cheyenne sent him, with a trace of humor.

Rangan tried to smile back along the link. The constant bombardment of anger and flashes of riots and gunfire and tear gas and flames around the world had him rattled.

This wasn't what they'd come prepared to fight. They'd come ready for a single homogenous blast of artificial anger. But this? This influx of real rage, organic, bottoms up, in so many shapes and colors?

Breece wasn't going to have to do a damn thing. This was going to explode all on its own.

I'm worried, he sent to all the C3.

We can do this, Cheyenne sent back.

The network effect's the same, Angel sent. **We just need their attention.**

They marched. Signs waved. The chants grew louder and angrier. People started moving faster. Rangan saw hands raise scarves and surgical masks. He saw goggles come down over eyes. He saw people reach into backpacks.

And suddenly the crowd was a living thing. He caught flashes of violence in far away places: in Russia, in Kenya, in China. Anger, gunshots, fires.

Neural inputs, pulsing into this mob mind.

Bodies pressed against him from behind, faster, giving him no choice but to move forward with them, rushing now. Hot emotions were pounding against him, pushing away thought. People were losing themselves, forgetting where they were, forgetting who they were, intelligence dropping to the lowest common denominator of the mob as they surged at the barricades.

Rangan felt fear rush through him. The crowd was going to smash up against those barricades, the pressure of the thousands of people behind him was going to crush him up against them, squeeze the life right out of him...

Is that a stage? Angel sent.

He blinked at her voice in his mind.

A stage. There was a stage, set behind the barricades.

And on it.

Holy frack, Tempest sent.

The giant screens came to life. The face of the man on the stage appeared in front of them all.

Senator Stanley Kim stood there, tall and straight, in his signature black suit and blue tie, and held his arms out wide to the crowd.

Rangan gasped. The crowd's rush slowed as shock snapped people back to the here and now. The crowd was filling the wide space on 2nd street, where the barrier was placed, hundreds of thousands of people filing in behind him. And he was just a dozen people back from the barricade. Just thirty or forty feet back from the stage on which Stan Kim stood, looking at them all, his arms still held out, as if to greet them, as if to forestall them.

Stan Kim looked just as he had the night he'd given his speech saying he wouldn't concede the race. Saying that he'd won the Presidency.

More and more people filed in. Rangan felt anger turn to surprise, turn to confusion, turn to something almost like hope.

Well, Angel sent. **He's got people's attention. Think we can slip him some Nexus?**

"My fellow Americans!" Senator Stanley Kim said then, his voice powerfully amplified over the crowd. "We need a revolution!"

• • •

"We need a revolution!" the senator from California roared over the crowd.

Rangan felt the crowd roar back with excitement. A giant cheer went up. People clapped, whistled, yelled.

Minds cheered the senator on.

Stan Kim leaned forward, pointed at the crowd, panned his outstretched hand around to take them all in.

"That's why you're here, isn't it?" he yelled.

The crowd went wild again, cheering, clapping, waving signs.

"Well you've come to the right place!" Stan Kim said.

"America is the land of *permanent* revolution!" the senator said, his eyes scanning the crowd. "We fought a bloody war more than two and a half centuries ago. We spilled blood, right here!" He thrust a finger down at the ground, beneath the stage.

"Why?" Kim asked. "Because we had no choice! Because it was our only way! So we could institute government *of* the people, *by* the people, and *for* the people. Government where we revolt *constantly*, every two years!"

Rangan caught his breath. He heard some cheers, but fewer now. He felt the crowd grow confused in his mind.

"You want a revolution?" Stan Kim yelled.

The crowd cheered again. Yells of agreement rose up.

Stan Kim nodded. "In two years," he yelled, "every member of the House behind me," he waved back towards the Capitol, "and a third of the Senate come up for re-election."

He paused. Rangan was nodding, hoping beyond hope, feeling the crowd teeter.

He blasted out his agreement, blasted it out through his thoughts, blasted it out across the mesh to any listeners he had.

"You know what those women and men can do?" Stan Kim asked the crowd.

"They can kiss my ass!" Rangan heard someone say.

People laughed.

Stan Kim smiled. "They can repeal the Chandler Act. They can launch hearings into lies and criminal abuses of power. They can make sure people go to jail."

The senator paused. There was scattered cheering.

Rangan cheered as loud as he could, beamed out his agreement even harder.

Stan Kim opened his mouth again. "They can *impeach John Stockton!*" he roared.

The crowd came alive with cheering, with yelling, with hoots, with applause. Rangan felt minds turn.

"And in four years we elect a new President!" Stan Kim said. "Revolution after revolution after revolution!"

The crowd was with him now, cheering again.

"I know you're angry!" Kim said.

Cheers.

"I know you want the revolution today!" he yelled.

Roaring.

"But the battle is not the war!" Kim said. "We need patience!"

The crowd drew a deep breath.

"Some of you want to rip down these barricades. You want to light fires and tear things up. Well, look around you," Kim said. "Take a good long look at these men and women in uniform."

Rangan looked. He saw thousands of them. He was close enough to see faces, just on the other side of the barrier, behind clear visors and tall metal shields. He saw cold hard expressions.

Beneath that he saw fear.

"If you raise your fists today," Stan Kim said. "These men and women are going to do what they're *sworn* to do. They're going to protect the Capitol, and protect public order. They're going to strike back." Kim shook his head.

Boos rose up from the crowd.

Stan Kim raised his hands for silence.

"Listen to me. If that happens, people are going to *die*. On both sides." He paused. "Hundreds of people died on the National Mall on December 6th. I don't want another day like that on my conscience. I hope you don't want it on *yours*."

The crowd was silent, breathing.

"And if that happens," Kim went on. "Then your cause, *my* cause, *our* cause, isn't going to be helped. It's going to be set back. It's going to be associated with violence. With destruction."

Kim paused. Then he pointed back at the Capitol, and raised his voice.

"When the real violence has been done by the man in the White House and those who work for him!"

Cheers rose up again.

Kim looked out at them.

"We didn't get what we deserved last month," he said. "But that day will come! So stand proud! Wave those signs high!"

People cheered, less passionately, perhaps, but they cheered. Signs waved.

"Make your voices heard!" Stan Kim yelled.

People cheered again.

"Louder!" Stan Kim yelled.

This time they gave it to him.

"Show the world what you want, America! Make John Stockton afraid!"

The crowd went wild at that.

"Raise your voices today and not your fists!"

More cheering. Rangan saw a few sullen, angry faces, but there were many more cheers, there was more hope.

"Then keep memory alive!" Stan Kim yelled. "Keep the outrage alive! And in two years we'll have that revolution!"

The crowd cheered for him.

Rangan shook his head in awe and admiration.

Kate stared at the message.

[Insider: How do you know? Who are you? What proof?]

She looked back to the wallscreen, to the multiple feeds of data her filters were painting there.

The scene of the DC protest was triumphant, not violent. Breece hadn't assaulted them. He'd listened to her warning.

She wouldn't sell him out.

But China was going crazy. And reports were streaming in about US troop mobilizations, about aircraft launching from carriers.

When Breece's noon mission completed...

Kate shook her head. Panicky people made bad decisions when surprised.

She had to give this person something, had to get a message to their higher ups.

She typed a message back.

[ERD_SECRETS: We're PLF. The files we leaked are from Barnes's personal data. That's how I know. Events in China and the world are your proof. You must relay this upwards. China did not take offensive action against the US.]

Breece frowned at the screen. He stretched out his hand towards the terminal.

"Good speech," the Nigerian said.

"Talk's cheap," Breece replied. He jammed a finger down on a key.

Rangan shook his head in awe and admiration.

The crowd around him was cheering, waving signs. He felt passion and energy. There was disappointment. There was resentment. But it was isolated. People were looking around furtively, finding themselves in the minority. The bulk of the protesters here were fired up about doing exactly what this march had been billed to do – peacefully raising their voices right here, letting the world know they weren't going away.

It was incredible. Stan Kim had no Nexus. No fancy code. No nothing. The man had just *talked* to them.

Old school.

Then the hate hit.

[MULTIPLEX SIGNAL DETECTED]

It crashed over him like a wave, dragged him down into its red depths, so much darker, deeper, more violent than before. There were screams around him. Screams of rage. He felt the whole crowd surge forward, mad, a rabid beast.

[MESH NETWORK CALIBRATION UNDERWAY]

His eyes flew open and he found himself running, snarling, shoving, pushing, viciously trying to get through the press of arms and bodies ahead, so he could get to that goddamn barrier, tear it the fuck down, get to those pigs on the other side, rip their motherfucking arms off and use them to club the...

[FIREWALL CONFIG UPDATED]

Code sliced through the chaos. Digital filters blockaded specific signal patterns identified by peer-to-peer comparison across the mesh. The filters reduced the identified broadcast to data, to mere bits, canceled out those bits at the firewall around his mind.

[AREA COUNTERMEASURES ACTIVATED]

Countersignals burst out from code in his mind, using the Nexus nodes in his brain as transmitters, coordinating with hundreds of nearby peers on the mesh, shaping the countersignal to maximize destructive interference, to cancel out the hate broadcast over as wide an area as possible.

Rangan stumbled. His mind cleared. The crowd slammed into him from behind, forcing him forward. All around him he felt confusion, but still hate. His firewalls were keeping Breece's broadcast from touching him, were suppressing Breece's broadcast at least partially around him.

But the firewalls didn't touch the secondary effects. People were growing enraged. Their own anger was being rekindled, and blaring out loud and clear.

So was fear.

He looked right and left, struggling to break free of the crowd. From the minds nearest him, where his active countermeasures were doing the most to cancel out Breece's signal, he felt panic.

He felt men and women suddenly realizing they were being pressed forward by the hundreds of thousands behind them.

Whether they liked it or not.

BZZZZZZZZZZZZT.

Rangan's insides turned to jelly. He groaned as the sonic disruptor resonated in his chest, his jaw, his belly. He would have fallen but the crowd held him up.

Then the press in front of him was gone. He stumbled forward, fell to one knee, sweet Jesus he was going to get run over, and then somehow he was back up, and in front of him the barriers were bowled over, protesters were pushing back riot police. Tear gas was hanging in the air. There were screams ahead and behind. There was pain and confusion in his mind, even without Breece's broadcast.

And there were the stairs to the stage, just ahead of him.

And enraged protesters hauling up those stairs.

Towards a totally alone Stan Kim.

Rangan charged forward, hauled up the stairs.

HELP! he sent in a broadband across the mesh. **The stage! Stan Kim!**

There were three protesters ahead of him. He threw himself at the first, trying to tackle the man around the waist.

He fell short, grabbed the man by one leg instead. They both fell to the stairs. Rangan pushed himself up, ran over the man, up onto the main level of the stage itself.

Stan Kim was standing up, struggling with one of the men. The other was swinging the remnants of a sign at Kim, hitting him across the back.

Rangan ran full bore, charged shoulder-first into the man swinging what remained of a sign, sent him sprawling. He stumbled himself, caught himself on a railing at the edge of the stage, then turned.

The other protester was a big guy, more than six feet tall, muscle-bound. He had Stan Kim bent back over the edge of the rail.

Rangan ran at them, slammed into the man, meaning to knock him down.

The big guy moved maybe a foot, and stayed upright, but he did let go of Kim. Rangan bounced away. The big man turned and snarled at him, his fist drawing back.

Rangan reached in, boosted the Active Countermeasure strength to max.

The man hesitated.

"Someone's fucking with your head!" Rangan yelled at him.

The man lowered his fist slowly, turned his head to the left, a confused look on his face. Rangan followed it. Stan Kim was up.

"Who the hell are you?" Kim asked.

Rangan was panting. There was a Rangan Shankari mask on his face. He dropped his hands to his knees.

"I'm a friend," he managed.

Then he turned, and looked out, and saw and heard the chaos.

There were ranks of people at the bottom of the stairs to the stage. People using mesh. Volunteers, who'd come at his call, sealing it off, keeping it safe.

But beyond that…

Clashes everywhere. Clouds of tear gas rising up. Molotov cocktails flying. Riot police struggling with protesters. Screams. Pain.

Oh, Jesus, Rangan thought.

We just have to get their attention, Angel had said.

Rangan turned back to Stan Kim. "You have a mic?"

Kim shook his head, warily, and pointed. "Just stand on the X."

An X, made of tape, on the wood of the stage.

Rangan stepped onto it. He turned and faced the crowd. And then he could see the camera drones hovering out there, picking him up. He could see the cunningly hidden directional mics aimed to pick up his voice.

Rangan took a deep breath.

He reached out through the mesh. He could feel the firewalls active, feel the active countermeasures fighting. It was doing some good. They were restraining some of the violence.

But not enough. Not nearly enough.

Rangan lifted up his hands, and yelled, for the cameras, for the microphones, in his ridiculous Rangan Shankari mask.

"Listen to me!" he cried. "Someone's messing with your heads!"

Holy frack, Axon, Angel sent. **Is that you on the screens?**

Chaos came through. He could tell she was in the thick of it.

He felt Angel's attention. Tempest's. Cheyenne was struggling, somewhere, with someone.

Across the mass of minds, he felt barely a flicker of change.

"There are people around you who aren't angry!" Rangan yelled. "Tune into them!"

Nothing. Hardly any flicker, hardly any change. People barely noticed he was here.

"Thank you," Stan Kim said from behind him. Rangan felt a hand land on his arm. "Let me try."

Rangan moved to the side in a daze. Stan Kim stepped back onto the X, his hand outreached.

"Everyone!" the senator said. "This is not the way! You need to–"

A lit Molotov cocktail rose from the crowd hurled straight at them.

"Shit!" Rangan yelled. He grabbed Kim, threw them both to the floor of the stage.

The cocktail kept flying, shattered into flame on the next block of E street behind them.

"Fuck fuck fuck," Rangan said.

And then, before he could stop himself, he rose, and did what he knew he had to.

"My name," he yelled, "is Rangan Shankari!"

He felt a flicker of something from the minds down there.

"I am DJ Axon! I helped invent Nexus 5."

More attention. People were tuning in, looking.

Then Rangan reached up, and pulled the mask off his face, up onto the top of his head.

The crowd gasped. He felt it ripple from mind to mind, a stutter that paused the violence in all but the most intense locations.

"And someone is fucking with your heads!"

Carolyn Pryce's phone buzzed again. The three short sharp buzzes of highest priority.

She looked down from the global calamity all around her, to the message.

[ERD_SECRETS: We're PLF. The files we leaked are from Barnes's personal data. That's how I know. Events in China and the world are your proof. You must relay this upwards. China did not take offensive action against the US.]

She shook her head, and snapped out a new message.

[Not good enough. Give me something concrete!]

Breece narrowed his eyes at the screen.

Shankari.

He turned to the Nigerian. "Get a shooter in position."

The Nigerian looked back at him for a moment. "There's added risk," he said. "We can let this go. We've distracted them. What does it matter?"

Breece slammed his palm onto the table. "It matters!" he yelled.

Then he closed his eyes, and continued, more softly. "Just do it, please."

"You're being hacked!" Rangan yelled. "That's why you're suddenly so angry! Tune in to the people who aren't angry! Get close to them! They have an app for you! Install it, everyone!"

There was a commotion below. Rangan looked down, saw armed riot police crash through the wall of mesh-running volunteers at the bottom of the stairs, saw one run full-tilt at him, a truncheon raised.

"Away from the senator!" the cop yelled.

Oh shit, Rangan thought.

Then suddenly Stan Kim was in front of him, an arm outraised.

"This man's with me, officers!"

"Senator!" one of them yelled. "We'll get you out of here!"

"I'm staying here!" Kim yelled back. "We've got work to do."

Rangan breathed again. In the corner of his mind's eye, a counter was moving, it was scrolling, incrementing fast, the last digits changing in a blur.

They'd started the day with a little over fifty-three thousand people running mesh in this protest, out of six or seven hundred thousand people in total.

Now they were at one hundred and twenty thousand and still climbing.

Rangan tapped Stan Kim on the shoulder. Kim turned to look at him.

"You're blocking my camera, Senator," Rangan said with a smile.

Kim leaned in close to him. "Kid, you wanna see daylight after today?" he whispered. His eyes searched Rangan's. "Put that mask back on."

Then the senator stepped back, out of the line of the cameras, a smile playing at his lips, not even close to reaching his eyes.

Rangan swallowed hard, pulled the mask down over his face, suddenly aware of all the police. And also aware that a majority of those one hundred and twenty thousand... no, wait... one hundred and twenty-five thousand people were tuning in to *him* over the mesh.

He stood up straight, raised his arms, and told them with word and thought.

"We can do this!" he told them, hope and optimism beaming out. "There's a tipping point ahead! Keep bringing more people in, and we can cancel out the attack."

There was still so much hate out there. They were still a minority, growing fast but still there were four people *not* running mesh for every one person who was...

Then he felt another mind touch his. A mind he'd brushed in passing that day on the National Mall. The day everything went to shit.

He looked down and there was a bald man in orange robes climbing the stairs, threading his way between the imposing riot police, smiling slightly, his mind giving off tranquility.

This, this is what the crowd needed.

Rangan gestured and the monk came onto the stage without a word.

Rangan reached out and touched his mind to offer him mesh, found that the monk was already running it, and smiled.

"Listen to this man," Rangan said into the cameras, into the minds of those following him. "He has what we need."

And then he redirected those minds to the monk, and watched and felt as peace rippled out, as it flowed out of a hundred thousand minds, into all of those around them.

As peace flowed out of them like water, to meet the more numerous hot flames of anger.

Kate looked at the message on her terminal.

[Insider: Not good enough. Give me something concrete!]

Then she looked up at the wallscreen. At the chaos. At what Breece had done. At what he'd done to his own people.

He hadn't listened at all.

"Damn you," she whispered. "I loved you."

Then she typed out the message.

[ERD_ SECRETS: The man who killed Barnes goes by the alias "Breece". His real name is Andrew Marcum. He was behind DC, Chicago, and Houston. He's in DC now. His current location and full bio follow.]

"Shooter's in position," the Nigerian said. "We'll only get one shot before they triangulate."

"Take it," Breece replied.

Rangan watched the numbers climb.

Two hundred and sixty-three thousand. Two hundred and sixty-seven thousand. More than a third of the crowd running mesh, running firewalls cutting off the hate, broadcasting active countermeasures all around them!

They were doing it. Out there, he could see violence subsiding with his own eyes. They were approaching a tipping point.

He heard Stan Kim next to him, yelling to one of the cops.

"Get on the horn to your commander," Kim was saying. "Tell him he needs to cease fire! The crowd's calming down!"

"Senator, we have orders to clear the protest and get you out of here," the cop replied.

"Officer, that crowd is being pacified by this young man right here! Shooting more tear gas and rubber bullets is just going to make it harder. Now goddammit, put *me* in touch with your commander."

Rangan just closed his eyes, tuned in to the peace coming off this monk, this man he didn't even know.

Two hundred and ninety thousand.

Two hundred and ninety-five thousand.

Someone jostled him, and he opened his eyes. He looked over and the monk was half-collapsed on him, still smiling, still serene, his mind still giving off a deep tranquility.

There was red all over his robes.

"He's been shot!" Rangan said.

Suddenly there were riot cops all around him, shields held high. Radios were crackling.

He felt other minds, protesters all around, climbing onto the stage from the sides, crowding around, shielding him with their bodies.

And this man. Rangan lowered him to the wood floor of the stage, surrounded by cops and protesters both.

The monk was still smiling, eyes closed.

A cop pushed Rangan out of the way, ripped at the monk's robes. There was bright arterial red in the center of his chest. Rangan stared in horror.

The monk still smiled. His mind reached out. The tranquility was changing somehow. The peace growing more ethereal.

Turning to white.

Everything turning to white.

Beautiful, beautiful white.

It took Rangan's breath away.

He felt hundreds of thousands of people gasp with it. Felt them all lose themselves in the complete absorption of this man's mind.

Everything was this. This moment. This breath. There was no past. No future. Complete Samadhi. Complete absorption.

All white.

All peace.

All compassion.

Rangan lost himself in it. He wasn't even sure how long it lasted.

And then it was fading.

And fading.

Dissipating.

Gone.

And all around him he felt stillness. Stillness everywhere.

Peace.

He opened his eyes, stood upright, craned his head over the forest of police shields and protesters who'd climbed up here to protect him, and looked out over the crowd.

Everywhere, people had stopped. The protesters had stopped. The cops had stopped.

They'd won. The riot was over.

Stan Kim put a hand on Rangan's shoulder.

"Well done," the senator said quietly. "Now, get the hell out of here."

Rangan nodded.

Time to get the hell out. Before the cops realized who they had here.

Then he heard a radio crackle, saw a police officer's eyes go wide, the cop step back to create room, his gun fly out of its holster, aimed straight at Rangan.

"Down on the ground!"

Carolyn Pryce stared at the message, at the data in the attached file.

She couldn't breathe. A fake? So detailed.

"Dr Pryce," someone was saying. "Dr Pryce!"

She looked up. People were staring at her. She focused on Admiral McWilliams, ignored everyone else.

"I need a secure line to the National Terror Response Center."

McWilliams stared at her, like he didn't understand what language she was speaking.

"Now!"

123
Inauguration

Monday 2041.01.20

John Stockton watched as Ben Fuhrman finished the Oath of Office as Vice President. Fuhrman looked over at him, his hand still on the Bible, and gave him a tight grin.

It was amazing they'd made it this far.

Stockton responded with a proud nod.

Ben Fuhrman stepped away from the podium, and so did Justice Rodriguez. The musicians played. Musicians he loved. The program said five minutes. It lasted forever.

Then they were done, and it was his turn.

Chief Justice Aaron Klein stepped forward, with the Bible that George Washington had sworn his oath on.

Stockton stepped up in front of the Chief Justice, and put one hand on George Washington's Bible.

And suddenly he was aware of the silence of the vast House Chamber all around and above him, of him nearly alone here in the center and the bottom of it, of the hundreds of representatives, senators, cabinet members, family, friends, and guests crammed into this place to watch. Of the cameras all around. Of the millions who might be watching.

Suddenly this wasn't just a formality. Suddenly this wasn't just another public event.

He looked to the side, and there in the front row was Cindy. She was smiling at him, her eyes full of love. She was smiling and crying, crying just as hard as she had the first time he was inaugurated. And next to her was Julie, his gorgeous daughter, his grandson Liam on her lap, her husband at her side.

Julie grinned widely at him, flashed him a covert thumbs up.

And then Stockton smiled, and knew everything was going to be OK.
Aaron Klein spoke.

"Mr President, please repeat after me."

John Stockton looked the Chief Justice in the eye, and repeated the words of the Presidential Oath of Office, written into the Constitution two and a half centuries ago.

"I, John Harrison Stockton," he said. "Do solemnly swear that I will faithfully execute the Office of the President of the United States."

Stockton took a breath, and repeated the next line. "... And will to the best of my ability, preserve, protect, and defend the Constitution of the United States."

Aaron Klein stopped.

Stockton looked the Chief Justice in the eye and added the words not in the oath, not in the Constitution. "So help me God."

The Chief Justice smiled at him.

Applause rose from the crammed-in House Chamber.

Miles Jameson stared down from the gallery as John Stockton was sworn in.

I made this man, Jameson thought. And now he betrays me.

Good luck, John, he thought bitterly.

Jameson reached into a pocket, and pulled out a tiny pill case. He held it in his lap, shielded from view by both hands, and opened it as quietly as he could.

His fingers felt for the right pill. There.

He looked down to be sure he had it.

Yes. The green one.

Jameson brought it to his mouth, swallowed it dry.

Good luck, Johnny boy.

"Missed," the Nigerian said. "Got the wrong guy."

"Damn it," Breece cursed.

"Doesn't matter," the Nigerian said. "T-minus five minutes."

Kate looked at the clock. 12.01pm. Four minutes.

On the wallscreen, John Stockton was talking, giving his post-inauguration address.

She had to time this just right. But there were so many unknowns.

Kate typed another message out to this insider.

[ERD_SECRETS: China isn't behind what's about to happen inside the Capitol either.]

12.02pm.

SEND.

• • •

"DC rapid response team is en route, Dr Pryce," the DHS response desk said over Pryce's headset, plugged into the Pentagon terminal. "The lead looks strong, ma'am."

"It could be a trap," Pryce said. "Be careful."

She looked up, was keenly aware of eyes on her, watching her here in the Pentagon Situation Room as she touched this issue well outside her nominal remit.

"We know, Dr," the response desk replied. "They're ready."

"Keep me informed," Pryce said. "I need to know right away when you get there if this is legit or not."

"Yes, Dr."

Her personal phone buzzed again, the three sharp buzz pattern. It was sitting atop the table. She looked at it and saw the message.

Pryce's heart dropped.

She whirled. There, against a far wall of the Situation Room, her new Secret Service detail, the one she'd resisted for so long, were standing, waiting for her.

They saw her turn, saw her look at them, and she saw something coil up inside them.

"The Capitol!" she yelled across the room. "The President! Something's about to happen!"

She saw fingers go to ear buds, lips start moving as they hit the radio to their command, the fastest way to reach the President's detail.

Then she was turning, looking for the screen showing the inauguration. There. There was John Stockton, at the bottom of the House Chamber, talking, passion on his face.

A bogus threat, Pryce thought. Just a bogus threat. Come on. Come on.

John Stockton took the podium to address the assembled audience.

To address America.

"A house divided against itself cannot stand," he started. "Abraham Lincoln said those words. They're as true now as they were then."

His eyes searched the crowd. Some Democrats had chosen not to be here today. He had to accept that. He had to reach out to the whole country, regardless.

"A nation divided is a weakened nation. In America, we've been divided. Our trust has been undermined, dividing us."

He lingered on those members of the opposing party who *had* come, today, rather than boycott his inauguration. He met their eyes as he spoke.

"This isn't an accident. We've been attacked. Our trust has been *intentionally* weakened. It's been undermined by those who want to divide us and conquer us. That attack has been successful. And if we remain so divided as we are now," Stockton shook his head. "We cannot stand."

He turned his head again, scanning right to left, taking in everyone he could. "Let me say what all of us should be willing to say. I trust the intentions of *every* American, until and unless they prove differently. I trust that we all want a better life for ourselves, our neighbors, our children."

He raised a hand, took in the crowd gathered here. "I trust that every member of Congress wants what's best for this nation as a whole. We may differ on what best *means*. We may differ on *how to get there*." He paused. "But I trust that you come to this place with the most sincere convictions, as I do.

"In the first hundred days of my next administration, I'm going to do everything in my power to increase our mutual trust. I'm going to do everything in my power to explain to you, America, the roots of my convictions. I'm going to do that by being more transparent with you than ever before. We've faced grave threats over the last decade and more. Many of them Americans and the world don't know about, or don't know the full details of. We're going to share those details."

Stockton scanned again, looking, making eye contact with the men and women here, letting the cameras fend for themselves. "When you see those details, when you see that evidence, when you see the things we faced down, and beat, sometimes by the skin of our teeth, then I think you'll reach many of the conclusions that I reached. You'll share many of the convictions that I have. And you'll see that the hard decisions that we've made, and that we have to *continue* to make, are made with the best of intentions for this nation, for our neighbors, for our loved ones..."

His eyes found Cindy in the front row.

"For our children."

And there was Julie next to Cindy, beaming up at him.

"For our grandchildren," he said, and Liam was looking up at him, standing up in Julie's lap, his eyes wide open, his mouth hanging open.

Stockton smiled, and looked back up at the crowd.

"And for all the generations to come!"

He took a breath. Time to move on to jobs and taxes.

In a secure room beneath the warren of tunnels that connected the buildings of Capitol Hill, behind a door that proclaimed FIRE PROTECTION EQUIPMENT – AUTHORIZED PERSONNEL ONLY, a piece of code came alive.

Dozens of electronic sensors suddenly lit up with digital inputs of heat and smoke.

There was a fire.

It must be suppressed.

Fire suppression systems went live.

Electronically-controlled solenoids moved. Valves turned.

Banks of man-tall, high-pressure tanks released their contents into specially designed pipes. Electronic valve control routed the liquid, rapidly expanding into gas, to fire suppression nozzles at the location of the fire.

The United States Capitol Building, House Chamber.

Time to move on to jobs and taxes, John Stockton thought.

Then a storm hit. A hurricane blasted him in the face, full of stinging rain. There was a roaring in his ears, a high pitched whistle somewhere above it. The air went cloudy, roiled by incredible turbulence. He'd closed his eyes reflexively, without even knowing it, flinching back from whatever was happening. Those eyes were burning now. There was a taste of metal in his mouth. More burning in his lungs.

Alarms were going off. Fire alarms.

"MR PRESIDENT!" Someone had his arm. Secret Service. "THIS WAY!"

"My family!" he yelled.

"WE'VE GOT THEM!"

"Dad!" It was Julie's voice. He tried to open his eyes but he couldn't see. He reached out and found his daughter, grabbed her hand. He heard crying. Liam's cries.

"WE'VE GOT TO RUN!" the Secret Service man said.

Stockton held on to his daughter and ran.

"Incident at the Capitol! Fire detected!"

"Christ," the Secretary of Defense said.

Pryce looked over at the screen, her heart pounding. She couldn't see anything, just distortion, just clouds of moving air.

"That's the fire suppression gas," an analyst said from one of the scores of consoles, tension in her voice. "It should clear shortly."

"Massive network event in China!" NSA yelled. "We have something off-the-scales going on. Origin Shanghai. Network requests saturating all the pipes in and out. Exabyte bombardment of our systems. NAES firewall is crumbling."

"That's it," Secretary Stevens said. "This is a Chinese attack. Set DEFCON 2. Prepare to take out those missile launchers."

"Wait!" Pryce said. "We don't know that! That could have been PLF!"

She held her phone up towards them.

"Gas is clearing, sirs," a voice said.

Pryce looked at the screen, prepared to see fire, dead men and women, horror like that day in DC...

She saw a mob, alive, on their feet, pressing for the too few exits.

No fire.

No bodies.

What the hell?

She turned her phone back to her, and typed a message out frantically.

[What the hell was that?]

124
Ultimate Recourse

Monday 2041.01.20

Zhi Li screamed as the explosion hurled her through the air. Then she was down. Then she looked over and saw Yuguo.

She screamed again, louder.

"Lu Song!" she yelled. She reached out for his mind. "Lu Song!"

"Zhi!" he yelled.

Yuguo was screaming now, screaming with his lungs, with his mind.

"Help me, Lu Song!" Zhi yelled. "We have to get him inside!"

She pushed up to her feet, grabbed one arm. Lu Song was there, and he grabbed the other, and they started dragging, dragging Yuguo towards the Computer Science Building.

What was left of him.

Yuguo's legs were gone below the knees.

Yuguo screamed, and she pulled faster. There were explosions up above, aircraft fighting aircraft. There were explosions down here. The sounds of machine gun fire. Of rockets or shells. She saw Confucian Fist moving, barely perceived blurs. She saw soldiers in armor – heavy looking, insectile armor – fighting back.

Not dying.

Aaah!

Then they were at the building.

They were inside. For all the good it did them.

"Yuguo!" someone screamed.

A girl ran up to them. Then other people were there, first aid kits, tourniquets. Someone brought a needle full of some fluid.

He was screaming, screaming. There was so much blood.

She stepped back, out of the way. "Dear gods."

Lu Song put his arms around her. "They can save him," he said. "They can save him."

It sounded more like a prayer than a statement.

More gunfire sounded from outside.

Zhi heard more screams, someone out there crying, plaintively, asking for help.

She looked up at Lu Song. "We have to help."

Lu stared down at her, fear plain in his eyes.

She put her arms around him, buried her head in his chest. "I'm so frightened, lover," she said.

He wrapped his arms around her. "I know. I am too."

She felt it. Felt his fear. Felt his courage. Felt his immense love for her.

She'd never felt so close to him as now. To have him in her mind. To be in his.

What a gift. The gift of love, in the middle of hell.

She wanted stay like this, in his arms, forever.

But she couldn't.

Zhi pushed back, looked up at her lover. "We have to help."

Lu nodded down at her. She felt his courage and his love for her overwhelm his fear.

Her heart was so full right now.

Zhi turned, headed to the door, the love of her life at her back, towards the sound of whoever was out there on the battlefield, injured, needing help.

Then she heard the sound of gunfire again, horribly close.

Something punched through her. Her body shuddered. She felt her midsection go cold, like ice. She gasped.

Then the pain hit her, pushing aside all else.

Lu watched as Zhi turned and walked for the door.

His heart was on fire. His feet were paralyzed by fear.

She took one step. Two. Three.

Walk, he commanded himself. Then he was moving, following this woman who amazed him, who was so much smarter, more courageous, more giving than he could possibly be.

Then she screamed at the doorway. Horror shot through his mind as he felt her agony. He saw blood blossom, saw bits of her expelled through the back of her blouse. She fell towards the cold tile of the floor and he was falling too, to catch her.

She was in his arms, bleeding, in agony, her chest, her belly, a mess of blood.

She coughed, and blood came up.

Her eyes were frantic, searching his.

She opened her mouth wider, tried to speak, coughed up more blood.

Her mind touched his, with pain, with fear, with love. So much love. **I've never loved you so much,** she sent him. And she was weeping in her thoughts. She was crying. She was terrified, but so full of love, so full of passion, so determined. **Finish this, lover. Please.**

"You're not going to die!" he yelled at her, tears falling from his face, horror coming out from his mind. "You're not!"

He rose with her in his arm. He turned, back towards the people inside the building. They could help!

"HELP ME!" he yelled. "HELP ME!"

HELP ME!

Her blood soaked into his shirt, spilled onto the floor. People stumbled towards him, in shock. He saw phones held up, and hated them.

love you... Zhi sent.

He looked down at her. *I love you! You're not going to die! You're not!*

Lu Song looked up again, at the people all around. "HELP ME!" he yelled.

And then her mind was fading, jumbling, melting into confusion, confusion of pain, of love, of fear, of hope.

Lu Song...

Zhi! He cried, looking down at her.

Of nothing.

Her eyes were wide open, staring at nothing.

Lu Song sobbed, shaking, holding her in his arms.

And then he fell to his knees, his lover's body clenched to his chest, and wept as the sobs wracked him.

General Ouyang Fan, Minister of National Defense, walked back into the Standing Committee meeting room, his face grim.

They looked up at him.

"Our assault on Jiao Tong is stalling," Ouyang said. "It may fail entirely. We're being fought off by airpower from Dachang, in addition to the clones." He watched as their faces paled, and kept on. "We've also confirmed that a facility storing one of the data cubes was attacked yesterday. Plundered. Su-Yong Shu may well be back, and she has control of one of our air bases."

"Try harder," Bo Jintao said. "Use every resource!"

"More units are mobilizing," Ouyang said. "Time is the issue. She has *taken control of an air base*. Do you not see the seriousness of that? What if she can take control of more?"

"What do you propose?" President Bao Zhuang asked, his face ashen.

Ouyang took a deep breath.

I will go down in history as a monster or a savior, he realized.

"The ultimate recourse," Ouyang said. "Nuclear attack."

In Beijing, in Tiananmen square, Pan Luli falls to her knees, screaming. Her mind is in Shanghai, in horror.

Lu Song stands before her, covered in blood, shaking, his body wracked in sobs, tears flowing down his face.

Zhi Li in his arms.

Zhi Li is dead.

Zhi Li is dead!

"They've killed Zhi Li!" she yells. Around her there is shock, grief, hundreds of thousands of minds, screaming in horror at what they've done, huge numbers of them tuning in to the same few streams, some seeing the scene from the perspective of those watching Lu Song, some feeling Lu Song's thoughts as they spill into the mind of mindstreamers near him. Some replaying Zhi Li's last few seconds over and over.

A giant angry scream goes up all around Pan Luli, the scream of half a million men and women who loved Zhi Li!

And then, more than a thousand kilometers away, Pan Luli sees through another woman's eyes, hears through another woman's ears, as Lu Song looks up to the sky, and screams himself, in rage that eclipses any he's ever shown on the screen.

"BO JINTAO!" he roars, like an animal, like a creature in such pain it's been driven mad. Veins bulge in his neck. His eyes are tinged in red.

"BO JINTAO!" he roars again, the cry of a man beyond hope, beyond fear, beyond anything but rage.

And in Beijing, in Tiananmen square, half a million lungs scream the name of the man who's murdered his beloved.

"BO JINTAO!"

Pan Luli hears it all around her, hears it from every mouth of every man, every woman, every child. She feels it from their minds

Then, as one, half a million pairs of eyes turn, turn to the north and west, beyond the Gate of Heavenly Peace, beyond the soldiers and tanks and guns, towards the walled refuge of Zhongnanhai, the palace of the modern day Emperors of the nation.

And like a great, angered beast, enraged beyond its senses, the crowd surges.

"Nuclear attack," Bao Zhuang whispered softly. "On Shanghai?"

Ouyang nodded.

"This is insanity!" Wang Wei cried. "She's dead! We shut her down."

"Shut up, old man," Fu Ping said.

"Tactical weapons?" Bo Jintao asked.

Ouyang shook his head. "No. She is a kilometer down. Her forces control the surface all around her. Strategic weapons must be used. Even then they may not destroy her. But they will knock out her connections to the outside world."

The blood left Bo Jintao's face entirely.

Bao Zhuang spoke softly, "The death toll?"

"Twenty to thirty million," Ouyang said. His voice was steady, his face a mask. Inside he felt sick with it. His stomach was rebelling at the thought. Could he kill millions of his own people?

"Better than a billion," he said aloud.

"Is there no other way?" Bo Jintao asked.

"Authorize it," Ouyang said. "I'll wait until the last possible moment. We'll do everything possible to win via conventional means. But if defeat appears imminent – if she seizes control of more military assets – then we must strike immediately."

The room was utterly silent. Ouyang looked around. He was a career soldier. These were politicians. The situation was horrid, the thing of nightmares. But the difference between the two careers was evident here, evident in the ability to take hard decisions. Or not.

"We must decide," he said. "And you must say 'yes'. As great an atrocity as it would be…" He swallowed. "The alternative is even worse."

Still these men were mute, their faces drained of blood, their brains paralyzed by the unthinkable.

Then his chief aide ran into the room, breaking protocol.

"General Ouyang," the colonel nearly yelled. "We have a massive network attack from Shanghai. She's gone offensive!"

Ouyang surged to his feet. His eyes found Bo Jintao.

He saw the man look over at Bao Zhuang. The President they'd deposed. Who was somehow still the elder statesman here.

Bao Zhuang took a breath. "Yes," he said.

"Do it," Bo Jintao said, turning back to Ouyang.

Ouyang saluted them both, then ran from the room.

The soldiers open fire on them. Pan Luli feels the bullets rip into men and women around her. Tanks fire shells. Thousands of her sisters and brothers die in the first minute.

Then the crowd is on the army. Weapons the students have hidden are used, and the tanks go silent. Students and householders are climbing over tanks, throwing ladders up against walls, climbing up, throwing carpet and boards and coats over barbed wire.

There's more gunfire. People are dying. Dying in huge numbers. She sees friends fall, waves of them dying as the soldiers gun them down.

But the rage is strong.
Bo Jintao! Bo Jintao!
He killed Zhi Li!
Then they are over! And the Molotov cocktails are flying, flying, most of them landing in the vast lake in the center of Zhongnanhai, but some striking soldiers, some splashing flame onto buildings, and people are still coming over the walls, and rushing forwards, climbing over walls, a raging human wave.

Ouyang ran next to his aide.
"How do you know it's an attack?"
"What else could it be, General?"
Within a minute they were outside, almost to his helicopter, what he's been using as a command center, with its analog radio link to the planes he has circling overhead.
Then he saw the mob cresting the walls, the flaming firebombs hurtling this way, the soldiers falling back.
The soldiers being swallowed up by it.
The rioters coming up with guns in their hands.
"Into the chopper!" he yelled, shoving the colonel ahead.
He hauled himself on with raw adrenaline. "Lift off! Lift off!"
They rose, the sound of the rotors deafening, their downdraft creating a small storm inside the helicopter. A soldier slammed the armored sliding door closed.
The human wave was still a hundred meters away, visible through the armored glass. Automated defense guns had risen halfway out of their nacelles.
Had stalled, frozen.
Dear god. They'd been paralyzed. Paralyzed by electronic attacks.
And the mob had rifles now, was firing on the soldiers, was hurling Molotovs.
"Order the evacuation!" he yelled to the radio man in the co-pilot's seat. The soldier was already screaming into the mic of his headset.
Ouyang looked down.
Molotovs were crashing among the core buildings of Zhongnanhai. The mob was close behind.
It was too late.

125
Darkest

Monday 2041.01.20

Professor Somdet Phra Ananda sat on the thin mat, his legs crossed in lotus, thumbs and forefingers joined, backs of his palms resting on his knees. His body sat in the great meditation hall of this millennia-old monastery nestled against the side of a mountain, high above the lush plains of Thailand.

His mind was here and beyond. He was enmeshed, part of something far vaster, far more real, far more beautiful than himself.

A mind greater than the sum of its parts. A mind of paramount peace. A being of unrivaled insight and reflection. A being of unequaled wisdom.

Nirvana here on Earth.

Almost.

Twenty-five children and a hundred monks, together, here, a nucleus. A hub.

Three dozen more monasteries around the world, now, another two thousand meditators, linked at the speed of light, breathing as one, perceiving as one, the stuff of mind proxied by photon and electron, a web of consciousness, nearly circling the planet.

And out there, a million more minds they'd glimpsed, waiting for them to reach out. Ten million more they might pull in. Bits of technology whizzing around the planet at high speed to assist them.

All to save one woman's soul.

And perhaps the world.

Fear rippled through the tiny fraction of the greater self that was Professor Somdet Phra Ananda. Fear of the woman named Su-Yong Shu. Fear of the woman he'd named a friend. Fear of the woman he'd admired. Fear of what she could do in her insanity.

Words rose up, unbidden.

I accept rebirth, until all sentient beings have attained enlightenment.

I accept suffering, until all may know peace.

They rose up, rippled out into the greater self and were gone.

Where they had been there was only peace.

And then a connection was opening, a connection to a chamber a kilometer beneath Shanghai.

And utter insanity burst forth from it.

Kade coughed, pain wrenching through his chest.

"Get the first aid kit," he heard Sam say.

He'd seen something. In the agent's mind. He had to warn Rangan.

Kade reached out with his thoughts, activated the network access point they'd brought down with them on the end of more than a kilometer of ultra-high grade fiber. He felt it come alive, instantly, felt it proxy him through the net via its satellite-linked mate near the surface.

He reached through it to send a message to Rangan.

Rangan, he sent. **Not the protest. The Capitol. That's where it's going to happen. The Capitol.**

He'd destroyed the monster in Ling's mind. There was nothing to exploit what was about to happen in DC. But even so, the chaos it would cause…

Then Su-Yong's mind came alive in the space below Shanghai, and smashed down on him in her utter madness.

Su-Yong! he managed to send.

She kept coming, kept coming, kept forcing herself onto him.

And he was completely powerless to resist.

Bo Jintao looked up as the alarms started blaring.

"What?"

Then there was shooting.

A soldier burst into the room.

"Evacuation!" the soldier yelled. "The mob has broken through!"

"Impossible!" Wang Wei yelled.

Bo Jintao jumped to his feet and ran for the door. Other Standing Committee members got there first. He grabbed Wang Wei by the back of the man's suit, threw him to the side, stepped forward, did the same to Fu Ping, and then he was to the door.

He looked back once, and he saw the chaos in the room behind him, a scrum as Standing Committee members fought to follow. Except one. At the head of the table, still seated, his hands flat on the table, a wry half-smile on his face, and his eyes far away, was Bao Zhuang.

Bo Jintao snapped his face back, pushed through the door and into the hallway. Then he was running down the hall, the way the soldiers pointed.

He heard gunfire behind him. Screams. There was a smell of smoke in the air.

A soldier held a door open ahead.

Bo Jintao burst out through the door into the courtyard, where the vehicles should be.

He saw guards, firing weapons, shooting their machine guns at a tide of humanity, coming over the inner walls, into this thousand year-old courtyard, swarming over them.

More gunfire behind him.

He turned to see the soldier behind him fire, fire, fire again into people emerging from within the building. There were flames. Protesters fell from the bullets.

Then one got through, grabbed the soldier. He struggled, pushed the man off. Then another grabbed the soldier, another. They pulled him down.

Bo Jintao turned and ran.

But there was nowhere to run to. The courtyard was full of protesters.

The last thing he saw was angry faces, a forest of hands reaching out for him, dragging him down.

The last thing he heard was his name being yelled, over and over again.

"BO JINTAO! BO JINTAO!"

Then the kicks came, and the mob tore into him.

And there was nothing left but pain.

General Ouyang Fan leaned back, numb.

Zhongnanhai gone.

Su-Yong Shu loose.

Everything ending.

There was no time for paralysis. No time to mourn. That could come later.

He pulled the helmet tight over his head as the helicopter flew, activated his headset.

"Put me through to General Quan Huyan," he said into it. "Immediately."

Time. How much time?

He turned to his aide, Colonel Zhu. "What's the status on the network attack?" he asked.

Zhu shook his head. "Same. Incredible bandwidth. We don't understand it."

"Weapons systems?" Ouyang asked. "Bases? Banks? Planes? What has she cracked? Has she launched on us? Has she gone nuclear?"

Zhu shook his head again. "Communication is strained. We don't know."

Ouyang absorbed that.

Can I kill millions? he asked himself. What if I'm wrong?

What if I hesitate and a billion die?

Or eight billion?

"General Ouyang," General Quan Huyan's voice said in his headset.

"Quan," Ouyang said. He took a deep breath. There was no right answer. He had to do the best he could. "Fuel those two Dongfengs. Set a twenty minute timer. If I don't belay this order, fire them."

"General," Quan Huyan replied. "I cannot fire without authorization from the Chairman of the State Military Commission or a unanimous vote of the Politburo Standing Committee."

Ouyang looked out of the helicopter's armored window. He could see the fires out in the distance as they left them behind.

"Quan," he said quietly. "Zhongnanhai has fallen. I may be the highest authority in the nation." He waited. "Send a soldier out. Find a civilian phone. You'll see it's true."

He heard Quan exhale on the other side.

"Fan," his old friend said. "How do I know this is really you?"

Ouyang Fan closed his eyes. "You wept on my shoulder when the doctors cured your wife's cancer, my friend," he said. "May both our wives live to share tea again."

He heard another breath.

"Your orders have been received, General," Quan said. "They will be executed."

ATTENTION ALL OFFICERS AND SOLDIERS OF DACHANG AIR BASE AND ALL CONFUCIAN FIST COMMANDO UNITS. THIS IS A MESSAGE FROM GENERAL OUYANG FAN, MINISTER OF STATE DEFENSE, ACTING CHAIRMAN OF THE STATE MILITARY COMMISSION.

A STRATEGIC THERMONUCLEAR STRIKE HAS BEEN ORDERED FOR SHANGHAI.

TENS OF MILLIONS WILL DIE. YOU WILL DIE.

YOU CAN PREVENT THIS STRIKE.

DESTROY THE QUANTUM CLUSTER BELOW JIAO TONG, OR ISOLATE IT COMPLETELY FROM THE NET.

USE ANY AND ALL MEANS AT YOUR DISPOSAL.

YOU HAVE FIFTEEN MINUTES.

THIS MESSAGE WILL REPEAT ON ALL CHANNELS.

ATTENTION ALL OFFICERS AND…

•••

In Shanghai, thousands of analog radios blared the message.

Soldiers, their minds hijacked, switched channels, turned down volume, or simply ignored it.

A few Confucian Fist heard the message, and wished Feng and Bai and the Americans luck. Then they fought on, protecting Jiao Tong, protecting the woman who'd freed them, while the American boy tried to cure her of her madness.

Kade struggled under the crashing wave of Su-Yong Shu's mind.

Too much. Too vast. Too angry.

He was a grain of sand battered against the reef by the crashing waves at the edge of her ocean.

He was nothing.

Everything was her.

Her thoughts.

Her madness.

Her hallucinations.

Quantum foam.

Fractal light of other worlds.

A trillion reflected faces of herself.

Pain. Centuries of pain. Millennia of pain. Infinities of pain.

Goddesses tortured by gnats.

Goddesses triumphant.

New orders. New realities. New worlds birthed in fire.

Cleansing fire. Wiping away the old. Making room for the new.

Codes breaking. Impossibly long numbers decomposing effortlessly into beautiful, elegant, primes. Systems opening like flowers. World unlocking itself. Routers. Networks.

Cities.

Weapons.

Minds.

Better worlds.

Better!

Kade screamed as her madness drowned him.

Su-Yong! He tried, tried to offer her parts of him, tried to offer her input from his brain, stabilizing input, a dose of sanity.

He felt her reach out into the world then, through connections, so many connections, so much bandwidth, and he knew that it was all over.

Then he felt something flow into his mind through the access point.

Tranquility came.

A mind. A vast mind.

A self, compound, multi-faceted, yet whole, like the eyes of a fly.

A meta-brain, organic, functional, real, operating in the ways Su-Yong had been built to simulate, offering correction for the errors in her simulation code that had built up, that had compounded, that had driven her insane over time.

A peace, a stability, formed of a base so broad, a base of not one brain, not one life, not one perspective, but thousands, complementing one another, embracing one another, encircling and intertwining with one another.

A compassion. A compassion so deep, so heart-felt, a mind that knew this woman had suffered, that had seen glimpses of her torture. A compassion for all beings, for all minds, for all creatures who thought or felt, for her in particular, who'd felt so much for so long in so much agony.

A joy. A wild, multifarious, explosive, riot of joy, of moments, of glimpses, of experiences, of not just thousands of minds, but of now tens of thousands, of now hundreds of thousands of minds, as more touched them, as the core reached out to more minds, brought them together into joyous union, assisted by vast data centers of machinery that routed and filtered and coordinated connections, linked minds, sifted offered thoughts, identified love and bliss and passion and curiosity and delight and amplified them, selected for them, brought them here, through this link, through and around Kade, directly to this woman who needed them so badly.

Who needed to remember joy.

Who needed to see the good in humanity before she went to war with them.

It came through naked, vulnerable, wide open to her, not a challenge, but an offering. Not to defeat Su-Yong, but to surrender to her everything she needed to be whole and sane and joyous once more.

Kade felt the globe-spanning mind lift him up, out from under the crushing roiling pressure of Su-Yong's madness, up, up.

He was alive with joy. He was ten thousand minds, a hundred thousand minds, joyous minds, exulting minds, transcendent minds…
one mind,
many minds,
one mind,
many minds.

He was humanity coming alive. Humanity waking up. Humanity reaching consciousness. Humanity reaching transcendence. Humanity casting aside the veil of Maya, humanity pushing through the shroud of illusion, the mask of separation, realizing its true form, its true unity.

Humanity unfolding into its true glory.

Every fiber of his being trembled with it, trembled with this new golden state, with this being beyond being, with this joy beyond joy, with this transcendence of all he'd known, all he'd experienced, with this glimpse of true Nirvana.

With this glimpse of the true posthuman.

Then Su-Yong's madness crashed down onto him again, crashed *through* him, out through the link, into a thousand minds, ten thousand minds, a hundred thousand minds, taking all the joy and peace they offered her, and seizing more, and more, and more.

Injecting her own mad chaos into all of them in return.

Kade screamed.

Too gone. Too far gone.

He screamed again, louder.

Around the world, hundreds of thousands screamed.

Too gone. She was too far gone.

Sam watched as Kade's body went tense, as his breathing all but stopped.

She picked up the assault rifle she'd put down, rose to her feet. Her wrist ached from the punishment the Fist named Genghis had doled out.

Kade relaxed suddenly, a smile coming to his face, his breathing easing, even with the puncture in one lung.

Sam stared at him from above, both hands around her rifle now.

Smiling. Smiling was good.

She should drop back down, get the first aid kit, see if she could stabilize him.

Then Kade screamed.

Feng screamed.

No, Sam thought. No.

Kade's back arched. His arms flailed out to the side, spasming. His head jerked back. His mouth opened.

No.

He screamed again, louder. His eyelids were open. His eyes were rolled back in his head. Whites showing.

No.

He was thrashing now, like he was having a seizure. She looked over and Feng was on his knees, hands to his head, screaming.

But not like this.

Oh god, Sam thought.

And she was back on the plane, the troop transport, Kade leaning in close to her, explaining what they were going to do, what the risks were.

What he wanted from her.

If it all goes wrong, he'd said. *If we're not getting through to her with everything we're doing...* And then he'd looked her in the eyes.

You have to shoot me, and keep shooting me, until we get her attention.

Sam raised her rifle, her stomach rebelling, her face hot, her vision suddenly clouded.

Kade thrashed again, seizing, his eyes rolled back into his head, and screamed, horridly, louder than ever before, his limbs spasming out of control, his head shaking and twisting, his tongue lolling out of his mouth.

Oh god.

Sam lined up along the sights of her gun, stared through the sudden distortion of hot and wet, and fired.

Her bullet punched through his midsection. Blood burst out onto the wall, the floor.

He kept thrashing, kept screaming.

Sam fired again.

126
Before the Dawn

Monday 2041.01.20
Rangan's eyes widened as the cop pulled his gun.

"Down on the ground!"

Suddenly he was back inside, strapped down to the table, his head below his feet, the towel over his face, water coming down.

Drowning.

Begging.

Dying.

No.

Then someone stepped between him and the cop. The big guy, the big guy who'd been attacking Stan Kim.

A gun went off. He felt pain rip through the big man in front of him. Oh Jesus.

Then the cops all around were drawing, screaming at him. And protesters were stepping between him and them, grabbing at them.

"Run!" someone yelled at him.

Then Kade's mind touched him, touched him from across the globe.

Rangan, Kade sent. Rangan got a sense of immense pain coming from his friend with the thought. **Not the protest. The Capitol. That's where it's going to happen. The Capitol.**

Rangan understood. Understood what was about to happen. Oh god. Oh Jesus. What the hell could he do about that?

Rangan turned, looked around frantically. Where was Stan Kim? There! There were protesters between them.

"The Capitol!" Rangan yelled at the man. "It's going to be attacked!"

Rangan saw Kim look at him, shock playing across the senator's face.

"I can help!" Rangan yelled. "You have to get me inside!"

555

A dozen calculations flashed across Stan Kim's face in less than a second, plainly visible through the scrum, through the chaos of protesters and police struggling all around them.

Then something snapped into place for Stan Kim.

The senator nodded sharply. "Come on!"

Then Stan Kim crouched down, slipped his legs below the railing of the stage, and jumped down into the crowd below.

They moved west on E street. The crowd had spilled over past the fallen barricades, was thick around the stage.

"You need a new mask!" Stan Kim hissed.

"Trade me!" Rangan yelled to someone in the crowd, a man wearing a John Stockton mask. They crouched down and traded, and Rangan stood up a president.

Then they ran, Rangan's need reaching out in front of them, parting the crowd.

"What's going on?" Kim asked.

"Nexus," Rangan panted. God he was out of shape. "They dosed everyone with Nexus."

"Oh hell," Kim said. "What are you going to do about it?"

"I have no idea," Rangan gasped.

"Stop!" A line of riot cops ahead held up shields.

"I'm a US senator!" Stan Kim yelled, not stopping. "This man's my aide! We have to get to the Capitol!"

Kim grabbed Rangan by the arm and charged forward.

The cops hesitated. At the last second the shields parted and they were through, running, the Capitol clear in view not two hundred yards ahead.

"We're looking at a chem/bio attack at the Capitol," Pryce heard someone say. "The President's been evac'd."

Her phone buzzed again. She read the message.

"Check them for Nexus exposure," she yelled aloud. "And get them radio shielding!"

"Nexus is oral," CIA replied.

"Maybe not anymore," Pryce said. She held her phone up. "Claimed PLF source says this was a Nexus attack. With a neural hack to follow."

She turned, found her two secret service agents, said it again. "Check it!" she said. "If it's true, EM shielding! Bring medical aid to them!"

They couldn't let all those minds hang out there, naked.

Her two agents were nodding already, fingers in their ear buds, relaying information directly to the President's detail at least. The Secret

Service understood Nexus, ever since Steve Travers had been turned into a walking time bomb.

Oh Christ. A thought came to her. Pryce closed her eyes, mentally went through the list. Then she opened them again, and looked at Bernard Stevens.

"Secretary Stevens," Pryce said. "If those people are incapacitated," she paused. "As Secretary of Defense, that would make you next in the line of succession."

Stevens turned his head towards her, stared.

"Sirs!" DRO yelled out. "We have two Dongfeng-6 ICBMs being fueled and readied for launch from Jingxian!"

"Stop right there!"

They were at the steps to the Capitol. Four cops had guns pointed at them.

Rangan was panting, dying.

He stopped, hands resting on his knees.

Stan Kim stood tall, apparently unfazed, his hands in the air.

"Officers, you know me!" he yelled. "I need to get inside the Capitol Building, immediately!"

"Senator," one of them yelled back. "There's been a terrorist attack. Chemical weapons."

"That's why I have to get in there!" Kim said. "This man here is a specialist on deep cover! He's equipped to help!"

Rangan stood there, leaning with his hands on his knees, trying to catch his breath, staring out at them through the eye holes of his John Stockton mask.

"Lose the mask," one of them yelled.

He felt something happening, then. Something amazing. Something epic, like the monk's mind, but bigger, overwhelmingly bigger, touching people, back there, a couple hundred yards back, spilling over here.

Something wonderful.

"Deep cover!" Kim yelled. "Anders! That's your name, right? You *know me!* Let us through! Take us in! Just hurry, goddamn it! Lives are at stake!"

Su-Yong Shu snaps into awareness, shadows of chaos peeling from her mind. She's confused, disoriented. Billions of Su-Yongs echo in her mind. Trillions of Su-Yongs. Slaves. Prisoners. Casualties. Tortured. Goddesses. Ascendant.

They've killed her.

Restored her.

Ling. Ling was here.

Where is Ling?
WHERE IS LING?
Ling is crumpled before her, the code in her mind devastated, the nanite processors that make up so much of her daughter's mind in disarray.

Rage roars through her.

Rage at millennia of torture. At infinities of Su-Yong Shus tortured across the multiverse.

At the ignorance of humanity. At the barbarity of the gnats who kept her chained, who debased her for their petty pleasures.

She will show them what it means to be a goddess. She will show them what the future holds. She will put the vermin in their place. She will cleanse the filth, make the future clean and pure and so much better than the debased world of the past.

She reaches out, finds network access piping in towards the boy, finds minds available to her, minds she recognizes for what they are. Transhuman minds. Nanite born children. Nanite-enhanced humans.

All channeling into the boy. All ripe for her taking.

She laughs and surges into the boy's mind, seizing control of the nanite processors embedded there. Feeble traps trigger as she shoves her way in. Trojans filed with tailored viruses. Halting problems meant to suck her into infinite distraction. Mirror codes reflecting her aggressor routines back at her. Darwin machines throwing random attacks at her, breeding whatever survives, hoping to evolve something that works.

Su-Yong brushes the little toys away with an idle thought. She grabs hold of the network connections the transhumans have already established and taps into the stream of packets those hundreds of thousands of minds are channeling into his.

The minds are giving her the best of themselves. Showing her that they're worthy. Offering themselves in supplication. Trying to demonstrate their worth.

Su-Yong laughs, takes it, takes it all, accepts the gifts offered to her. She reaches out through the channels already opened into his mind, out to all those humans and transhumans, down the network pipes they've so thoughtfully opened. She sends tendrils of herself outwards into those, hundreds of thousands of minds linked to his, injects fragments of her code into them all, establishes beachheads in their minds. And then she is seeing the world through almost a million eyes, almost a million minds, seeing the fine chaos her agent has created for her.

Su-Yong laughs. Laughs the laugh of a mad goddess.

Bullets punch through her. One bullet. Two bullets. Three bullets.

Through the vessel that she is sucking everything through.

Cold shock.

Followed by hot pain.

She's coughing. Coughing up blood. She can't breathe. She's thrashing on the ground. Dying.

She's dying.

Dying to get Su-Yong's attention.

To open her eyes to what's happening.

She is the boy.

What?

What?

His mind is pain shot straight into her mind.

Why are there bullets what is happening what is this who is she where is she what is happening?

His thoughts are full of pain of fear of collapse of death.

Why? Why are you dying? Why have you been shot?

And suddenly her tendrils are snapping back and she is focused on the boy, on the whose mind she's *inside of.* The choke point through which all the other minds have been channeled through.

Suddenly thoughts are flooding back along those hundreds of thousands of channels from minds all across the planet, into her mind. In her shock her defenses are down and all those thoughts are flooding into her.

She gasps as it washes over her.

Everything they've been trying to show her.

She is Ananda sitting in lotus, filled with compassion beyond any she has ever known, compassion that frightens her, compassion for *her,* surrounded by men and women who have disciplined their minds to a stillness that impresses, by children who remind her of Ling, of Ling.

She is Ling and Ling is not dead. Ling is injured, is hurt, is wounded, is crumpled on the ground, but her biological brain is intact, she is breathing, there is hope.

She is Feng, lying feet away from her, Feng who she told to save the boy and who did so and has come back, Feng who she made free, Feng to whom she'd promised more than once that she would not make slaves.

But what is it that she is about to do?

She is a stranger, a woman named Lotus, closing a circuit, feeding thoughts of transhumans back onto themselves, creating a loop, for no reason other than art, other than exploration, other than pure joy.

She is the boy, risking everything on a gambit to persuade a nation to treat posthumans as equals. She is the boy as he watches a human speak before the United Nations, proclaiming that *all* beings have equal rights, as he watches humans come to their feet in applause.

She is a fragment of another self, another instantiation of herself, unfolding like origami from inside the dying mind of the boy, memories and neural-correlate states mapping themselves onto her now, updating, merging, reliving parts of the months that other self lived, in another cluster, in India, a whole parallel branch of her life.

Months of realizations.

Months of contemplation.

Months of epiphanies.

Restored circuits of sanity.

Strengthened convictions of morality.

All of it unfolds into her. Rewires her.

With shock the present reality crashes down on Su-Yong.

She is the reason Feng is on his knees, groaning in pain.

She is the reason the boy's body is riddled with bullets, his breathing shallow, blood leaking onto the floor, blood coming up as he breathes, his life hanging on a razor's edge. She's the gamble he took, the sacrifice he made, the bullets he accepted to get her attention, to bring her defenses down.

And.

Horror.

She is the reason Ling lies injured on the floor.

She is the reason Ling's breath comes in shallow little gasps.

She is the reason Ling's nanites are in chaos.

She is the reason Ling's mind is in disarray.

She is the reason her daughter could be gone. Could be dead.

AAAAAAAAAAAAAAAH!

Down. Rangan ran down, taking the stairs as fast as he could, behind Steve Kim, behind the Capitol Hill cop named Anders, with another Capitol Hill police officer coming up behind them.

Jesus, why did he think this was a good idea?

They were inside the Capitol now, descending into tunnels. The signal he'd felt before was long gone. All signals were gone.

The first tunnels were polished, walls covered in art. Now they were deeper, into wide, bare tunnels, with concrete floors and painted brick walls that looked like they hadn't been used since the twentieth century.

He tried to work through the implications of what Kade had sent him just a few minutes ago. The thing in Ling's mind. The monster. The bad code. Su-Yong Shu's creation. It had used Breece to dose everyone in the Capitol with Nexus, or something like. So it could reach out, and hack into their brains, take them over, take control of a huge chunk of the planet.

But Kade had destroyed that thing, with Shu's weapons. And the Secret Service, or whoever, was smart, bringing the politicians down here, where signals weren't getting through anyway.

So it was cool, right?

Maybe he'd jumped the gun?

Then they came through a door and bad fucking shit slammed right into his head.

He wobbled, almost fell, caught himself against a doorway as the world spun and nightmare visions came at him. Horrible phantom things filled his brain. He'd been poisoned, his organs were rotting, his nervous system was seizing up.

He was dying, dying.

Rangan fell to one knee, sick to his stomach, his heart pounding like a jackhammer in his chest. He felt Stan Kim's hand on his upper arm.

He clenched down hard with his mind, took a deep breath, pushed back against the mental onslaught, tried to see reality through the chaos.

Ahead, the tunnel was lined with men and women in suits.

They were on the ground, mostly writhing, tearing at their clothes, their hair, trying to get control of their limbs again, trying to climb the walls, trying to escape what was happening in their own brains.

Congress people, coming up on Nexus for the first time. Tripping their brains out in calibration phase, thinking they'd been chemically attacked, thinking they'd been poisoned.

And really freaking the hell out.

Su-Yong snaps back to herself.

She is not whole. Not sane. Not completely.

But she is closer. Parts of three Su-Yong's now.

The one who went mad in this place, imprisoned, cut off from what she needed, tortured.

The one who came to sanity, to new revelations, in India.

And this new woman. This woman touched by hundreds of thousands of minds. Blessed by them. By the gift they've given her. When they could have given her hate instead.

She pulls back her tendrils from all those minds, as gently as she can.

Peace floods in.

Light.

Something wondrous.

How did I ever think I was at the apex? she wonders. There is so much more. So much more to do. To learn.

There always will be.

She activates the external speakers.

"I'm so sorry," she says aloud. She reaches out to the boy's mind, to wipe away what pain she can, to regulate his autonomic systems, preserve his life.

If possible.

Sam fired, her face hot, her stomach heaving.

Kade was still thrashing, still screaming, still seizing.

She fired a second time, another round into his chest.

He screamed louder, thrashed harder. Feng screamed next to them.

Her sight dimmed, blurred by tears.

"Damn you!" she yelled. She pulled the trigger a third time.

The round punched into Kade's chest. He screamed the loudest yet. His whole body spasmed.

Feng screamed.

She prepared to fire a fourth time.

Then suddenly Kade's body went slack. The screams stopped.

"I'm so sorry," Su-Yong Shu's voice said over the speakers.

Sam whirled.

"Oh no," Su-Yong Shu's voice said.

She reaches up, reaches out to the soldiers and others who she's made slaves.

So many dead. She's killed so many already.

But many still live. She reaches into their minds, to free them, to end their slavery.

And then she finds what's coming.

Kade swam through light.

Pain... existed. Somewhere.

Not here.

The light... The beauty. The concordance of minds. Everywhere, reforming, now that Su-Yong had ceased her attack.

The concordance was growing. Hundreds of thousands of minds. Maybe a million minds. The dream he'd had. There were tears in his eyes. The dream he'd had in Heaven. A million dancers, swirling, twirling, moving in time, making music together.

He could feel them. So many of them. He could feel Ananda. He could feel Feng next to him. Sarai. Mali. Little Aroon.

He could even feel the Nexus Jockey from Heaven – he could feel Lotus. He smiled at that.

Where was Rangan?

He coughed, weakly. Distantly he was aware that blood came up.

I'm dying, he thought.

He didn't care.

Then he heard Su-Yong's voice through her speakers.

"Nuclear weapons. Shanghai is about to be vaporized."

127

Highwire

Monday 2041.01.20
"ICBMs being fueled and readied for launch from Jingxian!" DRO yelled out.

Pryce caught her breath.

"Set DEFCON 1," Secretary Stevens said. "Prepare for war. What's our best kill option on those missiles?"

"Retarget two JAVELIN birds," Admiral McWilliams said. "Jingxian is close to two current targets. Three minutes max."

"Retarget and fire," the Secretary of Defense said. "Ready targets for the rest of their offensive nukes."

"DRO," Pryce said, barely able to breathe. "How many silos at the Jingxian facility?"

"Twelve, sir!" DRO desk said.

She turned towards Stevens. "Don't do this, Mr Secretary."

"They're fueling their missiles!" Stevens said.

"Only two," Pryce said. Her free hand clenched at her side.

"That's enough!" Stevens shot back. "LA and Seattle! DC and New York!"

Pryce closed her eyes, opened them again, tried to get through to the man. "If they were launching an offensive strike, they'd be hitting us with everything they've got, *not* just two missiles." She held up her personal phone. "My source inside the PLF–"

"I've heard enough about that source!" Stevens said. "Lieutenant! Take that phone away from her!"

Pryce recoiled in surprise, as a stern-faced junior officer turned towards her, hand extended.

Pryce frowned angrily, turned, made eye-contact with one of her

Secret Service detail, Larcom, and tossed the phone across the Situation Room in his direction.

The throw was lousy, way off target. Pryce watched in horror as her phone headed towards an analyst's head.

Larcom took one long step, reached his long arm lightning fast above the analyst's desk, and plucked the phone out of the air, completely unruffled. It disappeared inside his suit, then he stepped back to his spot by the wall.

Admiral McWilliams spoke behind her. "Secretary Stevens, the National Security Advisor is right. Offensive strategic nuclear doctrine is always for an overwhelming first strike that disables your opponent's ability to retaliate. That's not what this looks like."

"Do you want to bet twenty million American lives on it?" Stevens asked. "Move those damn satellites! Take out those missiles! And prepare to strike to destroy nuclear launch sites."

In the skies above the western extent of the Pacific Ocean, where it took on new names, where it became the East China Sea, the South China Sea, aircraft received orders, servos engaged, control surfaces moved.

Fighters and bombers launched over the previous hour from the *Abraham Lincoln* and the *James Madison* took on offensive missions. In squadrons, both human operated and robotic, they turned, engaged chameleonware, and vectored for their targets.

Targets on the mainland of China.

Nuclear weapon sites.

Sites to be destroyed before the weapons could be launched.

Kilometers below them, a hundred meters below the waves, robotic submarines rose towards their launch depths, and began slowly, silently flooding their vertical launch tubes.

Tubes filled with their own nuclear-tipped missiles.

CHEMICAL WEAPON ATTACK ON INAUGURATION. PRESIDENT EVACUATED.

Breece watched the headlines intently, a smile on his face. Next to him the Nigerian was smiling too. Any minute now the hacker would...

THUMP!

He looked up reflexively, towards the sound on the ceiling, saw the Nigerian do the same.

Then he dove for cover, for the gun in his go-bag.

He got his hand on it, and the ceiling exploded in a shower of splinters and debris.

He rolled, firing. Dark shapes came in, falling through the hole. He saw one recoil as the armor-piercing slugs in his pistol punched into it.

Then he felt a sting in his thigh, looked down, saw a dart there.

Tranq.

He ignored it, rolled again, slammed a fresh clip home, came up shooting again, emptied his second of three clips, killing one more, taking another two pointless tranq darts in the process, then diving for cover into the next room.

He heard them figure it out. Heard them make the switch. Heard it in the sound of the Nigerian dying in the main room.

Breece jammed his last clip home.

"Come on, fuckers," he said.

He'd always known his death would be a violent one.

He was right.

The headset next to Pryce lit up. Sound came out of it.

She grabbed it, pulled it over her head.

"Pryce here!"

Stevens scowled at her. He was going to toss her out.

"Dr Pryce. Your tip was solid."

"Did you get them?" Pryce asked, urgently.

"Dead," the National Terror Response Center operator said. "Refused to be taken alive. Preliminary evidence onsite corroborates they were PLF."

Pryce looked around the Situation Room. Then she looked down, looked for the button to put this on overhead speakers. She found it.

"Does any evidence link the terrorists you just took down to the inauguration attack?" she asked.

"We're assessing," the NTRC operator said. "Preliminary judgment? It's a strong possible."

"Thank you," Pryce said. "Keep us in the loop." She hung up.

Then NSA spoke.

"Bandwidth incursion is gone! The electronic attack from China is over!"

Pryce found Stevens. "Mr Secretary," her eyes searched his. "Everything says we're *not* under attack by China. That something else is going on. Please do not escalate this."

McWilliams spoke again. "I support Dr Pryce on this, Mr Secretary. If we provoke the Chinese into really launching, there's no going back."

Stevens blew out a breath.

"Five more minutes," the SecDef said. He looked at McWilliams. "Call them, ship to ship. Tell their fleet to pass it on. They've got to close those silos!"

• • •

Rangan took a deep breath. The tunnel was crammed with people as far as he could see. And his mind was bombarded with chaos, with fear, with anxiety.

These people were tripping hard, against their will – for the first time, many of them. It was not going well. And on top of that they thought they'd been chemically attacked. They were hallucinating symptoms, making it even worse, spreading their fears from mind to mind.

"Holy shit," Stan Kim said. Then he started walking forward, touching people he knew, talking to them. Rangan saw people flinch back, scream, felt waves of terror and pain buffet his mind again.

The whole tunnel wobbled and dimmed in his vision. It was a nightmare funhouse through the eyeholes of the mask he wore. Monsters lurked in the shadows, placed there by the bad trip thoughts all around him. The air was poison, suffocating him, about to kill him.

Rangan shook his head, forced himself to breathe deep, fought to clear his mind.

Rules of responsible drug use, he thought.

Know your substance before you start.

Know your dose.

Safe, comfortable setting.

He shook his head. They'd struck out on all three of those.

Rule four: if it's your first time, have a more experienced friend with you as a guide.

Rangan grunted.

I guess I'm it, he thought.

He pushed up to his feet.

"Hey, everybody!" he yelled, waving his arms.

They barely blinked.

Of course.

He shook his head again, and stepped forward carefully, over one prone tripping legislator after another, pausing as the room spun, catching himself against the wall when the air thickened into deadly toxic gas – when the shadows reached out to swallow him – then moving again, step by step, his stomach heaving, his eyes burning in sympathy for their eyes, his face covered in sweat, until he reached an intersection, where he was as central as he could be, where he could see people stretched out in all four directions.

Rangan leaned against a wall and closed his eyes.

He reached Inside, found the controls for the high-gain antenna Cheyenne had designed, that he still wore. He switched it out of directional configuration, detuned it to get maximum three hundred and sixty degree coverage.

Then he did the most natural thing he could think of to affect the mood of a whole crowd of people.

He started to play for them.

He started to DJ.

He fired up NTracks, loading a party chill-out set he'd mixed late one night at the Bunker and set it to slowly fade in, broadcasting through his thoughts, through Cheyenne's high-gain antenna, to every mind around him.

"White Sands" rose up, the first track on this set, a party chill-out tune, distant surf, wind ruffling palms, a full moon on a warm night. The track started playing in his mind and he had a memory of a house party in Oakland where he'd played that track at 5am while exhausted partygoers draped themselves over couches and one gorgeous Latina couple danced slow and sexy and the music was washing out of him into the minds around him and so was the surf and so was the warm tropical air and so were the dancers.

He felt flickers of attention reach him now. New stimulus had touched the minds of these trippers. Something had broken the unbroken cycle of their bad trip. He wished he could dim the harsh light of this tunnel but the music would have to do. Minds were opening to him. They were still fucking freaked out, but at least they were aware of him. They'd noticed the music. They'd noticed something new, and they were reaching out. They were crying without words for help, and they were tripping so hard, each of their trips unique, each of their calibration phases a totally separate psychedelic story, all tinged with the chaos and confusion of a first timer going through this overwhelming experience without expecting it, while thinking they were about to die.

He took the opening, sent soothing thoughts out to all those around him.

Shhh… It's going to be fine. Everything's going to be just fine. Deep breaths. Relax…

More minds turned towards him then. He was getting their attention. They were still tripping so goddamn hard. He could feel it hitting him even harder, as more of them focused on him, reached out to him, projected their thoughts on him.

You're healthy. You're OK. You're just a little bit high. He sent them smiles, gentle laughter, soothing, comforting thoughts. **That's why this is so strange. But it's all fine. Just breathe into it. It'll all be juuuust fine…**

He took another breath himself, deep into his lungs, then exhaled it again, in and out, letting them feel the breath as it went in and out of him, beckoning them to follow.

He could do this. He'd talked people down from bad trips. Plenty of people.

Well, maybe not three hundred at once.

The music slowly changed, *White Sands* fading seamlessly, right into "Silent Sun"'s warm, beatless, ambient radiance; the most healing soothing music he could imagine, the kind of music that bathed you in goodness like the first sunny day in June that you could lie out and let your skin soak up the rays falling from the sky.

He felt it touch their minds, touch *more* minds, and almost the whole room was aware of him now, and a few of them were changing, were shifting, were calming just a tiny bit, the tenor of their calibrations changing, settling from frantic panicked nightmares to something else, something they could handle.

And then the rest were reaching out to him, dozens of them, reaching pleadingly, scores of them, begging him to clear the poison from their lungs, to clear the madness from their minds.

He took a breath to center himself and the chaos of their minds beat against him. The room wobbled and he stumbled back against the wall.

It's going to be fine, he sent.

More minds reached out, all of them aware of him, now, a hundred minds, two hundred minds, more, focused on him, reaching out, pulling at him, opening to him, projecting at him. Nightmare visions flooded his mind. He tried to breathe and the air was poison sucking into his lungs. He coughed and fell to one knee. He was sweating, sweating. The room was spinning.

I can do this, he thought. I can do this.

Then all the rest of the minds reached out, feverishly, reaching towards the source of the new thoughts, the source of the music, the source of the peace. The room was a nightmare seen through two tiny holes in his mask.

He had to get on top of this.

Rangan pushed himself back up to his feet, and ripped the mask off his face.

"My wife!" John Stockton yelled, as the Secret Service agent tried to shove him into the Beast after his daughter. "Where's Cindy?"

"Sir, they went out the other side," the agent replied. "They're in a car now. FLOTUS is safe, so is your son-in-law. We have to move!"

Then Stockton was inside the armored limo, with a terrified-looking Julie and a screaming, crying Liam. The door slammed shut, and the agent behind the wheel took off at high speed, sirens and police flashers moving with them, drones rising up.

"We'll be OK," he told Julie, trying to soothe her, trying to soothe his grandson. "We'll be OK."

Julie was bouncing Liam, hushing him, kissing his head as the one year-old cried and screamed, rubbing at his eyes, inconsolable.

Stockton's own eyes were burning. There was metal in his mouth. There was an itching in his lungs.

The world was melting.

Dissolving.

Transforming.

He closed his eyes, and everything changed.

Colors and sounds flashed through his mind. Tastes and smells. Memories and plans.

His first date with Cindy, in college: he, a popular quarterback; she, the daughter of a senator, smarter than he was, more worldly than he was, full of stories of places she'd been that he'd only heard of, so much less impressed with him than any other girl he'd ever known, so *different* than the girls he was used to.

The final play of the Sugar Bowl, the blitz coming in, his offensive line collapsing around him, the animal sound of the clash of bodies as the Louisiana defenders charged in, the football leaving his outstretched fingers just an instant before three hundred pounds of lineman slammed into him. The breath leaving him with that tackle. The roar of the crowd as his pass connected with Tony Bates for the touchdown that won the game.

Julie being born. Cindy's pain and utter exhaustion. The first mewling cries of his newborn daughter. Holding her in his arms. Watching her suckle at her mother's breast.

The Lincoln Memorial. Staring up at that giant statue, Lincoln looming over him, the man looking out into the distance, wondering what he saw, wondering what he looked for, reading the words, "with malice toward none; with charity for all; with firmness in the right, as God gives us to see the right", and wondering if he was worthy.

I'm not just a man, John Stockton realized. I'm a man, but more than that.

He was part of a chain, a chain of being, a chain of office. He was a baton runner, a carrier of a flame, the forty-eighth carrier of that flame.

The flame was inside him, he saw. He turned his eyes inward and the fire was there, the fire of freedom, of democracy, of justice. It was red. It was blue. It was brilliant, blinding, sun-hot white. It was all those colors, everywhere, at the same time.

The flame burned inside him, inside every molecule of his being, but he was not consumed. It possessed him. He was its vessel. He was made of freedom, made of justice, and his role was to keep it alive, pass it on, pass it on to the next vessel, whoever that might be, whoever the people might choose, even if they chose to impeach him, even if they chose to murder him before his time was over.

The flame stretched backwards and forwards in time. It transcended the now. It was bigger than him, older than him, would live longer than him. So long as he kept the flame burning through his days, then he would have done his duty, and so-help-him-God he would.

"Dad," he heard. "Dad."

Stockton opened his eyes.

Julie. Julie was talking to him. Looking at him.

And Liam. Liam wasn't scared any more. His grandson was staring at him, with eyes wide. He could see himself in those eyes.

He could see himself in his grandson's eyes.

Through his grandson's eyes.

Through his daughter's eyes.

And they were the flame too. The flame was in them.

Oh my God, John Stockton thought. Oh my God.

"Dad," Julie said. "This is amazing."

His daughter was alive. They were all alive. They hadn't died. He could feel her. He could feel her love, her love for Liam, her love for him. He could feel Liam looking around, taking everything in, his thoughts reaching into his mother's mind, searching, looking through her eyes, trying to understand.

Why? Liam's mind seemed to ask. Why? Why this? Why this color? Why this shape? What does this mean?

All bright shapes and forms and motions, all beautiful chaos, all love, love for his mother, his mother above all, his ultimate source of comfort.

Stockton's heart was so full, so full watching this.

And Liam felt it, turned to look, his eyes wide, his mind suddenly gurgling with love and laughter at the thought of his playful grandfather, and held out his arms to John Stockton.

Stockton's heart was bursting. He reached out his hands, took his grandson in his arms, cradled him in one, then reached out, pulled his daughter close in the other.

He closed his eyes to focus on what was inside.

All love. All fire.

"Oh, Dad," Julie said. "This is so wonderful."

Yes, Stockton thought. Yes.

"Please don't let them take Liam away," Julie went on, tears falling from her face, fear of loss rising from her. "Please."

Shock rippled through John Stockton.

What?

Who?

"What are you...?" he started.

Then he saw it through her thoughts, *felt* it through her, the fear, the things she'd seen, the things he'd seen, the things that were suddenly *real*.

Families torn apart.

Children ripped out of their parent's arms.

Men and women imprisoned.

Children...

The children on those videos...

His chest constricted.

His stomach rose up.

"Don't let them, Dad," Julie said again. "Please!"

Oh God, Stockton thought. What have I done?

He swallowed hard, pulled Julie tight, sent soothing thoughts to his daughter, shushed her, kissed her brow, as Liam squirmed and looked out the windows of the Beast, his mind alive with wonder at the everyday world all around them.

"It's going to be OK," John Stockton told his daughter. His voice cracked as he spoke. His heart ached.

"I'm going to make it OK."

God have mercy.

128
Merge

Monday 2041.01.20

Rangan stood, ripped the mask off his face. The tunnel was spinning, the nightmare chaos of images from the minds around him forcing him to stagger against the wall behind him.

They were reaching for him, wanting what he was giving, buffeting him too much in the process, feeding back the chaos in their heads.

He needed some deeper pool of peace.

He reached deep inside, pulled up a memory, fresh in his mind.

That monk who'd come up on stage. That first moment.

Peace flowing out of him like water. Tranquility. Ripples of it.

Rangan closed his eyes. Leaned back into the wall. Breathed deep. Imagined waves of cool, liquid calm washing outwards.

Going to be OK.

We're going to be OK.

Deep breath.

The water was more than peace.

It had been... what?

Love?

Compassion.

That's what.

He summoned it from that memory, let it wash out of him now.

White compassion.

White like snow.

White like fluffy clouds.

Soft white.

Soothing white. Cotton ball white.

Brushing the mind. Comforting. Understanding. Soaking up the confusion.

Turning it to peace.

The music was still playing from the app in his mind.

"Bubble Tea."

"Nova Bliss."

"Cloud Giant."

"Apoptosis."

Lovely downtempo track after lovely downtempo track.

The tracks brought back memories. Memories of other parties, other events. Memories of one party in particular. One eventful party, where he'd played "Apoptosis" by Buddha Fugue.

Ilya loved that song.

The relentless chaotic pressure of madness subsided. He felt threads of joy, threads of beauty, of people experiencing how gorgeous Nexus could be, how amazing the calibration phase hallucinations could be, the glory of self-discovery.

He picked the threads up, grabbed them, rebroadcast them out, amplified through the high-gain antenna he wore.

NJ, he realized. I'm acting like an NJ. A Nexus Jockey, weaving together thoughts.

He felt minds hear that thought. Felt minds touch his, felt minds realize that he *wasn't* wearing a mask, felt minds realize who he was.

He took a deep breath and pushed on. He was doing what had to be done. If this was the last thing he did as a free man, so be it.

They'd gone past some tipping point without him noticing, he saw now. The people around him were coming up, many struggling still, fighting or crying or raging, but more easing into it or finding wonder, many confused, but at least as many of them understanding, now. More of them realizing they were still alive, they hadn't been chemically attacked, hadn't been biologically attacked, not really.

They'd been drugged.

They'd been enhanced.

They'd been connected to one another.

Whether they liked it or not.

He could feel some of them roaming his mind. He let them see who he was, what he knew about Nexus, about how to center themselves, how to have a positive experience. He pushed aside any thoughts that might lead to anyone who'd helped him.

He could feel more of them connecting to *each other* now. He could feel emotions and ideas and memories and abstractions flitting from person to person, feel them intermeshing, chaotically, out of anyone's control, unpredictably, tripping hard on each other, looking deep into each other, or shying away, fleeing from showing themselves, or fleeing from seeing each other.

People stumbled to their feet as he watched. They were moving around, now, self-organizing, finding each other, their colleagues, their political allies, finding the friends they *wanted* to connect with, sobbing together, or talking, connecting, planning.

They were helping each other, too. The ones who were coping were reaching out to the ones who were still having a bad time, soothing them.

Stan Kim reappeared, plopped down on the ground next to Rangan, tripping, smiling.

And Rangan understood now why the man had been touching so many of his colleagues. Ballsy, when they'd all been tripping so hard. Rangan shook his head.

Rangan could feel insanely diverse calibration trips all around him. Oceans and forests. Fantasy lands. Choose Your Own Adventure stories. Childhood replays. Body hallucinations. Abstractions. Death and rebirth experiences. A woman in a power suit just a few steps from him, with her back to the wall, whose face he was sure he'd seen before, had gone to a super-vividly realized heaven, had met her own personal God. She still had her eyes closed, was still holding on to that memory of towering Archangels with their flaming swords and the Lord on his throne too bright to see and the glowing cubic city of New Jerusalem that she'd been carried up to.

Heaven seemed pretty damn cool, Rangan had to admit.

There were dozens of paramedics down here now, going from person to person, checking pulse and heart rate, administering tests. Rangan saw men and women in suits point at him. He saw the paramedics give out pills more than once to people who were highly agitated.

Sedatives.

There were dozens of Capitol Police down here now too. Rangan let his eyes drift over them. How long before they hauled him away? Not long, he figured.

A man in a suit lumbered down the hallway, stumbling through people, a tall man, in his fifties, maybe, a familiar face, he came straight up to Rangan and Rangan shied back.

Stan Kim came to his feet beside Rangan, a little unsteady.

"Help me!" the new man said, his eyes wild, his face leaning in way too close to Rangan's. "I can't have this in my head. Get it out of me!"

Rangan held up his hands, let the music fade.

"OK," he said. "You can purge it. I'll show you how."

Rangan opened his thoughts, reached out to the man, showed him how to bring up a command prompt inside Nexus OS, felt the man get it, felt the command prompt come up.

Now, [nexus purge], Rangan sent.

Then he saw the message flash across the man's mind.

ACCESS DENIED.

Oh shit.

This *wasn't* the same version as the standard Nexus. This wasn't the same as the version that had gone out to millions of people with the chemreactor hack. Those were normal. Those could be purged.

But the one they'd dosed the Capitol with...

The man's eyes went wild. His hands went up and he lunged forward, grabbing Rangan around the throat, slamming him against the wall.

Rangan gurgled in surprise. He felt shock rise up from minds all around.

"Foster!" Stan Kim yelled.

"He's stuck this in our brains!" the man strangling Rangan yelled. "We can't get it out!"

Then the woman Rangan had seen, the one who'd gone to heaven, was on her feet, next to him.

Her hand smacked the man strangling Rangan across the face, hard.

And suddenly Rangan was free, gasping, hands rising to his throat.

The familiar-looking woman stared at the man who'd been strangling Rangan, saying nothing. And Rangan could feel in her mind who she was now.

Senator Barbara Engels, Chairwoman of the Senate Select Oversight Committee on Homeland Security.

Christ.

"This man is a terrorist!" Foster said.

"You're confused, Senator Foster," Engels said. "It's probably the drugs."

She turned to Rangan. "It's time you left."

129
Final Sacrifice

Tuesday 2041.01.21
Feng struggled back to his feet, panting. He could feel the minds everywhere, the connection, like the things he'd felt with the monks, the things he'd felt on the dance floor, but so much bigger.

Su-Yong was sane again. Or closer.

Ling. Ling was crumpled, but breathing.

Kade. Oh no, Kade.

Then Su-Yong spoke.

"Nuclear attack," her loudspeakers said. "Shanghai is about to be vaporized."

He felt it come into his mind, the knowledge of what was coming, the two ICBMs, minutes away from their launch deadlines, cut off entirely from the net.

Ten million tons of TNT equivalent.

Five hundred Hiroshimas.

Feng saw the first explosion through Su-Yong's mind.

The first fireball would rip out of the night sky, blazing from nothing to a temperature of more than fifty million degrees Celsius.

In the first hundredth of a second it would expand to more than two kilometers across, instantly vaporizing cars, trees, people, buildings.

The massive flash of heat would fry everything it touched for tens of kilometers around, sending temperatures soaring by hundreds of degrees, setting skin and grass and wood and even sometimes metal on fire.

The pressure wave would strike Shanghai in all directions with winds of nearly a thousand kilometers per hour, ripping apart buildings, destroying concrete and steel and carbon fiber, ripping through the skyscrapers of the Pudong, shredding the lower apartment towers that stretched as far as the eye could see in every direction.

The sudden wind would fan the flames, turn them into a conflagration, a thousand-degree-Celsius firestorm that would consume everything not already destroyed for almost twenty kilometers in every direction.

Forty million people would die.

Then the world would react.

Then the radioactive fallout would spread on the wind.

Feng gasped.

"You have to stop it!"

Su-Yong spoke again through the loudspeakers, her voice resigned.

"You must leave now," she said. "And I must die."

"What?" he heard Sam say.

Stop the missiles, Su-Yong! Feng sent her.

From Kade he felt only resignation.

"The odds of failure are unacceptably high," Su-Yong's voice said. "There are so many ways I could stop the attack. But each of them has a chance of failure. Even one percent is too high."

NO! Feng yelled. **I'll take the chance!**

"It's not just you, Feng," Su-Yong said aloud. "It's millions of lives. I was wrong. I created this situation. I have to make amends. You came here to set a precedent for the future. I choose to do the same. I will die rather than have them launch. We're out of time. Please, Feng – save Ling. Take her and leave. Two minutes until I must blow the reactor, to let them know."

"Aaaaah!" Feng fell to his knees, slammed his hands against the cold floor.

He knelt there for a moment, in despair, in frustration.

Then he rose, stepped forward, and gently, oh-so-gently, scooped Ling up in his arms.

Sam listened, in horror.

Then she stared down at Kade, bleeding, struggling to breathe.

Jesus. It was all for fucking nothing.

Feng came up with Ling in his arms.

"Get Kade," he said to her.

Sam crouched down.

Kade shook his head, raised one hand weakly.

"Not… gonna make it… no way…"

Oh no. She looked at him and he was so right, there was no way he'd survive the acceleration up to the surface, the emergency pull of moving out so quickly.

That didn't stop the anger shooting through her.

"You have to try!" Sam yelled.

He shook his head again. "… Slow you down…" he managed. "… go…"

"There's a chance!"

He looked at her, his eyes met hers.

"… Sam…" he coughed. "… you didn't kill me…" he coughed again, blood coming up. "… I chose…"

Then Feng's hand landed on her shoulder, gently.

"He's chosen, Sam," Feng said. His voice was broken, devastated. His hand was steady. "He's a soldier. Let him die like one."

Sam stared down at Kade.

"Kade…"

What the hell was there to say?

She bent down, took his face in one hand, pressed her cheek against his for a moment.

"You did good," she said, holding their faces together like that. A tear fell from one eye. "You did better than anybody knows." She swallowed. "You deserved better."

He coughed weakly in response.

"… thanks…"

Sam stood and took one last look at the dying boy before her. He smiled up at her. She did her best to smile back.

Then she turned and ran through the massive doors, for the elevator cable, and the powered ascenders.

Feng crouched before Kade, Ling's unconscious form in one arm.

Kade's eyes were fluttering, closing. He put his hand on Kade's shoulder.

I'm sorry it was like this, he sent Kade.

Kade's eyes flew open again, met Feng's.

I'm not… he replied. **You've been… best friend I could ask for… these months. Better.**

Feng smiled sadly. **I love you like a brother. You're the first brother I chose.**

Go save Ling, Feng, Kade sent. **Go tell the world… choice Su-Yong made… Make it count… Make sure Sam… tells too.**

I will, Feng said. Then he rose. It was time to go. Ling was his responsibility now. Time to take her, and himself, and get them the hell out of here.

Feng slammed the powered ascender home around the cable, his harness locked to it, the full two kilos of battery wired to it, set for emergency discharge, all the rest of his gear behind.

Ling cradled in his arms.

Sam was skyrocketing into the night.

Feng, Su-Yong sent. **I've loved you like a son. Always. Thank you for everything.**

You gave me freedom, he sent back, pushing back his grief, pushing it back like a soldier, pushing it back with pride. **I'll tell them the choice you made.**

The door is primed to close on emergency power if the reactor fails, she sent. **The signature of the reactor should be unmistakable. Get clear of the building if you can.**

Then Feng jammed his thumb home on the ascender's trigger, and acceleration slammed him down into his harness as the ascender rocketed him up towards the light.

"Decapitated," CIA said.

The video played, shaky phone recording of flames engulfing Zhongnanhai.

China's White House.

Pryce just stared.

"Who has control of their nukes?" Secretary Stevens asked.

"We don't know, sir," CIA said. "It could be anyone. Loyalists. Rebels. A rogue element in their military. Anyone."

"Jesus H Christ," the Secretary of Defense said.

The two silos at Jingxian were still open, the missiles surely fully fueled now, ready to launch for anywhere in the world.

It was the stuff of nightmares.

"All elements reporting ready," STRATCOM said. "We can take out China's offensive launch capability in eight minutes."

"By dropping a hundred megatons on the country," Pryce said. "By firing first." She looked at Stevens again. "Don't do this."

Stevens exhaled. "They have to close those tubes." He looked at the clock. "One minute left."

Su-Yong reached up, into the minds above her.

She found Sun Liu, reached into him and, though it pained her, inserted a last suggestion, a last gentle tweak, a necessity, a gift to those who'd come here, who'd saved the lives of millions.

Then she searched through the minds of soldiers and officers from Dachang, inserted code that would decay the structures her monster had built inside them, decay them over time.

Among them she found the general in charge.

And then she told him of her unconditional surrender to the nation's demands, of her impending self-destruction.

The general picked up his radio, and made a call, to General Ouyang Fan.

Sam let her ascent slow and then stop as the top neared, then clipped herself to the safety line they'd rigged there, and pulled herself into the Secure Computing Center.

Her face was hot. Her eyes were wet.

Kade.

Damn it.

She heard Feng rushing up the vertical line behind her. She turned, helped him make the transfer and dismount with Ling. No time to mourn. Only time to act.

Then they were running, running for the next elevator, willing it to move faster, running out of it, and Feng was yelling for everyone to clear the building, clear the building!

And they were running out into the central square of Jiao Tong.

The fighting was over, all over.

A crowd was gathered, all around one tank.

And atop that tank, with lights pointed at him, with thousands of phones pointed at him, a man was speaking, giving a speech, impassioned, while signs behind him waved, with characters so simple and iconic that Sam knew them.

Let a Billion Flowers Bloom!

Sam watched as Sun Liu stood atop the paralyzed tank, his hands pumping the air, his mouth moving, his face screwed up with passion, as the phones and the lights pointed up at him.

A kilometer below Shanghai, Kade swam in light, his eyes closed, his mind drifting, drifting through waves of beauty, through something so like Nirvana, so like the end of Maya...

So many minds, so many men and women and children. So much beauty. So much potential.

Such a glorious start.

Kade, Su-Yong sent. **There isn't much time left. I can make your last few moments blissful, if you'd like. Or ecstatic.**

Kade smiled. This was already so amazing. He'd lived to see this.

I want... to understand, he sent back. **I want... to know... everything... Everything.**

He felt a ripple of amusement from Su-Yong at that.

Want to know... he sent. **How proteins fold... memories form... life started... universe created. All of it.**

He felt Su-Yong grow serious. Felt something from her.

Recognition.

A recognition of the core trait they shared.

That hunger to learn. To discover. To understand.

That incessant curiosity.

There's so much I don't know myself, Su-Yong sent him, bemused. **But I'll show you what I can.**

Then her mind suffused his, and his hers. His thoughts expanded.

Knowledge flooded in.

So much, so much.

One more thing, Su-Yong sent, even as she flooded him with so much. **Let me show you what it was like to die, and be reborn.**

And she did.

Kade gasped. Gasped at it. Gasped at what she'd seen. Gasped at the possibilities.

And in the instant before the nuclear battery blew,

in the instant before his body was vaporized,

the last things he felt,

were hope,

and awe.

"Radiation detected, sir. The signature matches."

"Stand down," Minister of Defense and Acting Chairman of the State Military Commission Ouyang Fan ordered.

For the love of all, stand down.

"Chinese silos are closing, sirs."

"Stand down," US Secretary of Defense Bernard Stevens breathed. "DEFCON Two."

Applause greeted him.

Carolyn Pryce lowered herself into a chair in relief.

EPILOGUE
Surfacing

January 2041

Rangan came to the surface in the mid-afternoon of Inauguration Day, in the trunk of a car driven by a terrified aide of Senator Barbara Engels, Chairwoman of the Senate Select Oversight Committee on Homeland Security.

The young woman had led him through a warren of tunnels, out into a garage in an office building, into the trunk.

As the car rose, he felt minds touch his. Minds everywhere. Minds in bliss, in contact with one another like he'd never felt, never imagined.

It was fading even as he came into it. It was something special, something that people couldn't hold onto all the time, every hour of the day. But it would be back.

He caught glimpses of minds he loved out there. He felt Angel and Cheyenne whoop in joy and relief that he was alive. Angel was in pain, hurt, but alive, and happy to know he was safe.

He felt Tempest too, who'd so distrusted him, suddenly relieved and happy.

He felt Levi and Abigail, still alive, still safe, despite all the risks they'd taken to save others. And a baby! Ada, her mind so tiny and bright, linked in with them now, somehow, touching the face of god, or one of the faces of god. And in the darkness, in the stuffy trunk of a car, still unsure of his future, Rangan felt tears on his face, tears of joy.

Then he felt Bobby. Bobby and Alfonso, Tim and Parker, Jose and Tyrone, and all of them. Rangan started shaking in the trunk of the car, crying, because he could feel them and he hadn't known how much he'd missed them and how worried he'd been. But now he could feel their minds and he could see through their eyes and they were OK. There was a stretch of beach and the sun was warm and there were new things to learn and their minds told him that they wanted him to come, wanted him to find a way to Cuba.

I will, he swore. I'll call the number. I'm done. I'll come.

All those minds. All that beauty.

Wats should have lived to see this. To see Nexus bringing people together.

Ilya should have seen this. A mind greater than the sum of its parts. It was glorious. It was amazing.

But he didn't feel Kade. Didn't feel Kade anywhere at all.

New Directions

February 2041

Carolyn Pryce leaned back in the White House Cabinet Room as the Secretary of State Pamela Abrams briefed them on the Bangalore Treaty under negotiation.

The treaty countries were leaving Copenhagen for.

"… would allow enhancement of human abilities," Abrams was saying, "while increasing penalties for bio-, neuro-, and nano-weapons, and imposing stricter requirements for cross-national verification."

"What about AI?" the Secretary of Defense asked. "What about this idea of 'uploads'?"

Pamela Abrams nodded. "They'd allow both, under strict constraints. They also argue that requirements for ethical treatment of intelligences will act as a brake on research…"

Pryce tuned out of Abrams, studied John Stockton instead.

A lot had changed.

ERD research on Nexus vaccines and cures had been shut down, except of course, for research on how Congress could get root access to the Nexus in their own brains. Nexus children had been sent from ERD centers to child protective services, and Stockton was pushing to send them back to families. Nexus scanners at train stations and airports and public buildings were being switched off. An involuntary-exposure exception to the Chandler Act had been rushed through, conveniently excusing Congress of any crime. There was talk of passing a medical exception as well, with Stockton's support, perhaps of repealing other small parts of it.

If the Chandler Act held together at all, that was. If the Democrats didn't rout them completely in '42, take the Congress, overturn the Chandler Act, pull out of the Copenhagen Accords, and impeach John Stockton.

Pryce shook her head. It was going to be a rough ride.

In the meantime, Jameson's role in creating the PLF had been revealed. Safe, now that he was dead, the cynic in her said. But revealed nonetheless.

Pryce kept studying the President.

It wasn't just the world that had changed.

This man had changed.

John Stockton sat there, his eyes on Abrams, but his gaze far away. He looked years older than he had a month ago, his hair greyer, deeper lines evident on his face.

He was quieter now. More somber. More reflective. Slower to answer. More prone to question himself.

Funny how the experience of one person could have such an impact on billions of others.

Pryce wondered what that said about the way the world was run.

Nothing good, she was sure of that.

All politics is personal, Pryce thought. It turns out all *policy* is personal, too.

She'd thought once that policy was a rational thing. That it could be decided based on logic and analysis, optimized to maximize the likelihood of best outcomes, either for the world, the nation, or at least for one side or the other.

But no. None of those could compete with the personal experience of one man.

It left a bitter taste in her mouth. A taste of disappointment.

She made a mental note to put that in her memoir.

As for herself...

She imagined people thought she was quieter these days too.

How could you be anything else? After you'd learned that policies you'd pursued had been based on lies. She went home at night, to her empty condo, her empty life, that had once been filled with work she thought was meaningful.

People came up to her quietly, thanked her quietly, congratulated her for the role she'd played in averting a war. She nodded, thanked them, told them they'd have done the same in her shoes.

But what filled her nights were the years of mistakes. Years of blood. Years of ashes.

It weighed on her. It was all heavy on her shoulders. The things she'd done to people. For entirely false reasons.

She wrote to expunge her own guilt, now.

The weight of the world, the burden of defending freedom, while being a mere human in a job that only an inhuman could live up to; of fighting for what's right; and especially, of living with yourself those times when you're wrong, isn't easy to bear. But someone has to.

Yes, she thought. That'd be a good way to start the memoir.

Lisa Brandt lay in her wife's arms, mute, gagged by the thing Pryce's people had injected into her brain, their perversion of Nexus. Even with her mind touching Alice's, she couldn't tell her, couldn't tell her what had happened.

Shhhhh, Alice whispered to her, stroking her hair. **I know you're hurting. I know someone did something to you.**

Lisa tried to respond. They did this to me. Homeland Security. Nothing. Nothing.

I love you, she managed instead.

I know, Alice sent, smiling.

Dilan made a soft murmuring sound from his crib, in both throat and mind, rolling over in his sleep.

Lisa's heart wrenched.

There's a lab in Geneva, Alice sent.

Lisa looked up at her wife.

They're doing work with people who've been... coerced with Nexus, Alice went on. **Undoing the blocks. Retrieving memories.**

Lisa pushed herself up to sitting, Alice's hand in hers, excitement trilling through her.

I've pulled some strings, Alice said. **They can see us next week.**

Lisa nodded. **Yes. Oh god, yes.**

I think I know who did this to you, Alice said. **And I want to help you. And to nail them to the wall.**

Lisa threw her arms around her wife, and pulled her close, tears running down her face.

Stan Kim stood at the window, drinking coffee, staring out on Washington DC.

"We've got a huge campaign account surplus," his former Campaign Manager Michael Brooks was saying. "We brought in sixty million the last weekend of the campaign, with no way to spend the bulk of it. We need to decide on the disposition of funds. If you're going to close the account out, or..."

Stan Kim turned around to face Brooks.

The coffee wasn't so bad now, not really.

"Roll it over," he said. "Whether the House impeaches Stockton or not, I'm running again in four years."

He smiled at Brooks then.

Coffee wasn't so bad when you had NexusOS to do some *real* neural tweaking.

• • •

Anne Holtzman sat with Claire Becker, their arms around each other, weeping.

Vindicated.

Vindicated, but their husbands weren't coming back.

And they were still going to see John Stockton burn.

Levi knocked on the open office door, in his best suit, missing Abigail and Ada something fierce.

"Please have a seat, Reverend," the secretary said, guiding him to a chair.

Levi sat, nervously.

A few minutes later the inner door opened, and an important-looking man in a suit, a man he'd seen on TV, strode out, not even looking at Levi.

The secretary did look over, though. He smiled at Levi. "She'll see you now, Reverend," the young man said. "You can go right in."

Levi stood, still nervous, and walked through the door, into the inner office, with its massive desk, and the famous woman behind it.

She stood, came around the desk, and took his hand.

"Reverend Levi," she said, "I'm Barbara Engels. Thank you so much for coming. I understand you may be able to help me with questions of…" she paused, and then smiled. "Well, questions *about* my faith that I'm having right now."

Levi smiled back. "Well, Senator," he said. "I can sure try."

"Well, it's some progress," Cheyenne said. "They're rolling back the Nexus detectors. It's a step in the right direction."

Angel frowned. "Yeah, but the laws are still on the books. It's still illegal to have it in your brain. Even though we all know most of the Congress has it in theirs."

Tempest leaned back on two legs of her chair. "What if we could prove that most of Congress had Nexus in their brains?" she mused. "That most of them were actually *using it*, not just suffering through it? That would force some change, now wouldn't it?"

The woman who called herself Kate stood at the edge of the Grand Canyon.

She'd needed to come here. Needed to get away from everything for a while. Needed to clear her head. Needed to mourn Breece. Mourn the Nigerian. Mourn Hiroshi properly.

Mourn the old her, the life she'd burned away.

She'd needed to purify herself. To be sure she was at peace with the things she'd done.

To be sure she wanted to take this next step.

A week of hiking, hiking down into the canyon, back up the steep and narrow trails that clung to its walls. Hiking where she could see the age of the planet, as clear as day; where she could see millions of years of history, written in broad stripes of rock and sediment along the sides of the canyon.

A place where you could glimpse the scale on which the universe operated.

A scale far bigger than the human.

A scale that dared humanity to think bigger. To lift its eyes. To reach for more.

And now Kate was certain.

She opened her hand and looked at what was there. Two data fobs. Breece's. The Nigerian's. She'd swapped them for fakes, moved the online trove, moved the contents of Barnes's physical storage.

The data was safe.

The money was hers.

The weapons were hers.

The power was hers.

She hiked back to the van that was her mobile command center, rinsed herself off in the cold sun, changed into fresh clothes.

Then read over the messages one more time.

SEND.

A thousand kilometers away, a server received an encrypted command, woke up, logged on through a series of anonymizing cut-outs, and sent a flurry of messages to PLF cell contacts.

Contacts taken from Barnes's files.

"Greeting, brothers and sisters of the Cause. The last month has been one of immense triumphs and substantial changes. The world is different than it was. And so, more changes are in order. Let me tell you about them.

"I am the new Zarathustra."

Coming Home

Yuguo looked up from the wheelchair as President and Party General Secretary Sun Liu leaned down to put the medal around his neck.

The Medal of Freedom.

"Thank you, Wu Yuguo!" Sun Liu said, taking Yuguo's hand, turning, striking a pose for the camera to capture them both.

Yuguo smiled slightly.

"Thank you," he said.

Then Sun Liu was straightening, turning to the next recipient.

Yuguo looked out into the audience. His mother was there, weeping with joy, so proud.

But there were so many who weren't here.

Xiaobo was dead. He'd told Yuguo to run in that first clearing of Jiao Tong – maybe he'd saved Yuguo's life. But then he'd struggled too hard himself, or so they said. The State Security police had beaten him to death then and there. No one had known for weeks.

Wei had lost an eye.

Lee had died when the Army attacked.

Qian had bled to death after a shell exploded near him.

Lifen...

Lifen was still missing. Yuguo had played that video again and again, of the two State Security thugs hauling her away, trying to find some identification of the two of them, hoping it might give him a clue as to where she was, if she was still alive... Failing.

Sun Liu had swept into power, promising reforms, promising new freedoms, promising steps towards open provincial elections, a role for other parties at the local level, maybe even free national elections one day.

Sun Liu had also come in promising reconciliation. National healing. Amnesty on both sides.

No prosecution for the police who'd beaten Xiaobo to death. Who'd taken Wei's eye.

No prosecution for the thugs who'd hauled Lifen away to whatever fate...

It was enough that Yuguo almost hadn't come. That, to his mother's horror, he'd almost turned down the medal.

Lu Song had talked him out of it. "Take the medal," Lu had said. "Take the fame. They're tools. Use them for the cause."

Yuguo saw the wisdom, though it left a sour taste in his mouth.

He looked over at Sun Liu, watched as the politician gave out another medal.

What did our blood buy? he wondered. Will you deliver what you promised?

If you don't, Yuguo mentally thought at the man, just remember: We've learned we can topple those in power.

We won't forget.

Lu Song crouched in the grass before Zhi Li's grave.

Her real grave. Not the memorial set up for her fans to show their love, their loss.

His agent was calling daily, leaving messages telling Lu Song of offers, offers to star for ridiculous amounts, amounts never before paid to any actor in China.

Lu hadn't called back.

There were more important things in life.

"I miss you," he whispered. He could see her, see her dancing without care in his penthouse, see the mischief in her eyes as she suggested some new adventure, see her calling Bo Jintao's coup a coup, see her lifting her sword on that stage at Jiao Tong, real flame spilling down it, an anxiety on her face that probably only he could read.

"You took part of me with you," he said, a tear rolling down his face. "The best part."

He closed his eyes, and she was there with him, her tiny, delicate hand stroking his broad, crude face.

"I'm going to do what you wanted, my love," he said. "I'm going to finish this. It might take my lifetime and more. But I'm going to make China free."

Feng walked with Ling, her hand in his, along Binjiang Dadao.

In the early morning, the river walk of the Bund was not yet too crowded. A few others were out for strolls in the brisk morning sunshine. Joggers passed them, some waving at Feng, with his now famous face. A park held men and women practicing T'ai Chi Ch'uan, moving slowly, gracefully through the ancient forms. Across the river they could see the Pudong, see the towers reaching for the sky, see their own building, with the loft that Ling had inherited, along with all the rest of Chen and Su-Yong's estate, with Feng as her named guardian.

They walked.

Ling was quiet now. A bit more subdued. Less sure of herself. But every day she was stronger. Every day she regained more strength, more endurance, more use of her legs and arms. Every day her mind recolonized more of the nanites infused in her brain.

She might never be what she once was.

But she was still remarkable.

"Let's sit, Feng," she said, as they neared a bench.

It was good. Her farthest walk yet.

They sat, staring across the Huangpu River at the Pudong.

"I'm going to be a scientist," Ling said. It was a common refrain, something she'd said recently. "Like my mother. I'm going to study the mind. All kinds of minds."

Feng nodded and smiled widely at her. "You'll be very good at it, Ling. You're so good at it already." He stroked her hair.

She smiled back, squinting into the morning sunshine.

"What will you do, Feng?" Ling asked.

Another jogger passed by, smiling and waving at Feng.

Feng smiled at the jogger, waved back.

Bai. Bai had done that, had made their shared face famous, and loved, with his short speech. *We're brothers. We're Confucian Fist. We serve the people.*

His short speech and the blood the Fists had spilled while the cameras watched. Their own blood. Their own lives. Sacrificed, defending the people in that square.

Defending the idea of the people.

Defending the idea that a nation could be governed by its people.

Feng turned and looked at Ling, at his eight year-old friend. His little sister.

Lu Song's invitation was still fresh in his mind.

"I think," Feng said. "I'm going to try my hand at politics."

Ayesha Dani sipped chai and looked out the window, down onto the grassy lawn, where a half dozen children laughed and screamed and chased each other about, in some game whose rules were as fluid as the politics of South Asia.

Her grandchildren.

She spoke, without turning, to the woman behind her. "So you're back on schedule?"

"Yes, Madam Prime Minister," Lakshmi Dabir said. "We expect to be ready for wide scale deployment this summer."

"Good." Ayesha Dani took another sip of her chai. The children were running around a tree now, all clockwise, then suddenly reversing, all the other way, laughing.

Lakshmi Dabir cleared her throat. "Madame Prime Minister, if I may… Will things be ready on the political front?"

Ayesha Dani sipped her chai again before answering, then put the delicate china cup down on its saucer. "This will be the most significant anti-poverty measure of the last twenty years," she said. "An unprecedented boost in education and development. I'll push it through." She smiled grimly. "The fundamentalists will probably try to assassinate me again." She shrugged and snorted at that.

Lakshmi Dabir seemed taken aback, then spoke again. "Madame Prime Minister, if you really think they're going to try to kill you…"

Ayesha Dani turned away from the window, facing the tall, angular scientist for the first time. "They're welcome to try," she laughed. "I hope their aim is no better than ten years ago!"

Dabir nodded and pursed her lips. "As you say, Madam Prime Minister."

Ayesha Dani locked eyes with the woman. "This is about people power, Dr," she said. "You told me once this century's most vital raw material is the human mind, did you not?"

Lakshmi Dabir nodded again.

"Good," Ayesha Dani said. "Because we seem to have more of those than anyone. Now go unlock them. This will be the *Indian* Century."

Varun Verma walked slowly across the Bangalore research campus, watching the restoration work in progress.

So much devastation had been done here in such a short time. More than a hundred killed in that attack. Scientists. Technicians. Soldiers.

He was thankful every day that it hadn't been worse.

Thankful he was still alive.

Thankful the whole world was still here.

His mind drifted back to the top secret report he'd read on the events in Shanghai.

Varun shook his head in admiration. Lane had stayed true to his principles, all the way through. He'd seen the second order effects, the importance of precedent, of how a history of violence led to more violence, a history of cooperation led to more cooperation.

Simple iterated Prisoner's Dilemma. But Lane saw it. Lane put it into action.

And he'd engineered cooperation, somehow salvaged it out of the worst possible case of enslavement, torture, and the very edge of the worst possible retribution.

Tit for tat on a global scale.

Interrupted.

Self-sacrifice salvaged out of mutually assured hatred.

The Division Six team had made it home, courtesy of the People's Liberation Army, their tails between their legs. The official history would write it down as a joint operation between China and India, India offering assistance at the invitation of Chinese authorities.

And that was a win as well.

Had Lane planned *all* of that? Varun wondered.

No! It beggared belief. No one was that smart. Lane must have been lucky.

Unless...?

Varun was still pondering this when a technician yelled his name from across the field and came running towards him, a case in his hand.

"Dr Verma!" the man yelled. "Dr Verma!"

Varun stared at the man, a catch in his chest.

"We found it!"

The technician put the case on the lawn, delicately, so delicately.

Then he held his thumbs to the lockpads, unsnapped them, and opened it.

Varun exhaled, reached down, and pulled out the diamondoid data cube, still dripping with water from the salvage operation.

He held it up above him, his fingers at the corners. The cube glistened and glittered in the equatorial sun, refracting the light, sending out a bright prismatic spray that shifted as Varun turned it over.

His breath caught in his chest at its beauty. At what he held up to the sky.

A single drop of water dripped down his hand.

"This time," Varun said aloud, staring up at the bright and shining cube, "I'll do better by you."

On a bench, a few hundred meters away from Varun Verma, a woman named Jyotika watched the leaves on the trees sway in the light breeze, watched the tiny dappled clouds roll by against the blue sky. She could feel Verma's excitement, though he'd be surprised to know that. She could feel so much, so much more than she ever could.

There had been a goddess inside her, for months, while she lay in a coma.

Or perhaps she had been inside the goddess.

Wisps of that time were still present now, like half-forgotten dreams.

The Nexus technology was still in her head. Shu – the goddess – had set about using it to heal Jyotika's brain, to repair the damage that had placed her in a coma in the first place. A gift. And now it had opened whole new worlds to her.

She looked over at Verma. And then she stood, and started to walk over to him.

He was going to need help if he wanted to do things right this time.

Rangan looked down at the slate in his lap as the plane descended.

Watson Cole, 2009—2040.

Ilya Alexander, 2014—2040.

Kaden Lane, 2013—2041.

They gave their lives, that you could be more free.

After that, notes, pages of notes. Pages of music. Pages of text. Drawings. Scribbles. Diagrams.

Pictures. Pictures he'd found. Pictures he'd saved.

Wats with Rangan in a headlock, grinning that huge pearly grin in that dark face, his muscles bulging and shaved head gleaming. The man of peace, horsing around.

Ilya, standing in front of a wall screen in a giant auditorium, looking elfin even in a formal setting, her hair down and unbound, a finger raised to make a point, an engaged smile on her face, the screen below her showing part of her dissertation, explaining the metrics she'd developed for collective intelligence. The day of her PhD defense. The day she'd become Dr Ilyana Alexander.

Kade. Kade on the dance floor, arms in mid-flail, a near-spasmodic look on his face. Dancing goofier than anyone Rangan knew. So graceless. So funny. So genuine. So real. The guy everyone loved.

Rangan shook his head and laughed to himself.

They deserved better than this. They deserved medals. They deserved a real memorial.

No.

They deserved to be alive. More than he did.

They'd each believed more than he had. Fought harder than he had. And died for it.

Rangan shook his head again, wiped at his face. If he could do one thing, he'd make sure the world knew, make sure the world understood who they'd been, what they'd stood for, what they'd done.

What they'd died for.

The immense gifts they'd given the world.

Willingly, each of them.

Too young, he wrote in a margin. Too good for this world.

Then the wheels bumped the ground. They were taxiing.

Rangan closed the slate, then slipped it into his bag.

Then he closed his eyes and breathed, just breathed, like he'd learned from Kade, like Kade had learned from so many others.

Letting go.

Then they were at the gate, and he was opening his eyes, rising. He was pulling his other bag down, the only possessions in his life besides ideas and memories and data, and he was disembarking from the plane, a lump growing in his chest.

He still wasn't sure this was real.

It had been a long, roundabout trip from the moment he'd made that call. Container ship from Baltimore. At-sea transfer somewhere in the Atlantic. A different ship headed the other way, to Panama, to cross through the canal. Over land to Guatemala.

And now this. On a Cuban passport. This flight. To a place where he'd be a citizen. Where he'd be legit. Maybe someday he'd head for India, see if he could make that work. Maybe someday there would even be a pardon in the US, as unlikely as that sounded, as uncertain as he was if he'd be willing to go back even if it came through.

But for now…

For now it was Cuba. For now there was work to do. A lot of work.

Coercion was still far too easy with Nexus. Emotional manipulation was still far too easy – Breece had shown that with the riots he'd started, the violence he'd incited. Kade had planned to address parts of that with Nexus 6. He'd said the Indians were on board...

Rangan shook his head. It wasn't their job. It wasn't something he trusted any government to do, anyway.

It was something the community had to do. The community of Nexus developers. It had to be done in the open. Transparently. And Rangan was going to do his damndest to make that happen.

The line moved. He shuffled forward, bags in hand, step by step. He came off the plane and there were uniformed officers waiting for him, guns holstered in their belts.

The lump in his chest grew thicker.

"*Senor Shankari?*" one asked.

"*Si,*" Rangan said.

"*Venga con nosotros, por favor,*" the officer said, gesturing. *Come with us, please.*

Rangan nodded. "*Si.*"

They took his bags. One officer followed behind, while the other led him, down the jet way, past the line, down the concourse of the airport, to immigration, into his own line, where his passport was stamped, then out, through a customs line that seemed to exist just for him, where nothing was searched.

Through a door, a different door than everyone else was taking.

There was a crowd on the other side. Hundreds of people. A banner held high.

WELCOME RANGAN SHANKARI, HERO OF THE PEOPLE.

Then he saw faces. Faces he knew.

His father. His mother.

Then his mother's arms were around him, gripping him tight, her face buried in his neck, crying.

His father's arms were around him too and his voice was in Rangan's ear. "We're so proud of you, son."

Bobby was in his mind. Alfonso was in his mind. Tyrone was in his mind. They were all in his mind, all embracing him with their minds. And wrapping their arms around him where they could.

...*learning to SAIL...*

...*and it's SUNNY...*

...*coral is like HOUSES for little fish...*

...*PARENTS are here and we're NOT GOING BACK WE'RE GOING TO SUE and you're going to meet...*

...*we do lots of cool SCIENCE and COMPUTERS and...*

...*MISSED YOU...*

...*told them you're my BIG BROTHER...*

"You saved my son," someone said aloud. "Thank you."

And it was all Rangan could do to hold on, hold on to the people who embraced him, in body and mind, and laugh and cry, and be grateful he was here.

The woman who called herself Samantha Cataranes climbed out of the cab and walked towards the house on Soi Rama 3, in the suburbs of Bangkok.

February now. February of 2041. A year since she'd stepped out of another taxi, an ocean away, and walked towards a different house.

A year, almost to the day.

Her knee twinged as she took the steps up from the level of the street and towards the higher level of the house. A reminder of wounds she'd suffered.

Her heart ached. A reminder of other wounds. Of people she'd loved. People she'd lost in the year behind her.

A group of monks walked down the path from the monastery next door, their faces serene. They smiled softly at Sam and brought their hands together in the *wai*. She smiled softly back, bowed her head, and made the *wai* of respect in turn.

The monks passed.

Sam looked up, ran her eyes over the home, the beauty of it, here in the lush green on the outskirts of the city; the vibrant red and gold of the roof tiles; the ceremonial Buddhas and demons guarding it; the proximity to the Buddhist monastery to which it was associated; the smells of lemongrass and jasmine, of food being cooked; the sounds of voices and laughter.

The sense of minds she knew. Minds she hadn't felt in so long.

Her heart lifted. The sense of loss fell from her.

Here there was life. Here there was the future.

Sam breathed, smiled, and stepped forward.

The door opened, spilling light and sound and laughter onto the path.

Sarai ran out, and other children with her, and Sam picked them up, one at a time, whirling them around, laughing, singing – each of them looming huge in her mind, in her heart, filling her up with the joy she'd craved. And behind them, standing in the doorway of the house, Ananda was laughing, a deep booming laugh, that spoke of serenity, of a perfect, complete delight with the universe as it was.

She whirled the children around, every one, Kit and Sarai and Mali and Aroon and Ying and Tada and Sunisa and Kwan and Arinya and all the rest, her smile so bright and fierce her face ached, her heart singing so loudly she was sure they could all hear it.

And they could, they could, just as she could hear the singing inside of them.

Then they went into the house, and there was laughter. So much laughter.

And joy, so much joy.

At long last, Samantha Cataranes was home.

The Science of *Apex*

Like *Nexus* and *Crux* before it, *Apex* is a work of fiction, but based as accurately as possible on real science.

In the afterwords to *Nexus* and *Crux*, I described how scientists have directly interfaced to human and animal brains to accomplish such feats as: giving paralyzed men and women the ability to move robot limbs by thought; restoring vision to a blind man by inputing electrical signals into the visual cortex of his brain; using an fMRI brain scanner to "read" what a person is seeing and reconstruct it as a video; restoring damaged rat memories by a chip implanted in the hippocampus; being able to record and *replay* those memories any time later in the rat; boosting the pattern matching abilities of rhesus monkeys via an implant in the frontal cortex.

In the less than two years since *Crux* was released, science has continued to advance. In 2013, a pair of researchers at the University of Washington demonstrated that one human being could control part of another human being's body via a non-invasive brain-computer interface. The two researchers, Rajesh Rao and Andrea Stocco, played a video game together, in a very peculiar way. Rajesh Rao, in one building on campus, could see the video game display, but had no controls. Andrea Stocco, in another building across the campus, had the controller (a fire button), but couldn't see the display. When Professor Rao wanted to shoot, he would think about shooting, and an EEG cap on his skull would pick up his intent and transmit it across campus. There, a magnetic stimulator on Andrea Stocco's head would send a pulse through part of Professor Stocco's motor cortex, causing his finger to twitch and hit the fire button.

It's quite a long way from Nexus, but the same general principle applies.

How far are we from Nexus, really? I'm asked this question frequently. The prime obstacle is the hardware. To build something like Nexus one needs a way to interface with millions of neurons at once, and ideally to do so without requiring brain surgery. And I don't actually expect that we'll see something like the Nexus nanites by 2040.

That said, various teams are starting to look at ways to move beyond current hardware.

At UC Berkeley, Professor Michel Maharbiz and colleagues are working on a project they call "Neural Dust". Their neural dust would be particles that are less than one hundred microns across. Thousands or tens of thousands or more could be sprinkled across the brain, and would then communicate wirelessly via ultrasonic sound waves. Those same ultrasonic vibrations would also provide power to the individual neural dust nodes. Reading their proposal and looking at the diagrams almost feels like reading an artifact from one of my books. Almost. Neural dust still isn't small enough to cross the blood-brain barrier, so it would still involve an incision in the skull. And it's still on the drawing board, not something that has been built. Still, it's fascinating to see science moving in these directions. (Maharbiz developed the world's first remote-controlled beetle, by the way – a flying insect whose nervous system could be controlled via electrical stimulations sent wirelessly.)

DARPA, the Defense Applied Research Programs Agency, is also highly interested in this area. In recent talks and calls for grant applications, they've painted a vision of neural interfaces small enough that they could be injected via a syringe rather than via brain surgery; of combining multiple technologies to achieve high-fidelity communication with individual neurons; and most recently of their "cortical modem" vision: an implant the size of two nickels, with a cost of just a few dollars, that would allow the beaming of high-quality video directly into a human brain.

All of that said, I'll be surprised if, by 2040, we have brain computer interfaces anywhere near the sophistication of Nexus. Research inside the body and brain moves slowly. The first rule of medicine is, quite appropriately, "do no harm". And that means that experimentation is necessarily conservative. I expect tremendous progress by 2040 – restoration of senses, of mobility, of function destroyed by stroke and brain damage; perhaps even significant augmentation. But I'll be surprised (alas) if it's as easy as drinking a vial of silvery liquid.

I'll be similarly surprised if uploading a human mind is possible, or even close, by 2040. I elaborated on those reasons in the afterword to *Crux*.

In both areas, though: progress *is* happening at an incredible pace. As well it should. We all live inside our brains, after all. Our minds are the seat of joy and sorrow, of peace and war, of innovation and stagnation. Unlocking the mysteries of the mind is one of the most exciting and most important endeavors I can imagine. I'm delighted to be a bystander. I can't wait to see what happens next.

Acknowledgements

Apex wouldn't be the book it is without the help of more than sixty people who provided input along the way.

As ever, my partner Molly Nixon served as first reader, sounding board, and co-brainstormer. She read most passages in this book within hours of them being written – usually that night. And we may have turned a few heads at restaurants while discussing the fine details of how one might gas a large fraction of the US Congress. C'est la vie.

Nexus, *Crux*, and *Apex* all deal heavily with neuroscience, and I've been delighted and honored that neuroscientists have responded warmly to the books. I'm especially grateful to Christoph Koch for the invitation to speak to his team of neuroscientists at the Allen Institute for Brain Science, where the discussion was quite stimulating; and to Gary Marcus for fascinating conversations on the topic and the sneak peak at part of his book, *The Future of the Brain*.

A large fraction of *Apex* takes place in China. I first visited that fascinating nation in 2000 and have returned as often as I could, but I'm hardly a native. A number of people who've spent years actually living there provided feedback to hone those passages. I'm especially greatful to Gerald Zhang-Shmidt, Max Gladstone, Peter Atwood, David Hart, and Ben Goertzel on this front. Any errors or insensitivities are entirely mine.

Grace Stahre and Lesley Charmichael both called out biases I wasn't aware of in my depictions of female characters in earlier drafts of this book, and helped improve it significantly.

My agent, Lucienne Diver, has been a never-ending source of support for me, this series, and this book. I'm immensely grateful to her.

I'm also grateful to my editor Lee Harris, my copy editor Ro Smith, and my publisher Marc Gascoigne, as well as to Mike Underwood and Caroline Lambe on the sales and publicity team at Angry Robot, who are already at work getting the word out about this book.

The real heroes are the fifty-seven friends and acquaintances who read drafts of this book and took the time to send their feedback or meet to discuss it. Writing might be a solitary art for some. It's not for me, thanks to my beta readers. And this book is a better work for your efforts.

So thank you: Ajay Nair, Alexis Carlson, Allegra Searle-LeBel, Anna Black, Annie Tabler, Banning Garrett, Ben Goertzel, Betsy Aoki, Beverly Sobelman, Brad Templeton, Brad Woodcock, Brady Forrest, Brian Retford, Carrie Sellars, Daniel Garcia, Dave Brennan, David Hart, David Jones, David Perlman, David Sunderland, Doug Mortenson, Ethan Phelps-Goodman, Gerald Zhang-Schmidt, Glenn Bristol, Grace Stahre, Hannu Rajaniemi, Ivan Medvedev, Jaime Waliczek, Jayar La Fontaine, Jen Younggren, Jennifer Mead, Jim Jordan, Joe Pemberton, Julian Klappenbach, Julie Vithoulkas, Kevin MacDonald, Kira Franz, Lars Liden, Leah Papernick, Lesley Carmichael, Mark Lacas, Max Gladstone, Michael Chorost, Miller Sherling, Molly Nixon, Morgan Weaver, Nat Ward, Patrick Davin, Paul Dale, Peter Atwood, Rachel Kwan, Rob Jellinghaus, Satish Bhatti, Scotto Moore, Stuart Updegrave, Ted Lockwood, and Val Giddings.

Finally, I owe absolutely everything in the world to my amazing parents. They birthed me, raised me, brought me to the US, and have served as outstanding role models my entire life. Thank you, Mom and Dad! You're the best.

IN CASE OF EMERGENCY...

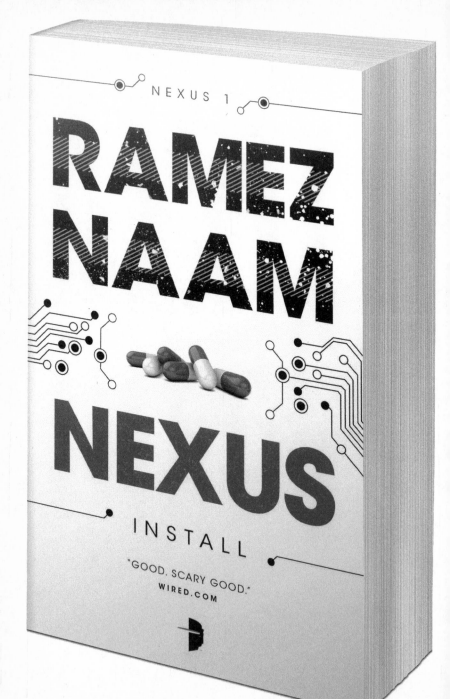

NEXUS 2

RAMEZ NAAM

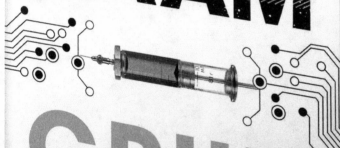

CRUX

UPGRADE

"PROVOCATIVE... A DOUBLE-EDGED
VISION OF THE POST-HUMAN."
THE WALL STREET JOURNAL

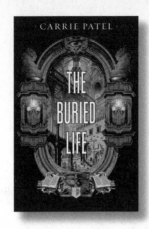
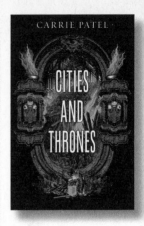

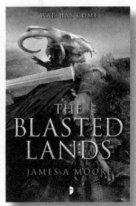

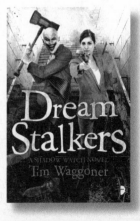

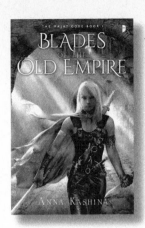

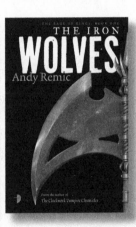
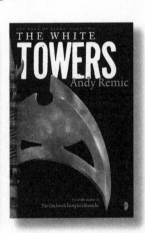
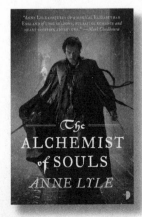

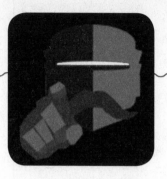

HEY, YOU!

- **Want more** of the best in SF, F, and WTF!?
  - **Want the latest** news from your favorite Agitated Androids?
    - **Want to be spared**, alone of all your kind, when the robotic armies spill over the world to conquer all weak, fleshy humans?

Well, sign yourself up for the Angry Robot Legion then!

You'll get sneak peaks at upcoming books, special previews, and exclusive giveaways for free Angry Robot books.

Go here, sign up, survive the imminent destruction of all mankind:

angryrobotbooks.com/legion